WAVE ME GOODBYE/HEARTS UNDEFEATED
OMNIBUS

Wave Me Goodbye

Hearts Undefeated

WAVE ME GOODBYE/HEARTS UNDEFEATED
OMNIBUS

Wave Me Goodbye
Stories of the
Second World War

Edited by
ANNE BOSTON

Hearts Undefeated
Women's Writing of
the Second World War

Edited by
JENNY HARTLEY

Virago

A *Virago* Book

This omnibus edition first published in Great Britain by Virago Press in 2003
Wave Me Goodbye/Hearts Undefeated Omnibus Copyright Collection,
Introduction and Notes © Anne Boston and Jenny Hartley 2003

Previously published separately:
Wave Me Goodbye first published in hardback in
Great Britain in 1988 by Virago Press
Published in Penguin Books in 1989
Published by Virago Press in 1999
Collection, Introduction and Notes copyright © Anne Boston 1988

Hearts Undefeated first published in large format paperback in
Great Britain in 1994 by Virago Press
Published by Virago Press 1999
Collection, Introduction and Notes copyright © Jenny Hartley 1994

A CIP catalogue record for this book
is available from the British Library

ISBN 1 84408 031 5

Typeset in Stempel Garamond by M Rules
Printed and bound in Great Britain by
Clays Ltd, St Ives plc

Virago Press
An imprint of
Time Warner Books UK
Brettenham House
Lancaster Place
London WC2E 7EN

www.virago.co.uk

Wave Me Goodbye

Stories of the
Second World War

Contents

For Annette and David

Acknowledgements

My thanks are due first to the late Elizabeth Berridge and Reginald Moore who kindly let me consult their library of wartime periodicals, pointed the way to many authors and sources, and offered invaluable encouragement. I am also grateful to Nicola Beauman, and to Ian Hamilton, for their helpful suggestions; and to Bridget Fisher, librarian at the University of East Anglia, who managed to call up material from halfway round the world. My thanks go too to Richard Boston, Simon Caulkin, and Alexandra Pringle of Virago Press for their help and advice.

Permission to reproduce the following stories is gratefully acknowledged: 'When the Waters Came' by Rosamond Lehmann from *Penguin New Writing*, edited by John Lehmann 1942, and from *The Gipsy's Baby*, first published by Collins 1946, reprinted by permission of The Society of Authors and Miss Rosamond Lehmann; 'Gas Masks' from *Mrs Miniver* by Jan Struther, published by Chatto & Windus 1939, copyright © Jan Struther 1939, reprinted by permission of Curtis Brown Ltd; 'I Was Too Ignorant' by Rosamond Oppersdorff from *New Writing and Daylight* Winter 1942–3, edited by John Lehmann, published by The Hogarth Press; 'Defeat' by Kay Boyle, from *Modern Reading 10* edited by Reginald Moore 1944, reprinted by permission of the Tessa Sayle Literary and Dramatic Agency on behalf of Kay Boyle; 'Goodbye, My Love' by Mollie Panter-Downes, reprinted by permission, © 1941,1969 The New Yorker Magazine, Inc; 'Night in the Front Line' by Molly Lefebure from *Selected Writing II*, edited by Reginald Moore, copyright © Molly Lefebure 1942; 'Miss Anstruther's Letters' by Rose Macaulay, from *London Calling*, edited by Storm Jameson, Harper NY 1942, reprinted by permission of A. D. Peters & Co Ltd; 'Face of My People' by Anna Kavan from *Horizon* 1944, edited by Cyril Connolly, and from *I am Lazarus* by Anna

'According to the Directive' by Inez Holden from *Cornhill Magazine* vol 163, 1947–49; 'Bread and Butter Smith' from *Mum and Mr Armitage* by Beryl Bainbridge, published by Gerald Duckworth 1985, reprinted by permission of Gerald Duckworth & Co Ltd; 'The Maiden' by Jean Stafford, copyright 1950 by Jean Stafford, renewed 1978 by Jean Stafford, reprinted by permission of Russell & Volkening as agents for the author, 'The Maiden' first appeared in *The New Yorker*; 'Gravement Endommagé' from *Hester Lilly and Other Stories* by Elizabeth Taylor, published by Peter Davies 1954, reprinted by permission of Virago Press Ltd.

Introduction

'Wish Me Luck As You Wave Me Goodbye', went the jaunty wartime song. That was the official brave face of women at war – the fond farewell, and then on with the uniform or overalls to join the battle on the Home Front. Sixty years after war was declared, the heroic myths are again brought out and dusted off for another round of anniversaries. Today those years when invasion could happen any moment and food and clothes and petrol were rationed, when nights meant the blackout and Anderson shelters and maybe the bomb which had 'your number on it', have acquired nostalgia with distance, like the notion that people were fighting for such unfashionable ideals as the New Deal and 'Fair Shares For All'. All the more reason, then, or so it seemed to me, to look at the short stories written by women when war was a way of life; for among the literature of guns and tanks and battle stratagems, their voices are too easily forgotten or ignored. They have a special relevance, too, in the wake of today's savage regional wars in which civilians are again the chief casualties.

The stories in this anthology are set in the decade between 1939 and 1949, and all but one were written around the same period; Beryl Bainbridge, writing retrospectively, seems to have soaked up the seedy post-war atmosphere to reproduce it as convincingly as stories published at the time. Five American writers are represented, but none from Australia, New Zealand or Canada – not for want of searching, though my access to wartime writing was limited to its availability in British libraries. The stories are roughly in chronological order, according to the events they describe and to a lesser extent when they were written; within that context they are arranged to offer as much contrast as possible in content and style. In the notes at the end, wherever possible I have added details of the authors' wartime circumstances and their bearing on the writing of these stories.

I was guided by two principles in making the selection principles which weren't always compatible, as it turned out: first, the story's literary qualities, and second, its historical interest. The best short-story writing, of course, is much more than the proverbial 'slice of life'; what turns it into art is the imaginative tension between surface, exterior events and the silent reality beneath; the dramatic insight implicit in the descriptive truth. At the same time, everyday human experience in wartime could be so extraordinary that it hardly needed to be embellished in fiction. Much of the writing was close to the rawness of journalism, and realism was often the most appropriate medium; it suited the urgency of the time. On a purely descriptive level I wanted the stories to cover as many aspects of 'the people's war' as possible. On those grounds, authenticity is given precedence over polished prose, and if a graphic semi-documentary sketch seemed a more truthful response than a highly crafted 'literary' exercise, or added a different aspect to the range of experience, I chose it. None the less I also looked for the widest variety of structure and approach: surreal interior accounts of fantasy and breakdown, popular romance, a black fable against war, a propaganda story written to commission – all have a place. The qualifying factor was that each story had to offer a particularly vivid glimpse into the special circumstances of wartime; not only physical conditions, but above all the territory of feelings, emotions and attitudes.

The fact that this collection could include so many of the finest women writers of their generation – among them several who had rarely, until then, used the short-story form – is itself a by-product of war. Short stories enjoyed an unexpected burst of popularity in wartime, when ordinary life was subject to constant interruption and time was at a premium. Most writers – like everyone else – were involved in war work of some kind, and the extended concentration novelists needed for creating full-length fiction was hard to come by. There were, also, overwhelming difficulties in encompassing events that were too huge and too close to bring into focus: as Elizabeth Bowen wrote, 'These years rebuff the imagination as much by being fragmentary as by being violent.' Short stories and poetry, with their snapshot immediacy, could capture a single incident in dramatic close-up – Rose Macaulay's 'Miss Anstruther's Letters' is an outstanding example of the wartime story's effectiveness in the hands of a novelist who rarely strayed into the genre.

At the same time, there was a growing audience. In the early stages of the 'phoney war' cinemas and theatres were closed, and with blackout enforcement and the disruption of normal social life people read more, and far more widely, than before. A collection of stories offered instant variety and could be read in short bursts in the endless waiting for All-Clear sirens, on long journeys or stuck in remote parts of the countryside. The lending libraries did record business, Forces libraries were set up for the armed services and paperbacks and periodicals were in unprecedented demand.

Because of the paper shortage, new magazines were prohibited from May 1940. But the ban did not apply to new publishing companies; some two hundred were set up in 1940 alone, producing dozens of 'little magazines' disguised in the form of anthologies of poems and prose. Paperback series like *Penguin New Writing*, edited by John Lehmann, and the indefatigable Reginald Moore's *Modern Reading*, *Selected Writing* and *Bugle Blast* (for the Forces), opened their pages to unknown and amateur writers along with the famous and established. Fiction in the women's magazines tended to follow the convention of romance backed up by a patriotic message, though there were exceptions – the stories and serials in *Woman's Journal*, for instance, contained hardly a single reference to the war throughout 'the duration'. (Fiction from women's magazines didn't survive the final selection process for this anthology, though I kept one romance, Pat Frank's 'five-minute story' 'The Bomb' from the *Strand Magazine*.)

I turned eagerly to *Horizon*, the leading wartime literary journal (and a familiar presence on the family bookshelves) as the first source for this anthology, only to be rebuffed by its editor Cyril Connolly's celebrated denunciation of 'experiences connected with the Blitz, the shopping queues, the home front, deserted wives, deceived husbands, broken homes, dull jobs, bad schools, group squabbles . . .' as too close to ordinary life to be worth recording. Apart from revealing Connolly's disenchantment with his own civilian circumstances, his statement shows how easy it was (and is) to dismiss at a stroke virtually every aspect of women's lives as subjects worth writing about, especially the domestic and personal areas where women writers tended to excel. Not surprisingly the two stories from *Horizon* included here – Diana Gardner's land girl disrupting a household like a cuckoo in the nest, and Anna Kavan's powerful impressionistic study of psychological war damage are each, in different ways, an antithesis of conventional 'women's' themes.

War, of course, had always been a masculine occupation, and from the first line of the *Aeneid* – 'Arms and the man I sing' – to Hemingway's *Men Without Women,* war fiction has been about men in uniform, men in action. The fine anthology edited by Dan Davin, *Short Stories from the Second World War,* is part of this tradition; all but four of the stories are by servicemen like himself, describing the terror, boredom, muddle and exhilaration of the battlefield. Men were brought up to be part of the ritual of war, and some writers accepted it almost as a need: F. J. Salfeld's story 'Fear of Death' begins 'Why did I want to join the Navy and fight? Mostly I wished to test the unknown in myself.'

But even in countries which escaped invasion women were very much participants in this war, and they too deserve a hearing. Total war was a great equalizer: children, the old and both sexes now took the brunt of slaughter and devastation along with the young men. It's salutary to remember that more British civilians than servicemen lost their lives by enemy action during the first three of its six years. At least now there was none of the terrible ignorance that had divided those at home from the men who fought in the Great War. Even so, despite the shared experience, war writing was still seen as the province of the serviceman: as the poet Keith Douglas put it, 'Whatever changes in the nature of warfare, the battlefield is the simple, central stage of the war; it is there that the interesting things happen.' The only woman represented in Dan Davin's anthology, Elizabeth Bowen, saw her war writing as outside the main tradition; in a postscript to her brilliant wartime collection *The Demon Lover* she distinguishes between *war* stories and *wartime* ones like her own, which 'are, more, studies of climate, war-climate, and of the strange growths it raised'. Her distinction equally applies to most of the stories in this anthology; the war is their environment, if not always their subject. Rosamond Lehmann's 'When the Waters Came' isn't ostensibly 'about' the war at all, yet it hangs like a darkening cloud over this subtle, sensitive account of a child saved from drowning, the violent thaw after the first grim winter bringing not relief but more omens of disaster. In Elizabeth Taylor's 'Gravement

Endommagé' the hostilities are over, but the after-effects are felt everywhere, in a marriage mortally damaged by long separation and in the shattered French landscapes the couple are driving through: 'Grass grew over grief, trying to hide collapse, to cover some of the wounds.'

The experience of war was as individual as it was universal, and one dubious advantage for writers was that its 'strange growths' produced any amount of narrative material. So we see an American bystander thrown into nursing injured and dying troops on the Front Line in France; a journalist caught up in the panic as Axis troops move into central Europe; women making bombs, practising air-raid drill, buried by rubble in the Blitz – and saying heartwrenching goodbyes, bringing up children alone, coming to terms with a husband who has turned into a stranger. That said, the stories are no more restricted to 'women's subjects', if they can be labelled as such, than they are to female protagonists: see Doris Lessing's savage impression of neo-Fascism in colonial Africa, the A. L. Barker story of a boy destroyed by his desire to be a war hero, the refugee Kling tortured by memories in Anna Kavan's 'Face of My People'; while at least half a dozen more are seen through the eyes of a male character.

As diverse as they are, almost without exception these stories are concerned with the personal and the particular – which may be more to do with the short story's general dictates than with the fact that they are by women. It's arguable, though, that writing turned more to introspection in wartime, when every aspect of personal life and self-expression was under attack. Given the grossly depersonalizing effects of violence and deprivation, fiction was a place of retreat to individual feelings and emotions – conserving, as V. S. Pritchett wrote, 'the human fragments in an iron age when human lives, what I feel and you feel, are considered to be shameful'.

Men who enlisted exchanged the peacetime world of work and family for other loyalties; for most women war meant going on as before, but with all the bulwarks of security that were normally taken for granted removed. No wonder so many of the stories remain stubbornly rooted in the domestic and personal – surrounded by destruction, women had the job of preserving life, of making do, keeping a brave face in front of the children. The absurd discrepancy between their attempts to hold on to ordinary existence while expecting the worst, gas attack and invasion included, is especially strong in the early 'phoney-war' stories by Rosamond Lehmann, Jan Struther and Mollie Panter-Downes. 'One had to laugh', says Mrs Miniver, and the contrast between everyday trivia and catastrophic events elsewhere is a recurring theme. Barbara Pym characteristically makes a poignant comedy out of non-events with faded, sweet-faced Laura dreaming of far-away drama, hemmed in all her life by disapproving relations and now by 'all the rather ludicrous goings-on of a country town that sees nothing of the war'. And Sylvia Townsend Warner has an unerring eye for the oddities and anomalies of hidden lives away from the 'central stage'. I included two of her stories, and was tempted to use more from a whole gallery of wartime character and incident, often wickedly funny and always alive with social insight and humane perception. (Other writers – notably Elizabeth Bowen and Rosamond Lehmann – equally deserve to be represented by more than one story; but space was short, and the consideration that Sylvia Townsend Warner's work is less widely read and less often included in anthologies was among my justifications for making her the exception.)

In the Blitz stories, any semblance of normality is lost and the writing becomes part of the process of intense struggle to stay whole as a person as a matter of survival. Rose Macaulay's story goes straight into the full shock of despair as the inhuman violence of an air raid destroys a woman's home, and in doing so dislodges all her pent-up anguish at the death of her lover. Her past reduced to ashes, she loses even the few pathetic possessions she has salvaged to looters and demolition men, deepening the horror. Under surreal conditions of danger and deprivation, Elizabeth Bowen's characters are dislocated from reality, creating their own worlds in visions of hallucinatory strength. The girl and her lover in 'Mysterious Kôr' have nowhere to stay together for the night; there is, too, the impossible strain of trying to stay detached from the person you love, for fear of what might happen to them. 'Think about people? How can anyone think about people if they've got any heart?' she bursts out. Denied even this emotional anchor, she retreats defiantly into fantasy: 'This war shows we've by no means come to the end. If you can blow whole places out of existence, you can blow whole places into it.'

Dreaming, she passes into the 'wide, void, pure streets' of her imaginary city.

Cut off from the future and the past, characters escape inward into themselves – sometimes, when conditions become unbearable, into madness. The nightmarish 'I Spy a Stranger' by Jean Rhys, like Anna Kavan's 'Face of My People', shows how the already insecure and alienated could be driven literally out of their minds by the conspiratorial, xenophobic war-climate. 'Inhuman', 'depersonalized', 'the impersonal machine' are the recurring language of paranoia in these two frighteningly convincing accounts of breakdown; they also accurately describe a society implacably geared to war.

The Anna Kavan and Jean Rhys stories express the profoundest alienation from the whole business of war, whatever the cause. To some extent this isolation was common to civilian writers and the 'intelligentsia' of either sex who held to any sort of independent critical stance; there was also a strong pacifist movement before and in the early stages of the war. But for women, brought up outside the masculine war tradition, the alienation could be doubly felt, and much of these writers' bitterest criticism is directed not at the enemy abroad, but at the disembodied system which makes conflagration part of accepted policy. Behind Stevie Smith's unquenchably spirited picture of two women friends crying companionably into their cocoa over 'the evil, and the cruelty, and the scientific use of force, and the evil' while the 'doodle bombs' sail down outside, is an eloquent sub-text of the connections between male chauvinism, religion, science and war. 'The Iconoclasts' by A. L. Barker leaves a horribly memorable afterimage of the way war feeds on myths, breeding violence into generations to come.

Only twenty years after the chauvinistic excesses of the First World War, the British exercised a good deal more caution about flag-waving in the second. Initial reluctance to accept its inevitability gave way to general agreement that this one was a necessary evil: Hitler had to be stopped, somehow. But acceptance didn't necessarily mean approval, and the stories by British writers in particular shy away from false heroics; their overriding tone is of scepticism, lack of illusion, the determination to register things honestly and faithfully. Even the frankly patriotic 'Mrs Miniver' stories are careful to avoid the 'licensed lunacy' of boycotting Grimm and

Struwwelpeter . . . to guard against that was the most important of all the forms of war work which she and other women would have to do'. The Hollywood screen version of *Mrs Miniver* was said to have helped galvanize American public opinion into joining the war – Churchill told Parliament it was worth a flotilla of battle-ships – but as Mollie Panter-Downes reported with typical understatement in the *New Yorker,* its rampant sentimentality made British audiences 'a trifle warm under the collar'. Ruth, the protagonist in her own story 'Goodbye, My Love', embodies the quintessential mixture of resignation, unspoken patriotism and quiet despair that seems to stand for British Everywoman in wartime.

By the time the Japanese attack on Pearl Harbor had brought in the United States, the British were exhausted by three gruelling years which on the Home Front alone had taken in near-defeat at Dunkirk, the air Battle of Britain and the recurring fury of the Blitz. Beside the self-deprecating irony of the British writing, the American stories by Edna Ferber and Dorothy Parker are full of vitality and conviction. It is doubtful whether any writer this side of the Atlantic could have carried off Edna Ferber's propaganda commission 'Grandma Isn't Playing', written to boost women's part in the war effort, with such bold and sympathetic credibility.

The Edna Ferber story is relatively unusual in making women at work its subject, which might seem surprising at a time when an army of Rosie the Riveters on both sides of the Atlantic found a new independence in war work of all kinds. This could be partly due to an inevitable class bias in these stories; writing was still essentially a middle-class occupation, whatever the democratizing effects of the war. Another notable exception is Pat Frank's 'The Bomb', which I included for its fascinating mixture of bomb-making technology with the language of formula romance; conventional 'femininity' still struggling for supremacy in a brave new world of overalls and high explosives. A girl and her boyfriend are almost killed by a German bomb aimed at the munitions factory where she works. Waiting for it to explode, she wonders 'whether the enemy also used liquid oxygen and lignite and carbon. How delicately one must handle it! Woman's work. It took a woman's gentle hands . . .' Her triumphant conclusion is that their salvation lay in the power (and incompetence) of love.

For the most part, though, women's work surfaces only in

asides, incidental to the overriding priorities of interior life and personal allegiances. The war changes everything and nothing; women (when they are honest enough to admit it) still feel left behind, left out while their men go off to the world of 'telegrams and anger'. The irrepressible young wife in Dorothy Parker's 'The Lovely Leave', who breaks all the rules of stiff-upper-lip decorum on her husband's brief homecoming, must have expressed the frustration of thousands of women when she erupts with her own. First she embarrasses him by being emotional, then she openly, unforgivably admits to feeling jealous of his new army loyalties. '"You see," she said with care, "you have a whole new life – I have half an old one. Your life is so far from mine, I don't see how they're ever going to come back together."'

Like Dorothy Parker, Sylvia Townsend Warner deals deceptively lightly with the chasms of incomprehension between men and women separated sometimes for years on end. In 'Sweethearts and Wives', William, coming home on leave from the Navy to a ramshackle cottage full of women and messy domesticity, can't help reflecting that 'children on a destroyer would be kept in better order and cleaned at regular intervals'. The second of her stories, 'Poor Mary', turns the husband-on-leave convention on its head with a rueful encounter between a conscientious-objector husband, working on the land, visited by his wife, grown plump and military after four years in the ATS; their wartime marriage, incongruous from the start, is now more improbable than ever. The role reversal is completed by Mary's thwarted longing for a heroic martial destiny, a neat comment on the limitations of women's aspirations at the time.

'Poor Mary', like the stories from the post-war years, is full of misunderstandings and doubts and ambiguities, as if the war had drained the world of certainty or happy endings. The impeccably constructed story by Jean Stafford, set in post-war Heidelberg, quietly exposes the barbarism of the victorious New World beside the monstrous refinements of the Old. Beryl Bainbridge's narrator has lined his pockets from the war, in 'a good line of business to be in if you didn't mind being called a racketeer, which I didn't'. The world is made shabbier, diminished by destruction. Elizabeth Taylor allows just a hint of hope to her couple contemplating their wrecked marriage in a battle-ruined French town: 'Oh, from the most unpromising material, he thought, but he did seem to see some glimmer ahead, if only of his own patience, his own perseverance, which appeared in this frame of mind, in this place, a small demand upon him.'

Elizabeth Bowen suggested that 'all wartime writing is ... resistance writing': interior life putting up its own resistance to the annihilating effects of war. In her own stories, her soaring imagination found its defence in 'resistance fantasies' against the pressures of reality. For other writers, that engagement meant simply registering events as honestly and directly as possible, without embellishing them with sentiment or melodrama or mock heroics. Self-expression could be an act of personal defiance against the weight of a world that seemed to be disintegrating; humour and irony, sympathy and rage continued to assert themselves in the battle for sanity and survival. Comic, stoical, compassionate, angry, subversive, these intensely individual voices bring a human proportion to the outsize events that reverberated round them; they speak for no one but themselves, yet each opens a window on to a hidden landscape of war.

Anne Boston

ROSAMOND LEHMANN

When the Waters Came

Very long ago, during the first winter of the present war, it was still possible to preserve enough disbelief in the necessity for disaster to waver on with only a few minor additions and subtractions in the old way. The first quota of evacuated children had meant a tough problem for the local ladies; but most of them, including her own, had gone back to London. Nothing very disturbing was likely to happen for the present. One thought, of course, of sailors freezing in unimaginable wastes of water, perhaps to be plunged beneath them between one violent moment and the next; of soldiers numb in the black-and-white nights on sentry duty, crammed, fireless, uncomforted on the floors of empty barns and disused warehouses. In her soft bed, she thought of them with pity – masses of young men, betrayed, helpless, and so much colder, more uncomfortable than human beings should be. But they remained unreal, as objects of pity frequently remain. The war sprawled everywhere inert: like a child too big to get born it would die in the womb and be shovelled underground, disgracefully, as monsters are, and after a while, with returning health and a change of scene, we would forget that we conceived it. Lovers went on looking on the bright side, stitching cosy linings, hopeful of saving and fattening all the private promises. The persisting cold, the catastrophes of British plumbing, took precedence of the war as everybody's topic and experience. It became the political situation. Much worse for the Germans, of course. Transport had broken down, there was no coal in Berlin. They'd crack – quite likely – morale being so low already.

The climax came one morning when the wind changed, the grey sky let out rain instead of snow. Then, within an hour, the wind veered round again to the north, the rain froze as it fell. When she went into the kitchen to order the day's meals, the first of the aesthetic phenomena greeted her. The basket of vegetables had come in folded in a crust of ice. Sprouts, each crinkled knob of green brilliance cased in a clear bell, looked like tiny Victorian paperweights.

The gardener scratched his head.

'Never seen nothink like it in fifty years. Better be careful walking out, M. There'll be some broken legs on the 'ill. It's a skating rink. I slipped up a matter of five times coming along. Young Bert's still trying to get up to the sheep at the top. He ain't done it yet.' He chuckled. 'It's a proper pantomime. The old Tabbies'll have to mind their dignities if they steps out today.'

The children ran in with handfuls of things from the garden. Every natural object had become a toy: twigs, stones, blades of grass cased in tubes of ice. They broke up the moulds, and inside were the smooth grooved prints of stems and leaves: a miracle.

Later she put on nailed shoes and walked with difficulty over the snowy field path to the post office. The wind was a steel attack; sharp knobs of ice came whirling off the elms and struck her in the face. She listened by what was once a bush of dogwood, now a glittering sheaf of long ice pipes that jangled and clashed together, giving out a musical ring, hollow, like a ghostly xylophone.

At the post office, the customary group of villagers was gathered, discussing the portents, their slow, toneless, deprecating voices made almost lively by shocked excitement. The sheep in the top field had been found frozen to the ground. Old Mrs Luke had slipped up on her doorstep and broken her thigh. The ambulance sent to take her to hospital had gone backwards into the ditch and overturned. Pigeons were stuck dead by their claws on branches. The peacock at the farm had been brought in sheathed totally in ice: that was the most impressive item.

'I *wish* I'd seen it!'

Stiff in its crystal case, with a gemmed crest, and all the blue iridescence gleaming through: a device for the birthday of the Empress of China.

That night was the end of the world. She heard the branches in the garden snapping and crashing down with a brittle rasp. It seemed as if the inside of the earth with all its roots and foundations had become separated from the outside by an impenetrable bed of iron; so that everything that grew above the surface must inevitably break off like matchwood, crumble and fall down.

Towards dawn the wind dropped and snow began to fall again.

The thaw came in February, not gradually but with violence, overnight. Torrents of brown snow-water poured down from the hills into the valley. By the afternoon, the village street was gone, and in its stead a turbulent flood raced between the cottages. The farm was almost beleaguered: water ran through the back door, out the front door. The ducks were cruising under the apple trees in the orchard. Springs bubbled up in the banks and ditches, gushed out among roots and ivy. Wherever you looked, living waters spouted, trickled, leaped with intricate overlapping voices into the dance. Such sound and movement on every hand after so many weeks of silence and paralysis made you feel light-headed, dizzy, as if you, too, must be swept off and dissolved.

'Oh, children! We shall never see the village looking like this again.'

She stood with them at the lower garden gate, by the edge of the main stream. There was nobody in sight.

'Why not?' said John, poking with the toe of his Wellington at the fringe of drifted rubbish. 'We might see it next year. No reason why not if we get the same amount of snow.'

Where were all the other children? Gathered by parents indoors for fear of the water? The cottages looked dumb.

'It's like a village in a fairy story.'

'Is it?' said Jane, colouring deeply. 'Yes, it is.' She looked around, near and far. 'Is it safe?'

'Of course it's safe, mutt,' said her brother, wading in. 'Unless you want to lie down in the middle of it and get drowned.'

'Has anything got drowned, Mummy?'

'No. The cows and horses are all safe indoors. Only all the old dead winter sticks and leaves are going away. Look at them whirling past.'

The water ran so fast and feverish, carrying winter away. The earth off the ploughed fields made a reddish stain in it, like blood, and stalks of last year's dead corn were mixed and tumbled in it. She remembered *The Golden Bough,* the legend of Adonis, from whose blood the spring should blossom; the women carrying pots of dead wheat and barley to the water, flinging them in with his images. Sowing the spring.

The children ran along the top of the bank, following the stream, pulling sticks from the hedge and setting them to sail.

'Let's race them!'

But they were lost almost at once.

'Mummy, will they go to the sea?'

'Perhaps. In time.'

Jane missed her footing and slithered down into the ditch, clutching at John, pulling him after her.

'It's quite safe!' he yelled. 'It only comes half-way up her boots. Can't we wade to the cross-roads and see what happens?'

'Well, be terribly careful. It may get deep suddenly. The gravel must be washing away. Hold her hand.'

She watched them begin to wade slowly down away from her, chattering, laughing to feel the push and pull of the current at their legs.

'It's *icy*, Mummy! It's lovely. Bend down and feel it.'

Moving farther away, they loosed hands and wandered in opposite directions, gathering up the piles of yellow foam-whip airily toppling and bouncing against every obstruction. She saw Jane rub her face in a great handful of it.

Oh, they're beginning to look very far away, with water all round them. It can't be dangerous, I mustn't shout. They were tiny, and separated.

'Stay together!'

She began to run along the bank, seeing what would happen; or causing it to happen. It did happen, a moment before she got there. Jane, rushing forward to seize a branch, went down. Perfectly silent, her astonished face framed in its scarlet bonnet fixed on her brother, her Wellingtons waterlogged, she started to sink, to sway and turn with the current and be carried away.

'How could you ... John, why didn't you? ... No, it wasn't your fault. It was mine. It wasn't anybody's fault. It's all right, Jane! What a joke! Look, I'll wrap you in my fleecy coat, like a little sheep. I'll carry you. We'll hurry home over the field. We'll be in hot baths in ten minutes. I'm wet to my knees, I've got ice stockings – and all of Jane is wet. How much of John is wet?'

'None of me, of course,' said John, pale and bitter. 'Have I got to have a bath?'

An adventure, not a disaster, she told herself unhopefully, stumbling and splashing up towards the garden over the ploughed field, weighed into the earth with the weight of the child, and of her ever more enormous clogged mud-shoes that almost would not move; and with the weight of her own guilt and Jane's and John's, struggling together without words in lugubrious triangular reproach and anxiety.

But by the end of the day it was all right. Disaster had vanished into the boothole with the appalling lumps of mud, into the clothes-basket with sopping bloomers and stockings, down the plug with the last of the mustard-clouded bath water. Jane lay wrapped in blankets by the nursery fire, unchilled, serene and rosy. John toasted the bread and put on his two yodelling records for a celebration. Adventure recollected in tranquillity made them all feel cheerful.

'I thought I was done for that time,' said Jane complacently.

'It'll take more than that to finish you – worse luck,' said John, without venom. 'We haven't had a moment's peace, any of us, since you were born. Tomorrow I'm going to make a raft and see how far I can get.'

'I'm afraid by tomorrow it'll all be dry land again.'

She looked out of the window and saw that the water in the fields had almost disappeared already. After countless white weeks, the landscape lay exposed again in tender greens and browns, caressing the eye, the imagination, with a promise of mysterious blessing. The air was luminous, soft as milk, blooming in the west with pigeon's breast colours. In the garden the last of the snow lay over flower-beds in greyish wreathes and patches. The snowman stood up at the edge of the lawn, a bit crumpled but solid still, smoking his pipe.

What will the spring bring? Shall we be saved?

'But you were wrong about one thing, Mummy,' said Jane, from the sofa. 'You know what you said about . . . you know.'

'About what? Go *on*. Cough it up.'

'About nothing being . . . you know,' said Jane with an effort. 'Drowned.'

'Oh dear, was I wrong?'

'Yes, you were wrong. I sor a chicking. At least, I think so.'

JAN STRUTHER

Gas Masks

Clem had to go and get his mask early, on his way to the office, but the rest of them went at half past one, hoping that the lunch hour would be less crowded. It may have been: but even so there was a longish queue. They were quite a large party – Mrs Miniver and Nannie; Judy and Toby; Mrs Adie, the Scots cook, lean as a winter aspen, and Gladys, the new house-parlourmaid: a pretty girl, with complicated hair. Six of them – or seven if you counted Toby's Teddy bear, which seldom left his side, and certainly not if there were any treats about. For to children, even more than to grown-ups (and this is at once a consolation and a danger), any excitement really counts as a treat, even if it is a painful excitement like breaking your arm, or a horrible excitement like seeing a car smash, or a terrifying excitement like playing hide-and-seek in the shrubbery at dusk. Mrs Miniver herself had been nearly grown-up in August 1914, but she remembered vividly how her younger sister had exclaimed with shining eyes, 'I say! I'm in a war!'

But she clung to the belief that this time, at any rate, children of Vin's and Judy's age had been told beforehand what it was all about, had heard both sides, and had discussed it themselves with a touching and astonishing maturity. If the worst came to the worst (it was funny how one still shied away from saying, 'If there's a war', and fell back on euphemisms) – if the worst came to the worst, these children would at least know that we were fighting against an idea, and not against a nation. Whereas the last generation had been told to run and play in the garden, had been shut out from the grown-ups' worried conclaves: and then quite suddenly had all been plunged into an orgy of licensed lunacy, of boycotting Grimm and Struwwelpeter, of looking askance at their cousins' old Fraulein, and of feeling towards Dachshund puppies the uneasy tenderness of a devout churchwoman dandling her daughter's love-child. But this time those lunacies – or rather, the outlook which bred them – must not be allowed to come into being. To guard against that was the most important of all the forms of war work which she and other women would have to do: there are no tangible gas masks to defend us in wartime against its slow, yellow, drifting corruption of the mind.

The queue wormed itself on a little. They moved out of the bright, noisy street into the sunless corridors of the Town Hall. But at least there were benches to sit on. Judy produced pencils and paper (she was a far-sighted child) and began playing Consequences with Toby. By the time they edged up to the end of the corridor Mr Chamberlain had met Shirley Temple in a Tube lift and Herr Hitler was closeted with Minnie Mouse in an even smaller rendezvous.

When they got into the Town Hall itself they stopped playing. Less than half an hour later they came out again into the sunlit street: but Mrs Miniver felt afterwards that during that half-hour she had said goodbye to something. To the last shreds which lingered in her, perhaps, of the old, false, traditional conception of glory. She carried away with her, as well as a litter of black rubber pigs, a series of detached impressions, like shots in a quick-cut film. Her own right hand with a pen in it, filling up six yellow cards in pleasurable block capitals; Mrs Adie sitting up as straight as a ramrod under the fitter's hands, betraying no signs of the apprehension which Mrs Miniver knew she must be feeling about her false fringe; Gladys's rueful giggle as her elaborate coiffure came out partially wrecked from her ordeal; the look of sudden realization in Judy's eyes just before her face was covered up; the back of Toby's neck, the valley deeper than usual because his muscles were taut with distaste (he had a horror of rubber in any form); a very small child bursting into a wail of dismay on catching sight of its mother disguised in a black snout; the mother's muffled reassurances – 'It's on'y Mum, duck. Look – it's just a mask, like at Guy Fawkes, see?' *(Mea mater mala sus est.* Absurdly, she remembered the Latin catch Vin had told her, which can mean either 'My mother is a bad pig' or 'Run, mother, the pig is eating the apples.')

Finally, in another room, there were the masks themselves, stacked close, covering the floor like a growth of black fungus. They took what had been ordered for them – four medium size, two small – and filed out into the street.

It was for this, thought Mrs Miniver as they walked towards

the car, that one had boiled the milk for their bottles, and washed their hands before lunch, and not let them eat with a spoon which had been dropped on the floor.

Toby said suddenly, with a chuckle, 'We ought to have got one for Teddy.' It would have been almost more bearable if he had said it seriously. But just as they were getting into the car a fat woman went past, with a fatter husband.

'You did look a fright,' she said. 'I 'ad to laugh.'

One had to laugh.

ROSAMOND OPPERSDORF

I Was Too Ignorant

There is nothing new or startling in the introduction to this story, yet a word of explanation is needed.

The scene is laid in a Military Camp in Brittany. It begins with the Battle of Flanders, and ends with the Battle of France. The old story of refugees will be omitted. Silence also over the collapse of France. That this, too, is ancient history, does not matter.

I was on this particular and very remote spot because of my husband. I was trapped there because of the war. I had never in my life done any hospital work. I had never had the least desire to. In fact I had always kept away from blood or anything to do with sickness.

There were four hospitals in the camp. These were full almost at once, before the Battle of Flanders was even over. A fifth hospital, known as the G5, was hastily slung together, and in no time this, too, was full. Two hundred and fifty more beds.

It was at this moment, with every hour, for me, dragging in impotent idleness and inside agony, that I offered my services for what they were worth, and was accepted. They had no choice.

For the 250 beds in the G5 there were at first four nurses, not including myself, who could hardly be called a nurse. In the end, when everything went from bad to worse, we were three, including myself.

I have travelled a long way since that first day when I entered G5. I do not think that I was either heroic or brave. On the contrary, I was a coward and wanted to run. But I couldn't run.

Fright is based on ignorance. I hope no one will ever be caught in such ignorance as I was.

Eight forty-five a.m. Nanotte is at the main door of the G5 to greet me. I'm to stick to Nanotte. She is my boss.

Eyes stare at the new nurse. There is no escape from those eyes. Can they guess that in spite of the white dress and veil, the new nurse is absolutely ignorant? That the sight of blood, running or coagulated, makes her wince? That pus and sour smells make her sick?

Beds are easy to make. Anyone can make beds. Physical work is an outlet, also a shield. I go at it with a vengeance, but very definitely trying not to look too closely. Coward . . . you asked for this, now face it. But no. The eye is like a butterfly, flitting here and there, yet never lighting. And if it lights . . . then off again, as far as it can go. More beds. Now a pail of water and some rags. Scrub the shelves and floor. Upstairs for this. Down for that. Up again. Keep going. The first day is over. The first day of sights and smells.

The second day. Already a feeling of rhythm and routine. The long lines of eyes don't bother to stare. Your own eye is less of a butterfly. It lingers here and there, timidly, but with a desire to get acquainted. Nanotte is massaging. Surely I can do that. The swollen ankle and misshapen foot, full of corns and bunions, stinks. I swallow hard, and try to think of something else, as dirt plus ointment rolls off into thin black worms, but I am ashamed of my feelings. I must be inhuman to be such a hot-house flower. Nanotte is 'cupping'. That doesn't look very difficult. Just needs a steady, quick hand. I will try. A thin crust of courage is forming. There is already a bridge, although a shaky one.

The third day. I accompany the doctors and Nanotte from bed to bed, in the three ground-floor wards which are in her care. She with her charts, I with my notebook. The notebook is a camouflage behind which I hide. The butterfly is astonishingly brave today. Trying to show off, no doubt, because the doctor is there. A few more pegs are driven into the bridge. Each day brings healing.

One thing leads to another. No. 8, in Ward 2, the Belgian, has a drain from his stomach. The dressing doesn't hold. Yellow ooze leaks out. He asks . . . will I change the dressing? Yes . . . of course, immediately. But inside . . . no, I won't. This is still too much. The smell alone. Flies hover over the spotted sheets. You shoo them off, but back they come, drugged, to the same spots. Nanotte . . . No. 8, the peritonitis fellow, must have pads, another bandage. It's quite a mess. I'll get the things. I'll watch . . . then I can do it next time. Steady, butterfly.

Please . . . may we have clean sheets for 5 and 6? They're absolutely black and stiff with blood. Sorry, they'll have to stay black – and stiff.

Please . . .14 is in great pain. Can I have a pillow to ease his back? A real pillow . . . not one of those bolster things. My dear, what do you think this is . . . a luxury hospital?

Where are the towels? *Towels,* did you say? There are none. And soap? You'll have to bring your own, we don't supply it. I've told you before . . . this is not a luxury place, so stop asking for impossible things.

But *please* . . . where can one get tea? The doctor has ordered it for some of the Moroccans. Oh . . . tea . . . You'll have to run over to the kitchens for that. They're out there (a wave of the arm) . . . just beyond H3. (Approximately three city blocks away.)

And from these kitchens, twice a day, the food is brought in, in pails. Great lumpy goulashes and green greasy soups that always look the same and smell the same, and are still more lumpy and revolting by the time they are dumped on to the aluminium dishes that are greasy too.

One day slides into another without much room for thought. The faces beneath the numbers on the cots change, and change again. The Moroccans are now all bunched together in one ward and can keep each other company in their semi-convalescence. They sit cross-legged on the beds, playing cards, jabbering in their own language, sometimes chanting weird nostalgic tunes. They use their beds like tents. Amazing what one finds in them. All sorts of hidden food reserves to nibble on at odd hours. Bits of half-chewed cheese, biscuits, coloured candies, a square of mangey chocolate tediously wrapped up in newspaper, a broken comb, a piece of mirror.

We can't get Allah up. We can't do anything with Allah. He has his own ideas. He lies all day long with the covers pulled over his head, and his dirty yellow feet protruding well beyond the bed.

Ali Ben Hassam can be dismissed tomorrow, for convalescent leave. But Ben Ali doesn't want to go. His friends are all here . . . why should he go away? Next morning, just before the doctor's round, he starts moaning and groaning, and develops a terrible pain in his stomach. It works. The doctor orders tea only, but under the cover of the sheets he stuffs all that his comrades have stolen for him . . . a meal in itself. The next day at the appointed hour the terrible pain has shifted mysteriously to his head, and is accompanied by frenzied dirges to Allah (the real Allah, of course). The doctor smiles. The third day he is sternly ordered out. The last I saw of Ali Ben Hassam was his back, and the sad droop and pinched look of his shoulder blades as he trudged down the road, quite alone . . . and very far from his native land.

Several weeks have passed, and we get our first breathing spell. Many of the men are up. Some of the beds are empty.

We have time now for flowers. Each ward has its bunch of daisies, long-stemmed buttercups or foxgloves. In the late afternoons, we go with our sewing things and repair tears on blood-stained uniforms that smell strongly of sweat. These are the gracious tasks. Flowers always bring cheers and thanks. Magazines too, even though they are torn and smudged. The only two puzzles are put together, pulled apart, put together again and again. But it is our sitting there with our sewing that the men love the most.

Reliving this first period, which at the time I thought such a terrible trial and so full of heartaches over the hopelessness of the conditions, I realize now that it was mere child's play, and in view of what followed, it was just an initiation.

For suddenly, our few days of respite were at an end. Orders came through to make ready. A new lot were on the way.

Midnight past. Still waiting for the ambulances. They were due at ten. It has been a long day, and a hard one, with so many beds to shift around, and everything to make ready. Now the place is quiet. In the wards the men doze fitfully. Subconsciously, they too are waiting. Our new blackout shades throw rings of pale sickly light on the concrete floor. We talk in hushed voices with the doctors and orderlies, smoking innumerable cigarettes and taking turns to sit on the two wooden benches in the entrance.

Here they come . . . the first ambulance . . . second, third, tenth, seventeenth. How many are there? One by one the men are lifted out and the stretchers laid on the floor. The entrance is filled. The corridors too . . . The ghastly, unbelievable suffering. The cries. The groans. The distorted, dilated eyes. No words can describe this scene, nor will any amount of time ever efface it from my memory. Six in the morning. We have just left G5. No question of sleep. Even if one wanted to, one couldn't. Besides, we must be back in a few hours.

I have had a bath. That is to say, I have sat cross-legged in my rubber tub, and poured a pitcher of lukewarm water over me. There is no running water where I live. The lack of rain has dried the wells, and we are limited to two small pitchers a day. This is uncomfortable enough at any time, but in the heat, and today of all days, it is a calamity. Water can wash away so many things.

Eight-thirty. I linger over coffee. Pour a second cup. Light a second cigarette. I've got to go back up there. No use thinking that something will happen to save me. Nothing will. I really am a coward. Now I know it for sure. Slowly, very slowly . . . up the hill, to G5.

One look over the wards is enough. Enough to make one want to run. The further away the better.

I don't know much about a dying man, but No. 19 is going to die. Can't call for Nanotte, she's been transferred to the sterilization room. I'll get the Polish nurse, who has the last three wards on the ground floor. Mustn't run. Must walk. No one has told me this, but I'm sure. The others mustn't know what's happening, mustn't sense my panic. The Polish nurse also says he's dying. We must get him out of the ward. We must have a doctor's permission to move him. The doctors are operating. Can I open the door . . . and just go in? Every moment counts. I open the door, step inside, close it quickly. Help. What are they doing to this one. Another leg I guess, but I can't quite see. He is surrounded. The basins are full of blood. The heat and stench are nauseating. Strangely enough, the butterfly doesn't turn a hair. The doctor has seen me at last, but he is still intent. Finally: well, what is it? Doctor, No. 19 in Ward 1, the man with the leg off at the hip, is dying. Will you give me permission to get him out of the ward? Yes – go ahead – I'll come up when I can. But he never came. There was nothing he could have done, and he knew it.

Upstairs, in a little bedroom, with windows tightly closed, Charvet, the Infirmier Major, who was a soldier and not a doctor, and myself, waited and watched No. 19 struggle to die. It took about an hour, and I was foolish enough to think all the time that, in spite of everything, I could *will* him to live.

And a few moments later, the blood donors arrived. If they had come sooner . . . but no use thinking that now. There are others. Six more in my wards who need transfusions. Remember: walk, don't run.

That night, after more than twenty-six hours on duty, I slept. But even in sleep, the nightmare didn't let me go. My dying fellow was with me all the time, squashing May-bugs between his fingers, and calling for Jeanette. Next morning, the same heavy feeling of dread. With faltering steps, faltering heart, and precious little courage . . . back to G5.

Since Nanotte's desertion, I'm all alone. Alone in the same three wards (sixty beds in all), and because these wards are nearest to the air-raid shelters, all the worst wounded are there. No one to tell me anything now, neither how nor what nor why. All I know is that the doctors rely on me to keep cool and clear.

Charts and temperatures come first, of course. I had done these with Nanotte, but never alone. Then, the washing, which alone is also a job. And all the time, through everything, a traffic of stretchers going to and coming from the dressing room, all in prescribed order. And . . . those beds which for a time are empty, to make over quickly. And then always be there when the poor devil is brought back, usually with undried tears on his cheeks. From another list, others who must be X-rayed, and sent to another building altogether. Luckily I do not have to go into the dressing-room often . . . but one can't help hearing.

This way, stretcher-bearers. Easy now . . . legs first . . . and by inches, the rest of the body. Be careful going out the door, I tell you. Too late. They've bumped him. Brutes. And on the top of everything, they have the nerve to grumble.

No. 15 is twenty years old, and has hardly more than a torso left to him. No. 8 is amputated below the knees, and his two stumps stick up in the air. No. 16 is much older. He was a stretcher-bearer. He has lost one arm, and has a bad bullet wound in the other shoulder. And so on.

Listen to them talk, only three days later . . . and know what kept me going and why I didn't run away.

No. 15 (the legless fellow) has decided to be a ballet dancer – no, a tight-rope walker. No. 16 (without an arm) is going in for boxing. No. 8 (also amputated) thinks that a bit of skiing would do him a world of good. Nos. 11 and 9 (each lacking a foot) pipe up and decide that tap dancing will be their cup of tea. And so on. Jokes of this sort are tossed back and forth across the wards, and we all laugh. Pity is the one thing which one cannot offer.

No. 7 is finally beginning to register, and take note of his surroundings. He had lost his speech and senses, and has been
lying there for five days in an open-eyed gaze, which was getting us all down, who by now were prone to chatter.

Speaking of washing: it takes days of hard scrubbing to get the
blood off their hands, and it's almost impossible to get it out of
their nails, so deeply is it lodged. Hair is matted and clotted with
it.

Some of the old ones are still with me, including Allah, who has
turned into an angel. *'Bonjour La Ma Sœur. Allah très sage. La
Ma Sœur beaucoup à faire. Allah aide La Ma Sœur.'* He fetches
water, carries things, is always hanging around to do odd jobs,
and trots off with a beaming face, full of importance to do them.
The same with Napoleon, the Corsican and Buddah, the Indo-
Chinaman.

In the outside world, so mixed up with ours, the air is full of
goodbyes. The Poles are off, singing as usual. Belgians and French
are coming in. There is confusion in the camp. The other night the
French Battalion of Tanks had moved up to the Front. All day
they have thundered past, shaking the bowels of the earth, pow-
dering the dust to smaller and ever smaller atoms. The
Commanding Officer was our friend, and many others, so we
went down to the next junction to see them off. The tanks were
strung with branches of laurel and yellow gorse. All the men were
singing. One would have thought that they were off to the Battle
of Flowers at Nice. The evening sky was cloudless. The singing
went zigzagging off into the night, and we were left, at least I was,
remembering the men at G5, with an unwanted and silly choke
caught somewhere in my throat.

Thank God for work. I go back to G5 after supper, and in the
mornings rise earlier, hardly able to wait, for I am only happy
when I am there. In between times, I bathe my feet and swollen
ankles with the water left over in my hot water bottle – a little
trick I've devised, a way of cheating, to get more water, for we are
down to one small pitcher a day now. The heat is terrific.

I have found a refuge of quiet. It is a miniature valley beyond
the refuse dump back of the cafe. The wheat is up to my waist.
Cherry trees come bursting over the top, like giant old-fashioned
bouquets. There are daisies too, very white, and swaying slightly
in the moonlight.

Five hundred more wounded have just come in. I do not know where they will be put. But this is no business of mine. All my beds are full.

You from G5, where are you today? You who called me l'Ange Rose . . . how could I have deserted you as I did? Walked out five minutes before the Germans walked in? You who had no one, who were powerless to move, what did you think and feel that morning of 18 June? Did Nanotte go, as she promised me to do, from bed to bed (this was the only thing I had time to arrange), telling you each in turn that I was forced to leave, that my husband, who was a Pole, had come back at the last minute – dropped mysteriously from the blue – and taken me away, that I had no choice? By now, you have understood no doubt . . . and perhaps you have forgiven me. But will you ever, ever know what this cost me? Or how much I loved you . . . all your queer mutilated shapes which I know by heart, but which frightened me so much at first?

More than a year has passed since then, yet time and distance do not take you from me. Wherever you are, believe me, I am still with you. And may God forgive me that I wasn't even capable of treating your bed-sores, which were wounds in themselves, open and festering. *I was too ignorant.*

KAY BOYLE

Defeat

Towards the end of June that year and through July, there was a sort of uncertain pause, an undetermined suspension that might properly be called neither an armistice nor a peace, and it lasted until the men began coming back from where they were. They came at intervals, trickling down from the north in twos or threes, or even one by one, some of them prisoners who had escaped and others merely a part of that individual retreat in which the sole destination was home. They had exchanged their uniforms for something else as they came along – corduroys, or workmen's blue, or whatever people might have given them in secret to get away in – bearded, singularly and shabbily outfitted men getting down from a bus or off a train without so much as a knapsack in their hands and all with the same bewildered, scarcely discrepant story to tell. Once they had reached the precincts of familiarity, they stood there a moment where the vehicle had left them, maybe trying to button the jacket that didn't fit them or set the neck or shoulders right, like men who have been waiting in a courtroom and have finally heard their names called and stand up to take the oath and mount the witness stand. You could see them getting the words ready – revising the very quality of truth – and the look in their eyes, and then someone coming out of the post office or crossing the station square in the heat would recognize them and go towards them with a hand out, and the testimony would begin.

They had found their way back from different places, by different means, some on bicycle, some by bus, some over the mountains on foot, coming home to the Alpes-Maritimes from Rennes, or from Clermont-Ferrand, or from Lyons, or from any part of France, and looking as incongruous to modern defeat as survivors of the Confederate Army might have looked, transplanted to this year and place (with their spurs still on and their soft-brimmed, dust-whitened hats), limping wanly back, half dazed and not yet having managed to get the story of what happened straight. Only, this time, they were the men of that tragically unarmed and undirected force which had been the French Army once but was no longer, returning to what orators might call reconstruction but which they knew could never be the same.

Wherever they came from, they had identical evidence to give: that the German ranks had advanced bareheaded, in short-sleeved summer shirts – young blond-haired men with their arms linked, row on row, and their trousers immaculately creased, having slept all night in hotel beds and their stomachs full, advancing singing and falling singing before the puny coughing of the French machine-guns. That is, the first line of them might fall, and part of the second, possibly, but never more, for just then the French ammunition would suddenly expire and the bright-haired blond demi-gods would march on singing across their dead. Then would follow all the glittering display: the rust-proof tanks and guns, the chromium electric kitchens, the crematoriums. Legends or truth, the stories became indistinguishable in the mouths of the Frenchmen who returned – that the Germans were dressed as if for tennis that summer, with nothing but a tune to carry in their heads, while the French crawled out from under lorries where they'd slept maybe every night for a week, going to meet them like crippled, encumbered miners emerging from the pit of a warfare fifty years interred with thirty-five kilos of kit and a change of shoes and a tin helmet left over from 1914 breaking them in two as they met the brilliantly nickelled Nazi dawn. They said their superiors were the first to run; they said their ammunition had been sabotaged; they said the ambulances had been transformed into accommodations for the officers' lady friends; they said *Nous avons été vendus* or *On nous a vendu* over and over, until you could have made a popular song of it – the words and the music of defeat. After their testimony was given, some of them added (not the young but those who had fought before) in grave, part-embittered, part-vainglorious voices, 'I'm ashamed to be a Frenchman,' or, 'I'm ashamed of being French today,' and then gravely took their places with the others.

There was one man, though, who didn't say any of these things, probably because he had something else on his mind. He was a dark, short, rather gracefully made man, not thirty yet, with hot, handsome eyes and a cleft chin. Even when he came back without his uniform and without the victory, a certain air of responsibility, or authority, remained because he had been the chauffeur of the mail bus before the war. He didn't sit talking in the bistro about what he had seen and where he had been, but he got the black beard off his face as quickly as he could, and bought a pair of new shoes, and went back to work in stubborn-lipped, youthful, almost violent pride. Except one night he did tell the story; he told it only once, about two months after he got back, and not to his own people or the people of the village but, as if by chance, to two commercial travellers for rival fruit-juice firms who were just beginning to circulate again from town to town in the Unoccupied Zone. They sat at the Café Central together, the three of them, drinking wine, talking about the anachronism of horse-and-mule-drawn cannon in Flanders and the beasts running amok under the enemy planes, and saying how they had all believed that the French line was going to hold somewhere, that it wasn't going to break.

'At first we thought it would hold at the Oise,' one of the travelling men said. 'We kept on retreating, saying the new front must be at the Oise, and believing it too, and then when we dropped below the Oise, we kept saying it would hold at the Marne, and believing it, and then we thought it would be the Seine, and even when we were south of Paris we kept on believing about some kind of a line holding the Loire . . .'

'I still don't know why we stopped retreating,' said the other commercial traveller. He sat looking soberly at his glass. 'We can't talk about the Italians any more. I still don't see why we didn't retreat right down to Senegal. I don't see what stopped us,' he said. Then the quiet-mouthed little bus-driver began telling them about what had happened to him on 14 July.

He had been told, he said, that in some of the cities the enemy hadn't taken or had withdrawn from, processions formed on the 14th and passed through the streets in silence, the flagstaffs they carried draped with black and their heads bowed. In some of the villages, the mayor, dressed in mourning, laid a wreath on the monument to the last war's dead while the peasants knelt about him in the square.

'I was in Pontcharra on the 14th,' said one of the travelling salesmen, 'and when the mayor put the wreath down and the bugle called out like that for the dead, all the peasants uncovered themselves, but the military didn't even stand at attention.'

'By that time none of the privates were saluting their officers in the street anywhere you went,' said the other salesman, but the bus-driver didn't pay any attention to what they said. He went on telling them that he'd been taken prisoner near Rennes on 17 June, and that there he saw the tracts the Boche planes had showered down the week before. The tracts said, 'Frenchmen, prepare your coffins! Frenchwomen, get out your ball dresses! We're going to dance the soles off your shoes on 14 July!' He told the commercial travellers exactly what use they made of the tracts in the public places there. He was more than three weeks in the prison camp, he said, and on the night of 12 July he and a *copain* made their escape. They went in uniform, on borrowed bicycles. They kept to the main road all night, wheeling along as free and unmolested in the dark as two young men cycling home from a dance, with their hearts light, and the stars out over them, and the night air mild. At dawn they took to the side roads, and towards eight o'clock of the new day they saw a house standing alone, a little in advance of the village that lay ahead.

'We'll ask there,' the bus-driver had said, and they pushed their cycles in off the road and laid them down behind a tree. The house, they could see then, was the schoolhouse, with a sign for '*Filles*' over one door and for '*Garçons*' over the other. The *copain* said there would be nobody there, but the bus-driver had seen a woman come over to the window and look at them, and he walked up to the door.

The desks were empty because of what had happened and the time of year but the bus-driver said he knew it must have been the schoolmistress who was standing in the middle of the room between the benches, a young woman with fair, wavy hair, eyeing them fearlessly and even sharply as they came. The bus-driver and his *copain* said good morning, and they saw at once the lengths of three-coloured stuff in her hands and the work she had been doing. They looked around them and saw four French flags clustered in each corner of the classroom and great loops of bunting that were draped along three sides of the room. The first thing the bus-driver thought was that she ought to be warned, she ought to be told, and then, when he looked at her face again, he knew she knew as much as or more than they.

'You ought to keep the door locked,' he had said, and the schoolmistress looked at him almost in contempt.

'I don't care who comes in,' she said, and she went on folding the bunting into the lengths she wanted to cut it to drape across the farthest wall.

'So the village is occupied?' the bus-driver said.

'Yes,' she said, but she began cutting the tricolour bunting.

'There's one thing,' said the *copain*, looking a little bleakly at the two others. 'If you give yourself up, at least you don't get shot.'

The schoolmistress had put her scissors down and said to the bus-driver, 'You'll have to get rid of your uniforms before there's any chance of your getting through.' She glanced around the classroom as though the demands of action had suddenly made it strange to her. 'Take them off and put them in the cupboard there,' she had said, 'and cover yourselves with this stuff while you wait,' and she heaped the blue, white and red lengths upon the desks. 'In case they might come in,' she said. She took her hat and filet off the hook as she said, 'I'll come back with other clothes for you.'

'If there would be any way of getting something to eat,' the bus-driver had said, and because he asked this, the tide of courage seemed to rise even higher in her.

'Yes,' she said, 'I'll bring back food for you.'

'And a bottle of pinard,' said the *copain*, but he didn't say it very loud.

When she was gone, they took their uniforms off and wrapped the bunting around themselves, doing it for her and modesty's sake, and then they sat down at the first form's desks, swathed to their beards in red, white and blue. Even if the Boches had walked into the schoolroom then, there probably wasn't any military regulation made to deal with what they would have found, the bus-driver had said to his *copain* – just two Frenchmen in their underwear sitting quietly inside the colours of their country's flag. But whether he said the other thing to the teacher as soon as she brought the bread and sausage and wine and the scraps of other men's clothing back, he didn't know. Sometimes, when he thought of it afterwards, he wasn't quite sure he had ever got the actual words out, but then he remembered the look on her face as she stood by the tree where the bicycles had lain and watched them pedalling towards the village just ahead, and he knew he must have said it. He knew he must have wiped the sausage grease and the wine off his mouth with the back of his hand and said, 'A country isn't defeated so long as its women aren't' or 'until its women are' or 'as long as the women of a country aren't defeated, it doesn't matter if its army is' – something like that, perhaps saying it just before they shook hands with her and cycled away.

That was the morning of the 13th, and the bus-driver told how they rode all day in the heat, two what-might-have-been-peasants cycling slowly hour after hour across the hushed, summery, sunny land. The war was over for them, for this country the war was over; there was no sound or look of it in the meadows or the trees or grain. The war was finished, but the farmhouse they stopped at that evening would not take them in.

'Have you got your bread tickets with you?' the peasant said, and even the white-haired sows behind his legs eyed them narrowly with greed.

'We're prisoners escaped. We've got a bit of money,' the bus-driver said. 'We'll pay for our soup, and maybe you'll let us sleep in the loft.'

'And when the Boches come in for the milk they'll shoot me and the family for having taken you in!' the peasant said, and the bus-driver stood looking at him bitterly a moment before he began to swear. When he had called the man the names he wanted to, he said, 'Look here, we were soldiers – perhaps you haven't got that yet? We haven't been demobilized; we were taken prisoner, we escaped. We were fighting a little war up there.'

'If you'd fought it better, the Boches wouldn't have got this far,' the peasant said. He said it in cunning and triumph, and then he closed the door.

They slept the night at the next farm (the bus-driver told the commercial travellers), eating soup and bread and drinking red wine in the kitchen, and when they had paid for it they were shown up to the loft. But they were not offered the side on which the hay lay; the farmer was thinking of next winter and he told them they could lie down just as well on the boards. They slept heavily and well, and it was very light when they woke in the morning, and so that day, the day of the 14th, they did not get far. By six that night they were only another hundred kilometres on, and then the *copain*'s tyre went flat. But a little town stood just ahead and they pushed their bicycles towards it through the summer evening, and down its wide, treeless street. They hadn't seen the uniform yet, but they knew the Germans must be there. Even on the square in the heart of town they saw no sign, but still there was that unnatural quiet, that familiar uneasiness on the air, so they pushed their wheels through the open doors of a big garage, past the dry and padlocked petrol pumps, and stood them up against the inside wall. There, in the garage's half-security and semi-dark, they looked around them; twenty or more cars stood one beside the other, halted as if forever because of the lack of fluid to flow through their veins. Overhead the glass panes of the roof were still painted blue; the military and staff cars parked in the shadowy silence still bore their green-and-khaki camouflage. The war was over, everything had stopped, and out beyond the wide-open automobile doorway they saw the dance platform that had been erected in the square, and the dark, leafy branches twined on its upright beams and balustrade, and the idle people standing looking. There were no flags up, only this rather dismal atmosphere of preparation, and it was then the bus-driver and his *copain* had remembered it was the 14th.

'It's a national holiday and we haven't had a drink yet,' the *copain* said. He stood there in the garage with his hands in the pockets of the trousers that didn't belong to him, staring bleakly out across the square. Even when two German soldiers who were putting electric wiring up in the dance pavilion came into view, his face did not alter. He simply went on saying, 'We haven't had the apéritif all day.'

The bus-driver took a packet of cigarettes out of his jacket pocket and put one savagely on his lip. As he lit it, he looked in hot, bitter virulence out to where the Germans were hanging strings of bulbs among the fresh, dark leaves.

'"Frenchmen, prepare your coffins!"' he had said, and then he gave a laugh. 'They've made only one mistake so far, just one,' he said, and as he talked the cigarette jerked up and down in fury on his lip. 'They've got the dance-floor and the decorations all right, and they've probably got the music and maybe the refreshments too. So far so good,' he said. 'But they haven't got the partners. That's what's going to be funny. That's what's going to be really funny.'

The bus-driver sat there in the Café Central telling it to the two commercial travellers, perhaps because he had had more to drink than usual, telling them the story, or perhaps because it had been weighing long enough heavy on his heart. He told them about the dinner the garage owner gave him and his *copain:* civet and fried potatoes and salad and four kinds of cheese and armagnac with the coffee. He said they could scarcely get it all down and that then their host opened a bottle of champagne for them. That's the kind of man the garage owner was. And during the dinner or afterwards, with the wine inside of him, it seems the bus-driver had said it again. He had said something about as long as the women of a nation weren't defeated the rest of it didn't matter, and just as he said it the music struck up in the dance pavilion outside.

The place the garage owner offered them for the night was just above the garage itself, a sort of storeroom, with three windows overlooking the square. First he repaired the *copain*'s tyre for him, and behind him on the wall as he worked they read the newspaper cutting he had pinned up, perhaps in some spirit of derision. It exhorted all Frenchmen to accept quietly and without protest the new regulations concerning the circulation of private and public vehicles.

'Without protest!' the garage owner had said, taking the dripping red tube out of the basin of water and pinching the leak between his finger and thumb. 'I'll have to close this place up, and they ask me to do it without protest.' He stood rubbing sandpaper gently around where the imperceptible hole in the rubber was. 'We weren't ready for war and yet we declared it just the same,' he said, 'and now we've asked for peace and we aren't ready for that, either.' When he had finished with the tyre he showed them up the stairs.

'I'll keep the light off,' he said, 'in case it might give them the idea of coming up and having a look,' but there was no need for any light, for the illumination of the dance pavilion in the square shone in through the windows and lit the rows of storage batteries and the cases of spare parts and spark plugs. From outside, they heard the music playing – the exact waltz time and the quick, entirely martial version of swing.

'Somebody ought to tell them they're wasting their time,' the bus-driver had said, jerking one shoulder towards the windows.

He could have burst out laughing at the sight of them, he explained, some with white gloves on even, waiting out there, to the strains of music for what wasn't going to come.

The garage owner shook out the potato sacks of waste on the floor and gave them the sacks to lie down on, and then he took one look out of the window at the square and grinned and said good night and went downstairs. The *copain* was tired and he lay down at once on the soft rags on the floor and drew a blanket up over him, but the bus-driver had stood a while at one side of the window, watching the thing below. A little group of townspeople was standing around the platform where the variously coloured lights hung, and the band was playing in one corner of the pavilion underneath the leaves. No one was dancing, but the German soldiers were hanging around in expectation, some standing on the steps of the platform and some leaning on the garnished rails.

'For a while there wasn't a woman anywhere,' the bus-driver told the commercial travellers. 'There was this crowd of people from the town, perhaps thirty or forty of them looking on, and maybe some others further back in the dark where you couldn't see them, but that was all,' and then he stopped talking.

'And then what happened?' said one of the travelling men after a moment, and the bus-driver sat looking in silence at his glass.

'They had a big, long table spread out with things to eat on it,' he said in a minute, and he didn't look up. 'They had fruit tarts, it looked like, and sweet chocolate, and bottles of lemonade and beer. They had as much as you wanted of everything,' he said. 'And perhaps once you got near enough to start eating and drinking, then the other thing just followed naturally afterwards – or that's the way I worked it out,' he said. 'Or maybe, if you've had a dress a long time that you wanted to wear and you hadn't had the chance of putting it on and showing it off because the men were away – I mean if you were a woman. I worked it out that maybe the time comes when you want to put it on so badly that you put it on just the same whatever's happened, or maybe, if you're one kind of a woman, any kind of a uniform looks all right to you after a certain time. The music was good, it was first class,' he said, but he didn't look up. 'And here was all this food spread out and the corks popping off the bottles, and the lads in uniform, great big fellows, handing out chocolates to all the girls . . .'

The three of them sat at the table without talking for a while after the bus-driver's voice had ceased, and then one of the travelling men said, 'Well, that was just one town.'

'Yes, that was just one town,' said the bus-driver, and when he picked up his glass to drink, something as crazy as tears was standing in his eyes.

MOLLIE PANTER-DOWNES

Goodbye, My Love

Adrian's mother welcomed them as though this were just an ordinary visit, with nothing particular about it. They found her, as they had found her so many times before, working in the big herbaceous border facing the sea, crouching girlishly with a frail little green plant in the palm of one earthy hand. She greeted them abstractedly, pushing back her wispy grey hair with the back of the hand that held the trowel and leaving a smudge. While they talked, Ruth looked at the border, which Adrian had built for his mother on a ledge of the cliff garden, facing it with a paved path beside which the rosemary and the seeded mulleins sprang. Even now, in late autumn, with the sea mist hanging in drops on the spiders' webs that festooned the last red-hot pokers, it was beautiful. Sometimes Ruth wondered if the cold woman, her mother-in-law, didn't express some secret frustration in these savage reds and yellows, these sullen purples, which she caused to gush out of the warm Cornish earth.

Ruth was grateful now for the lack of outward emotion which had so often chilled her. When Mrs Vyner asked Adrian, as they walked back to the house, 'Which day do you go?' she might have been asking about some weekend visit he was going to make. He said, 'Wednesday', and she repeated, 'Wednesday' in a vague voice, her attention wandering to a bough of japonica which the wind had loosened from the wall they were passing. She sat down on the porch to unlace her shocking old gardening boots.

'I suppose you don't know where you're going to be sent,' she said. 'I know it has to be very secret nowadays, because of the submarines.'

'I think it's Syria,' Adrian said. 'From the stuff we're taking, I'm pretty certain.'

'You can't be sure,' Mrs Vyner said. 'There's a Mrs Mason who's come to live at the Cross Glens. You know, Adrian, where old Colonel Fox used to live. Well, Captain Mason went off with a topee and shorts, poor man, and the next thing she heard was that he was sitting up on a fjord in Iceland. It's all done to put the spies on the wrong track. I'll point Mrs Mason out to you in church tomorrow.'

Later, when the Rector came in, he made more of an occasion of it than his wife had. He gave Ruth a heartier kiss than usual. 'It's good of you to think of the old people when you've got so little time left,' he said. Ruth disliked the phrase 'so little time left'. Suddenly she was inordinately conscious of time. The house was full of it, ticking between simpering shepherdesses on the mantelpiece, grumbling out of the tall mahogany case in the hall, nervously stuttering against Adrian's wrist. The church clock, just across the rectory garden, struck every quarter. Ruth thought, 'Four days, and one of them nearly gone.'

After dinner the Rector got out *The Times* atlas and pored over it with Adrian, while Mrs Vyner sat knitting a sock and talking about the garden and the village. The Rector's broad thumb, tracing the possible course that a convoy would take out into the Atlantic, swooped down upon the Cape. He and Adrian sounded quiet and contented, as though they were plotting a fishing holiday.

Ruth and her mother-in-law sat knitting a little apart, chatting in low voices.

'The black spot has been dreadful on the roses this year,' Mrs Vyner said. 'Really dreadful. What do you plan to do after he's gone?'

'I shall get a job,' Ruth said. 'I thought I might go into one of the services. Shorthand and typing ought to be useful. Anyway, I'm going to do something.'

'That's sensible,' Mrs Vyner said. 'After all, you'll be perfectly free, won't you? It isn't as though you have any ties.'

'No, I've got no ties at all,' Ruth said.

When they were undressing in the big, chilly guest room, she said to Adrian, 'Somehow, now that you're going I wish we'd had a child. You know, the Sonnets and all that – "And nothing 'gainst Time's scythe can make defence, Save breed, to brave him when he takes thee hence."'

'I'm not sorry,' Adrian said. 'This way I shan't be missing anything. When I get back we'll have the fun of kids together.'

'Yes, we will,' Ruth said, raising her voice slightly, as though she were talking to someone behind him. 'How long do you think the war's going to last?' she asked, picking up her hair-brush.

'Darling! As though it matters a damn what I think. I don't know – maybe another couple of years or so.'

'Some people say it will be over next spring.'

'Some people talk a hell of a lot of nonsense,' he said.

The bed was a big, old-fashioned double, its mattress divided into two gentle troughs where successive generations of guests had lain. Ruth got in and pulled the covers up to her chin. She watched Adrian moving around the room. 'They were an awful long time demobilizing people after the last war, weren't they?' she said. 'Maybe the firm would make a special application for you, or whatever they do. After all, they'll be terribly anxious to get you back. Mr Hobday told me himself that he didn't know how they were going to get on without you.'

'Oh, they'll manage,' Adrian said.

At intervals all through the night, Ruth kept waking up and listening to the sea. She pictured it running up the jagged inlets of the long, cruel coast, along which she and Adrian had often sailed in his little boat. He was asleep, breathing softly and lightly, his face close to her shoulder. She lay thinking this way until it began to get light and the birds started shouting in Mrs Vyner's wild garden.

They went to church next morning, walking through the gate in the yew hedge into the bleak little churchyard. The congregation that had come to hear the Rector preach was small and badly dressed, for the parish was thinly populated and poor. It was easy, without Mrs Vyner's whisper, to identify the more prosperous Mrs Mason, tweedy in a front pew, with a plain little girl on either side. Captain Mason had at least provided her with two defences 'gainst Time's scythe, hideous though they were in their spectacles and with gold bands round their teeth, before he took himself off to his Icelandic fjords. Ruth looked across the aisle at Mrs Mason, who was cheerfully singing the Te Deum. 'I'll get used to it, too,' she thought. The only other representative of the local gentry in church was Major Collingwood, who read the lessons in a voice beautifully husky with Irish whiskey and buttonholed Adrian afterwards in the porch. 'Well, my boy! Just off, I hear,' he said. 'Going East, I suppose? No, no, don't tell me – mustn't ask, mustn't ask. Well, it looks like a big showdown there this winter. Hitler's going to try and break through. Yes, we've got to be prepared for heavy fighting, heavy fighting.'

'The old fool,' Ruth thought. She walked away and began reading some of the inscriptions on the crosses of local grey stone at the heads of the few green mounds in the churchyard. Most of the men were fishermen who had been drowned in winter storms along the coast. 'John Tregarthen, who lost his life off Black Point, 10 December 1897,' she read. 'Samuel Cotter, drowned in the wreck of the *Lady May*, 25 January 1902.'

Adrian came up and took her arm. 'Hungry?' he asked. She shook her head, and he saw that there were tears in her eyes. 'Damn that old idiot!' he said. 'Darling, it's going to be a quiet winter. What do you bet? We'll be stuck in some bloody desert, eating our heads off with boredom. We're going to be forgotten men, forgotten by Hitler, forgotten by the General Staff, forgotten by –'

'It's all right,' she said.

Mrs Vyner came up, fastening her shabby fur round her long, thin neck, and the three of them walked back into the rectory garden.

Next day, Ruth and Adrian went back to London. That night they went out with friends and had plenty to drink. Ruth was able to sleep that night. The next evening, their last, they dined quietly in the flat. She had cooked the things he liked best, but neither of them had much appetite. At last they gave up trying. The one clock in the flat went on sucking time, like an endless string of macaroni, into its bright, vacant face. Every clock in London seemed to crash out the quarters outside their drawn curtains. When the telephone rang as they sat over their coffee, Adrian got up to answer it as though he were glad of the interruption. It turned out to be a man who used to be in love with Ruth and who had been out of England for some time. Adrian had always disliked him, but he sounded very cordial now. Afterwards he said, 'I'm glad Mike has turned up again. I want you to go out with him. That's why I said to him just now, "When I'm gone I'd take it as a personal favour if you'd give Ruth a ring now and then and take her out and give her a good time."'

'I don't want to go out with Mike,' she said.

'Please do,' he said. 'It will make me feel better to think of you looking pretty, out dancing and enjoying yourself.'

The following morning there was plenty to do – breakfast, a taxi, last-minute things. Meeting at some moment in the bustling, efficient nightmare, Adrian said, 'I don't suppose I'll be able to wire you, but I'll give someone a letter to post from the port after we sail,' and Ruth said, 'That will be fine.' She felt cold and frightened and a little sick, as though this were the morning fixed for a major operation. She wasn't going to the station, so they said goodbye in the hall, a tiny cupboard built for a man to hang his hat in, for a woman to read a telephone message in – not for heroic partings.

'Well, take care of yourself,' Adrian said. 'Don't forget what we said last night. If the bombings start again, you go down to Cornwall, you go anywhere. Anyway, you get out of here. Promise? Otherwise I won't be able to keep my mind on this war.'

'I promise,' Ruth said, smiling. Language was inadequate, after all. One used the same words for a parting which might be for years, which might end in death, as one did for an overnight business trip. She put her arms tightly round him and said, 'Goodbye, my love.'

'Darling,' he said. 'I can't begin to tell you –'

'Don't,' she said. 'Don't.'

The door shut, and presently Ruth heard the taxi driving away. She went back into the living room, sat down, and looked at the breakfast things. Adrian's cup was still half full of coffee, a cigarette stubbed out in the wet saucer. The cigarette seemed to have acquired a significance, to be the kind of relic which in another age would have been put carefully away in a little box with the toenail parings of a dead man, the hair clippings of a dead woman.

The next two days were bad. Ruth felt that the major operation had come off but that she still had not come round from the anaesthetic. She pottered about the flat, went for a walk, bought some things she wanted, dropped in at a movie and a concert. Time now seemed to have receded, to be an enormous empty room which she must furnish, like any other aimless woman, with celluloid shadows of other people's happiness, with music that worked one up for nothing. An hour or so after Adrian left, she put through a call to Cornwall. 'Adrian's gone,' she said, and across the bad line, across a rival conversation between two men who were trying to arrange a board meeting, she heard her mother-in-law's calm, tired voice saying, 'Yes, it's Wednesday, isn't it? I knew he was going on Wednesday.' As she hung up the receiver, she suddenly remembered a French governess out of her childhood who used to rage, weeping with anger, 'Oh, you British, you British!' Her friends rang her up with careful, planned kindness. Their stock opening was 'Has he gone? Oh, you poor darling! But aren't you terribly relieved it's over?' and then they would date her up for a dinner or a theatre. Their manner was caressing but sprightly, as though she were a stretcher case who mustn't be allowed to know that she was suffering from shock. She slept very badly and had terrible dreams, into which the sea always seemed to come. She went to sleep picturing the blacked-out ship creeping out cautiously into the dark sea. The girl who washed her hair had once told her that her brother had been torpedoed off Norway and that he had been rescued, covered with oil from the explosion. In one of Ruth's dreams Adrian was struggling in a sea of oil while Mrs Vyner, watching from her cliff garden, said 'Yes, it's Wednesday, isn't it? I knew he was going to drown on Wednesday.'

On the third day, Ruth woke up feeling different. It was a queer feeling, exhausted but peaceful, as though her temperature had fallen for the first time after days of high fever. The end of something had been reached, the limit of some capacity for suffering. Nothing would be quite as bad again. She thought, 'After all, there are thousands of women going through what I'm going through, and they don't make a fuss.' She got up and dressed, with particular care, because she planned to go round to one of the women's recruiting stations today and find out about a job. It would be important to make a good impression at the first interview. Afterwards she would write a funny letter about it to Adrian, she thought. Although it would probably be months before any mail caught up with him, she would write tonight and tell him not to worry, that she had finished making a fuss and was being sensible, like all the other women in England – like Mrs Mason, the jolly woman in tweeds singing away at the Te Deum as though there were still something to be thankful about.

She was out all day, and when she put her latchkey in the door she was humming. As she took off her hat, the telephone rang, and she went to it, still humming, and said 'Hello?' Adrian's voice said 'Darling?' and her knees went weak. She sat down suddenly, while his voice raced on, sounding excited and a bit blurred, as though he had had two or three drinks. 'I'm at the station, I'll be right round. Got to the port, but something went wrong. We all waited, then the message came through that it was cancelled. I wasn't allowed to phone you.'

'Cancelled?' she said stupidly. 'You're not going?'

'Not for another week,' he said. 'Maybe ten days. God, what luck. I'm going out to find a taxi. Darling, don't move until I get there.'

Ruth heard the click as he hung up, and she hung up slowly, too. For a moment she sat quite still. The clock on the table beside her sounded deafening again, beginning to mark off the ten days at the end of which terror was the red light at the end of the tunnel. Then her face became drawn and, putting her hands over it, she burst into tears.

MOLLY LEFEBURE

Night in the Front Line

''Alf a mo, 'Itler, 'alf a mo,' said Mrs Minnow as the remains of her former staircase descended upon her, burying her in a welter of wood, dust and plaster.

She struggled and groped in the darkness, her one thought to find the attaché case of valuables which she had placed handy when she had retired under the stairs for refuge at the commencement of the raid. As she groped she talked.

'Wot the b— 'ell. I've been bombed that's wot. Well, nothing like it. Where'd I put that case? Well I'll be blowed. 'Ere it is, just where I thought.' And clutching the case tightly she heaved, scrambled and fought her way out from the debris surrounding her, and stumbling over many unexpected and unseen obstacles for several desperate moments, found herself in the brick-littered street.

'I been bombed that's wot,' said Mrs Minnow once again. 'Lucky I'm not 'urt and lucky I was under them stairs.'

'You all right, ma?' said a man's voice. It was the warden. Mrs Minnow staunchly replied yes. He told her to wait a tick and disappeared again. Mrs Minnow, recovered from her first shock, was now able to take stock of the world about her. It was a very confused world. The night was furiously bloodstained by the blazing docks and quivering in the echoing blasphemy of the guns. Great flashes of searing gunfire rick-racked across the sky and the exploding shells burst there like burning and passionate kisses. Below this vast dome of sound and fury seethed a human clamour; shouting, crying, screaming, traffic hooting and ambulance bells clanging, footsteps racing in the dark; people colliding, searching, cursing, dying.

Mrs Minnow was most intensely aware of another sound which grew closer every minute ... a steady, belly-thumping, rhythmic, slow, low throb, gaining upon the ear till it was directly overhead, beating the world out; then three long streaks of sound, like the tearing of three long strips of silk, and Mrs Minnow was crouching beside what had been left of her front doorstep, with the world rumbling, tumbling around her again. Another warden helped her up and she dusted herself down. She tried to say something appropriate to his kindness and the occasion, but only managed to gasp, 'Getting a bit too much if you ask me.'

'You all right?' asked the warden.

'Yes,' said Mrs Minnow.

'All right, you trot along to the school, they'll take care of you there. Mind the 'ose pipes.'

Clutching her case Mrs Minnow started to grope her way to the school. The pavements were littered with debris and hose pipes snaked across them. Now and then she was obliged to make detours. She overtook Mr and Mrs East, also bound for the school. Mrs East was weeping bitterly. Mr East carried the canary and wore his old straw hat.

''Ouse is gone,' he said laconically. 'Direct it on Mason's. All killed they say. Three little kids there.'

'It's a bloody shame to leave kids in this,' said Mrs Minnow. ''Ell it is, proper 'ell. Blimey, 'ere comes Jerry again.'

'Oh, never mind 'im,' said Mr East with superb scorn. 'Where was you, in the Anderson?'

'No, under the stairs. The others all went along to the Landers' Anderson . . . I say I 'ope they're all right . . . no, I was under the stairs. I'd took a look at the fire and didn't like the look of things so I went under the stairs. Always reckoned safe in the last war stairs was . . .'

'Bombs is different this war,' said Mr East. 'Where's old Jim?'

'Down at the docks 'elping put out the fire.'

'All that nice furniture gone and the nice new clock wot our Jack give us,' wailed Mrs East. 'Oh, lemme die, lemme die.'

'Now 'old on, Liza,' said Mr East. 'Cheer up, Liza. We're nearly there now. Oughta be glad you're alive you ought. Downright ungrateful that's wot you are.'

They came to the school. The big hall was crowded with people, most of them lying upon rugs and mattresses on the floor. The lights had gone out and lamps were being used. Somebody gave Mrs Minnow a cup of hot tea and a biscuit. She sat on a canvas stool drinking the tea and nibbling the biscuit.

'Don't think much of that biscuit,' she remarked presently to a small woman beside her. 'Government oughter be able to give us a better biscuit 'n that.'

'My Joey's gone,' said the small woman, in a monotonous voice. 'I've lost my Joey.'

'What 'appened, duck?' asked Mrs Minnow kindly.

'My Joey's gone,' said the small woman again. 'I've lost my Joey.'

'Nutty,' observed the stout lady on Mrs Minnow's right.

'You oughta go to 'ospital,' said Mrs Minnow to Joey's mother. 'Ain't there nobody to take care of 'er proper?' she asked.

'She'll be orright. We'll all be orright in the morning or else we'll be bleeding well dead.'

Mrs Minnow finished her biscuit and went in search of Mrs East. She was still weeping and did not respond to Mrs Minnow's kindly attentions. 'Blooming downpour,' said Mrs Minnow, a trifle disgusted. 'Blimey, I'll be glad to get outa this. Wot's the good of crying over spilt milk.' She felt cold and weary. The hall was packed with people and she found a place on the floor in the corridor. A woman with two small boys gave her a blanket to wrap up in.

'We was in a shelter,' she told Mrs Minnow. ''Ad our blankets there and our clothes.' She indicated the bulging pillow-cases her children rested their heads upon. 'Blasted bomb dropped near the shelter. We was about the only ones to get out all right.'

'Musta been a nasty shock.'

'Not 'alf,' said the mother. She didn't say much more, but looked nervously at her children now and again. Mrs Minnow saw her extend a furtive hand and run it over the smallest child's slumbering body.

They lay there. It was chilly and dark. Around them the murmuring of many voices, sounds of broken weeping and low moaning. Heavy raucous snores. Again and again the engines of German planes thumping and circling overhead, the screaming of falling bombs, dull shattering explosions . . . Mrs Minnow's heart pounding in pulpy dread as she pressed her stout person as flat as possible against the hard unyielding floor as if she would burrow a shallow hole there and in it hide.

Presently, through sheer exhaustion, she slept. Her sleep was thick, murky and blotched with the dust of debris and the smoke of fire. She would suddenly start awake, to find her stomach cold and sick and her hip-bone sticking sharply into the floor. Then she would mutter, sigh heavily and sleep again.

In the early hours of the morning she was once more flung awake, her head splintering into many little pieces, her brain ripped into fragments by the agonized shrieking of many persons. Something stifling was pressing her down, there was a vast roaring and the sliding shaking of buildings collapsing.

Her first instinct was to lie quite still, while the floor seemingly tilted and retilted beneath her. Then it steadied. Something warm trickled down her left leg. A woman's voice yelled in agony. 'Get me out! Get me out!'

Mrs Minnow began to heave and struggle. She rose and fell in the debris like an ooze-embedded prehistoric monster reincarnating. More plaster, more dust, more splintering wood. After long suffocating moments of kicking and clawing, panting and groaning, a hand seized her shoulder and a rough voice said, ''Old on ma, we've got you.'

She emerged. She noticed, without realizing the full meaning of her escape, that a great lump of stone had fallen a few feet from her. Beside her, beneath broken rafter and rubbish, something moaned and moved. Her shivering mind recalled her case. She cried, 'My case, my case,' and tried to stoop to search for it in the dust and muck at her feet, but somebody took hold of her and led her into the playground. She sat on some stone steps. She felt inside her blouse where she had pinned her purse and old-age pension book and they were still there. She held her hands close to her face . . . inspected them . . . they were black with grime. She pulled up her torn skirt and looked at her leg; it bore a slight cut.

She sat very still. The guns thundered and exhorted; she paid them no heed. Then a picture flashed before her eyes, a sound cut her ears: the mother of the two little boys, following a man carrying one of them. She uttered strange shrill cries. Her face was white and open like a window when the curtains blow through. Her hands drooped in front of her, lacerated and bloodstained from her wild efforts to dig out her children.

Mrs Minnow recoiled. Then she got up. She was going to clear out of this. She was going to find a nice deep shelter and stay there till it was all over. Get away. Hide and get right away from it all. Her brain sagged as though the elastic had gone from an old pair of knickers. She mooched across the playground, down the street. She narrowly escaped being knocked over by an ambulance.

A policeman stopped her. 'Where are you going, mother?'

'A shelter,' said Mrs Minnow. 'I wanta shelter. A deep shelter.'

The policeman took her to a shelter; he was a kind man. Mrs Minnow descended into that humid atmosphere and there, huddled on a bench below ground, inert and motionless, she waited for the morning. When the All Clear sounded she ascended into the desolate, smoking, reeking wasteland which had been her world and was now a dark pile of ruins. She thought only of getting out of the place and going to her sister in Chingford. She felt dimly that first she should look for her old man, though what would be the good? However, she made her way towards the docks, but was stopped by a police barricade. She was told they were still putting out the fire. She turned to go back home, but remembered home was no more, and reaching the end of her street one glance told her it was of no use to stop there. She said to a warden she knew, 'If my Jim comes 'ome tell 'im I've gone to Elsie's at Chingford.'

The warden said he would.

She was given a lift on a coster's pony-cart to Bow Road. Here the coster met his brother's wife who was evacuating with his own family to Ilford, and as there was not enough room on the cart for them all Mrs Minnow was put down on the pavement, expressing her thanks and saying she hoped they would all meet again in better times. Then she walked on, along Bow Road to Stratford.

On either side walked people like herself; some wheeling their salvaged belongings in prams, others pushing little hand carts such as children play with in the streets, others carrying cases or stuffed pillow-cases, others just like Mrs Minnow with only themselves rescued from the bombs.

Along the roadway streamed a constant procession of little carts, cars, lorries, vans, conveying escaping families with their hastily snatched belongings; some had even managed to bring away bedding and furniture. Buses also passed, packed with paper-faced children.

A young woman carrying a baby and followed by a girl of ten and a little boy, struggling to bear between them a bulging old case, approached Mrs Minnow and asked, 'Got a pram?'

'No,' said Mrs Minnow.

'Know anybody 'oo 'as?'

'No.'

'This case is bleeding 'eavy,' said the young woman plaintively.

Mrs Minnow shook her head and walked on. She felt as though her feet would drop off and decided to hitch-hike, so she stopped on the kerb edge and raised a forlorn thumb to a passing lorry. It did not stop.

'Blooming 'ard-'earted un-Christian be'aviour,' said Mrs Minnow bitterly, turning to a young woman waiting at the nearby bus stop. The buses and trolley-buses were few and far between, and when they came they were filled to overflowing. Mrs Minnow tried boarding one or two but retired defeated. Suddenly she wanted to talk. To talk and go on talking. She turned once more to the young woman and recited her woes in a blank abandoned monologue.

'Bombed twice I been. Once in me own 'ouse . . . then in the school. School full of people . . . nearly all killed. Oh, terrible it's been, terrible. But I'm getting out of it, going to me sister's at Chingford. Couldn't bear another night I couldn't, drive me mad. Wouldn't go through that again not for a 'undred pounds. All night at it they was. Never stopped. All me 'ome gone. Not much I 'ad, but it was me little all. Everythink gone. Look at me. Look at the sight I am! Look at me 'ands! No water to wash 'em with. No light. No gas. Nothink left to me but me purse and pension book. Nothink. My God, what a blooming awful world it is.'

The young woman leapt at a passing bus and was borne away arguing violently with the exasperated conductor. Mrs Minnow stared vacantly after her, muttered, 'My God,' once more, then slowly turned to continue her journey to Chingford.

Another lorry approached. She hailed it dispiritedly, it drew up. It was carrying coals. The driver thrust out a blackened face.

'Give us a lift, mate,' said Mrs Minnow.

The driver hesitated. Then he opened the door of his driving-cabin. 'All right, ma,' he said. ''Oist yerself up now. 'Ere, give us yer 'and.'

ROSE MACAULAY

Miss Anstruther's Letters

Miss Anstruther, whose life had been cut in two on the night of 10 May 1941, so that she now felt herself a ghost, without attachments or habitation, neither of which she any longer desired, sat alone in the bed-sitting-room she had taken, a small room, littered with the grimy, broken and useless objects which she had salvaged from the burnt-out ruin round the corner. It was one of the many burnt-out ruins of that wild night when high explosives and incendiaries had rained on London and the water had run short: it was now a gaunt and roofless tomb, a pile of ashes and rubble and burnt, smashed beams. Where the floors of twelve flats had been, there was empty space. Miss Anstruther had for the first few days climbed up to what had been her flat, on what had been the third floor, swarming up pendent fragments of beams and broken girders, searching and scrabbling among ashes and rubble, but not finding what she sought, only here a pot, there a pan, sheltered from destruction by an overhanging slant of ceiling. Her marmalade for May had been there, and a little sugar and tea; the demolition men got the sugar and tea, but did not care for marmalade, so Miss Anstruther got that. She did not know what else went into those bulging dungaree pockets, and did not really care, for she knew it would not be the thing she sought, for which even demolition men would have no use; the flames, which take anything, useless or not, had taken these, taken them and destroyed them like a ravaging mouse or an idiot child.

After a few days the police had stopped Miss Anstruther from climbing up to her flat any more, since the building was scheduled as dangerous. She did not much mind; she knew by then that what she looked for was gone for good. It was not among the massed debris on the basement floor, where piles of burnt, soaked and blackened fragments had fallen through four floors to lie in indistinguishable anonymity together. The tenant of the basement flat spent her days there, sorting and burrowing among the chaotic mass that had invaded her home from the dwellings of her co-tenants above. There were masses of paper, charred and black and damp, which had been books. Sometimes the basement tenant would call out to Miss Anstruther, 'Here's a book. That'll be yours, Miss Anstruther'; for it was believed in Mortimer House that most of the books contained in it were Miss Anstruther's, Miss Anstruther being something of a bookworm. But none of the books were any use now, merely drifts of burnt pages. Most of the pages were loose and scattered about the rubbish-heaps; Miss Anstruther picked up one here and there and made out some words. 'Yes,' she would agree. 'Yes, that was one of mine.' The basement tenant, digging bravely away for her motoring trophies, said, 'Is it one you wrote?' 'I don't think so,' said Miss Anstruther. 'I don't think I can have . . .' She did not really know what she might not have written, in that burnt-out past when she had sat and written this and that on the third floor, looking out on green gardens; but she did not think it could have been this, which was a page from Urquhart's translation of Rabelais. 'Have you lost *all* your own?' the basement tenant asked, thinking about her motoring cups, and how she must get at them before the demolition men did, for they were silver. 'Everything,' Miss Anstruther answered. 'Everything. They don't matter.' 'I hope you had no precious manuscripts,' said the kind tenant. 'Books you were writing, and that.' 'Yes,' said Miss Anstruther, digging about among the rubble heaps. 'Oh yes. They're gone. They don't matter . . .'

She went on digging till twilight came. She was grimed from head to foot; her only clothes were ruined; she stood knee-deep in drifts of burnt rubbish that had been carpets, beds, curtains, furniture, pictures, and books; the smoke that smouldered up from them made her cry and cough. What she looked for was not there; it was ashes, it was no more. She had not rescued it while she could, she had forgotten it, and now it was ashes. All but one torn, burnt corner of note-paper, which she picked up out of a battered saucepan belonging to the basement tenant. It was niggled over with close small writing, the only words left of the thousands of words in that hand that she looked for. She put it in her note-case and went on looking till dark; then she went back to her bed-sitting-room, which she filled each night with dirt and sorrow and a few blackened cups.

She knew at last that it was no use to look any more, so she went to bed and lay open-eyed through the short summer nights. She hoped each night that there would be another raid, which should save her the trouble of going on living. But it seemed that the Luftwaffe had, for the moment, done; each morning came, the day broke, and, like a revenant, Miss Anstruther still haunted her ruins, where now the demolition men were at work, digging and sorting and pocketing as they worked.

'I watch them close,' said a policeman standing by. 'I always hope I'll catch them at it. But they sneak into dark corners and stuff their pockets before you can look round.'

'They didn't ought,' said the widow of the publican who had kept the little smashed pub on the corner, 'they didn't ought to let them have those big pockets, it's not right. Poor people like us, who've lost all we had, to have what's left taken off us by *them* . . . it's not right.'

The policeman agreed that it was not right, but they were that crafty, he couldn't catch them at it.

Each night, as Miss Anstruther lay awake in her strange, littered, unhomely room, she lived again the blazing night that had cut her life in two. It had begun like other nights, with the wailing siren followed by the crashing guns, the rushing hiss of incendiaries over London, and the whining, howling pitching of bombs out of the sky onto the fire-lit city. A wild, blazing hell of a night. Miss Anstruther, whom bombs made restless, had gone down once or twice to the street door to look at the glowing furnace of London and exchange comments with the caretaker on the ground floor and with the two basement tenants, then she had sat on the stairs, listening to the demon noise. Crashes shook Mortimer House, which was tall and slim and Edwardian, and swayed like a reed in the wind to near bombing. Miss Anstruther understood that this was a good sign, a sign that Mortimer House, unlike the characters ascribed to clients by fortune-tellers, would bend but not break. So she was quite surprised and shocked when, after a series of three close-at-hand screams and crashes, the fourth exploded, a giant earthquake, against Mortimer House, and sent its whole front crashing down. Miss Anstruther, dazed and bruised from the hurtle of bricks and plaster flung at her head, and choked with dust, hurried down the stairs, which were still there. The wall on the street was a pile of smoking, rumbling rubble, the Gothic respectability of Mortimer House one with Nineveh and Tyre and with the little public across the street. The ground-floor flats, the hall and the street outside, were scrambled and beaten into a common devastation of smashed masonry and dust. The little caretaker was tugging at his large wife, who was struck unconscious and jammed to the knees in bricks. The basement tenant, who had rushed up with her stirrup pump, began to tug too, so did Miss Anstruther. Policemen pushed in through the mess, rescue men and a warden followed, all was in train for rescue, as Miss Anstruther had so often seen it in her ambulance-driving.

'What about the flats above?' they called. 'Anyone in them?'

Only two of the flats above had been occupied, Miss Anstruther's at the back. Mrs Cavendish's at the front. The rescuers rushed upstairs to investigate the fate of Mrs Cavendish.

'Why the devil,' inquired the police, 'wasn't everyone downstairs?' But the caretaker's wife, who had been downstairs, was unconscious and jammed, while Miss Anstruther, who had been upstairs, was neither.

They hauled out the caretaker's wife, and carried her to a waiting ambulance.

'Everyone out of the building!' shouted the police. 'Everyone out!'

Miss Anstruther asked why.

The police said there were to be no bloody whys, everyone out, the bloody gas pipe's burst and they're throwing down fire, the whole thing may go up in a bonfire before you can turn round.

A bonfire! Miss Anstruther thought, if that's so I must go up and save some things. She rushed up the stairs, while the rescue men were in Mrs Cavendish's flat. Inside her own blasted and twisted door, her flat lay waiting for death. God, muttered Miss Anstruther, what shall I save? She caught up a suitcase, and furiously piled books into it – Herodotus, *Mathematical Magick,* some of the twenty volumes of *Purchas his Pilgrimes,* the eight little volumes of Walpole's letters, *Trivia, Curiosities of Literature,* the six volumes of Boswell, then, as the suitcase would not shut, she turned out Boswell and substituted a china cow, a tiny walnut shell with tiny Mexicans behind glass, a box with a mechanical bird that jumped out and sang, and a fountain pen. No use bothering with the big books or the pictures. Slinging the suitcase across her back, she caught up her portable wireless set and her typewriter, loped downstairs, placed her salvage on the piled wreckage at what had been the street door, and started up the stairs again. As she reached the first floor, there was a burst and a hissing, a huge *pst-pst,* and a rush of flame leaped over Mortimer House as the burst gas caught and sprang to heaven, another fiery rose bursting into bloom to join that pandemonic red garden of night. Two rescue men, carrying Mrs Cavendish downstairs, met Miss Anstruther and pushed her back.

'Clear out. Can't get up there again, it'll go up any minute.'

It was at this moment that Miss Anstruther remembered the thing she wanted most, the thing she had forgotten while she gathered up things she wanted less.

She cried, 'I must go up again. I must get something out. There's time.'

'Not a bloody second,' one of them shouted at her, and pushed her back.

She fought him. 'Let me go, oh let me go. I tell you I'm going up once more.'

On the landing above, a wall of flame leaped crackling to the ceiling.

'Go up be damned. Want to go through that?'

They pulled her down with them to the ground floor. She ran out into the street, shouting for a ladder. Oh God, where are the fire engines? A hundred fires, the water given out in some places, engines helpless. Everywhere buildings burning, museums, churches, hospitals, great shops, houses, blocks of flats, north, south, east, west and centre. Such a raid never was. Miss Anstruther heeded none of it; with hell blazing and crashing round her, all she thought was, I must get my letters. Oh dear God, my letters. She pushed again into the inferno, but again she was dragged back. 'No one to go in there,' said the police, for all human life was by now extricated. No one to go in, and Miss Anstruther's flat left to be consumed in the spreading storm of fire, which was to leave no wrack behind. Everything was doomed – furniture, books, pictures, china, clothes, manuscripts, silver, everything: all she thought of was the desk crammed with letters that should have been the first thing she saved. What had she saved instead? Her wireless, her typewriter, a suitcase full of books; looking round, she saw that all three had gone from where she had put them down. Perhaps they were in the safe keeping of the police, more likely in the wholly unsafe keeping of some rescue-squad man or private looter. Miss Anstruther cared little. She sat down on the wreckage of the road, sick and shaking, wholly bereft.

The bombers departed, their job well done. Dawn came, dim and ashy, in a pall of smoke. The little burial garden was like a garden in a Vesuvian village, grey in its ash coat. The air choked with fine drifts of cinders. Mortimer House still burned, for no one had put it out. A grimy warden with a note-book asked Miss Anstruther, have you anywhere to go?

'No,' she said, 'I shall stay here.'

'Better go to a rest centre,' said the warden, wearily doing his job, not caring where anyone went, wondering what had happened in North Ealing, where he lived.

Miss Anstruther stayed, watching the red ruin smouldering low. Sometime, she thought, it will be cool enough to go into.

There followed the haunted, desperate days of search which found nothing. Since silver and furniture had been wholly consumed, what hope for letters? There was no charred sliver of the old locked rosewood desk which had held them. The burning words were burnt, the lines, running small and close and neat down the page, difficult to decipher, with the o's and a's never closed at the top, had run into a flaming void and would never be deciphered more. Miss Anstruther tried to recall them, as she sat in the alien room; shutting her eyes, she tried to see again the phrases that, once you had made them out, lit the page like stars. There had been many hundreds of letters, spread over twenty-two years. Last year their writer had died; the letters were all that Miss Anstruther had left of him; she had not yet re-read them; she had been waiting till she could do so without the devastation of unendurable weeping. They had lain there, a solace waiting for her when she could take it. Had she taken it, she could have recalled them better now. As it was, her memory held disjointed phrases, could not piece them together. Light of my eyes. You are the sun and the moon and the stars to me. When I think of you life becomes music, poetry, beauty, and I am more than myself. It is what lovers have found in all the ages, and no one has ever found before. The sun flickering through the beeches on your hair. And so on. As each phrase came back to her, it jabbed at her heart like a twisting bayonet. He would run over a list of places they had seen together, in the secret stolen travels of twenty years. The balcony where they dined at the Foix inn, leaning over the green river, eating trout just caught in it. The little wild strawberries at Andorra la Vieja, the mountain pass that ran down to it from Ax, the winding road down into Seo d'Urgel and Spain. Lerida, Zaragoza, little mountain-towns in the Pyrenees, Jaca, Saint Jean Pied-du-Port, the little harbour of Collioure, with its painted boats, morning coffee out of red cups at Villefranche, tramping about France in a hot July; truffles in the *place* at Perigueux, the stream that rushed steeply down the village street at Florac, the frogs croaking in the hills about it, the gorges of the Tarn, Rodez with its spacious *place* and plane trees, the little walled town of Cordes with the inn courtyard a jumble of sculptures, altar-pieces from churches, and ornaments from chateaux; Lisieux, with ancient crazy-floored inn, huge four-poster and preposterous little saint (before the grandiose white temple in her honour had arisen on the hill outside the town), villages in the Haute-Savoie, jumbled among mountain rocks over brawling streams, the motor bus over the Alps down into Susa and Italy. Walking over the Amberley downs, along the Dorset coast from Corfe to Lyme on two hot May days, with a night at Chideock between, sauntering in Buckinghamshire beech-woods, boating off Bucklers Hard, climbing Dunkery Beacon to Porlock, driving on a June afternoon over Kirkdale pass . . . Baedeker starred places because we ought to see them, he wrote, I star them because we saw them together, and those stars light them up for ever . . . Of this kind had been many of the letters that had been for the last year all Miss Anstruther had left, except memory, of two-and-twenty years. There had been other letters about books, books he was reading, books she was writing; others about plans, politics, health, the weather, himself, herself, anything. I could have saved them, she kept thinking; I had the chance; but I saved a typewriter and a wireless set and some books and a walnut shell and a china cow, and even they are gone. So she would cry and cry, till tears blunted at last for the time the sharp edge of grief, leaving only a dull lassitude, an end of being. Sometimes she would take out and look at the charred corner of paper which was now all she had of her lover; all that was legible of it was a line and a half of close small writing, the o's and a's open at the top. It had been written twenty-one years ago, and it said, 'Leave it at that. I know now that you don't care twopence; if you did you would' ... The words, each time she looked at them, seemed to darken and obliterate a little more of the twenty years that had followed them, the years of the letters and the starred places and all they had had together. You don't care twopence, he seemed to say still; if you had cared twopence, you would have saved my letters, not your wireless and your typewriter and your china cow, least of all those little walnut Mexicans, which you know I never liked. Leave it at that.

Oh, if instead of these words she had found light of my eyes, or I think of the balcony at Foix, she thought she could have gone on living. As it is, thought Miss Anstruther, as it is I can't. Oh my darling, I did care twopence, I did.

So each night she cried herself to sleep, and woke to drag through another empty summer's day.

Later, she took another flat. Life assembled itself about her again; kind friends gave her books; she bought another typewriter, another wireless set, and ruined herself with getting necessary furniture, for which she would get no financial help until after the war. She noticed little of all this that she did, and saw no real reason for doing any of it. She was alone with a past devoured by fire and a charred scrap of paper which said you don't care twopence, and then a blank, a great interruption, an end. She had failed in caring once, twenty years ago, and failed again now, and the twenty years between were a drift of grey ashes that once were fire, and she a drifting ghost too. She had to leave it at that.

ANNA KAVAN

Face of My People

Before they took over the big house and turned it into a psychiatric hospital, the room must have been somebody's boudoir. It was upstairs, quite a small room, with a painted ceiling of cupids and flowers and doves, the walls divided by plaster mouldings to simulate pillars and wreaths, and the panels between the mouldings sky blue. It was a frivolous little room. The name Dr Pope looked like a mistake on the door and so did the furniture, which was not at all frivolous but ugly and utilitarian, the big office desk, the rather ominous high, hard thing that was neither a bed nor a couch.

Dr Pope did not look at all frivolous either. He was about forty, tall, straight, muscular, with a large, impersonal, hairless, tidy face, rather alarmingly alert and determined-looking. He did not look in the least like a holy father, or, for that matter, like any sort of father. If one thought of him in terms of the family he was more like an efficient and intolerant elder brother who would have no patience with the weaknesses of younger siblings.

Dr Pope came into his room after lunch, walking fast as he always did, and shut the door after him. He did not look at the painted ceiling or out of the open window through which came sunshine and the pleasant rustle of trees. Although the day was warm he wore a thick dark double-breasted suit and did not seem hot in it. He sat down at once at the desk.

There was a pile of coloured folders in front of him. He took the top folder from the pile and opened it and began reading the typed case notes inside. He read carefully, with the easy concentration of an untroubled singlemindedness. Occasionally, if any point required consideration, he looked up from the page and stared reflectively at the blue wall over the desk where he had fastened with drawing pins a number of tables and charts. These pauses for reflection never lasted more than a few seconds;

he made his decisions quickly and they were final. He went on steadily reading, holding his fountain pen and sometimes making a note on the typescript in firm, small, legible handwriting.

Presently there was a knock and he called out, 'Come in.'

'Will you sign this pass, please, for Sergeant Hunter?' a nurse said, coming up to the desk.

She put a yellow slip on the desk and the doctor said, 'Oh, yes,' and signed it impatiently, and she picked it up and put a little sheaf of handwritten pages in its place and he, starting to read through these new papers with the impatience gone from his manner, said, 'Ah, the ward reports,' in a different voice that sounded interested and eager.

The nurse stood looking over his shoulder at the writing, most of which was her own.

'Excellent. Excellent,' Dr Pope said after a while. He glanced up at the waiting nurse and smiled at her. She was his best nurse, he had trained her himself in his own methods, and the result was entirely satisfactory. She was an invaluable and trustworthy assistant who understood what he was trying to do, approved of his technique and cooperated intelligently. 'Really excellent work,' he repeated, smiling.

She smiled back, and for a moment the identical look of gratification on the two faces gave them a curious resemblance to one another, almost as if they were near-relatives, although they were not really alike at all.

'Yes,' she said. 'We're certainly getting results now. The general morale in the wards has improved enormously.' Then her face became serious again and she said, 'If only we could get ward six into line.'

The smile simultaneously disappeared from the doctor's face and a look that was more characteristic appeared there; a look of impatience and irritation. He turned the pages in front of him and reread one of them and the irritated expression became fixed.

'Yes, I see. Ward six again. I suppose it's that fellow Williams making a nuisance of himself as usual.'

'It's impossible to do anything with him.' The nurse's cool voice contained annoyance behind its coolness. 'He's a bad type, I'm afraid. Obstructive and stubborn. Unfortunately some of the youngsters and the less stable men are apt to be influenced by his talk. He's always stirring up discontent in the ward.'

'These confounded trouble-makers are a menace to our whole work,' Dr Pope said. 'Rebellious undesirables. I think friend Williams will have to be got rid of.' He pulled a scribbling-pad across the desk and wrote the name Williams on it, pressing more heavily on the pen than he usually did so that the strokes of the letters came very black. He underlined the name with deliberation and drew a circle round it and pushed the pad back to its place and asked in a brisker tone:

'Anyone else in six giving trouble?'

'I've been rather worried about Kling the last day or two.'

'Kling? What's he been up to?'

'He seems very depressed, Doctor.'

'You think his condition's deteriorating?'

'Well, he seems to be getting more depersonalized and generally inaccessible. There's no knowing what's in his head. It's not the language difficulty, either: his English is perfectly good. But he's hardly spoken a word since that day he was put in the gardening squad and got so upset.'

'Oh yes; the gardening incident. Odd getting such a violent reaction there. It should give one a lead if there were time to go into it. But there isn't, of course. That's the worst of dealing with large numbers of patients as we are.' A shade of regret on the doctor's face faded out as he said to the nurse still standing beside him:

'You see far more of Kling than I do. What's your own opinion of him?'

'I think, personally, that he's got something on his mind. Something he won't talk about.'

'Make him talk, then. That's your job.'

'I've tried, of course. But it's no good. Perhaps he's afraid to talk. He's shut up like an oyster.'

'Oysters can be opened,' the doctor said. He twisted his chair round and smiled directly up at the good nurse he had trained.

He was very pleased with her and with himself. In spite of troublesome individuals like Williams and Kling the work of the hospital was going extremely well. 'Provided, naturally, that one has the right implement with which to open them.'

He got up and stood with his back to the window which, to be in keeping with the room's decoration, should have had satin curtains but instead was framed in dusty black-out material. He had his hands in his trouser pockets and he was still smiling as he went on:

'We might try a little forcible opening on oyster Kling.'

The nurse nodded and made a sound of agreement and prepared to go, holding the signed pass in her hand.

'Lovely day, isn't it?' she remarked on her way, in order not to end the interview too abruptly.

Dr Pope glanced into the sunshine and turned his back on it again.

'I'll be glad when the summer's over,' he said. 'Everyone's efficiency level drops in this sort of weather. Give me the cold days when we're all really keen and on our toes.'

The nurse went out and shut the door quietly.

The doctor swung round again in his energetic fashion and opened the window as wide as it would go, looking out over grassy grounds dark with evergreens. On a hard tennis court to the right a circle of patients in shorts clumsily and apathetically threw a football about and he watched them just long enough to observe the bored slackness of their instructor's stance and to note automatically that the man was due for a reprimand. Then he went back to his desk under the smiling loves.

As if he were somehow aware of the doctor's censorious eye, the instructor outside just then straightened up and shouted with perfunctory disgust, 'You there, Kling, or whatever your name is; wake up, for Christ's sake, can't you?'

The man who had not been ready when the ball was thrown to him, who had, in fact, altogether forgotten why he was supposed to be standing there on the hot reddish plane marked with arbitrary white lines, looked first at the instructor before bending down to the ball which had bounced off his leg and was slowly spinning on the gritty surface in front of him. He picked up the big ball and held it in both hands as though he did not know what to do with it, as though he could conceive of no possible connection between himself and this hard spherical object. Then, after a moment, he tossed it towards the man standing next to him in the ring, not more than two yards away, and at once forgot it again, and nothing remained of the incident in his mind except the uneasy resentment that always came now when anyone called out to him.

For many months he had been called Kling, that being the first syllable and not the whole of his name, which was too difficult for these tongues trained in a different pronunciation. To start with, he had not minded the abbreviation, had even felt pleased because, like a nickname, it seemed to admit him to comradeship with the others. But now, for a long time, he had resented it. They've taken everything from me, even my name, he thought sometimes when the sullen misery settled on him. By 'they' he did not mean the men of another race with whom he shared sleeping room and food and daily routine, or any particular individuals, but just the impersonal machine that had caught and mauled him and dragged him away from the two small lakes and the mountains where his home was, far off, to this flat country across the sea.

And then there was that other reason why the sound of the short syllable was disturbing.

The game, if it could be called that, came to an end and the patients slowly dispersed. There was a little free time left before tea. Some of the men walked back to the hospital, others lighted cigarettes and stood talking in groups, several lay full length on the grass or dawdled where ilexes spread heavy mats of shade.

Kling sat down by himself on the top of a little bank. He was young, very big and broad, very well-built if you didn't mind that depth of chest, dark, his hair wiry like a black dog's, arms muscled for labour, his eyes only slightly decentred. He did not look ill at all, he looked enormously strong, only his movements were all rather stiff and slow, there was a marked unnatural rigidity about the upper part of his torso because of the lately healed wound and because of that heavy thing he carried inside him.

The bank was in full sunshine. Kling sat there sweating, dark stains spreading on his singlet, under the arms, sharp grasses pricking his powerful, bare, hairy legs, his breast stony feeling, waiting for time to pass. He was not consciously waiting. His apathy was so profound that it was not far removed from unconsciousness. A breeze blew and the tall grass rippled gently but he did not know. He did not know that the sun shone. His head was bent and the only movements about him were his slow breaths and the slowly widening stains on the singlet. His chest was hot and wet, and gloom ached in the rocky weight the black stone weighed under his breastbone, and his big blackish eyes, dilated with gloom, stared straight ahead, only blinking when the sun-dazzle hurt, and sweat stood in the deep horizontal lines on his forehead.

While he sat there a row of patients with gardening tools, spades, rakes, hoes, on their shoulders came near. They walked in single file in the charge of a man walking alongside, himself in hospital clothes, but with stripes on his sleeve. Kling watched them coming. All of him that still lived, resentment, gloom, misery, and all his clouded confusion, slowly tightened towards alarm. He could see the polished edges of spades shining and he shuddered, all his consciousness gathering into fear because of the danger signals coming towards him across the grass. As he watched, his breathing quickened to heave his chest up and down, and, as the gardening squad reached the foot of the bank, he made a clumsy scramble and stood up.

Standing, he heard the clink of metal, and saw a shiny surface flash in the sun. The next moment he was running; stumbling stiffly, grappling the weight inside him, running from the men with the spades.

He heard the *Kling!* of his name being shouted, and again a second clattering *kling!* and, running, heard the spade kling-clink on the stone, he seemed to be holding it now, grasping the handle that slipped painfully in his wet hands, levering the blade under the huge ugly stone and straining finally as another frantic *kling!* came from the spade, and the toppling, heavy, leaden bulk of the stone fell and the old, mutilated face was hidden beneath, and Kling, stopping at the door of ward six where he had run, choking with strangled breath, while two men passing gazed at him in surprise, felt the dead mass of stone crushing his own breast.

He went into the ward and lay down on his bed and closed his eyes against the drops of sweat which trickled into the ends of his eyes. Then for a time there was nothing but the soreness of breath struggling against the stone.

This was what he had known a long while, ever since the truck had been blown thirty feet down into a ravine and he had seen the falling stone and felt it strike, felt it smash bone, tearing through muscle, sinew and vein to lodge itself immovably in his breast. Ever since then the stone had been there inside him, and at first it had seemed a small stone, just a dead spot, a sort of numbness

under the breastbone. He had told the MO* about it and the MO
had laughed, saying there was no stone or possibility of a stone,
and after that he had not spoken of it again; never once. But from
the start he had been very uneasy, oppressed by the stone and by
the heaviness that could come from it suddenly to drive away
laughter and talk. He had tried not to think of the stone, but it
had grown heavier and heavier until he could not think of anything else, until it crushed everything else, and he could only
carry it by making a very great effort. That was not so bad really
because with the weight of the stone crushing him he was nothing, and that was not painful or frightening, it was just a waiting
and that was nothing as well. But sometimes, perhaps at the
moment of going to sleep, the dead weight lifted a little and then
there were all the uncovered faces, the stone and the digging, and
the old man would come back.

And so he lay very still on the bed, waiting for the deadness to
overlay him, lying there in the knowledge that, if the dead-weight
of the stone lifted to let him breathe, the old man would come.

Strange how it was always this one who came and never one of
the others.

The stone weight was lifting now and Kling, who had dozed a
little while after his breath had stopped struggling, woke suddenly, frightened by the return of the bloody-faced man lying in
brown leaves with hairs growing out of his nostrils and a torn
shirt fluttering.

That was his father who had lain dead in the room beside the
Blue Lake. No, not that man. When he thought of his home he
couldn't see any faces, only the jagged line of the mountains like
broken egg-shell against the sky; and the two lakes, the Blue Lake
and the lake shaped like a harp. That, and sometimes the inn with
the acid wine of the district greenish in thick glasses, the swarming trout in the small tank on the wall, crowded sleek fish-bodies,
slithering past the glass. But no faces ever. The stone blocked out
all the home faces.

When he thought of the war it was always the digging he
thought of because, seeing him so strong and used to work with

---

*   Medical Officer

a spade, they had put him on that job from the beginning; and then there were faces, wrecked or fearful or quiet or obscene faces, far too many of them; how he had laboured and toiled till his saliva ran sour, desperate to hide the faces away from the brutal light.

How many faces had he covered with earth and stones? There surely were thousands; and always thousands more waiting: and he all the time digging demented, always the compulsive urge in him like a frenzy, to hide the ruined faces away. And sometimes he remembered that officer in charge of the burying party, the one who joked and sang all the time, he must have been a bit cracked really, boozed or something; but they had dug and shovelled till their hands were raw and blistered and hardly noticed the pain because of his Hey! Hi! Ho! and the jolly loud voice that he had.

There had been no singing that afternoon in the gully where the corpses, boys' and old men's among them, sprawled in the withered oak leaves between the rocks. Only haste then and the bitter taste in the mouth and the aching lungs, hacking the stony ground that was hard like iron to the weak bite of the spade, and the sky grey and muggy and flat and quiet. In the end someone had shouted and the others all started running back to the truck; and he had run too, and just then he had seen the old man lying flat on his back with blood congealing all down one side of his shattered face and the dry leaves gummed and blackening the blood.

Kling was looking now at this object that the stone had rolled aside to reveal. There was no stone weighting him any more as he watched the object, feeling the bed shake under him as he shook and the muscles twitching in his forearms and thighs.

Then, watching the object while his heart pounded, he saw the hairs sprouting at his father's nostrils as he lay dead on the wooden bed that was like a wagon without wheels, he saw a movement detach itself from this man in the gully, or perhaps it was the torn shirt which flapped in the wind, only there was no wind, and he did not stop to investigate but, knowing only the obsessional urge to hide at all costs that which ought not to be exposed to the level light, hoisted his spade and shoved and battered and fought the top-heavy rock until he heard a grinding crash and knew the torn face bashed out of sight, shapeless – smashed and hidden under the stone: and was it the same stone that burst his own chest and sank its black, dead heaviness in his heart?

The weight fell again now so that there was no more pain or fright and the bed did not shake; there was only the waiting that was nothingness really, and the men in blue talking and moving about the ward.

That was all that he knew, sweat slowly drying as he lay on the bed, and the old man mercifully buried by the stone. The others took no notice of Kling, nor he of them, and he heard their talk and did not know that he heard until a woman's voice cut through sharp. 'Williams, and the rest of you, why are you hanging about in the ward?' He turned his head then to the nurse who had just come in, she was speaking to him, too, 'Kling, you're to go to Dr Pope after tea. You'd better get up and make yourself decent,' and he saw her flat, cold eyes linger on him as she went out of the door.

'Get up and make yourself decent,' the man called Williams said. 'That's no way to talk to a fellow who's sick.'

Kling said nothing but looked up at him, waiting.

'To hell with them,' Williams said. 'To hell with the whole set-up. Bloody racket to get sick men back into the army. Cannon-fodder, that's all they care about. Taking advantage of poor mugs like us. Pep talks. Pills to pep you up. Dope to make you talk. Putting chaps to sleep and giving them electric shocks and Christ knows what. Lot of bloody guinea-pigs, that's what we are. Bloody, isn't it?'

Kling was staring at him with blank eyes.

'Look at Kling here,' Williams said. 'Any fool can see he's as sick as hell. Why can't they leave him in peace? Why should he go back into their bloody army? This isn't his country anyway. Why should he fight for it?'

From the far reaches of his non-being Kling looked at the faces round him. They were all looking at him but they had no meaning. Williams had no meaning any more than the others. But he heard Williams go on.

'Damned Gestapo methods. Spying and snooping around listening to talk. Bitches of nurses. Why the hell do we stand for it?'

A bell was ringing and the patients started to move out of the ward. Kling, staring up, saw the meaningless shapes of their faces receding from him. He looked at Williams who was still there and Williams looked back at him, smiling, and said, 'Coming to tea, chum?' And in the words Kling half recognized something forgotten and long-lost, and some corresponding thing in him which had died long ago almost revived itself; but the stone was too heavy for that resurrection, and he could not know that what he wanted to do was to smile.

'So long, then, if you're stopping here,' Williams said. He pulled a packet of Weights out of his pocket and put a cigarette on the bed beside Kling's hand, which did not move. 'Don't let that bastard of a doctor put anything over you,' Kling heard Williams, walking towards the door, call back to him as he went.

Kling did not smoke the cigarette, or pick it up even; but after a time rose, and with those stiff motions which seemed to be rehearsing some exercise not well remembered, washed, dressed himself in shirt and blue trousers, combed his thick hair, and went along corridors to the door upon which was fastened the doctor's name.

There was a bench outside the door, and he sat down on it, waiting. The passage was dark because the windows had been coated with black paint for the black-out. Nothing moved in the long, dark, silent passage at the end of which Kling sat alone on the bench. He sat there bending forward, his hands clasped between his knees, his red tie dangling, his eyes fixed on the ground. He did not wonder what would happen behind the door. He waited without speculation or awareness of waiting. It was all the same to him, outside or here in the ward, he did not notice, it made no difference to his waiting.

A nurse opened the door and called him and he got up and stepped forward, and, looking past her along the wall of the corridor, thought: how many stones are there in this place; so many faces and stones: and lost the thought before it meant anything, and went into the room.

'I want you to lie on the couch,' Dr Pope told him. 'We're going to give you a shot of something that will make you feel a bit sleepy. Quite a pleasant feeling. It won't hurt at all.'

Obedient, null, with that unnatural stiffness, Kling laid himself down.

Lying on the high couch he looked at the exuberant ceiling without surprise. The flowers and the crowding cherubic faces did not seem any more strange to him than anything else. The ceiling did not concern him any more than the doctor concerned him. Nothing concerned him except the heaviness in his breast.

He waited, looking at the doctor as if he had never seen him before, the nurse busy with swab and spirit and tourniquet, and he felt far off on his arm the tourniquet tightening, the bursting pressure of flesh against tightening fabric, and then the small sharp sting as the needle entered the vein.

'Just try to relax,' the doctor said, watching, while the fluid in the hypodermic went down, the blank waiting face with wide-open extremely dilated eyes.

He smiled his professional smile of encouragement and looked from the face at the chest and the massive shoulders bulked rigid under the white shirt that they stretched tight, at the clenched strong hands, the rough blue cloth strained on the tensed thigh, the stiffly upthrust boots not neatly laced, and back to the blank face again. He noticed on the face how the deep tan of the outdoor years was starting to turn yellowish as it slowly faded inside hospital walls.

'Well, how do you feel now?' he asked, smiling, of the man who stared up at him without answering.

'I want you to talk, Kling,' he said. 'I want you to tell me what's worrying you.'

Kling, his patient, looked away from him and up at the ceiling.

'What is it you've got on your mind?' asked the doctor.

Kling stared upwards without speaking, and now his limbs started twitching a little.

'You'll feel better after you've talked,' Dr Pope said.

The nurse finished the long injection and withdrew the syringe adroitly. A single drop of blood oozed from the pierced vein and she dabbed a shred of cotton wool on to it and silently carried her paraphernalia into the background and stood watching.

'You've got to tell me what's making you miserable,' the doctor said, speaking loudly. He bent down and put his hand on Kling's shoulder and said loudly and very distinctly, close to his ear, 'You are very miserable, aren't you?'

Kling looked at him with his wide, black, lost animal's eyes and felt the hand on his shoulder. His shoulder twitched and something inside him seemed to be loosening, he felt sick in his stomach, and a sleepy strangeness was coming up at him out of nowhere, turning him tired, or sick.

'Why are you miserable?' he heard the question. 'Something happened to you, didn't it? Something you can't forget. What was that thing?'

Kling saw the doctor standing far too close, bending down almost on top of him. The hand that had hold of his shoulder gripped hard like a trap, the distorted face looked monstrous, foreshortened and suspended beneath painted faces, the eyes glaring, the threat of the mouth opening and shutting. Kling groaned, turning his head from one side to the other to escape from the eyes, but the eyes would not let him go. He felt the strangeness of sleep or sickness or death moving up on him, and then something gave way in his chest, the stone shifted, and sleep came forward to the foot of the couch, and he groaned again, louder, clutching his chest, crumpling the shirt and the red tie over his breastbone.

'Was it something bad that was done to you?' he heard the doctor's voice shout in his ear.

He felt himself turning and twisting on the hard bed, twisting away from the eyes and the voice and the gripping hand that was shaking him now. He shut his eyes to escape, but a salt prick of tears or sweat forced them open, he did not know where he was or what was happening to him, and he was afraid. He was very frightened with the strange sleep so near him, he wanted to call for help, it was hard for him to keep silent. But somewhere in the midst of fear existed the thought, they've taken everything; let them not take my silence. And the queer thing was that Williams was somehow a part of this, his smile, the cigarette and what he had spoken.

'Was it something bad that *you* did?' Kling heard.

He did not feel the hand that was shaking his shoulder. He only felt his face wet, and on the other side of sleep a voice kept on moaning while another voice shouted. But he could not listen because, just then, the stone moved quite away from his breast and sleep came up and laid its languid head on his breast in place of the stone.

He tried to look at the strange sleep, to know it, but it had no form, it simply rested sluggishly on him, like gas, and all he could see above was a cloud of faces, the entire earth was no graveyard great enough for so many, nor was there room to remember a smile or a cigarette or a voice any more.

The old man was there and had been for some time, not sprawled in leaves now but standing, bent forward, listening; and Kling knew that this time something must pass between them, there was something which must be said by him, in extenuation, or in entreaty, to which the old man must reply: though what it was that had to be said, or what words would be found to express it, did not appear yet.

The old man bent over him and blood dripped on to his face and he could not move because of what lay on his breast, and when the old man saw he could not move he bent lower still and Kling could see the tufts of bristly hairs in his father's nostrils. He knew he would have to speak soon, and, staring wildly, with the old man's face almost on his, he could see the side of the face that was only a bloodied hole and he heard a sudden frantic gasp and gush of words in his own language, and that was all he heard because at that moment sleep reached up and covered his face.

Dr Pope and the nurse had both seen that Kling was going to start talking. The doctor had seen it coming for about half a minute and waited intently. The nurse looked expectant. When the first sounds came both of them had moved forward at once and the doctor had bent lower over his patient, but now they stepped back from the couch.

'I was afraid that might happen,' Dr Pope said in his irritable voice. 'Damned annoying. I suppose there's no one in the place who could translate?'

'I'm afraid not,' the nurse said.

'Exasperating,' the doctor said. 'So we can't get anything out of him after all.'

'I'm afraid not,' the nurse said again.

'Most frustrating and disappointing,' said Dr Pope. 'Oh, well, it's no good trying to work on him now.'

OLIVIA MANNING

A Journey

Mary Martin, setting out to report the Hungarian occupation of
Transylvania*, believed that journalists were magically immune
from danger. Another woman, a journalist, had asked her to go to
Cluj, while she herself remained to see how things went in
Bucharest. 'I wouldn't do anything for her if I were you,' said one
of the newspaper men in the Athenée Palace bar. 'It's pretty risky
and you'll get no thanks.' Mary's husband, an oil engineer, was
even less enthusiastic. 'The plane service has stopped. You'll have
to go by train. It'll be a grim journey.' But she had made up her
mind to go and it was too late to start the process of altering it.

The train was crowded. The peasants stood tightly packed in
the corridors gazing out with their solemn faces at the wildly-
moving crowds on the platforms. They would stand so, gazing
for hours as though they saw no difference between stations and
the varying countryside. Mary found a seat in the restaurant-car.
Here the sun poured through hotly on to dishevelled businessmen sleeping with their heads on the tables among crumbs and
spilt wine. The train stood another two hours before moving out.
As the shadows slid across the tables and things began to shake
and rattle, the men roused themselves. The majority of them were
Hungarians. Mary could not understand what they said, but from
the malicious pleasure of their tone and gestures she guessed they
were imagining the discomfort of the Romanians running from
Cluj.

The sun slowly moved off the tables. The atmosphere remained
stifling. It was heavy with tobacco smoke. They were soon off the

---

* To appease Germany, Romania was forced to cede territory to the
Soviet Union, Bulgaria and Hungary. Transylvania, including Cluj,
was annexed by Romania's old enemy Hungary in August 1940.

Bucharest plain where the oil derricks stood in hundreds, spidery in the hard light, and climbing the foothills into the mountains. At the first skiing village Mary took a walk on the platform. Outside the air sang past her face with a startling freshness. Among the dark-peaked pines that covered the hills were trees already turning yellow, patching the green like lion-skins. She had to get back inside the train, where the heat carried up from the summer-hot capital was stupefying.

More people crowded into the carriage at every station, but the restaurant-car, where no one dared enter who could not pay for a meal, remained half-empty. Twilight fell. At stations faces came against the window, seemed to stick a moment as though blown there like leaves, and then whisked away again. Dinner was served; meat that a few months before would have been thrown back at the waiters was accepted without comment. Everyone knew the best meat now had to go as a bribe to Germany.

By dark they were on the great Transylvanian plateau. The train was very late. The men fell asleep one by one, collars undone, coats off, hair tousled. Mary began to feel anxious about arriving so late. She had wired a hotel, but received no reply. She did not know if a room were booked for her or not. She knew only one person in Cluj – an English governess whom she had met once in Bucharest. Now that the carriage was quiet she could hear two Romanian Jews talking in half-whispers at the table behind her. They were, she gathered, going to settle some business in Cluj before the barrier of a new frontier came down. One was apparently of Austrian origin; the other from the Bukhovina. One of them said: 'Much use it is now, a Romanian passport.' The other said: 'The sooner one changes it, the better.'

At last some time in the middle of the night they reached Cluj. The station was deserted and glossy-looking in the meagre electric light. Half a dozen soldiers with rifles stood at the station entrance. Some of the businessmen forced their way out first, as though in a panic. Outside, Mary realized their eagerness had been to get one of the half-dozen rickety horse-carriages that had been waiting for the train. There were no taxis. All petrol had been requisitioned by the Romanian army, so the Hungarians could get none of it. Mary changed her suitcase into her right hand and set out to walk the two miles from the station to the main square. A line of lights in frosted globes stretched down the centre of the road. People hurried darkly on the pavements as though to get out of sight, to get under cover.

A dim light came from the hotel in the square. Some people were leaving as Mary entered. The clerk shook his head at her before she spoke. She was near to tears from anxiety and tiredness.

'But I sent a wire,' she said.

'We have had many wires. There is not a bed to be found in the town.'

She sat down on her suitcase as though broken at the waist. After some moments, she said in a small voice: 'Can you suggest anything?'

'Shall I telephone the British consul for you?'

'It's too late. He'd be asleep.'

'No matter,' said the clerk. 'It is his business. But if you prefer I could telephone the sanatorium. They don't like it but perhaps as a concession for a young foreign lady.' He dialled a number and Mary, as though through the haze of a drug, listened to one side of a conversation in German. 'They agree,' said the clerk. 'Now if you will come to the door I will show you the road you must take. I regret I cannot come with you.'

He refused to accept any reward and Mary, startled, said: 'You must be a Saxon.'

'I'm a German. I come from Coblenz. Good night.'

She found the sanatorium at last. An elderly night nurse opened the door and put out a hand as though she needed to be helped in. She followed the nurse down a white passage lit with red buttons. The door of one of the rooms opened and another nurse hurried out. From within came the sound of a deep, harsh voice rambling in Hungarian. There was, Mary felt, something peculiarly horrible about delirium in a foreign language.

'He is very ill,' said the nurse. 'Dying, we fear.'

Mary could still hear the man's voice in the distance as she sat down on her iron bedstead with its thin, sterilized covers. A temperature chart hung on the wall. Dimly lit, in one corner of the room, stood a chromium-plated surgical machine of some sort. A little black-shaded reading-lamp lit the pillow. She thought of her own bed that she shared with her kindly, comfortable husband and wondered why she had ever come here.

Next morning her mood had changed. The strange town was full of the movement of a break-up. There was a tenseness and suspicion in the atmosphere. The shop windows had their shutters up against riots. Some were shut, others had their doors half open on the chance of somebody at such a time giving thought to purchase of furniture, shoes and books. Women crowded round the grocery stores asking one another when life would be organized again and bread, milk and meat reappear for sale. Only the large café on the square, that baked its own rolls, was open. A waiter stood at the door holding the handle and only opening for those whose faces he knew. Curiosity persuaded him to let Mary in. When she had eaten her rolls and drunk a pint of strong, sweet coffee, she felt life regaining its charm. Through the large café window, in the centre of the square, stood the cathedral, new and uninteresting, rebuilt after fire. Around the cathedral went the traffic – the only petrol-driven vehicles were the military cars filled with the dressy, anxious, little Romanian officers. Everything else – carriages, motor-cars, tractors, buses, carts – was being pulled by men or horses. They were laden with Romanian goods being hastily got out of the way of the coming Hungarians. Mary had nothing definite to do – only wander around and notice things and get people talking. She wanted first to find the English governess, Ellie Cox, who might be able to tell her a great deal.

The Hungarian Jewish family with which Ellie had worked were delighted when Mary telephoned. One female voice after another came to the telephone and chatted delightedly in English – but Ellie was not there. No, she had gone to Bucharest. She had married. She had married a Hungarian, a doctor, and now lived at the hotel in the square with her husband. Mary, making excuses to the family that would have had her come to luncheon, went to the hotel in the square. The German clerk was not on duty, but another told her that the English lady had gone out. They were sure she had gone to visit her new flat, which was in Strada Romano. Mary found the flat – one floor of an enormous eighteenth-century Hungarian mansion. Ellie was measuring the windows in the main room. She gave a friendly squeal when she saw Mary.

'You lucky woman,' said Mary at the door.

Ellie's eyes followed Mary's round the big white room. 'Not what you'd call homey,' she said. 'Not what I'd have chosen myself.'

'It's wonderful. We've had to live in such awful places. We'd have given anything to find a place like this.'

'My hubby found it.'

They stood together by one of the big windows watching the flight of the Romanians. A farm motor-tractor went past laden with bedding and pulled by an old horse. Ellie gave a giggle.

'Look at that,' she said. 'You can't help laughing – but it's an awful nuisance all this happening just now when we want to get our flat ready. We've got a lot of stuff waiting to come here and we can't get a furniture van for love nor money.'

'It doesn't worry you – the idea of being left alone here in the centre of Europe?'

'Well, I won't be exactly alone. I've got my husband. And the people I used to work for are ever so decent.'

'Are there any other English people here?'

'Only the consul. He's a nice little chap. He's been ever so kind and he told me to keep my British passport in case I want to leave – but why should I? I'm all right here. But he'll have to go soon. You know, we'll probably have the Germans here.'

'I see the shops are boarded up.'

'Oh it's been awful. Shocking, it's been. Crowds rushing about the streets and fighting and throwing stones. It really wasn't safe to go out. What's the good of their behaving like that? And of course the Romanian army – army! I ask you! – just stood and grinned. Anybody could take anything for all they cared. Then the Germans said they'd come in to restore order and that pulled them up with a jerk. They got busy taking the stuff out before someone stopped them. And it's all Hungarian stuff, too – all left after the last war. Yesterday they dismantled the telephone exchange.'

'Can't I telephone Bucharest?'

'Doubt it.' Ellie started laughing again as another ridiculous conveyance went past. She was a tall, large-boned, blonde girl. Her face was very English. Mary suddenly felt a deep affection for her.

'What made you come here in the first place?' she asked her. 'It's such a long way from home.'

'I don't quite know. I was doing some classes at the Polytechnic, just for fun, and these people wrote wanting a young lady who'd go and live with them and teach them all English.

The letter was put up on the board and I read it. I didn't give it a thought. My friend Addie Clay said just for a joke: "Why don't you go, Ellie, you're always wanting to see the world." "What, me!" I said. "Out in the wilds. Not likely." Then I began to think about it and it began to get me – and here I am.'

'The English are like that,' said Mary, thinking of a memorial she had seen in the English port where she had been born – erected to ships' crews, to ordinary Englishmen who might have stayed comfortably at home and instead had gone to the ends of the earth to die of yellow-fever or cholera or at the hands of enemies about whom they knew nothing.

There were footsteps echoing up the empty stairway. A handsome, middle-aged man entered the room. Ellie's confidential seriousness of manner dissolved into playfulness.

'What do you think of my hubby?' she asked.

'Perhaps he can give me the latest news,' said Mary.

'News,' the Hungarian looked her up and down, and laughed. 'What about? The fashion in hats?'

Ellie put on a severe look: 'Don't you be so silly. You always think women can't understand anything. Mary's come here for a newspaper. She's a reporter.'

The Hungarian became serious, as was required of him. He had been taking lessons from Ellie and spoke English with a stiff precision. The latest news was that Manu, the Transylvanian leader, had arrived – but he had arrived too late. Two days before, when the riots were at their height, the peasants had held the post office for a short time and had telephoned Manu in Bucharest: 'Come and save us from the Germans,' they begged. He had answered: 'Don't be foolish. Go back to your work and I will come later.' For a day they had hung round the station expecting him by every train. What a welcome he would have received! What a hero he would have been! But now, enthusiasm had died; the riots were suppressed. There had been no one at his house when he arrived by car, and no one had cared. A small crowd had gathered outside when his arrival became known and he had gone out and said: 'Have patience. Now we can do nothing, but our time will come. I return now to Bucharest to work for our cause.' Then he had gone inside to pack his goods.

'I'll have to go,' said Mary. 'I must try and see Manu. Perhaps I can send a telegram.'

'It will be delayed for days,' said Ellie's husband.

She walked through the bare-looking, comfortless town to the post office that was still the centre of activity. It was crowded; the telephone boxes were being dismantled and the Romanian police were holding back groups of indignant Hungarians. Mary waved her British passport and was allowed to enter. Inside people were fighting for telegraph forms. She struggled through to the counter and asked how long it would take a telegram to get to Bucharest. 'Two, three, four days,' said the clerk. She decided to go back with her news that night.

She hurried to police headquarters to report her entry into the town and get permission to leave it. All doors lay wide open and men hurried past her too busy to notice her. She wandered in and out of empty rooms and up to the iron gallery running round the central court yard. Here the police were throwing down bundles of papers to the lorries below. Furniture, typewriters, the glass from the windows, the handles from the doors, the radiators, the shutters were all stacked up awaiting transport. Only the shell of a building remained.

A clerk leaning against a doorway patted Mary on the shoulder. 'This time it does not matter,' he said. 'Everyone is coming and going without permits.'

Mary set out to find Manu's house. None of the carriages would leave the centre of the town, so she walked to the outskirts to which she had been directed. The town thinned out quickly into the rich, flat countryside. Manu's house looked to her like the setting for a Russian play. It stood back in its garden, square and naked-looking with a small porch flanked by nineteenth-century stone nymphs. The door of the house lay open. Within the wide hallway the furniture was covered with sheets, and crowded around it were ornaments, mirrors, oil paintings in heavy oval frames, and suitcases. Two busy young men were in the old-fashioned depths of the house. Mary called to them. They gazed at her without understanding. 'Manu,' she insisted. '*Journal Londres*.' They grasped it at last and one sped up the great curve of the staircase. At once Manu appeared on the upper landing, made a little gesture of pleasure as though Mary were an old friend, and, fixing her with a steady glare of pleasure, surprise and questioning, descended the long flight of stairs with the competent grace of an actor. At the bottom he flung out a hand, then hurrying to her, took hers and held it.

Wave Me Goodbye

'Journal? London?' he inquired eagerly.

'Yes,' Mary nodded.

'Ah!' he smiled with great charm.

Mary knew only that he was notable in Bucharest as the one, the only, honest Romanian politician. He was a short, sturdy, middle-aged man with a long nose and a bright, empty stare. He wore an outdoor cape and carried a wide-brimmed hat which he put on as he stepped into the air.

'Do you speak French or English?' asked Mary.

No, he spoke only Romanian, Hungarian and German. And she? Only French and a little Romanian. They looked at one another, silenced, but smiling. Mary watched a large, silvery butterfly that had settled on his shoulder. A smell of apples came from the trees.

'What now?' she asked in Romanian.

Ah! He lifted a hand and replied rapidly: 'We must have patience. Now we can do nothing, but our time will come. I return now to Bucharest to work for our cause.' She nodded her recognition of the sentence. He took her hand again and patted it, then bowed very low over it. She went down the flight of steps from the porch and looked back. He took off his hat and waved it a little towards her. His smile was brilliant.

She was relieved the interview was safely over, but she felt a little dazzled, as though she had come for a moment within the aura of a distinguished actor.

The Istanbul Express was said to be arriving at Cluj at eight o'clock. She went down to the station in the afternoon to get her ticket stamped. The offices, waiting-rooms and buffets were all shut and padlocked. A telephone was ringing urgently within. She found an official who told her that the Istanbul Express would not stop there that evening because it had been besieged the evening before. She said she would come to the station nevertheless, and asked him to stamp her ticket. He took it, stared at it as though he did not know what it was, then pushed it back into her hand and walked away.

Under the brilliant sunlight stood half a dozen trucks laden with rich furniture. In one truck was a gilded French suite upholstered in red satin. There was nothing else but the naked rails, the grit heaps and the shut, dusty, dispirited-looking station. The peasants who had been cleared off the station lay in heaps around the square outside.

Back in the town Mary saw Ellie rushing towards her: 'What a life!' Ellie cried and rushed past, beaming and excited by something. At Cook's Agency Mary found that not only was the train expected to stop at Cluj, but an extra wagon-lit was being put on. People were snatching over each other's shoulders to get berths. Mary got the last and feeling like someone who has just taken out an insurance policy against life, faced the rest of the day. She found a large bookshop modelled on German lines. Inside she discovered it was kept by the family that had employed Ellie. The mother questioned her when she was leaving and how? Who was looking after her? Who would take her to the station? She said she supposed she would go alone.

'Ah!' she said. 'We would take you were we not forced to an engagement tonight. But I will give you this boy,' she called to a small messenger-boy, 'he will carry the trunk.'

'But I can carry it; it is only a light suitcase.'

'No, he will take it. He can go now and get it for you and when you come he will be waiting for you.'

This kindness lessened a little for Mary the star of anxiety that was burning in her solar plexus.

By twilight crowds of incipient rioters had collected again, but they had no leader. Manu had left Cluj and now people did not know what they wanted. They moved about in shadowy groups, rushing suddenly this way and that in pursuit of a rumour. They seemed harmless. No one took much notice of them. A tremendous rose-and-violet sunset stretched up from behind the cathedral. Clouds were flung in semicircles as though by a sower. The streets were fading in a misty, greenish light through which groups of youths drifted out of side-streets and round corners and were lost in the distance. The lorries were still dragging past with their loads of furniture. The Hungarians were gathered on the pavements to watch the flight of the Romanians. Sometimes a military car went past at important speed, hooting unceasingly. Only a few street lamps were coming on. The electricity plant was being disabled. People were saying that the water was cut off. Some of the grocery shops had opened and women were queueing outside them. A Romanian aeroplane sped at an angle round the square a few feet above the house-tops.

Mary had arranged to see Ellie at the hotel and found her sitting crocheting in a comfortless little private sitting-room; her husband was lying down in the bedroom beyond.

'Did you hear the latest?' she asked. 'No water and they're drawing water from the old well. Not very nice, I don't think. Not very safe.'

At that moment there was a rapid knock on the door. A man entered without waiting to be called and asked for Ellie's husband. Ellie motioned him into the inner room. The two men began talking furiously while Ellie's husband put on his outdoor shoes.

'Did you ever!' said Ellie, with a shocked, excited gasp.

'What is the matter?' asked Mary.

'Those Romanians! They're taking away all the instruments and things from the hospital. And in 1918, when it was handed over, everything there was complete to the last needle. My hubby says the doctors stood like soldiers and handed over everything complete to the last needle . . . There! You don't understand, do you? He's just saying that they're taking the beds and bedding from under the patients; they're even taking the chromium handles off the doors . . . My hubby says perhaps if all the doctors go and reason with them, it may shame them. What a hope!'

The two men hurried out. Ellie clicked her tongue as the door shut and started a new row of her crochet. She was about thirty, but looked much younger.

Mary said: 'I wonder how long it will be before we meet again? It looks as though we may have to make a getaway soon.'

'Yes,' Ellie shook her head over her work. 'Things don't look too good. It's all right for me now, being married to a Hungarian – but it's awful for you being cut off from England like this. Where will you go?'

'We don't know. Perhaps we can get to Egypt.'

'Bit of a journey.'

'Yes.' Mary could only think of Ellie left alone here in all her Englishness as the English retreated out of Europe. 'Where is your family?'

'Highgate. My pop's got a shop there. I've written them that I'm married and won't be leaving like the other people. The consul put it in the bag for me. Very decent he's been. I hope they won't worry about me. They'll know I'll be all right.'

It was time for Mary to go to the station.

'I wish I could go with you. But I've got my in-laws coming to dinner. They're nice old things, but they don't know a word of English.'

'You've been very kind.' There was a strong sympathy between them there in the foreign hotel-room in the centre of Europe as the time came to separate.

'I haven't got my Hungarian passport yet,' said Ellie. 'They don't half make a fuss about giving you one.'

'They won't touch you – a young woman alone here. If you were a man . . .' Mary, thinking of her husband, caught her breath and said quickly: 'We must get away soon.'

Ellie said nothing for a moment, then: 'You're English. That means a lot.'

'After France fell, they made us realize it meant a lot less.'

Ellie came down to the hotel door. The bat-black plane was still swooping above the square. The little boy with the suitcase was waiting for Mary. She set out with him down the long, wide road to the station. There were crowds of other people carrying bags and parcels. Mary, half in panic, began hurrying and the small boy, changing the bag from one hand to the other, manfully hurried too. When she wanted to take a turn in carrying the bag he would not give it up. In the distance there was a dark wavering movement of people packed round the station. She began to feel sick with apprehension. At the third-class entrance the peasants were fighting to get in.

Romanians and Jews were moving steadily through the first and second-class entrances. The half-lit station was a desolate place in spite of the crowds. The peasants were settling down prepared for a long wait. Some were cooking their messes of maize over spirit-stoves. They remembered the cruelty with which they had driven out the Hungarians and they were not waiting to give them revenge. The parents-in-law of some who had married into the enemy were trying to persuade them to remain, but their instincts advised them more soundly. Groups of women were weeping together. Furniture heaped across the platform formed a barricade over which people climbed to get from one end to the other.

Mary tried to make inquiries of a porter. She spoke in Romanian, then French. He brushed past her roughly, saying: 'Speak Hungarian.' She spoke to one of the Romanians in the crowd. He told her they were all expecting the express, which had now been signalled two hours late. It should be in at ten. She found some seats among the heaped furniture and settled down like the peasants to wait. She tried to persuade the small boy who had carried the bag to go home to bed, but he refused. She gave him a hundred-lei piece, thinking he might then go more willingly, but he remained. Every few moments he opened his small, dirty hand, took a glimpse at the coin, then quickly closed his fingers over it. Suddenly, amazingly, a train came in. It was a wooden, third-class local train. The peasants flung themselves to their feet and ran madly, from carriage to carriage. The doors were locked. They climbed in through the glassless windows, hauling one another up by arms and legs until the carriages were choked. Then they climbed on to the roof. While some were still only half in and half on, the train suddenly moved out. Bunches of people fell off like lice. Others ran along the line yelling madly. From one of the bridges came the crackle of rifle fire. The peasants panicked back to the platform and huddled against the wall.

It was now half past ten. Mary again tried to persuade the boy to go. He shook his head. She showed him by pantomime that he should be asleep – he smiled with a thin, tired cynicism.

Some time after eleven a second local train came in. The peasants rushed at it. A few minutes later there was the sound of another train coming in on the line behind. People shouted to one another that this was the express, but for some moments they stood uncertainly, expecting the local train to move away. Then someone shouted that the express was leaving. People began to run to the end of the platform to get round the local train to the rail behind. Mary ran too, and the small boy who would not give up the suitcase came after her. When they rounded the engine of the local train they were in complete darkness. Tripping over slag-heaps and rails they got into the space between the two trains. The doors of the express were locked. People climbed up the steps and thumped on the windows, but no one attempted to open for them. The express engine had been uncoupled. Suddenly it spurted forward. Mary and the boy threw themselves back against the local train and felt the heat of the passing engine. She caught the boy's hand and ran round to the other side of the express carriages. At the end there was an open door from which a light fell across the line. She ran madly for it and leapt up the steps. The boy handed up her bag and, as she took it, the train moved, pulling away his hand, and she did not see him again.

She was, she found, at the kitchen door of the restaurant-car. Trembling, nearly sobbing, she leant for some moments staring into the kitchen, stunned as though she had come in out of a storm. Inside, the cook, a remote, dark little man, was sharpening his knives. He was absorbed, as though by a work of creation. When he glanced at her she gave him a smile that was almost affectionate. Gentle and humble with relief at her escape, she asked if she could pass through to the dining-car. He made way for her at once. Inside the car the tables were occupied, mostly by men, dissociated like the whole train from the chaos outside. In a few moments Mary had adjusted herself and was as dissociated as they. The train shunted back to the station. She lifted the blind and glanced out at the faces lifted a moment to the patch of light. There was a sound of shots, some cries and a heavy pelting of feet. The train started again. A stone struck the window glass and she lifted the blind. People were running beside the train, waving their hands, shouting unheard, trying to jump on the steps to the kitchen door. As the train gathered speed they fell back one by one. A waiter started serving the third dinner.

BARBARA PYM

Goodbye Balkan Capital

The six o'clock news blared out, crowding the already over-crowded little drawing room with all the horrors of total war in 1941. The photographs on the piano shook with the noise. The Archdeacon's face, or as much of it as was not concealed in his bush of beard, seemed to express distaste at the vulgarity of it all. Mrs Arling looked as she had in life, meek and resigned. Thirty years of her husband's thundering sermons had hardened her to loud voices and violent opinions. And anyway, all this that was happening was no concern of theirs. They had both died in the 1920s, when Hitler was writing *Mein Kampf*, and the Archdeacon, also a disappointed man, had turned to preparing a collected edition of his sermons as a consolation for a vacant Bishopric which he had failed to get.

The Misses Arling, accustomed to these horrors, sat quietly listening. Janet, the elder sister, was knitting a khaki sock. A cigarette jutted from her square face, and she held her head thrust up to avoid getting the smoke into her eyes. Her fingers went on mechanically with the knit-two, purl-two ribbing. There would be no need to look until she started to turn the heel.

Laura Arling was arranging some polyanthus in a bowl. She was dim and faded, with a face that might once have been pretty in her distant Edwardian youth. It was an unfashionable face, but somehow nostalgic and restful in a world so full of brutality and death. If anyone troubled to look at her they might say that she had a sweet expression, if, indeed, that phrase is ever used ser-iously now.

She had spread a sheet of *The Times* on the round mahogany table, and the flowers, crimson, purple, yellow and creamy white, were scattered all over the Deaths column, so that as Laura picked up a flower her eyes would light on a death and then go all down the column, looking fearfully for the words 'by enemy action'. She wished Janet wouldn't have the wireless quite so loud. It must be because of her deafness, although she would never admit it. The words seemed to lose all their meaning when they were blared out like this. It reminded Laura of the police car which had come round on that dreadful September evening, telling them to get ready for five hundred evacuee children who had arrived at the station. Laura smiled as she remembered the sad little procession dragging through the garden gate, labels tied to their coats, haversacks and gas masks trailing on the ground. Janet had been so splendid. She had sent them all to the lavatory, which was just what they wanted, if only one had been able to think of it, for after that they had cheered up and rushed shouting about the garden until it was time for bed. It seemed such a long time since those first days of the war. The children had all gone back after a month or two and the house had seemed unnaturally quiet until April, May and June, when the distorted voice of the wireless had flung so many terrible pieces of news at them, that now, a year later, it seemed hardly possible that they had survived it all and were still here.

Now it was the Balkans, the *Drang nach Osten,* Janet said, and she always knew about things like that. At the beginning of the war she had got a translation of *Mein Kampf* out of Boots. Of course, as everyone said, the Balkans didn't seem quite so bad. They were further away, for one thing, and after the collapse of France one no longer had the same high hopes of other people. Also, it was mildly comforting to feel that the Germans were going in the opposite direction. Now after the usual War of Nerves, German troops had begun to enter another Balkan Capital. But this time it seemed more real and important. Laura stopped arranging the polyanthus and listened. This was *his* Balkan Capital, her dear Crispin's. He was First Secretary at the Legation there, and they were saying that the British diplomats were ready to leave at any moment.

'You can't trust these Balkan people. No guts,' said Janet, brushing a wedge of ash off her knitting. She got up and turned the wireless off with a snap.

Laura did not protest. She was remembering Crispin at a Commemoration Ball in Oxford, when she was eighteen and he twenty-one. They had danced together an improper number of times, having somehow got separated from the decorously chaperoned party in which they had started the evening, and at six o'clock, when the dance was over, they had gone on the river in a punt and had breakfast. It had been like a dream, walking down the Banbury Road in the early morning sunshine, wearing her white satin ball gown and holding Crispin's hand. Even Aunt Edith's anger and her threat to Tell the Archdeacon had failed to terrify her, because she was remembering Crispin's kisses and the beautiful things he had said. It had been their first and last meeting, for she had never seen him again after that morning. She supposed that she must have been a little unhappy at parting, she must surely have longed for letters which never came, but her memory did not help her here. It had kept only the happiness, enshrined in all its detail like those Victorian paperweights which show a design of flowers under glass, and which are now sought again, in days when Victorian objects are comforting relics of a period when the upper-middle classes lived pleasant, peaceful lives, and wars were fought decently in foreign countries by soldiers with heavy drooping moustaches. Laura had never loved anyone else, not even in the last war, when officers used to come to supper on Sunday nights, and her poor mother had dared to hope that it might not be too late even then. Crispin had gone into the Diplomatic Service after leaving Oxford and it had been quite easy to get news of him. Laura had been able to imagine him in Madrid, in Washington, in Peking, in Buenos Aires and now in this stormy Balkan Capital, where he had been First Secretary for several years. Indeed, she was expecting that he might be made Ambassador or Minister somewhere, although she feared that there must be a lot of unemployment among diplomats, with the Germans occupying so many countries.

Laura's imagination and *Harmsworth's Encyclopaedia* had helped to give her quite a vivid picture of the town where Crispin now lived. She could see its fine modern buildings, the streets all glass and steel and concrete skyscrapers, with brilliant neon lighting flashing out foreign words into the darkness, and the fine Art Gallery and Museum were as familiar to her as if she had really trudged round them on a wet afternoon. The British Legation was in the old part of the town, near to the famous Botanical Gardens. Laura often thought of Crispin walking there on fine spring mornings, perhaps sitting on a seat reading official documents, with lilacs, azaleas, and later, scarlet and yellow cannas making a fitting background for his dark good looks. For she could not think of him as fat or bald, the brightness of his hazel eyes dimmed or hidden behind spectacles, his voice querulous and his fingers, gnarled with rheumatism, tapping irritably on his desk. Devouring Time might blunt the Lion's paws; these things could happen to other people, but not to Crispin.

'I've got a WVS* meeting tonight,' said Janet brusquely. 'We're going to divide the town into districts and get somebody to canvass each street.'

'What for?' asked Laura vaguely.

'Pig swill,' said Janet briefly. 'There's still far too much food being wasted, especially among the poorer classes.'

Laura studied her sister dispassionately. She was so formidable in her green uniform, or splendid, that was what one really meant, what everyone said. She was like the Archdeacon, firm as a rock, much more efficient than poor Laura, who took after their mother and was dreamy and introspective. Perhaps it's because I haven't got a proper uniform, thought Laura, who, as a member of the ARP† Casualty Service, had only a badge and an armlet. Uniform made such a difference, even to women.

The next day the news was worse. The perfidious Balkan State had signed the Axis Pact, the British Legation was leaving, and there was a talk on the wireless about what happens when diplomatic relations are broken off. Laura now imagined Crispin in his shirt sleeves, burning the code books, stuffing bulky secret documents into the central heating furnace, a lock of dark hair falling over one eye. She was sure he would be doing something really important, for he had always seemed so fine and exciting to Laura, shut in then by the Archdeacon and North Oxford aunts in Edwardian England, and now by Janet and all the rather ludicrous goings-on of a country town that sees nothing of the war.

In the Balkans, in the dangerous places,
Where the diplomats have handsome faces . . .

*   Women's Voluntary Service
†   Air Raid Precautions

she thought, as she walked along with her shopping basket. But that wasn't right at all. It was the Highlands and the country places, and Highlands brought her back to porridge and oatmeal. Lord Woolton had said that we must make more use of oatmeal. Janet had got some recipes from the WVS and they were going to have savoury oatmeal for supper tonight.

One couldn't honestly say that it was very nice, but it was filling and made one feel virtuous and patriotic, especially when eggs or something out of a tin would have been so much more tasty. But Janet had banned all tin opening and the eggs were being pickled for next winter, when they would be scarce, or *difficult*, that was the word she had used.

They had just finished supper when the siren went. Laura's stomach always turned over when she heard the wailing, although this was the fifteenth time this year, according to her diary. Still, it was eerie when it went at night, and one never knew for certain that the planes were just passing over on their way to Liverpool. Sometimes they sounded as if they were right over the house, and, as the Head Warden had said, not without a certain professional relish, two or three well placed HE* bombs could practically wipe out their small town.

'What a good thing you've had supper,' said Janet, splendidly practical as always. 'I should change out of that good skirt if I were you.'

Janet ought really to have been the one to go out, thought Laura, but she had resigned from ARP after a disagreement with the Head of the Women's Section. It had started with an argument about some oilcloth and had gone on from strength to strength, until they now cut each other in the street. And so it was Laura, always a little flustered on these occasions, who had to collect her things and hurry out to the First Aid Post.

She came downstairs carrying her gas mask and a neat little suitcase, in which she had packed her knitting, *Pride and Prejudice*, some biscuits and a precious bar of milk chocolate. On her head she wore a tin hat, painted pale grey and beautiful in its newness. They had been given out at the practice that evening, but

---

*   High Explosive

Laura had hidden hers in her room, wanting to surprise Janet with it the next time she had to go out.

Janet seemed rather annoyed when she saw it. It made Laura look quite important and professional. 'I should think it must be very heavy,' she said grudgingly. 'I'll leave a thermos of tea for you, though I suppose you'll get some there.'

'Well, expect me when you see me, dear,' said Laura, her voice trembling a little with excitement. Going out like this and not knowing when she would return always made her feel rather grand, almost noble, as if she were setting out on a secret and dangerous mission. The tin hat made a difference, too. One felt much more *splendid* in a tin hat. It was almost a uniform.

Laura went out and switched on her torch, being careful to direct the beam downwards. The bulb was swathed in tissue paper and tied as on a pot of jam, so that she wanted to write on it 'Raspberry, 1911,' as their mother used to. After a while her eyes got used to the darkness, and she could see that it was a lovely night with stars and a crescent moon. The planes were still going over, a sinister purring sound somewhere up there among the stars. Laura hurried on. Her tin hat was loose and heavy on her head, making it feel like a flower on a broken stalk.

'Liverpool again,' said a calm, melancholy voice behind her. She recognized the shape of a woman she knew.

'Yes, I'm afraid it must be. It's so terrible,' said Laura helplessly, wishing there were something adequate one could say. But there was nothing. It was of no consolation to the bombed that the eyes of women in safe places should fill with tears when they spoke of them. Tears, idle tears were of no use to anyone, not even to oneself. This oppressive sorrow could not be washed away in the selfish indulgence of a good cry.

At the First Aid Post everything was jolly and bustling. Stretcher bearers and First Aid parties in dark blue boiler suits were filling water bottles and collecting blankets. Women were hurrying to and fro carrying large bottles, dressings and instruments. An efficient girl was at the telephone and the doctor, stout and reassuring, was hanging his coat on a peg and looking forward to a game of bridge later on. Everything was ready for the casualties that might be brought in.

Laura put on her overall. It was of stiff blue cotton, voluminous and reaching to her ankles. It had full, short sleeves, a neat collar and ARP embroidered on the bosom in scarlet letters. She got out her knitting and sat down on the bed with the nurse and the friend she had walked up with.

At first they were all very jolly and talkative. These nocturnal meetings were a social occasion enjoyed by everybody. The most unlikely people were gathered together, people who would otherwise never have known each other, bound as they were by the rigid social conventions of a small country town. Conversation was animated and ranged over many topics, horrible stories of raid damage, fine imaginative rumours, titbits about the private lives of the Nazi leaders gleaned from the Sunday papers, local gossip and grumblings about ARP organization. Time passed quickly, an hour, two hours. The throb of enemy planes was drowned with voices until everything was quiet, except for the chatter and the welcome hissing of the Primus from another room. When this sound was heard everybody began to get out their little tins of biscuits, rare blocks of chocolate were broken up and shared, like the Early Christians, Laura thought, having all things in common. At last somebody came round with cups of tea on a tray and thick triangular slices of bread and margarine, with a smear of fish paste on each. No banquet was ever more enjoyed than this informal meal at one o'clock in the morning. Whatever would poor Father and Mother have thought of this gathering? Laura wondered. Perhaps it was a good thing that they had not been spared to see it. Laura had always thought that the shock of a Labour Government in office had hastened the Archdeacon's end.

After the meal everyone settled into lethargy. Conversation died down to a few stray remarks. The doctor's voice was heard saying, 'Double five hearts', and there was a hum of voices from the decontamination room. The women knitted rather grimly, and the men, already tired after a day's work, dozed and smoked. The room was very hot and people were seen dimly through a haze. Laura thought longingly of rivers, pools and willows, of her own linen sheets, or plunging one's face under water when swimming, even of the inside of a gas mask, with its cool rubbery smell and tiny space of unbreathed air.

They had turned the light out now and the room was in darkness, except for the glowing ends of cigarettes and a Dietz lantern which flickered on the table. The scene would have made a good subject for a modern painter; there was nothing in Dali and the

Surrealists more odd than this reality, the smoky room crowded with silent men and women, lying or sitting on beds, chairs or the floor, some covered with dark army blankets, others with coats, one or two faces with mouths a little open, defenceless in sleep, one man, surprisingly, for it was very hot, clasping a stone hot-water bottle with 'HM Govt' stamped on the end. As still life garnishings there were the tables covered with dressings, bottles and instruments, with all that their presence implied, long metal Thomas splints lying on top of a cupboard, heavy wooden walking sticks and crutches crowded into a corner. In a hundred years' time this might be a problem picture. What were these people doing and why?

Laura sat bolt upright, leaning against the wall. She closed her smarting eyes and tried to sleep. But she found herself thinking about Crispin in the Balkans, wondering what he was doing at this minute. He was probably lying down in a comfortable sleeper in a special diplomatic train, like the luxurious Nord or Orient Expresses, which glide silently into stations at night, their dark windows shuttered, conveying their rich sleeping passengers with the least possible disturbance across a sleeping Europe. But Europe was never sleeping, and now less than ever. Things happened in these hours when human vitality was at its lowest ebb; bombers rained death between one and four in the morning, troops crossed the frontiers at dawn. Crispin was probably awake too, looking through important documents, perhaps even dictating to a secretary, while the great train, diplomatically immune from the inconveniences of *Zoll* and *Douane*, carried him eastwards to Moscow or Istanbul, further and further away from his Legation. Laura saw it as a large suburban house, built in continental wedding-cake style, a magnolia tree, impersonal in its beauty, in bud in the garden, and inside all the desolation of a house whose occupants have had to leave it in a hurry. Drawers open and empty, out-of-date foreign newspapers on the floor, dead flowers in the vases, dust on the rococo furniture and the massive square stoves, their pretty majolica tiles cold now and stuffed with the dead ashes of the code books and secret documents. The keys had been left with the kind, homely American Ambassador, who had promised to keep an eye on the things that couldn't be taken away, like the valuable paintings and the stuffed eagle shot by the Minister on a hunting tour in the mountains, just as if they were going to the seaside for their summer holidays and would be back in a month. But it was 'Goodbye Balkan Capital!' and the train was rushing through the darkness to deposit its important passengers, blinking like ruffled owls in the early morning sunshine, on the platform of some other foreign capital, where Great Britain still had a representative to greet them. And then, after a cup of tea, so to speak, they would be pushed on to another train or boat, always on the move like refugees, except that they had their own country waiting for them at the end of the journey, houses in Mayfair or Belgravia and loving friends to welcome them, servants to put cool, clean sheets on their beds . . .

A beautiful note sounded through the room, piercing and silvery as the music of the spheres must sound. It was the All Clear. In a surprisingly short time the blanket-covered shapes became human and active, everything was put away and they walked out into the sharp, cold air, their voices and footsteps ringing through the empty streets. They were all much jollier and noisier than they normally would have been, because they were up at such an odd hour of the morning and they felt the glow of virtue which comes from duty done. There had been no bombs and no casualties but they had been standing by. They had missed their night's rest so that if anything *had* happened they would have been there to deal with it.

Laura let herself into the house very quietly. She went into the drawing room and sat by the dead fire, drinking the tea that Janet had left for her. It wasn't very hot and had that tinny taste peculiar to thermos tea, but Janet would be hurt if she left it. It did not occur to Laura that she could pour it away.

It was an exquisite pleasure to turn over in the cool sheets and stretch her tired limbs. She remembered some lines from Sir Philip Sidney:

Take thou of me smooth pillows, sweetest bed,
A chamber deaf of noise and blind of light,
A rosy garland and a weary head . . .

It was as if she had never really been tired before.

Outside the first birds began to sing. It would soon be dawn.

How thrilling one's first sight of Moscow must be, Laura thought. All those curiously shaped domes and towers, the Kremlin, Lenin embalmed . . .

Eventually, as Laura gathered from much anxious listening to the news, the Legation staff did arrive in Moscow. They were to take the Trans-Siberian railway back to England. This journey was so great and so amazing that even Laura could hardly conceive what it would be like. A journey to the moon would have been easier to imagine. She studied her atlas carefully, but it was all too vague to be real except for the ending, the eventual safe arrival in England on a sunny day in June, July or August – she had no idea how long it would take – with the plane trees in the squares in full, dusty leaf. She wondered whether Crispin had a house in London and where it was. She hoped that it had not been bombed, and even began the futile occupation of studying the addresses of people in *The Times* killed 'by enemy action' to see what parts of London might be supposed to be in ruins.

It was while she was doing this one day that she came across it, *his* obituary among the long, impersonal list. She read it through mechanically, attracted by the name Crispin, without at first realizing that it was anybody she knew. He had died at the house of his sister Lady Hinge, in a village in Oxfordshire. It didn't say anything else, but Laura discovered a small paragraph about him on one of the inner pages. 'Since leaving Oxford,' it said, 'he had been in the Diplomatic Service, retiring from it in 1936.' Five years ago! Laura was annoyed to think that she had missed that information, if, indeed, it had ever been mentioned anywhere. The paragraph ended with three dry words: 'He was unmarried.' Laura had somehow thought that he would not be married. Her reading and imagination had given her a picture of diplomats which did not include wives, although she had not been so unworldly as to suppose that there could not be substitutes which were just as good. And at the back of her mind there may have been a hope that he would one day come back to England and the romantic first meeting would happen all over again.

When she had recovered from the first shock Laura found herself grieving not so much for his death, as that could make no practical difference to her, but for the picture she had had of him. The remembrance of her wonderful imaginings about his journey made her feel foolish and a little desolate, when all the time he had been perfectly safe in an Oxfordshire village, his life as dull as hers. He might even have been an Air Raid Warden. She paused, considering this possibility for Crispin with amusement and dismay.

She cut out the notice with her embroidery scissors. It was sad to think that the only tangible souvenir she had of Crispin was the bald announcement of his death. And yet her memory had a great deal. She found it hard to look forward to the future and a New Social Order, when there had been so much happiness in the past, the bad old days, as she had heard them called. Surely *they* (by whom she usually meant people like Mr Herbert Morrison and Mr Ernest Bevin) would leave her that, her Victorian paper-weight, with its bright and simple design of flowers? Perhaps she had already been punished for her self-indulgent dreaming by her disillusionment about Crispin. No dramatic 'Goodbye Balkan Capital!' but a quiet death in a safe part of England. It was even possible that *her* end might be more violent and exciting than his.

Why, she thought, when the siren went that evening, I might get killed by a bomb! And yet that would not be right. It was always Crispin who had had the dramatic adventures, and after all these years Laura did not want it to be any different. In life or in death people are very much what we like to think them. Laura knew that she might search in vain in the Oxfordshire churchyard among the new graves with their sodden wreaths to find Crispin's. But it would be easy in the Balkans, in the dangerous places. There would always be something of him there.

JEAN RHYS

I Spy a Stranger

'The downright rudeness I had to put up with,' Mrs Hudson said, 'long before there was any cause for it. And the inquisitiveness! She hadn't been here a week before they started making remarks about her, poor Laura. And I had to consider Ricky, hadn't I? They said wasn't his job at the RAF Station supposed to be so very hush-hush, and that he oughtn't to be allowed –'

While her sister talked Mrs Trant looked out of the window at the two rose beds in the front garden. They reassured her. They reminded her of last summer, of any day in any summer. They made her feel that all the frightening changes were not happening or, if they were happening, that they didn't really matter. The roses were small, flame-coloured, growing four or five on the same stalk, each with a bud ready to replace it. Every time an army lorry passed they shivered. They started shivering before you could see the lorry or even hear it, she noticed. But they were strong; hardened by the east coast wind, they looked as if they would last for ever. Against the blue sky they were a fierce, defiant colour, a dazzling colour. When she shut her eyes she could still see them as plainly as if they were photographed on her eyelids.

'They didn't stop at nasty remarks either,' said Mrs Hudson. 'Listen to this:

> People in this town are not such fools as you think and unless you get rid of that crazy old foreigner, that witch of Prague, who you say is a relative, steps will be taken which you will not like. This is a friendly warning but a good many of us are keeping an eye on her and if you allow her to stay . . .
>
> This time next year . . .
> You'll be all very much the worse for wear.

'That was the first,' she said. 'But afterwards – my dear, really! You think who, in a small place like this, who?'

'I might give a guess.'

'Ah, but that's the worst of it. Once start that and there's no end. It's surprising how few can be trusted. Here's a beauty. Written on quite expensive paper too.'

'"A Gun for the Old Girls . . ." A gun for the old girls?' Mrs Trant repeated. 'What's that mean?'

'There's a drawing on the other side.'

'*Well!*'

'Yes. When that came Ricky said, "I can't have her any longer. You must tell her so."'

'But why on earth didn't you let me know what was going on? Malvern isn't the other end of the world. Why were you so vague?'

'Because it *was* vague. It was vague at first. And Ricky said, "Take no notice of it. Keep quiet and it'll all blow over. And don't go and write a lot of gossip to anybody, because you never know what happens to letters these days. I could tell you a thing or two that would surprise you." So I said, "What next? This is a free country, isn't it?" And he said there wasn't much free nowadays except a third-class ticket to Kingdom Come. And what could you have done about it? You couldn't have had her to stay. Why, Tom detests her. No. I thought the best thing was to advise her to go back to London.'

And hadn't she tried to be as nice as possible and speak as kindly as she could?

'Laura,' she had said, 'I hate to tell you, but Ricky and I think it best that you should leave here, because there's such a lot of chatter going on and it really isn't fair on him. The Blitz is over now, and there are all these divan rooms that are advertised round Holland Park or the Finchley Road way. You could be quite comfortable. And you can often find such good little restaurants close by. Don't you remember the one we went to? The food was wonderful. The one where the menu was in English on one side and Continental on the other?'

'What do you mean by Continental?'

'Well, I mean Continental – German, if you like.'

'Of course you mean German. This Anglo-German love-hate affair!' she had said. 'You might call it the most sinister love affair of all time, and you wouldn't be far wrong . . .!'

'She could be very irritating,' Mrs Hudson continued. 'She

went on about London. "I daresay, Laura," I said, "I daresay. But London's a big place and, whatever its disadvantages, it has one advantage – there are lots of people. Anybody odd isn't so conspicuous, especially nowadays. And if you don't like the idea of London, why not try Norwich or Colchester or Ipswich? But I shouldn't stay on here." She asked me why. "Why?" I said – I was a bit vexed with her pretending as much as all that, she must have known – "Because somebody has started a lot of nasty talk. They've found out that you lived abroad a long time and that when you had to leave – Central Europe, you went to France. They say you only came home when you were forced to, and they're suspicious. Considering everything, you can't blame them, can you?" "No," she said, "it's one of the horrible games they're allowed to play to take their minds off the real horror." That's the sort of thing she used to come out with. I told her straight, "I'm sorry, but it's no use thinking you can ignore public opinion, because you can't." "Do you wish me to leave at once?" she said, "or can I have a few days to pack?" Her face had gone so thin. My dear, it's dreadful to see somebody's face go thin while you're watching. Of course, I assured her she could have all the time she wanted to pack. If it hadn't been for Ricky I'd never have asked her to go, in spite of that hound Fluting.'

'Oh Lord,' said Mrs Trant, 'was Fluting mixed up in it?'

'Was he? Was he not? But it was her own fault. She got people against her. She behaved so unwisely. That quarrel with Fluting need never have happened. You see, my dear, he was dining here and he said some of the WAAFs* up at the Station smelt. And he was sarcastic about their laundry allowance. "Pah!" he said. Just like that – "Pah!" *Most* uncalled for, I thought, especially from a man in his position. However, what can you do? Smile and change the subject – that's all you can do. But she flew at him. She said, "Sir, they smell; you stink." He couldn't believe his ears. "I *beg* your pardon?" – you know that voice of his. She said, "Inverted commas." He gave her *such* a look. I thought "You've made an enemy, my girl".'

---

* Women's Auxiliary Air Force

'I call that very tactless – and badly behaved too.'

'Yes, but tactless and badly behaved on both sides, you must admit. I told her, "It's better not to answer to them. Believe me, it's a mistake." But she thought she knew better. It was one silly thing like that after another, making enemies all over the place . . . And she brooded, she worried,' said Mrs Hudson. 'She worried so dreadfully about the war.'

'Who doesn't?'

'Yes, but this was different. You'd have thought she was personally responsible for the whole thing. She had all sorts of cracky ideas about why it started and what it meant.'

'Trying to empty the sea with a tin cup,' Mrs Trant said sadly.

'Yes, just like that. "It's too complicated," I said to her one day when she was holding forth, "for you to talk about the why and wherefore." But she had these cracky ideas, or they'd been put into her head, and she wanted to try to prove them. That's why she started this book. There was no harm in it; I'm sure there was no real harm in it.'

'This is the first I've heard about a book,' said Mrs Trant. 'What book?'

Mrs Hudson sighed. 'It's so difficult to explain . . . You remember all those letters she used to write, trying to find out what had happened to her friends? Through the Red Cross and Cook's and via Lisbon, and goodness knows what?'

'After all, it was very natural.'

'Oh yes. But suddenly she stopped. She never had any news. I used to wonder how she could go on, week after week and month after month, poor Laura. But it was curious how *suddenly* she gave up hope. It was then that she changed. She got this odd expression and she got very silent. And when Ricky tried to laugh her out of it she wouldn't answer him. One day when he made a joke about the Gestapo getting her sweetheart she went so white I thought she'd faint. Then she took to staying in her room for hours on end and he didn't like it. "The old girl's got no sense of humour at all, has she?" he said. "And she's not very sociable. What on earth does she do with herself?" "She's probably reading," I said. Because she used to take in lots of papers – dailies and weeklies and so on and she *hung* about the bookshops and the library, and twice she sent up to London for books. "She was always the brainy one of her family." "Brainy?" he said. "That's one word for it." I used to get so annoyed with him. After all she paid for the room and board and the gas meter's a shilling in the slot. I didn't see that it was anybody's business if she wanted to stay up there. "If you dislike her so much, it's all to the good, isn't it?" I said. But that was the funny thing – he disliked her, but he couldn't let her alone. "Why doesn't she do this, and why doesn't she do that?" And I'd tell him, "Give her time, Ricky. She's more unhappy than she lets on. After all, she'd made a life for herself and it wasn't her fault it went to pieces. Give her a chance." But he'd got his knife into her. "Why should she plant herself on us? Are you the only cousin she's got? And if she's seen fit to plant herself on us, why can't she behave like other people?" I told him she hadn't planted herself on us – I invited her. But I thought I'd better drop a hint that was the way he felt. And there she was, my dear, surrounded by a lot of papers, cutting paragraphs out and pasting them into an exercise-book. I asked what she was doing and if I could have a look. "Oh, I don't think it will inter-est you," she said. Of course, that was the thing that, when the row came, they had most against her. Here it is – the police brought it back. Ricky said I must destroy it, but I wanted to show it to you first.'

Mrs Trant thought, 'First those horrible anonymous letters, now a ridiculous exercise-book!' She said, 'I don't understand all this.'

'It's what I told you – headlines and articles and advertisements and reports of cases in court and jokes. There are a lot of jokes. Look.'

The exercise-book began with what seemed to be a collection of newspaper cuttings, but the last pages were in Laura's handwriting, clear enough at first, gradually becoming more erratic, the lines slanting upwards, downwards, the letters too large or too small.

'It was only to pass the time away,' Mrs Hudson said. 'There was no harm in it.'

'No, I suppose not.' Mrs Trant turned to the handwriting at the end. She said, 'The top part of this page has been torn out. Who did that?'

'I don't know. The police, perhaps. It seems they had a good laugh when they read it. That must have been one of the funniest bits.'

Mrs Trant said, 'A forlorn hope? What forlorn hope?'

... a forlorn hope. First impressions – and second?

An unforgiving sky. A mechanical quality about everything and everybody which I found frightening. When I bought a ticket for the Tube, got on to a bus, went into a shop, I felt like a cog in a machine in contact with others, not like one human being associating with other human beings. The feeling that I had been drawn into a mechanism which intended to destroy me became an obsession.

I was convinced that coming back to England was the worst thing I could have done, that almost anything else would have been preferable. I was sure that some evil fate was in store for me and longed violently to escape. But I was as powerless as a useless, worn-out or badly-fitting cog. I told myself that if I left London I should get rid of this obsession – it was much more horrible than it sounds – so I wrote to the only person whose address I still had, my cousin Marion Hudson, hoping that she would be able to tell me of some place in the country where I could stay for a while. She answered offering me a room in her house. This was at the end of what they called the 'phoney war' ...

'But she seems to be writing to somebody,' said Mrs Trant. 'Who?'

'I've no idea. She didn't tell me much about herself.' Mrs Hudson added, 'I was pleased to have her. She paid well and she was good about helping me in the house, too. Yes, I was quite pleased to have her – at first.'

... the 'phoney war', which was not to last much longer. After I realized I was not going to get answers to my letters the nightmare finally settled on me. I was too miserable to bear the comments on what had happened in Europe – they were like slaps in the face.

I could not stop myself from answering back, saying that there was another side to the eternal question of who let down whom, and when. This always ended in a quarrel, if you can call trying to knock a wall down by throwing yourself against it, a quarrel. I knew I was being unwise, so I tried to protect myself by silence, by avoiding everybody as much as possible. I read a great deal, took long walks, did all the things you do when you are shamming dead.

You know how you can be haunted by words, phrases, whole conversations sometimes? Well, I began to be haunted by those endless, futile arguments we used to have when we all knew the worst was coming to the worst. The world dominated by Nordics, German version – what a catastrophe. But if we were dominated by Anglo-Saxons, wouldn't that be a catastrophe too? Then, of course, England and the English. Here everybody, especially Blanca, would become acrimonious. 'Their extraordinary attitude to women.' 'They're all mad.' 'That's why.' And so on. Blanca's voice, her face, the things she used to say haunted me. When I had finished a book I would imagine her sharp criticisms. 'What do you think of that? Isn't it unbelievable? What did I tell you? Who was right?' All these things I could hear her saying.

And I began to feel that she wasn't so far wrong. There is something strange about the attitude to women as women. Not the dislike (or fear). That isn't strange of course. But it's all so completely taken for granted, and surely that is strange. It has settled down and become an atmosphere, or, if you like, a climate, and no one questions it, least of all the women themselves. There is *no* opposition. The effects are criticized, for some of the effects are hardly advertisements for the system, the cause is seldom mentioned, and then very gingerly. The few mild ambiguous protests usually come from men. Most of the women seem to be carefully trained to revenge any unhappiness they feel on each other, or on children – or on any individual man who happens to be at a disadvantage. In dealing with men as a whole, a streak of subservience, of servility, usually appears, something cold, calculating, lacking in imagination.

But no one can go against the spirit of a country with impunity, and propaganda from the cradle to the grave can do a lot.

I amused myself by making a collection of this propaganda, sometimes it is obvious, sometimes sly and oblique, but it's constant, it goes on all the time. 'For Blanca.' This is one way they do it, not the most subtle or powerful way of course.

Titles of books to be written ten years hence, or twenty, or forty, or a hundred: *Woman an Obstacle to the Insect Civilization? The Standardization of Woman, The Mechanization of Woman, Misogyny* – well, call it Misogyny – *Misogyny and British Humour* will write itself. (But why pick on England, Blanca? It's no worse than some of the others.) *Misogyny and War, the Misery of Woman and the Evil in Men or the Great Revenge that Makes all other*

Revenges Look Silly. My titles go all the way from the sublime to
the ridiculous.

I could have made my collection as long as I liked; there is any
amount of material. But why take the trouble? It's only throwing
myself against the wall again. You will never read this, I shall not
escape.

Mrs Trant, who had been frowning at the words *Misogyny and
War*, exclaimed indignantly, 'Couldn't she find something else to
occupy her mind – now, of all times?'

'Do you know,' said Mrs Hudson, 'there are moments – don't
laugh – when I see what she meant? All very exaggerated, of
course.'

'Nonsense,' Mrs Trant repeated, examining sketches of sharp-
nosed faces in the margins of the last few pages.

I am very unpopular in this damned town – they leave me in no
doubt about that. A fantastic story about me has gone the rounds
and they have swallowed every word of it. They will believe anything, except the truth.

Sometimes people loiter in the street and gape up at this house.
The plane tree outside my window has been lopped and they can
look straight into my room, or I think they can. So I keep the curtains drawn and usually read and write in a very bad light. I
suppose this accounts for my fits of giddiness.

Why do people so expert in mental torture pretend blandly
that it doesn't exist? Some of their glib explanations and excuses
are very familiar. I often think there are many parallels to be drawn
between –

Here the sentence broke off. Mrs Trant shook her head and shut
the exercise-book. 'What a stifling afternoon!' she said. 'Too
much light, don't you think?'

She glanced at the roses again and decided that their colour
was trying. The brilliant, cloudless sky did that. It made them
unfamiliar, therefore menacing, therefore, of course, unreal.

'It's all very well to say that nobody liked Laura,' she thought.
'Judy liked her.'

Judy was her youngest daughter and the prettiest. But too
moody, too fanciful and self-willed. She had stood up to her

father about Laura. It had been amusing at the time, but now she
wasn't so sure – a girl ought to play safe, ought to go with the
tide, it was a bad sign when a girl liked unpopular people. She
imagined Judy growing up to be unhappy and felt weak at the
knees, then suddenly angry.

She must have said 'Judy' aloud, because Mrs Hudson remarked,
'You worry too much about Judy. She's all right – she's tough.'

'She's *not* tough,' thought Mrs Trant. 'She's the very reverse of
tough, you sterile old fool.'

She moved her chair so that she could not see the rose beds and
said, 'Well, if you told Ricky about these hallucinations, I don't
wonder there was a row.'

'I never told him.'

'Well, why was there all this trouble? Did she seem crazy? Did
she look crazy?'

'No, not exactly. Only a very strained expression. I don't know
why they made such a dead-set at her. Her *gift* for making enemies, I suppose.'

'Fluting?'

'Not only Fluting. She was so careless.'

– Careless! Leaving the wretched book lying about, and that
daily woman I had spread a rumour that she was trying to pass
information on to the enemy. She got on the wrong side of everybody – everybody –

'You know old Mr Roberts next door – well, she quarrelled
with him. You can't imagine why. Because his dog is called
Brontë, and he kicks it – well, pretends to kick it. "Here's Emily
Brontë or my pet aversion," he says, and then he pretends to kick
it. It's only a joke. But Ricky's right; she has no sense of humour.
One day they had a shouting match over the fence. "Really,
Laura," I told her, "you're making a fool of yourself. What have
you got against *him*? He's a dear old man." She gave me such a
strange look. "I don't know how you can breathe after a lifetime
of this," she said . . .

'Well, things did go very wrong, and after the anonymous letters came, Ricky said I must get rid of her. "When is she going?"
he would say, and I would tell him, "One day next week." But the
next week came and she didn't go, and the week after that and she
didn't go . . .'

– I should have insisted on her leaving, I see that now. But somehow I couldn't. And it wasn't the three guineas a week she paid. I said two, but she said it wasn't enough. Three she gave me, and goodness knows it's nice to have a little money in your pocket without asking for it. Mind you, I wouldn't say that Ricky is a mean man, but he likes you to ask; and at my age I oughtn't to have to ask for every shilling I spend, I do think. But it wasn't that. It went right against the grain to turn her out when she was looking so ill. Seven stone ten she weighed when she left. Even the assistant in the chemist's shop looked surprised.

Then the day when I was going to give her another hint, she said, 'I've started packing.' And all her things were piled on the floor. Such a lot of junk to travel about the world with – books and photographs and old dresses, scarves and all that, and reels of coloured cotton.

A cork with a face drawn on it, a postcard of the Miraculous Virgin in the church of St Julien-le-Pauvre, a china inkstand patterned with violets, a quill pen never used, a ginger jar, a box full of old letters, a fox fur with the lining gone, silk scarves each with a history – the red, the blue, the brown, the purple – the green box I call my jewel case, a small gold key that fits the case (I'm going to lock my heart and throw away the key), the bracelet bought in Florence because it looked like a stained glass window, the ring he gave me, the old flowered workbox with coloured reels of cotton and silk and my really sharp scissors, the leather cigarette case with a photograph inside it . . . Last of all, the blue envelope on which he wrote 'Listen, listen', in red chalk . . .

'When I told Ricky "She's going, she's packing her things," he said, "Thank God. That's the best news I've heard for a long while." But it was the next night that it happened. We were down in the kitchen. The worst raid we've had – and no Laura. I said, "Do you think she's asleep?" "How could anybody sleep through this? She'll come when she's ready. I expect the zip in her ruddy siren suit's got stuck," Ricky said, and I had to laugh . . . You know, he really was horrid to her. "What's the old girl want to clutter up the bathroom for?" he'd say, and I'd say, "Well be fair, Ricky, she must wash, whatever her age is. If she didn't it would only be another grievance against her" . . . She had some good clothes when she first came and she used to make the best of herself. "These refugees!" he'd say. "All dressed up and nowhere to go." Then she got that she didn't seem to care a damn what she looked like and he grumbled about that. She aged a lot too. "Ricky," I said, "if you do your best to get people down you can't blame them when they look down, say you?" Sometimes I wonder if she wasn't a bit right – if there isn't a very nasty spirit about.'

'But there always has been,' Mrs Trant said.

'Yes, but it's worse now, much worse . . . Well, when the lull came I rushed upstairs. She was smoking and playing the gramophone she'd bought, and as I came in the record stopped and she started it again. "Laura," I said, "is this the moment to fool about with *music*? And your black-out's awful." While I was fixing it I heard the warden banging at the door and shouting that we were showing lights. "I thought so," she said. "The Universal Robots have arrived," and something about *RUR*. Then she went to the head of the stairs and called out to the warden "The law? The law! What about the prophets? Why do you always forget them?" In the midst of this the All Clear went. Ricky said to me "That's enough now. She's as mad as a hatter and I won't stand for it a day longer. She *must* get out." I decided not to go to bed at all, but to do my shopping early for once, and as soon as I was in the butcher's I knew it had got round already – I knew it by the way people looked at me. One woman – I couldn't see who – said, "That horrible creature ought to be shot." And somebody else said, "Yes, and the ones who back her up ought to be shot too; it's a shame. Shooting's too good for them." I didn't give them any satisfaction, I can tell you. I stood there with my head up, as if I hadn't heard a word. But when I got back here the police were in the house. They'd been waiting for a pretext – not a doubt of that. They said it was about the lights, but they had a warrant and they searched her room. They took the book and all her letters. And at lunch-time Fluting telephoned to Ricky and said there was so much strong feeling in the town that something must be done to get her away at once . . . I don't know how I kept so calm. But I look older too, don't you think? Do you wonder? . . . After the police left she went upstairs and locked herself into her room and there she stayed. I knocked and called, but not a sound from her. When Fluting telephoned Ricky wanted to break the door down. I've never seen him in such a state my dear, green with rage. I said No, we'd get Dr Pratt, he'd know what to do.'

'And did Dr Pratt say she was insane? What a terrible thing!'

'No, he didn't, not exactly. She opened the door to him at once and when he came downstairs Ricky talked about getting her certified. "I'll do nothing of the sort," Pratt said. "There's too much of that going on and I don't like it."'

'Pratt's an old-fashioned man, isn't he?'

'Yes, and obstinate as the devil. Try to rush him and he'll go bang the other way. And I got a strong impression that somebody else has been on at him – Fluting, probably. "She's been treated badly," he said, "from all I can hear." "Well," Ricky said, "why can't she go somewhere where she'll be treated better? I don't want her here." Pratt said he knew that the police weren't going to press any charge. "They hadn't any charge to press," I said, "except the light – and goodness knows it was the *merest glimmer.*" And he smiled at me. But he told us it was advisable for Laura to leave the town. Wasn't there any friend she could go and stay with, because it would be better for her not to be alone? We said we didn't think there was – I remembered what you told me about Tom – and we all went up to her room. Pratt asked her if she was willing to go to a sanatorium for a rest and she said, "Why not?" Ricky shouted at her, "You get off to your sanatorium pronto. You ought to have been there long ago." "You're being inhuman," Pratt said. Ricky said, "Well, will the bloody old fool keep quiet?" Pratt told him he'd guarantee that.'

'Inhuman,' said Mrs Trant. 'That's the word that keeps coming into my head all the time now – inhuman, inhuman.'

Her sister went on, 'And she was perfectly all right until the last moment. The taxi was waiting and she didn't come down, so I thought we'd better go and fetch her. "Come along, old girl," Ricky said. "It's moving day." He put his hand on her arm and gave her a tug. That was a mistake – he shouldn't have done that. It was when he touched her that she started to scream at the top of her voice. And swear – oh my dear, it was awful. He got nasty, too. He dragged her along and she clung to the banisters and shrieked and cursed. He hit her, and kicked her, and she kept on cursing – oh, I've *never* heard such curses. And I wanted to say, "Don't you dare behave like that, either of you," but instead I found I was laughing. And when I looked at his face and her face and heard myself laughing I thought, "Something has gone terribly wrong. I believe we're all possessed by the Devil . . ." As soon as we got into the garden Ricky let go of her, a bit ashamed of himself, I will say. She stood quietly, looking around, and then – d'you know what? – she started talking about the roses and in quite a natural voice, "How exquisite they are!" "Aren't they?" I said, though I was shaking all over. "They weren't here," she said, "last time I went for a walk." I said, "They come out so quickly, so unexpectedly. Have one for your buttonhole." "No, let them live," she said. "One forgets the roses – always a mistake." She stood there staring at them as if she had never seen roses before and talking away – something about how they couldn't do it, that it wouldn't happen. "Not while there are roses," she said two or three times. Quite crazy, you see, poor Laura, whatever Pratt's opinion was. "The taxi's waiting, dear," I said, and she got in without any fuss at all.'

'Is this the place?' Mrs Trant said.

There was a photograph on the cover of a prospectus showing a large, ugly house with small windows, those on the two top floors barred. The grounds were as forbidding as the house and surrounded by a high wall.

'I don't like this place.'

'What was I to do, my dear? The sanatorium Pratt suggested was far too expensive. She's got hardly any money left, you know. I had no idea how little she had. What will happen when it's all gone I daren't think. Then Ricky got on to this place near Newcastle. I showed her the prospectus. I asked her if she minded going and she said "No". "You do realize you need a rest, don't you?" I said. "Yes," she said, "I realize that." She can come away if she wants to.'

'Can she, do you think?'

'Well, I suppose she can. I must say the doctor there doesn't seem – I know I ought to go and see her, but I dread it so. I keep on putting it off. Of course, there's a golf links there. Not much of a garden, but a golf links. They can play golf as soon as they are getting better.'

'But does she play golf?' said Mrs Trant.

'Let's hope,' said Mrs Hudson, 'let's hope . . .'

EDNA FERBER

Grandma Isn't Playing

She should, by now, have been a wrinkled crone with straggling white hair and a dim eye. Certainly her mother in the Old Country had been that at forty. Yet here was Anna Krupek, a great-grandmother at sixty, with half a century of backbreaking work behind her, her lean hard body straight as a girl's, her abundant hair just streaked with iron grey, her zest for life undiminished. The brown eyes were bright and quizzical in the parchment face; the whole being denoted a core of soundness in a largely worm-eaten world. Not only did this vital sexagenarian enjoy living; she had the gift of communicating that enjoyment to others. When, with enormous gusto, she described a dish she had cooked, a movie she had seen, a flower that had bloomed in her garden, you vicariously tasted the flavour of the dish, you marked the picture for seeing, you smelled the garden blossom.

She never had been pretty, even as a girl in her Old World peasant finery, bright-hued and coquettish. But there was about her a sturdy independence, an unexpected sweetness such as you find in a hardy brown sprig of mignonette.

On first seeing Anna Krupek in her best black, you were plagued by her resemblance to someone you could not for the moment recall – someone as plain, sustaining and unpretentious as a loaf of homemade bread. Then memory flashed back to those photographs of that iron woman Letizia Bonaparte, mother of the ill-starred Emperor – she who, alone of all that foolish family, had been undeceived and unimpressed by the glittering world around her.

It wasn't that Anna didn't show her years. She looked sixty – but a salty sixty, with heart and arteries valiantly pumping blood to the brain. Her speech still was flavoured with the tang of her native tongue, though forty-four years had passed since she had crossed the ocean alone to marry Zyg Krupek and live with him in Bridgeport, Connecticut. This linguistic lack was only one of many traits in Anna which irked her daughter-in-law Mae, and rather delighted her grandson, Mart, and her granddaughter Gloria.

'Heh, Gram, that's double talk,' Mart would say.

Anna's son, Steve, would rather mildly defend his mother from the waspish attacks of his wife, Mae. 'Now, Mae, leave Ma alone. If you don't like the way she does things why'n't you do 'em yourself?'

For Anna Krupek lived in that household and the household lived on Anna, though none of them realized it, least of all she. It was Anna who kept the house spotless; it was Anna who cooked, washed, darned, mended. But then, she had been used to that all her life; she was a dynamo that functioned tirelessly, faithfully, with a minimum of noise and fuss, needing only a drop or two of the oil of human kindness to keep her going.

Mae, the refined, the elegant, perhaps pricked a little by her conscience would say, perversely, 'I wish I had your energy. You never sit still, makes me tired just to watch you rushing around.'

'Inside is only,' Anna would say above the buzz of the vacuum or the whir of the mixer, for Mae's house was equipped with all the gadgets of the luxury-loving American home.

'"Inside is only." Only what, for God's sake! Drives me crazy the way you never finish your sentences. Fifty years in this country and you'd think you landed yesterday. Inside is only what?'

Mildly Anna would elaborate. 'Your legs and arms isn't tired, and back, like is good tired from work. Inside you only is tired because you ain't got like you want. You got a good husband, Steve, you got Mart and Glory, is swell kids, you got a nice house and everything fixed fine, only is like all the time fighting inside yourself you would like big and rich like in the movies. Is foolish.'

'I don't know what you're talking about.'

But she knew well enough. Mae Krupek definitely felt she had married beneath her when she, with generations of thin native blood in her veins, had condescended to Steve Krupek, son of that Bohunk Anna Krupek. Steve had been all right, a nice boy, and earning pretty good money in the Bridgeport General Electric, but everybody knew his mother had supported herself and her children and educated them by doing scrubbing and washing for Bridgeport's comfortable households. Before her marriage to

Steve twenty years ago, Mae had taken the secretarial course in a Bridgeport business school, but she never could learn to spell and her typed letters looked like sheet music. She never kept a job more than a week or two. But she knew what was what; she never had worn white shoes to work; and now her nails were maroon, she pronounced 'and' with two dots over the a, her picture even sometimes appeared in the club and society page of the *Bridgeport Post* when there were local drives or community doings or large municipal activities of an inclusive nature. Still, she wasn't a complete fool. Though she thought it would be wonderful to have the house to herself with her husband, Steve, and her son, Mart, and her daughter, Gloria, she knew, did Mae, that her mother-in-law was a pearl of great price when it came to cooking the family meals, doing the family dishes, scrubbing the family floors, all of which tasks are death on maroon nail-polish.

But if the second generation, embodied in Anna Krupek's son and his wife, took her for granted or grudgingly accepted her, the third generation, surprisingly enough, seemed to meet her on common ground. Mae had managed to get herself and her husband on the membership roll of a second-rate country club. Mart and Gloria never went near it. Mae and Steve, in the century's twenties and thirties, had dutifully followed the pattern of hip flask and high speed and cheap verbal cynicism. Theirs had been a curious grocer's list vocabulary of rejection: 'Nuts!' 'Applesauce!' 'Banana oil!' 'Boloney!' To the ears of Mart and Gloria this would have sounded as dated and ineffectual as the 'nit', 'rubberneck', 'skiddoo' of a still earlier day.

When Gloria Krupek had been born, almost eighteen years ago, the first thing that struck her family's eye was her resemblance to her Grandmother Krupek. It was fantastic – the little face with its wrinkles and its somewhat anxious look; thin, wiry, independent. The Connecticut neighbours said, 'She's the spit of her grammaw, the way she looks at you. Look, she's trying to set up!'

They had named her Gloria (influence of the movies on Mae), and Anna Krupek had not interfered, though her nice sense of fitness told her that it somehow didn't sound well with Krupek. She thought that a plain name like Sophie or Mary or Anna would have been better. She did not know why.

Perhaps the day and age into which they were born had given

young Mart and Gloria their curiously adult outlook, their healthy curiosity about the world. The years of the Depression had been followed by the war years. These two young things never had known a world other than that. Emotional, economic, and financial turmoil, all were accepted by them as the normal background to living. They had been catapulted into chaos and had adjusted themselves to it. Their parents, Mae and Steve, were like spoiled, foolish children to them. They were fond of them, tolerant of them, but not impressed. But the old woman of peasant stock – hardy, astringent, shrewd, debunked – this one they understood and respected. They knew the simple story of her early days – a trite enough story in American annals. They never thought of it, consciously, but they knew her for a courageous human being who had faced her fight with life, and fought it. She didn't bore them as she bored Mae and – sometimes – Steve. Mae and Steve were impatient and even contemptuous: 'Oh, Ma, you're a pain in the neck! This isn't the Old Country!'

The Old Country. Anna Krupek never thought of it now, except when she saw the familiar name in the newspapers. War-torn now, the peaceful village in which she had been born. Ravaged, blood-sodden, gruesome. Anna had been fourteen when Zyg Krupek sailed away to America. She would have married him before he left, but he had no money for her passage and her parents forbade his marrying her and leaving her, though he had promised to send the passage money as soon as he should begin to work in the rich New World overseas.

'Yes, a fine thing!' they scoffed. 'Marry and off he goes and that's the last of him. And then you'll be here on our hands with a baby more likely than not, and who will marry you then!'

They had tried to make her marry Stas after Zyg had gone – Stas, who was an old man of thirty or more, with a fine farm of his own and cows and pigs and God knows what all besides, and a silk dress and gold earrings and a big gold brooch containing a lock of his first wife's hair – she who had died giving birth to her fifth. It was the old plot of a trite story, but it wasn't trite to Anna. She had held out against them in the face of a constant storm of threats and pleadings. For months she wept until her eyes were slits in her swollen face, but her tears were shed only in the privacy of her pillow and quietly, quietly, so that the other seven children should not hear. And then when she was sixteen and faced with spinsterhood in that little village from which the young strong men had fled to the golden shores of the New World – then Zyg's letter had come with the passage money. It was like a draught of new life to one dying. Pleadings and remonstrance meant nothing now. The child of sixteen packed her clothes and the linen she herself had woven and she embarked alone on the nightmarish journey.

Conn-ec-ti-cut. Bridgeport, Conn-ec-ti-cut. A place you couldn't say, even. She stepped off the gangplank in New York Harbour in her best dress, very full-skirted and tight-bodiced, with six good petticoats underneath and her bright shawl over her hair and the boots that came up to her shins. And there in the crowd stood a grand young man who looked like Zyg, but older, in a bright-blue suit and a fashionable hat with a brim and a white linen shirt and a blue satin necktie and yellow leather shoes and a gold ring on his finger. When he saw her he looked startled and then his face got red and then for one frightful moment she thought he was about to turn and run through the crowd, away from her. But then he laughed, and as she came toward him his face grew serious and then he took her in his arms and he was Zyg again, he was no longer the startled stranger in the splendid American clothes, he was Zyg again.

Sixteen to sixty. There was nothing startling or even fresh about the story. The Central European peasant girl had joined her sweetheart in America, had married him, had borne four children, all sons, and had settled in a community in which there were many from her own native land, so that she spoke with them, and her English remained bad. She had lived her lifetime, or most of it, an hour's train ride from the dazzling city of New York; she had never seen it, for you could not count that brief moment of her landing when she had been too blinded by love, happiness, bewilderment, weariness, and the effects of three weeks of seasickness in an unspeakable steerage to see or understand anything.

She had been widowed at twenty-six. Then life would have been a really grim business for anyone but a woman of Anna Krupek's iron determination. Strong, young, bred to physical labour, with centuries of toiling ancestors in her bones and blood and muscles, she had turned scrubwoman, washerwoman, cleaning woman, emergency cook for as many Bridgeport families as her day would allow. She had fed her four, she had clothed them, sent them to school; they had turned out well, not a black sheep among the lot of them. Sig, the firstborn, had settled in the West and Tony had followed him and both had married. Anna had never seen their children, her grandchildren. She had thought to see them next year and next year and next, but she never had. Andy had a farm in Nebraska. None of these three of peasant farm stock had found the rocky soil of New England to their liking. Only Steve, of the four, had stayed in Bridgeport and had married there.

It was Mae who had stopped the scrubbing and the washing and the cooking and cleaning by the day.

'She's got to stop it, I tell you, Steve Krupek! It isn't fair to the children having a washwoman for a grandmother. When Gloria grows up and marries –'

'Oh, now, listen! She's five years old!'

'What of it! She won't stay five forever. She'll be going to school and everything and the other girls won't have anything to do with her.'

'Well, if they're stinkers like that I don't care if they don't.'

'You don't know what you're talking about. I know, I tell you. And I just won't have people saying that my children's grand-mother is a common washwoman!'

'Just take that back, will you!'

'All right then. Washwoman. An elegant washwoman.'

'I can't support two households, not the way things are now.'

'What about those brothers of yours?'

'They're having a tough time, crops and prices and weather and all. You only have to read the papers. Fifty dollars every three months for her would look big to them. Me too, for that matter.'

So it was that Anna Krupek had come to live with her son Steve, and her daughter-in-law Mae, and her grandchildren Martin and Gloria, in the neat white house with the bright-blue shutters and the garage attached and the four trim tall cedars and the single red maple in the front yard. It was then situated on a new street in what had been a subdivision of the sprawling smoke-etched factory town; but the town had crept up on them. It still was a neat street of comfortable six or seven-room houses with a garage for every house and a car for every garage. Lawn-mowers whirred, radios whanged, vacuums buzzed, telephones rang, beef roast or chicken or loin of pork scented the Sunday noontime air.

Anna Krupek's group of Bridgeport households had been stricken at her abandoning them. 'What'll we do without you, Anna! The washing! The cleaning! Your cakes! Who'll iron my net curtains?'

'You get somebody all right.'

'Not like you, Anna.'

'Maybe I come and help for fun sometime, I don't say nothing to my folks.'

But she never did. Mae wouldn't have it. Besides, there was enough to keep Anna busy the whole day through in the house on Wilson Street. Hers was the little room off the kitchen in which Mae had fondly hoped to have a maid installed when Steve's income should soar to meet her ambitions. The maid never had materialized, but the room was a bright, neat little box, and after Anna's green thumb had worked its magic in the back yard, the hollyhocks and delphiniums and dahlias looked in at her window.

Anna Krupek had made this adjustment as she had all her life surmounted adverse or unfamiliar circumstance. She missed her independence, but she loved the proximity of her grandchildren. When, in the beginning, it had been explained to her that a grandmother who went out to clean by the day was not considered a social asset in Mae's set she had turned bewildered eyes on her son Steve.

'All my life I work.' She looked down at her gnarled brown hands, veinous, big-knuckled. She looked at them as you would look at two faithful friends who have served you a lifetime. 'I worked you and the boys should have everything nice, school and nice shoes and good to eat so you grow big, like your pa wanted.' It was not said in reproach. It was a simple statement of fact uttered in bewilderment.

'I know, Ma. I know.' Steve was shamefaced. 'You been swell. It's only that Mae thinks – we think you've worked hard enough all your life and now you ought to take it easy.'

'I got no money to take it easy.' This, too, was not said in reproach. The truth only, spoken by a realist.

Then Mae took matters in hand. The children of the people you scrub and wash for . . . same school as Gloria and Martin . . . it isn't

fair to them . . . won't want to play with a washwoman's grandchildren . . .

Anna turned and looked at her son, and his eyes dropped and
a sick feeling gripped him at the pit of his stomach. A little silence
beat in the room. Hammered. Pounded. Then Anna Krupek's
hands that had been fists of defiance opened, palms up, on her
knees in a gesture of acceptance.

'I don't want I should do anything would hurt Glory or Mart.
I guess things is different. I been so used to work all the time, but
maybe I like to play like a lady now.'

'Sure, Ma. Sure!' Steve, hearty and jocular so that the hurt look
might vanish from her eyes.

She had five dollars each month from one of the four sons,
turn and turn about, and usually ten dollars from each of them at
Christmastime. Her wants were few. Her neat starched gingham
dresses in the house, her black for best, a bus into Bridgeport's
Main Street for a little shopping and an occasional motion picture.
Ten cents for an ice-cream cone for Glory; a quarter surreptitiously slipped to Marty for one of his mechanical contraptions.

For a time, in her late forties and early fifties, she had felt very
shaky and queer; there were times when she could scarcely get
through a day's work. But that passed and then a new strength
had seemed to flow back into her body; it was almost as if she
were young again. There seemed little enough that she could do
with this new energy. The housework had become routine, the
rooms shone, the meals were hot and punctual, the flowers
bloomed in the garden, she even planted some vegetables each
year because she loved to tend them and to pluck the succulent
leaves and roots and pods.

A shining car in the garage – two, in fact, if you counted the
rackety, snorting vehicle that Mart had contrived out of such parts
and pieces as he could collect from derelict and seemingly dead
motors of ancient vintage. Overstuffed furniture in the living
room. A radio that looked like a book-case. Silk stockings so
taken for granted that Gloria never had heard of anything else.
Movies. They never walked. They jumped into the car to go
down to the corner to get a loaf of bread, to buy a pack of cigarettes at the neighbourhood drugstore.

Anna should have been content and happy, but she was uneasy.
Here was more of luxury than she and her compatriots had ever

dreamed of in the days of the Central European village, even when they had talked of the wonders of the golden New World. Something was missing, something was wrong. She began to be fussy, she was overneat, the two women bickered increasingly. But there was Mart and there was Gloria. Anna drank new life and new meaning in life from the wellspring of their youth and vitality.

Mart, from his fourteenth year, had lived a mysterious life of his own in a world made up of mechanical things that inhabited a corner of the cellar. He was nearly twenty now. Bolts, nuts, screws, rods, struts, engines, fuselages, jigs, tanks, wings, presses, drills, filled his life, made up his vocabulary. Food scarcely interested him except as fuel. He stoked absentmindedly and oftenest alone and at odd hours, his face turned away from his plate as he read the latest magazines on mechanics. His boyish incisive voice would be heard from the cellar depths.

'I can't come up now. I'm busy. Put it on a plate somewhere, will you, Gram?'

'Everything gets cold.'

'Naw.' When he emerged an hour later, grease-stained and sooty-faced, there was his food, neatly covered over and somehow miraculously hot and succulent, awaiting him.

'Is good?'

'Huh? Oh. Yeah. Swell.' His eyes on the book, his mouth full, his legs wound round the chair rungs. But, finished, he would carry his plate to the kitchen and scrape it neatly and even make as though to wash it.

'Go away. I do that.'

'I might as well learn kitchen police right now.'

Suddenly he would grab her, he would twist his lean frame into the latest jitterbug contortions, he would whirl her yelping through space. He would set her down carefully, soberly, and disappear into the cellar workshop, where a single bulb lighted the metal-strewn bench.

Breathless, enchanted, she would screech down the cellar stairs, 'Crazy fool! I tell your pa!'

'Madam, close that door. Visitors not allowed in private office of aviation experts.'

Gloria, going on eighteen, was a modern streamlined version of her grandmother; the firm chin, the clear-eyed look, the mouth that curled up a little at the corners. Usually her dark hair hung softly to her shoulders, but sometimes, busy at some task, she slicked it away from her face and then the resemblance between the old and the young was startling. In shorts or slacks, uncorseted, bare-legged, sandalled, Gloria moved with the freedom of a winged thing.

'Skinny is all the go now,' Anna Krupek would say, her fond eyes following the girl. 'Your age I used to cry I was so thin. Zyg, your grampaw, he made fun; he said I was like a chicken, scrawny. It was then stylish to be fat. Now girls got legs like boys, thinner even, and on top too.'

The two were like the upper and lower halves of a wholesome bread sandwich, and between them was Mae Krupek of the middle generation, a limp lettuce leaf spiked with factory mayonnaise, serving only to bind the two together.

There were plans of great elegance for Gloria. Mae wanted her to attend a private school after she had finished at the high school. 'Well, I guess I could swing it,' Steve said, 'if she wants it. I didn't know there was a place in Bridgeport where –'

'Not Bridgeport,' Mae interrupted, and trying to make it sound casual. 'There's a lovely girls' school in Boston, near Harvard; that Denning girl went there, she married Christopher Houghton, Third; they live in New York.'

'You're crazy,' Steve said, but without heat, as one would state a fact.

'I knew you'd say that. What chance has she got in a town like this! We're nobody. Away at a good school they meet other girls, and they have brothers, and Gloria meets them and she's invited to their houses, weekends and everything.'

'Yeah. Only maybe it would work in reverse, see. Gloria's got a brother too, you know. And maybe one of these dames would meet him, low as we are, and she might fall for him, and then you'd have nothing but a daughter-in-law on your hands instead of What's-his-name Third.'

But as it turned out they needn't have bothered. The neat white house on Wilson Street began to shake and tremble with the roar of traffic. Trucks, cars, jeeps, buses packed with workingmen and – a little later – women, all headed for the aeroplane factory that was two miles distant. Until now it had been rather a modest plant, an experimental thing, really, reached by way of another street. Now it had doubled, trebled, quadrupled in size; its hum could be heard for miles; it was served not by hundreds but by thousands, and you could hardly tell which were men and which women, for they all wore pants and shirts and the girls had their heads bound in snoods or kerchiefs. 'Like was in the Old Country, only not pants,' Anna Krupek said interestedly. She followed the news avidly; she read of the country of her birth, of the horror that had befallen it; her kind eyes were stern. 'We've got to do something. Quick we got to do or is here in America like over in Old Country, people is killed, people is hungry, everything goes in pieces, houses, and towns and churches and schools. We got to do quick.'

Young Mart did quick. He came in at suppertime one evening with a young fellow in uniform.

'Them wings is pretty,' Anna Krupek said. 'You get a suit like that, Marty, and I make you embroidery wings on it the way this young man is got.'

They had roared at that.

'Yup, I'm getting me a suit, Gram,' Mart said. 'And I hope I'll have the wings, too. Only they come already embroidered.'

The young fellow with him was Lieutenant Gurk; the family gathered that he had been stationed in Texas, he was out at Mitchell Field on some special mission, he hoped to go overseas very soon. He was unloquacious, like Mart. He and Gloria seemed to know a number of people in common, which was strange.

'Gurk,' said Mae, pronouncing the name with considerable distaste. 'From Texas?'

'No, ma'am, I'm –'

'There were some Gurks – let me see – they had a garage and filling station – remember, Steve? We pass it near the bridge – Gurk's Garage. But of course you wouldn't be re—'

'Yes. That's me, Mike Gurk. That's my father's place.'

Mae was furious. She spoke to Mart about it later, after the young man had gone. She addressed herself not only to Mart but to her husband and to Gloria and even Anna, as one who knows herself to be right and expects the support of the family against an erring member of the group.

'I'm upset enough about your being in it and risking your life, and goodness knows aviation's the most dangerous – but at least there are wonderful boys in it of the best families, and why you have to pick one like that to bring home, a common mechanic out of a garage in greasy overalls!'

'Hi, you're getting mixed, Mom.' His tone was light, but his face was scarlet.

'You could think of your sister once in a while. There are perfectly stunning aviators. This is a wonderful chance for Gloria – and you too, for that matter – to meet the most—'

But he left the room then, to Mae's chagrined bewilderment. Gloria was about to follow him. Then she began to laugh; she laughed as you would at a vexatious but dear child. 'Look, cooky, this war wasn't arranged so that I could meet dazzling members of the Air Force, exactly.'

'But it wouldn't hurt the war if you did! And I don't need you to tell me about the war, thank you. I'm doing my share.'

Mae was serving on committees, she was busy at jobs that entailed calling people on the telephone or going to their houses. She seemed particularly occupied with the war work which necessitated canvassing the houses in the more impressive residence sections – Brooklawn, the more fashionable end of old South Park Avenue, and the tree-shaded, sizeable houses on Toilsome Hill. She would return to her own home after one of these sorties, her mood gay or sullen depending on what she had seen or heard. She would glance with new eyes at the interior of the house on Wilson Street, and even at its outside aspect.

'Well, I wouldn't have believed it. With all their money, and the place looks like a junk shop. Not even good antiques.' Or, with a baleful look around the living room, 'These curtains are dated and stuffy. They don't use that heavy material any more. Chintz, or silk with net glass curtains, or that cream kind of linen stuff, or wool. That's what's smart now. Those old things are hideous!'

Steve's job with the GE was a war job now, automatically. He worked early, he worked late, he looked tired and older, but he had the air of one who knows that his work is good and useful. Gloria said she was going to be a Wave,* she was going to join the WACs;† she applied for Red Cross Motor Service, she worked as

---

* Women Accepted for Volunteer Emergency Service

† Women's Army Corps

Nurse's Aide, she gave her fresh young blood to the blood bank; she collected this and that, she was on committees, she grew thinner, her eyes were bigger, but there was a sort of bloom about her, too. She said, 'This is no damn good, this is silly, I'm not really doing anything, I wish I could be a ferry bomber pilot, I wish I could go overseas, I wish, I wish, I wish.'

Anna Krupek was not one to avoid fundamental truths. 'You wish, you wish – I know what you wish. You wish you got a husband and baby, that is what you wish.'

A look of desperation leaped into Gloria's eyes. 'They're all going away, the men. Pretty soon there won't be any to marry.'

Anna Krupek, standing at the stove, stirring something in a pot like a benevolent witch, said comfortably over her shoulder, 'They come back. You wait.'

'I don't want to wait.'

'Or you go where he is. Like me. I betcha I cried like anything, my folks was mad with me, but I went where Zyg was, across the ocean even I went.'

'That was different. You were different.'

'Nothing is different. On top only.'

Mae confronted Gloria one day. 'Who was that man in uniform I saw you with on Fairfield Avenue?'

Gloria flushed, but she was unable to resist paraphrasing the classic reply. 'That wasn't no man in uniform, that was my beau.'

'It looked like that Gurk.'

'It was Lieutenant Gurk.'

'How did you happen to run into him?'

'I didn't. I telephoned him.'

'I thought he was at Mitchell Field, or Texas, or – didn't he say he was going overseas?'

'He's being sent to Seattle, Washington, first. And then probably Alaska – the Aleutians – up where—' She turned her face away.

'Gloria, I hope to goodness you haven't been seeing that – that – I hope you haven't been seeing him, even with Mart.'

Gloria's voice had an even edge like cold steel. 'You couldn't call it just seeing him, exactly. I've been chasing him. I've been breaking my legs running after him.'

'You must be out of your mind!'

'You never said a truer word.'

Mae started to make a thing of it, a family to-do, with tears, reproaches and name-calling, but then Lieutenant Gurk vanished not only physically but in all his manifestations so far as Mae was concerned, because Mart went, too; he wasn't Mart any more, he was Martin Krupek of the American Air Force. The psychopathic dreams of a mad paperhanger had reached across thousands of miles of ocean and land and had changed the carefree boy into a purposeful man.

Each member of the family took it in his or her own way.

Mae moped and cried and put up photographs of him all over the house, including rather repulsive studies taken at the age of two months. Steve looked older and more careworn than ever, but there was nothing of age or care in his voice when he spoke of him. 'My son, Martin. He's in the Air Force, you know. Aviation. Don't know yet whether he's going to be a pilot or a bombardier. Yep, aviation. That's the thing. God, if I was twenty years younger! But it's kids these days. Boys.'

Gloria said little. She was working hard in a confused and scattered effort. She was gone from morning until night. She spent her free time writing letters, and all her small change on air-mail stamps.

Anna Krupek went about her business. She was quieter. She was alone in the house now for the greater part of the day. Mae did practically nothing in the way of household work. 'My Red Cross,' she said possessively as she whisked out of the house, usually taking the car for her exclusive use. 'My Bundles Committee. My Drive Committee.'

Then a queer thing happened. The neighbours noticed that the house seemed closed almost daily for hours during the middle of the day. Anna Krupek would board a bus after the others had breakfasted and gone. She would return in mid afternoon or even later sometimes.

'Where were you, Ma? I tried to get the house on the phone and no answer.'

'Maybe out in the yard or to the store.'

The meals were prompt and good in spite of the rationing. When they complained about meat shortage she said, 'We cook *haluski* in Old Country, not meat all the time like here. Morning it would be dark yet. The men would get up and go to the farm, it was miles away, not like here in America, farmers live on the farm like Sig and Tony and Andy got it good. We would get up too, pitch-black, and make the housework and cook *haluski*, it was like little noodles, only cut with a spoon in little pieces, not like noodles with a knife. And we would put in pot hot with hot stones and we take it out to the men, miles, and they would eat it for their breakfast and it was good.'

'Sounds awful,' Mae said.

'You yell about no coffee. Maybe once a week we had coffee, it was out of barley roasted in our oven, not real coffee like you got. It tasted fine I can tell you. We had only Sunday. Meat once a month, it taste like a piece of cake, so sweet.'

'Well, thank God Mart's getting meat; steaks and things.'

'Plenty of food,' Steve said, crossly for him. 'People bellyaching. Ought to be working. Planes, that's what we need. They could use twice the help they've got. Men and women.'

'You betcha!' Anna Krupek said with enormous energy. Then again in what amounted almost to a shout, 'You betcha!'

She jumped up from the table and brought in the meat. She had managed to get a ham, juicy and tender; she served with it a hot sauce blended of homemade grape jelly and prepared mustard; it was smooth and piquant on the tongue. It was like a Sunday dinner, or a holiday.

'Gosh, you certainly did yourself proud, Ma,' Steve said. 'I'll bet there's no other country in the world where a family can sit down to a meal like this, middle of the week. Is it somebody's birthday or something I've forgotten?'

'No,' said Anna Krupek, and brought in a lemon chiffon pie.

There was nothing to warn them. When Mae Krupek came home next day at five her mother-in-law was not there. Gloria had just come in, the early spring day was unseasonably hot, there was no dinner in preparation, the kitchen was silent except for the taunting whir of the refrigerator.

'Well, really!' Mae snatched off her hat, ran a hand through her hair, and glared at the white enamel cabinets which gave her as good as she sent, glare for glare. 'After five! Your father'll be home and no dinner. She's probably gone to a movie or something, or running around with those everlasting points. I'm dead. Simply dead.'

Gloria, sprawled on the couch in the living room, jumped up and came into the kitchen. 'Well, let's get things started. I hope nothing's happened to Gram.'

'Never fear,' Mae retorted.

'If it weren't for Gram you'd have to get dinner every day, and breakfast too, and everything.'

'And how about yourself!'

'Oh, me too. Sure. I'd like to learn to cook.'

'Why?' snapped Mae, whirling on her.

'Well, my goodness, why not?' Gloria said, reasonably enough. 'Anyway, Gram's a kind of unpaid slavey around here.'

'She gets her room and board and everything.'

'So do you.'

'You're crazy. I happen to be your father's wife.'

'Gram's his mother.'

The heat, the annoyance, and the prospect of wrestling with the contents of the refrigerator caused Mae's taut nerves to snap. 'Oh, shut up!' she yelled, her refinement temporarily cast off like a too-tight garment. Steve Krupek, coming in at that moment, blinked mildly.

'What's the ruckus?'

'Nothing. Dinner'll be late. Your ma isn't home.'

'OK. Too hot to eat, anyway. Wonder where Ma is.'

The three stood there in the clean, white kitchen with its gay, painted border and its polka-dotted, ruffled curtains and its geranium blooming in the window pot. Queer not to see the neat, deft figure performing expert magic with pots and pans and spoons.

Someone passed the kitchen window. Grandma Krupek always came in the back way. The kitchen door was locked. You heard her key click.

Grandma Krupek stood framed in the doorway with the new green of the backyard lawn behind her. Then she stepped into the kitchen.

They stared at her, the three of them. It is noteworthy that not one of them laughed. It was not only amazement that kept them from this; it was something in her face, a look of shyness, a look of courage, a look of resolve, a curious mixture of all three that blended to make an effect of nobility.

Then, 'Well, my God!' said Mae Krupek, and dropped a pan in the sink with a clatter and spatter.

Anna Krupek was dressed in slacks and shirt, the one blue, the other grey, and her hair was bound in a coloured kerchief. On her feet were neat, serviceable, flat-heeled shoes, in her hand was a lunch box such as workmen carry.

'Hello,' said Grandma Krupek inadequately. She put down her lunch box, went to the sink and retrieved the pan and its contents.

Between them Steve and Mae said all the things that people say in astonishment, disapproval, and minor panic: 'What does this mean!' 'Have you lost your mind!' 'You can't a thing like this!' 'What will people say!' 'We'll put a stop to it.' 'You're making a fool of yourself and all of us.'

Only Gloria, between tears and laughter, kissed her grandmother and gave her a hearty smack behind and said, surveying the slim little figure in trousers and shirt, 'Sexagenarian is right!'

Anna Krupek stood her ground. Quietly, stubbornly, over and over again she said, 'I work in aeroplane factory. Is defence. Is fine. I like. I make planes for Mart. In a week only I learned so quick.'

'You can't do that kind of work. You're too old. You'll be sick.'

Anna's was a limited vocabulary, but she succeeded in making things reasonably plain.

'Say, in factory is a cinch. Easier as housework and cooking, you betcha.' Then, fearful of having hurt them, 'I cook again and make everything nice in the house after we fight the war, like always. But now I make aeroplane for Mart.' She just glanced at Gloria. 'For Mart and other boys.'

Mae drew a long breath, as though she had come up after being under water. 'We'll see about that. Steve, you've got to speak to them. You have her fired. I won't stand for it.'

'My boss is Ben Chester. I don't get fired. Years and years I work for his ma, cleaning and washing. Ben, he is crazy for me. I don't get fired. No, sir!'

Mae's lips were compressed. She was too angry for tears. 'The neighbours! And everybody laughing at us! At your age!'

Grandma Krupek wagged her head. 'Oh, is plenty old ladies working in aeroplanes.' She shot another lightning glance at Gloria. 'Old ladies and kids too. Next to me is old lady she is getting new false teeth for hundred and fifty dollar! And her hair marcel each week. I save my money, maybe I travel.'

'Travel!' echoed Mae, weakly.

But Gloria leaped the gap at last. 'Could I get a job there, do you think? Could I do it?'

'Sure thing. Two, three weeks you could travel – oh – New York or – uh – Seattle – or – 'with elaborate carelessness. 'And back.'

Mae turned to Steve. 'Well, your mother won't stay here any longer, that's one sure thing. I won't have it.'

'OK,' said Anna Krupek, without rancour.

Steve spoke quietly. 'You're staying here, Ma. This is your home.'

Anna's face was placid but firm. 'On day shift I am through I am home five o'clock. I help you, Mae. You ain't such a bad cook; you got to learn only. I was afraid in factory first, but I learn. Like when I cross the ocean alone to come to this country. I was afraid. But I learn.'

She looked at her two hands as she had once before, almost as though they belonged to someone else. She looked at them and turned them as she looked, palms in and then palms out, curiously, as at some rare jewels whose every facet reflected a brilliant new light.

'What you think! I make aeroplane. I sit in chair, comfortable, I put a little piece in a little hole it should fit nice, and for this I am pay fifty dollars a week.' She shook her head as though to rid it of a dream. 'Zyg, he won't believe it.'

DOROTHY PARKER

The Lovely Leave

Her husband had telephoned her by long distance to tell her
about the leave. She had not expected the call, and she had no
words arranged. She threw away whole seconds explaining her
surprise at hearing him, and reporting that it was raining hard in
New York, and asking was it terribly hot where he was. He had
stopped her to say, look, he didn't have time to talk long; and he
had told her quickly that his squadron was to be moved to
another field the next week and on the way he would have
twenty-four hours' leave. It was difficult for her to hear. Behind
his voice came a jagged chorus of young male voices, all crying
the syllable 'Hey!'

'Ah, don't hang up yet,' she said. 'Please. Let's talk another
minute, just another –'

'Honey, I've got to go,' he said. 'The boys all want a crack at
the telephone. See you a week from today, around five. 'Bye.'

Then there had been a click as his receiver went back into place.
Slowly she cradled her telephone, looking at it as if all frustrations
and bewilderments and separations were its fault. Over it she had
heard his voice, coming from far away. All the months, she had
tried not to think of the great blank distance between them; and
now that far voice made her know she had thought of nothing
else. And his speech had been brisk and busy. And from back of
him had come gay, wild young voices, voices he heard every day
and she did not, voices of those who shared his new life. And he
had heeded them and not her, when she begged for another
minute. She took her hand off the telephone and held it away
from her with the fingers spread stiffly apart, as if it had touched
something horrid.

Then she told herself to stop her nonsense. If you looked for
things to make you feel hurt and wretched and unnecessary, you
were certain to find them, more easily each time, so easily, soon,
that you did not even realize you had gone out searching. Women

alone often developed into experts at the practice. She must never join their dismal league.

What was she dreary about, anyway? If he had only a little while to talk, then he had only a little while to talk, that was all. Certainly he had had time to tell her he was coming, to say that they would be together soon. And there she was, sitting scowling at the telephone, the kind, faithful telephone that had brought her the lovely news. She would see him in a week. Only a week. She began to feel, along her back and through her middle, little quivers of excitement, like tiny springs uncoiling into spirals.

There must be no waste to this leave. She thought of the preposterous shyness that had fallen upon her when he had come home before. It was the first time she had seen him in uniform. There he stood, in their little apartment, a dashing stranger in strange, dashing garments. Until he had gone into the army, they had never spent a night apart in all their marriage; and when she saw him, she dropped her eyes and twisted her handkerchief and could bring nothing but monosyllables from her throat. There must be no such squandering of minutes this time. There must be no such gangling diffidence to lop even an instant from their twenty-four hours of perfect union. Oh, Lord, only twenty-four hours . . .

No. That was exactly the wrong thing to do; that was directly the wrong way to think. That was the way she had spoiled it before. Almost as soon as the shyness had left her and she felt she knew him again, she had begun counting. She was so filled with the desperate consciousness of the hours sliding away only twelve more, only five, oh, dear God, only one left – that she had no room for gaiety and ease. She had spent the golden time in grudging its going.

She had been so woebegone of carriage, so sad and slow of word as the last hour went, that he, nervous under the pall, had spoken sharply and there had been a quarrel. When he had had to leave for his train, there were no clinging farewells, no tender words to keep. He had gone to the door and opened it and stood with it against his shoulder while he shook out his flight cap and put it on, adjusting it with great care, one inch over the eye, one inch above the ear. She stood in the middle of the living-room, cool and silent, looking at him.

When his cap was precisely as it should be, he looked at her.

'Well,' he said. He cleared his throat. 'Guess I'd better get going.'

'I'm sure you had,' she said.

He studied his watch intently. 'I'll just make it,' he said.

'I'm sure you will,' she said.

She turned, not with an actual shrug, only with the effect of one, and went to the window and looked out, as if casually remarking on the weather. She heard the door close loudly and then the grind of the elevator.

When she knew he was gone, she was cool and still no longer. She ran about the little flat, striking her breast and sobbing.

Then she had two months to ponder what had happened, to see how she had wrought the ugly small ruin. She cried in the nights.

She need not brood over it any more. She had her lesson; she could forget how she had learned it. This new leave would be the one to remember, the one he and she would have to keep forever. She was to have a second chance, another twenty-four hours with him. After all, that is no short while, you know; that is, if you do not think of it as a thin little row of hours dropping off like beads from a broken string. Think of it as a whole long day and a whole long night, shining and sweet, and you will be all but awed by your fortune. For how many people are there who have the memory of a whole long day and a whole long night, shining and sweet, to carry with them in their hearts until they die?

To keep something, you must take care of it. More, you must understand just what sort of care it requires. You must know the rules and abide by them. She could do that. She had been doing it all the months, in the writing of her letters to him. There had been rules to be learned in that matter, and the first of them was the hardest: never say to him what you want him to say to you. Never tell him how sadly you miss him, how it grows no better, how each day without him is sharper than the day before. Set down for him the gay happenings about you, bright little anecdotes, not invented, necessarily, but attractively embellished. Do not bedevil him with the pinings of your faithful heart because he is your husband, your man, your love. For you are writing to none of these. You are writing to a soldier.

She knew those rules. She would have said that she would rather die, and she would have meant something very near the words, than send a letter of complaint or sadness or cold anger to her husband, a soldier far away, strained and weary from his work, giving all he had for the mighty cause. If in her letters she could be all he wanted her to be, how much easier to be it when they were together. Letters were difficult; every word had to be considered and chosen. When they were together again, when they could see and hear and touch each other, there would be no stiltedness. They would talk and laugh together. They would have tenderness and excitement. It would be as if they had never been separated. Perhaps they never had been. Perhaps a strange new life and strange empty miles and strange gay voices had no existence for two who were really one.

She had thought it out. She had learned the laws of what not to do. Now she could give herself up to the ecstasy of waiting his coming.

It was a fine week. She counted the time again, but now it was sweet to see it go. Two days after tomorrow, day after tomorrow, tomorrow. She lay awake in the dark, but it was a thrilling wakefulness. She went tall and straight by day, in pride in her warrior. On the street, she looked with amused pity at women who walked with men in civilian suits.

She bought a new dress; black – he liked black dresses – simple – he liked plain dresses – and so expensive that she would not think of its price. She charged it, and realized that for months to come she would tear up the bill without removing it from its envelope. All right – this was no time to think of months to come.

The day of the leave was a Saturday. She flushed with gratitude to the army for this coincidence, for after one o'clock, Saturday was her own. She went from her office without stopping for lunch, and bought perfume and toilet water and bath oil. She had a bit of each remaining in bottles on her dressing table and in her bathroom, hut it made her feel desired and secure to have rich new stores of them. She bought a nightgown, a delightful thing of soft chiffon patterned with little bouquets, with innocent puffs of sleeves and a Romney neck and a blue sash. It could never withstand laundering, a French cleaner must care for it – all right. She hurried home with it, to fold it in a satin sachet.

Then she went out again and bought the materials for cocktails and whiskies-and-sodas, shuddering at their cost. She went a dozen blocks to buy the kind of salted biscuits he liked with drinks. On the way back she passed a florist's shop in the window of which were displayed potted fuchsia. She made no attempt to resist them. They were too charming, with their delicate parchment-coloured inverted cups and their graceful magenta bells. She bought six pots of them. Suppose she did without lunches the next week – all right.

When she was done with the little living-room, it looked gracious and gay. She ranged the pots of fuchsia along the window sill, she drew out a table and set it with glasses and bottles, she plumped the pillows and laid bright-covered magazines about invitingly. It was a place where someone entering eagerly would find delighted welcome.

Before she changed her dress, she telephoned downstairs to the man who tended both the switchboard and the elevator.

'Oh,' she said, when he eventually answered. 'Oh, I just want to say, when my husband, Lieutenant McVicker, comes, please send him right up.'

There was no necessity for the call. The wearied attendant would have brought up anyone to any flat without the additional stress of a telephoned announcement. But she wanted to say the words 'my husband' and she wanted to say 'lieutenant'.

She sang, when she went into the bedroom to dress. She had a sweet, uncertain little voice that made the lusty song ludicrous.

> Off we go into the wild blue yonder,
>   Climbing high into the sun, sun, sun, sun.
> Here they come: zooming to meet our thunder—
>   At 'em boys, give 'er the gun!

She kept singing, in a preoccupied way, while she gave close attention to her lips and her eyelashes. Then she was silent and held her breath as she drew on the new dress. It was good to her. There was a reason for the cost of those perfectly plain black dresses. She stood looking at herself in the mirror with deep interest, as if she watched a chic unknown, the details of whose costume she sought to memorize.

As she stood there, the bell rang. It rang three times, loud and quick. He had come.

She gasped, and her hands fluttered over the dressing table. She seized the perfume atomizer and sprayed scent violently all about her head and shoulders, some of it reaching them. She had already perfumed herself, but she wanted another minute, another moment, anyway. For it had taken her again – the outrageous shyness. She could not bring herself to go to the door and open it. She stood, shaking, and squirted perfume.

The bell rang three times loud and quick again, and then an endless peal.

'Oh, *wait*, can't you?' she cried. She threw down the atomizer, looked wildly around the room as if for a hiding-place, then sternly made herself tall and sought to control the shaking of her body. The shrill noise of the bell seemed to fill the flat and crowd the air out of it.

She started for the door. Before she reached it, she stopped. There he stood in the brightly lighted little hall. All the long sad nights, and all the strong and sensible vows. And now he had come. And there she stood.

'Well, for heaven's sake!' she said. 'I had no idea there was anybody out here. Why, you were just as quiet as a little mouse.'

'Well! Don't you ever open the door?' he said.

'Can't a woman have time to put on her shoes?' she said.

He came in and closed the door behind him. 'Ah, darling,' he said. He put his arms around her. She slid her cheek along his lips, touched her forehead to his shoulder. And broke away from him.

'Well!' she said. 'Nice to see you, Lieutenant. How's the war?'

'How are you?' he said. 'You look wonderful.'

'Me?' she said. 'Look at you.'

He was well worth looking at. His fine clothes complemented his fine body. The precision of his appointments was absolute, yet he seemed to have no consciousness of it. He stood straight, and he moved with grace and assurance. His face was browned. It was thin; so thin that the bones showed under the cheeks and down the jaws; but there was no look of strain in it. It was smooth and serene and confident. He was the American officer, and there was no finer sight than he.

'Well!' she said. She made herself raise her eyes to his and found suddenly that it was no longer difficult. 'Well, we can't just stand here saying "well" at each other. Come on in and sit down. We've got a long time ahead of us – oh, Steve, isn't it wonderful! Hey. Didn't you bring a bag?'

'Why, you see,' he said, and stopped. He slung his cap over on to the table among the bottles and glasses. 'I left the bag at the station. I'm afraid I've got sort of rotten news, darling.'

She kept her hands from flying to her breast.

'You – you're going overseas right away?' she said.

'Oh, Lord, no,' he said. 'Oh, no, no, no. I said this was rotten news. No. They've changed the orders, baby. They've taken back all leaves. We're to go right on to the new field. I've got to get a train at six-ten.'

She sat down on the sofa. She wanted to cry; not silently with slow crystal tears, but with wide mouth and smeared face. She wanted to throw herself stomach-down on the floor, and kick and scream, and go limp if anyone tried to lift her.

'I think that's awful,' she said. 'I think that's just filthy.'

'I know,' he said. 'But there's nothing to do about it. This is the army, Mrs Jones.'

'Couldn't you have said something?' she said. 'Couldn't you have told them you've had only one leave in six months? Couldn't you have said all the chance your wife had to see you again was just this poor little twenty-four hours? Couldn't you have explained what it meant to her? Couldn't you?'

'Come on, now, Mimi,' he said. 'There's a war on.'

'I'm sorry,' she said. 'I was sorry as soon as I'd said it. I was sorry while I was saying it. But – oh, it's so hard!'

'It's not easy for anybody,' he said. 'You don't know how the boys were looking forward to their leaves.'

'Oh, I don't give a damn about the boys!' she said.

'That's the spirit that'll win for our side,' he said. He sat down in the biggest chair, stretched his legs and crossed his ankles.

'You don't care about anything but those pilots,' she said.

'Look, Mimi,' he said. 'We haven't got time to do this. We haven't got time to get into a fight and say a lot of things we don't mean. Everything's all – all speeded up, now. There's no time left for this.'

'Oh, I know,' she said. 'Oh, Steve, don't I know!'

She went over and sat on the arm of his chair and buried her face in his shoulder.

'This is more like it,' he said. 'I've kept thinking about this.' She nodded against his blouse.

'If you knew what it was to sit in a decent chair again,' he said.

She sat up. 'Oh,' she said. 'It's the chair. I'm so glad you like it.'

'They've got the worst chairs you ever saw, in the pilots' room,' he said. 'A lot of busted-down old rockers – honestly, rockers – that big-hearted patriots contributed, to get them out of the attic. If they haven't better furniture at the new field, I'm going to do something about it, even if I have to buy the stuff myself.'

'I certainly would, if I were you,' she said. 'I'd go without food and clothing and laundry, so the boys would be happy sitting down. I wouldn't even save out enough for air-mail stamps, to write to my wife once in a while.'

She rose and moved about the room.

'Mimi, what's the matter with you?' he said. 'Are you – are you jealous of the pilots?'

She counted as far as eight, to herself. Then she turned and smiled at him.

'Why – I guess I am –' she said. 'I guess that's just what I must be. Not only of the pilots. Of the whole air corps. Of the whole Army of the United States.'

'You're wonderful,' he said.

'You see,' she said with care, 'you have a whole new life – I have half an old one. Your life is so far away from mine, I don't see how they're ever going to come back together.'

'That's nonsense,' he said.

'No, please wait,' she said. 'I get strained and – and frightened, I guess, and I say things I could cut my throat for saying. But you know what I really feel about you. I'm so proud of you I can't find words for it. I know you're doing the most important thing in the world, maybe the only important thing in the world. Only – oh, Steve, I wish to heaven you didn't love doing it so much!'

'Listen,' he said.

'No,' she said. 'You mustn't interrupt a lady. It's unbecoming to an officer, like carrying packages in the street. I'm just trying to tell you a little about how I feel. I can't get used to being so completely left out. You don't wonder what I do, you don't want to find out what's in my head – why, you never even seem to ask how I am.'

'I do so!' he said. 'I asked you how you were the minute I came in.'

'That was white of you,' she said.

'Oh, for heaven's sake!' he said. 'I didn't have to ask you. I could see how you look. You look wonderful. I told you that.'

She smiled at him. 'Yes, you did, didn't you?' she said. 'And you sounded as if you meant it. Do you really like my dress?'

'Oh, yes,' he said. 'I always liked that dress on you.'

It was as if she turned to wood. 'This dress,' she said, enunciating with insulting directness, 'is brand new. I have never had it on before in my life. In case you are interested, I bought it especially for this occasion.'

'I'm sorry, honey,' he said. 'Oh, sure, now I see it's not the other one at all. I think it's great. I like you in black.'

'At moments like this,' she said, 'I almost wish I were in it for another reason.'

'Stop it,' he said. 'Sit down and tell me about yourself. What have you been doing?'

'Oh, nothing,' she said.

'How's the office?' he said.

'Dull,' she said. 'Dull as mud.'

'Who have you seen?' he said.

'Oh, nobody,' she said.

'Well, what do you *do*?' he said.

'In the evenings?' she said. 'Oh, I sit here and knit and read detective stories that it turns out I've read before.'

'I think that's all wrong of you,' he said. 'I think it's asinine to sit here alone, moping. That doesn't do any good to anybody. Why don't you go out more?'

'I hate to go out with just women,' she said.

'Well, why do you have to?' he said. 'Ralph's in town, isn't he? And John and Bill and Gerald. Why don't you go out with them? You're silly not to.'

'It hadn't occurred to me,' she said, 'that it was silly to keep faithful to one's husband.'

'Isn't that taking rather a jump?' he said. 'It's possible to go to dinner with a man and stay this side adultery. And don't use words like "one's". You're awful when you're elegant.'

'I know,' she said. 'I never have any luck when I try. No. You're the one that's awful, Steve. You really are. I'm trying to show you a glimpse of my heart, to tell you how it feels when you're gone, how I don't want to be with anyone if I can't be with you. And all you say is, I'm not doing any good to anybody.

That'll be nice to think of when you go. You don't know what it's like for me here alone. You just don't know.'

'Yes, I do,' he said. 'I know, Mimi.' He reached for a cigarette on the little table beside him, and the bright magazine by the cigarette box caught his eye. 'Hey, is this this week's? I haven't seen it yet.' He glanced through the early pages.

'Go ahead and read if you want to,' she said. 'Don't let me disturb you.'

'I'm not reading,' he said. He put down the magazine. 'You see, I don't know what to say, when you start talking about showing me glimpses of your heart, and all that. I know. I know you must be having a rotten time. But aren't you feeling fairly sorry for yourself?'

'If I'm not,' she said, 'who would be?'

'What do you want anyone to be sorry for you for?' he said. 'You'd be all right if you'd stop sitting around alone. I'd like to think of you having a good time while I'm away.'

She went over to him and kissed him on the forehead.

'Lieutenant,' she said, 'you are a far nobler character than I am. Either that,' she said, 'or there is something else at the back of this.'

'Oh, shut up,' he said. He pulled her down to him and held her there. She seemed to melt against him, and stayed there, still.

Then she felt him take his left arm from around her and felt his head raised from its place against hers. She looked up at him. He was craning over her shoulder, endeavouring to see his wrist watch.

'Oh, now, really!' she said. She put her hands against his chest and pushed herself vigorously away from him.

'It goes so quickly,' he said softly, with his eyes on his watch. 'We've – we've only a little while, darling.'

She melted again. 'Oh, Steve,' she whispered, 'dearest.'

'I do want to take a bath,' he said. 'Get up, will you, baby?'

She got right up. 'You're going to take a bath?' she said.

'Yes,' he said. 'You don't mind, do you?'

'Oh, not in the least,' she said. 'I'm sure you'll enjoy it. It's one of the pleasantest ways of killing time, I always think.'

'You know how you feel after a long ride on a train,' he said.

'Oh, surely,' she said.

He rose and went into the bedroom. 'I'll hurry up,' he called back to her.

'Why?' she said.

Then she had a moment to consider herself. She went into the bedroom after him, sweet with renewed resolve. He had hung his blouse and necktie neatly over a chair and he was unbuttoning his shirt. As she came in, he took it off. She looked at the beautiful brown triangle of his back. She would do anything for him, anything in the world.

'I – I'll go run your bath water,' she said. She went into the bathroom, turned on the faucets of the tub, and set the towels and mat ready. When she came back into the bedroom he was just entering the living-room, naked. In his hand he carried the bright magazine he had glanced at before. She stopped short.

'Oh,' she said. 'You're planning to read in the tub?'

'If you knew how I'd been looking forward to this!' he said. 'Boy, a hot bath in a tub! We haven't got anything but showers, and when you take a shower, there's a hundred boys waiting, yelling at you to hurry up and get out.'

'I suppose they can't bear being parted from you,' she said.

He smiled at her. 'See you in a couple of minutes,' he said, and went on into the bathroom and closed the door. She heard the slow slip and slide of water as he laid himself in the tub.

She stood just as she was. The room was lively with the perfume she had sprayed, too present, too insistent. Her eyes went to the bureau drawer where lay, wrapped in soft fragrance, the nightgown with the little bouquets and the Romney neck. She went over to the bathroom door, drew back her right foot, and kicked the base of the door so savagely that the whole frame shook.

'What, dear?' he called. 'Want something?'

'Oh, nothing,' she said. 'Nothing whatever. I've got everything any woman could possibly want, haven't I?'

'What?' he called. 'I can't hear you, honey.'

'Nothing,' she screamed.

She went into the living-room. She stood, breathing heavily, her finger nails scarring her palms, as she looked at the fuchsia blossoms, with their dirty parchment-coloured cups, their vulgar magenta bells.

Her breath was quiet and her hands relaxed when he came into the living-room again. He had on his trousers and shirt, and his necktie was admirably knotted. He carried his belt. She turned to him. There were things she had meant to say, but she could do nothing but smile at him, when she saw him. Her heart turned liquid in her breast.

His brow puckered. 'Look, darling,' he said. 'Have you got any brass polish?'

'Why, no,' she said. 'We haven't even got any brass.'

'Well, have you any nail polish – the colourless kind? A lot of the boys use that.'

'I'm sure it must look adorable on them,' she said. 'No, I haven't anything but rose-coloured polish. Would that be of any use to you, heaven forbid?'

'No,' he said, and he seemed worried. 'Red wouldn't be any good at all. Hell, I don't suppose you've got a Blitz Cloth, have you? Or a Shine-O?'

'If I had the faintest idea what you were talking about,' she said, 'I might be better company for you.'

He held the belt out toward her. 'I want to shine my buckle,' he said.

'Oh … my … dear … sweet … gentle … Lord,' she said. 'We've got about ten minutes left, and you want to shine your belt buckle.'

'I don't like to report to a new CO* with a dull belt buckle,' he said.

'It was bright enough for you to report to your wife in, wasn't it?' she said.

'Oh, stop that,' he said. 'You just won't understand, that's all.'

'It isn't that I won't understand,' she said. 'It's that I can't remember. I haven't been with a Boy Scout for so long.'

He looked at her. 'You're being great, aren't you?' he said. He looked around the room. 'There must be a cloth around somewhere – oh, this will do.' He caught up a pretty little cock-tail napkin from the table of untouched bottles and glasses, sat down with his belt laid over his knees, and rubbed at the buckle.

She watched him for a moment, then rushed over to him and grasped his arm.

---

*   Commanding Officer

'Please,' she said. 'Please, I didn't mean it, Steve.'

'Please let me do this, will you?' he said. He wrenched his arm from her hand and went on with his polishing.

'You tell me I won't understand!' she cried. 'You won't understand anything about anybody else. Except those crazy pilots.'

'They're all right!' he said. 'They're fine kids. They're going to make great fighters.' He went on rubbing at his buckle.

'Oh, I know it!' she said. 'You know I know it. I don't mean it when I say things against them. How would I dare to mean it? They're risking their lives and their sight and their sanity, they're giving everything for –'

'Don't do that kind of talk, will you?' he said. He rubbed the buckle.

'I'm not doing any kind of talk!' she said. 'I'm trying to tell you something. Just because you've got on that pretty suit, you think you should never hear anything serious, never anything sad or wretched or disagreeable. You make me sick, that's what you do! I know, I know – I'm not trying to take anything away from you. I realize what you're doing, I told you what I think of it. Don't, for heaven's sake, think I'm mean enough to grudge you any happiness and excitement you can get out of it. I know it's hard for you. But it's never lonely, that's all I mean. You have companionships no – no wife can ever give you. I suppose it's the sense of hurry, maybe, the consciousness of living on borrowed time, the – the knowledge of what you're all going into together that makes the comradeship of men in war so firm, so fast. But won't you please try to understand how I feel? Won't you understand that it comes out of bewilderment and disruption and – and being frightened, I guess? Won't you understand what makes me do what I do, when I hate myself while I'm doing it? Won't you please understand? Darling, won't you please?'

He laid down the little napkin. 'I can't go through this kind of thing, Mimi,' he said. 'Neither can you.' He looked at his watch. 'Hey, it's time for me to go.'

She stood tall and stiff. 'I'm sure it is,' she said.

'I'd better put on my blouse,' he said.

'You might as well,' she said.

He rose, wove his belt through the loops of his trousers, and went into the bedroom. She went over to the window and stood looking out, as if casually remarking the weather.

She heard him come back into the room, but she did not turn around. She heard his steps stop, knew he was standing there.

'Mimi,' he said.

She turned towards him, her shoulders back, her chin high, cool, regal. Then she saw his eyes. They were no longer bright and gay and confident. Their blue was misty and they looked troubled; they looked at her as if they pleaded with her.

'Look, Mimi,' he said, 'do you think I want to do this? Do you think I want to be away from you? Do you think that this is what I thought I'd be doing now? In the years – well, in the years when we ought to be together.'

He stopped. Then he spoke again, but with difficulty. 'I can't talk about it. I can't even think about it – because if I did I couldn't do my job. But just because I don't talk about it doesn't mean I want to be doing what I'm doing. I want to be with you, Mimi. That's where I belong. You know that, darling. Don't you?'

He held his arms open to her. She ran to them. This time, she did not slide her cheek along his lips.

When he had gone, she stood a moment by the fuchsia plants, touching delicately, tenderly, the enchanting parchment-coloured caps, the exquisite magenta bells.

The telephone rang. She answered it, to hear a friend of hers inquiring about Steve, asking how he looked and how he was, urging that he come to the telephone and say hello to her.

'He's gone,' she said. 'All their leaves were cancelled. He wasn't here an hour.'

The friend cried sympathy. It was a shame, it was simply awful, it was absolutely terrible.

'No, don't say that,' she said. 'I know it wasn't very much time. But oh, it was lovely!'

ELIZABETH BOWEN

Mysterious Kôr

Full moonlight drenched the city and searched it; there was not a niche left to stand in. The effect was remorseless: London looked like the moon's capital – shallow, cratered, extinct. It was late, but not yet midnight; now the buses had stopped the polished roads and streets in this region sent for minutes together a ghostly unbroken reflection up. The soaring new flats and the crouching old shops and houses looked equally brittle under the moon, which blazed in windows that looked its way. The futility of the black-out became laughable: from the sky, presumably, you could see every slate in the roofs, every whited kerb, every contour of the naked winter flowerbeds in the park; and the lake, with its shining twists and tree-darkened islands would be a landmark for miles, yes, miles, overhead.

However, the sky, in whose glassiness floated no clouds but only opaque balloons, remained glassy-silent. The Germans no longer came by the full moon. Something more immaterial seemed to threaten, and to be keeping people at home. This day between days, this extra tax, was perhaps more than senses and nerves could bear. People stayed indoors with a fervour that could be felt: the buildings strained with battened-down human life, but not a beam, not a voice, not a note from a radio escaped. Now and then under streets and buildings the earth rumbled: the Underground sounded loudest at this time.

Outside the now gateless gates of the park, the road coming downhill from the north-west turned south and became a street, down whose perspective the traffic lights went through their unmeaning performance of changing colour. From the promontory of pavement outside the gates you saw at once up the road and down the street: from behind where you stood, between the gate-posts, appeared the lesser strangeness of grass and water and trees. At this point, at this moment, three French soldiers, directed to a hostel they could not find, stopped singing to listen derisively to the waterbirds, wakened up by the moon. Next, two wardens coming off duty emerged from their post and crossed the road diagonally, each with an elbow cupped inside the slung-on tin hat. The wardens turned their faces, mauve in the moonlight, towards the Frenchmen with no expression at all. The two sets of steps died in opposite directions, and, the birds subsiding, nothing was heard or seen until, a little way down the street, a trickle of people came out of the Underground, around the anti-panic brick wall. These all disappeared quickly, in an abashed way, or as though dissolved in the street by some white acid, but for a girl and a soldier who, by their way of walking, seemed to have no destination but each other and to be not quite certain even of that. Blotted into one shadow, he tall, she little, these two proceeded towards the park. They looked in, but did not go in; they stood there debating without speaking. Then, as though a command from the street behind them had been received by their synchronized bodies, they faced round to look back the way they had come.

His look up the height of a building made his head drop back, and she saw his eyeballs glitter. She slid her hand from his sleeve, stepped to the edge of the pavement and said: 'Mysterious Kôr.'

'What is?' he said, not quite collecting himself.

'This is –

> Mysterious Kôr thy walls forsaken stand,
> Thy lonely towers beneath a lonely moon –

– this is Kôr.'

'Why,' he said, 'it's years since I've thought of that.'

She said: 'I think of it all the time –

> Not in the waste beyond the swamps and sand,
> The fever-haunted forest and lagoon,
> Mysterious Kôr thy walls –

– a completely forsaken city, as high as cliffs and as white as bones, with no history –'

'But something must once have happened: why had it been forsaken?'

'How could anyone tell you when there's nobody there?'

'Nobody there since how long?'

'Thousands of years.'

'In that case, it would have fallen down.'

'No, not Kôr,' she said with immediate authority. 'Kôr's altogether different; it's very strong; there is not a crack in it anywhere for a weed to grow in; the corners of stones and the monuments might have been cut yesterday, and the stairs and arches are built to support themselves.'

'You know all about it,' he said looking at her.

'I know, I know all about it.'

'What, since you read that book?'

'Oh, I didn't get much from that; I just got the name. I knew that must be the right name; it's like a cry.'

'Most like the cry of a crow to me.' He reflected, then said: 'But the poem begins with "Not" – "*Not in the waste beyond the swamps and sand* –" And it goes on, as I remember, to prove Kôr's not really anywhere. When even a poem says there's no such place –'

'What it tries to say doesn't matter: I see what it makes me see. Anyhow, that was written some time ago, at that time when they thought they had got everything taped, because the whole world had been explored, even the middle of Africa. Every thing and place had been found and marked on some map; so what wasn't marked on any map couldn't be there at all. So *they* thought: that was why he wrote the poem. "*The world is disenchanted*," it goes on. That was what set me off hating civilization.'

'Well, cheer up,' he said; 'there isn't much of it left.'

'Oh, yes, I cheered up some time ago. This war shows we've by no means come to the end. If you can blow whole places out of existence, you can blow whole places into it. I don't see why not. They say we can't say what's come out since the bombing started. By the time we've come to the end, Kôr may be the one city left: the abiding city. I should laugh.'

'No, you wouldn't,' he said sharply. '*You* wouldn't – at least, I hope not. I hope you don't know what you're saying – does the moon make you funny?'

'Don't be cross about Kôr; please don't, Arthur,' she said.

'I thought girls thought about people.'

'What, these days?' she said. 'Think about people? How can anyone think about people if they've got any heart? I don't know how other girls manage: I always think about Kôr.'

'Not about me?' he said. When she did not at once answer, he turned her hand over, in anguish, inside his grasp. 'Because I'm not there when you want me – is that my fault?'

'But to think about Kôr *is* to think about you and me.'

'In that dead place?'

'No, ours – we'd be alone there.' Tightening his thumb on her palm while he thought this over, he looked behind them, around them – even up at the sky. He said finally: 'But we're alone here.'

'That was why I said "Mysterious Kôr".'

'What, you mean we're there now, that here's there, that now's then? . . . *I* don't mind,' he added, letting out as a laugh the sigh he had been holding in for some time. 'You ought to know the place, and for all I could tell you we might be anywhere: I often do have it, this funny feeling, the first minute or two when I've come up out of the Underground. Well, well: join the Army and see the world.' He nodded towards the perspective of traffic lights and said, a shade craftily: 'What are those, then?'

Having caught the quickest possible breath, she replied: 'Inexhaustible gases; they bored through to them and lit them as they came up; by changing colour they show the changing of minutes; in Kôr there is no sort of other time.'

'You've got the moon, though: that can't help making months.'

'Oh, and the sun, of course; but those two could do what they liked; we should not have to calculate when they'd come or go.'

'We might not have to,' he said, 'but I bet I should.'

'I should not mind what you did, so long as you never said, "What next?"'

'I don't know about "next", but I do know what we'd do first.'

'What, Arthur?'

'Populate Kôr.'

She said: 'I suppose it would be all right if our children were to marry each other?'

But her voice faded out; she had been reminded that they were homeless on this his first night of leave. They were, that was to say, in London without any hope of any place of their own. Pepita shared a two-roomed flatlet with a girl friend, in a by-street off the Regent's Park Road, and towards this they must make their half-hearted way.

Arthur was to have the sitting-room divan, usually occupied by Pepita, while she herself had half of her girl friend's bed. There was really no room for a third, and least of all for a man, in those small rooms packed with furniture and the two girls' belongings: Pepita tried to be grateful for her friend Callie's forbearance – but how could she be, when it had not occurred to Callie that she would do better to be away tonight? She was more slow-witted than narrow-minded – but Pepita felt she owed a kind of ruin to her. Callie, not yet known to be home later than ten, would be now waiting up, in her housecoat, to welcome Arthur. That would mean three-sided chat, drinking cocoa, then turning in: that would be that, and that would be all. That was London, this war – they were lucky to have a roof – London, full enough before the Americans came. Not a place: they would even grudge you sharing a grave – that was what even married couples complained. Whereas in Kôr . . .

In Kôr . . . Like glass, the illusion shattered: a car hummed like a hornet towards them, veered, showed its scarlet taillight, streaked away up the road. A woman edged round a front door and along the area railings timidly called her cat; meanwhile a clock near, then another set further back in the dazzling distance, set about striking midnight. Pepita, feeling Arthur release her arm with an abruptness that was the inverse of passion, shivered; whereat he asked brusquely: 'Cold? Well, which way? We'd better be getting on.'

Callie was no longer waiting up. Hours ago she had set out the three cups and saucers, the tins of cocoa and household milk and, on the gas-ring, brought the kettle to just short of the boil. She had turned open Arthur's bed, the living-room divan, in the neat inviting way she had learnt at home – then, with a modest impulse, replaced the cover. She had, as Pepita foresaw, been wearing her cretonne housecoat, the nearest thing to a hostess gown that she had; she had already brushed her hair for the night, rebraided it, bound the braids in a coronet round her head. Both lights and the wireless had been on, to make the room both look and sound gay: all alone, she had come to that peak moment at which company should arrive – but so seldom does. From then on she felt welcome beginning to wither in her, a flower of the heart that had bloomed too early. There she had sat like an image, facing the three cold cups, on the edge of the bed to be occupied by an unknown man.

Callie's innocence and her still unsought-out state had brought her to take a proprietary pride in Arthur; this was all the stronger, perhaps, because they had not yet met. Sharing the flat with Pepita, this last year, she had been content with reflecting the heat of love. It was not, surprisingly, that Pepita seemed very happy – there were times when she was palpably on the rack and this was not what Callie could understand. 'Surely you owe it to Arthur,' she would then say, 'to keep cheerful? So long as you love each other –' Callie's calm brow glowed – one might say that it glowed in place of her friend's; she became the guardian of that ideality which for Pepita was constantly lost to view. It was true, with the sudden prospect of Arthur's leave, things had come nearer to earth: he became a proposition, and she would have been as glad if he could have slept somewhere else. Physically shy, a brotherless virgin, Callie shrank from sharing this flat with a young man. In this flat you could hear everything: what was once a three-windowed Victorian drawing-room had been partitioned, by very thin walls, into kitchenette, living-room, Callie's bedroom. The living room was in the centre; the two others opened off it. What was once the conservatory, half a flight down, was now converted into a draughty bathroom, shared with somebody else on the girls' floor. The flat, for these days, was cheap – even so, it was Callie, earning more than Pepita, who paid the greater part of the rent: it thus became up to her, more or less, to express good will as to Arthur's making a third. 'Why, it will be lovely to have him here,' Callie said. Pepita accepted the good will without much grace – but then, had she ever much grace to spare? – she was as restlessly secretive, as self-centred, as a little half-grown black cat. Next came a puzzling moment: Pepita seemed to be hinting that Callie should fix herself up somewhere else. 'But where would I go?' Callie marvelled when this was at last borne in on her. 'You know what London's like now. And, anyway,' – here she laughed, but hers was a forehead that coloured as easily as it glowed – 'it wouldn't be proper, would it, me going off and leaving just you and Arthur; I don't know what your mother would say to me. No, we may be a little squashed, but we'll make things ever so homey. I shall not mind playing gooseberry, really, dear.'

But the hominess by now was evaporating, as Pepita and Arthur still and still did not come. At half past ten, in obedience to the rule of the house, Callie was obliged to turn off the wireless, whereupon silence out of the stepless street began seeping into the slighted room. Callie recollected the fuel target and turned off her dear little table lamp, gaily painted with spots to make it look like a toadstool, thereby leaving only the hanging light. She laid her hand on the kettle, to find it gone cold again and sigh for the wasted gas if not for her wasted thought. Where are they? Cold crept up her out of the kettle; she went to bed.

Callie's bed lay along the wall under the window: she did not like sleeping so close up under glass, but the clearance that must be left for the opening of door and cupboards made this the only possible place. Now she got in and lay rigidly on the bed's inner side, under the hanging hems of the window curtains, training her limbs not to stray to what would be Pepita's half. This sharing of her bed with another body would not be the least of her sacrifice to the lovers' love; tonight would be the first night – or at least, since she was an infant – that Callie had slept with anyone. Child of a sheltered middleclass household, she had kept physical distances all her life. Already repugnance and shyness ran through her limbs; she was preyed upon by some more obscure trouble than the expectation that she might not sleep. As to *that*, Pepita was restless; her tossings on the divan, her broken-off exclamations and blurred pleas had been to be heard, most nights, through the dividing wall.

Callie knew, as though from a vision, that Arthur would sleep soundly, with assurance and majesty. Did they not all say, too, that a soldier sleeps like a log? With awe she pictured, asleep, the face that she had not yet, awake, seen – Arthur's man's eyelids, cheek-bones and set mouth turned up to the darkened ceiling. Wanting to savour darkness herself, Callie reached out and put off her bedside lamp.

At once she knew that something was happening – outdoors, in the street, the whole of London, the world. An advance, an extraordinary movement was silently taking place; blue-white beams overflowed from it, silting, dropping round the edges of the muffling black-out curtains. When, starting up, she knocked a fold of the curtain, a beam like a mouse ran across her bed. A searchlight, the most powerful of all time, might have been turned full and steady upon her defended window; finding flaws in the black-out stuff, it made veins and stars. Once gained by this idea of pressure she could not lie down again; she sat tautly, drawn-up knees touching her breasts, and asked herself if there were anything she should do. She parted the curtains, opened them slowly wider, looked out – and was face to face with the moon.

Below the moon, the houses opposite her window blazed back in transparent shadow; and something – was it a coin or a ring? – glittered half-way across the chalk-white street. Light marched in past her face, and she turned to see where it went: out stood the curves and garlands of the great white marble Victorian mantelpiece of that lost drawing-room; out stood, in the photographs turned her way, the thoughts with which her parents had faced the camera, and the humble puzzlement of her two dogs at home. Of silver brocade, just faintly purpled with roses, became her housecoat hanging over the chair. And the moon did more: it exonerated and beautified the lateness of the lovers' return. No wonder, she said herself, no wonder if this was the world they walked in, if this was whom they were with. Having drunk in the white explanation, Callie lay down again. Her half of the bed was in shadow, but she allowed one hand to lie, blanched, in what would be Pepita's place. She lay and looked at the hand until it was no longer her own.

Callie woke to the sound of Pepita's key in the latch. But no voices? What had happened? Then she heard Arthur's step. She heard his unslung equipment dropped with a weary, dull sound, and the plonk of his tin hat on a wooden chair. 'Ssshsssh!' Pepita exclaimed. 'She *might* be asleep!'

Then at last Arthur's voice: 'But I thought you said –'

'I'm not asleep; I'm just coming!' Callie called out with rapture, leaping out from her form in shadow into the moonlight, zipping on her enchanted housecoat over her nightdress, kicking her shoes on, and pinning in place, with a trembling firmness, her plaits in their coronet round her head. Between these movements of hers she heard not another sound. Had she only dreamed they were there? Her heart beat: she stepped through the living-room, shutting the door behind her.

Pepita and Arthur stood the other side of the table; they gave the impression of being lined up. Their faces, at different levels – for Pepita's rough, dark head came only an inch above Arthur's khaki shoulder – were alike in abstention from any kind of expression; as though, spiritually, they both still refused to be here. Their features looked faint, weathered – was this the work of the moon? Pepita said at once: 'I suppose we are very late?'

'I don't wonder,' Callie said, 'on this lovely night.'

Arthur had not raised his eyes; he was looking at the three cups. Pepita now suddenly jogged his elbow, saying, 'Arthur, wake up; say something; this is Callie – well, Callie, this is Arthur, of course.'

'Why, yes, of course this is Arthur,' returned Callie, whose candid eyes since she entered had not left Arthur's face. Perceiving that Arthur did not know what to do, she advanced round the table to shake hands with him. He looked up, she looked down, for the first time: she rather beheld than felt his red-brown grip on what still seemed her glove of moonlight. 'Welcome, Arthur,' she said. 'I'm so glad to meet you at last. I hope you will be comfortable in the flat.'

'It's been kind of you,' he said after consideration.

'Please do not feel that,' said Callie. 'This is Pepita's home, too, and we both hope – don't we, Pepita? – that you'll regard it as yours. Please feel free to do just as you like. I am sorry it is so small.'

'Oh, I don't know,' Arthur said, as though hypnotized; 'it seems a nice little place.'

Pepita, meanwhile, glowered and turned away.

Arthur continued to wonder, though he had once been told, how these two unalike girls had come to set up together – Pepita so small, except for her too-big head, compact of childish brusqueness and of unchildish passion, and Callie, so sedate, waxy and tall – an unlit candle. Yes, she was like one of those candles on sale outside a church; there could be something votive even in her demeanour. She was unconscious that her good manners, those of an old-fashioned country doctor's daughter, were putting the other two at a disadvantage. He found himself touched by the grave good faith with which Callie was wearing that tartish house-coat, above which her face kept the glaze of sleep; and, as she knelt to relight the gas-ring under the kettle, he marked the strong, delicate arch of one bare foot, disappearing into the arty green shoe. Pepita was now too near him ever again to be seen as he now saw Callie – in a sense, he never *had* seen Pepita for the first time:

she had not been, and still sometimes was not, his type. No, he had not thought of her twice; he had not remembered her until he began to remember her with passion. You might say he had not seen Pepita coming: their love had been a collision in the dark.

Callie, determined to get this over, knelt back and said: 'Would Arthur like to wash his hands?' When they had heard him stumble down the half-flight of stairs, she said to Pepita: 'Yes, I was so glad you had the moon.'

'Why?' said Pepita. She added: 'There was too much of it.'

'You're tired. Arthur looks tired, too.'

'How would you know? He's used to marching about. But it's all this having no place to go.'

'But, Pepita, you –'

But at this point Arthur came back: from the door he noticed the wireless, and went direct to it. 'Nothing much on now, I suppose?' he doubtfully said.

'No: you see it's past midnight; we're off the air. And, anyway, in this house they don't like the wireless late. By the same token,' went on Callie, friendlily smiling, 'I'm afraid I must ask you, Arthur, to take your boots off, unless, of course, you mean to stay sitting down. The people below us –'

Pepita flung off, saying something under her breath, but Arthur remarking, 'No, I don't mind,' both sat down and began to take off his boots. Pausing, glancing to left and right at the divan's fresh cotton spread, he said: 'It's all right is it, for me to sit on this?'

'That's my bed,' said Pepita. 'You are to sleep in it.'

Callie then made the cocoa, after which they turned in. Preliminary trips to the bathroom having been worked out, Callie was first to retire, shutting the door behind her so that Pepita and Arthur might kiss each other good-night. When Pepita joined her, it was without knocking: Pepita stood still in the moon and began to tug off her clothes. Glancing with hate at the bed, she asked: 'Which side?'

'I expected you'd like the outside.'

'What are you standing about for?'

'I don't really know: as I'm inside I'd better get in first.'

'Then why not get in?'

When they had settled rigidly, side by side, Callie asked: 'Do you think Arthur's got all he wants?'

Pepita jerked her head up. 'We can't sleep in all this moon.'

'Why, you don't believe the moon does things, actually?'

'Well, it couldn't hope to make some of us *much* more screwy.'

Callie closed the curtains, then said: 'What do you mean? And – didn't you hear? – I asked if Arthur's got all he wants.'

'That's what I meant – have you got a screw loose, really?'

'Pepita, I won't stay here if you're going to be like this.'

'In that case, you had better go in with Arthur.'

'What about me?' Arthur loudly said through the wall. 'I can hear practically all you girls are saying.'

They were both startled – rather that than abashed. Arthur, alone in there, had thrown off the ligatures of his social manner: his voice held the whole authority of his sex – he was impatient, sleepy and he belonged to no one.

'Sorry,' the girls said in unison. Then Pepita laughed soundlessly, making their bed shake, till to stop herself she bit the back of her hand, and this movement made her elbow strike Callie's cheek. 'Sorry,' she had to whisper. No answer: Pepita fingered her elbow and found, yes, it was quite true, it was wet. 'Look, shut up crying, Callie: what have I done?'

Callie rolled right round, in order to press her forehead closely under the window, into the curtains, against the wall. Her weeping continued to be soundless: now and then, unable to reach her handkerchief, she staunched her eyes with a curtain, disturbing slivers of moon. Pepita gave up marvelling, and soon slept: at least there is something in being dog-tired.

A clock struck four as Callie woke up again – but something else had made her open her swollen eyelids. Arthur, stumbling about on his padded feet, could be heard next door attempting to make no noise. Inevitably, he bumped the edge of the table. Callie sat up: by her side Pepita lay like a mummy rolled half over, in forbidding, tenacious sleep. Arthur groaned. Callie caught a breath, climbed lightly over Pepita, felt for her torch on the mantelpiece, stopped to listen again. Arthur groaned again: Callie, with movements soundless as they were certain, opened the door and slipped through to the living-room. 'What's the matter?' she whispered. 'Are you ill?'

'No; I just got a cigarette. Did I wake you up?'

'But you groaned.'

'I'm sorry; I'd no idea.'

'But do you often?'

'I've no idea, really, I tell you,' Arthur repeated. The air of the room was dense with his presence, overhung by tobacco. He must be sitting on the edge of his bed, wrapped up in his overcoat – she could smell the coat, and each time he pulled on the cigarette his features appeared down there, in the fleeting, dull reddish glow. 'Where are you?' he said. 'Show a light.'

Her nervous touch on her torch, like a reflex to what he said, made it flicker up for a second. 'I am just by the door; Pepita's asleep; I'd better go back to bed.'

'Listen. Do you two get on each other's nerves?'

'Not till tonight,' said Callie, watching the uncertain swoops of the cigarette as he reached across to the ashtray on the edge of the table. Shifting her bare feet patiently, she added: 'You don't see us as we usually are.'

'She's a girl who shows things in funny ways – I expect she feels bad at our putting you out like this – I know I do. But then we'd got no choice, had we?'

'It is really I who am putting you out,' said Callie.

'Well, that can't be helped either, can it? You had the right to stay in your own place. If there'd been more time, we might have gone to the country, though I still don't see where we'd have gone there. It's one harder when you're not married, unless you've got the money. Smoke?'

'No, thank you. Well, if you're all right, I'll go back to bed.'

'I'm glad she's asleep – funny the way she sleeps, isn't it? You can't help wondering where she is. You haven't got a boy, have you, just at present?'

'No. I've never had one.'

'I'm not sure in one way that you're not better off. I can see there's not so much in it for a girl these days. It makes me feel cruel the way I unsettle her: I don't know how much it's me myself or how much it's something the matter that I can't help. How are any of us to know how things could have been? They forget war's not just only war; it's years out of people's lives that they've never had before and won't have again. Do you think she's fanciful?'

'Who, Pepita?'

'It's enough to make her – tonight was the pay-off. We couldn't get near any movie or any place for sitting; you had to fight into the bars, and she hates the staring in bars, and with all that milling about, every street we went, they kept on knocking her even off my arm. So then we took the Tube to that park down there, but the place was as bad as daylight, let alone it was cold. We hadn't the nerve – well, that's nothing to do with you.'

'I don't mind.'

'Or else you don't understand. So we began to play – we were off in Kôr.'

'Core of what?'

'Mysterious Kôr – ghost city.'

'Where?'

'You may ask. But I could have sworn she saw it, and from the way she saw it I saw it, too. A game's a game, but what's a hallucination? You begin by laughing, then it gets in you and you can't laugh it off. I tell you, I woke up just now not knowing where I'd been; and I had to get up and feel round this table before I even knew where I was. It wasn't till then that I thought of a cigarette. Now I see why she sleeps like that, if that's where she goes.'

'But she is just as often restless; I often hear her.'

'Then she doesn't always make it. Perhaps it takes me, in some way – well, I can't see any harm: when two people have got no place, why not want Kôr, as a start? There are no restrictions on wanting, at any rate.'

'But, oh, Arthur, can't wanting want what's human?'

He yawned. 'To be human's to be at a dead loss.' Stopping yawning, he ground out his cigarette: the china tray skidded at the edge of the table. 'Bring that light here a moment – that is, will you? I think I've messed ash all over these sheets of hers.'

Callie advanced with the torch alight, but at arm's length: now and then her thumb made the beam wobble. She watched the lit-up inside of Arthur's hand as he brushed the sheet; and once he looked up to see her white-nightgowned figure curving above and away from him, behind the arc of light. 'What's that swinging?'

'One of my plaits of hair. Shall I open the window wider?'

'What, to let the smoke out? Go on. And how's your moon?'

'Mine?' Marvelling over this, as the first sign that Arthur remembered that she was Callie, she uncovered the window, pushed up the sash, then after a minute she said: 'Not so strong.'

Indeed, the moon's power over London and the imagination

had now declined. The siege of light had relaxed; the search was over; the street had a look of survival and no more. Whatever had glittered there, coin or ring, was now invisible or had gone. To Callie it seemed likely that there would never be such a moon again; and on the whole she felt this was for the best. Feeling air reach in like a tired arm round her body, she dropped the curtains against it and returned to her own room.

Back by her bed, she listened: Pepita's breathing still had the regular sound of sleep. At the other side of the wall the divan creaked as Arthur stretched himself out again. Having felt ahead of her lightly, to make sure her half was empty, Callie climbed over Pepita and got in. A certain amount of warmth had travelled between the sheets from Pepita's flank, and in this Callie extended her sword-cold body; she tried to compose her limbs; even they quivered after Arthur's words in the dark, words *to* the dark. The loss of her own mysterious expectation, of her love for love, was a small thing beside the war's total of unlived lives. Suddenly Pepita flung out one hand: its back knocked Callie lightly across the face.

Pepita had now turned over and lay with her face up. The hand that had struck Callie must have lain over the other, which grasped the pyjama collar. Her eyes, in the dark, might have been either shut or open, but nothing made her frown more or less steadily: it became certain, after another moment, that Pepita's act of justice had been unconscious. She still lay, as she had lain, in an avid dream, of which Arthur had been the source, of which Arthur was not the end. With him she looked this way, that way, down the wide, void, pure streets, between statues, pillars and shadows, through archways and colonnades. With him she went up the stairs down which nothing but moon came; with him trod the ermine dust of the endless halls, stood on terraces, mounted the extreme tower, looked down on the statued squares, the wide, void, pure streets. He was the password, but not the answer: it was to Kôr's finality that she turned.

MARGERY SHARP

Night Engagement

The trouble with this shelter life (said Mrs Catchpole) is that a girl don't get a chance to make steady friends. All the regulars bringing their wives and families, nice young fellows just passing through on leave, here today and gone tomorrow, a girl that respects herself doesn't know where to turn.

Take my Doris: time and again she's come back to our corner and said, 'Mum, there's ever such a nice young fellow just been chatting to me, but he isn't a regular.'

'Bring him over,' I say, 'and let's have a look at him.' So she brings him over, and we pass a pleasant evening and then the minute the All Clear goes he says, 'It's been a great pleasure meeting you, now I'm off to Aberdeen,' and a fat lot of good that is to a girl that lives in SW1.

'Take heart, Doris,' I say, 'there's a Mr Right somewhere.'

'Not in this shelter,' says Doris, 'not for a girl that respects herself; I think I'll try the Tube'; so the next night, off she goes in her siren-suit with half the sandwiches and a bottle of tea.

Well, I don't see her again till next morning when I find her at home in the scullery having a wash before she goes to work.

'Well, Doris,' I say, 'how's the Tube?'

'Well, Mum,' she says, 'I really can't tell. I met ever such a nice young fellow, works in the Post Office, stood me a cup of coffee and everything, only then a Warden butted in, said I better look out he had quite a name in the shelter and no companion for a girl that respects herself; so I really can't tell.'

'Will he be there tonight?' I ask.

'Oh, yes,' says Doris, 'we made a date after the Warden cleared off.'

'Then you better take me along with you,' I say, 'and let me have a look at him.' So that night off we trek, bed and bedding, and there sure enough is Doris's new friend – ever such a nice young fellow, though not so young at that, and not what you'd call delighted to see me.

'Harry,' says Doris, 'this is Mum.'

'Pleased to meet you,' I say, 'perhaps we may offer you a sandwich?'

'Thank you very much,' says he, 'perhaps in return I may offer you a coffee?' And off he goes to fetch it, and we never see him again. Well, Doris blames me, of course, says I oughtn't to have come in my curlers, but what I say is if a fellow's put off by curlers he don't know the facts of life and you're better without him. However, Doris takes umbrage, says she thinks she'll go along to the Fire Station and see if they want a mascot.

Well, she never got there, lucky as it turned out, because they'd an Alsatian dog already, but what did happen was the Blitz got something fierce, Doris popped into a cellar and down came the whole place on top of her.

Well, I know nothing about it till she doesn't turn up in the morning, and when a girl respects herself like Doris that means something, so I trot off to the Fire Station (that's when I found out about the dog), but they hadn't seen her.

So then I went round and about, and I don't mind telling you I was worried to a rind, and at last I find a whole demolition squad digging Doris out. I know it's Doris because they can hear her voice faint through the ventilator, and they let me creep in to have a chat.

'Are you all right, Doris?' I call.

'Oh, yes, Mum,' she says, 'there's ever such a nice young fellow down here with me, works on the Railway, and would you believe it, he knows Auntie Flo.'

'You bring him along,' I say, 'and let's have a word with him.' So along he comes to the ventilator, and I call down again.

'That's my daughter, Doris,' I say, 'I'm her Mum, and when you get out I'll be very pleased to meet you.'

'Mrs Catchpole,' he says, 'that goes for me too.' So I creep out again and ask the squad how long they'll be at it. They say they can't tell, they'll be as quick as they can; so I say, if there's no danger not to hurry themselves, because it does look as though Doris is on to something at last, though I don't say that last bit aloud, perfect gentleman as the officer was; called me 'Madam' and everything.

Well, I went along and got some cigarettes and made some tea in a bottle and the lady next door very kindly let me have a tin of salmon and back I went to pass them down to Doris, who says I better go round to her office and tell them she'll have to have the day off.

The squad wasn't looking too happy and the house next door had caved in as well, but Doris says they're still quite OK, plenty of air and no gas, and her new friend had shored up the ceiling with a bedstead they found.

'Best use for it,' I think, and as I can't do anything more off I go to the office, very nice about it they were, and then on to my sister Flo.

'Do you know a fellow,' I ask, 'works on the Railway?'

'What name?' she asks.

'I don't know his name,' I say, 'but he works on the Railway and he's buried along of my Doris.'

'Well, that's either Ted Parker,' she says, 'married and three kids, or Arthur Greenway, nice young fellow lives with his Mum.'

'Well, let's hope and pray it's Arthur,' I tell her, and I think it would be a kind and neighbourly act to go and have a word with Mrs Greenway, in case she doesn't know what's happened to him. And sure enough she doesn't, worried to a rind she was, and ever so glad to hear he was safe and sound along of my Doris.

We had a cup of tea together, and I took a good look over the house. Mrs Greenway said Arthur was a teetotaller and Primitive Methodist, didn't go with the girls because he liked them steady and said that to find a girl that was steady was like getting a camel through the eye of a needle.

'Why, he ought to meet my Doris!' I say, and we both have to laugh because of course he *had* met her.

So we have a bit more pleasant chat, and I tell her about Doris, how she was a girl that always respected herself and then off we go together to where they're still digging Doris and Arthur out. A different officer, not a patch on the first, kept telling us to stand back because it was near black-out and if the Blitz started there was no knowing what might happen.

'That's all very well,' I say, 'but that's my Doris down there, and this lady's Arthur, and we want to have a word with them.'

'You stand back and have a word with your Maker,' he says, really hardly polite.

Well, I don't know about Mrs Greenway, but as a matter of fact I did do a bit of praying, and it may have been that or it may not, but just as the first Jerries came over one of the men crawled in through a hole and crawled out again dragging Doris after.

Doris had a lot of plaster and such in her hair, but her siren-suit had stood up wonderful. And young Arthur too, though no beauty, had brought out a cat he found down there, which showed he had a kind nature. Well, by this time we were quite like old friends, so we thanked the squad and the officer, I also sent my best wishes to the first officer and back we went to the Greenways' and had some tea.

By this time the Blitz was in full swing, so I say to Doris, 'Well, Doris, is it to be the Tube or the shelter?'

'Oh, no,' says young Arthur, 'we've got an Anderson in the yard, you must stay with us.'

'That's right,' says Mrs Greenway, 'you must stay with us like Arthur says.'

'Well, if we don't intrude,' I say.

'You must come to us regular,' says Arthur, 'for I don't like to think of Miss Catchpole in a public shelter; you never know who you may meet.'

'Oh, I've never met anyone,' says Doris.

'Until last night,' says Arthur, with a meaning look; and though maybe he didn't know his fate, I and Doris and his Mum did all right, and it's lucky Mrs Greenway and me get on so well so the young people can have the place to themselves.

PAT FRANK

The Bomb

They had walked past the last row of bungalows skirting the village, and through the pines, and were within sight of the barbed-wire barricade enclosing the sprawling munitions factory, when they saw it first. It was very high, only a silver splinter except when the sun struck sparks from its wings.

The man squinted into the sun. 'Eight or nine thousand feet,' he estimated aloud. It was so high, and so far distant, that it seemed to crawl across the pale blue background. But Alan March knew, because he was of the Air Force and knew the deception of the sky when it is deep and measureless, that it was racing towards them at two hundred, perhaps two-fifty. Even at that height he caught the bulges of four engine nacelles, and knew it for a bomber.

'It must be one of ours,' the girl said. 'They only get here at night, so it must be one of ours.'

His right arm coiled round the girl's slender shoulders. 'I don't know, Pinky,' he said. 'I can't catch the silhouette yet. What do you think?'

'My eyes aren't good enough to make it out. It's the bad light in the factory at night. My eyes have lost their feel for daylight.'

'Let's not take a chance,' he said, his fingers tightening round her arm. 'Nothing must happen to us, not now, Pinky. Let's foot it for the factory, and duck into the shelter.' Even as he spoke he knew there wasn't time. It was a quarter of a mile to the factory gates.

'Why should there be war when people are in love?' she asked, and he felt her small, supple hands clinging to his shirt front and her warm head snuggling against the inside of his arm.

'We won't let the war bother us,' he said. 'The war will have to stop for a while.'

'The war won't stop just for us, Alan. Wars have never stopped because of love of women.'

He didn't speak, for the bomber was much closer. It would pass directly over the plant, and over them. Three tiny white clouds blossomed under the bomber, and then three more miraculously appeared above it. 'Anti-aircraft!' Alan said. 'It's theirs!' He saw the plane's belly gape open.

'Look!' the girl half-whispered. 'A bomb!'

A dot appeared below the plane, for the space of a breath seemed part of it, and then with seeming leisure disassociated itself from the larger shape above. It grew, and its nose began to slant downward. Then, like a black teardrop, it was outlined alone against the sky, and the plane had passed on, leaving only the bomb.

'Down! Down!' shouted Alan. 'Down on your face!'

Pinky was on the ground. She bent her neck, put her hands over her head, and drew up her knees until she was a small, quivering human ball.

Now I am going, she thought. I never again will bury my head in his neck, or feel the bristles on his chin, or feel his kisses on my eyes. She was an intimate of bombs. That's what they made at the factory, bombs. Five-hundred-pounders like the one diving at them. The bomb began to sing. It sang first in a low, penetrating whine. It was thus a bomb was designed to sing. Its guiding tail was fluted, so that it would whine, and shriek, and scream, and spread fear over a space of time before it killed.

For months she had helped make bombs like that. They moved along on a conveyor belt, each in its niche, each seven feet long and eighteen inches through. How they nicknamed them, and joked about them, at the factory!

'Minnie here will slap a dent in somebody's head.' That's what Helen always said, and she would pat their round, smooth aluminium-alloy surfaces. Helen worked beside her. She called all the bombs 'Minnie'.

The whine sharpened. She wanted to scramble to her feet and run, run, anywhere. She felt Alan's big arm pulling her to the ground again. 'Steady!' he commanded. 'Steady!'

Pinky wondered whether the enemy also used liquid oxygen and lignite and carbon. How delicately one must handle it! Woman's work. It took a woman's gentle hands. On the other side, some woman had fitted together this bomb calling to her. What sort of woman? Grey-haired, bent and slow? Middle-aged, and stiff as a bayonet, and methodical? Or young, and sometimes given to dreaming, as she herself was?

Only yesterday, she thought, Mr Gordon, the assembly superintendent, had bawled at her. He had snatched a fuse cylinder from her hands and shouted: 'What sort of a hodgepodge is this? Wires to the detonator aren't secured. What good is it? I ask you, what good is it? Young lady, keep your mind on your job!'

And Helen had snickered and said: 'She can't help it, Mr Gordon. She's in love. He's coming to see her this evening.'

Like a fire siren in the next block, the bomb was screeching now. She wanted to look up, but dared not. How long it took to fall!

The tone of the bomb grew deeper. She edged closer to Alan, and felt his arms going round her head. He is trying to save me from the blast, she thought, and then it struck.

It struck with a thick thud, as if a giant had driven a pick into the solar plexus of the earth.

Her small teeth ground together, her insides contracted, her breath was still, every muscle waited for the explosion. It did not come, but she dared not raise her eyes. She knew that if the fuse was set for penetration work it would be three or four seconds between impact and explosion – time enough to smash through ten stories of a building, or seek out the vitals of a bombproof shelter.

She found she was counting 'twelve, thirteen, fourteen' as Alan lifted her to her feet.

'Look, Pinky,' he was yelling, 'it's a dud. It didn't go off, Pinky, it's a dud!' She saw it, its snout and half its length buried in the earth between two saplings thirty yards distant. She knew it would never explode now.

'Alan,' she breathed, 'some other woman must be in love.' He did not know what she meant.

DIANA GARDNER

The Land Girl

I have Jersey cream for breakfast here on the farm. It is thick enough to spread on my porridge. Unfortunately, there is not enough sugar to go with it because of the rationing, which is rather a curse. What I'd like would be oceans of brown-sugar crystals of the kind we used to have at my guardian's. As it is, I have to take it surreptitiously when Mrs Farrant goes to the kitchen for the kettle. She's very severe and down on land girls altogether. She's also against me because I'm a 'lady', or I am when compared with her. She's a hard-bitten, crusty, thin woman and I don't think she and her husband get on particularly well together. She never calls him by his name or anything else, and refers to him as 'Mr Farrant'.

They don't half work the land girls. You are expected to do a man's work right enough. Not that I mind: it's fun being out in the open all day, even if it is blasted cold. Today we fallowed a field the size of the hall at college and it took five hours. About mid-afternoon, Mr Farrant came over and gave me a cigarette. I'm not allowed to smoke at the farmhouse because of Mrs F., so I have one now and again in the fields. It's decent of him to understand. I should say he's a man of about fifty-six, tall, very thin, and his face is lined with tiny red veins. He has whitish hair and blue, amused eyes. I wish he wouldn't wear leather gaiters: they make his legs look far too thin.

'We'll make you into a farmer yet, Miss Una,' he said.

I laughed at the idea. If there weren't a war on I'd never be doing landwork. I don't believe I've got the patience. Farming is a dull game: you have to wait so long for things to grow. I like action. It was that which got me expelled from school – I used to sneak into the town to buy sweets after 'lights out'. I've also got strong feelings, with decided likes and dislikes. Which reminds me, I don't think I'm going to like Mrs F. at all.

There's a thick frost today. Miller, the cowman, says it went down to 27 degrees last night. I was late for breakfast because it was so hard getting out of bed. Mr Farrant was on the farm and Mrs F. was busy in the scullery. It was quite nice to eat alone. I didn't have to be endlessly on my best behaviour. Believe me I was in a rage when I discovered that Mrs F. had left only a tea-spoonful of sugar in the bowl for both tea and porridge. Mean old pig! I thought. I'll pay you out. Before I went on the farm I unset my tea over the tablecloth.

Miller was detailed for two hours to teach me how to manage the tractor. When the weather breaks we'll be busy. Miller is a bad teacher, or I'm a dud. I expect I shall understand in time.

Mr Farrant gave me my lesson this morning. He explains things very well. He took the whole carburettor to pieces and showed me how it worked.

The weather is still midwinter. Today I felt very bored, going up and down among the cabbages. If the war goes on much longer I shall be sick of this game. Nobody of my own age to talk to, only the farmhands and their wives, and I bet they laugh and imi-tate me behind my back. To tell the truth I don't feel I'm all that popular, and this makes me seem affected. Am beginning to wonder why I ever came here at all.

This morning Mr Farrant took me in his gig to market. The town looked like a Christmas card by Raphael Tuck; people were climbing the hill bent double for fear of falling on the ice, and one or two women wore red woollen caps with lipstick to match.

I enjoy going around with Mr Farrant. He's a nice old boy and treats me well. He was shy at first about taking me into the Drovers, because he said I was a lady. It was very hot and farmer-ish in there. I must say I enjoyed drinking a glass of good old brown ale with the locals. These togs, breeches and coat, etc. are very comfortable. Thank goodness I don't bulge out in the wrong places.

When we got home Mrs F. didn't seem particularly pleased to see us. She spilled my tea pouring it out, so I refused to thank her for it. When she went to lock up the fowls I am afraid I pulled a face at Mr Farrant, but he didn't seem to mind.

There has been another fall of snow. My room is in the attic and, after Mr Farrant called me to get up, I lay quite a while looking at it reflected on the ceiling.

Practically all day I was clambering about with Miller searching for a pair of ewes which have lambed too early. After we'd found them, Mrs Miller made tea for us at their cottage. It was the queerest place inside. The 'parlour' was fixed from top to bottom with pictures of the seaside and china 'gifts', mostly from Brighton. She was very pleasant and had only two teeth in the top front. I wonder what happened to the others. Miller is a robust, earnest sort of fellow, and good-looking, if you like the earthy type.

Mrs Farrant made a scene today. I have come to loathe her.

When I came in I shook off all the snow I could in the scullery before going into the sitting-room. Mr Farrant was doing accounts. I could see she was in a vile temper; her hair was screwed into a tighter knot than ever.

I sat in an armchair and took up the *Daily Mail*.

Presently she looked across.

'Why didn't you take off your boots?' she said.

Before answering I laid the paper down very deliberately, and looked her over. 'Because I've been out all day on the farm and I'm dog-tired. I shook the snow off as I came in.'

'The snow's all over the carpet, and you'll take off those boots,' she said.

She came and stood over me so menacingly that my gorge rose.

'My good woman,' I said, 'I haven't taken up farming to be ordered about by you.'

'This is my house and I'll be obeyed in it.'

'No one could mistake that,' I replied curtly, and I admit I looked meaningly at Mr Farrant.

'You'll kindly leave this room,' Mrs F. said. She's certainly got a shrill voice.

'I'm going to, thanks,' I said, and I took the *Daily Mail* with me. As I climbed to my room I brushed off as much snow as I could on the stairs.

When I came down for supper I found Mrs F. had gone to bed.

Mr Farrant was quiet all through the meal. I am afraid he was upset about it all.

Mrs F. is scarcely civil when I address her now. She has also taken to giving me small helpings at meals. When I object she refers to the strict rationing. I don't believe it; we live on a farm where there's plenty of food, and I tell her so.

This morning she had taken away the cream and left no milk for the porridge. She was making her bed upstairs.

I must say I wouldn't like to have a wife like Mrs F.

Last night I went to a Temperance Dance with the Millers. Mrs Miller doesn't dance, so I waggled a toe with him. It was a tiring affair. It's hard to get drunk on lemonade. When we got back to the farm after a three-mile walk through the snow, I found that damned woman had locked me out. All the doors were bolted and the place in darkness. I threw snowballs at Mr Farrant's window – they have separate rooms – and presently he came down, looking very sleepy, poor man, and let me in.

As I passed her door her room was suspiciously quiet. I am afraid I made no apology for getting him out of bed. He ought never to have married a woman like Flo Farrant.

This morning, when I accused her of locking up the house, she had the rotten taste to reply, 'Oh, I thought you'd be out all night.'

'What the hell do you mean by that?' I asked.

I think she was frightened because she did not answer.

'Come on,' I said. 'Explain yourself.'

But she wouldn't.

I'm going to get even with her for this.

I spent the whole of today carting hay for the cattle. I can't help thinking of what that bitch said yesterday.

It's open war between Mrs F. and me in this house now. I don't know how Mr Farrant can put up with it. I talk only to him. Mrs F. and I have put each other into Coventry.

*

I must think clearly about this evening to know what exactly happened. I admit I did it in an inexplicable, mad moment and I suppose I shall live to regret it, but I do feel Mrs F. is entirely to blame for the atmosphere which has grown up between us.

As it was Sunday she caught the early bus into town and went by train to her mother's farm.

She was gone all day.

At lunchtime Mr Farrant and I got on particularly well together. We laughed a good deal at his jokes and he seemed relieved that she was out of the way, and shy that he and I were alone, which was funny, because around the farm and all the time we are at work he treats me as if I were a sort of refined workman. In the afternoon he dozed, the newspaper over his face and his gaiters off. I was dressed in a frock for a change and feeling no longer a farm labourer.

Over tea we got on still better. I know Mr Farrant likes me quite a lot; I'm sensible and reasonably attractive. I like him in lots of ways. He's friendly and has a sense of humour.

As I poured the tea, sitting in Mrs F.'s chair, I must admit I was glad she was out of the house for once.

But not a shadow of what happened later entered my head at any time during the afternoon. I wrote some letters to one or two people I'd met at the agricultural college and amused Mr Farrant with tales about them. He thought they sounded great jokes.

When suppertime came he insisted that he should prepare it.

'After all, we're both farmers,' he said, 'so why shouldn't I get a meal for a change?'

He opened a tin of tongue and made some sandwiches. The tea was dreadfully strong. Afterwards he smoked some of my cigarettes and told me about his youth. He must have been a lad. Why on earth he had to marry Flo Farrant only the stars can tell.

As she was due on the ten o'clock bus, I decided to go to bed before she arrived. Just before nine-thirty, Mr Farrant made the fire up and went into the kitchen to make some tea. While he was gone I put the room to rights, and presently he returned with a thermos and laid it on the table.

It was then something took possession of me. The sight of the old, chipped thermos on the orange tray and his spent, thin shoulders bent over it, caused my dislike of Mrs Farrant to well up into a sudden storm of hatred. I don't remember ever having experienced such rage, and no one can accuse me of being sweet-tempered. I felt choked with hatred. As I watched the nape of his neck I gripped the back of a wooden chair so hard that my hands were bloodless. Yet despite the ferocity of this feeling I don't think it could have lasted a second. I relaxed my grip on the chair and sat down.

He looked up, alarmed.

'Are you feeling all right?'

'Yes . . . th-thanks,' I stammered.

'Not ill or anything? You're so white.'

'It must be the heat of the room,' I said, and pulled myself together. I got up. 'I'm going to bed.'

'Right you are,' he said. 'I'm turning in, too.'

He went into the kitchen and I heard him stoking the 'Ideal' boiler.

Suddenly my brain began to work at a great speed. Now that I think about it I suppose my subconscious had already worked out a plan. My movements became swift and furtive. I went quickly to the door, looked to right and left in the hall and then, as softly as I could, sped up the stairs. The way I knew what to do next was quite peculiar. I went straight to Mr Farrant's bedroom and switched the light on. His bed was over in the corner. I went straight over and lay on it. I even shook off my shoes as I climbed up – a funny thing to do when I had only a few moments to spare. I could hear him moving about downstairs and I knew the bus with Mrs Farrant in it would be arriving at any minute. I lay on my back and rolled about from side to side to deepen my impression in the feather mattress. It very soon became disordered. Then I got up, took off a blue Tyrolean brooch I always wear and laid it beside his brushes on the dressing-table. Grabbing my shoes in my hand I made my way onto the landing and up the stairs to the attic.

Once in my own room I stood with my head pressed against the door, listening for the sound of his movements. I heard him lift the lid of the letter-box and let it drop. He paused by the stairs to wind the grandfather clock.

At that moment I heard the bus. It pulled up and then started off noisily. Mrs Farrant was at the gate.

He climbed the stairs softly. I don't think he heard the bus. As he came to the linoleum on the landing, his steps grew louder. He crossed to his room and went in.

Hardly breathing, I came out of mine and ran stealthily down the stairs. My eyes must have been fixed and frightening. When the front door handle turned, I gave a little gasp; nothing must prevent my plan from succeeding. If I were not wrong, Mrs Farrant would say goodnight to her husband before she drank her tea.

I slipped into his room as quickly and quietly as I could. Once inside I appeared to be in no hurry. He stood in the middle of the room in his shirt sleeves. He appeared not to have noticed the state of the bed, and was staring pensively at his feet. He looked up, surprised.

'I'm sorry,' I said, and I can't think what I must have looked like, 'but I've left a brooch on your dressing-table.' I spoke slowly. 'It's a little Austrian brooch my guardian gave me years ago.'

I began to play for time.

'Stupid of me to have left it. There it is – on the little china tray' – I heard footsteps on the stairs – in a slightly higher key I said, 'On the china tray, beside your brushes.'

'Oh,' he said, vaguely, and took it up in his hands. He was stupefied and tired. 'I don't quite understand.' He looked down at it in the palm of his hand and then at me. 'How did it get there?'

But I had no need to reply. Mrs Farrant stood in the doorway, her dark clothes part of the shadow in the landing, her face compressed and challenging. She looked at her husband, at the brooch in his hand, at me and, finally, at the disarranged bed.

I don't know what I looked like but I can remember the sensation of rising triumph as I met her eyes. He was too befuddled to know what to say and I made no effort to help him.

I waited an age for her to speak, but she said nothing. Her face became completely expressionless. She looked again at the brooch in Farrant's hand and then turned on her heel. We heard her cross the landing to her own room and close the door sharply behind her.

I must confess I didn't know what to do when he turned and looked at me in a bewildered sort of way. I snatched the brooch from his hand and rushed upstairs to my room.

*

This morning it is still very cold. As I lay in bed unable to sleep, a good deal of noise was going on in the house below. Eventually I got up and stared at the outbuildings of this blasted farm. Presently, Miller led the pony out and harnessed him to the gig. Almost at once Mrs Farrant piled it high with some tattered luggage. Without saying anything to Miller she climbed in and jerked the reins. The pony moved forward, through the gate and on to the highroad, his breath misty in the frozen morning air. I got cold watching her back-view until it was out of sight; the thin body and that frightful bun. That was the last I shall ever see of her, thank God.

After that I dressed and went downstairs.

As I went into the kitchen with a jauntiness I was far from feeling, Mr Farrant was making his own breakfast. He looked up with a numbed expression. I had expected reproaches: it put me off my stroke not to get any.

'She's gone,' he said, wearily. 'Nothing I could say made any difference.'

I said nothing.

Here I am waiting for the bus. It's so cold I have to run up and down beside my suitcases to keep warm. I am in my best clothes, but I do not know where I am going or what I shall do. All I am certain of is, I must get out of that house.

After all, I couldn't stay there alone with Mr Farrant. Even though he's been an awful dear to me, he's old enough to be my father. And my life has only just begun.

SYLVIA TOWNSEND WARNER

Sweethearts and Wives

Sometimes Justina and Midge discussed what would happen if all their husbands came on leave together. Lettice could go to her grandmother's – but then William would not see her, and really she was now a nice, displayable baby. The Sheridans might find a double bed at the farm – but that would not take away Roy and the twins, and if Mrs Sheridan slept out, one could not expect her to be back in time to get breakfast. Justina and Tom might have a little honeymoon at The Griffin – but that, as Midge said, would break up the household.

Without husbands the household consisted of three women and four children. Justina, who liked figures, had worked out that the average age of the party was thirteen. If one left out Mrs Sheridan, who was over thirty, the average age fell to eight years and nine months; but to leave out Mrs Sheridan except arithmetically was inconceivable, for Mrs Sheridan was the king-pin and glory of the establishment; she cooked.

Both Justina and Midge had married early in 1940. To their respective mothers it seemed natural, since both husbands were in the Forces, that they should stay on at home, keeping their spirits up, poor little things, by giving a helping hand in country houses suddenly denuded of servants and enlarged by such creative activities as organizing First-Aid Points, entertaining Polish officers and breeding table rabbits. When they decided to set up house together in Badger Cottage, it seemed hopefully probable that the poor darlings would soon tire of cooking for themselves – the more so as Badger Cottage was such a disadvantageous dwelling, lonely, ugly, derelict, miles from any shop, and all the water needing to be pumped by hand. But the discovery of Mrs Sheridan quenched this hope. Mrs Sheridan was also married to a fighting man; he had been a circus hand, now he was in the

RASC.* Mrs Sheridan, bombed out of Mitcham, had come to Suffolk to find a home for herself, her three children, her Alsatian dog and her horse. The horse had associations. Mrs Sheridan could not bear to be parted from it. The billeting officer had washed his hands of her when a fight between the Alsatian and Justina's two poodles elicited the fact that Mrs Sheridan would do anything and everything for whoever made a kind home for her and her beautiful Shirley. Midge's baby immunized her from conscription, but the poodles could not do the same for Justina, who had been directed to replace an auctioneer's clerk in the local town. By privily dismembering her bicycle, hiding the fragments in a fox covert, and declaring it stolen, she was in a position to claim Shirley as an essential means of transport. The horse thereby received a ration, Mrs Sheridan was able to live with them and be their cook, and when the Alsatian was reconciled to the poodles the compound household worked perfectly.

Another of Mrs Sheridan's beauties was her farmer friend, Mr Cuffey. Until Shirley had become an essential means of transport he had kept her going with oats, and he still stabled her. For Mr Cuffey (though a grimly married man who had never been out of Suffolk in his life, and regularly taking the collection at a Methodist Chapel) had a romantic streak in his nature which made him the slave of Mrs Sheridan's black eyes, purple velveteen trousers and *haute école* graces. At dusk Mr Cuffey would materialize to woo Mrs Sheridan with illegal cream and extra butter, and sometimes a nice little bit of pork, and sometimes a pheasant which had been foolish enough to get itself entangled in a rabbit snare; and having a generous circus-like outlook on windfalls Mrs Sheridan would share these courtesies with Midge and Lettice and Justina.

Arriving on the heels of his telegram, Midge's William found himself being conducted, as it were, on a tour through the Sheridans: Mrs Sheridan, Pamela, Gloria, and Roy Sheridan, Driver Sheridan (by proxy of photographs and such a wonderful likeness to the boy), the Alsatian and the horse. But unfortunately he had come on a day which was not the morrow of one of Mr Cuffey's more impassioned dusks.

---

* Royal Army Service Corps

'If only we had known you were coming, we could have feasted you on the wages of sin,' remarked Midge. 'As it is, it must be fish.'

'I expect William gets a lot of fish in the Navy,' said Justina. 'I expect he's sick of fish. Midge, come outside one minute.'

William heard some serious murmurings, and the sound of damp, flat objects being turned over. Then they reappeared.

'Darling, I'm afraid it won't be fish after all. You see, Justina brought back what she could get, and what she could get was one largish sole and a plaice. And we were to share the sole and Mrs Sheridan was to have the plaice. She prefers plaice. But the sole isn't big enough for three, and if we had the plaice too there would be no fish for Mrs Sheridan. So we think she had better have the sole and we'll have toasted cheese.'

Justina said: 'Fortunately there's quite a lot of cheese.'

'My only criticism is, that you don't seem to have accounted for the plaice,' said William.

'Oh, Mrs Sheridan will have it for her breakfast.'

'She likes plaice, she likes it better than sole,' Midge said. 'It would be a shame to deprive her of her plaice.'

'Especially as she will have been so obliging about the sole,' added Justina.

At breakfast (tea, toast, apple jelly, and the smell of Mrs Sheridan's plaice) and at intervals during the rest of his leave William Corby reminded himself that it is ridiculous to think much about food, that by virtue of his profession he was better fed than any civilian, that it was very handsome of Mrs Sheridan to share the wages of sin with his daughter as well as with her own children, and that it was marvellous for his Midge to have a cook. If she had not got a cook, Midge explained, she would never have time to make so much jam. Midge's jams seemed to be the mainstay of every meal; though this, as Midge also explained, was partly because if you made jam without as much sugar as the book said, it had to be eaten down immediately or it mildewed.

On Sunday, too, he got a little riding, as Mrs Sheridan lent him her horse.

'But oughtn't she to have a rest?'

'My Shirley is a professional horse. She's never missed a performance, bless her!' said Mrs Sheridan, who, as it was Saturday evening, had an agreeable odour of gin about her.

The Alsatian and the two poodles came along too, and killed and ate several rabbits. Justina's Tom, so he had heard, was a good shot. Every man, thought William, at any rate every husband, should be able to shoot; and he reproached himself that he was incapable of shooting anything except stationary bottles at fairs. One is not a good shot unless one can shoot something edible. He would like to meet Tom Debenham and have some shooting lessons. It would be fun if Tom's next leave should coincide with a leave of his own. It might mitigate, too, this disquieting impression of having four children at Badger Cottage, and two, or possibly three, wives. Yet democracy is desirable; we must all aim at a future of more equality and less formality, and the household at Badger Cottage was a step towards such a future. It was probably reactionary of him to dislike seeing so much of Mrs Sheridan's purple trousers and never feeling sure whether it was Lettice wearing Pamela's rompers or Gloria clasping Lettice's teddy bear who needed picking out of the pond. If he had spent the last three years at home instead of at sea, he would be better at recognizing his own child. Meanwhile, he was riding Mrs Sheridan's horse, and Lettice and Midge were sharing in Mr Cuffey's love-gifts, and the joint households of early Soviet days must have been more ill-assorted and infinitely hungrier.

These reflections were cut short by the necessity for galloping across a field in order to deter the two poodles from pulling down a sheep. The fact that the Alsatian had taken no part in this assault but was virtuously engaged in hunting another rabbit was a further reminder that it is the more privileged classes who have most to learn in the matter of citizenship.

Badger Cottage was going on much as usual when a parcel came for Midge containing a large tin of olives and a note from William hoping that they might come in handy. As going on much as usual meant just then that Roy and Lettice had whooping cough and that Gloria had eaten the greater part of an indelible pencil, Midge remarked that dear William must be at Gibraltar, didn't Justina think, and the tin of olives was put by in the store cupboard. Midge was too loyal to voice the wish that William had sent tinned salmon instead, Justina was too polite to say so either and Mrs Sheridan only said: 'Well, thank God it's in a tin, anyway. Which reminds me, Midgie, my twins have got at the jam you put in the attic; at first I thought it was mice, but it's too sticky for mice.'

It might have been expected that Tom, coming on leave so soon after this, would have eaten the olives. William had allowed for it. Besides having heard that Tom was a good shot, he had heard that Tom was something of an epicure; and he had said to himself a trifle wistfully: 'To each according to his need' – being, as his father-in-law said, a damn sight too well up in all that anti-God sort of stuff. Tom did not eat the olives because, after his first meal, during which Gloria sat on his knee, toyed with his hair and addressed him with purple lips as Daddy, he announced that he was going to take Justina to London to see some shows and have her nails cleaned.

Driver Sheridan, on the other hand, entered at once into the spirit of Badger Cottage, arriving with a goose, twenty-four kippers, several tins of army stew, two bottles of whisky, four hundred cigarettes, six yellow dusters and an invaluable collection of nails, screws, bolts and washers, the property of HM Government. During his stay he undertook a number of repairs and improvements, mended the meat-safe, washed and clipped the poodles, lifted the main-crop potatoes several weeks too early, repainted the dog kennel and part of the front door, hung a swing for the children, fixed an aerial to the wireless and did things to the pump. On his last evening, too, he further asserted himself as a practical man by fighting Mr Cuffey, and spent the remaining hours alternately beating and embracing Mrs Sheridan. Bruised and admiring, she passed the next day wandering among his incompleted works, saying dreamily: 'There'll be something to show for this, I shouldn't be surprised.'

The first perceptible aftermath of Driver Sheridan, however, was the cessation of cream and butter, and Mr Cuffey's inability to go on stabling Shirley; never in all his days had he known such a messy horse. It is difficult to place a full-sized horse with delicate lungs: circus life, as Mrs Sheridan explained, the draughts playing on open pores, always weakens the lungs – think of monkeys. Finally, Shirley was accommodated at the Vicarage, where the sound of the organ, said Mrs Sheridan, would be like old times for her. Justina more moodily remarked that she would now be more than a mile from her essential means of transport, and that the Transoms would henceforth expect a regular supply of prizes for their incessant Church Roof Restoration Fund whist drives – as was indeed the case.

Other tokens of Driver Sheridan's manliness were still lying around when William came on his next leave: festering heaps of wood and wire that only needed a few finishing touches to become a rabbit-hutch, rusty bolts and cog-wheels which should have been put back in the mangle, but somehow got overlooked, and several fresh neuroses in the pump.

'Come just when you're wanted,' said Mrs Sheridan warmly. 'You sailor-men are always so handy.'

If he had not been so obliteratingly in love with his wife William Corby would have remembered to arrive as a good provider. As it was, he just got into the first train with nothing more than love, lemons, silk stockings, presents for the children and good intentions. The presents for the children were eaten in a flash, the stockings were put away, love is always impalpable, one cannot live on lemons – he did as best he could with the good intentions. There was certainly a great deal to do. It seemed to him that Badger Cottage was much dirtier and more disarrayed than the passage of six months and the transit of Driver Sheridan could justify. But then, as he told himself, he came off a ship, a childless, melancholy world of its own. Four children would no doubt make a destroyer look as tousled as Badger Cottage; and he thrust down the inward retort to this, that children on a destroyer would be kept in better order and cleaned at regular intervals.

Women, he also told himself, are less fussy than men: it is a wise, natural provision to fit them for the inevitable mess and confusion of maternity. Women, too, are braver, more adaptable, probably hardier, certainly less self-indulgent. They are more primitive and so better attuned to the primitive state of the universe when, as the scriptures so acutely remark, the earth was without form, or void, and the waters brooded on the face of the earth; which reminded him he must try to do something about the bathroom. But the brave, adaptable, hardy, self-disciplined and primitive Midge had spots on her chin, moaned in her sleep and smoked more than was good for her. As for Justina, she had a cold in her head. It was so violent that she did not go to work, so instead Mrs Sheridan rode into town and did the shopping. Mrs Sheridan was a somewhat erratic shopper, but she always remembered the children; and it was so nice for her, Midge pointed out, to be reunited with Shirley. To give Mrs Sheridan more time to enjoy this reunion, Justina cooked.

Justina had been taught cooking at a domestic college for young ladies. She knew how to make omelets, fudge, several kinds of soufflé, coffee and – theoretically – soap. Unfortunately omelets and soufflés cannot be made without breaking real eggs, so Justina's home-lore chiefly expressed itself in coffee. For the rest there was always cheese, and Midge's jams, and the national loaf now so vitaminous that it was almost as ready to ferment as the jams. Why on earth, thought William, didn't I have at least the foresight to bring them some ships' bread? Busy himself as he might in being a man about the house, his thoughts dwelt increasingly on food. But he did not realize how enchained he was to sensual lures till the message came from Mrs Transom to say that after all she could not have them to supper as the vicar had just gone down with mumps.

'Mumps! O my God,' wailed Midge. 'None of them has had mumps! O Justina, why did we let them go to the children's service?'

(Mumps, thought William. I've had mumps. I could perfectly well have gone to that supper.)

'I expect he was in his pulpit all the time,' replied Justina. 'It isn't as if he'd been confirming them or christening them. And somebody had to go to church after they'd been so obliging about Mrs Sheridan's horse.'

Damn Mrs Sheridan, thought William.

'What's mumps?' asked Mrs Sheridan; and answered herself by adding that mumps was all in a day's work. She could afford to be philosophical, thought William: she had not lost a supper, she had been staying at home anyway to look after the children. Which, of course, was very good of her.

Justina remarked that there was still quite a lot of the beetroot soup left. Midge said she didn't wonder. William didn't wonder either.

'And there is any amount of oatmeal. Isn't there something called brose that's made of oatmeal – with cabbage in it? Didn't Robert Burns sup brose?'

Mrs Sheridan opined that there was more than that in Robbie Burns' brose.

'What a pity we gave the remains of the rabbit to the dogs!'

The word *olives* began to shape itself in William's mind, but he said nothing.

'It's the very devil,' mused Midge, 'feeding the dogs. They're much fussier than the children. Or us.'

'They don't appreciate the war, poor things,' said Mrs Sheridan. 'Do you think a jam roly-poly? That would be filling. And we must browse down that elderberry jam that wouldn't set.'

The word *olives* now thundered in William's brain. His tongue was swollen with keeping silence. Some flash of his electrical agony must have reached Justina, for suddenly her face became illumined with intellect, and she said:

'I know! I've got it! We'll open that tin of olives that William sent us.'

'O Justina, we can't! It's gone.'

'Gone? Have those blasted children . . .'

'No, it's not the children this time. It's me. I gave it to the Transoms for a whist-drive prize.'

She spoke to Justina exactly as the conventional wife confesses to her husband that she has given his trousers to the jumble sale. Amid everything else that he was feeling, William was able to notice this.

'Damn! What on earth came over you? No one in this village would know what to do with an olive.'

'But you don't like them, Justina. I'm not all that fond of them, really. And Zoe doesn't like them either, for I asked her.'

'I can *eat* them,' said Mrs Sheridan. 'But that's not to say I actually enjoy it.'

Midge lit another cigarette. She was still looking like a guilty wife and spoke savagely.

'What else could I do, Justina? You know how those black-mailing Transoms hound us for their whist drives. It's all very well for you, you are out all day, you don't know much about real life. But I can assure you, what with thinking about food for the dogs, and washing for the children, and prizes for the Transoms, real life isn't worth living!'

The ensuing silence was broken by Roy Sheridan, who strolled in carrying a tin chamber-pot in which there were some baby mice. He had found the mice in Daddy's rabbit hutch, he explained. There had been lots more, but they had got away. Now could he have some cotton-wool to make a nest for them? Presently William was able to suggest that, since they could not sup at the Vicarage (where at this moment, he said to himself, those Transoms are devouring olives like quails and manna), they should walk the four miles into town and have dinner at The Griffin and try for a bottle of whisky for Justina's cold . . . that is, if Mrs Sheridan would stand by her generous offer to keep an eye on the children. It was a lovely frosty night, the walk would be fun.

'We shall get up our appetites,' he concluded.

Mrs Sheridan was quite ready to stay at home, so William set out with his two wives.

The dinner and the whisky cost in all four pounds seventeen shillings. Both Midge and Justina got slightly drunk and were much improved by it. In fact, it might have been called a successful evening if it had not been riddled by a tendency to remember Mrs Sheridan and feel how unselfish she was, and what a pity it was that she had been left out of it.

ANN CHADWICK

The Sailor's Wife

The sky lay blue between showers, giving a sharpness to the shadows in the dirty town behind her as she climbed. The water shone blue, and the little ships rode like toys on a still backwater, swinging slowly on their anchors. She climbed up past the council houses to the last street, thinking in her surface mind that these were semi-detached houses, larger than any she had tried; thinking under that that she was getting hungry; feeling under that the stares of children, the window curtains screening casual eyes: a stranger in the neighbourhood.

The woman who came to the door set her aproned front in the opening and looked out of her shut face with two small brown eyes. Yes! she said. I'm sorry to bother you, began the sailor's wife. The other woman opened her face tentatively, like a hungry clam. Not at all, she said. The sailor's wife shifted her tired feet and tried to sound conversational. I was wondering if you might know someone in this neighbourhood who lets rooms? The clam reconsidered and fixed its jaws ajar, immobile. Oh no, I'm afraid not. I can't think of a soul. Some do let, mind you – Mrs Carstairs next door – but she's full up. Full up and booked ahead. Yes, said the sailor's wife. Pause. You'll find the town's fair packed out, said the other woman – what with the shipping and the RAF station and the torpedo factory – I can't think where you'll get in. Long pause.

Was it just for yourself? she asked. The sailor's wife smiled tightly. For myself, she said, and my husband when he's on leave. And a ten months' baby, she added. But he's out in the pram all day and I have his cot with me. He's very good. But the clam had shut like a trap. Ah well, said the woman who had come to the door. Ah well, echoed the sailor's wife. You barnacled old bitch, she thought. Sorry I can't help you, said the woman, and moved back longingly from the door. The sailor's wife smiled. Well, thank you very much, she said. She went slowly back to the pavement.

She walked stumpingly on the outside of her swollen feet. Four-thirty. Time to be starting back to the hotel. The baby would be crying and annoying people by five. I'll try two more houses in this street, she thought. That would make it up to sixteen. Then I'll take the bus back.

Cute the kid had been this morning. Kicking on the bed while she washed nappies in the hand-basin. Should be crawling by now. Thank God he wasn't. Hanging out the nappies and getting the pram ready on the green behind the hotel. Tying his toys in, and settling him. That chambermaid. Telling the chambermaid she would be back for lunch and what to do if it came on to rain. That chambermaid, laughing out of her pale face. A double coping of round curls, red and light – flashing as new farthings shaking all round her head. Hanging and brushing together silently like copper feathers on a cockerel's neck. Laughing – I never seen a like baby! Sitting there hours and never a whisht out of him – Poor wee soul. People liked babies.

Looking over her shoulder she could see the ships below her in the river. Nice to find a place up here where you could watch them in and out. Little carrier down there now. Wrong camouflage markings. Besides it had only been a week. Four or five weeks to go anyhow. There were some of the right sort of houses at the end of the row. Try this one.

She went quickly up the walk, watching the dog messes carefully, seeing the wet primroses and crocuses dismally gleaming. A large dirty brass plate under the bell said Mrs Garbutt. She rang. The milk had not been taken in yet. No one came. She rang again and turned to look out over the roofs at the slow ships moving greyly. Another shower was coming round the circle of hills. It had rained every single day so far – five days – still no place to live. She would give the baby bread and milk and the last orange. No one had come. I'll try the back door, she decided. Now that five minutes had been wasted here already – made you persistent. She went round.

Mrs Garbutt stood at her cluttered back door in an inadequate skirt and a vast, sloppy jumper belted in. She started when the sailor's wife came round the corner. Spare us! she said rhetorically, and returned to her fixed scrutiny of a pen with ducks in it that extended over most of her ruined garden. The sailor's wife looked too. There was nothing to see but filthy, stained, awkward ducks moving unceasingly in greedy circles. Mrs Garbutt said, There's been an egg missing every morning for weeks and I'm watching to see where she lays it, the besom.

A large puppy that had been under an overturned box at the corner of the house lolloped silently up behind the sailor's wife and thrust a cold wet nose up her skirts. Ah-ft! said the sailor's wife. My, my – come here you, said Mrs Garbutt absently. The puppy flung himself on his back and waved his filthy fool's paws. The sailor's wife rubbed his stomach with her foot defensively. I couldn't get an answer at the front so I came round, she said. Ah well, said Mrs Garbutt, I've been out here all the day waiting for her to lay, the tramp. This is one day I swore I'd not be fooled and neither I will. What was it you were wanting, my dear?

I was wanting to know do you know anyone around here who lets rooms, said the sailor's wife. Hm? said Mrs Garbutt, giving all her attention to the pen. The sailor's wife breathed deeply and spoke slowly and distinctly. I thought perhaps you might know someone in this neighbourhood who would let me have rooms. She fenced herself from the puppy's advances, bending over with extended hands. She wanted suddenly to cry from weariness and impatience. I hate puppies, she thought fiercely.

Well, my dear, you're asking me, said Mrs Garbutt meaning-lessly. Come here you. That's a question, she added with an air of finality. I think she goes up into the hedge, the bird. Well my dear, you want what everyone in this town wants. Have you tried at the shops?

I've tried every shop in town, said the sailor's wife. They haven't even a list to give folk. She thought to herself, and you know it, or why would I be tramping the streets on the off-chance. The puppy bounced off and she straightened up.

There's a fact, said Mrs Garbutt. The town's full and more than full for a fact. She knows I'm watching, the fox. She'll not lay the day. Well, my dear, and is it just yourself you want for?

My husband comes home on leave occasionally for a day or so, and we've a baby. But he's too young to run about and break things, and I've got his cot with me, said the sailor's wife. She thought – that's my family I'm talking about, brushing over. My own family – the only thing. Poor thing, you'll have a job with a baby, said Mrs Garbutt looking at her suddenly quite softly, with a morbid sympathy. No one will take you I'll allow. The sailor's wife laughed and said nothing. The last people I had fair drove me crazy with their wild ways and I'm having no more naval people, there's a fact.

The sailor's wife made the last effort of the day. You can't judge all by one, she appealed, looking as sweet as she could, what with her sore feet and thinking about the baby. Aye, but that I can, my dear, said Mrs Garbutt. She looked at the sailor's wife sharply. I don't envy your job for a fact, my dear, she said. You must expect hard hearts and robbing fingers in this town, for that's what you'll find. Where's your baby now? He's in his pram at the hotel. I'm going back to feed him now, said the sailor's wife. Left him all alone? The sailor's wife nodded. He's very good. Mrs Garbutt shook her head.

I'm glad you won't have me, thought the sailor's wife, you sloppy old duck-watcher. The puppy was gambolling back. She turned to escape. Thank you, she said loudly as she went. It was like struggling out of a swamp to leave the place. Its gloom clung to her. The smell of ducks followed sadly.

There wasn't enough time to do another house. She tried slow and fast steps alternately to ease her feet. Margot loves Alan, was written in chalk on the pavement. There was a portrait of Margot and someone else had drawn hop-scotch squares over it. The sky was clear again and the dark was already coming down.

The baby. It was almost five minutes' walk down the hill to the bus stop. She tried very long rhythmic strides and was getting on famously when right at the very bottom, what with looking to see if a bus was coming, she caught her heel on the kerb and stumbled awkwardly into the street. And there was a lorry looming along. She thought – it must have hit me – the bright colours – I've been carried quite a distance. It was as quick as that.

First of all there were just colours – sickening because they were whirled so – green, yellow, red, orange. Then darkness and that sweeping back, back, back feeling like drunkenness. Then colour again, moving slowly in sheets and planes and curtains – crimson, grey, violet. Reaching and squeezing her in. And then sounds began. Infinite ones. Whispers. Voices crowding, drowning, rising. Well, my dear? Ah well. The besom, the bird. Sorry I can't help. Sorry. Sorry. No babies. No naval people. No English people. No human beings. No one. No one. Sorry. Can't help, can't help.

Margot loves Alan. This is Margot's face. As well as white chalk can show. Margot's face loves Alan's face. Alan's face is a hop-scotch square. Margot loves it. Margot loves. Loves.

Emergency cards? No permanent residence. Can't give you eggs on those. Not enough for registered customers. You service wives should stick at home. Should. Ought . . . Should stick. War won't last forever. One year. Don't marry before the peace. Wait. Don't start babies in war-time. Wait. Wartime. Four years. Don't live in war-time. Wait. Stick. Sorry I can't help. Can't give you eggs. Sorry, only for registered customers. Sorry no life going on in war-time. Wait . . . Only four or five years.

The baby's crying. Crying? Where is he? It's dark. Where did I leave him. He's lost, Christ he's lost. He's crying. Where? I left him in rooms. After the liberty boat left I went back the way I had come. But the rooms were gone. The baby is lost. Hungry and crying in strange rooms. Lost. Oh God help me, the baby's gone.

She wept. The tears were warm and salt. People soothed her. Pay no attention. No one cares. Just sympathies to get rid of you. Cry like hell. Make them listen. Demand a place to stay – demand your baby. Weep. Weep.

Can you stand up? insisted a man's heavy voice. Rough, clumsy arms tried to support her. Don't move her – maybe she's broke something, said a woman. She realized something had happened. What's the matter? she demanded, resisting.

Then her arm hurt suddenly, enough to make her sick. Everyone was asking questions. She tried to think quickly so that she could take time for the next step. I want to go to the Bay Hotel, she said, because the baby's there.

Then suddenly the sickness went and she saw the people round her. First the policeman, anxious, clumsily helping her to stand, forgetting he was a policeman. An errand boy, white, big-eyed, silent. The loud women, frowning, exclaiming, arguing among themselves as to what had happened, waving their fat and thin hands. The silent staring women. The men turning to go about their business, others still leering, others offering. These were the people who lived in this town – thought the sailor's wife clearly. She had their attention. Well, quick.

For a horrible moment she couldn't think of anything to say. Then because she was afraid they would all lose interest and go away, she said loudly – I did it on purpose! She started to cry again. The policeman clung to his duty. Now, my girl, he said firmly, no hysterics. I *did*, she said, I definitely did. The policeman succeeded in righting her in spite of herself. But it's against the law, he warned, and a daft thing. He gave her his handkerchief.

Crying seemed quite enjoyable. She leaned against the policeman for dizziness and tried to concentrate on what she was doing. No one will give me rooms – she sobbed as loudly as she could. The policeman was embarrassed. People were taking renewed interest. Come along quietly now, he said. I'll take you to the hotel. She looked at the beautiful sleek police car. I've nowhere for my baby to live! she wailed. And then she felt sick again and couldn't think at all.

When they got to the hotel the lorry driver had come to have a paper signed that it was the sailor's wife's own fault. He was a little worried man, thin and anxious. Then a doctor came, and prodded around until he was sure nothing was broken, and put her to bed. Then everyone threatened to go away and let her recover from the shock. Even the lorry driver wanted to go and come back tomorrow. The chambermaid was feeding the baby corn flakes. Let me see the paper I have to sign, said the sailor's wife. I must stick to the point, she thought, reading it.

Can you find me rooms in town? said the sailor's wife to the driver. He looked suspicious. The sailor's wife sighed, wishing there were more covers on the bed, wishing she could feel strong and warm and accomplish something. If you can find me rooms, I'll sign it, she said laboriously. The lorry driver smiled suddenly, pleased. Oh, you can stay with my sister, he said. She sometimes takes folk though it's not that she has to. Just wouldn't see a body stuck. I'll fix it. She smiled and accepting the driver's pen, signed the paper. It seemed to take a long, long time. The policeman was pretending he hadn't heard what they were saying. Now I've got a place, thought the sailor's wife. I have. I've got a place. She fell asleep half smiling.

STEVIE SMITH

Sunday at Home

Ivor was a gigantic man; forty, yellow-haired, grey of face. He had been wounded in a bomb experiment, he was a brilliant scientist.

Often he felt himself to be a lost man. Fishing the home water with his favourite fly Coronal, he would say to himself, 'I am a lost man.'

But he had an excellent sardonic wit, and in company knew very well how to present himself as a man perfectly at home in the world.

He was spending this Sunday morning sitting in his bedroom reading Colonel Wanlip's 'Can Fish Think?' letter in *Angling*. '… the fallacious theory known as Behaviourism'.

As the doodle bomb* came sailing overhead, he stepped into the airing cupboard and sighed heavily. He could hear his wife's voice from the sitting-room, a childish, unhappy voice, strained (as usual) to the point of tears.

'All I ask,' sang out Ivor, 'is a little peace and quiet; an agreeable wife, a wife who is pleasant to my friends; one who occasionally has the room swept, the breakfast prepared and the expensive bric-a-brac of our cultivated landlord *dusted*. I am after all a fairly easy fellow.'

'I can't go on,' roared Glory. She waved her arms in the air and paced the sitting-room table round and round.

Crump, crump, went the doodle bomb, getting nearer.

'Then why,' inquired Ivor from the cupboard (where he sat because the doodle bombs reminded him of the experiment), 'did you come back to me?'

---

* V–1 flying bombs, usually known as 'doodle bugs' or 'buzz bombs' because of the noise they made. V–2s were pilotless flying bombs. The V–1s were launched on Britain in June 1944, the V–2s in September.

Glory's arms at shoulder height dropped to her side. There was in this hopeless and graceful gesture something of the classic Helen, pacing the walls of Troy, high above the frozen blood and stench of Scamander Plain. Ten years of futile war. Heavens, how much longer.

She ran to the cupboard and beat with her fists upon the door. 'You ask that, you . . . you . . . you . . .'

'Why yes, dear girl, I do. Indeed I do ask just that. Why did you come back to me?'

'Yesterday in the fish queue . . .' began Glory. But it was no use. No use to tell Ivor what Friedl had said to her in the fish queue . . . before all those people . . . the harsh, cruel words. No, it was no use.

The doodle bomb now cut out. Glory burst into tears and finished lamely, 'I never thought it was going to be like this.'

Crash. Now it was down. Three streets away perhaps. There was a clatter of glass as the goldfish bowl fell off the mantelpiece. Weeping bitterly Glory knelt to scoop the fish into a half-full saucepan of water that was standing in the fender.

'They are freshwater fish,' said Ivor stepping from the cupboard.

Glory went into the kitchen and sat down in front of the cooking stove. How terrible it all was. Her fine brown hair fell over her eyes and sadly the tears fell down.

She picked up the french beans and began to slice them. Now it would have to be lunch very soon. And then some more washing up. And Mrs Dip never turned up on Friday. And the stove was covered with grease.

From the sitting-room came the sound of the typewriter. 'Oh God,' cried Glory, and buried her head in her arms. 'Oh God.'

Humming a little tune to himself, Ivor worked quickly upon a theme he was finishing. 'Soh, me, doh, soh, me. How happy, how happy to be wrapped in science from the worst that fate and females could do.'

'If only I had science to wrap myself up in,' said poor Glory, and fell to thinking what she would wish, if she could wish one thing to have it granted. 'I should wish,' she said, 'that I had science to wrap myself up in. But I have nothing. I love Ivor, I never see him, never have him, never talk to him, but that the science is wrapping him round. And the educated conversation of the clever girls. Oh God.'

Glory was not an educated girl, in the way that the Research Persons Baba and Friedl were educated girls. They could talk in the informed light manner that Ivor loved (in spite of Friedl's awful accent). But she could not. Her feelings were too much for her; indeed too much.

'I do not believe in your specialist new world, where everybody is so intelligent and everybody is so equal and everybody works and the progress goes on getting more and more progressive,' said Glory crossly to Friedl one day. She shook her head and added darkly, 'There must be sin and suffering, you'll see.'

'Good God, Glory,' said Ivor, 'you sound like the Pythoness. Sin and suffering, ottotottoi; the old bundle at the cross roads. Dreams, dreams. And now I suppose we shall have the waterworks again.'

'Too true,' said Friedl, as again Glory fled weeping.

'Sin and suffering,' she cried now to herself, counting the grease drips down the white front of the stove. 'Sin, pain, death, hell; despair and die. The brassy new world, the brassy hard-voiced young women. And underneath, the cold cold stone.'

Why only the other day, coming from her Aunt's at Tetbury, there in the carriage was a group of superior schoolgirls all of the age of about sixteen. But what sixteen-year-olds. God, what terrible children. They were talking about their exams. 'Oh, Delia darling, it was brilliant of you to think of that. Wasn't it brilliant of Delia, Lois? But then I always say Delia is the seventeenth century, if-you-see-what-I-mean. And what fun for dear old Bolt that you actually remembered to quote her own foul poem on Strafford. No, not boring a bit, darling, but sweet and clever of you – especially sweet.'

At the memory of this atrocious conversation between the false and terrible children, Glory's sobs rose to a roar, so that Ivor, at pause in his theme, heard her and came storming into the kitchen.

'You are a lazy, slovenly, uncontrolled female,' he said. 'You are a barbarian. I am going out.'

'Round to Friedl's, round to Friedl's, round to Friedl's,' sang out Glory.

'Friedl is a civilized woman. I appreciate civilized conversation.' Ivor stood over Glory and laughed. 'I shall be out to lunch.'

He took his hat and went out.

'The beans,' yelled Glory, 'all those french beans.' But it was no good, he was gone.

Glory went to the telephone and rang up Greta.

Greta was lying in bed and thinking about hell and crying and thinking that hell is the continuation of policy. She thought about the times and the wars and the 'scientific use of force' that was the enemy's practique. She thought that evil was indivisible and growing fast. She thought that every trifling evil thing she did was but another drop of sustenance for the evil to lap up and grow fat on. Oh, how fat it was growing.

'Zing,' went the telephone, and downstairs padded Greta, mopping at her nose with a chiffon scarf which by a fortunate chance was in the pocket of her dressing-gown. The thought of the evil was upon her, and the thought that death itself is no escape from it.

'Oh yes, Glory, oh yes.' (She would go to lunch with Glory.)

The meat was overcooked and the beans were undercooked. The two friends brought their plates of food into the sitting-room and turned the gas fire up. Two of the asbestos props were broken, the room felt cold and damp.

'It is cold,' said Greta. 'Glory,' she said, 'I like your dressing-gown with the burn down the front and the grease spots, somehow that is right, and the beastly dark room is right, and the dust upon the antique rare ornaments; the dust, and the saucepan with the goldfish in it, and the overcooked meat and the undercooked beans, it is right; it is an abandonment. It is what the world deserves.'

'Let us have some cocoa afterwards,' said Glory.

'Yes, cocoa, that is right too.'

They began to laugh. Cocoa *was* the thing.

'When you rang up,' said Greta, 'I was thinking, I said, Hell is the continuation of policy. And I was thinking that even death is not the end of it. You know, Glory, there is something frightening about the Christian idea, sometimes it is frightening.' She combed her hair through her fingers.

'I don't know,' said Glory, 'I never think about it.'

'The plodding on and on,' went on Greta, 'the de-moting and the up-grading; the marks and the punishments and the smugness.'

'Like school?' said Glory, waking up a bit to the idea.

'Yes, like school. And no freedom so that a person might stretch himself out. Never, never, never; not even in death; oh most of all not then.'

'I believe in mortality,' said Glory flippantly, 'I shall have on my tombstone, "In the confident hope of Mortality". If death is not the end,' she said, an uneasy note in her voice, 'then indeed there is nowhere to look.'

'When I was studying the Coptics,' said Greta, 'do you know what I found?'

'No, Greta, what was that?'

'It was the Angels and the Red Clay. The Angels came one by one to the Red Clay and coaxed it saying that it should stand up and be Man, and that if the Red Clay would do this it should have the ups and downs, and the good fortune and bad fortune, and all falling haphazard, so that no one might say when it should be this and when that, but no matter, for this the Red Clay should stand up at once and be Man. But, No, said the Red Clay, No, it was not good enough.'

Glory's attention moved off from the Coptics and fastened again upon the problem of Ivor and herself. Oh dear, oh dear. And sadly the tears fell down.

Greta glanced at her severely. 'You should divorce Ivor,' she said.

'I've no grounds,' wailed Glory, 'not since I came back to him.'

'Then you should provoke him to strangle you,' said Greta, who wished to get on with her story. 'That should not be difficult,' she said, 'and then you can divorce him for cruelty.'

'But I love Ivor,' said Glory, 'I don't want to divorce him.'

'Well, make up your mind. As I was saying,' said Greta, '… so then came the Third Angel. "And what have you got to say for yourself?" said the Red Clay. "What have you to promise me?" "I am Death," said the Angel, "and death is the end." So at this up and jumps the Red Clay at once and becomes Man.'

'Oh Glory,' said Greta, when she had finished this recital, and paused a moment while the long tide of evil swept in again upon her, 'Oh Glory, I cannot bear the evil, and the cruelty, and the scientific use of force, and the evil.' She screwed her napkin into a twist, and wrung the hem of it, that was already torn, quite off. 'I do not feel that I can go on.'

At these grand familiar words Glory began to cry afresh, and

Greta was crying too. For there lay the slop on the carpet where the goldfish had been, and there stood the saucepan with the fish resting languid upon the bottom, and there too was the dust and the dirt, and now the plates also, with the congealed mutton fat close upon them.

'Oh, do put some more water in the fish pan,' sobbed Greta.

Glory picked up the pan and ran across the room with it to take it to the kitchen tap. But now the front door, that was apt to jam, opened with a burst, and Ivor fell into the room.

'They were both out,' he said. 'I suppose you have eaten all the lunch? Oh, hello Greta.'

'Listen,' said Glory, 'there's another bomb coming.'

Ivor went to the cupboard.

'Do you know, Ivor,' screamed Greta through the closed door, 'I had a dream and when I woke up I was saying, "Hell is the continuation of policy".'

'You girls fill your heads with a lot of bosh.'

Glory said, 'There's some bread and cheese in the kitchen, we are keeping the cocoa hot. Greta,' she said, 'was telling me about the Coptics.'

'Eh?' said Ivor.

'Oh do take those fish out and give them some more water,' said Greta.

'The story about the Angels and the Red Clay.'

'Spurious,' yelled Ivor, 'all bosh. But how on earth did you get hold of the manuscript, Greta, it's very rare.'

'I don't think there's much in it,' said Glory, 'nothing to make you cry. Come, cheer up Greta. I say Ivor, the doodle has gone off towards the town, you can come out now.'

Ivor came out looking very cheerful. 'I tell you what, Greta,' he said, 'I'll show you my new plastic bait.' He took the brightly coloured monsters out of their tin and brought them to her on a plate. 'I use these for pike,' he said.

There was now in the room a feeling of loving kindness and peace. Greta fetched the cheese and bread from the kitchen and Glory poured the hot cocoa. 'There is nothing like industry, control, affection and discipline,' said Greta.

The sun came round to the French windows and struck through the glass pane at the straw stuffing that was hanging down from the belly of the sofa.

'Oh, look,' said Glory, pointing to the patch of sunlight underneath, 'there is the button you lost.'

Silence fell upon them in the sun-spiked room. Silently, happily, they went on with their lunch. The only sound now in the room was the faint sizzle of the cocoa against the side of the jug (that was set too close to the fire and soon must crack) and the far off bark of the dog Sultan, happy with his rats.

SYLVIA TOWNSEND WARNER

Poor Mary

At the last minute he remembered flowers. He went out and gathered some primroses from the hedgerow, hardening himself not to notice the snap of their stems. It was one of his fidgets to dislike picking flowers.

The track sloped away downhill. Here and there the leafless hedge was tufted with white where the blackthorns had come into bloom. It was like a black wave breaking into lips of foam. Down in the valley a plume of white steam rose up, its summit catching the pink light of sunset. It was still hanging there when he heard the train go on. And Mary, shouldering her pack, had handed in her ticket and joined the nondescript civilian group waiting for the bus. The white plume thinned out, the train gathered speed, snorting on towards London. But Mary had got out at East Wickering, junction for Stoat and Saint Brewers.

I want to spend this leave at home, she had written; *unless you'd rather not. It's more than time I saw you in your hermit cell.* If it had not been for the last sentence he would have supposed she wanted to spend her leave with her family.

'Flowers for the guest-room,' he said to himself, setting down the spotted mug in the centre of the bureau. The bed, an old-fashioned double bed with brass end-rails and a white quilt, suddenly seemed a bed in which he had never slept. It looked like Wordsworth's bed, so monumentally domestic. He must contrive that she saw the camp-bed first. For the last week he had spent his spare time preparing for her, scrubbing the floors, polishing the windows, putting away his clothes, his books, his papers, so that his dwelling might offer its most impersonal face to her inspection. Now that he had remembered flowers everything seemed ready. The food on the table was covered with a napkin to keep flies off it, the kettle was in a state to boil when he wanted it to, the watercress was keeping cold in a damp cloth. He snuffed at his fingers' ends, and once more washed his hands very carefully. He had been cleaning out pigsties all the morning. Then he set off to meet his wife.

He had not seen her since 1941. A conscientious objector, he had applied for exemption from military service. The day after the tribunal had granted him exemption provided he worked on the land Mary volunteered for the ATS.* They had never agreed about war, so neither was surprised by the other.

'But as we are bound to argue,' she said, 'and people will only laugh at you if you have a military wife coming on visits, I shan't come. Unless you are ill, of course. Then I will apply for compassionate leave.'

One of the things he had learned in four years spent as a farm labourer was an exact computation of time. So he met her where he had intended to meet her, fifty yards from where the bus had set her down. Though he knew she would be wearing uniform, it was a surprise to see that part of the uniform was a skirt. He had been similarly astonished on their wedding-day when apparently he had been assuming that she would come up the aisle wearing white satin trousers. Seeing the skirt he also saw her legs below it, and that they were fatter than they used to be.

'Hallo, Nicholas!'

'Hallo, Mary!'

She smells of metal, he thought, as much as I smell of dung. We are subdued to what we work in. He had smelled her, he had seen her legs. He did not seem to have seen her face. He took her pack, and said: 'Look! There's a hawk.'

'I suppose they do a lot of harm to the crops,' she replied.

'Wood-pigeons are worse.'

She set off, walking with quick resolute steps. Marching, in fact. So why on earth should she know about hawks? The thought prompted an enquiry about the V-2, and they went up the trackway talking of air raids and air-raid damage. Just as there was a difference between their smells and a difference in their gait there was a difference in their manner of speech. Her voice had grown rather common and twanging, it sounded uncared for, and she jumped from one subject to another. She seemed to preface every remark with *Gosh!* and he to inaugurate every reply

---

*   Auxiliary Territorial Service

with *Um*. Listening to himself he thought, Do I sound more like the village schoolmaster or the village idiot?

A melancholy tenderness that was almost entirely the April dusk suffused him. Blackbirds shot across the path from hedge to hedge, scolding at them, beyond the hedges lambs bleated and rushed away at a ghostly gallop. He had been working from six in the morning, and was tired, and craved for tea. Yet each time that they paused for Mary to recover her breath he was glad to postpone the moment of reaching his house, and when the one chimney-pot reared into view above the hedge and beneath the evening star he said gloomily: 'Here's where I live.'

'It's nice. And all to yourself? Lucky bastard!'

'There are only two rooms,' he said defensively. 'The third one leaks.'

'Is it old?'

'Run up after the last war by a chicken-farming ex-serviceman. When he was ruined the farmer bought it. As he bought it very cheap, naturally he doesn't trouble to keep it in repair. So we sit in the kitchen. But I've got a chemical closet.'

It was strange to hear her feet on the floor of concrete slabs. Not strange to her, though, who had been living for four years in army constructions. The only strange thing to her would be to hear two pairs of feet instead of many. He moved the kettle forward on the range and lit the candles.

'Candles!' she said appreciatively.

'Because it's a party. Ordinarily I use an oil lamp.' His voice was still heavy with gloom.

'What queer squat candlesticks! They're clay, aren't they? Did you make them?'

'No. I bought them at a sale. They're called corpse candlesticks. The idea is that you leave them by the body all night, you see, and the rats can't knock them over.'

'I wonder you don't use them every night,' she said. 'Have you got any other cheerful curiosities?'

She had taken off her cap and unbuttoned her tunic. The candlelight softened the contest between her natural high colour and the too tawny make-up she had applied to it. If one were tracking her down in Roget's *Thesaurus,* the word would be *comely.*

Seeing that he was looking at her she said: 'Isn't it calamitous how fat I've grown? It's that army food, incessant gorges of starch. Gosh! Those puddings! Enough to make any girl look like a prize ox.'

'When I first came here I was covered with spots and boils,' he said consolingly. 'I thought I'd caught it from the pigs, till I discovered it was my well. Now I boil it.'

'I'd hate to have to do with pigs.'

'They're clean animals, really. It's just that they are overcrowded, and dirty feeders.'

'Sounds like the ATS.'

He cut more bread, reflecting that he would need to bake again on the morrow. Habit, of course, and mass-feeding, and the goaded appetite of the disciplined: though that would not account for the scatteration of egg-shell, the jam spooned on to a salted plate, the wide periphery of crumbs and cigarette ash. Nerves, he thought. Poor Mary's nerves are strained. His own strained nerves obliged him to sip his tea as though it were Napoleon brandy and frown at the iron-mould on the cloth.

'Lovely bread, Nicholas.'

'Soda bread. I bake it myself.'

'You seem to have a lot of time. Don't you ever do any work?'

'Fifty-six hours a week. Sometimes overtime. Pigs on Sunday. But it fits in somehow, and I don't dislike it. And the alternative would be to have a woman in.'

He had not meant this. She did not perceive it. Staring round her as though in a foreign country she said: 'And the polish on everything, too! You're wasted, Nicholas. You ought to be in the army.'

'Yes, sergeant.'

But more concerned than he had been over his own maladroit remarks she flushed, and refused to eat anything more, like an abashed child.

'Walk round and see the rest of it. Here's your room.'

'Pretty flowers.'

Glaring at the bed he remarked: 'I've got a bed in the third room.'

'But that's the room that leaks. You said so.'

She had turned around from the mirror, and it was as though the mirror had given back to her her former countenance, at once innocent and domineering.

'It doesn't leak in dry weather,' he said. 'I expect the cat's there now. She comes in and out by the window.'

'Cat? Why, you used to hate cats. You said they tortured birds.'

'So they do. So I do hate them. But I must needs find this animal in a gin, and dress its paw, and the damned beast has adopted me. It's a female, too.'

'Life's harder in the country, I expect,' she commented. It was for such slanting ironies that he had first loved her; for that, and for smelling of geraniums, and for the chivalrous quarrelsome disposition which had kept her at his side before his exemption was assured, saying hopefully that he might need someone to scrap with the authorities. But unseeing she went on to undo it by saying: 'You know, a lot of people are awfully interested when I tell them my husband is a CO. You'd be surprised how many feel the same way. All these murder cases, you know. Everyone's dead against the death sentence.'

'It doesn't surprise me very much,' he said. 'I was in the train the other day, I had to go to a dentist. And there was a bomber crew in the same carriage, and they were talking about a murder. They all agreed that it was wrong to take human life. I asked one of them why, and he said because you can't know what you're meddling with.'

'Exactly! I've heard dozens say the same thing. I'm beginning to think so myself. I think they ought to abolish it. I expect they will after the war.'

'They'll abolish war, my dear. Belligerents always abolish war after a war. It's harder to part with a death sentence. And impossible to give up hunting and shooting because hunting and shooting make us what we are. Have a cigarette?'

'I don't think you've grown any pleasanter,' she said. 'Is that an owl? Let's go back to the other room.'

In the other room the clock was ticking, the kettle was boiling. Three hours earlier the bed had not seemed his own, now his living-room was not his either, but some sort of institutional waiting-room where two people had made an inordinate mess of a meal. At last, irked beyond bearing, he rose and began to clear the table and to wash up. The hot water in the bowl, the feeling of the crockery, dried and still warm as he stacked it on the dresser, the reassumption of his ordinary evening routine began to console him. He moved to and fro more nimbly, preparing for the two breakfasts he would get in the morning, pouring the remains of the tea into the bottle he would carry to work with him – he had grown to enjoy cold tea – rinsing out the teapot and standing it on its head, throwing out the slops and bringing in the kindling for the morrow's fire, winding the clock and putting the cat's saucer down on a sheet of newspaper. Now, had he been by himself, he would have raked out the fire and gone off to read in bed. Instead, hospitality constrained him to say: 'Have you brought a hotwater bottle?'

She did not answer. With a kettle in one hand and the wood-basket in the other he glanced at her. But she was not asleep. She was openly and directly crying.

He built up the fire and put on the kettle. This, whatever it was about, would mean more tea. Then he patted her shoulder and said: 'Poor Mary!' She put up her hand that was so plump and so demonstrably manicured, and clung to his wrist. She's going to have a baby, he thought. The cat in the gin that had clawed him to the bone, clawed and clung, had been within a few days of giving birth. He had made her a nest in the wood-house, but she had limped off to hide under a gorse-brake. The kittens had grown up and gone their wild way, and now she was pregnant again. But for poor Mary there was nothing but some sort of nursing-home.

She clung to his wrist and rubbed her head against his arm. Moulting, he thought, still clinically remembering the cat. She was going to have a baby, no doubt of it. It accounted for every-thing, for her nerves, for her legs, for her appetite, for her coming. Poor Mary, patriotism had not been enough, she had had no hatred in her heart for anybody, and so she was going to have a baby. The fortunes of war. Some get killed, some get maimed, some are got with child. There ought to be a pension from the War Office. And in that dreadful uniform, too, that pitiable skirt turned up. I hope to God, he thought, I shall not have to meet the father, one of those strenuous noodles, I suppose, who think badly of the death sentence. I'm damned if I will. And the next instant he was thinking, My poor Mary, I hope it wasn't a rape. Meanwhile his indifferent body was complying with the routine of his daily life, and he felt himself to be growing more and more sleepy and knew that unless he spoke he might yawn.

'If you'll let go a minute, Mary, I'll make some tea.'

She let go. The hand that had been so strong fell on her lap and crept into the other hand. Presently it moved again and pulled out a khaki handkerchief, and she began to mop her eyes and snort back her tears.

'This damned war! It's this damned war, Nicholas.'

He groaned assentingly.

'Now that it's nearly over, how I hate it!'

With an effort he refrained from pointing out that it was only in Europe that the war might be said to be nearly over.

'If they'd let me fight, as I wanted to, I might be killed by now. If we'd stayed in London and I'd driven an ambulance or a pump I might be killed by now. As it is I've never been so healthy in all my life.'

'You don't look well,' he said. 'I noticed at once that you looked tired. And you got frightfully out of breath walking up the hill.'

'Fat! My healthy army fat! When I come out of the army, Nicholas, I shall come out healthy, hideous, middle-aged and without an interest in life. And there will be hordes and hordes of me, all in the same boat. Gosh, what a crew!'

Giving up the hypothesis of a baby he realized how much he was relinquishing. Once it was born, she would have been happy enough.

'We shall all be in that boat, dear. Besides, you're a sergeant, aren't you? That's something. You'll soon get thin, once you're out in the rough and tumble of civilian life. Once you're thin, you'll take hold, you'll get interested in something or other. Probably you'll fall in love, and make a fresh start.'

The kettle was boiling, he began to prepare for more tea.

'Fall in love? Fall in love? Not again. You see, I did it.'

He paused, kettle in hand. (Would nothing rid him of these turbulent kettles?)

'And he was killed? I'm sorry, Mary.'

'He wasn't killed. He chucked me, and now he's married to another bitch.'

'And that's all?'

'And that's all.'

He glanced towards the clock. It felt like midnight, but it was only half past ten. If he could give her something stronger, some whisky, some rum. A little rum, now, in her tea . . . But a pigeon-shooting party last week had cleaned out the Red Lion of everything except aniseed cordial.

'Sugar?' he inquired.

She looked at him.

'I'm sorry. I'm sorry! I asked you that only three hours ago, didn't I? I am an insensate clod.'

'That's all right, Nicholas. Actually, I don't take sugar. You could have had all mine, you see. Think what you've missed. Actually, why I came back was to see if you'd ever want to live with me again. Not that I thought it likely. Why should you? Anyhow, it's plain you don't. So that's over. What good tea you make.'

She drank in gulps, swallowing violently, swallowing tea and tears.

'You were always domestically inclined, weren't you? It will be a comfort to me, yes, really it will, to think of you being so happy and tidy and self-contained, with your cat and your corpse-candles and your books and your flowers. Did Robinson Crusoe have flowers on his table, as well as his old cat sitting up to it like a Christian? I can't remember. Perhaps when we are both very old I may come and spend the afternoon with you on your island. And you can make me some of your nice tea, and ask me if I take sugar with it. But of course I'll give you ample warning. I won't be a disquieting footprint. I *did* warn you this time, you know.'

She had risen, she had picked up her cap and her pack and her cigarette-case and her lighter and her lipstick and all her bits and pieces.

'I think I'll go to bed. I've got rather a headache.'

'Yes. We'll go to bed.'

Leaving the room all anyhow, he thought, staring at her submissive military back in the doorway. Whether it made things better, whether it made them worse, it was the only thing he could do, the only way he could comfort her. They would lie in the Wordsworthian bed, their smells of dung and of metal would mingle, her shoulder would feel like greengages and her hair would get in his mouth, and she would be silent. It was one of her graces that she was silent in bed. And afterwards, when she had gone to sleep, he would straighten himself and lie on his back, letting the day's fatigue run out of his limbs as the fleas run out of the body of a shot rabbit. And probably his last waking thought would be of the alarm clock, poised to wake him at five-thirty, and of the limpid innocent morning in which he would go out to his work.

DORIS LESSING

The Black Madonna

There are some countries in which the arts, let alone Art, cannot be said to flourish. Why this should be so it is hard to say, although of course we all have our theories about it. For sometimes it is the most barren soil that sends up gardens of those flowers which we all agree are the crown and justification of life, and it is this fact which makes it hard to say, finally, why the soil of Zambesia should produce such reluctant plants.

Zambesia is a tough, sunburnt, virile, positive country contemptuous of subtleties and sensibility: yet there have been states with these qualities which have produced art, though perhaps with the left hand. Zambesia is, to put it mildly, unsympathetic to those ideas so long taken for granted in other parts of the world; to do with liberty, fraternity and the rest. Yet there are those, and some of the finest souls among them, who maintain that art is impossible without a minority whose leisure is guaranteed by a hard-working majority. And whatever Zambesia's comfortable minority may lack, it is not leisure.

Zambesia – but enough; out of respect for ourselves and for scientific accuracy, we should refrain from jumping to conclusions. Particularly when one remembers the almost wistful respect Zambesians show when an artist does appear in their midst.

Consider, for instance, the case of Michele.

He came out of the internment camp at the time when Italy was made a sort of honorary ally, during the Second World War. It was a time of strain for the authorities, because it is one thing to be responsible for thousands of prisoners of war whom one must treat according to certain recognized standards. It is another to be faced, and from one day to the next, with these same thousands transformed by some international legerdemain into comrades in arms. Some of the thousands stayed where they were in the camps; they were fed and housed there at least. Others went as farm labourers, though not many; for while the farmers were as always short of labour, they did not know how to handle farm labourers who were also white men: such a phenomenon had never happened in Zambesia before. Some did odd jobs around the towns, keeping a sharp eye out for the trade unions, who would neither admit them as members nor agree to their working.

Hard, hard, the lot of these men, but fortunately not for long, for soon the war ended and they were able to go home.

Hard, too, the lot of the authorities, as has been pointed out; and for that reason they were doubly willing to take what advantages they could from the situation, and that Michele was such an advantage there could be no doubt.

His talents were first discovered when he was still a prisoner of war. A church was built in the camp, and Michele decorated its interior. It became a show-place, that little tin-roofed church in the prisoners' camp, with its whitewashed walls covered all over with frescoes depicting swarthy peasants gathering grapes for the vintage, beautiful Italian girls dancing, plump dark-eyed children. Amid crowded scenes of Italian life, appeared the Virgin and her Child, smiling and beneficent, happy to move familiarly among her people.

Culture-loving ladies who had bribed the authorities to be taken inside the camp would say, 'Poor thing, how homesick he must be'. And they would beg to be allowed to leave half a crown for the artist. Some were indignant. He was a prisoner, after all, captured in the very act of fighting against justice and democracy, and what right had he to protest? – for they felt these paintings as a sort of protest. What was there in Italy that we did not have right here in Westonville, which was the capital and hub of Zambesia? Were there not sunshine and mountains and fat babies and pretty girls here? Did we not grow – if not grapes, at least lemons and oranges and flowers in plenty?

People were upset – the desperation of nostalgia came from the painted white walls of that simple church, and affected everyone according to his temperament.

But when Michele was free, his talent was remembered. He was spoken of as 'that Italian artist'. As a matter of fact, he was a bricklayer. And the virtues of those frescoes might very well have been exaggerated. It is possible that they would have been overlooked altogether in a country where picture-covered walls were more common.

When one of the visiting ladies came rushing out to the camp in her own car, to ask him to paint her children, he said he was not qualified to do so. But at last he agreed. He took a room in the town and made some nice likenesses of the children. Then he painted the children of a great number of the first lady's friends. He charged ten shillings a time. Then one of the ladies wanted a portrait of herself. He asked ten pounds for it; it had taken him a month to do. She was annoyed, but paid.

And Michele went off to his room with a friend and stayed there drinking red wine from the Cape and talking about home. While the money lasted he could not be persuaded to do any more portraits.

There was a good deal of talk among the ladies about the dignity of labour, a subject in which they were well versed; and one felt they might almost go so far as to compare a white man with a kaffir, who did not understand the dignity of labour either.

He was felt to lack gratitude. One of the ladies tracked him down, found him lying on a camp-bed under a tree with a bottle of wine, and spoke to him severely about the barbarity of Mussolini and the fecklessness of the Italian temperament. Then she demanded that he should instantly paint a picture of herself in her new evening dress. He refused, and she went home very angry.

It happened that she was the wife of one of our most important citizens, a general or something of that kind, who was at that time engaged in planning a military tattoo or show for the benefit of the civilian population. The whole of Westonville had been discussing this show for weeks. We were all bored to extinction by dances, fancy-dress balls, fairs, lotteries and other charitable entertainments. It is not too much to say that while some were dying for freedom, others were dancing for it. There comes a limit to everything. Though, of course, when the end of the war actually came and the thousands of troops stationed in the country had to go home – in short, when enjoying ourselves would no longer be a duty, many were heard to exclaim that life would never be the same again.

In the meantime, the tattoo would make a nice change for us all. The military gentlemen responsible for the idea did not think of it in these terms. They thought to improve morale by giving us some idea of what war was really like. Headlines in the newspaper were not enough. And in order to bring it all home to us, they planned to destroy a village by shell-fire before our very eyes.

First, the village had to be built.

It appears that the general and his subordinates stood around in the red dust of the parade-ground under a burning sun for the whole of one day, surrounded by building materials, while hordes of African labourers ran around with boards and nails, trying to make something that looked like a village. It became evident that they would have to build a proper village in order to destroy it; and this would cost more than was allowed for the whole entertainment. The general went home in a bad temper, and his wife said what they needed was an artist, they needed Michele. This was not because she wanted to do Michele a good turn; she could not endure the thought of him lying around singing while there was work to be done. She refused to undertake any delicate diplomatic missions when her husband said he would be damned if he would ask favours of any little wop. She solved the problem for him in her own way: a certain Captain Stocker was sent out to fetch him.

The captain found him on the same camp-bed under the same tree, in rolled-up trousers, and an uncollared shirt; unshaven, mildly drunk, with a bottle of wine standing beside him on the earth. He was singing an air so wild, so sad, that the captain was uneasy. He stood at ten paces from the disreputable fellow and felt the indignities of his position. A year ago, this man had been a mortal enemy to be shot at sight. Six months ago, he had been an enemy prisoner. Now he lay with his knees up, in an untidy shirt that had certainly once been military. For the captain, the situation crystallized in a desire that Michele should salute him.

'Piselli!' he said sharply.

Michele turned his head and looked at the captain from the horizontal. 'Good morning,' he said affably.

'You are wanted,' said the captain.

'Who?' said Michele. He sat up, a fattish, olive-skinned little man. His eyes were resentful.

'The authorities.'

'The war is over?'

The captain, who was already stiff and shiny enough in his laundered khaki, jerked his head back frowning, chin out. He was a large man, blond, and wherever his flesh showed, it was brick-red. His eyes were small and blue and angry. His red hands, covered all over with fine yellow bristles, clenched by his side. Then he saw the disappointment in Michele's eyes, and the hands unclenched. 'No it is not over,' he said. 'Your assistance is required.'

'For the war?'

'For the war effort. I take it you are interested in defeating the Germans?'

Michele looked at the captain. The little dark-eyed artisan looked at the great blond officer with his cold blue eyes, his narrow mouth, his hands like bristle-covered steaks. He looked and said: 'I am very interested in the end of the war.'

'Well?' said the captain between his teeth.

'The pay?' said Michele.

'You will be paid.'

Michele stood up. He lifted the bottle against the sun, then took a gulp. He rinsed his mouth out with wine and spat. Then he poured what was left on to the red earth, where it made a bubbling purple stain.

'I am ready,' he said. He went with the captain to the waiting lorry, where he climbed in beside the driver's seat and not, as the captain had expected, into the back of the lorry. When they had arrived at the parade-ground the officers had left a message that the captain would be personally responsible for Michele and for the village. Also for the hundred or so labourers who were sitting around on the grass verges waiting for orders.

The captain explained what was wanted. Michele nodded. Then he waved his hand at the Africans. 'I do not want these,' he said.

'You will do it yourself – a village?'

'Yes.'

'With no help?'

Michele smiled for the first time. 'I will do it.'

The captain hesitated. He disapproved on principle of white men doing heavy manual labour. He said: 'I will keep six to do the heavy work.'

Michele shrugged; and the captain went over and dismissed all but six of the Africans. He came back with them to Michele.

'It is hot,' said Michele.

'Very,' said the captain. They were standing in the middle of the parade-ground. Around its edge trees, grass, gulfs of shadow.

Here, nothing but reddish dust, drifting and lifting in a low hot breeze.

'I am thirsty,' said Michele. He grinned. The captain felt his stiff lips loosen unwillingly in reply. The two pairs of eyes met. It was a moment of understanding. For the captain, the little Italian had suddenly become human. 'I will arrange it,' he said, and went off downtown. By the time he had explained the position to the right people, filled in forms and made arrangements, it was late afternoon. He returned to the parade-ground with a case of Cape brandy, to find Michele and the six black men seated together under a tree. Michele was singing an Italian song to them, and they were harmonizing with him. The sight affected the captain like an attack of nausea. He came up, and the Africans stood to attention. Michele continued to sit.

'You said you would do the work yourself?'

'Yes, I said so.'

The captain then dismissed the Africans. They departed, with friendly looks towards Michele, who waved at them. The captain was beef-red with anger. 'You have not started yet?'

'How long have I?'

'Three weeks.'

'Then there is plenty of time,' said Michele, looking at the bottle of brandy in the captain's hand. In the other were two glasses. 'It is evening,' he pointed out. The captain stood frowning for a moment. Then he sat down on the grass, and poured out two brandies.

'Ciao,' said Michele.

'Cheers,' said the captain. Three weeks, he was thinking. Three weeks with this damned little Itie! He drained his glass and refilled it, and set it in the grass. The grass was cool and soft. A tree was flowering somewhere close – hot waves of perfume came on the breeze.

'It is nice here,' said Michele. 'We will have a good time together. Even in a war, there are times of happiness. And of friendship. I drink to the end of the war.'

Next day the captain did not arrive at the parade-ground until after lunch. He found Michele under the trees with a bottle. Sheets of ceiling board had been erected at one end of the parade-ground in such a way that they formed two walls and part of a third, and a slant of steep roof supported on struts.

'What's that?' said the captain, furious.

'The church,' said Michele.

'Wha-at?'

'You will see. Later. It is very hot.' He looked at the brandy bottle that lay on its side on the ground. The captain went to the lorry and returned with the case of brandy. They drank. Time passed. It was a long time since the captain had sat on grass under a tree. It was a long time, for that matter, since he had drunk so much. He always drank a great deal, but it was regulated to the times and seasons. He was a disciplined man. Here, sitting on the grass beside this little man whom he still could not help thinking of as an enemy, it was not that he let his self-discipline go, but that he felt himself to be something different: he was temporarily set outside his normal behaviour. Michele did not count. He listened to Michele talking about Italy and it seemed to him he was listening to a savage speaking; as if he heard tales from the mythical South Sea islands where a man like himself might very well go just once in his life. He found himself saying he would like to make a trip to Italy after the war. Actually, he was attracted only by the north and by northern people. He had visited Germany, under Hitler, and though it was not the time to say so, had found it very satisfactory. Then Michele sang him some Italian songs. He sang Michele some English songs. Then Michele took out photographs of his wife and children, who lived in a village in the mountains of North Italy. He asked the captain if he were married. The captain never spoke about his private affairs.

He had spent all his life in one or other of the African colonies as a policeman, magistrate, native commissioner or in some other useful capacity. When the war started, military life came easily to him. But he hated city life, and had his own reasons for wishing the war over. Mostly, he had been in bush-stations with one or two other white men, or by himself, far from the rigours of civilization. He had relations with native women; and from time to time visited the city where his wife lived with her parents and the children. He was always tormented by the idea that she was unfaithful to him. Recently he had even appointed a private detective to watch her; he was convinced the detective was inefficient. Army friends coming from L— where his wife was, spoke of her at parties, enjoying herself. When the war ended, she would not find it so easy to have a good time. And why did he not simply live with her and be done with it? The fact was, he could not. And his long exile to remote bush-stations was because he needed the excuse not to. He could not bear to think of his wife for too long; she was that part of his life he had never been able, so to speak, to bring to heel.

Yet he spoke of her now to Michele, and of his favourite bush-wife, Nadya. He told Michele the story of his life, until he realized that the shadows from the trees they sat under had stretched right across the parade-ground to the grandstand. He got unsteadily to his feet, and said: 'There is work to be done. You are being paid to work.'

'I will show you my church when the light goes.'

The sun dropped, darkness fell, and Michele made the captain drive his lorry to the parade-ground a couple of hundred yards away and switch on his lights. Instantly, a white church sprang up from the shapes and shadows of the bits of board.

'Tomorrow, some houses,' said Michele cheerfully.

At the end of a week, the space at the end of the parade-ground had crazy gawky constructions of lath and board over it, that looked in the sunlight like nothing on earth. Privately, it upset the captain: it was like a nightmare that these skeleton-like shapes should be able to persuade him, with the illusions of light and dark, that they were a village. At night, the captain drove up his lorry, switched on the lights, and there it was, the village, solid and real against the background of full green trees. Then, in the morning sunlight, there was nothing there, just bits of board stuck in the sand.

'It is finished,' said Michele.

'You were engaged for three weeks,' said the captain. He did not want it to end, this holiday from himself.

Michele shrugged. 'The army is rich,' he said. Now, to avoid curious eyes, they sat inside the shade of the church, with the case of brandy between them. The captain talked, talked endlessly, about his wife, about women. He could not stop talking.

Michele listened. Once he said: 'When I go home – when I go home – I shall open my arms . . .' He opened them, wide. He closed his eyes. Tears ran down his cheeks. 'I shall take my wife in my arms, and I shall ask nothing, nothing. I do not care. It is enough to be together. That is what the war has taught me. It is enough, it is enough. I shall ask no questions and I shall be happy.'

The captain stared before him, suffering. He thought how he dreaded his wife. She was a scornful creature, gay and hard, who laughed at him. She had been laughing at him ever since they married. Since the war, she had taken to calling him names like Little Hitler, and Storm-trooper. 'Go ahead, my little Hitler,' she had cried last time they met. 'Go ahead, my Storm-trooper. If you want to waste your money on private detectives, go ahead. But don't think I don't know what you do when you're in the bush. I don't care what you do, but remember that I know it . . .'

The captain remembered her saying it. And there sat Michele on his packing-case, saying: 'It's a pleasure for the rich, my friend, detectives and the law. Even jealousy is a pleasure I don't want any more. Ah, my friend, to be together with my wife again, and the children, that is all I ask of life. That and wine and food and singing in the evenings.' And the tears wetted his cheeks and splashed on to his shirt.

That a man should cry, good Lord! thought the captain. And without shame! He seized the bottle and drank.

Three days before the great occasion, some high-ranking officers came strolling through the dust, and found Michele and the captain sitting together on the packing-case, singing. The captain's shirt was open down the front, and there were stains on it.

The captain stood to attention with the bottle in his hand, and Michele stood to attention too, out of sympathy with his friend. Then the officers drew the captain aside – they were all cronies of his – and said, what the hell did he think he was doing? And why wasn't the village finished.

Then they went away.

'Tell them it is finished,' said Michele. 'Tell them I want to go.'

'No,' said the captain, 'no, Michele, what would you do if your wife . . .'

'This world is a good place. We should be happy – that is all.'

'Michele . . .'

'I want to go. There is nothing to do. They paid me yesterday.'

'Sit down, Michele. Three more days, and then it's finished.'

'Then I shall paint the inside of the church as I painted the one in the camp.'

The captain laid himself down on some boards and went to sleep. When he woke, Michele was surrounded by the pots of paint he had used on the outside of the village. Just in front of the captain was a picture of a black girl. She was young and plump. She wore a patterned blue dress and her shoulders came soft and bare out of it. On her back was a baby slung in a band of red stuff. Her face was turned towards the captain and she was smiling.

'That's Nadya,' said the captain. 'Nadya . . .' He groaned loudly. He looked at the black child and shut his eyes. He opened them, and mother and child were still there. Michele was very carefully drawing thin yellow circles around the heads of the black girl and her child.

'Good God,' said the captain, 'you can't do that.'

'Why not?'

'You can't have a black Madonna.'

'She was a peasant. This is a peasant. Black peasant Madonna for black country.'

'This is a German village,' said the captain.

'This is my Madonna,' said Michele angrily. 'Your German village and my Madonna. I paint this picture as an offering to the Madonna. She is pleased – I feel it.'

The captain lay down again. He was feeling ill. He went back to sleep. When he woke for the second time it was dark. Michele had brought in a flaring paraffin lamp, and by its light was working on the long wall. A bottle of brandy stood beside him. He painted until long after midnight, and the captain lay on his side and watched, as passive as a man suffering a dream. Then they both went to sleep on the boards. The whole of the next day Michele stood painting black Madonnas, black saints, black angels. Outside, troops were practising in the sunlight, bands were blaring and motorcyclists roared up and down. But Michele painted on, drunk and oblivious. The captain lay on his back, drinking and muttering about his wife. Then he would say, 'Nadya, Nadya', and burst into sobs.

Towards nightfall the troops went away. The officers came back, and the captain went off with them to show how the village sprang into being when the great lights at the end of the parade-ground were switched on. They all looked at the village in silence. They switched the lights off, and there were only the tall angular boards leaning like gravestones in the moonlight. On went the lights – and there was the village. They were silent, as if suspicious. Like the captain, they seemed to feel it was not right.

Uncanny it certainly was, but *that* was not it. Unfair – that was the word. It was cheating. And profoundly disturbing.

'Clever chap, that Italian of yours,' said the general.

The captain, who had been woodenly correct until this moment, suddenly came rocking up to the general, and steadied himself by laying his hand on the august shoulder. 'Bloody wops,' he said. 'Bloody kaffirs. Bloody . . . Tell you what, though, there's one Itie that's some good. Yes, there is. I'm telling you. He's a friend of mine, actually.'

The general looked at him. Then he nodded to his underlings. The captain was taken away for disciplinary purposes. It was decided, however, that he must be ill, nothing else could account for such behaviour. He was put to bed in his own room with a nurse to watch him.

He woke twenty-four hours later, sober for the first time in weeks. He slowly remembered what had happened. Then he sprang out of bed and rushed into his clothes. The nurse was just in time to see him run down the path and leap into his lorry.

He drove at top speed to the parade-ground, which was flooded with light in such a way that the village did not exist. Everything was in full swing. The cars were three deep around the square, with people on the running-boards and even the roofs. The grandstand was packed. Women dressed as gipsies, country girls, Elizabethan court dames and so on, wandered about with trays of ginger beer and sausage-rolls and programmes at five shillings each in aid of the war effort. On the square, troops deployed, obsolete machine-guns were being dragged up and down, bands played and motorcyclists roared through flames.

As the captain parked the lorry, all this activity ceased, and the lights went out. The captain began running around the outside of the square to reach the place where the guns were hidden in a mess of net and branches. He was sobbing with the effort. He was a big man, and unused to exercise, and sodden with brandy. He had only one idea in his mind – to stop the guns firing, to stop them at all costs.

Luckily, there seemed to be a hitch. The lights were still out. The unearthly graveyard at the end of the square glittered white in the moonlight. Then the lights briefly switched on, and the village sprang into existence for just long enough to show large red crosses all over a white building beside the church. Then moonlight flooded everything again, and the crosses vanished. 'Oh, the bloody fool!' sobbed the captain, running, running as if for his life. He was no longer trying to reach the guns. He was cutting across a corner of the square direct to the church. He could hear some officers cursing behind him: 'Who put those red crosses there? Who? We can't fire on the Red Cross.'

The captain reached the church as the searchlights burst on. Inside, Michele was kneeling on the earth looking at his first Madonna. 'They are going to kill my Madonna,' he said miserably.

'Come away, Michele, come away.'

'They're going to . . .'

The captain grabbed his arm and pulled. Michele wrenched himself free and grabbed a saw. He began hacking at the ceiling board. There was a dead silence outside. They heard a voice booming through the loudspeakers: 'The village that is about to be shelled is an English village, not as represented on the programme, a German village. Repeat, the village that is about to be shelled is . . .'

Michele had cut through two sides of a square around the Madonna.

'Michele,' sobbed the captain, '*get out of here.*'

Michele dropped the saw, took hold of the raw edges of the board and tugged. As he did so, the church began to quiver and lean. An irregular patch of board ripped out and Michele staggered back into the captain's arms. There was a roar. The church seemed to dissolve around them into flame. Then they were running away from it, the captain holding Michele tight by the right arm. 'Get down,' he shouted suddenly, and threw Michele to the earth. He flung himself down beside him. Looking from under the crook of his arm, he heard the explosion, saw a great pillar of smoke and flame, and the village disintegrated in a flying mass of debris. Michele was on his knees gazing at his Madonna in the light from the flames. She was unrecognizable, blotted out with dust. He looked horrible, quite white, and a trickle of blood soaked from his hair down one cheek.

'They shelled my Madonna,' he said.

'Oh, damn it, you can paint another one,' said the captain. His own voice seemed to him strange, like a dream voice. He was certainly crazy, as mad as Michele himself . . . He got up, pulled Michele to his feet, and marched him towards the edge of the field. There they were met by the ambulance people. Michele was taken off to hospital, and the captain was sent back to bed.

A week passed. The captain was in a darkened room. That he was having some kind of a breakdown was clear, and two nurses stood guard over him. Sometimes he lay quiet. Sometimes he muttered to himself. Sometimes he sang in a thick, clumsy voice bits out of opera, fragments from Italian songs, and – over and over again – 'There's a Long Long Trail'. He was not thinking of anything at all. He shied away from the thought of Michele as if it were dangerous. When, therefore, a cheerful female voice announced that a friend had come to cheer him up, and it would do him good to have some company, and he saw a white bandage moving towards him in the gloom, he turned over on to his side, face to the wall.

'Go away,' he said. 'Go away, Michele.'

'I have come to see you,' said Michele. 'I have brought you a present.'

The captain slowly turned over. There was Michele, a cheerful ghost in the dark room. 'You fool,' he said. 'You messed everything up. What did you paint those crosses for?'

'It was a hospital,' said Michele. 'In a village there is a hospital, and on the hospital the Red Cross, the beautiful Red Cross – no?'

'I was nearly court-martialled.'

'It was my fault,' said Michele. 'I was drunk.'

'I was responsible.'

'How could you be responsible when I did it? But it is all over. Are you better?'

'Well, I suppose those crosses saved your life.'

'I did not think,' said Michele. 'I was remembering the kindness of the Red Cross people when we were prisoners.'

'Oh shut up, shut up, shut up.'

'I have brought you a present.'

The captain peered through the dark. Michele was holding up a picture. It was of a native woman with a baby on her back smiling sideways out of the frame.

Michele said: 'You did not like the haloes. So this time, no haloes For the captain – no Madonna.' He laughed. 'You like it? It is for you. I painted it for you.'

'God damn you!' said the captain.

'You do not like it?' said Michele, very hurt.

The captain closed his eyes. 'What are you going to do next?' he asked, tiredly.

Michele laughed again. 'Mrs Pannerhurst, the lady of the general, she wants me to paint her picture in her white dress. So I paint it.'

'You should be proud to.'

'Silly bitch. She thinks I am good. They know nothing – savages. Barbarians. Not you, captain, you are my friend. But these people, they know nothing.'

The captain lay quiet. Fury was gathering in him. He thought of the general's wife. He disliked her, but he had known her well enough.

'These people,' said Michele. 'They do not know a good picture from a bad picture. I paint, I paint, this way, that way. There is the picture – I look at it and laugh inside myself.' Michele laughed out loud. 'They say, he is a Michelangelo, this one, and try to cheat me out of my price. Michele – Michelangelo – that is a joke, no?'

The captain said nothing.

'But for you I painted this picture to remind you of our good times with the village. You are my friend. I will always remember you.'

The captain turned his eyes sideways in his head and stared at the black girl. Her smile at him was half innocence, half malice.

'Get out,' he said suddenly.

Michele came closer and bent to see the captain's face. 'You wish me to go?' He sounded unhappy. 'You saved my life. I was a fool that night. But I was thinking of my offering to the Madonna – I was a fool, I say it myself. I was drunk, we are fools when we get drunk.'

'Get out of here,' said the captain again.

For a moment the white bandage remained motionless. Then it swept downwards in a bow.

Michele turned towards the door.

'And take that bloody picture with you.'

Silence. Then, in the dim light, the captain saw Michele reach out for the picture, his white head bowed in profound obeisance.

He straightened himself and stood to attention, holding the picture with one hand, and keeping the other stiff down his side. Then he saluted the captain.

'Yes, sir,' he said, and he turned and went out of the door with the picture.

The captain lay still. He felt – what did he feel? There was a pain under his ribs. It hurt to breathe. He realized he was unhappy. Yes, a terrible unhappiness was filling him, slowly, slowly. He was unhappy because Michele had gone. Nothing had ever hurt the captain in all his life as much as that mocking Yes, *sir*. Nothing. He turned his face to the wall and wept. But silently. Not a sound escaped him, for fear the nurses might hear.

A. L. BARKER

The Iconoclasts

The top step was sacred. To tread on it was not only a crime but a deliberate thumbing at fate. Of course a lot of people did – his parents, the occasional gardener and visitors who were being shown the paved walk under the lime trees. It worried Marcus to think what a lot of trouble they were storing up for themselves, until he decided that as they were adults, they had graduated out of the power of the step. One day, he too would be beyond it, he would be able to tread there without his footstep shaking loose some dreadful animus.

Just now it was necessary to stretch his legs from the penultimate step to the square of turf beyond the top, and Marcus, small for his five years, found the reach considerable. That was as it should be, he wouldn't want it to be easy, any more than one would wish the lion one had defeated to be tame.

With the pail of earth he was carrying, the step was doubly difficult to avoid, and he had to take the secondary route up the bank and under the flowering currants. Already there was quite a beaten track there. His father didn't like him to go in under the bushes, he said Marcus must have the proclivities of a cat and would probably take to the tiles in due course. Marcus had explained, he was always explaining, that it was a matter beyond his control – the detour was as much of a nuisance to him as it was to everyone else. But they never seemed to catch the gravity of the situation, and to Marcus's father it was just a source of humour.

On the paved part at the back of the toolshed was quite a pile of earth which Marcus had carried there. He was going to make a castle, like his seaside ones, and irrigate it. That was ambitious, especially as he had only inferior materials – earth and tap-water instead of sand and sea.

Marcus thought he had enough earth now, but before he started work there was a routine job to be done. Puffing and severe, he climbed to the top of the rockery and stared between the garden trees to a sloping brown field, stitched all over with green. There was a scarecrow among the furrows, a poor trashy thing of sticks, sacking and a yellow trilby. At sight of the trilby, Marcus's frown relaxed and he nodded approvingly.

Some boys had once stolen the scarecrow's hat and the farmer said jokingly that in future perhaps Marcus would keep an eye on the new one. Marcus accepted the commission in all seriousness; twice a day he made sure that the turnip head was decently covered.

He went back to the toolshed. Boddy was propped against a flower-pot, and a big beetle which had crawled out of the loose earth was advancing on him. It looked too large to squash, no doubt it would crackle and spread out on the paving. But Boddy had to be saved, and not by retreat, either. Marcus shovelled up the beetle and threw it on to the flower-bed.

When the danger was past, he said sternly to Boddy, 'You'll have to be more careful. I haven't got time to turn around today.'

Marcus turned his back then, and Boddy, whose salient feature was his big lolling head, sat meekly by, grinning his golliwog's grin. His was the function of the subordinate, the apprentice. Marcus used him without mercy and it was only because he was made of good durable leather with a head full of straw shavings and thatched with nothing more sensitive than dusty wool that he had survived.

Marcus was much attached to him because Boddy did what no one else did, he went in awe of Marcus. That made a full circle – Marcus's father looked up to his superior at the office. Marcus's mother looked up to Marcus's father, Marcus's grandmother looked up to them both, Marcus had to look up to everybody and Boddy looked up to Marcus.

There was a worm in the pile of earth. Marcus showed it to Boddy. 'That's a snake. It's not safe just here, you'd better tuck your legs in.'

He thought he might keep the worm and let it swim in the moat of his castle, so he put it under a flower-pot.

'This is very important,' he said, making the earth into a tight pile and cutting it with his spade. 'It's a secret.'

The new venture was now on a par with treaties and plans, the movement of armies and the sinking of oil-wells. For Marcus, frowning, absorbed, the world had very properly dwindled, it waited on his monumental mud just as it waits – for the single-minded – on diplomacy, the invention, the battle, the fortune in the making. Only Boddy, as the onlooker, could be expected to know that it never waited for anything.

As castles go, it was not a success. Marcus would not admit that it looked like a nasty chocolate pudding. He put the worm in the moat and told Boddy that it was better than any at the seaside. It was guarded by a sinister serpent and when the sun came out it would get hard as iron and no one would ever be able to knock it over. It would still be there by his next birthday – there could be no longer period of time than that. Secretly, Marcus was so disgusted with it that he couldn't stop saying what a wonderful castle it was, and pushed Boddy into the laurel bushes for not looking impressed.

After that, he gave way to baser instincts, flattened the castle, worm and all, and made some really excellent mud-pies. He chatted amiably, forgetting that Boddy was flat on his face under the ugly spotted laurels. That was the best of Boddy, whether he was there or not, he always listened.

Marcus was extremely busy when he heard his grandmother in the garden. She was calling him to lunch – that was the signal for him to double up like a jack-knife and creep through the shrubbery, away from the direction of her voice. Not because he was furtive or guilty, but simply because it was part of his policy to be elusive, not easily found – in fact, not to be found at all. He preferred to turn the tables and seek the seeker.

Coming into the shadow of the garden wall, he suddenly drew himself up, lifted one leg and began solemnly to hop. In one corner opposite him was the husk of a summerhouse. Once it had stood on a pedestal and revolved so that anyone inside could always arrange to face the sun. That had been long before Marcus's time, and rain and frost had rotted the flimsy wood. It leaned against the wall, in the winter drenched black, in the summer whitey-grey like an old bone. When Marcus looked inside, he saw the dark glint of water that had driven in through the roof, and something with fierce red eyes set it trembling.

Marcus had skipped off quickly. Whatever it was in the summerhouse, he believed it preferred him to hurry by and not stare too much. For dignity's sake he could not run past; he always, however sober his pace, began to skip and hop when he came in sight of the hut, thus placating its creature without loss of prestige. So the skipping and hopping became a ritual and after the manner of ritual, had a definite form. Two hops, three skips and a short jump, took Marcus on a level with the summerhouse door. He was then entitled to assert himself and his command of the ritual by a deliberate stare. Two hops, three skips and a short jump took him well out of the creature's jurisdiction again.

Marcus had this belief in ceremony. It did not constrain him, rather was it a bone in his amorphous world. True, there existed a rigid routine, imposed on him from outside, and cutting the day which should have been elastic, into sections of food, play and sleep. Yet he felt the need of something immutable and his own, and ceremony had the sure reciprocal action of a slot-machine.

Marcus crept up behind his grandmother as she stood on the lawn. She looked as if she had forgotten all about him, so he hooted in a deep, frightening voice.

'Good heavens, Marcus, must you do that? Where on earth do you get to? I can never find you.' But she wasn't really interested. She was tapping her small rounded chin and looking at the grass. 'We ought to get the lawn re-laid before next summer,' she said to herself, and nodded with the same seriousness Marcus had shown towards his castle.

During lunch, Marcus learned that Neil Farncombe was coming to spend the afternoon. He was the son of a business friend of Marcus's father and he had come to visit once before, some two years ago, when Marcus was still addicted to teddy bears and flop-eared rabbits. There had been a great deal of trouble, everyone except Marcus remembered it.

'But they'll get on better now,' said his grandmother. 'Marcus isn't such a baby.'

Neil was ten. He had a small angular face, high cheekbones and eyes of a particular burning blue. Without waiting until they were out of hearing of the grown-ups, he said, 'What's that in aid of?' and nodded at Marcus's clothes.

Marcus looked down at his green boiler-suit with the tool pockets on the bib. 'Huh?' he said, frowning.

'Oh, forget it.' Neil strolled off, casual and self-possessed in his zipped leather jacket and grey shorts. Marcus made to go in the opposite direction, but was called back by his grandmother.

'Go with Neil,' she said.

Reluctantly, Marcus trailed after the elder boy.

'No doubt,' said Marcus's grandmother, 'we shall have to buy the child a zipped leather jacket now.'

Neil mooched through the shrubbery and stopped at the bottom of the steps. He stared up at the sky from under his hand, they both heard a distant mumbling.

'Now what's that?' grunted Neil, squinting fearfully against the sunlight.

'It's an aeroplane,' said Marcus, pleased at being able to offer the information.

Neil's high cheekbones burned scarlet. He glared at Marcus from under his shading hand. 'Don't try to be funny with me,' he said. 'Just don't try.'

Marcus was both offended and bewildered. To relieve his feelings he kicked viciously at the path.

'Blenheim,' said Neil laconically. 'It might be one of ours.'

'If it isn't, shall we go into the shelter?' Marcus was thrilled at the possibility.

Neil turned on him with the air of an officer about to rend a very raw recruit. 'What did I say that plane was?'

'Benim.'

'And a Blenheim's a British kite, isn't it? Don't you even know that? When I said it might be one of ours I meant it might have come from our field.'

'Your field?'

Neil turned away impatiently. 'Our aerodrome at Haydown.'

Marcus lost his temper. 'It's not yours! It's not your aerodrome!'

'It's as much mine as anybody else's.' Neil was still staring up from under his hand. 'I live right by it and I'm there nearly every day and I know all the men on it and all the planes. That's a Blenheim all right.'

'It's not!' shouted Marcus, red-faced and ridiculous. 'It's not! It's not!'

The visitor put his hands in his pockets, rocked to and fro on his heels and spoke with absolute authority. 'It's a twin-engined

Blenheim bomber with "Mercury" engines and five machine-guns – one in the port wing, two in the turret and two in the blister under the nose. It can carry a thousand pounds of bombs, but I expect it's on a training trip now.'

Marcus looked sulky, yet he was impressed. Under his breath he muttered, 'It's not,' just once, without conviction.

As Neil watched the plane out of sight, he looked almost homesick. He glowered at Marcus. 'Don't you know anything about planes?'

'Course I do! I've got a plane of my own!'

'What – a toy?' Neil turned away.

Marcus danced earnestly beside him. 'It flies! It flies over the house!'

Neil said nothing. He was moodily climbing the steps. Marcus, in a passion to be first, wriggled past him and went on ahead. When he stretched over the final step he almost lost his balance. Neil put his foot squarely on the sacred stone.

'No!' shrieked Marcus.

'Eh?'

'No! No!'

Neil came on to the top of the steps. 'Are you crazy?'

'You shouldn't have trod on that step!'

Neil looked at it. 'Why not?'

'Something will happen to you!'

'Eh?'

Marcus backed away, wildly mysterious. 'The awfullest thing that could happen!'

'Guff,' declared Neil and deliberately went back and jumped about on the sacred step. 'How's that?'

They stood staring at each other in the sunshine, Marcus open-mouthed, horrified; Neil with eyebrows raised, hands in pockets, feet squarely on the forbidden stone.

'It'll get you – it'll be so angry!'

'What will? The bogey under the step? Pouf!' Neil gave it a final kick and strolled on. 'There's no such thing as bogeys. Of course,' he looked grave, 'there *are* gremlins. You have to watch out for them all right.'

'What's gremlins?'

'I say!' Neil stopped to look hard at Marcus. 'Your number's still pretty wet, isn't it? You don't know anything.'

'I do! I do! I know more than you! I know more than anyone!'
But Marcus was not absolutely convinced. He catapulted fiercely
to and fro across the path to hide his doubts.

'You don't either,' declared Neil crushingly. 'You don't even
know what a gremlin is.'

'What is it?'

'It's a – well, it makes things go wrong.'

'Is it alive?'

'Of course it's alive. How could it upset things and get people
into trouble if it was dead? It's something to be scared of, I can tell
you. Not like an old step!'

'Has it got red eyes?'

'Some of them have. Some've got green eyes and horns.
There're lots of them at our airfield.'

Marcus looked smug. 'I've got one!'

Neil sneered openly. 'Where? Under the step?'

'Course not! In the summrouse.'

'That's a load of guff! You only get them on airfields – anywhere where there's planes. What d'you think *you'd* have a
gremlin for?'

'I've got one. In the summrouse.'

'Guff.'

Marcus danced with fury. 'I'll show you! I'll show it you then!'

'All right, I'll take a look-see.'

'You be careful! It'll bite your head off –'

Neil frowned irritably. 'Oh get on with it! Beetle.'

'Ah?'

'Go on, show me – if you can.'

Fuming, but uneasy, Marcus led the way to the summerhouse.
That dark corner of the garden was already in shadow, and to
Marcus the chill in the air was sufficient warning. He hung back,
pointing quite unnecessarily.

'Pouf! What a ropey old place!' Neil strolled towards it.

Marcus valiantly ran after the elder boy and dragged his arm.
'You mustn't go in! It's inside.'

Neil looked down at him, his blue eyes were suddenly fierce.
'You're scared!'

'I'm not!'

'You are! Scared stiff of a dirty old hut! Well, I'm not!'

He shook off Marcus's hand and strode up to the summerhouse.

At the doorway he stopped, one foot on the threshold, and muttered, 'There is something in here.'

Marcus's green boiler-suit swelled with pride. 'It's a gemlin!' he shouted. 'Jus' you come back –' He broke off, clapping one hand over his mouth in curiously feminine consternation.

Neil had disappeared inside. Next moment the boiler-suit wilted as there sounded a dreadful roar from the summerhouse – a stamping and shouting and a hollow clanging noise. Marcus was petrified, but when a long grey shape leapt from the hut and vanished into the shadows, he screamed at the top of his voice.

Neil, appearing at the summerhouse door, with a rusty spade in his hand, gave him one contemptuous glance. 'A gremlin says you – just a dirty old rat. I'd have flattened it if it hadn't been so dark in there.'

Marcus licked his lips and looked at Neil with new humility. He wouldn't have cared to face a rat any more than a gremlin.

Neil strolled off, looking moody and discontented. Marcus trotted at his heels. They came to the toolshed and Neil passed the mud-pies without a word. Marcus hoped he hadn't noticed them.

'What's this?'

Neil swooped into the bushes and dragged out poor forgotten Boddy. Dangling by one leg in mid-air, the limp arms flapped, the golliwog's grin and the white boot-button eyes looked frankly imbecile.

Marcus felt his cheeks burn, his eyes pricked with tears of shame as Neil swung the doll to and fro on a level with his face.

'This yours?'

'No!'

Neil's lips twisted. Tauntingly he swung the golliwog closer so that it brushed against Marcus's nose. 'Whose is it then?'

Marcus thought desperately. 'A little gurl's.'

'Yours, more likely. Got a teddy bear, too?'

'It's not! It's not! It's not!' Scarlet-faced, Marcus backed away, stamping and shouting. 'Not! Not! Not!'

Smiling thinly, Neil let the doll drop, his foot met it squarely as it fell, and poor, grinning Boddy went sailing over the shrubbery and out of sight.

'Pancaked,' said Neil obscurely, and Marcus was too deep in shame to ask what he meant.

They came out on to the lawn again. Neil threw himself down

and tore up handfuls of grass. He spoke more to himself than to Marcus. 'Why shouldn't they let me go up to the airfield instead of coming here? I asked enough times!'

'There's an aeroplane coming!' Marcus stood over him, earnestly pointing in the wrong direction. Neil rolled on his back, shaded his eyes and located the plane at once.

'It's a Benim,' declared Marcus, also squinting up from under his hand, but seeing nothing.

'It is not. It's a Bristol Beaufighter back from a recco. You don't know one kite from another.'

Marcus opened his mouth and shut it again. Even he had to admit that as an aircraft spotter he had his shortcomings.

Neil hugged his knees and chewed grass. Marcus plumped down close by, hugged his knees and chewed a gritty mouthful of grass which he had mistakenly grubbed up by the roots. The plane mumbled off into silence and the enormous province of the sun. After a while, Marcus grew bored and began to tumble laboriously about on the grass.

Neil took no notice until, in the middle of a somersault, Marcus felt a hand seize the slack of his boiler-suit and pull him upright. He swayed and blinked, Neil's fierce blue eyes, the sky and the green garden were see-sawing all together.

'The windmill – 'Neil was saying, 'where is it?'

Dizzy with tumbling, Marcus could only open his mouth and say 'Ah?' very stupidly.

Neil shook him. 'The windmill! I saw it from the bus – which way is it?'

Marcus took a chance and pointed to one corner of the tipping world. Unfortunately it was in the direction of the house and Neil let go his hold on the green boiler-suit. Marcus sat down with a bump and stayed there waiting for things to sober up. Neil stood over him, scowling.

'You're the biggest dope I was ever stuck with. It's no matter, I'll find things out for myself.'

He stalked off. Marcus scrambled up and followed, conscious that once again he had cut rather a poor figure.

Neil must have had a knack of finding his way, for he went at once to the highest point in the garden – the top of the rockery – climbed it, and stared round like a sailor scanning the seas. 'There it is – about a mile away. Just right.'

He jumped from the rockery, landing lightly on all fours and springing upright almost in the same movement.

Marcus beamed. 'Are you going to the windmill?'

'Yes, I am. If anyone asks where I am, say we're playing hide-and-seek and I'm hiding. See?'

Marcus shook his head, still beaming. 'I'm coming too.'

'You're not.'

'I am!' His voice bellowed in the silence and seemed to echo against the dazzling windows of the house. Neil gripped him by the shoulder.

'Shut up! You're not coming.'

Marcus shut his mouth, but he looked mulish, and as soon as Neil moved off along the lime-walk, he trotted after, his lower lip jutting ominously. Neil knew he was being followed, but said nothing till they came to the arched door set in the garden wall. He pulled back the bolt, then turned.

'Go on back now. I'm doing this on my jack. Go on!'

'No! Won't. I'm coming too.'

Neil let the open door swing shut again. He advanced on Marcus, his long fingers twitching. 'You're asking for it! Will you go back or do I have to make you?'

Marcus was quite frightened. There was something of the piti-less stoop of a hawk in those bladed cheek-bones, the blue, burning eyes. But he could be obstinate, and even though he quailed, he planted his feet wide apart in desperation. 'If you don't let me come, I'll shout till they come and then I'll tell where you're going. I'll tell! I'll tell!'

So great was his awe of Neil that his voice grew louder and louder and he had to stamp to bolster up his courage.

Neil looked murderous, his face reddened with fury, he gathered himself as if to swoop on the yelling Marcus. And then all he did was to clap one hand over the younger boy's open mouth.

'All right! Come on – I'll settle with you later. Only shut up!'

Marcus obeyed at once and they went out into the lane. Some two or three fields and a paddock separated them from the wind-mill. Neil hauled Marcus bodily over the first stile and they began to tramp through the long lush grass minted with buttercups. Marcus was soon dusted in yellow pollen up to his waist, and Neil's long brown legs with the socks draggling round his ankles, glinted with rich butter gold.

It was difficult to keep up with Neil because he didn't allow for anyone else having shorter legs or less wind. Marcus dared not complain, and anyway, he was husbanding his breath in order to ask two very important questions. He seized his chance when they were clambering over the gate into the second field.

'What are we going to the windmill for?'

'Wait and see,' was all the information he got.

The next field was full of dry, bristly grass that made little knocking noises against their legs. Marcus was so fascinated by it and by the faded blue flowers growing among it, that he forgot all about his question until Neil turned and curtly told him to get a move on.

Then he said breathlessly, and with just the right degree of deference and eagerness which even Neil could not resist, 'What you going to be when you grow up?'

Neil made a sound half-laugh, half-snort. 'That's a good one! What am I going to be when I grow up? I'll be a driver, of course.'

'An engine-driver?'

Neil hooted so loudly that there came a frightened scuttling in the undergrowth.

'Engine-driver! You must be the biggest swede in the world. Don't you even know what a driver is? It's the same as a peelo. Know what a peelo is?'

Marcus took the only course open to him. He stuck his hands in the patch pockets on the front of his boiler-suit and sulked. Neil spat out the piece of grass he was chewing and strode on.

'All right – if you don't know, I'll tell you. A driver's a pilot – he takes the plane up and he's got to bring it down in one piece. Doesn't matter if it's a monoplane or a Halifax with nine machine-guns and five and a half tons of eggs – and that means bombs, not hen-fruit – the driver's the boss and what he says goes. But I'm going to be a fighter-pilot and make smoke-rings round every Messerschmitt they put up. As for Heinkels – I'll pop them off like paper bags.'

Neil was walking so fast that Marcus had to run to keep near. Suddenly he stopped and swung round.

'D'you say your prayers at night?'

Marcus nodded breathlessly.

'Then you pray for the war to go on for years – till I'm old enough to fly. If two people pray it might do more good than one.' He added threateningly: 'Will you do it?'

Marcus promised earnestly and Neil plunged on again. A blackberry trailer snaking out from the hedge caught him squarely across his bare leg and almost tripped him. He trampled it down but Marcus was petrified at sight of the blood streaming from the lacerations of the thorns. In the sunlight, against the pale grass, it looked bright and terrible.

Neil hardly glanced at it. 'Pah! Anyone that wanted to be a pilot wouldn't bother about that!'

As they were crossing the paddock, Marcus, who had been dedicated to the trade of milkman for years, called out importantly, 'I'm going to be a pilot too!'

But Neil took no notice. He was intent on the windmill just ahead. Marcus looked at it too. Sometimes he was brought here by his mother – she would sit and try to paint. She was never pleased with what she did, she said the windmill was like an old bloated moth, it was all wrong.

Something in the grass caught Marcus's eye. He stepped aside to look, and Neil, turning to hurry him on, saw him stooping over a tiny rabbit caught in a trap. It was dead and its long ears were pressed back by the fear which had finally killed it. The small forepaws were daintily composed side by side, but the dark bubble eyes still stared – with death behind as well as before them. One hind leg, caught and smashed, had sprinkled the white scut with colour bold and incompatible among the fair grass and the faded blue flowers.

Marcus's eyes filled with tears. Gently he stroked the soft, cold fur. 'Poor rabbit, poor, poor rabbit!'

Neil's shadow fell across the grass. 'Are you coming or are you going to stay there all day?'

Marcus looked up, horrified. 'But the rabbit! The poor, poor rabbit – it's hurt!'

Neil frowned impatiently. 'Don't be daft – it's dead.'

'Dead?'

Marcus's smooth brows drew together as he pondered. He had encountered that word before. Roughly, he understood it to mean 'gone away'. When people were dead, they went away and you didn't see them any more.

'Can't you see it's dead?' Neil made as if to nudge the rabbit with his foot, but Marcus flung out his hands in protection.

'You're not to! You're not to hurt it!'

Neil's brown pointed face darkened, and as quickly cleared again. Shrugging, he looked down at Marcus with curling lip and chilly, remote scorn.

'You're soft,' he said, as one might to a worm. 'You're pappy. You'll never be a pilot. Go back and play with your dolls.'

He turned and strode off. Marcus looked down at the rabbit. It couldn't be dead because he could still see it, it hadn't disappeared as the kitten had last year, and old Mr Philpotts. He tried to pull the trap away and felt sick.

Neil had climbed over the gate and was out of sight. Marcus scrambled up, telling himself he would see to the rabbit on his way back. It was resting quietly, perhaps it would go to sleep until he returned.

He walked away carefully, so as not to disturb it. One or two black flies came and settled on the torn leg and crawled round the dark convex abyss of the staring eyes.

Neil was standing looking up at the windmill as Marcus came trundling across the field. It was built of wood, all bleached and bare like the walls of the summerhouse. Where the nails had given way, slats hung down so that you could see right through into the mill, and if you walked round, you caught twinkles of light where the holes linked up with other holes on the far side. The great sails had only their bones left, even these were snapped and shredded like the flimsiest cane – they lay back against the mill building with the exhaustion of broken mechanical things. Time had stripped off every vestige of use, rotted the last grain, blacked into cobwebs the honest crust of flour; the marks of labour were all lost in dissolution and decay.

Neil glanced at Marcus but hardly seemed to see him. He had eyes only for the windmill, he stared at it, and his queer blue eyes blazed above his high Slav cheek-bones. Marcus couldn't see what there was to be so excited about, but he was excited all the same. He trotted behind Neil, chattering and undismayed when the other boy never said a word.

Neil ignored Marcus until he wanted to go inside the mill. Then he said, 'Wait here,' and his tone was such that Marcus never thought of disobeying. Neil vanished silently into the blackness of the mill.

He was a long time gone. Marcus hopped first on one leg then on the other to occupy himself. He found a grasshopper and lost it immediately. He did somersaults until the mill took to dancing sombrely in the background. Marcus preferred it still, so he sat on the grass and listened.

There was no sound of Neil moving about inside. Marcus shouted, but no one answered. He decided that Neil was doing this on purpose to see how quickly he would get frightened. Then he would jump out and say that Marcus could never be a pilot.

That thought kept the green boiler-suit very still for a while. He sat bolt upright, chewing a stalk of grass as Neil had done. The slow, leathery flapping of a great black bird was the only sound in the afternoon quiet. If he had not been so excited, he might have gone to sleep.

And then Neil came suddenly out of the mill. Marcus ran up to him, chattering and effusive after his enforced silence. Neil took no notice of what Marcus said. He was whistling softly and looking at the mill-sails. His leather jacket was grey with dust, and the scummy fabric of a cobweb clung to his sleeve. Across the back of one hand was a long, important scratch. Marcus observed it with envy.

Neil flung himself down on the grass. 'See that sail – the top one on this side? I'm going to get out through a hole in the boards and hang on it and make it swing round. When it's pointing down at the ground, I'll let go and make a four-point landing.'

Marcus didn't understand just what Neil meant to do, but it sounded reckless and exciting beyond his dreams of adventure. He was completely carried away by the prospect of danger.

'Me too!' He stooped over Neil. 'I'll make a point landing too!'

'You will not.' Neil stood up and calmly stripped off his jacket. 'You can stay here and mind this and watch what I do.'

'I'm going to do it too!'

Marcus was jumping up and down in a frenzy. Neil gripped and held him. 'You fool! You can't do what I do. It's a test, don't you understand – I have to test my nerve. I'm going to be a fighter-pilot, I've got to have nerve, I've got to be tough and take risks and keep cool. I might not be good enough. I've got to find out, I've got to keep testing myself.'

Marcus was too young to know what fanaticism was, or he might have seen in Neil's face the fatal unity, feral and precipitate, and no more amenable than flame. The clear, freckled brow, gathered and jutting over those oddly empty blue eyes, the firm, intolerant mouth, were dominated by an ardour so extreme, so pitiless that it chilled and almost repelled.

Marcus was sobered by it. He wriggled free of Neil's grasp and drew away, wary as an animal at another's oddity.

'All right.' Neil brushed aside Marcus and his change of heart like a bothersome gnat. He stood there rolling up the sleeves of his grey flannel shirt. Marcus watched, frowning. He felt unsure of himself. He did not properly understand what Neil meant to do, and the desire to emulate fought with his natural caution. It would be as well, perhaps, to see just what the feat might be before doing it himself. Besides, once Neil was busy with it, he wouldn't be so free to stop Marcus from doing as he wanted. So Marcus reasoned, scowling under the weight of his own cunning.

Neil nodded towards the windmill. 'It's not such a wonderful test at that. I guess anyone could do it.' All at once he looked quite miserable; driving his hands deep into his trousers pockets, he went off without another word.

Marcus waited until he had vanished inside the mill, then, carrying Neil's jacket, he found a point of vantage and settled himself with all the fuss of an audience in a theatre.

For a long while nothing happened. Marcus sat gravely attentive for a few moments, and then as there was nothing to attend to, began to swivel round and round on his seat – to the detriment of the boiler-suit. When that amusement palled, he wandered over to the hedge and pulled up armfuls of rank grass in a search for frogs. Soon his fingers were stained green. He smelt them curiously and in a spirit of strict empiricism, sucked his thumb. It tasted bitter and he began to feel irritable and thirsty and the corners of his mouth turned down in a sudden mood of discontent.

He would have gone on to the next stage of intoning wearily, over and over again, his need to go home, and from there proceeded to a restricted but persistent grizzle, had not a slight sound made him look towards the windmill.

In relation to the mill itself, the sails stood at the angle of an 'X'. Neil had emerged – miraculously as it seemed to Marcus, although in fact he had crept through a gap in the boarding which was hidden from below – and was now braced in the angle between the two right-hand sails. The lower sail looked fairly sound, but the upper one had been slashed by the winds until it was twisted and hung askew.

Marcus's mouth opened slowly. Weariness forgotten, he scrambled out of his ditch and ran back to the mill for a closer view of this performance. Neil had his back to Marcus, but he was manoeuvring to turn sideways, his left shoulder outwards, and his right to the mill. Chips of dry, rotten wood flaked from under his feet and dropped softly to the grass. He glanced down once and called, 'It's a piece of cake!' and Marcus's mouth watered. He hoped Neil would save him some because he wasn't so sure, now, that he wanted to go and do what Neil was doing, even for a piece of cake.

The sails did not move, they hadn't changed their position since the boys came; but then there was no wind, so it was silly to expect them to turn. Neil moved out from the angle of the sails as far as he could, until the lower one sloped too much for him to reach it. Then he took a firm grip on the under edge of the upper sail; swinging up his feet, he caught and held with his hands so that he was strung along it, monkey-wise. In this position, he began to work his way up to the tilted tip of the sail. He was about ninety feet from the ground, Marcus could not have been more impressed if he had been a thousand feet up. From being merely a subject of imitation, with contagious habits and rare knowledge, Neil had become a hero. Blinking upwards, Marcus surrendered his own considerable ego to unquestioning devotion. He did not suppose now that he could do what Neil did. He would have to wait years before he was so tall and strong, before he would be able to test his nerve like this.

Marcus looked distastefully at his plump arm. It hadn't got any bronze hairs on it like Neil's had, and he hadn't any hairs on his legs, either. He pulled up one leg of the boiler-suit and looked hopefully, but his knee was smooth as ivory, and the whole leg still had its generous baby curves. Frowning, Marcus blinked up again at the mill.

He forgot all about his unsatisfactory self at once; Neil had almost reached his objective. He was now over a hundred feet from the ground, at the highest point of the sail, still moving easily. Marcus almost forgot to breathe in his excitement.

The feat looked spectacular, yet it would have been straightforward enough for an agile boy with no fear of heights, had it not been for something which meant nothing to Marcus, but wherein lay the real unobtrusive danger.

The sails were rotten. They hardly supported their own weight; time and the winds had wilted them like sad feathers. The top right-hand sail juddered under Neil's weight, now and then chips of grey wood came away in his hands. Neil knew all about it, he regarded it as the saving danger which made this test of his nerve worth the while. When he reached the tip of the sail, he rested for a moment.

Marcus felt his heart beating so hard against his chest that he had to fold his arms to keep it quiet. He thought that Neil, with his pilot's magic, meant to jump from where he was and thus make the mysterious 'four-point' landing.

What Neil had planned was that his weight on the end of the sail would cause it to swing downwards and he would be taken within jumping distance of the ground. But he had reckoned without the axle being jammed and out of true, he had not thought of the years of binding rust. The sails would never turn again, they were splayed and fixed at the mercy of every gale. Neil thought only that they must be made to move, and he thought that he could do it. He did not care for the alternative of going back the way he had come. Besides, that would be an admission of defeat.

Marcus blinked as Neil let his feet drop and hung by his hands. He swung a little at first, then steadied himself. It was a sight Marcus could recall ever afterwards – the gaunt mill with the daylight in its broken sails, and that remote, impersonal figure dangling in the blue air.

Neil began to try to shift the sail. He could not bear that any obstacle should impede and change the course of his test. He believed that his weight would alter the balance, would drag his sail down according to plan. He had not understood the greater art of adapting plans to the speed of changing circumstance.

Again and again he tried to break down the rigidity of the sail and set it swinging. He drew himself up by his hands and then let himself drop, in the hope that the sudden jerk would disengage the cogs so that at least one half turn might be accomplished. That was all he needed – one half turn.

But the sails were fixed and the muscles of his arms already ached unbearably from his climb. He thought he might not be able to hold on much longer, he had strength enough for only one more effort. In a sort of bitter frenzy, his sight blurred by tears of pain and impotence, he drew himself up until his waist was on a level with his hands. His teeth bit deeply into his lip, the sweat shone on his pale forehead. The sail was an enemy which he must subdue or be subdued by it. When he could draw himself no higher, he hung there poised for a second to gather his strength and reinforce his grip. Then, savagely, he threw himself down from his hands.

Marcus was puzzled because Neil had not jumped and made his four-point landing. So, when after his last jerk, Neil parted company with the sail and came hurtling down, Marcus thought he was at last carrying out his plan, and in his opinion, the shrill cracking sounds which accompanied the fall greatly improved it as a spectacle.

And in fact, Neil seemed intent on making the performance as exciting as possible. He did not come straight to the ground. Instead, he fell on the lower right-hand sail, lay across it for a second or so as if to prove his mastery, and then, almost languidly, tipped over and continued his journey to the ground.

He landed on his back. The ground shook him once, flinging up his arms and legs like a doll's, then he lay still. Marcus ran over to him, shouting, 'I saw the point landing! I saw it! I saw it!'

Delightedly he capered round Neil, fulfilling the desire and purpose of the celebrant who marks a victory and honours a hero.

Neil did not move. He was so still that Marcus checked his dance with sudden misgivings. The performance might not be finished, or worse – he might have offended against the etiquette of the four-point landing. He had to admit that it was a far more impressive adventure than any of his own, it might well have a certain form which Neil would presently demonstrate.

So he waited patiently. It was quite silent now, the big black bird had flapped away; the sunlight, like a bright empty gas under a glass bowl, had dissolved all motion, even the crepitant motion of the beetles.

Neil said nothing. He did not even look at Marcus. His head was tilted back so that from where Marcus stood, only the under part of his chin and his brown throat were visible. Legs and arms were flung out just as Marcus had seen Boddy's arms and legs spread wide when he was thrown on the floor.

It was odd. On tiptoe, stretching his neck as if to peer over a fence, Marcus moved closer to Neil. He looked down at his face. The elder boy's eyes were closed and his skin, which had been brown and warm, was a cold creamy colour. A grey shadow seemed to be creeping over his jaw, changing his face. His lips were pale and dry like paper, his wide nostrils pinched.

Marcus stooped down, hands on his knees, deferential.

'Neil.'

No movement, no sign that he had even heard.

'Neil!' Marcus stooped lower, frowning. 'Neil – what you doing?'

Only one of the grasses by Neil's ear moved under Marcus's breath. Disapprovingly, he sat back on his heels, noting fragments of dry wood still gripped between the pale fingers. It was obvious then what had happened. Neil had gone to sleep, forgetting about everything, even forgetting to put down the bits of wood he had brought back.

Neil's head rolled a little to one side, his eyelids moved, lifted unwillingly; he looked out from under them like someone in a blessedly dark room looking out at the blaring daylight.

'You mustn't go to sleep,' said Marcus reprovingly. 'It's not night.'

Neil's eyes opened wider. It seemed as if he had to force himself to see Marcus, although he was only such a little way away. Marcus obligingly bent closer and touched his hand.

The touch troubled the elder boy. His whole body shuddered. He drew his arms slowly in to his sides and tried to raise himself. His head lifted slightly from the ground, then fell back. He did not move again, only the grey shadow deepened across his mouth.

'Aren't you going to get up?'

Neil licked his lips, looking at Marcus almost furtively. 'No, I – think I'll stay here a bit.'

'I saw you do the point landing!'

Neil closed his eyes and began to mutter. 'I came a crumper. The sail was stuck. I couldn't get it to turn like I wanted – I wanted it to turn –'

He moved his head restlessly from side to side. Marcus couldn't think why he didn't get up.

'Let's go home now.'

'I don't want to go home.' Neil felt around with his hand, picked a stalk of grass and stuck it in the side of his mouth. His lips closed on it, pressed together so tightly that his chin wrinkled. He did not chew the grass, he made it a gesture of defiance, and once it was made, seemed unable to carry it to any conclusion. The stalk just stayed there, straight and still, in the corner of his mouth.

Marcus wandered about, moodily kicking the ground with his heels. He could not understand this turn of events, it made him irritable that there was neither point nor pleasure in it.

'I want to go home now!' he shouted from a little way off and stamped.

Neil looked at him with hatred. But he spat out the grass, put his arms flat against the ground and pressed on them. His head lifted, his lower lip drew in under his teeth and even the grey shadow was dredged from his face. It was as if he had no flesh, only bone.

A sound came from deep in his throat, and with it, his rigidity collapsed. He fell back, gasping. Suddenly his eyes were dark and fierce with terror, they shone like the rabbit's eyes, rounded and brittle as a bubble. His fingers unclenched and let fall the chips of dry wood from the mill sail.

Marcus was deeply puzzled. He picked up the wood and examined it politely. It wasn't at all unusual – only out of deference to Neil he stowed two pieces away in the pocket of his boiler-suit. After that he sat down and waited patiently for orders.

But Neil gave no orders. He lay there staring at Marcus, and now the shadow had come back. He had a grey-cloth face. He never looked away, and the terror in his eyes was so violent and so inexplicable that Marcus was frightened too. He glanced round about; there was only the bland empty sunshine and the stooping mill. There was nothing to be afraid of – that made Marcus more frightened than ever. He began to whimper.

'I want to go home.'

The other boy moved his lips and Marcus stopped grizzling to listen hopefully. A rustle, as of some slight insect slipping through the dry grasses, was the only sound Neil made.

At that Marcus lost patience.

'I want to go home!' He seized Neil's arm to try to pull him up. Neil seemed to flatten himself to the ground, his lips drew back, baring his teeth in another extreme of fear, both savage and agonized.

Marcus stepped back. Quite obviously Neil didn't want to get up. He had no intention of going home, he meant to stay here and sleep. Marcus's lower lip jutted. Never had home and tea seemed so important. Neil was trying to stop him, just because he wanted to go to sleep in the daytime.

He glared at the still figure on the ground – then caught sight of the wilting sails of the mill and remembered the four-point landing, how Neil had even paused in his descent to balance casually on the lower sail. Humility and deference returned immediately.

Pondering, he decided that this wish to sleep at a time so inappropriate, might be the habit of heroes. Perhaps it was a ritual to lie down on the ground and shut your eyes after an adventure. Marcus wondered if he ought to do the same. He thought not. He was too hungry and besides, it hadn't been his adventure. Instead, he would prove to Neil that he wasn't so soft and go home by himself, leaving Neil to follow when he was ready.

'I'm going home now,' he said and beamed with self-sufficiency. He would have turned and marched off, had not Neil reached out to hold him by the ankle. Marcus skipped back, frowning. An odd qualm chilled him as he looked into Neil's face.

There was something wrong with his eyes. They had been blue before, Marcus could remember just how blue and fierce they had been. Now they were dark and they shone into the full glare of the sun without blinking or once looking away from Marcus. Yet he had a cold feeling that the darkness in the eyes was also outside them, so that Neil couldn't see properly. He kept moving his lips, they moved all the time as if he were speaking, but didn't say anything. He didn't even whisper.

Marcus backed away. Neil's hand, flung out on the ground towards him, opened and shut like a crab. It puzzled Marcus that the look on Neil s face was of fear, and the dark, unblinking eyes were never turned away from him as if Neil dreaded being left alone.

But that could not be, Neil was never frightened, and there was nothing to be frightened of here. Besides – Marcus turned stoutly on his heel – Neil hadn't asked him to stay. He could have said if that was what he wanted.

At the gate into the paddock he stopped to look back. Neil had not moved. His body was spilled negligently on the grass, one arm still stretched towards Marcus, his face blurred by distance but turned the way Marcus had gone. The mill drooped behind him, the shadow would soon lie across him and he would be out of the sun.

There was something else on the grass near the mill. It was Neil's leather jacket. Marcus wrinkled his nose. He still thought it a funny time and place to go to sleep. Perhaps Neil would like his jacket as a pillow. He hesitated, on the verge of going back. But then he had a vision of Neil's scorn, his 'You're soft! You'll never be a pilot!' Neil would be contemptuous, and rightly so, if he went back for such a womanish gesture. Fighter pilots probably never used pillows but just stretched out on the hard ground. Marcus was impressed by this Spartan routine, he knew he would find it very difficult to keep as still as Neil had for such a long time.

He waved to Neil and scrambled under the gate. Very soon he came to the place where the rabbit lay. He stalked past, head averted. Neil had said it was soft to worry about the rabbit, Neil had shown how to be tough and daring. He was going to be like Neil and some day test his nerve by doing a four-point landing.

It was the first time he had been out for a walk by himself, he felt grown-up and independent. He walked through the field of knocking grasses and his legs struck them stoutly aside.

In the last field he stopped, lifting his pink damp face to the sky. A far-off bumbling, filling the air, filling every nook and cranny, every mouse-hole, every fold in every shrivelled leaf – and there were three shapes, tiny against the blue – Oriental, precise.

'Benims,' said Marcus, and stood looking from under his hand, paying them due reverence until they were out of sight.

MALACHI WHITAKER

The Mandoline

The morning was still, bright yet ethereal, and an elderly sun had warmed the dead bracken on the hillside so that already it glowed golden brown. For a few days there had been fog and a blanketing silence and drops of moisture hanging stagnant from the leafless twigs, so that now in the sunlight, although it was only November, spring seemed to be poised, motionless but sure, over the far hills.

Two figures were approaching the long, low, stone farmhouse which stood in the middle of the common, one of them wearing nankeen trousers banded against the mud, an earth-coloured jerkin and a newish dark blue cap. He had a broken nose and friendly brown eyes and gesticulated with hands and arms as he walked.

His companion was a very pale, thin youth with an almost expressionless face, his eyes partially enlarged by thick-lensed glasses. His features were small and delicate, his teeth regular but yellowish. He wore the grey-green uniform of a German prisoner, a loose-brimmed cap, the crown of which fitted tightly, and large, heavy boots which seemed to drag along behind him.

The first man, who was a kind of foreman-guard, opened the iron gate of the farmyard, and walking up to the door, knocked in a light, hesitant way. The prisoner stood behind him, looking like some tall, stupid bird. He had not spoken except to say yes or no.

In the low, dark farmhouse kitchen, which opened straight on to the yard, an elderly man and his wife were working, the woman washing cans and the man carefully mending a cracked pipe stem with thin string. They looked an old couple, bent and grey-haired, but neither of them had yet reached sixty years of age. As they heard the low knocking, they turned and went to the door together, being full of curiosity about the two men, one of whom they knew well, the other not at all.

A new road, which ran a lane's-length from the farm, was being built by German prisoners, still retained though the war was long over, and from eight in the morning until dusk there was the sound of continuous noisy activity about the moorland farm, as the grey-green figures broke up the stones which were brought in by lorries from the neighbouring stone quarries. The old people, who were called William and Mary Illingworth, had often seen the prisoners, but had not yet spoken to one of them.

The woman dried her hands and opened the door, looking out past the men into the still autumn morning. The foreman, Sam Proudle, smiled and moved his arms about uncertainly.

'Good morning, Mrs Illingworth. I've come to ask you a favour,' he said, 'but I don't know if you'll grant it.'

'What is it?' asked the woman quickly. In some way, she was afraid. She could not think what a prisoner could require of her, and searched her mind timorously.

'Well, it's a funny request,' went on the foreman slowly, 'I don't know whether I ought to ask you. But I know you've got a mandoline; and this gentleman' – he waved a couple of fingers at the prisoner – 'wants to know if he can borrow it for one of his *kamerads* for the camp concert. For Sunday, he wants it, for next Sunday, and a few days to practise in.'

The farmer stood with his hands on the table, looking mildly at the pair.

'Can you play it?' the woman asked the prisoner.

He stood up more straightly, opened his mouth once or twice, and said, 'No, no.'

The foreman explained hurriedly, 'This gentleman plays the piano. It's one of his *kamerads* that plays the mandoline. VERY GOOD,' he suddenly shouted at the prisoner. He had evidently grown so used to shouting simple English words at the prisoners that for the moment he had forgotten something. In a much lower tone he continued, 'This is our interpreter. I'll leave him with you to explain.' And he went away.

The couple stared dumbly at the tall youth, who looked back at them, his eyes very wide behind his army spectacles.

'Come in,' the woman said suddenly; and to her husband she said: 'He wants to borrow our Godfrey's mandoline.'

The boy stepped over the threshold and stood motionless upon a stone flag of the floor. The old man had retreated behind the kitchen table and remained there without speaking, only looking at the young German with calm eyes. The thin string slowly unwound itself from the pipe in his hand. The woman began bustling about and talking in a high-pitched voice, and outside, in the walled garden which was a continuation of the yard, the sun searched the wet, brown, withered bushes, the dying Michaelmas daisies, and the two heaps of garden refuse beneath the aged pear tree.

'I have been in hospital,' said the boy suddenly, 'for a long time.'

'Sit down,' said the woman, motioning towards a wooden chair.

He sat abruptly, looking at his muddy boots, the marks from which remained where he had stood. His hands lay lax on his knees. He had not removed his cap. He did not notice the flickering fire, the red grandfather clock in one corner of the room, the two brass candlesticks on the high, narrow mantelshelf.

'What do you do? In Germany?' the farmer asked in a very loud, careful voice.

'I am a schoolmaster.'

'My son is – was – going to be a teacher.'

'The one who played the mandoline,' the woman broke in. 'Our Godfrey. He played the mandoline.'

The boy looked round, but could not see the mandoline. It was not in the kitchen. He looked towards the farmer.

'Your son?' he asked, searching for words with some difficulty, apologizing. 'I only know English these few months, since I kom heer. Your son, does he not wish to lend the mandoline to my *kamerad*?'

'My son was killed,' said the farmer harshly. 'In Germany.'

'Oh!' said the prisoner. A pale flush ran slowly over his paler face, and drained away. There was a long silence.

The woman broke it. 'Come into the parlour,' she said. 'We have a piano. Come and play it.'

'The parlour?' asked the boy. He did not understand.

'Come and play the piano,' said the woman, bright-eyed with nervous haste. 'Come with me.'

The boy followed her out of the kitchen, over the flagged hall to a small sitting-room. The sunlight showed crude colour-patches in a faded carpet. Across one corner of the room stood a shiny, walnut-veneered piano, with pleats of green silk showing under an ornamental lattice at the front. The piano was open, and upon the stand lay a cheap copy of some music on which was printed Gem No. 79, Strauss Waltz Medley.

The woman pointed to it. 'Play that,' she said.

The boy peered at the simple music, and sitting down on the piano stool, put his muddy boots on the pedals. His cap was still upon his head.

'It is a long time since I played the piano,' he said.

'Go on. Go on. Play it,' said the farmer who had come through from the kitchen and was now sitting stiffly in a corner, still holding in his hand the half-mended pipe with its dangling string.

There were many pages of music, and the boy played steadily through them. Here and there he struck a false note, and said 'Oh!' in quick shame. The woman had gone back into the kitchen, where she drew down from a high shelf in the cupboard an old coffee-grinding machine. There were a few beans in the brass cup. She ground them, and making one cup of coffee with milk from a jug on the table, took it into the parlour. The boy was still playing.

She put down the coffee on a small table beside him.

'Here,' she said gently, 'drink this.'

At her words, the boy stopped playing in the middle of a bar, and turning, thanked her. The old man had left his chair and could be heard moving in the bedroom above the parlour.

'You will take care of Godfrey's mandoline?' asked the woman anxiously. 'Yes, yes,' answered the boy, drinking his coffee.

'Godfrey played the mandoline. He played the piano, too. We bought the piano for him.' She smiled slightly at her own work-worn hands. 'But now he is dead. The war.' She looked full at the boy.

Again the pale flush broke over his thin face.

After a little while, 'I have had a letter from home,' he said. 'The first in a year. All is well.'

'All is well,' she repeated after him.

'All is well,' he said. And there was again silence until the old man came slowly downstairs, carrying the mandoline in a shiny black case.

He handed the case to the boy, who stood abruptly. Some of the mud on his boots had dried, and fell off in small clumps, silently, as he moved his feet.

'What do they call you?' asked the farmer in the same loud, careful voice he had used before. 'What is your name?'

'My name is Adolf,' said the boy, 'Adolf Klein.'

And for the third time his face flushed.

'Klein. That, in German, means little, I think.' He smiled, as if it were a joke being called little, who was so tall. But Klein was only a foreign word to the farmer and his wife, and meant nothing.

'Now I shall have to go. They might miss me. Thank you very much for the coffee, and for the piano, and for the mandoline.'

They moved awkwardly to let him pass through to the kitchen and out of the door.

'Come again and play the piano,' said the woman. She touched his sleeve gently, wonderingly, as he crossed the flagged passage again. And as he walked through the house, the boy looked around at everything, at the grandfather clock ticking away the years, at the brass candlesticks polished to a rounded fineness. He seemed to be looking for a picture of Godfrey. But there was no picture, no sign of his death anywhere. Godfrey seemed to be alive in the kitchen, in the parlour, at the piano playing the Strauss Waltz Medley, even carrying the mandoline.

'Yes, come again,' said the old man in his strange, loud voice.

He walked across the yard to the iron gate and opened it, to let the prisoner through, and then looked across the common to the bracken-brown hill, lying drenched in yellow light. His wife joined him, and they stood together in the silence until the tall boy carrying the mandoline was out of sight.

INEZ HOLDEN

According to the Directive

The day the Information Officer brought a journalist to the camp a lorry was waiting in the yard to take some of the Displaced Persons away.

Those who were leaving stood shoulder to shoulder in the back of the lorry clasping the packets of chocolates and cigarettes which had been given for the journey. Some of them also carried bunches of flowers which they held, like Victorian posies, closely to their chests.

Some wooden steps had been placed against the back of the lorry. The last man to walk wearily upwards wore a long grey overcoat, a peaked cap and dark blue civilian trousers; he carried a cheap cardboard suitcase and he smiled as the others moved to make room for him beside them.

A man in uniform stood by with a list; when the last Displaced Person had answered, and had his name checked against the list, the steps were taken away. A little group waited in the yard to wave goodbye to their friends as they drove out of the camp.

Lisa Wilson asked where the people were going. 'Are they all on the way home?' she said.

'On the way home,' Edward Syler repeated. 'No, I don't think so. The lorry's on the way to Hanover, maybe there's a convoy going from there and perhaps a few will be repatriated, but I reckon the majority are just planning to link up with friends in other camps. No doubt they've all got permission to visit relatives in some distant DP Assembly Centre, but of course you can't believe everything they say.'

'No, I suppose not.'

Edward Syler, the Information Officer, wore pince-nez but they were strong pince-nez, bridged together with a tough piece of metal. His shirt had been washed so often and so earnestly that it had lost its original khaki and become almost cream coloured; he wore a faded field-jacket and he had a shouting manner as if he was forever lecturing to a group of deaf foreigners.

'Well now, Miss Wilson, you've come here to write a feature on DPs,' he said. 'So you just go ahead and ask me any questions you like.'

'What about the last man in the lorry,' Lisa said. 'Wasn't that a Wehrmacht coat he was wearing?'

'Yes, I guess so. As I told you I used to be in this camp myself as a Welfare Officer. That Italian guy was already here when I arrived, I remember he had some story about being forced into the German Army – anyhow, he went on wearing his Wehrmacht overcoat on cold days because he didn't have any other coat – of course he must have been an ex-enemy alien when he first came into the camp and according to the directive he wouldn't have been entitled to DP status – we used to get all sorts here you know, Poles, Balts, Turks and one or two types claiming British or American citizenship. Why, we even had Menonites.'

'Menonites, what are they?'

'Oh, they're an agricultural community, they mostly came from Russia, they'd been driven right across two continents and finally landed up here. They don't believe in war.'

'How do you mean they don't believe in war? They must have noticed that something of the sort was going on around them.'

'Oh, sure, they noticed that there was some shooting, many of them were killed, but they don't take an active part in war themselves. Their religion forbids it.'

As Syler and Lisa walked slowly across the courtyard Syler said, 'I thought we'd go across to the Sick Bay, you might get a story there.' He rattled through some statistics and then he said, 'Well, I reckon you're familiar with the overall DP situation in Germany right now.'

Lisa wondered where Syler came from. 'Are you an American?' she asked him.

'An American? Hell no,' he said. 'I was born in Tokyo and educated in Heidelberg, but both my parents were of British nationality, though I've spent a number of years in the United States. My second wife came from Florida. I've never regretted marrying an American.'

'Is your wife in Europe now?'

'I dunno,' Syler said. 'We were divorced some while back. Well, here's the Camp Sick Bay, but of course there are only convalescents here. We have a directive to send all serious cases straight to the hospital in the town.'

There were sixteen beds in the Sick Bay but only four of them were occupied. One man was sitting on the edge of his bed, he wore a check shirt and grey flannel trousers. His black hair was parted in the middle, his eyes were dark with a melancholy expression, but he smiled all the time as if to show that he knew, more than anyone else, what was going on around him.

'Another Italian?' Lisa asked.

'No, a Frenchman,' Syler said.

At the far end of the room a man with a blackened face and close-cropped hair leant back against the coarse cotton of his pillow reading in a low tone from a book which he held in both hands as if afraid that someone might try to take it from him. He did not look up as Edward and Lisa came in but continued to read, his lips moving rapidly and his eyes, which were red-rimmed and distressingly bloodshot, staying open all the time.

On the other side of the room a fair-haired boy, propped up by two pillows, lay back with both his eyes closed.

Near the entrance, and opposite the check-shirted Frenchman, an old man, with frail transparent hands and a long thin face, was sitting up in bed. Edward Syler walked over to him.

'Well, Monsieur Dumaine,' Syler said. 'How are you getting on?'

Dumaine inclined his head graciously and answered in French. He said that he was not getting the right diet. 'Some of the food I eat now is not at all good for me in my enfeebled state.'

The check-shirted convalescent on the bed opposite gave a contemptuous smile.

The old man went into elaborate explanations of the kind of diet which, he believed, would suit him best. 'Diet,' he said, 'is a very subtle and important thing. We live by what we eat, and, in fact, it affects all our thoughts. But I shall recover quickly when I have all I need. On Monday I take the train to Paris.'

'But it is not certain that you will be able to go to France,' Syler told him.

'Why not?' Dumaine asked sharply.

Syler looked round the room as if seeking some help from the convalescents, but the man with the blackened face still muttered

on at the same speed and in the same tone, the fair-haired boy
kept his eyes closed and the man in the check shirt did not give up
his sneering smile.

'Well, Monsieur Dumaine,' Syler said. 'You had better see the
French liaison officer, he will explain all the circumstances.'

'Circumstances,' Dumaine said. 'I have no need to be told anything about them. I know my own circumstances only too well –
who better?' But after these words the old man's thoughts seemed
to wander away from the camp and the convalescents' room. He
began to talk about his farm in France. 'We had plenty of cheese
there,' he said. 'Cheese and butter,' and with one thin hand he
made a swirling movement round and round as if he was churn-
ing butter in a bowl. 'And when I am there again I shall make
more cheese and butter and look after animals and so become a
farmer as before.'

The check-shirted convalescent on the bed opposite laughed
softly.

The fair-haired boy had opened his eyes and he was leaning on
his elbow staring. Syler walked over to him. 'Well, Harry,' he
said. 'How's the rheumatism?'

'It's better, thank you,' the boy answered. 'But I sleep a lot.'

'Ah, that's what you want,' Syler said in his shouting manner.
'Plenty of rest and you'll soon be all right. Now here is Miss
Wilson, a journalist from London, to see you.'

'I'm from London, too,' said the boy. 'I was born there in
Castle Street.' He was silent for a few moments nervously touching the covers of a book lying on the bed.

'What have you been reading there?' Syler asked.

'World history,' the boy told him. 'But in the Red Cross Club
last month I was reading an illustrated paper. There were some
pictures of cadets training. It shows that they do accept boys of
my age as soldiers. I should like to join the British Army now.'

'He's been reading about Sandhurst,' Syler explained. 'It's true,
isn't it, Harry, that you walked here all the way from Danzig?'

'From Danzig. Yes.'

'Without food or water?'

'No,' the boy said. 'I had some water to drink on the way.'

'How many days did it take?'

'It took ten days,' Harry answered.

'A long journey.'

'Yes, it was a long journey.'

The camp doctor came in. The check-shirted man stood up. Dumaine, looking forward to further conversations about his diet, waved his hand in greeting, but the man with the blackened face went on reading aloud.

'Come on,' Syler said. 'Let's get out of here.'

As they walked across the courtyard Syler said, 'I keep asking them questions. Maybe you can pick up a story from some of their talk.'

'Yes,' Lisa said. 'Maybe I can. Will the boy Harry be able to go back to England soon?'

'No, I don't think so. You see,' Syler said, 'his father was killed in the Wehrmacht, his mother died during an air raid on Hamburg, the boy says he was born in Castle Street, London, but there's no trace of him in that district at all. The British haven't accepted him for citizenship, he has no relatives, no friends, no proof of how his early life was spent, so he must wait in the camp till all these questions have been cleared up.'

'How old is he?'

'It is believed that he has just passed his fourteenth birthday.'

'Oh, I see. Too young to decide his own future.'

'It's not so much a question of age as of nationality. You see, he's the son of a German father, and, as far as we know, of a German mother, he speaks perfect English and he wants to be British, but that doesn't make him British. If there was no definite ruling on this sort of thing we'd be snowed under with Germans claiming to be British. You'd be surprised how many Germans want to be British, nowadays.'

'I daresay. What about Dumaine? He seems to think he'll be going back to France on Monday.'

'Yes, he thinks so, but he won't be going. You see, according to an USFET* directive, all western nationals must return to their homes before the fifteenth of this month. That's next Monday. Their alternative is to join the German economy with its certainty of lower rations and likelihood of unemployment.'

---

* United States Forces European Theatre.

'It sounds harsh.'

'Yeah, but it isn't. It only applies to a few hundred DPs, French, Dutch, Belgians and so on. They can't have any reason for staying here unless they've been collaborators.'

'Then why can't Dumaine go back?'

'Because he's a collaborator. In any case there's some uncertainty about his nationality, it's being investigated right now. He speaks French and German equally well. Mostly he speaks a mixture of both. He may be German. Of course it's true what he says about his farm in France. But I don't suppose he'll ever see it again.'

'But surely a feeble old man of eighty years old wouldn't be likely to start a Fascist revival wherever he went?'

'No, but you see Dumaine's war work rules him right out. He was employed by the Todt Organization. He's quite frank about it himself, he says, "I needed a job so I offered my services to the Germans as an interpreter." Well, the Todt Organization was a Nazi set-up, so Dumaine couldn't be accepted in France now.'

'No, I see that. What will happen to him?'

'If it's proved that he's a German he will be moved to the German refugee hospital about a quarter of a mile from here. Wherever Dumaine goes he'll be the hell of a nuisance. I remember when he came into the camp. He refused, at first, to go through the usual de-lousing process and he wanted a room of his own and all that sort of thing.'

The winter was over and the sun was shining through the black boughs of three slender trees which had survived the bombardment, grass was already struggling up through the uneven ground giving the edge of the courtyard a green and hopeful look.

'Well, what do you think of the DP Camp?' Syler said. 'Can you get a story out of it?'

'I don't know yet,' Lisa answered. 'I was still thinking about the convalescents' room. What about the man in the end bed?'

'Oh, you mean the Bible reader? No one knows who he is. He arrived in the camp with a completely burnt and blackened face and red-rimmed eyes. He still looks the same way, but he was much worse then. He had a brown paper parcel with him and he could only say, "I was in the centre of an explosion." He said it over and over again, in perfect Polish without any accent. The brown paper parcel contained some clean underclothes and a

Bible in German – nothing else. So that guy just lies there all day reading the holy scriptures in German, but we think he may be Polish.'

'Will he be sent back to Poland then?'

'Well, according to the directive nationals can return to the country of their origin but we don't know anything of this man's origin – neither does he. A Pole must prove he's a Pole before he can go to Poland. We haven't been able to find anyone who knows the Bible reader and it's doubtful if they could recognize him the way he is now, and of course we can't expect any help from him, his memory's gone. He is, in fact, now mad.'

'He's a bit beyond the reach of directives then?'

Syler seemed to feel affronted, as if he were a man of honour whose sister had just been insulted in public. 'Nothing's beyond the reach of directives,' he said. 'The directives are OK. They've all been planned on a high level.'

As they made their way towards the Assembly Room they passed a long wooden corridor which connected the sick bay with the main building. The corridor had been divided into a series of small offices and in the centre there was a larger room with wide windows.

'See that room?' Syler said. 'I was responsible for that when I was here. I had it made into a little library.'

There were only two people in the wide windowed room, a young man wearing a Norfolk jacket, and the boots and breeches of the continental refugee, and a girl with long straight hair who held a book in her hand but did not appear to be reading.

'Of course, there's nobody much there now,' Syler said. 'The rest are working outside, or in the administration of the camp, but that little library has been a big success. The DP Committee said it was a grand idea. I fixed for the bookshelves to be six foot along the back and eight foot four along the side walls. We painted them white.'

'Who's the girl in there?' Lisa asked.

'The girl? Oh, she's Polish, she used to belong to a large family. She told me how they all used to go to a country house each summer – all the aunts, uncles, nephews, nieces, cousins and grandparents – they were thirty-seven in all. What d'you know about that? Thirty-seven in one family. But now none are left – all killed or lost, deported by the Russians, killed in air raids or in the

Warsaw Rising. 'Course the majority were murdered by the SS. The girl and her sister were liberated from Auschwitz by the Allies but the sister committed suicide a few weeks later. This girl won't go back to Warsaw, she says she'd be willing to go to the United States but there's no one to sponsor her. I guess she'll have to wait for mass emigration.'

'What about the man – the other DP in there?'

'Oh, he's not a DP, he's an Infiltree. He was in this camp as a DP but he was repatriated to Poland, then he came back here. Maybe he's holding out for Palestine.' Edward Syler peered into the library room. 'Some of the paint's got scratched,' he said sadly. ''Course we were very short of paint in this camp; and that's how it is that some of the Germans' slogans are still up in the passages. This place used to be one of Ley's Labour Ministries you know.'

When Syler took Lisa into the Assembly Room she saw that there was a frieze round the wall of square-shouldered German workers painted in pastel colours, some with hammers or spanners, some with pick-axes and others with spades.

Lisa stared at the large-limbed lifeless figures. 'A bit depressing, aren't they?'

'Sure they're depressing, but we'd need the hell of a lot of paint to paint them out.'

At the end of the room there was a noticeboard. 'Reminds me of school,' Lisa said.

'Oh, the noticeboard. There's all kinds of notices up there, the concerts the DPs organize for themselves, the elections for the DP Commandant, the classes in the DP school and now this census they're planning to take on how many of those who come from Russian occupied territory are willing to go back there.'

Lisa looked at the notice and saw that someone had scribbled on it in pencil. 'No. Don't want to go back because they take away your food card, and also they hang you.'

Syler stared closely at the noticeboard through his pince-nez. 'They're very confused right now,' he said. 'We may as well leave this camp if we want to get to the other camp in good time. It's mainly a Transit Camp.'

As they walked towards Syler's car Lisa said, 'What about that dark man in the convalescents' room. I mean the Frenchman – is he going back to France on Monday?'

'Oh, yeah. The guy in the check shirt. Sure he's going, but he doesn't want to. He says he served five years in the French navy and he's been in the French police force too, but the authorities in France sent for him – that was during the occupation, of course – there was some doubt about his activities and they informed him that he wasn't a Frenchman – it seems his mother was Italian. When he told me this story he said, "I can stand a good deal, but when they told me I wasn't a Frenchman that was another matter – I didn't hesitate an instant, I thought if they say I'm an Italian all right I'll be an Italian, and I came voluntarily into Germany." Of course none of this was official – off the record you know – don't quote me. As a matter of fact I wasn't very clear about what had happened to him and nothing he told me made much sense.'

'It looks as if he was as much a collaborator as Dumaine.'

'Oh, no, he comes into the category of "forced worker". There's no evidence that he collaborated with the Germans, he's not a political type at all. He belongs to the criminal class really. You can't believe much he says, he's an experienced liar and very bitter because his nationality was called into question.'

As they entered the yard two men were coming back into the camp from work in the fields, they both wore military mackintosh capes which did not fit them very well and gave them a comic air.

'See those two men?' Syler said.

'Yes.'

'Menonites. Don't believe in war. See?'

When they had been driving for a little while and the camp was out of sight Syler stopped the car and said that he had two bottles of cognac with him. 'Wouldn't go on a trip without liquor,' he said. 'I've brought a glass for you.' He opened the bottle and poured some out for Lisa, but he himself drank out of the bottle, throwing his head back as if he was a GI drinking Coca-Cola.

'The mortality rate amongst the Anglo-American personnel in Berlin is very high just now,' he said.

'What do they die of?'

'Oh, "mortality rate" – that's just a figure of speech. I mean the guys that get sent home with DTs.'

After Syler had drunk some more he began to talk, in a soft voice, about a woman he was planning to meet in Berlin. 'You ought to meet my girlfriend,' he said. 'You'd like her, you know, she's sympathetic, that's what she is, sympathetic. To tell you the truth, I aim to marry her.'

'Another American?' Lisa asked.

'No, she's German. Most of her relatives are interned or something, so she's all alone now. She hasn't got anyone but me.' Syler sighed deeply. 'Still, she'll be all right when we're married.'

'Have you got permission already?' Lisa asked.

'Permission?'

'Yes, you do have to get permission before you can marry a German national, don't you? I mean the official consent of your superior officer, according to the directive.'

Syler stared at the bottle of cognac as if it was an enemy. Then he shouted, 'Aw, to hell with the directive. What do I care about directives?' He started up the car, and, peering through his pince-nez at the long white road before him, he drove on in silence to the Transit Camp.

BERYL BAINBRIDGE

Bread and Butter Smith

Whenever the Christmas season approaches I always think of the good times we had, my wife and I, at the Adelphi Hotel just after the war. When I say 'times' I wouldn't like to give the impression that we were regular visitors to the hostelry at the foot of Mount Pleasant – that would be misleading. As a matter of fact we only stayed there twice. Before and in between those occasions we put up at the Exchange Hotel in Stanley Street, next door to the station.

Though born and brought up in Liverpool, I had crossed the water and gone to live on the Wirral at the earliest opportunity – you did if you came from Anfield – but I was in the habit of popping over on the ferry each Christmas to carve the turkey, on Boxing Day, for my sister Constance. She was, apart from my wife, my only surviving relative. Leaving aside the matter of Mr Brownlow, Constance's house in Belmont Road wasn't a suitable place to stay – to be accurate, it was one up and one down with the WC in the back-yard – and as the wife and I found it more convenient to occupy separate bedrooms I always booked into an hotel. I could afford it. I was in scrap metal, which was a good line of business to be in if you didn't mind being called a racketeer, which I didn't. The wife minded, but as I often tell her, where would she be today if I hadn't been. She'd soon buck up her ideas if she found herself languishing in the public ward of a National Health hospital.

If it hadn't been for Smith, we'd have stuck with the Exchange and not gone on switching hotels the way we did. Not that it achieved anything; he always ferreted us out. I fully believe that if we had changed venues altogether and given Blackpool or Hastings a whirl he'd have turned up in the grill room on the night before Christmas Eve, wearing that same crumpled blue suit, as though drawn by a magnet. I don't want to malign the poor devil, and don't think I'm being wise after the event, but I always found him a bit of a strain, not to mention an aggravation, right from the moment we met him, which was that first year we stayed at the Exchange.

We'd had our dinner, thank God, main course, pudding and so forth, and the waiter had just brought us a bowl of fruit. No bananas or tangerines, of course – too soon after the end of hostilities – but there was half a peach and a few damsons and some apples nicely polished.

'Shall I have the peach?' my wife said.

'Have what you like,' I told her. I've never been enamoured of fruit.

It was then that this fellow at the next table, who seemed to have nothing in front of him but a plate of bread and butter, leaned forward and said to me: 'The waiter is doing what King Alcinous may have done to the storm-beaten Greeks.'

That's exactly what he said, give or take a few words. You meet a lot of loopy individuals among the educated classes, and at the time I mistook him for one of those. Loopy, that is.

I ignored him, but the wife said: 'It's a thought, isn't it?' She was nervy that far back. Once she'd been foolish enough to respond, we couldn't get shot of him. I'm an abrupt sort of person. I don't do things I don't want to do – never have – whereas the wife, long before her present unfortunate state manifested itself, is the sort of person who apologizes when some uncouth lout sends her reeling into the gutter. Don't get me wrong, Smith was never a scrounger. He paid his whack at the bar, and if he ever ate with us it was hardly an imposition because he never seemed to order anything but bread and butter. Even on Christmas Day all he had was a few cuts of the breast and his regular four slices. He wasn't thin either. He had more of a belly on him than me, and he looked well into his fifties, which I put down to his war experiences. He was in the desert, or so he told the wife, and once saw Rommel through field glasses.

All along, I made no bones about my feelings for Smith. That first night, when he intruded over the fruit, I turned my face away. Later on, whenever he began pestering us about the Maginot line, or the Wife of Andros, or his daft theory that the unknown soldier was very probably a woman who had been scurrying along the hedgerows looking for hens' eggs when a shell had blown her to pieces at Ypres, I just got to my feet and walked away. My wife brought it on herself. She shouldn't have sat like Patience on a monument, listening to the fool, her left eyelid twitching the way it does when she's out of her depth. His conversation was right over her head.

Not that he seemed to notice; he couldn't get enough of us. When we said we wouldn't be available on Boxing Day, he even hinted that we might take him along to Belmont Road. I was almost tempted to take him up on it. Mr Brownlow was argumentative and had a weak bladder. Constance had picked him up outside the Co-op in 1931. It would have served Smith right to have had to sit for six hours in Constance's front parlour, two lumps of coal in the grate, one glass of port and lemon to last the night, and nothing by the way of entertainment beyond escorting Mr Brownlow down the freezing backyard to the WC.

The following year, to avoid the possibility of bumping into Smith, we went to the Adelphi. And damn me, he was there. There was a dance on Christmas Eve in the main lounge, and I'll never forget how he and the wife began in a melancholy and abstracted manner to circle the floor, her black dress rustling as she moved, and he almost on tiptoe because he was shorter than her. Every time he fox-trotted the wife in my direction he gave an exaggerated little start of surprise, as though I was the last person he expected to see. When he fetched her back to the table, he said, 'I do hope you have no objection to my dancing with your lady wife. I wouldn't like to give offence.'

'No offence taken,' I said. I've never seen the point of dancing. 'Do as you please.'

'We shall, we shall,' the wife said, laughing in that way she has.

We had to play cards with the blighter on Christmas Day. On Boxing Day it was almost a relief, which was saying something, to travel out on the tram to Anfield for the festivities with Constance and Mr Brownlow.

The next year we tried the Exchange again, never thinking that lightning would strike twice, or three times for that matter, but blow me, it did. Smith turned up an hour after we arrived. I did briefly begin to wonder who was avoiding who, but it was obvious that he was as pleased as punch to see us.

'My word,' he cried out. 'This is nice. My word, it is.'

I sensed he was different. There was nothing I could put my finger on; his suit was the same and he still blinked a lot, but something had changed in him. I mentioned as much to the wife. 'He's different, don't you think?' I said.

'Different?' she said.

'Cocky,' I said. 'If you know what I mean?'

'I don't,' she said.

'Something in the eye,' I insisted.

But she wouldn't have it.

All the same, I was right. Why, he even had the blithering nerve to give me a present, wrapped up in coloured paper with one of those damn soft bows on the top. It was a book on golf, which was a lucky choice, inspired almost, as I'd only taken up the game a few months before. I didn't run amok showing my gratitude, nor did I scamper upstairs and parcel up one of the handkerchiefs the wife had given to me. To be frank, I didn't even say thank you.

I didn't need acquaintances, then. As long as I had the wife sitting there, reading a library book and smoking one of her Craven A cigarettes, I didn't have to go to the bother of being pleasant. Not that Smith noticed my lack of enthusiasm for his company. It appeared to me that no matter where I was, whether in the corridor minding my own business, or coming out of the lift, or having a quiet drink in the Steve Donoghue Bar, he was forever bobbing up alongside me, or behind me – and always a mine of useful information. 'Are you aware,' he'd ask, eyeing the beer pitching in my glass as a train rumbled out of the station below, 'that the first locomotive was so heavy that it broke the track beneath it?'

He didn't seem to know anybody in the city, but a couple of times I saw him going down in the lift very late at night with his hat and coat on. God knows where he was off to. Once, I saw him in the deserted booking-hall of the station. I was on the fourth floor of the hotel, in the small hours, looking out of the back windows at the arched roof beneath, estimating what price, per ton, the cast-iron ribs would fetch on the scrap market. It was raining and Smith was perambulating up and down, hatless, holding an umbrella in a cock-eyed way, followed by a flock of pigeons. While I was watching, Smith suddenly spun round and flourished his brolly at the pigeons. I took it that he was drunk. The birds flapped upwards in alarm. There wasn't a pane of glass left intact in the roof – it had all been blasted to smithereens during the Blitz. One of the pigeons in attempting to escape through the ribs must have severed a wing on the shards of glass. It sort of staggered in mid-air and then dropped like a lump of mud to the granite floor of the booking-hall. I couldn't hear the noise it made, flopping down like that, but it obviously gave Smith quite a turn. He froze, his gamp held out to one side like some railway guard waiting to lower his flag for a train to depart. I couldn't see his face because I was looking down on him, but I could tell by the stance of the man, one foot turned inwards, one arm stuck outwards, that he was frightened. Then he took a running kick at the thing on the ground and sent it skidding against the base of the tobacco kiosk. After a moment he went over to the kiosk and squatted down. He stayed like that for some time, rocking backwards and forwards on his haunches. Then he took out his handkerchief, laid it over the pigeon, and walked away. He was definitely drunk.

That final year, 1949, I switched back to the Adelphi. You've never clapped eyes on anything like that hotel. It's built like a Cunarder. Whenever I lurched through the revolving doors into the lobby, I never thought I'd disembark until I'd crossed the Atlantic. The lounge is the size of a dry dock; there are little balconettes running the entire length of it, fronted by ornamental grilles. Sometimes, if the staff dropped a nickel-plated teapot in the small kitchen behind the rostrum, I imagined we'd struck an iceberg. I never used to think like that until Smith put his oar in. It was he who said that all big hotels were designed to resemble ocean liners. On another occasion – because he was a contrary beggar – he said that the balconettes were modelled after confessionals in churches. I never sat in them after that.

We arrived at four o'clock on 23 December and went immediately into the lounge for tea and cakes. I had just told the wife to sit up straight – there's nothing worse than a slouching woman, particularly if she's got a silver fox fur slung round her shoulders – when I thought I saw, reflected in the mirrors behind the balconettes, the unmistakable figure of Smith. I slopped tea into my saucer.

'What's up?' asked my wife.

'I could swear I just saw that blighter Smith,' I said. 'Could I have been mistaken, do you think?'

'What?' she said. 'You? Surely not.' She was lifting up her veil and tucking it back over the brim of her hat, and you could tell how put out she was; both her cheeks were red with annoyance.

The odd thing was that he never came into the grill room that night. 'Perhaps it wasn't him,' I said. 'Perhaps it was a trick of the light.'

'Some trick,' she said.

'If he has the effrontery to present me with another little seasonal offering,' I warned her, 'I'll throw it back in his face.'

After we had finished our pudding my wife said she was off to her bed.

'You can't go up now,' I said. 'I've paid good money to be here.'

'If I'm to live through the excitement of visiting Constance and Mr Brownlow,' she said, 'I'll need all the rest I can get.' She fairly ran out of the grill room; she never had any staying power.

I had a drink in the bar and asked the fellow behind the counter if he'd seen Smith, but he didn't seem to know who I was talking about. That's the trouble with shifting from one hotel to another – none of the staff know you from Adam. I looked into the smoking-room about ten o'clock and he wasn't there either. I could have done with Smith. The hotel was crowded with guests, some in uniform, full of the Christmas spirit and anxious that everyone should join in. Several times I was almost drawn into one of those conversations about what branch of the services I'd been in during the hostilities. I'll say that much for Smith; he never asked me what I'd done in the war. At a quarter past ten I went into the lounge and ordered myself another drink. There weren't too many people in there. A dance was in progress in the French room; I could hear the band playing some number made popular by Carmen Miranda. The waiter had just set my glass down in front of me when the doors burst open at the side and a line of revellers spilled into the lounge and began doing the conga down the length of the pink carpet towards the Christmas tree at the far end. They wound in and out of the sofas and the tables, clasping each other at the waist and kicking up the devil of a noise. Mercifully, having snaked once round the tree, showering the carpet with pine-needles, they headed back for the dance floor. And suddenly, for a split second, before he disappeared behind the tree, I thought I saw Smith near the end of the line, clutching hold of a stout individual who was wearing a paper hat. The fat man appeared again, but I was mistaken about Smith. Oddly enough, he must have been on my mind because for the rest of the evening I fancied I caught glimpses of him – coming out of the gents, going into the lift, standing at the top of the stairs looking down into the lounge – but it was never him.

Shortly after midnight I went upstairs to unpack my belongings. My room was on the first floor and overlooked Lewis's department store. I'd changed into my pyjamas – such as they were – and was putting my Sunday suit on a hanger when I realized that my wife had forgotten to include my grey spotted tie among the rest of my things. It wasn't that I gave a tinker's cuss about that particular tie, it was just that Mr Brownlow had bought it for me the previous Christmas and my not wearing it on Boxing Day would undoubtedly cause an uproar.

I went out into the corridor, determined to ask the wife what she meant by it. It wasn't as if she had a lot on her mind. Unfortunately, I forgot that the door was self-locking and it shut behind me. I rapped on my wife's door for what seemed like hours. I've never seen the point of chucking money away on pyjamas; the drawstring had gone from the trousers and there wasn't one button left on the jacket. When my wife finally deigned to open up, she too stepped over the threshold, and in an instant her door had slammed shut as well. I admit I lost my head. I ran up and down, swearing, trying to find a broom cupboard to hide in; any moment those blighters from the French room could have come prancing along the corridor.

'Fetch a porter,' advised my wife.

'Not like this,' I shouted. 'I'm not fit.'

'Here,' she said, and she took off her dressing-gown – it had white fur round the sleeves – and handed it to me.

I had crept half-way down the stairs when I heard carol singing one floor below. I just couldn't face anyone, not wearing that damn-fool dressing-gown and my trousers at half mast. I hopped back upstairs and at that moment the wife called out to me from the doorway of her room; apparently her door hadn't been locked after all.

I spent an uncomfortable night in the wife's bed – I don't sleep well – and when I switched on the light to see if I could find anything to read, there was only the Bible. The room was a pig-sty; she hadn't emptied her suitcase or hung anything up, and there was a slice of buttered bread on top of her fox fur. I woke her and asked if she had a library book handy.

'For God's sake,' she said, 'I'm worn out.'

I was having afternoon tea the following day, on my own – the wife had gone window-shopping in Bond Street – when Smith arrived at the hotel. He said a relative had been taken ill and he'd had to visit them in hospital. Being Smith, he couldn't leave it at that. He had to give me a lecture on some damn-fool theory of his that we thought ourselves into illnesses. Our minds, he said, controlled our bodies. Some blasted Greek or other had known it centuries ago.

Faced with him, and realizing that he'd be dogging my footsteps for the next forty-eight hours, I grew irritated. Don't forget, I hadn't had much sleep, and there was some sort of expression on his face, some sort of light in his eyes that annoyed me. I don't know how to explain it; he looked foolish, almost happy and it rubbed me up the wrong way. I wanted to get rid of him once and for all. It was no use insulting the man; I had done that often enough and it was like water off a duck's back. Then an idea came to me. I had recognized right from the beginning that he was a prudish sort of fellow. I knew that he had never married, and I had never seen him strike up a conversation with an unescorted woman, apart from the wife. He preferred the company of married couples, providing they were respectable.

'Blow me down,' I said. 'I've been getting pains in my legs for the past eight years. Now I know why.'

'Why?' he asked.

'On account of the wife,' I said.

'Your wife?' he said, tugging at his little ginger moustache.

I implied that the wife had led me something of a dance. She was under the doctor for it, of course. It had gone on for years. She couldn't be blamed, not exactly. That's why I was forced to keep changing hotels . . . there had been various incidents of a somewhat scandalous nature with various men. As I spoke I stumbled over the words – I knew he wasn't a complete fool. I expressed the hope that he wouldn't betray my confidences. I didn't feel bad telling lies about my wife. It wouldn't get back. There was no danger of Smith repeating it to somebody he knew, who might repeat it to somebody we knew, because none of us knew anybody. It shut him up all right. The light went out of his eyes.

At seven o'clock that evening, according to the waiter on duty, Smith came into the smoking-room and ordered a pot of tea. The waiter noticed that he kept clattering the ash-tray up and down on the table. When the tea was brought to him, he said, 'Oh, and I'll need some bread and butter if it's all the same to you.' While the waiter was gone Smith took out his service revolver and shot himself in the head. He died almost at once. He must have been more upset about his relative being ill than he let on.

We never went back to the Adelphi, or to the Exchange for that matter. Not because of anything to do with Smith, but because less than a year later the wife began to show signs of instability; in any case the following August Constance passed on and there was certainly no call to clap eyes on Mr Brownlow ever again.

One could say that my wife has passed on too, only in her case it's more that she's wandered out of reach. As Bread and Butter Smith might have put it: 'All the world's against her, so that Crete (alias Rainhill Mental Institution) is her only refuge.'

JEAN STAFFORD

The Maiden

'I bought the pair of them in Berlin for forty marks,' Mrs Andreas was saying to Dr Reinmuth, who had admired the twin decanters on her dinner table. 'It sickens me, the way they must let their treasures go for nothing. I can take no pride in having got a bargain when I feel like a pirate.' Evan Leckie, an American journalist who was the extra man at the party, turned away from the woman on his right to glance at his hostess to see if her face revealed the hypocrisy he had heard, ever so faintly, in her voice, but he could read nothing in her bland eyes, nor could he discover the reaction of her interlocutor, who slightly inclined his head in acknowledgement of her sympathy for his mortified compatriots but said nothing and resumed his affectionate scrutiny of the decanters as Mrs Andreas went on to enumerate other instances of the victor's gains through the Germans' losses. Evan, just transferred to Heidelberg from the squalor and perdition of Nuremberg, joined in the German's contemplation of these relics of more handsome times. One of the bottles was filled with red wine, which gleamed darkly through the lustrous, sculptured glass, chased with silver, and the other with pale, sunny Chablis. The candlelight invested the wines with a property beyond taste and fluidity, a subtle grace belonging to a world almost imaginary in its elegance, and for a moment Evan warmed towards Mrs Andreas, who had tried to resuscitate this charming world for her guests by putting the decanters in the becoming company of heavy, florid silverware and Dresden fruit plates and a bowl of immaculate white roses, and by dressing herself, a plump and unexceptional person, in an opulent frock of gold brocade and a little queenly crown of amethysts for her curly, greying hair.

The double doors to the garden were open to admit the moonlight and the summer breeze, and now and again, in the course of the meal, Evan had glanced out and had seen luminous nicotiana and delphiniums growing profusely beside a high stone wall.

Here, in the hilly section of the city, it was as quiet as in the country, there was not a sound of jeeps or drunken GIs to disturb the light and general conversation of Americans breaking bread with Germans. Only by implication and indirection were the war and the Occupation spoken of, and in this abandonment of the contemporary, the vanquished, these charming Reinmuths, save by their dress and their speech, could not be distinguished from the conquerors. If chivalry, thought Evan, were ever to return to the world, peace would come with it, but evenings like this were isolated, were all but lost in the vast, arid wastes of the present hour within the present decade. And the pity that Mrs Andreas bestowed upon her German guests would not return to them the decanters they had forfeited, nor would her hospitality obliterate from their hearts the knowledge of their immense dilemma. Paradoxically, it was only upon the highest possible level that Germans and Americans these days could communicate with one another; only a past that was now irretrievable could bring them into harmony.

For the past month in Nuremberg, ever since Evan's wife, Virginia, had left him – left him, as she had put it in a shout, 'to stew in his own juice' – Evan had spent his evenings in the bar of his hotel, drinking by himself and listening, in a trance of boredom, to the conversations of the Americans about him. The mirrored walls and mirrored ceilings had cast back the manifold reflections of able-bodied WACs in summer uniforms, who talked of their baseball teams (once he had seen a phalanx of them in the lobby, armed with bats and catchers' mitts, looking no less manly than the Brooklyn Dodgers) and of posts where they had been stationed and of itineraries, past and future. 'Where were you in '45?' he had heard one of them cry. 'New Caledonia! My God! So was I. Isn't it a riot to think we were both in New Caledonia in '45 and now are here in the Theatre?' Things had come to a pretty pass, thought Evan, when *this* was the theatre of a young girl's dreams. They did not talk like women and they did not look like women but like a modern mutation, a revision, perhaps more efficient and sturdier, of an old model. Half hypnotized by the signs of the times, he had come almost to believe that the days of men and women were over and that the world had moved into a new era dominated by a neuter body called Personnel, whose only concerns were to make history and to snub the history that had already been made. Miss Sally Dean, who sat across from him tonight, had pleased him at first glance with her bright blonde hair and her alabaster shoulders and the fine length of her legs, but over the cocktails his delight departed when, in the accents of west Los Angeles, she had said she wished General MacArthur were in Germany, since he was, in her opinion, a 'real glamour puss'. The woman on his right, Mrs Crowell, the wife of a judge from Ohio in the judiciary of the Occupation, was obsessively loquacious; for a very long time she had been delivering to him a self-sustaining monologue on the effronteries of German servants, announcing once, with all the authority of an anthropologist, that 'the Baden mind is *consecrated* to dishonesty'. He could not put his finger on it, but, in spite of her familiar housewife's complaints, she did not sound at all like his mother and his aunts in Charlottesville, whose lives, spun out in loving domesticity, would lose their pungency if cooks kept civil tongues in their heads and if upstairs maids were not light-fingered. Mrs Crowell brought to her housekeeping problems a modern and impersonal intellect. 'The Baden mind', 'the Franconian mind', 'the German character' were phrases that came forth irrefutably. And the bluestocking wife of a Captain McNaughton, who sat on Evan's left and who taught library science to the wives of other Army officers, had all evening lectured Dr Reinmuth on the faults (remediable, in her opinion) of his generation that had forced the world into war. Dr Reinmuth was a lawyer. She was herself a warrior; she argued hotly, although the German did not oppose her, and sometimes she threatened him with her spoon.

It was the German woman, Frau Reinmuth, who, although her grey dress was modest and although she wore no jewels and little rouge, captivated Evan with her ineffable femininity: she, of all the women there, had been challenged by violence and she had ignored it, had firmly and with great poise set it aside. To look at her, no one would know that the slightest alteration had taken place in the dignified *modus vivendi* she must have known all her life. The serenity she emanated touched him so warmly and so deeply that he almost loved her, and upon the recognition of his feeling he was seized with loneliness and with a sort of homesickness that he felt sure she would understand – a longing, it was, for the places that *she* would remember. Suddenly it occurred to him that the only other time he had been in Heidelberg, he had been here with his wife, two years before, and they had gone one afternoon by trolley to Schwetzingen to see the palace gardens. Virginia had always hated history and that day she had looked at a cool Louis Quatorze summerhouse, designed for witty persiflage and premeditated kisses, and had said, 'It's so chichi it makes me sick.' And she had meant it. How she had prided herself on despising everything that had been made before 1920, the year of her birth! Staring at the wines aglow in their fine vessels, Evan recaptured exactly the feeling he had had that day in Schwetzingen when, very abruptly, he had realized that he was only technically bound for life to this fretful iconoclast; for a short while, there beside the playing fountains, he had made her vanish and in her place there stood a quiet woman, rich in meditations and in fancies. If he had known Frau Reinmuth then, she might have been the one he thought of.

Evan watched Dr Reinmuth as he poured the gold and garnet liquids, first one and then the other, into the glasses before his plate. The little lawyer closely attended the surge of colour behind the radiant crystal and he murmured, in a soft Bavarian voice, 'Lovely, lovely. Look, Liselotte, how beautiful Mrs Andreas' *Karaffen* are!' Frau Reinmuth, wide-faced, twice his size, turned from her talk of the Salzburg Festival with Mr Andreas and cherished both her husband and the decanters with her broad grey eyes, in whose depths love lay limitlessly. When she praised the design of the cut glass, and the etching of the silver, and the shape of the stoppers, like enormous diamonds, she managed somehow, through the timbre of her voice or its cadences or through the way she looked at him, to proclaim that she loved her husband and that the beauty of the bottles was rivalled and surpassed by the nature of this little man of hers, who, still fascinated, moved his handsome head this way and that, the better to see the prismatic green and violet beams that burst from the shelves and crannies of the glass. His movements were quick and delicately articulated, like a small animal's, and his slender fingers touched and traced the glass as if he were playing a musical instrument that only his ears could hear. He must have been in his middle forties, but he looked like a nervous, gifted boy not twenty yet, he was so slight, his hair was so black and curly, his brown face was so lineless, and there was such candour and curiosity in his dark eyes. He seemed now to want to carry his visual and tactile encounter with the decanters to a further point, to a completion, to bliss. And Evan, arrested by the man's absorption (if it was not that of a child, it was that of an artist bent on abstracting meanings from all the data presented to his senses), found it hard to imagine him arguing in a court of law, where the materials, no matter how one elevated and embellished justice, were not poetry. Equally difficult was it to see him as he had been during the war, in his role of interpreter for the German Army in Italy. Like every German one met in a polite American House, Dr Reinmuth had been an enemy of the Third Reich: he had escaped concentration camp only because his languages were useful to the Nazis. While Evan, for the most part, was suspicious of these self-named martyrs who seemed always to have fetched up in gentlemanly jobs where their lives were not in the least imperilled, he did believe in Dr Reinmuth, and was certain that a belligerent ideology could not enlist the tender creature so unaffectedly playing with Mrs Andreas' toys, so obviously well beloved by his benevolent wife. Everyone, even Mrs Crowell, paused a second to look from the man to the woman and to esteem their concord.

Frau Reinmuth then returned to Mr Andreas, but it was plain to see that her mind was only half with him. She said, 'I envy you to hear Flagstad. Our pain is that there is no music now,' and in a lower voice she added, 'I have seen August bite his lip for sorrow when he goes past the opera house in Mannheim. It's nothing now, you now, but a ruin, like everything.' Glancing at her, Evan wondered whether she were older than her husband or if this marriage had been entered upon late, and he concluded that perhaps the second was true, for they were childless – the downright Mrs McNaughton had determined that before the canapés were passed – and Frau Reinmuth looked born to motherhood. But even more telling was the honeymoon inflection in her voice, as if she were still marvelling now to say the name 'August' as easily as she said 'I' and to be able to bestow these limnings of her dearest possession generously on the members of a dinner party. It was not that she spoke of him as if he were a child, as some women do who marry late or marry men younger than themselves, but as if he were a paragon with whom she had the remarkable honour to be associated. She, in her boundless patience, could endure being deprived of music and it was not for herself that she complained, but she could not bear to see August's grief over the hush that lay upon their singing country; she lived not only for, she lived *in*, him. She wore her yellow hair in Germanic braids that coiled around her head, sitting too low to be smart; her hands were soft and large, honestly meriting the wide wedding band on the right one. She was as completely a woman as Virginia, in spite of a kind of ravening femaleness and piquant good looks, had never been one. He shuddered to think how she must be maligning him in Nevada to the other angry petitioners, and then he tried to imagine how Frau Reinmuth would behave under similar circumstances. But it was unthinkable that she should ever be a divorcée; no matter what sort of man she married, this wifely woman would somehow, he was sure, quell all disorder. Again he felt a wave of affection for her; he fancied drinking tea with her in a little crowded drawing-room at the end of one of these warm days, and he saw himself walking with both the Reinmuths up through the hills behind the Philosophenweg, proving to the world by their compassionate amity that there was no longer a state of war between their country and his.

But he was prevented from spinning out his fantasy of a friendship with the Reinmuths because Mrs Crowell was demanding his attention. Her present servant, she told him, was an aristocrat ('as aristocratic as a German can be', she said *sotto voce*, 'which isn't saying much') and might therefore be expected not to steal the spoons; now, having brought him up to date on her belowstairs problems, she changed the subject and drew him into the orbit of her bright-eyed, pervasive bustling. She understood that he had just come from Nuremberg, where she and the judge had lived for two years. 'Isn't it too profoundly *triste*?' she cried. 'Where did they billet you poor thing?'

'At the Grand Hotel,' said Evan, recollecting the WACs with their moustaches and their soldierly patois.

'Oh no!' protested Mrs Crowell. 'But it's simply *overrun* with awful Army children! Not children – brats. Brats, I'm sorry to say, is the only word for them. They actually roller-skate through the lobby, you know, to say nothing of the *ghastly* noise they make. I used to go to the hairdresser there and finally had to give up because of the hullabaloo.'

At the mention of Nuremberg, Dr Reinmuth had pivoted around towards them and now, speaking across Mrs McNaughton, he said dreamily, 'Once it was a lovely town. We lived there, my wife and I, all our lives until the war. I understand there is now a French orchestra in the opera house that plays calypso for your soldiers.' There sounded in his voice the same note of wonder that he had used when he acclaimed the decanters that he could not own; neither could he again possess the beauties of his birthplace. And Evan Leckie, to whom the genesis of war had always been incomprehensible, looked with astonishment at these two pacific Germans and pondered how the whole hideous mistake had come about, what Eumenides had driven this pair to hardship, humiliation, and exile. Whatever else they were, however alien their values might be, these enemies were *sub specie aeternitatis*, of incalculable worth if for no other reason than that, in an unloving world, they loved.

Mrs Andreas, tactfully refusing Dr Reinmuth's gambit, since she knew that the deterioration of the Nuremberg Opera House into a nightclub must be a painful subject to him, manoeuvred her guests until the talk at the table became general. They all continued the exchange that had begun with Frau Reinmuth and Mr Andreas on the Salzburg Festival; they went on to speak of Edinburgh, of the *Salomé* that someone had heard at La Scala, of a coloratura who had delighted the Reinmuths in Weimar. Dr Reinmuth then told the story of his having once defended a pianist who had been sued for slander by a violinist; the defendant had been accused of saying publicly that the plaintiff played Mozart as if the music had been written for the barrel organ and that the only thing missing was a monkey to take up a collection. This anecdote, coinciding with the arrival of the dessert, diverted the stream of talk, and Judge Crowell, whose interest in music was perfunctory and social, revived and took the floor. He told of a murder case he had tried the week before in Frankfurt and of a rape case on the docket in Stuttgart. Dr Reinmuth countered with cases he was pleading; they matched their legal wits, made Latin puns and so enjoyed their game that the others laughed, although they barely understood the meanings of the words.

Dr Reinmuth, who was again fondling the decanters, said, 'I suppose every lawyer is fond of telling the story of his first case. May I tell mine?' He besought his hostess with an endearing smile, and his wife, forever at his side, pleaded for him, 'Oh, do!' and she explained. 'it's such an extraordinary story of a young lawyer's first case.'

He poured himself a little more Chablis and smiled and began. When he was twenty-three, in Nuremberg, just down from Bonn, with no practice at all, he had one day been called upon by the state to defend a man who had confessed to murdering an old woman and robbing her of sixty pfennigs. The defence, of course, was purely a convention, and the man was immediately sentenced to death, since there was no question of his guilt or of the enormity of his crime. Some few days after the trial, Dr Reinmuth had received an elaborate engraved invitation to the execution by guillotine, which was to be carried out in the courtyard of the Justizpalast one morning a day or so later, punctually at seven o'clock. He was instructed, in an accompanying letter, to wear a Prince Albert and a top hat.

Mrs Andreas was shocked. 'Guillotine? Did you *have* to go?'

Dr Reinmuth smiled and bowed to her. 'No, I was not required. It was, you see, my *right* to go, as the advocate of the prisoner.'

Judge Crowell laughed deeply. 'Your first case, eh, Reinmuth?' And Dr Reinmuth spread out his hands in a mock gesture of deprecation.

'My fellow-spectators were three judges from the bench,' he continued, 'who were dressed, like myself, in Prince Alberts and cylinders. We were a little early when we got to the courtyard, so that we saw the last-minute preparations of the stage before the play began. Near the guillotine, with its great knife – that blade, my God in Heaven! – there stood a man in uniform with a drum, ready to drown out the sound if my client should yell.'

The dimmest of frowns had gathered on Judge Crowell's forehead. 'All this pomp and circumstance for sixty pfennigs?' he said.

'Right you are, sir,' replied Dr Reinmuth. 'That is the irony of my story.' He paused to eat a strawberry and to take a sip of wine. 'Next we watched them test the machine to make sure it was in proper – shall I say decapitating? – condition. When they released it, the cleaver came down with such stupendous force that the earth beneath our feet vibrated and my brains buzzed like a bee.

'As the bells began to ring for seven, Herr Murderer was led out by two executioners, dressed as we were dressed. Their white gloves were spotless! It was a glorious morning in May. The flowers were out, the birds were singing, the sky had not a cloud. To have your head cut off on such a day!'

'For sixty pfennigs!' persisted the judge from Ohio. And Miss Dean, paling, stopped eating her dessert.

'Mein Herr had been confessed and anointed. You could fairly see the holy oil on his forehead as his keepers led him across the paving to the guillotine. The drummer was ready. As the fourth note of the seven struck in the church towers, they persuaded him to take the position necessary to the success of Dr Guillotin's invention. One, he was horizontal! Two, the blade descended! Three, the head was off the carcass and the blood shot out from the neck like a volcano, a geyser, the flame from an explosion. No sight I saw in the war was worse. The last stroke of seven sounded. There had been no need for the drum.'

'Great Scott! said Mr Andreas, and flushed.

Captain McNaughton stared at Dr Reinmuth and said, 'You chaps don't do things by halves, do you?'

Mrs Andreas, frantic at the dangerous note that had sounded, menacing her party, put her hand lightly on the lawyer's and said, 'I know that then you must have fainted.'

Dr Reinmuth tilted back his head and smiled at the ceiling. 'No. No, I did not faint. You remember that this was a beautiful day in spring? And that I was a young man, all dressed up at seven in the morning?' He lowered his head and gave his smile to the whole company. 'Faint! Dear lady, no! I took the tram back to Fürth and I called my sweetheart on the telephone.' He gazed at his wife. 'Liselotte was surprised, considering the hour. "What are you thinking of? It's not eight o'clock," she said. I flustered her then. I said, "I know it's an unusual time of day to call, but I have something unusual to say. Will you marry me?"'

He clasped his hands together and exchanged with his wife a look as exuberant and shy as if they were in the first rapture of their romance, and, bewitched, she said, 'Twenty years ago next May.'

A silence settled on the room. Whether Evan Leckie was the more dumbfounded by Dr Reinmuth's story of a majestic penalty to fit a sordid crime or by his ostentatious hinting at his connubial delights, he did not know. Evan sought the stunned faces of his countrymen and could not tell in them, either, what feeling was the uppermost. The party suddenly was no longer a whole; it consisted of two parts, the Americans and the Germans, and while the former outnumbered them, the Germans, in a deeper sense, had triumphed. They had joyfully danced a *Totentanz*, had implied all the details of their sixty-pfennig marriage, and they were still, even now, smiling at each other as if there had never been anything untoward in their lives.

'I could take a wife then, you see,' said Dr Reinmuth, by way of a denouement, 'since I was a full-fledged lawyer. And she could not resist me in that finery, which, as a matter of fact, I had had to hire for the occasion.'

Judge Crowell lit a cigarette, and, snatching at the externals of the tale, he said, 'Didn't know you fellows used the guillotine as late as that. I've never seen one except that one they've got in the antiquarian place in Edinburgh. They call it the Maiden.'

Dr Reinmuth poured the very last of the Chablis into his glass, and turning to Mrs Andreas, he said, 'It was nectar and I've drunk it all. *Sic transit gloria mundi.*'

ELIZABETH TAYLOR

Gravement Endommagé

The car devoured the road, but the lines of poplars were without end. The shadows of sagging telegraph wires scalloped the middle of the road, the vaguer shadows of the pretty telegraph posts pleased Louise. They were essentially French, she thought – like, perhaps, lilies of the valley: spare, neatly budded.

The poplars dwindled at intervals and gave place to ruined buildings and pock-marked walls; a landscape of broken stone, faded Dubonnet advertisements. Afterwards, the trees began again.

When they came to a town, the cobblestones, laid fan-wise, slowed up the driving. Outside cafés, the chairs were all empty. Plane trees in the squares half hid the flaking walls of houses with crooked jalousies and frail balconies, like twisted birdcages. All had slipped, subsided.

'But it is so *dead*!' Louise complained, wanting to get to Paris, to take out from her cases her crumpled frocks, shake them out, hang them up. She dreamed of that; she had clung to the idea across the Channel. Because she was sick before the boat moved, Richard thought she was sick deliberately, as a form of revenge. But seasickness ran in her family. Her mother had always been prostrated immediately – as soon (as she so often had said) as her foot touched the deck. It would have seemed an insult to her mother's memory for Louise not to have worked herself up into a queasy panic at the very beginning. Richard, seeing walls sliding past portholes and then sky, finished his drink quickly and went up on deck. Hardier women than Louise leaned over the rails, their scarves flapping, watching the coast of France come up. The strong air had made him hungry, but when they had driven away from the harbour and had stopped for luncheon, Louise would only sip brandy, looking away from his plate.

'But we can never get to Paris by dinner-time,' he said, when they were in the car again. 'Especially driving on the wrong side of the road all the way.'

'There is nowhere between here and there,' she said with authority. 'And I want to *settle.*'

He knew her 'settling'. Photographs of the children spread about, champagne sent up, maids running down corridors with her frocks on their arms, powder spilt everywhere, the bathroom full of bottles and jars. He would have to sit down to telephone a list of names. Her friends would come in for drinks. They would have done better, so far as he could see, to have stayed in London.

'But if we are pushed for time . . . Why kill ourselves? . . . After all, this is a holiday . . . I do remember . . . There is a place I stayed at that time . . . When I first knew you . . .' Only parts of what he said reached her. The rest was blown away.

'You are deliberately going slow,' she said.

'I think more of my car than to drive it fast along these roads.'

'You think more of your car than of your wife.'

He had no answer. He could not say that at least his car never betrayed him, let him down, embarrassed him, because it constantly did and might at any moment.

'You planned this delay without consulting me. You planned to spend this night in some God-forsaken place and sink into your private nostalgia while my frocks crease and crease . . .' Her voice mounted up like a wave, trembled, broke.

The holiday was really to set things to rights between them. Lately, trivial bickering had hardened into direct animosity. Relatives put this down to, on his part, overwork, and, on hers, fatigue from the war, during which she had lived, after their London house was bombed, in a remote village with the children. She had nothing to say of those years but that they were not funny. She clung to the children and they to her. He was not, as he said – at first indulgently but more lately with irritation – in the picture. She knit them closer and closer to her, and he was quite excluded. He tried to understand that there must be, after the war, much that was new in her, after so long a gap, one that she would not fill up for him, or discuss. A new quirk was her preoccupation with fashion. To her, it was a race in which she must be first, so she looked *outré* always, never normal. If any of her friends struck a new note before her, she by-passed and cancelled out that particular foible. Men never liked her clothes, and women only admired them. She did not dress for men. Years of almost exclusively feminine society had set up cold antagonisms.

Yes, hardship had made her superficial, icily frivolous. For one thing, she now must never be alone. She drank too much. In the night, he knew, she turned and turned, sighing in her sleep, dreaming bad dreams, wherein she could no longer choose her company. When he made love to her, she recoiled in astonishment, as if she could not believe such things could happen.

He had once thought she would be so happy to leave the village, that by comparison her life in London after the war would seem wonderful. But boredom had made her carping, fidgety. Instead of being thankful for what she had, she complained at the slightest discomfort. She raised her standards above what they had ever been; drove maids, who needed little driving, to give notice; was harried, piteous, unrelaxed. Although she was known as a wonderful hostess, guests wonderfully enjoying themselves felt – they could not say why – wary, and listened, as if for a creaking of ice beneath their gaiety.

Her doctor, advising the holiday, was only conventional in his optimism. If anyone were benefited by it, it would be the children, stopping at home with their grandmother – for a while, out of the arena. What Richard needed was a holiday away from Louise, and what Louise needed was a holiday from herself, from the very thing she must always take along, the dull carapace of her own dissatisfaction, her chronic unsunniness.

The drive seemed endless, because it was so monotonous. War had exhaled a vapour of despair over all the scene. Grass grew over grief, trying to hide collapse, to cover some of the wounds. One generation hoped to contend with the failure of another.

Late in the afternoon, they came to a town he remembered. The small cathedral stood like torn lacework against the sky. Birds settled in rows on the empty windows. Nettles grew in the aisle, and stone figures, impaled on rusty spikes of wire, were crumbling away.

But it looks too old a piece of wreckage, he thought. That must be the war before last. Two generations, ruined, lay side by side. Among them, people went on bicycles, to and fro, between the impoverished shops and scarred dwellings.

'After wars, when there is so little time for patching up before the next explosion, what hope is there?' he began.

She didn't answer, stared out of the window, the car jolting so that her teeth chattered.

*

When Richard was alone in the hotel bedroom, he tried, by spreading about some of Louise's belongings, to make the place seem less temporary. He felt guilty at having had his own way, at keeping her from Paris until the next day and delaying her in this dismal place. It was destined to be, so far as they were concerned, one of those provincial backgrounds, fleeting, meaningless, that travellers erase from experience – the different hotel rooms run together to form one room, this room, any room.

When he had put the pink jars and bottles out in a row above the hand basin, he became dubious. She would perhaps sweep them all back into her case, saying, 'Why unpack before we reach Paris?' and he would find that he had worsened the situation, after all, as he so often did, meaning to better it.

His one piece of selfishness – this halt on the way – she had stubbornly resisted, and now she had gone off to buy picture-postcards for the children, as if no one would think of them if she did not.

Because he often wondered how she looked when he was not there, if her face ever smoothed, he went to the window, hoping to see her coming down the little street. He wanted to catch in advance, to be prepared for, her mood. But she was not moody nowadays. A dreadful consistency discoloured her behaviour.

He pulled the shutters apart and was faced with a waste of fallen masonry, worse now that it was seen from above, and unrecognizable. The humped-up, dark cathedral stood in an untidy space, as if the little shops and cafés he remembered had receded in awe. Dust flowed along the streets, spilling from ruined walls across pavements. Rusty grasses covered debris and everywhere the air was unclean with grit.

Dust, he thought, leaning on the iron rail above window-boxes full of shepherd's-purse – dust has the connotation of despair. In the end, shall we go up in a great swirl of it? He imagined something like the moon's surface, pock-marked, cratered, dry, deserted. When he was young, he had not despaired. Then, autumn leaves, not dust, had blown about these streets; chimes dropped like water, uneven, inconsequential, over rooftops; and the lime-trees yellowed along neat boulevards. Yet, in the entrancement of nostalgia, he remembered, at best, an imperfect happiness and, for the most part, an agony of conjecture and expectancy. Crossing the vestibule of this very hotel, he had turned; his eyes had always sought the letter-rack. The Channel lay between him and his love, who with her timid smile, her mild grimace, had moaned that she could not put pen to paper, was illiterate, never had news; though loving him inordinately, could not spell, never had postage stamps; her ink dried as it approached the page; her parents interrupted. Yes, she had loved him to excess but had seldom written, and now went off in the dust and squalor for picture-postcards for their children.

At the window, waiting for her to appear, he felt that the dust and destruction had pinned down his courage. Day after day had left its residue, sifting down through him – cynicism and despair. He wondered what damage he had wreaked upon her.

Across the street, which once had been narrow and now was open to the sky, a nun went slowly, carrying bread under her arm. The wind plucked her veil. A thin cat followed her. They picked their way across the rubble. The cat stopped once and lifted a paw, licked it carefully, and put it back into the grit. The faint sound of trowel on stone rang out, desultory, hopeless, a frail weapon against so convincing a destruction. That piteous tap, tap turned him away from the window. He could not bear the futility of the sound, or the thought of the monstrous task ahead, and now feared, more than all he could imagine, the sight of his wife hurrying back down the street, frowning, the picture-postcards in her hand.

Louise was late. Richard sat drinking Pernod at a table in the bar where he could see her come into the hotel. There was only the barman to talk to. Rather clouded with drink, Richard leaned on his elbow, describing the town as it had been. The barman, who was Australian, knew only too well. After the '14–'18 war, he had put his savings into a small café across the road. 'I knew it,' Richard said eagerly, forgetting the lacuna in both years and buildings, the gap over which the nun, the cat had picked their way.

'I'll get the compensation some day,' the Australian said, wiping the bar. 'Start again. Something different.'

When a waiter came for drinks, the barman spoke in slow but confident French, probably different from an Englishman's French, Richard thought, though he could not be sure; a Frenchman would know.

'She gets later and later,' he said solemnly.

'Well, if she doesn't come, that's what she's bound to do,' the barman agreed.

'It was a shock to me, the damage of this town.'

'Twelve months ago, you ought to have seen it,' the barman said.

'That's the human characteristic – patience, building up.'

'You might say the same of ants.'

'Making something from nothing,' Richard said. 'I'll take another Pernod.'

The ringing sound of the trowel was in his ears. He saw plodding humanity piling up the bricks again, hanging sacking over the empty windows, temporizing, camping-out in the shadow of even greater disaster, raking ashes, the vision lost. He felt terribly sorry for humanity, as if he did not belong to it. The Pernod shifted him away and made him solitary. Then he thought of Louise and that he must go to look for her. Sometimes she punished him by staying away unaccountably, but knowing that did not lessen his anxiety. He wished that they were at peace together, that the war between them might be over for ever, for if he did not have her, he did not have all he had yearned for; steadied himself with, fighting in the jungle; holding fast, for her, to life; disavowing (with terrible concentration) any danger to her.

He wondered, watching the barman's placid polishing of another man's glasses, if they could begin again, he and Louise, with nothing, from scratch, abandoning the past.

'First I must find her,' he thought. His drinking would double her fury if she had been lingering to punish him, punishing herself with enforced idling in those unfestive streets; a little scared, he imagined; hesitantly casual.

She came as he was putting a foot unsteadily to the floor. She stood at the door with an unexpectant look. When he smiled and greeted her, she tried to give two different smiles at once – one for the barman to see (controlled, marital), the other less a smile than a negation of it ('I see nothing to smile about').

'Darling, what will you have?'

She surveyed the row of bottles hesitantly, but her hesitation was for the barman's benefit. Richard knew her pause meant an unwillingness to drink in such company, in such a mood, and that in a minute she would say 'A dry Martini,' because once he had told her she should not drink gin abroad. She sat down beside him in silence.

'A nice dry Martini?' he suddenly asked, thinking of the man with the trowel, the nun with the bread, the battered cathedral, everybody's poor start. Again she tried to convey two meanings; to the barman that she was casual about her Martini, to her husband that she was casual about him.

Richard's head was swimming. He patted his wife's knee.

'Did you get the postcards all right?'

'Of course.' Her glance brushed his hand off her knee. 'Cheers!' she held her glass at half-mast very briefly, spoke in the most annulling way, drank. Those deep lines from her nose to her mouth met the glass.

'Cheers, my darling!' he said, watching her. Her annoyance froze the silence.

Oh, from the most unpromising material, he thought, but he did seem to see some glimmer ahead, if only of his own patience, his own perseverance, which appeared, in this frame of mind, in this place, a small demand upon him.

Notes on the Authors

BERYL BAINBRIDGE was born in Liverpool in the 1930s and spent her early working years there as an actress in repertory. She took up writing after leaving the theatre to have a baby. Several of her novels, including *The Dressmaker* and *A Quiet Life*, are set against an unobtrusive but impeccably realized wartime or post-war background. Her recent fiction – notably *The Birthday Boys, Every Man for Himself* and *Master Georgie* – has been based on historical events. Among the finest British novelists writing today, she has won many literary awards and has been shortlisted five times for the Booker Prize. She has also written five plays for stage and television. 'Bread and Butter Smith' appeared in *Mum and Mrs Armitage* (1985); her collected stories were published in 1995.

A. L. BARKER has been writing since the age of nine. She worked in a City office after leaving school, and spent six months in the Land Army and three years working for the National Fire Service during the war before joining the BBC. *Innocents*, her first book of stories including 'The Iconoclasts', was published in 1947. Several more volumes of stories followed, including *Life Stories*, in which fiction is juxtaposed with fragments of autobiography as they shaped her writing, and *Element of Doubt*, a collection of ghost stories. Her stories are masterpieces of economy and precision, often compacted with shocking intensity. Her novel, *John Brown's Body* (1969), was shortlisted for the Booker Prize and is being reissued with another novel, *The Gooseboy* by Virago (1999) who are also publishing her most recent book, *The Haunt*.

ELIZABETH BOWEN (1899–1973), one of this century's finest novelists and short-story writers, was born in Dublin but brought up in England; *Bowen s Court* (1942) recounts the history of her family and their home in County Cork. Her first book of short stories, *Encounters*, was published in 1923, the year of her marriage. The war years could justifiably be called the peak of her life; she was at the height of her writing powers, identified closely with England in crisis, and she was also deeply in love. She stayed on in London throughout the Blitz, working as an air-raid warden in between journalistic assignments and her 'Activities' for the Ministry of

Information, which involved reporting on Irish attitudes to the war. Her novel *The Heat of the Day* (1949), and collection of stories, *The Demon Lover* (1945), both written and set in wartime, are among the most memorable British fiction from this era. Her many other works include *The Death of the Heart* (1938) and *Look at All Those Roses* (stories, 1941).

KAY BOYLE (1902–1992) was born in Minnesota, and travelled to Europe in 1922. In Paris she became friends with a group of expatriate artists and began writing for avant-garde magazines. Her first novel, *Plagued by the Nightingale,* was published in 1930; since then she has written, edited and translated more than thirty books, including short stories, poetry and essays. In 1941 she left occupied France to return to America, but was back in Paris as correspondent for the *New Yorker* in 1945. She was awarded the 1941 O. Henry Memorial Prize for her story 'Defeat'.

ANN CHADWICK (1921–1997) had stories published in several 'little magazines' during a peripatetic wartime spent in London, Gloucestershire and Scotland. The sailor she was married to when she wrote 'The Sailor's Wife' was Lynn Chadwick, the sculptor. The story was published in *English Story* VI, edited by Woodrow Wyatt. She stopped writing while bringing up a family of five children, and latterly lived in Wales.

EDNA FERBER (1887–1968), American novelist and playwright, a vivid and powerful storyteller in the traditional mould. The daughter of a Hungarian storekeeper, she started out as a journalist and went on to write a string of bestselling novels including *Showboat, Cimarron* and *Giant,* all later made into films, and several plays. Her central characters are strong pioneer women, dedicated to their families and the land: there is often an underlying anti-racial theme. 'Grandma Isn't Playing' was written in 1942 in response to the war, whose aftermath left her deeply disillusioned. She introduced the story as follows in her collection *One Basket:* 'Only during World War I and World War II have I ever written according to plan or theme ordered or suggested by someone else . . . In "Grandma Isn't Playing", one can detect . . . the somewhat heavy tool of propaganda. A necessary and an important wartime weapon, but often unwieldy in unaccustomed hands.'

PAT FRANK's story 'The Bomb' appeared in the *Strand Magazine,* 1941.

DIANA GARDNER (1913–1997) was the youngest of three, with two brothers; her mother died when she was nine. She became a dedicated short-story writer from the age of eleven, and her work appeared in nearly every literary review, including *Horizon,* during the Second World War. In 1947 Tambimuttu of Poetry London Editions published a collection of her stories *Halfway Down the Cliff,* and her novel *The Indian Woman,* based on one of her stories, was published in 1953. She also studied art, and several one-person exhibitions of her watercolours were held in London and out of town.

INEZ HOLDEN, journalist and writer, was a contributor to vários periodicals during and after the war. She was a special correspondent in Germany just after the war, covered the Nuremberg Trials, the Slansky Tribunal and other events and wrote two books about her experiences during the war in an aircraft factory and a Royal Ordnance Factory. Perhaps her best-known novel is *The Owner* (1952). She was a close friend of Stevie Smith, and each based fictional characters on the other – Inez appears as Lopez in Stevie Smith's third novel *The Holiday* and 'The Story of a Story' (see under Stevie Smith), while Inez Holden's character Felicity strongly resembles Stevie Smith in the fictionalized diary *It Was Different at the Time.*

ANNA KAVAN (1901–68), née Helen Ferguson, was born of English parents in France; she wrote several conventional novels under her original name in the 1920s and 30s. She took the name of Anna Kavan by deed poll, and after a breakdown and treatment in a mental hospital wrote the remarkable series of sketches *Asylum Piece* (1940). During the war she worked on *Horizon,* and 'Face of My People' is one of several stories in *I am Lazarus* (1945) which first appeared in the magazine. The rich, strange, visionary qualities of her writing – notably in *Ice,* a novel, and *Julia and the Bazooka,* posthumously published stories – have given her a cult following. She was a heroin addict for over thirty years, and died in London holding her 'bazooka' – a plastic syringe.

MOLLY LEFEBURE was born in London, her studies at London University were interrupted by war, and she became a reporter in east London and the first regular woman police-court reporter. She was then taken on as secretary to Home Office pathologist Keith Simpson and spent most of the war working with him in public mortuaries (another first, if not an enviable one, for a woman); she wrote an account of this work in *Evidence For the Crown* (1954). She married at the end of the war, and had two children. After working for fifteen years with the GLC youth service she took to full-time writing; her books include lives of Samuel Taylor Coleridge and Sara Coleridge. Her novel *Blitz!* (1988) was based on 'Night in the Front Line'.

ROSAMOND LEHMANN (1901–1990), novelist and short-story writer, was born in Buckinghamshire and studied at Girton, Cambridge. Her first novel *Dusty Answer* caused a sensation when it was first published in 1927; it was followed by *A Note in Music,* then by *Invitation to the Waltz* and its sequel *The Weather in the Streets,* all written during the thirties, which established her as a leading novelist of her generation. Her finest achievement, *The Echoing Grove,* appeared in 1953. A writer of great subtlety and sensitivity, she was outstandingly perceptive on the pains of women in love. During the war her brother, John Lehmann, persuaded her to write stories for *Penguin New Writing,* which he edited; 'When the Waters Came' was among them. They were collected in *The Gipsy's Baby* (1946).

DORIS LESSING (1919–) was born of British parents in Iran; the family emigrated to a farm in Rhodesia when she was five. She came to England in 1949 with the manuscript of her first novel, *The Grass Is Singing;* it was published in 1950, and became an international success. This prolific and highly influential writer has since written 21 novels, including the seminal *The Golden Notebook, Memoirs of a Survivor* and two five-volume novel cycles, the *Children of Violence* series and the futuristic *Canopus in Argos: Archives* (1979–83). She has also written eleven short-story collections, three plays, an opera libretto, eight non-fiction books and two volumes of autobiography. Her stories about Africa are collected in *This Was the Old Chief's Country* and *The Sun Beneath Their Feet.*

ROSE MACAULAY (1881–1958) lived in Italy for seven years as a child and never lost her thirst for travel. She studied history at Oxford and subsequently produced a steady flow of novels, poetry and non-fiction which won her high literary standing, although her prevailing dry, satirical tone is less popular today. Among her best novels are the historical *They Were Defeated* (1932), and *The World My Wilderness* (1950), set in post-war London and France. She was created a Dame Commander of the British Empire in 1958, shortly before her death. The war years were deeply troubled for her personally. In 1939 her married lover was seriously injured in a car crash while she was driving. 'Miss Anstruther's Letters' was written when he was dying of cancer in 1942, shortly after her flat and all her possessions were destroyed in an air raid. She wrote few short stories; this outstanding exception, which she described as 'unoriginal, but veracious (mainly)', was written at the request of Storm Jameson for *London Calling,* an anthology of British writing for American publication after the US entered the war.

OLIVIA MANNING (1908–80) was the daughter of a naval officer and an Irish mother: born in Portsmouth, she came to London in her early twenties after an art-school training. Her first novel, *The Wind Changes*, was published in 1937. The war years were the subject of much of her later fiction, including her two best-known works, the *Balkan Trilogy* and *Levant Trilogy*. Just before war was declared she married R. D. Smith, a British Council lecturer (her friend Stevie Smith was a bridesmaid) and went with him to Bucharest; they went on to Greece, to be evacuated to Egypt as the Nazis moved in. From 1941 to 1945 she worked in Jerusalem at the Public Information Office and for the British Council. The death of her brother at sea in 1941 was a source of lasting grief. After the war she moved back to London. As well as twelve novels she wrote two collections of short stories, *Growing Up* (1948) from which 'A Journey' is taken, and *A Romantic Hero* (1967). 'A Journey' is characteristic of her comment that 'My subject is simply life as I have experienced it, and I am happiest when I am writing of things I know.'

ROSAMOND OPPERSDORFF was an American by birth who until the war lived most of her life in Paris. Her husband was Polish, and after leaving France in 1940 she worked in a Polish military hospital in Scotland. 'I Was Too Ignorant' was published in *New Writing and Daylight*, edited by John Lehmann, in 1942.

MOLLIE PANTER-DOWNES (1906–1997), Anglo-Irish writer whose first novel was published when she was eighteen. She wrote four more, but referred to *One Fine Day* (1947) as her 'only novel'. Certainly it is a fine achievement; a subtly evocative picture of an ordinary middle-class household coming to terms with post-war life made shabbier, harder, yet imbued with quiet optimism. She described herself first and foremost as a reporter; she was the London correspondent for the *New Yorker* for some forty years from 1939, and her wartime 'Letters from London', collected in *Letters from England* for American publication, enjoyed a success similar to Jan Struther's *Mrs Miniver*. 'Goodbye, My Love' appeared in the *New Yorker* in 1941.

DOROTHY PARKER (1893–1967): born Dorothy Rothschild in West End, New Jersey. Her bittersweet verse and stories, collected in *The Portable Dorothy Parker* in 1944, evoked the bright, brittle, wisecracking pre-war era which had brought her fame as a contributor to *Vogue, Vanity Fair* and the *New Yorker* and as a central figure of the celebrated Algonquin Hotel Round Table. 'The Lovely Leave' was one of the last stories she wrote; it appeared in 1943, and is cruelly apposite in the light of her own experience. Her first husband, Edwin Parker, was posted overseas in the First World War and they divorced after years of separation; her second marriage to Alan Campbell was also a war casualty (though they remarried in 1950).

BARBARA PYM (1913–80) was born in Oswestry, Shropshire and educated at St Hilda's, Oxford. During the war she served in the WRNS in Britain and Naples. Her first novel, *Some Tame Gazelle*, was published in 1950, followed by four others within the next decade. After her publishers turned down her seventh novel she had nothing published for sixteen years, until the *Times Literary Supplement* asked selected critics to nominate the most underrated writer of the past seventy-five years. She was the only author to be mentioned twice – notably by Philip Larkin. A new book, *Quartet in Autumn*, was accepted for publication; she took up writing again, and two more novels followed, the last published posthumously. 'Goodbye Balkan Capital' first appeared in 1988.

JEAN RHYS (1894–1979) was born Gwendolyn Williams, in Dominica. She was sent to England at sixteen, and ran away from drama school to join the chorus line in a touring theatre production. Her first book of stories, *The Left Bank* (1927), written in Paris after the break-up of her first marriage, was followed by four novels in the next decade, all with a similar tough-talking yet intensely vulnerable heroine. Their passivity is old-fashioned, but the cool, laconic treatment is entirely modern. The Second World War, for her, 'smashed everything'; she had lost touch with her daughter in Holland, and her second husband had joined the air force, leaving her alone. 'I Spy a Stranger' is one of several stories from this time describing nervous breakdown. With the failure of *Good Morning, Midnight* (1939) her work went out of print and it was only after nearly twenty reclusive years that she was 'rediscovered' and her last, best-known novel, *Wide Sargasso Sea*, published. A third book of stories, *Sleep It Off Lady*, was published in 1976.

MARGERY SHARP (1905–1991), English novelist, playwright and short-story writer, popular in 1930s Britain and America for her light comedies with ingenious plots. After the success of *The Nutmeg Tree* (1937), her cheerfully loose-living heroine Julia Packett enjoyed further adventures in the *Saturday Evening Post*. 'Night Engagement' was written for the wartime magazine *Lilliput* (1941).

STEVIE SMITH (1902–71) was born in Hull; when she was three her mother brought her and her sister to live with her aunt in Palmer's Green, North London, where she stayed for the rest of her life. She wrote three novels: *Novel on Yellow Paper* (1936), *Over the Frontier* (1938) and *The Holiday* (1949), and nine volumes of poetry, in which the idiosyncratic blend of black humour and childlike directness are underlined by her constant preoccupation with death. By the 1950s she was much in demand for live performances, reading and singing her poems to her own music. 'Sunday at Home' caused a permanent breach between Stevie (who appears in the story as 'Greta') and the married friends on whom she based the main characters, even after she changed the title from its original and more pointed 'Enemy Action'. It was broadcast on radio in 1949. After the falling-out she wrote an account of the difficulties of making 'these transcripts from life' in 'The Story of a Story'.

JEAN STAFFORD (1916–79) was brought up in Colorado, the daughter of a western writer and a nurse. In 1936 she won a travelling scholarship to Heidelberg, and on her return to America settled on the east coast. In 1940 she married the poet Robert Lowell, against the wishes of his patrician Boston family; the theme of the misfit in urbane establishment society recurs in her fiction. Her first novel, *Boston Adventure*, was published in 1944, and became a bestseller; at the same time her marriage became a disastrous private battleground, and she and Lowell were divorced in 1950. She married twice more, the third time to the journalist and critic A. J. Liebling. Her later novels, *The Mountain Lion* and *The Catherine Wheel,* were less popular than the first and she switched to writing her stylish, elaborately crafted short stories many of which, including 'The Maiden', first appeared in the *New Yorker.* Her *Collected Stories* won the Pulitzer Prize in 1970.

JAN STRUTHER (1901–53), pen-name of Joyce Anstruther, later Joyce Maxtone Graham – she took the pseudonym because both her mother and mother-in-law were writers. In the 1930s her mainly humorous articles and light verse were published in *Punch,* the *Spectator* and other magazines. The *Mrs Miniver* sketches based on her own family life first appeared weekly in *The Times* in 1938–9, and the book became a bestseller. Mrs Miniver's patriotic sentiments notwithstanding, Jan Struther was criticized in Britain for her departure to America with her two younger children soon after war was declared; she stayed there for the duration.

ELIZABETH TAYLOR (1912–75): her subtle and delicate craft, and the small worlds she chose to portray, belie the work of a major artist. She was born Elizabeth Coles in Reading, Berkshire; the daughter of an insurance inspector, she worked as a governess and in a library before marrying at twenty-four. She wrote her first novel, *At Mrs Lippincote's* (1945), while her husband was in the air force during the war; eleven more novels followed, the last published posthumously. Her stories appeared in leading magazines including the *New Yorker* and the *Saturday Evening Post,* and were collected in four volumes: *Hester Lilly and Other Stories* (1954) (from which 'Gravement Endommagé' is taken), *The Blush and Other Stories* (1958), A *Dedicated Man and Other Stories* (1965) and *The Devastating Boys* (1972).

SYLVIA TOWNSEND WARNER (1893–1978) had no formal education though she was the daughter of a housemaster at Harrow school. After working in a munitions factory in the First World War she spent ten years as an editor on a ten-volume project, *Tudor Church Music,* for Oxford University Press. The success of her first novel *Lolly Willowes* (1926) encouraged her to take up full-time writing. During the 1930s she became active in politics in response to events in Spain and Nazi Germany, and in 1937 she worked briefly for the Red Cross Bureau in Barcelona. Her writing was by then known in the United States as well as Britain and many of her stories first appeared in the *New Yorker.* She was in New York for a writers' conference when war was declared, but returned to England soon afterwards. After the war she added an acclaimed biography of T. H. White to her novels, stories, journalism and poetry. Two of her eight short-story collections, *A Garland of Straw* (1943) and *The Museum of Cheats* (1947), are full of witty, compassionate glimpses into wartime life.

MALACHI WHITAKER (1895–1975) – 'the Bradford Chekhov', as one critic called her – made her name with four books of stories, all published before the Second World War, and then declared herself 'written out'. Born Marjorie Olive Taylor, she left school early to work in her father's bookbinding business, and married a Yorkshire businessman. She was a self-taught writer, and wrote prolifically as a child, throwing everything away. Under the pen-name of Malachi Whitaker she sent a story to Middleton Murry at the *Adelphi,* a magazine she had admired in the public library. He printed her stories, and her first collection was published to literary acclaim in 1929. The vivid, spare, unsentimental stories are perfectly matched to her first subject, the people and landscapes of her native Yorkshire.

Hearts Undefeated

Women's Writing of the
Second World War

Here there are broken homes, burnt homes,
But hearts undefeated to meet each day.
F. Tennyson Jesse, 1940

For Anne Stern

Contents

Abbreviations

AFS   Auxiliary Fire Service
ARP   Air Raid Precautions
ATS   Auxiliary Territorial Service
BEF   British Expeditionary Force
BUF   British Union of Fascists
CO   Commanding Officer
ENSA Entertainments National Service Association
FANY First Aid Nursing Yeomanry
LDV   Local Defence Volunteers (later Home Guard)
MT   Motor Transport
NAAFI Navy, Army and Airforce Institutes (operated canteens)
POW   Prisoner of War
WAAF Women's Auxiliary Air Force
WLA   Women's Land Army
WRNS Women's Royal Naval Service (known as Wrens)
WVS   Women's Voluntary Service

[...]   indicates a cut made by the editor

Small changes in spelling and punctuation have been made for the
sake of consistency

Introduction

Journalism has become the eyes of modern writing.
DIANA TRILLING, *HARPER'S MAGAZINE*, MAY 1944.

The act of keeping the record straight is valuable in itself.
MARTHA GELLHORN, *THE FACE OF WAR*, 1959.

Any authentic record seems valuable because from thousands of [. . .] stories we can construct a picture out of the jigsaw of formless details.
BRYHER, *LIFE AND LETTERS TODAY*, OCTOBER 1941.

The Second World War inspired an outburst of women's writing, creating a rich and moving legacy for readers in the years to come. In books and magazines, letters and diaries, countless women – some of them writers by profession but many of them not – put down on paper their versions of the war. A selection of that material is reproduced here, telling us what the war felt and looked like to the women experiencing it. 'Fiction pales by comparison,' wrote Diana Trilling in 1944. Non-fiction was acknowledged as the best medium for keeping 'the record straight', as Martha Gellhorn put it. But the record of the war is not one record. An anthology with its 'jigsaw of details' can help to give a more complete picture, a fuller record than a single account. It can also try to do justice to the immense variety of experience that opened up to women at the time, as well as to the extraordinary literary talent that took this opportunity to flourish.

The Function of Writing in Wartime

This is just a typical experience of hundreds of simple people who never thought they would have to face anything like it. So I record it.
VERE HODGSON, 4 JANUARY 1942, *FEW EGGS AND NO ORANGES*

The memories being recorded and published in recent years add immeasurably to our understanding of the war. This anthology contains no oral accounts because it has a different emphasis. It shows how women wrote the war at the time, what it looked like from their perspective as they tried to shape and make sense of their experiences. How did they want to present the war to themselves and others at the time? How were they constrained by that very war itself in how they might write it? Memory has its own controlling pressures, some of them nostalgic; the writing of a particular moment is born out of different needs.

For some women, writing itself became an imperative and symbolic act, keeping 'alive something that is vital to us', and now 'needed more than ever', as Rumer Godden wrote to her sister in April 1940.[1] Freedom of expression was frequently extolled as one of the principles the Allies were fighting for, and the pen was a weapon available to both sexes. At the beginning of the war Virginia Woolf used an uncharacteristically bellicose image about her writing when she described 'the little pitter patter of ideas' as 'my whiff of shot in the cause of freedom'. 'Thinking', she wrote in 1940, 'is my fighting.'[2] This desire also lies behind Elizabeth Bowen's suggestion that all wartime writing is 'in a sense [...] resistance writing'.[3]

Writing filled many needs. For some, 'keeping the record straight' became an obsession. 'I am hardly awake in the morning when I reach for this book to write in it,' noted Sarah Gertrude Millin in 1942.[4] She published a book for each year of the war, mixtures of news reporting and personal commentary, which were her way of imposing order on the war. Leonora Eyles, another professional writer, had a more specific obligation. *For My Enemy Daughter* was the letter that could not be sent to her

---

1. Letter of April 1940, quoted in Rumer Godden, *A Time To Dance, No Time To Weep*, Macmillan, 1987.

2. Entries for 16 September 1939 and 15 May 1940, *The Diary of Virginia Woolf*, Vol. V 1936–1941, ed. A.O. Bell, The Hogarth Press, 1984.

3. Elizabeth Bowen, Preface to the American edition of *The Demon Lover*, 1945, reprinted in *Collected Impressions*, Longmans, 1950.

4. Sarah Gertrude Millin, *The Pit of the Abyss*, Faber and Faber, 1946.

daughter who had married an Italian and was living in Italy. Julia Tremayne was also cut off from her daughter, and her as yet unseen granddaughter. Living on the German-occupied Channel Island of Sark, she could not send letters to England, but wrote to her daughter frequently. The letters were then hidden carefully, 'and as shooting seems to be the penalty for most things I must make my cubby-hole very safe.'[5] Writing letters, even if they could not be sent, created a reassuring fantasy of communication.

Others used writing to keep in touch more directly, the war making letter-writers out of many who had not been accustomed to express themselves on paper. This was the last great age of letter-writing between families split up by evacuation, military service and war work. The collections of letters in the Imperial War Museum testify to the literary powers developed by many women who often wrote as the family's correspondent to absent members. Women's particular skills as letter-writers were recognized in the practice which spread among servicemen abroad of asking visiting female celebrities to write home for them. Elsie and Doris Waters ('Gert and Daisy'), Joyce Grenfell, Eleanor Roosevelt and Adele Astaire were all inundated with requests and complied good-naturedly. Joyce Grenfell tried 'hard to make each one different and try to imagine the homes the letters are going to. But it takes time. However, it seems, mysteriously, to give pleasure.'[6]

With personal letters written to strangers, the traditional categories of letters (written to others you know), books (written to others you do not know) and diaries (written for yourself) started to blur. The movement seemed to have been towards the public. The private form of the diary sometimes took on the function of a letter. Vere Hodgson started her diary in order to send it to her cousin in Rhodesia; Hilda Silberman duplicated her letters to friends in America 'as a general news-letter from England in wartime'. She must have been one of the pioneers of this new form of letter, and was 'gratified' when recipients forwarded them

---

5. Julia Tremayne, *War on Sark*, Webb & Bower, 1981.

6. Joyce Grenfell, Hyderabad, 18 December 1944, *The Time of My Life*, *Entertaining the Troops, Her Wartime Journals*, ed. J. Roose-Evans, Hodder & Stoughton, 1989.

to the local press. 'Thus a wider circle gets direct news from Britain.'[7] Books, on the other hand, often seemed to want to forge a more personal note, to close the distance between author and reader into an intimate conversation between two people. In 1940 Naomi Jacob began *Me – In War-Time*: 'You must take it as a very ordinary woman, trying to discuss with you her everyday problems, which, it may be, are the same problems as you, yourself face.' Two years later Vera Brittain cast her controversial pacifist pamphlet, *Humiliation with Honour*, in the form of letters addressed to her fifteen-year-old son. Letters were a powerful wartime form. Vera Lynn's popular radio programme 'Sincerely Yours' was billed in the *Radio Times*, 'To the men of the Forces: A letter in words and music from Vera Lynn.'

Naomi Jacob 'trying to discuss with you', Vere Hodgson sending her diary abroad, Joyce Grenfell writing to the 'wives, mothers and a sweetheart of four of the very ill boys in the big orthopaedic ward' – whether they broaden or contract the traditional form, they all illustrate the same phenomenon: the function of women's wartime writing as friendship. It is not surprising that friendship should be particularly important in wartime, and writing could sustain and develop comforting relationships. Anne Frank's *Diary*, perhaps the most famous of all women's wartime writing, is addressed to Kitty, the diary with its own status as the best friend much needed during Anne's time in hiding from the Nazis. In June 1942, when Anne received the diary, she wrote on the flyleaf: 'I hope I shall be able to confide in you completely, as I have never been able to do in anyone before, and I hope that you will be a great support and comfort to me.' By September the *Diary* was addressed to other friends as well as Kitty, and Anne added to the flyleaf:

> I have had a lot of support from you so far, and also from our beloved club to whom I now write regularly, I think this way of keeping a diary is much nicer and now I can hardly wait for when I have time to write in you. *I am, Oh, so glad that I took you along.*

The diary remained vital. 'I will write my diary and keep

---

7. Hilda Silberman, *Unimportant Letters of Important Years 1941–1951*, The Favil Press, 1951.

sane' was Naomi Mitchison's resolution at the beginning of the war.[8] Like many others, she recognized how helpful writing could be in affording her a measure of control over her life. Joan Veazey strapped her diary to her wrist so that she could write as she worked through the Blitz in her husband's London parish,[9] an ingenious device but presumably a bit awkward. It shows how important keeping a diary must have been to her. Others faced more than awkwardness for the sake of their diaries. Bessy Myers was imprisoned by the Germans in France in 1940, and realized what an incriminating document hers was – 'I must be mad, mad, mad'.[10] Before the war was over women were rereading their diaries to remember themselves as they had been, and the selves they had written and created in the earlier years of the war.

There was another impulse for some of these wartime writers, as the subtitle of Vere Hodgson's *Few Eggs and No Oranges* suggests: 'A Diary Showing how Unimportant People in London and Birmingham Lived through the War Years 1939–1945'; Hilda Silberman's title, too, *Unimportant Letters of Important Years*. The word 'unimportant' appears again and again in women's descriptions of themselves. So does 'ordinary'. Why this insistence? In part, it seems to be a signal, a woman declaring her place in the ranks of the People's War. Partly too, it was a recognition of the significance of this particular moment in history, when ordinary existence was intersected by the extraordinary phenomenon of war. It was also a flag waving in celebration of ordinary life, those virtues of British life to be valued, defended, fought for, and carefully documented. The writer needed to make the ordinary visible and therefore valuable. Margaret Robson explained that she was publishing her late husband's letters 'because I thought that there was room for a war book which was not written

---

8. Naomi Mitchison, *You May Well Ask, A Memoir 1920–1940*, Gollancz, 1979.

9. See Michael Moynihan, *People At War 1939–1945*, David and Charles, 1974.

10. Bessy Myers, *Captured, My Experiences as an Ambulance Driver and as a Prisoner of the Nazis*, George Harrap, 1941.

around some exciting incident or escape, but showed war as it really was from the point of view of the ordinary front-line soldier'.[11]

Through writing, then, women could memorialize. They could also reach out, personalize, soften the sharp edge of war. ATS women who packed spares for tank repairs going overseas often included personal notes, a practice frowned on by the army. Landgirls put messages in sacks of potatoes and Red Cross knitters tucked notes into the toes of socks going out to India. Children's clothes and shoes coming to Britain from America sometimes held a letter and a prayer or a blessing for the recipient.

Writing could also help to keep the war at bay; which could be one reason why wartime writing is often more light-hearted and flippant than we might expect. Anita Leslie worked as an ambulance driver in France, a harrowing experience, yet her accounts came as a surprise to her family: 'We were rather shocked, dear, by your very frivolous letter.'[12] Writing could offer a useful turning away from war. Anne Lee-Michell commented later on her wartime diary: 'Many entries now seem to me facetious. I think we craved humour during our anxieties and that I recorded anything that made us laugh.'[13]

To write is also to have a voice for others. Some of the women in this collection have written on behalf of others who were unable to do so: those in concentration camps, those who died, those living in unbearable conditions, and especially those too young to write for themselves. They also wrote to protest against anti-semitism and racism.

Women and the Literature of War

You would need to be half-dead not to feel observant and curious *now* about the general scene – and all our note-taking, the good

---

11. Postscript to Walter Robson, *Letters from a Soldier*, Faber and Faber, 1960.
12. Anita Leslie, *Train to Nowhere*, Hutchinson, 1953.
13. Quoted in Moynihan, *People At War*.

with the bad, will be useful some day, to those whose job it will be to 'compose' this time, in terms of history or of art.

KATE O'BRIEN, *THE FORTNIGHTLY*, 1941.

As truthful as history but as readable as fiction.

VERA BRITTAIN, *TESTAMENT OF EXPERIENCE*, 1957.

Women have always had a role in war and the literature of war. From *The Iliad* onwards, when Hector tells his wife Andromache how she will grieve and 'ache again' after his death in battle, women have had their place as watchers and mourners, and as symbols of what men are fighting for. These are passive roles; until this century women were rarely involved in war and rarely wrote about it. It was with the First World War that they entered the arena of war, nursing and driving ambulances near the front lines, making munitions and filling men's jobs at home. These new experiences laid the foundations for the new genre of women's war writing, which rapidly established itself with a crop of poems, journals and novels.[14] With the Second World War the relation between women and war expanded and intensified dramatically. For the first time in this country the whole population was involved in the war, the women and children as well as the men. Bombs are no respecters of age or sex. And for the first time in the history of this country, women were conscripted into the forces or war-related jobs.

These new and stirring times for women had to be recorded, and in new ways. Choices were made on the first day of the war, as Virginia Woolf's diary for 3 September 1939 shows: 'M(abel) said train very empty. I believe little exact notes are more interesting than reflections.' They certainly were, and Woolf was not alone in her appreciation of the small facts rather than the large acts of war. It was the effects rather than the deeds of war which interested women writers. War was forcing new conjunctions

---

14. See Claire Tylee, *The Great War and Women's Consciousness*, Macmillan, 1990.

between public and private in their own lives, and these conjunctions called for expression. New hybrids emerged as women writers blended previously discrete genres such as journalism, fiction and autobiography. Sometimes they anticipated later literary developments. Clare Boothe's description of her writing looks towards the New Journalism of the 1960s: 'I was interested far less in events themselves than in the effect they had on people's hearts and minds. Above all, I was interested in how *I* felt about how they felt, which is a highly emotional and egoistic approach that would disqualify anybody at once as an "objective journalist".'[15] She and other women used their brief to exploit the 'personal angle' in order to explore the effects of the war upon the individual.

Vera Brittain's success with her First World War *Testament of Youth* had shown how a 'new type of autobiography', as she called it, could do justice to women's experience of war. This autobiographical impulse combined with women's traditional propensity towards the novel, and with the documentary styles of the 1930s, to initiate some strikingly apt innovations. In 1941 Inez Holden published *Night Shift*, a highly acclaimed series of sketches of work in an aircraft factory. It is narrative by snapshot, setting up and wilfully shattering the expectations of fiction. At the end it abruptly shatters itself when the factory is suddenly blown to pieces. Kay Boyle's novel, *Primer for Combat* (1943), parallels a sympathetically observed report of the fall of France with a more bitterly described story of a marital break-up. Sarah Gertrude Millin's books put detailed journalism alongside disjointed accounts of her own experience and opinions, while Amy St Loe Strachey's *Borrowed Children* (1940) mixes diary and case-history, story and sociology. Stratchey's hope seems to be that the intractable problems created by evacuation will be dissolved by the wish-fulfilling structures of romance. Edith Olivier and Storm Jameson provided themselves with fictional personae for their wartime diaries, and Gertrude Stein brandished her own wonderful mixture of history, geography, and stream of idiosyncrasy in *Wars*

---

15. Clare Boothe, *European Spring*, Hamish Hamilton, 1941.

I Have Seen (1945). Elizabeth Bowen said that she wrote short stories instead of novels because 'during the war [. . .] it would have been impossible to have been writing only one book'.[16] Some of these books *do* seem to be more than one book, as they stretch and improvise in order to accommodate and express new experiences.

Grief and Women's Writing

Denny took the measurements (for the blackout) and began to add them up. Seeing the tea-table with [. . .] the children and the big boys still there I began to cry. I had to keep on going out during tea-time to cry on the stairs.

NAOMI MITCHISON, *YOU MAY WELL ASK, A MEMOIR 1920–1940*, 1979.

The girl in the green-grocer's shop was red-eyed this morning: her husband had been killed in Germany. I didn't sympathise: that would have seemed bathetic, somehow impertinent. Another assistant mentioned it. The girl said briefly: 'Worse has happened to others,' and walked off.

MARY SEATON, 'THOUGHTS FROM HOME', *LEAVES IN THE STORM*, SCHIMANSKY AND TREECE (EDS), 1947.

I am very much aware that I am not describing the emotional aspect of all this but it is not easy.

MARGERY ALLINGHAM, *THE OAKEN HEART*, 1941.

In men's war writing women mourn, but grief seems to be strangely absent from women's war writing. In the public arena at least, women seem to have felt the pressure of male codes of behaviour, to the extent of being unable or unwilling to show grief openly. Even the customary forms of condolence were infected by this reticence, as Virginia Woolf noticed: '"Please, no letters" I read this twice in *The Times* Deaths column from

---

16. Elizabeth Bowen, op. cit.

parents of dead officers.'[17] Woolf saw this as part of 'the myth making stage of the war we're in', in which women seemed to be caught up in the myth of the British stiff upper lip. Public grief would have been unpatriotic, feminine, weak. Writing towards the end of the war, Mary Seaton commented on 'the lack of ostentation in today's grief. It isn't just that mourning arm bands and memorial services in the village church are out of fashion. People's feelings are becoming more proudly their own affair.'[18]

The low visibility of grief in their published writing shows how women's values and emotions can never wholly enmesh with those of a nation at war. Part of women's public war language must be silent. This was almost national policy, with restraint and suppression impressed upon wives writing to their husbands away on active service. Women's magazines advised their readers not to worry their menfolk with tales of hardship or confessions of infidelity. Suppression becomes a characteristic mode for women in wartime. Perhaps this accounts for some of the popularity of the 1945 film *Brief Encounter*, a celebration of heroic suppression.

With careful attention, however, the significant gaps and silences reveal themselves: those moments, for example, when Naomi Mitchison and others go off to cry on the stairs. Or there may be a brief, painful revelation, such as the parenthesis which punctures a breezy letter about a son's departure for training: '– the nightmare I have envisaged ever since he was born: that the youth of his generation should be ruined as was my own.–'[19] Books with titles like *No Time for Tears* and *No Time to Weep* remind us of the presence of tears and weeping, even while stoically brushing them aside.

17. Virginia Woolf, entry for 3 June 1940, *The Diary of Virginia Woolf*, Vol. V.

18. Mary Seaton, 'Thoughts from Home', *Leaves in the Storm*, eds Schimansky and Treece, Lindsay Drummond, 1947.

19. Quoted in Naomi Royde Smith, *Outside Information, Being a Diary of Rumours*, Macmillan, 1941.

War from the Women's Perspective

> Didn't women have their war as well?
> VERA BRITTAIN, *TESTAMENT OF EXPERIENCE*, 1957.

The women's perspective of the Second World War seems to have three distinctive hallmarks. First, it is largely anti-war, although in a submerged way. In 1938 Virginia Woolf published *Three Guineas*, which starts from the question 'how are we to prevent war?' This would have been the desire of practically all the writers in this anthology, many of whom would also have agreed with her about the relationship between war and the construction of gender: 'No, I don't see what's (to) be done about war. It's manliness; and manliness breeds womanliness – both so hateful.'[20] War is, then, basically a male activity, to which women must always stand at an angle, however implicated they are.

Secondly, at the time, women recognized the transience of their wartime experiences. Hilary Wayne was speaking for many women when she said that 'in the ATS one felt one was suspended – disconnected from pre and post-war life'.[21] It was this very sense of disconnection, of difference whether for good or bad, which impelled women to record what they knew would be the most highly charged moments of their lives. They did not know when the war would end but they acknowledged its status in their lives as an exceptional parenthesis.

The third characteristic of the women's perspective is that it was largely outlawed by the literary world of the time. The proliferation of small magazines has often been noted, but there were surprisingly few contributions in them by women. The explanation for this was given by the leader of the pack, Cyril Connolly, editor of *Horizon*:

> We take the line that experiences connected with the blitz, the shopping queues, the home front, deserted wives, deceived husbands, broken homes, dull jobs, bad schools, group squabbles,

---

20. Letter to Shena, Lady Simon, 25 January 1941, *Leave The Letters Till We're Dead, The Letters of Virginia Woolf 1936–1941*, ed. Nigel Nicolson, The Hogarth Press, 1980.
21. Hilary Wayne, *Two Odd Soldiers*, George Allen & Unwin, 1946.

are so much a picture of our ordinary lives that unless the work-manship is outstanding we are prejudiced against them.[22]

This list effectively bans most female experience. Luckily, the women themselves did not take the Connolly line, and reached for their pens.

In compiling this collection I have, with a few exceptions, included only published materials, most of it now out of print. Given the demands of war work and the shortages of paper, the amount that was written and published during the war is astounding. But reading was of course a good way to get through some of the tedium of the war, and books and articles about the war were popular. There was, according to the official historians, 'a striking increase in the expenditure on books'.[23] 'New books appear daily,' Hilda Silberman noted in 1942, 'but in small editions and are quickly out of print.' This anthology is an attempt to rescue a fraction of the ephemeral literature of wartime books and magazines, letters and diaries.

I have chosen only what was originally published in English, and mainly from the standpoint of Britain. Boundaries had to be drawn somewhere. There are a few accounts from France, but the Far East is almost entirely missing. I have included some American women as the relationship between Britain and America was such an important part of the experience of the war in Britain.

The Imperial War Museum keeps a huge collection of unpublished writing available for public inspection. Between eight and nine hundred items on the Second World War, ranging from a single letter to multi-volume memoirs, are by women. Retrospective memoirs predominate, but there are some contemporary letters and diaries. The unpublished pieces in this anthology come from or via the Imperial War Museum: private voices of love or grief which are missing from the published accounts.

I have tried to choose what was written during the war or soon afterwards, but this has not always been possible; there are inevitably some exceptions, and also some gaps. Accounts of top secret work, for example, would have to be left till later. Sexual revelations would for the most part come later too, although the

---

22. *Horizon*, January 1944.
23. E.L. Hargreaves and M.M. Gowing, *Civil Industry and Trade*, HMSO & Longmans, 1952.

collections of personal letters in the Imperial War Museum show women writing about sex with admirable openness and frankness when they can be sure of a sympathetic reception. But on the whole there is little overt sex in this version of the war, and there is little from working class women either.

The American Martha Gellhorn listened to two WAAFs at work in a control tower and commented on 'the girls' voices that sound so remarkable to us (it is hard to decide why, perhaps because they seem so poised, so neat)'. So poised, so neat: these words could well describe much of the prose in this anthology. It is for the most part the prose of middle-class women. Many people hoped that the war would break down class barriers, and to some extent it did, with middle-class women going into factories, extending their limited circles of acquaintance and so on. But as can be seen from the paragraph in which Rose Macaulay welcomed the way the war would 'resolve class distinctions', and yet at the same time remarked how 'the less well instructed pronounced "*sireen*" for "siren",'[24] the barriers could not come down overnight. Nor would working-class women unused to writing suddenly rush to put down their experiences in print. Some of their accounts are coming out now, and a missing part of the picture is being completed.

This anthology's version of the war may, then, be an incomplete one; nevertheless it offers a wonderful body of literature to appreciate, and a way into women's wartime life as it seemed at the time. The value of this contemporary perspective is highlighted with particular neatness by the cover picture,[*] the meaning of which has shifted considerably over the years. Abram Games's recruitment poster for the ATS is one of the war's most famous images of women. At the time it was highly controversial: there was too much lipstick, too much glamour. This was not how wartime women should be depicted. The uproar reached the House of Commons and the poster was withdrawn. Fifty years later the Blonde Bombshell, as she was known, returns to grace a collection of her contemporaries' writings. She seems now not so much provocative as confident and assured, just the image to represent the millions of women who responded to the war with 'hearts undefeated'.

---

24. Rose Macaulay, *Life Among The English*, Collins, 1942.
*   Used for a different edition

CHAPTER ONE

Prelude

Throughout the 1930s Germany was re-arming. Most people in Britain hoped to avoid a war, but felt it was inevitable after the 1938 Munich Crisis. Thirty-eight million gas masks were issued, and trenches dug for air-raid shelters. Many women writing at this time were sceptical of all politicians, and women's magazines often made the point that with more women in power, war could be averted. But although there were some famous pacifist exceptions, such as Vera Brittain and Sybil Thorndike, most came to agree with the view that Nazism must be resisted by force.

With the approach of war came the urge to write. Reporters such as Martha Gellhorn, Virginia Cowles and Clare Hollingworth were already covering the European scene; but the idea of reporting a war also appealed to women who were not journalists. Polly Peabody was a young American Red Cross worker who managed to get herself to Norway at the beginning of the war. From there she filed her first newspaper story: 'It was terribly exciting, and I felt as if I were a character in a Hollywood movie. The word "scoop" became a thrilling new addition to my vocabulary. Writing had always been a day-dream on which I had dwelt during solitary hours.' The war made Peabody's dream come true; she worked as a war reporter and published *Occupied Territory* in 1941.

Other women with no such ambitions for professional careers as writers also reached for their pens; many diaries were started in 1939. Some of these, including Nella Last's, were kept for Mass Observation, the social survey organization set up by Charles Madge and Tom Harrisson in 1937. Why did women bother to sit up late with their diaries, and add to the labour of their wartime days? A good reason is suggested by one diarist, Anne Lee-Michell: 'Perhaps I felt dimly that we were assisting, however remotely, in historic events.' And as the war went on those left feeling lonely and vulnerable found comfort in confiding in their diaries.

VIRGINIA COWLES

The 1938 Nuremberg Rally

I saw the spirit of Nazi Germany flowing through the ancient streets of Nuremberg like a river that had burst its dams. A million red, white and black swastikas fluttered from the window-ledges, and the town, swollen to three times its normal size, resounded to the ring of leather boots and blazed with a bewildering array of uniforms.

Although the vast regimentation of modern Germany was a phenomenon which only the machine age could produce, at night the medieval background became curiously real. The clock swung back to the Middle Ages. The long red pennants, fluttering from the turreted walls of Nuremberg Castle, shone in the moonlight like the standards of an old religious war; the tramp of marching feet and the chorus of voices chanting the militant Nazi hymns had all the passion of an ancient crusade. It was only when you heard the sudden whine of a silver-winged fighter, travelling at three hundred miles an hour, that you were jerked back to the grim reality of 1938.

That grim reality had cast a dread shadow over the Party Congress, for this was 'crisis week'. Never in history had a crisis been more cold-bloodedly manufactured. For days the world had known the exact form it would take, even the date of its culmination. It had watched the attack against Czechoslovakia growing in violence, and now, with the German Army mobilized, it waited for the crescendo to be sounded by Hitler's speech, dramatically planned for the last day of the Congress. [...]

The idea of the superman was encouraged by the vast displays in Nuremberg. Everything that was done was done on a gigantic scale. The power of the spectacles lay not so much in their ingeniousness but in their immensity. The keynote was always repetition and uniformity. Instead of a few gilt eagles there were hundreds; instead of hundreds of flags there were thousands; instead of thousands of performers there were hundreds of thousands.

At night the mystic quality of the ritual was exaggerated by huge burning urns at the top of the stadium, their orange flames leaping into the blackness, while the flood-lighting effect of hundreds of powerful searchlights played eerily against the sky. The music had an almost religious solemnity, timed by the steady beat of drums that sounded like the distant throb of tom-toms.

One night I went to the stadium with Jules Sauerwein to hear an address Hitler was making to Nazi political leaders gathered from all over Germany. The stadium was packed with nearly 200,000 spectators. As the time for the Führer's arrival drew near, the crowd grew restless. The minutes passed and the wait seemed interminable. Suddenly the beat of the drums increased and three motor cycles with yellow standards fluttering from their windshields raced through the gates. A few minutes later a fleet of black cars rolled swiftly into the arena: in one of them, standing in the front seat, his hand outstretched in the Nazi salute, was Hitler.

The demonstration that followed was one of the most extraordinary I have ever witnessed. Hitler climbed to his box in the Grand Stand amid a deafening ovation, then gave a signal for the political leaders to enter. They came, a hundred thousand strong, through an opening in the far end of the arena. In the silver light they seemed to pour into the bowl like a flood of water. Each of them carried a Nazi flag and when they were assembled in mass formation, the bowl looked like a shimmering sea of swastikas.

Then Hitler began to speak. The crowd hushed into silence, but the drums continued their steady beat. Hitler's voice rasped into the night and every now and then the multitude broke into a roar of cheers. Some of the audience began swaying back and forth, chanting 'Sieg Heil' over and over again in a frenzy of delirium. I looked at the faces round me and saw tears streaming down people's cheeks. The drums had grown louder and I suddenly felt frightened. For a moment I wondered if it wasn't a dream; perhaps we were really in the heart of the African jungle. I had a sudden feeling of claustrophobia and whispered to Jules Sauerwein, asking if we couldn't leave. It was a silly question, for we were hemmed in on all sides, and there was nothing to do but sit there until the bitter end. [...]

The most fashionable gathering-place in Nuremberg was the Grand Hotel. [...] Outstanding in the English group were Lord and Lady Redesdale and their daughter, the Honourable Unity Valkyrie Mitford. [...] To Unity, National Socialism was a Left Wing revolution and Hitler the champion of the downtrodden masses. There was no doubt that the latter was flattered by her admiration and sincerely fond of her. He often telephoned her, gave her presents, and in public treated her with deference. Although the Nazi Party leaders fawned over her in public, in private they were jealous of the friendship. Tom Mitford told me that when Unity went to Germany they often refused to tell Hitler she had arrived. The only way she could get into communication with him was to wait in the street, sometimes for hours, hoping to catch his eye when he passed. [...]

Her rather naive observations on Hitler were at times strangely revealing. When I asked her what she talked with him about, she replied, 'Gossip'. He liked to hear the anecdotes his advisers were apt to overlook. For instance, when Madame de Fontanges, the French journalist, fired a revolver at Count de Chambrun, the French Ambassador in Rome, declaring that the latter had tried to thwart her romance with Mussolini, Unity related the episode to Hitler. She said he thought it very funny and laughed delightedly, saying what a narrow squeak it might have been for 'poor old Mussolini'.

According to her, Hitler had a sense of humour and liked company. [...] The remark that struck me most was her comment on Hitler's talent as an imitator. She claimed that if he were not the Führer of Germany, he would make a hundred thousand dollars a year on the vaudeville stage. He often did imitations of his colleagues – Goering, Goebbels and Himmler – but, best of all, he liked to imitate Mussolini. This always provoked roars of laughter. 'And sometimes,' added Unity, 'he even imitates himself.'

BELLA FROMM

Flight from Germany

Paris, 6 September 1938:
The last two days were a nightmare: At the last minute I discovered that I needed a Belgian visa, because of the one hour's ride at night through that country. I could not get it without photographs. It took a great deal of scurrying around, but it was all finally arranged.

At nine o'clock the night express came thundering into the station. Farewells and tears. At the far end of the platform, in

civilian clothes, was Rolf. We had agreed that he was not to run
the risk of being seen with me at the train. Blurred by my tears, I
could hardly see his face. The train had already started. Goodbye, Rolf . . . God bless you . . .

Four and a half years ago my child, Gonny, had left on the
same train, from the same station, in her adventure in search of
freedom and a new life. And now, I too was going on the same
quest.

The heavy luggage was booked, sealed, and stamped. My few
suitcases were in the rack above me. The passport was in order. I
traveled luxuriously in a Pullman sleeper. Perhaps for the last
time. I had not spared money, because I had to leave the rest in
Germany anyway. Exhausted, I went to bed.

About 2 A.M. I was badly frightened by the sudden apparition
of two uniformed figures. Drugged by my first sound sleep in
weeks, my senses momentarily reeled with terror.

'Frontier pass control,' one of them announced gruffly.

I asked them to let me put on some clothes, but they made me
leave the door open while I dressed.

'Emigrant's passport!' announced one. 'Jewish bitch! Trying
to smuggle out her valuables, I suppose.'

I kept my mouth shut. They turned everything inside out.
They took the soles from my bedroom slippers. They squeezed
the toothpaste from the tube.

'Have you anything that should not be taken out of the country?' demanded one.

'You've seen for yourself everything I have,' I said.

'You Jewish whore!' one shouted at me. 'Trying to smuggle
out all that jewelry.' He pointed to the little heap that had been
emptied out on the bed.

'I am not trying to smuggle anything out,' I said. 'All that has
been the property of my family for generations. Here is the
permit issued by the Foreign Exchange Office.'

'We'll have to check on that with Berlin,' said he. 'We reach the
frontier in half an hour. You'll have to get off the train.'

My protests were futile. I said I should miss the boat.

'Then take the next one.'

They seemed to be deliberately unaware of how hard it was to
obtain passage. Cancellation or even delay was impossible, with
so many hundreds eagerly awaiting their turn. I had a vision of

being sent back to Germany and having to go through the business of laboriously collecting my exit papers all over again. My heart almost stopped.

The two went outside for a whispered consultation. When they returned, they submitted a statement for me to sign:

'I am a Jewish thief and have tried to rob Germany by taking German wealth out of the country. I hereby confess that the jewels found on me do not belong to me and that in trying to take them out I was eager to inflict injury on Germany. Furthermore, I promise never to try to reenter Germany.'

I signed. I had to get out of this country. This was a country to get out of if you had to do it naked.

Half an hour later the train crossed the border. I was in safety. My heart was pounding and I began to cry. Tears of liberation. But I was still uneasy until the train stopped at the Gare du Nord.

The statement, together with my jewels, had gone into the pockets of my tormentors. I am sure they will go no farther up the line. If they reappear, it will be in the shop of a pawnbroker.

9 September 1938. S.S. Normandie:
Safe aboard this gorgeous boat! It is almost too much for me to believe. Then, when I do become acutely aware of my good fortune, I feel almost guilty, remembering the unfortunate ones who wait, trembling, desperately hoping for their chance to get out. There *must* be a way to help.

The magnificent ship glides through the waters to the new land. I cannot get myself to join in the gay cheerfulness on board. There is an atmosphere of luxury and freedom from care, but I am not yet in a mood to breathe this air. I find I cannot yet stand fun and laughter.

STEVIE SMITH

Where is Czechoslovakia?

1939
Friendship and the revolt from friendship is the stuff of life. I am so grateful to my darling friends, to all my darling friends, but for the moment adieu. When I get home my noble aunt is reading the

papers. At the time I was writing this the number of people reading the papers was more than usual. To keep out or not to keep out of war, that was at that time the question. Now, perhaps we are already again at war, perhaps not. My aunt is a staunch Tory, and equally staunchly she is regarding Germany as the ultimate enemy. Unlike many of the people who live in my own high-class suburb, she is well read in the political game. To-night is the night of the announcement of the flight of the Premier. Flight into darkness, say some, echoing the beautiful title Schnitzler chose for his suicide novel. I am listening at the house of a friend, an old mamma, she is really the church friend of my aunt, or the church sweet enemy, since my aunt carries on her church work in a fury of disagreement with the other ladies. Mrs A., we will call her, has a radio, which my aunt and I have not. My aunt does not like 'the noise.' Mrs A.'s radio announces the flight. On this great day of stress Mrs A. has not seen a paper. She has been too busy. So I say: 'The news looks serious. Japan is coming in with Germany. That will be not so hot for Australia.'

Mrs A. pants rather; she is making a wool rug and the colours must be matched nicely. She pants: 'Oh, yes, Australia! Mr A. has bought a new car.' So now the great news comes through that the Premier is flying to Berchtesgaden. 'So that is the best news I have heard today.' 'What is?' says Mrs A. 'That the Premier is flying to Berchtesgaden.' 'Oh,' Mrs A. says. 'Oh.' Then she says: 'Mr Parker was just in. He said: "Why are we interfering in Czecho-Slovakia?"' I am rather intrigued by this piece. Bottle Green, I guess, is calling all suburbs. Now, I hurry to say to you that I am not high hatting the suburbs; suburbs are very OK in many ways. I use the term spiritually, not geographically. I am thinking of the people who say: 'Where the hell is Czecho-Slovakia?' These people often don't live in suburbs at all; suburbs (it is unfortunate for suburbs) is a term of abuse, and these people earn abuse. Their forefathers, I guess they said: 'Where the hell is Waterloo?' 'Where the hell is Trafalgar?' But they would have known what the hell all right if Napoleon had invaded England. So they will know what the hell all right if Germany goes on her *Drang nach Kolonien*, like hell they will, like hell. So Mrs A. has two sons just down from Oxford, just the right age. I said, *just the right age*. So Mrs A. says now something so sad to make the angels weep, and so ridiculous. Alas, that human beings have the special privilege to be so often at the same time ridiculous and sad. So what does Mrs A. say? 'Whatever happens my boys will not be involved – because we have all signed the Peace Pledge.' Oh, sad echoing of fiendish laughter! Oh, the hollow laughter that goes echoing round the halls of hell upon these words. 'We have signed the Peace Pledge.' And already upon my eyes there is darkness and a great wind blowing over dead battlefields, and the stench of death without honour, and the ridiculous sad cry: We never knew. 'Oh, now I must go!' I say. 'Yes, you have heard the news,' says Mrs A. with a meaning note. Oh, yes, I suppose I am very rude, to hear the news and go.

CICELY MCCALL

The Women's Institutes' Annual General Meeting, Earl's Court

This was June 1939. England was still at peace.

In this year only a few months after Munich, only three months before the invasion of Poland, the Associated Countrywomen of the World, the international body which binds together Women's Institutes all over the world, had held a week of meetings in London. Twenty-three countries had been represented, and nine of these representatives came to Earl's Court. One by one they were called to the front of the platform. Some wore national dress. Some neither spoke nor understood English. But all of them understood the applause and the smiles which greeted each fresh announcement.

America, Sweden, India. One by one they came forward, made their bow, and sometimes said a few words.

Latvia, Norway . . . Germany!

She was a tall woman. Her shoulders were flung back, her face set as she stepped on to the platform. There was a second's tense silence, as though suddenly nine thousand pairs of lungs had contracted, and their hearts too. Then came deafening applause. It rang round the hall tumultuously. It fell, then grew again in increasing volume as though each perspiring delegate on that very hot June morning could not enough say:

'Welcome! We are all countrywomen here today. We are non-party, non-sectarian. We wish for peace, goodwill and co-operation among nations. You have had the courage to come here in spite of rumours of wars. We bid you welcome!'

The strained look had gone from the German delegate's face. Amazement had taken its place. Amazement and pleasure. As she stepped off the platform she hesitated, almost stumbled. Perhaps she could not see very well. We shall never know what message she carried back to her country when her eyes were dried. Now, in this fourth year of war, is she still alive? Does she remember?

CHAPTER TWO

The Outbreak of War

Britain declared war on Germany on 3 September 1939. The most immediate effect on the women of Britain was the mass evacuation that then followed: one and a half million mothers and children were removed from supposed danger areas and sent into the country.

In this way the war forced itself dramatically into the homes of many, whether they were evacuees or what were hopefully called 'hostesses'. The 'home front' would become one of the great phrases – one of the great monuments even – of the war, but the home itself was one of the war's first casualties. It was broken into and broken up by evacuation, and by conscription too, as husbands and sons were called up to active service. Further problems faced women at work. Figures for women's employment went down at the beginning of the war, as the government adopted a policy of limiting 'non-essential' production not related to the war effort to a few firms. Industries such as textiles and pottery, which traditionally employed a large number of women, were cut back, but the new jobs in munitions were slow in coming. Professional women lost ground too. Elaine Burton, an administrator dismissed from her job at the beginning of the war, wrote her well-researched book *What of the Women?* (1941) to argue for the more efficient use of women's labour.

The favoured tone for women's writing at the outbreak of war seems to have been one of determined light-heartedness, combined with a desire to show some practical spirit. Jan Struther's Mrs Miniver and E.M. Delafield's Provincial Lady both dash gallantly up to London to search for worthy war work – 'Driving, for choice' according to Mrs Miniver. *The Provincial Lady in Wartime* chronicles the doings of September and October 1939: 'Spend large part of the day asking practically everybody I can think of, by telephone or letter, if they can suggest a war job for me. Most of them reply that they are engaged in similar quest on their own account.'

MARGERY ALLINGHAM

Evacuation, Day One in the Country

I don't know what sort of invasion we all had in mind, but we were not unduly optimistic. We had certainly been warned. From the beginning the evacuation scheme had come in for criticism. To read the country letters in the newspapers just after the Munich crisis you would have thought that everybody in the towns was a vermin-infested T.B. carrier; and naturally in the face of such a howl of fury the newspapers did what they always do when confronted by the really unpopular and shut down on the whole story like a clam. This was particularly unfortunate, because the scheme could have done with an airing, especially that part of it which affected adults. [. . .]

We all agreed there was no need to worry anyone who didn't want evacuees. I was particularly vehement about this, I remember, because I felt with a passion left over from my own childhood that the important thing was to put the youngster where someone wanted him first and worry about his living space afterwards. 'Better a dinner of herbs . . .' in fact, every time. And there were in Auburn literally dozens of people who said yes yes, they thought they had room for another little old boy or a nice little girl.

Meanwhile the time went on and on. One by one we slipped home for lunch and raced back again, but still no one came. I was frankly fascinated by the evacuation scheme, and had been from the beginning because it seemed to me to be the most revolutionary of all the Government measures, not excluding conscription. After all, one's own fireside is the citadel of freedom, and it did seem extraordinarily dangerous if any local authority could legally invade it. However, since the art of being governed is to do the necessary voluntarily and in one's own way before anyone starts shoving, and since Britain has that art at her finger-tips, I did not anticipate any real trouble; but I did feel the whole scheme might have been better had it been given the usual thorough shaking out in the high winds of Parliament and Press before it became law.

At that time no one knew much about it, for it had never been published out of Hansard as far as I could find out. All we knew then, and that mainly from hearsay, was that when an adult was billeted on you you got five shillings a week from the Post Office, and she was expected to buy her own food and cook it on your stove if you let her. It was made pretty clear that you were expected to let her do that, but no other details appeared to have been considered at all. Nothing about washing up, nothing about bedding, nothing about fuel, nothing about cooking utensils. It sounded like a fine source of trouble and quarrels all round to us, 'worse than the war,' and we congratulated ourselves on the ninety children. Whatever a child does you can't very well quarrel with it, and in our experience in Auburn half the trouble in a lifetime comes from quarrels.

Meanwhile it was nearly three o'clock in the afternoon, very hot and very dusty. We began to worry they would not get down in time for them to have their tea and get safely installed before the black-out. Mrs Moore hoped they hadn't been travelling all day and wondered if they wouldn't be starving, and Doey said he'd been informed that they would all have rations.

Presently Mr Moore shouted from the playground, and we all popped out; but it was only a big coloured van arriving. It swung down through the elm avenue and pulled up outside the school. The driver and his mate turned out of their seats like automatons, opened the doors, and began to drag out wooden food cases. They did not smile or speak or look at us. They brought the stuff straight in, dumped it in a corner and went back for more, moving quickly and as if they were working in their sleep. It was the first time war strain had come to Auburn, and it was odd and impressive, like the first puff of ack-ack fire in a blue sky. They looked as though they had been at work for seventy-two hours, as they probably had. There were red rims round their eyes, and their faces were grey and dirty. When someone asked them about the evacuees they snapped at us, and one man took off his coat, rolled it in a ball and threw it in a corner. Then he put his head on it and went to sleep.

Thinking it over, we were curiously unexcited by all this when one considers how interested we usually are when anything a little bit different arrives. We expected excitement, I suppose, and were saving it for the children. At any rate we took no notice of the sleeping man or his lorry, as far as I remember, apart from regarding them both stolidly. We examined the stores. There were quantities of it; bully beef, two sorts of tinned milk, and a considerable number of tins of biscuits as well as several quires of brown paper shopping bags.

Doey said suspiciously, 'There's a lot there, isn't there?' But at that moment a message came over from the Lion to say that eight buses were on their way. This delighted us all, and Mrs Moore got the kettles boiling. We were fidgeting about making last-minute preparations, when Doey, who had been thinking over the message, suddenly said, '*Eight* buses?'

I said, 'Oh, they'll be those little old-fashioned charabanc things.' And he said, 'Very likely.'

I was wrong. Mrs Moore, who was by the big window which looks on to the road, saw them first. There they were, as foreign-looking as elephants. There were eight of them, big red double-decker London buses, the kind that carries thirty-two passengers on each floor, and as far as we could see they were crowded. They pulled up, a long line all down the road, with a London taxicab behind them. A small army of drivers and officials sprang out, shouting instructions to their passengers.

It was a difficult moment. We locals were all doing arithmetic. Twice thirty-two is sixty-four; eight times sixty-four is five hundred and twelve; and the entire population of Auburn is under six hundred and fifty. We hoped, we trusted, there had been some mistake.

It was at this point that Doey made the second discovery. *They weren't children.* They were strange London-dressed ladies, all very tired and irritable, with babies in their arms.

We attempted to explain to the drivers, but all the time we were doing it it was slowly dawning upon us that we should never succeed. The drivers and the officials expected us to be hostile. They had read the newspapers. They were very tired, and moreover they were so nervy and exhausted, more with the emotional effort than anything else, that they were raw and spoiling for trouble. Doey and I, on the other hand, were just plain terrified. Finally we persuaded them to wait for just ten minutes while we found out if there had been a mistake, and we all went into the Lion to telephone authority at Fishling.

Authority at Fishling sounded a bit rattled also, and we gathered that our difficulties were as nothing beside the troubles of others, and that we'd kindly get on with what God and the

German Chancellor had seen fit to send us. So we said 'All right,' and went back. It was the beginning of the war for us in Auburn, the first real start of genuine trouble.

Fortunately there was plenty to do. As a reception committee we had hardly shone, and the immediate need seemed to be to remove any unfortunate first impressions.

To our intense relief the buses proved to be not quite full. There were just over three hundred souls altogether, many of them infants, but they looked like an army. They trooped into the school, spread over the rooms and the playground and sat down, all looking at us with tired, expectant eyes.

There appeared to be no one actually in charge of them now they had arrived. The bus drivers went away with the buses, and the two school-masters and one young school-mistress who had come down with them were due to rush back as soon as possible to rejoin their own schools evacuated somewhere else in the east country.

The utter forlornness of the newcomers was quite theatrical. To our startled country eyes their inexpensive but very fashionable city clothes were grand if unsuitable, and with the myriads of babies in arms and the weeping toddlers hanging to their skirts they looked like everybody's long-lost erring daughter turned up to the old homes together in one vast paralysing emotional surprise.

They did not talk much, except to catch one's arm and say, 'Get me off soon, please. I'm very done up,' which was piteous in the circumstances. They had no luggage except brown paper carriers containing the babies' immediate necessities, which was fortunate, for they had had an air-raid warning or two on the way down and had been bundled into shelters and out again. Moreover, they were not the ordinary East End cockneys, with whom we have some kinship and whom we had expected. These girls came from the suburbs well our side of the city, and most of them were obviously better off in actual spending money than the majority of Auburn families. Somehow this made it more difficult.

What we did not understand at all at the time, and which would never have occurred to us if some of them hadn't told us about it afterwards, was that they were nearly all great cinema-goers and had been seeing newsreel pictures of refugees for months, so that when their turn came they dropped into the part more or less automatically. To us who did not know this, of course, their silent hopeless gloom, indicative of utter exhaustion, was terrifying and incomprehensible. After all, they had only come thirty-five miles, and that in a bus. In normal times they might easily have done the trip for pleasure. We wondered what in God's name was happening up there in London.

Meanwhile, of course, our position (Doey's and mine) was rather delicate. It's one thing to arrange with a valued neighbour and client to receive two small girls, and another to send her instead two weeping young women and eight children under seven between them.

Also another problem had arisen. It was Anne who produced it. This was the first time I ever saw Anne. She came up, forcing her way through the crush and roaring with laughter. Her gaily painted face was quite different in its happiness from almost everyone else's, and she was hatless. She touched my arm, and I saw that she was wearing a wildly patterned green and purple silk dress, which, like the lady's in the ballad, was 'narrow . . . that used to be sae wide.' Tony, nearly two, clung to her neck and screamed with delight.

She said, 'Here, I say, where's the clinic?'

The word rang a faint bell. As far as I could remember there was a welfare clinic at Flinthammock which was held every Thursday afternoon, or something like that. This did not sound as if it was going to be much use to Anne, however, for she said she was 'due' in ten days or so, and that there were about twenty others like her. They 'had ought' to have had pink tickets, she said, but what with the rush and one thing and another they'd come along without.

Since it seemed to be our business, I assured her it would be quite all right. I had come to the conclusion that this was probably the end of the world, and that Dante was evidently going to have a hand in it, as I had always feared he might. I also felt wildly indignant that it should be Englishwomen who were being herded about in this abominable way. I do not defend this insular and prideful reaction, which shocked me out of the corner of my eye, so to speak, at the time; but I feel bound to mention it because it was so strong.

Meanwhile we were getting a move on as best we could. I sent as many people as I dared over to Margaret and Christine, and

Doey sent some home to Mrs Doe. Mrs Moore and Mrs Gager somehow got tea for everybody, and at the same time we sent out a general SOS. There was nothing formal or resounding about it, as far as I remember, but rather an agonized shout of 'Somebody come!'

Miraculously Auburn responded. It turned up like the Navy or the Fire Brigade or one's parents and, having taken one horrified, outraged look at the scarifying sight in the big schoolroom, it took the situation in hand.

It was extraordinary. People who had no room, who loathed the idea of strangers, and who had declared in all honesty that while they were prepared if necessary to die for their country, they could not and would not stomach a child in their house for ten minutes, came up to the sunny playground with unwilling, conscience-driven steps, paused at the doorway of the big school aghast, and then went in and collected some weeping young mother and her infants and carried them home with tight lips and grim eyes.

The entire business became more and more unreal as it went on. We went back into a Bret Harte or Dickensian world in which stony hearts dissolved in acid tears and piteous rosy-faced babies smiled their way into private fortresses. It was a frightening experience, a sort of return to simplicity by way of an avalanche; or as though God, tiring at last of our blasted superiority, had taken us and banged our heads together. [. . .]

It occurred to me at this point that we were only one village out of hundreds, probably thousands, all suddenly confronted by this remarkable invasion, and that all over the country startled people must be opening their doors like this to tired and sometimes angry strange girls and their heavy-eyed children. Somehow that reflection did not make our immediate problem seem any more simple.

Meanwhile Jane had discovered the Ring Farmers. They were not called that yet, of course; that came later. At this time they were just one vast loving family who did not want to be separated even for a night. There were nineteen of them: a matriarch who had been married twice and her younger children, two families of her married daughters, a daughter-in-law and at least one baby apiece. Most of the girls were remarkably pretty, Jessie Matthews types, and they were very smart if in a rather dressed-up way for

Auburn. They all had soft voices and that delightful impudent direct intelligence which belongs to the city. Mama outshone them all, however. She was well over fifty, and looked like some fine Shakespearean actress playing the Queen of Denmark before the trouble started. Her expression was imperious and her carriage regal. She was wearing a black halo hat which suited her, and she drew me away from the others and said, 'How about letting us stay here till the morning? You know what the girls are. We ought to get the kids to sleep. We'll be all right by ourselves. We don't *want* billets, my dear, not to-night. Just find us a few necessities, and we'll manage.'

Well, of course they couldn't stay there because there was no black-out in the big room for one thing; but we did fit them up for the night in the schoolroom behind the chapel, and the big old-fashioned pew forms fitted together made cribs for the babies. Mr Spooner, who looks after the chapel, worked like a slave to make them comfortable. Bill got out his lorry, and Albert and Charlotte, and Alan their eldest, loaded it with camp beds dug out from the junk cupboard and mended at speed. Everybody lent something, blankets or crocks or food, for the night.

Mama received everything with the gracious ease of a Duchess at a bazaar. She was never hurried, never hesitant, and always charmingly smooth and polite. If she needed anything we had forgotten, she indicated it rather than mentioned it. Someone said she couldn't have taken in things better if she'd been a sausage machine.

When the flow ceased she dismissed us gently with thanks and a Mona Lisa smile. There was no need for us to think of them for quite a time, she said. They'd manage.

As I came back I saw Albert and Charlotte in the Queen's yard, and we eyed each other very thoughtfully for a minute before we all burst out laughing at the same thing. The old woman thought she was pretty smart. The joke was, of course, that we weren't being done; we were just being generous. I wondered if the old lady, with all her town intelligence, would ever get the exquisite subtlety of that one.

This slightly peculiar humour of ours, which is scarcely ever understood or even suspected by the townsfolk, may be a little hard to follow, because of course on the surface the townee always appears to come off best. On this occasion Mama had our crocks, our beds, our blankets and our food, and we had no means of knowing if we should ever see any of them again. However, the whole thing goes far deeper than that and is the outcome of a thousand years' experience of living next door to the same families. We had certainly risked a few odds-and-ends, but think of the position in which she had put herself. If she and her family were proposing to live amongst us for any length of time the definite information we should have in a few days' time about her innate honesty, her reliability as a borrower, her generosity and her cleanliness was practically beyond price.

STORM JAMESON

City Without Children

1939

The children were sent out of London over the weekend. [. . .] Over half a million children were hurried out of the city. Some further hundreds of thousands went independently, packed off to relatives and boarding schools in the country. On Wednesday, September 6, London looked as it would look if some fantastic death pinched off the heads under fifteen. [. . .]

In the centre of London, the City proper, there are squares that have changed little if at all since the eighteenth century. The houses have become the offices of sedate firms. Unless they shout, little marble-playing boys are not ordered off, and not many weeks since I watched children playing in one of these squares a game with flat stones that was probably old in Troy. The children have vanished. Two big paunchy business men, carrying rolled copies of *The Times*, self-conscious with gas masks in canvas boxes slung on their shoulders, stroll across in the sun. The steps going down into a small church are well sand-bagged. It is as dark as a crypt in this sunken place, and nearly full of people praying, as people have prayed here for five centuries, for help in the day of trouble and lamentation. Without looking up, a woman said in a loud voice: 'My son! Oh, my son!' To what listener?

The streets are lively with typists and office girls, going home. Many of these girls are only two years older than a sister who has been evacuated. On one side of an age line you are still a child who must be protected. A step, and you have become a young woman with handbag, toeless sandals, and gas mask, who must go to the office as long as the office is there. It seems a pity. But one cannot save everybody. So these older children walk jauntily on their long thin legs, carrying their masks with a touch of coquetry.

F. TENNYSON JESSE

A Letter to The Times

1939

'Sir,

'While from all my friends in the country comes praise of many town-children evacuees – and, without exception, praise of all the secondary-school children – complaints are pouring in about the half-savage, verminous and wholly illiterate children from some slums who have been billeted on clean homes. Stories with which one cannot but sympathise are told of mattresses and carpets polluted, of wilful despolation and dirt that one would associate only with untrained animals. The authorities, with plenty of time to prepare, seem to have failed both in the physical and psychological examination of the evacuees, although the mechanics of the great trek have been so well ordered.

'Now one hears that both women and children of the roughest and uncleanest types are going back to their own "homes". At the present time, when Britain is fighting for liberty, no Briton would suggest dictatorship methods, but surely something short of these can be evolved to prevent these unfortunate children from being allowed to return to the appalling conditions whence they have been rescued? It is not fair that they should disrupt small houses, but is it not possible to cause (to coin a phrase) "grass-orphanages" under the care of skilled and sympathetic teachers, to come into being? Let the mothers go back if they will. It does not matter so much what happens to adults, but surely children should not be allowed to go back to conditions which shame a nation fighting for civilization.

'In the course of my work I have, in the last few years, attended many trials at the Central Criminal Court, and am nearly always horrified by the low physical and mental standards of the accused persons. Stunted, misshapen creatures, only capable of understanding the very simplest language and quite incapable of thought, moved by impulses at the best sentimental, at the worst brutal. During a trial when accused and witnesses are of this sub-human sort, it is as though a flat stone in the garden had been raised and pale wriggling things that had never seen the light, were exposed. No one who knows anything of Criminal Courts will contradict me.

'These children, of whom the country residents so reasonably complain, are bound to grow up into just such sub-human savages, unless we seize this opportunity of saving them. I do not, of course, say that all crime is due to the appalling conditions in which most men and women who find their way to our courts live when young – there have been several trials in the last two years which have shown that men, who have had every advantage in youth, can be brutal, treacherous and base. But I do say that no child who has not been shown the rudiments of decency and in whom imagination has not been encouraged, stands a chance of being a good and happy citizen.

'War has lifted the flat stone – these disgraces to our educational system have been forced out into the light. Do not let us, even though a certain amount of arbitrary arrangements may be needed, let them creep back beneath their stone. This is, and I repeat it with every emphasis of passion at my command, an opportunity which, if we miss it, we do not deserve to have given to us again.'

I could have written more forcibly, but after all one has to be careful of the words one uses to Auntie *Times*.

NELLA LAST

A Son's Last Day At Home

Thursday, 14 September 1939
The last day of having a 'little boy' – for so my Cliff has seemed, in spite of being twenty-one at Christmas. He has been so thoughtful and quiet these last few days, and so gentle. I watched

his long sensitive fingers as he played with the dog's ears, and saw the look on his face when someone mentioned 'bayonet charging'. He has never hurt a thing in his life: even as a little boy, at the age when most children are unthinkingly cruel, he brought sick or hurt animals home for me to doctor, and a dog living next door always came for a pill when it felt ill – although as Cliff used to complain, it never noticed him at other times! It's dreadful to think of him having to kill boys like himself – to hurt and be hurt. It breaks my heart to think of all the senseless, formless cruelty. I looked at his room to-day: he and his brother, though deeply attached, like their separate rooms and, although it meant more work, I like privacy myself too much to have denied them it. I thought of the crowd he would have to live in, and of how, unless for an occasional dance etc., he prefers a tramp over the hills with a pal – or even just aunt Sarah's old dog. He likes to sit before the fire with his legs stretched out, munching an apple and reading, sitting for hours on end, designing and making his Christmas or birthday cards and little witty tags for Christmas presents.

He always likes a few flowers in an old tankard on his bedside table, a clean serviette, the cat on the window sill at his elbow and the dog by his feet while having meals – such little unimportant things to ask, and yet to be denied for only God knows how long. We who remember the long drawn-out agony of the last war feel ourselves crumble somewhere inside at the thoughts of what lies ahead.

Tonight I looked a bit washed out, so after tea I changed into my gayest frock and made up rather heavily. When Cliff came in with his friend, he said 'Oho!' and raised my face with his finger: 'Hm! Quite good but just a *wee* bit tartish!' – and he wiped my lips and cheeks, kissed me on the tip of my nose and turned me round to see if Jack approved. Jack and he insisted on making toast and scrambling eggs – I think they are proud of this little accomplishment! No one could eat it though, and I felt myself going cold – a funny little sign that I'm best to be in bed.

JAN STRUTHER

Mrs Miniver's 'Peace-In-War'

London, 5 October 1939

Dearest Susan,

I have come back here to find a job, as Starlings now seems to be running perfectly all right, nursery, evacuees, and all. I don't know yet what kind of job I can get, if any. Driving, for choice. What I hanker for, of course, is to be put at the beck and call of some very important hush-hush sort of man who needs to be driven very fast in a long-nosed powerful car to mysterious destinations. From time to time my passenger would glance down at his watch, then backwards over his shoulder, and say briefly, 'Step on it, Mrs M.' And I should see in the driving-mirror a supercharged straight eight, disguised as a grocer's van, rapidly gaining on us ... Yes, definitely, that would be just my cup of tea. But either this type of man is dying out – which I should deplore – or else, which is more likely, he does his own driving.

In the meanwhile I am helping at whatever odd jobs I can find – addressing envelopes, rolling bandages, &c. – and enjoying, more than I can say, being back in London, which is unbelievably impressive.

The funny thing is that although the floodlighting experiments used to reveal a whole lot of architectural beauties which one didn't know, the black-out reveals even more. One loses the details of buildings, but sees their outlines properly for the first time. That is, when there's any vestige of a moon. And even when there isn't, one still discovers new things by hearing, touch, and smell. For instance, I had never noticed before that the area railings in this Square were of such a pleasing design. Now I know them intimately, by touch. And I can tell when I'm getting near to the Air Raid Shelter at the corner by the damp jutey smell of the sandbags. In fact, the whole of London now smells most pleasantly of jute – even indoors, because of the stuff one uses for undercurtains. It is one of the best scents in the world: partly, I suppose, because it reminds one of those rickety tents one made out of sacking as a child.

As for the balloons – you've probably read a lot about them in the papers already, but I can't help that, I have *got* to talk about them. They are the most delightful and comforting companions in the world. You see, I hadn't been in London at all since war broke out, and when I travelled up five days ago, by the late train, I don't mind admitting I was feeling rather jittery. There was a serene gold sunset, with oast-houses sticking up against it like black cats, and all the way up in the train that wretched lovely line from *Antony and Cleopatra* kept running in my head:–

> Finish, good lady; the bright day is done,
> And we are for the dark.

I went to bed very sore about the shins from falling over a station barrow, and hating the house with neither Clem nor the children in it, and with Mrs A. looking more than ever like John Knox; and altogether everything was rather grim. But when I looked out of my window early next morning and saw all those fat little silver watch-fish floating overhead in a clear sky, I felt completely reassured. They really are quite beautiful, although – like puppies – they manage to combine this with being intrinsically comic. From time to time they are taken down: ostensibly to refill them with gas, but really, I suspect, to scrape off the barnacles. I only wish, once they've got them down, they'd paint faces on them like Chinese dragons. I'm sure it would add to their deterrent effect. The best thing of all, which nobody had prepared me for, is that on windy nights they *sing*. It's like going to sleep on a ship at anchor, with the sound of wind in the rigging. Only, thank goodness, London doesn't rock – yet.

There, I have finished letting off steam about the balloons. *Liberavi animam meam*, as Uncle John always used to say when he had just been particularly offensive to poor Aunt Sarah. Like many well-read but ill-tempered people, he thought a Latin tag excused everything. But Aunt Sarah didn't know any Latin. Bad Luck.

As for other things, all I can say is that Hitler, poor misguided man, has made the biggest mistake of his life in giving us a month of this kind of peace-in-war in which to become calm, collected, and what's more, *chic*. Of course, the people who are natural born dowds still manage to make their gas masks look dowdy, but those who are normally well-turned-out somehow contrive to make them into a positive decoration. It isn't only a question of having one of the many expensive and pansified cases which are on the market, though I admit they help: it's more that most people have now learned to carry the things with an air – with *panache*. You might think, walking about London, that everybody was going off to a picnic with a box of special food.

Another thing: you know how in normal times, when they come back to London in the autumn, English women make no attempt to keep on wearing light, bright colours. They just mutter 'Fogs' in a defeatist manner, put away their summer handbags, gloves, scarves, and so forth, and then throw up their arms and drown in a sea of black, navy, dark brown, bottle, and maroon, as the fashion catalogues would say. This year, wearing white 'accessories' has become literally a matter of life and death – or at any rate, of wholeness and injury; and you've no idea how much more cheerful the place looks. But it's odd, isn't it, that the aim of 'protective colouring' should now be to detach us from our background, not to melt us into it? This war will have to introduce a new word for that process, just as the last one introduced 'camouflage'.

Talking of stockings, I remember Teresa saying last year that one of the most awful minor catastrophes in the world was when one's suspender gave way at a party: how one felt quite discomfited, and lop-sided, and altogether at a loss until it was done up again. Well, I think that's the main difference between September, 1938, and now. Then, we felt only too distinctly the uncomfortable *ping*! of the elastic. But now we've had time to do it up again; and we feel more than equal to coping with the party, however long and strenuous it may be.

How silly it was of him to allow us to become not only angry but bored. This nation is never really dangerous until it's bored.

Yours ever, with much love,

Caroline.

ROSAMOND LEHMANN

A Review of Mrs Miniver

1939

Here are the sayings and doings of Mrs Miniver, familiar to some of us in more ephemeral form in *The Times*, now collected all together in one pretty pink and blue volume, so that her countless admirers may derive a more permanent pleasure from her charm, her wit and wisdom. 'Boxed, and in a gay binding,' this work seems destined for the drawing-room table, or for the best spare room, where the perusal of one or two of her little adventures should help the week-end guest to drop off at night soothed, smiling and serene.

Mrs Miniver is, we know, secure in the heart of the majority of her public; and I must be taken as speaking only for a minority, upon which she exercises an oppression of spirits which, since it is caused by such a charming person, appears at first sight due to mere jealousy and spite. Yet surely it is odd that anyone so tactful, kind, tolerant, popular, humorous and contented, should arouse such low feelings, even in the ever-dissatisfied minority? And then, if one happens to dislike the spectacle of so much success, why not simply ignore it, and turn away? Why read, as one must, with exasperation, the column she has with such modest triumph made her own? Why does one look out for her next appearance with such feelings as the deserving poor must entertain for the local Lady Bountiful, or the inmates of a Borstal Institute for a certain kind of official visitor?

One trouble is, one can't ignore the successful; and to enable one to forgive them there is needed some quality alien to Mrs Miniver. It is not so much that we are irritated by her being pleased with herself: blissfully married, mother of three, well off, well read, she has a right to be pleased: is it perhaps the way she has of masking her colossal self-satisfaction with tender self-depreciation? 'See what a silly I am!' It is in her humility that we suspect her most. [. . .]

Now the war is upon Mrs Miniver, as it is upon all of us. But whoever is defeated, she'll come through. Having plenty of courage and common sense, she will cope successfully with evacuees and increased taxation, even if necessary with bombs. The airy balloon that hovers so lightly above our heads may shrivel a little, but it won't collapse. Inheriting (despite her tendentious name) no long traditions, or rather inheriting only mixed bits and pieces of outworn and debased ones, she will be adaptable, and come up shaken but intact, whatever new society emerges. For whether Right wing or Left wing, the right are always right, and always with us.

Competition and Correspondence in the New Statesman

16 December 1939
Professor Harold Laski has written a book entitled *The Danger of Being A Gentleman*. The usual prizes for not more than 200 words from a book of that title.

Second Prize
Curious, thought Mrs Miniver, pensively nibbling a *langue-de-chat*, how difficult life was becoming for people who happened to have come out of the top drawer.

She poked the fire, tilting the tarred logs until a stream of molten lava poured down. Yes – that was symbolic . . . The black stream (or would it, perhaps, be a Red one?) would soon pour ruthlessly down over the Clems and the Carolines, the Tobys, Judys and Vins; over their luncheon-parties and shooting-parties, and all the civilized fun which they had so long and so lightheartedly enjoyed.

Unless – unless what? Wasn't there something they could do about it, some means of preserving all that was gay and lovely in their tradition, while purging it of all that was dangerous and bad? She felt a faint stirring in the back of her mind, as of some small wood animal waking from its winter sleep. . . .

But just then the telephone rang. The trouble was, thought Mrs Miniver as she reached out to answer it, that one never quite had time to get to the bottom of one's deeper thoughts. That, perhaps, was the Danger of being a Gentleman. . . .

K. Watkins

23 December 1939

Correspondence
SIR, – I am afraid I must plead guilty to a slight deception.

When I saw the announcement of your competition No. 512, I felt pretty sure that I could write a far crueller satire on 'Mrs Miniver' than could any of my detractors. I therefore tried my hand at it, and sent in the result over beyond my wildest hopes, and as my close connection with Mrs Miniver precludes me from accepting the prize, I have no choice but to reveal myself.

Would you be so good as to send the prize to the competitor who was next in order of merit – or, if you prefer it, to the Association for the Relief of Distressed Gentlewomen?

17 Halsey Street, S.W.3.

Jan Struther

F. TENNYSON JESSE

It is a Very Queer War

11 September 1939

It is a very queer war. Our little social life, such as it was – quiet but pleasant – has come to a complete end. Noel Streatfeild, complete with gas mask and tin helmet, dashed in for lunch, full of stories about the firemen and ambulance drivers at the station where she is an A.R.P. warden. She was going down in the pitch black the other night, dressed in her slacks and dark blue sweater, when a voice with a French accent murmured to her: 'Would you not like to come home with me, pretty boy?' It was one of the French Bond Street tarts. 'Shut up, you fool!' said Noel.

'*Mon dieu!*' said the tart.

4 November 1939

The A.R.P. authorities informed us that it is very important during an aerial bombardment to sit with a cork in your mouth, as the blast from a shell (even a long way off) may snap your jaws to and then, not only may your tongue be cut off, but your ear-drums are blown in. So we ordered our old man to produce us three corks for us to take upstairs, and when he served the coffee after dinner he solemnly presented Tottie with three corks on a little tray in the most correct manner imaginable, remarking: 'Your corks, sir!'

VERILY ANDERSON

A FANY is Court-Martialled

My plans for concealing my fears under a dashing adventurous life came to nothing. For one thing, now that war had been declared, there was nothing for the moment to fear. Eagerly I volunteered to be sent abroad; but when the time came to be posted from London I found myself instead back in Sussex in a house I knew well, with about thirty other FANYs, including Elizabeth with her unstuffed palliasse.

We were commanded by a bubbly-haired old actress who, as the niece of a senior army officer, took her position very seriously. In her talk she mingled a certain amount of army jargon, picked up at her uncle's breakfast table, with the normal chatter we understood of hats and actors and horses. Sometimes, judging by her modes of addressing us, she saw us as Mayfair Debutantes and sometimes as Men Going Over The Top.

The idea behind our camping in this big and beautiful house was that we should be able to drive ambulances for the army. At first we had no ambulances, and hung about wistfully wishing we had. Then we were allotted an assortment of commandeered furniture-vans, fish-carts, and carriers.

Within a week of our collecting them, I had the misfortune to be the first FANY to crash one into a gatepost.

The C.O. came running out to look at the damage. Several army expressions must have floated up from her subconscious, but for the moment all she could say was a reproving,

'Really, Bruce, it's too tiresome!'

She went back to her office, which she called The Orderly Room, and must have sat down to think hard of something with more of a military tang.

A few minutes later, while I was getting ready for lunch, two FANYs of the quiet, useful, obedient type came into the bedroom which I shared with four others (including one whose claim to fame was that her husband had been fallen on by Queen Mary in her recent motor accident). The two FANYs stood in a waiting attitude, one each side of me.

'Want to borrow a comb?' I asked affably.

'You're under arrest,' said one.

'I'm what?' I asked.

'Under arrest. We've had orders to close in on you and march you to the orderly room without your cap or belt.'

I giggled. This was just the sort of joke Elizabeth and I had with each other, but it was funnier coming from these two.

'Oh,' said one to the other, 'she can't. The C.O. never thought of that. Our belts are stitched on to our tunics.'

'Then, without your cap, fall in!' said the other.

'I say, are you serious?' I asked with some surprise, now remembering the episode of the fallen gate-post.

'C.O.'s orders. Quick march.'

I put on my tunic and, still buttoning it, trotted merrily along between them, hoping to meet Elizabeth on the way downstairs. But Elizabeth was not about. To my amazement, everybody we passed turned away as though in shame. I had knocked a good many gate-posts down in my time, but nobody had ever before felt so deeply about it as this.

In the orderly room I had an idea which I felt might interest our dramatic C.O. I saluted her.

'You can't salute without a cap on,' she remembered, and then gave various conflicting orders to my escorts.

'The Prisoner To Be Confined In A Cell,' she ended up and I was marched away to the green dressing-room which I had known as such since I was a child. I sat down on the bed waiting to see what would happen next. I could hear my escorts moving about outside as they guarded me.

Soon one of them brought my lunch on a tray. Her eyes were downcast and the tray shook a little. After all that ceremonial, I expected dry bread and water, which is what we were given as children when we were sent to bed in disgrace. I was quite surprised to be allowed ordinary sausages and mash, which was followed by apple tart brought by the other escort.

To my intense delight, secreted in the apple tart was a slip of paper on which dear Elizabeth had written, '*Keep a stiff upper lip for the honour of the Third.*' I was glad her eyes were not downcast.

A few minutes later I heard weeping outside, followed by muffled footsteps.

The gardener's wife came in to take my tray away. She handed me a box of chocolates.

'I dunno, I'm sure,' she said. 'One of the young ladies give me this to give you. The one outside was crying her eyes out and saying she couldn't go on. And half of them downstairs wouldn't touch their lunch. You'd think there'd been a murder. Three left the table sudden-like, and that pretty young Lady Victoria burst into tears and ran upstairs in a dreadful state.'

'But what's it all about?' I asked. 'What's happened?'

'Haven't they told you?'

'No.'

'You're going to be court-martialled.'

'Oh, dear!' I said, 'Then I'd better clean my buttons.'

My next visitor was the M.T. sergeant, a tough-looking lady who was rarely seen out of oily overalls.

'Please tell me,' I asked her anxiously, 'did I kill somebody?'

'Who? You? Not that I know of.'

'Then what's this all about?'

'You've done something serious, my gal,' she said, taking her cigarette out of the corner of her mouth. 'You've damaged government property.'

'But this place belongs to my father's churchwarden.'

'As far as we're concerned, it's government property. What I want to know is, would you prefer to be tried by men or women?'

'Men,' I said, 'every time.'

'I think the C.O. would prefer to keep this to ourselves. So I'll tell her you'd rather have women. I shall be on your side, of course.'

This was something new. So far the sergeant had never found herself able to be on my side.

'I'm the prisoner's friend,' she said, smoothing down her Eton crop and wiping her hand on the seat of her overalls.

'Oh,' I said. 'Who'll be my enemy?'

'The president of the court. That's the C.O. Rather fun, eh?' She rollocked out of the room.

As my guard had mutinied, it was the M.T. sergeant who escorted me down to what used to be, before the arrival of the FANYs, the small drawing-room. The C.O. had herself chosen a jury and three witnesses, who had been nowhere near the gate-post at the time of the impact.

I thought of Elizabeth's message and tried to see how funny it all was. But the jury and the witnesses were all so painfully embarrassed that I began to feel as though I was having my appendix out in a public waiting-room. The only person who appeared to be enjoying herself was the prisoner's friend. She seized the opportunity of making hay with her senior officer, whom I found myself feeling quite sorry for. After all, the C.O. had obviously set out to do what she felt was her duty to the country.

Two greyhounds wandered in and, rather as though they had come into church, were hustled discreetly out.

My mind wandered off on to other things while the president and the prisoner's friend became more and more irrelevant, only occasionally attracting the unwilling attention of the jury.

I was surprised out of my reverie by the pronouncement,

'Not guilty.'

'But surely –' I started to object, then thought better of it. If the gate-post had been proved still intact, let it rest at that. I was dismissed.

The tension was broken. I was surrounded by FANYs, jury and otherwise, shaking my hand and congratulating me as though I had shot the winning goal in a school match. One of the dormitories instantly gave a feast for me, delving under their beds to produce drinks and cakes and fruit. The C.O., delving back again into her subconscious for an appropriate term, brought out a beauty.

'If you'd been found guilty, there would of course have been The Question of Mitigation Of Sentence.'

NELLA LAST

Whistling up the Spirits

Wednesday, 1 November 1939
I know by Cliff's letters it's the little simple things of home and his former life before he was a soldier that are dearest. I often wonder what his thoughts have been when he was writing my letters.

He said he liked the snap of him and me together. It was like his 'own picture' of me – always gay and kind and 'firm'. He felt I was one of the things to 'hold on to' and know I would never change. Wonder what had gone 'agley' – he does not often show his feelings. Odd he should think I am always gay. Come to think of it, down at the W.V.S. Centre they think I'm a 'mental tonic', as old Mrs Waite put it.

I must be a very good actress, for I don't feel gay often. Perhaps, though, I'm like the kid who whistled as he went past the churchyard to keep his spirits up, for down in my heart there is a sadness which never lifts and, if I did not work and work till I was too tired to do anything but sleep when I went to bed, would master me. Like the little Holland boy who put his hand in the hole in the dyke and kept back the trickle of water that would have quickly grown to a flood, I *must* keep my dykes strong enough – or else at times I'd go under.

I got a dozen chintz bags made tonight – such pathetic, brave little bags with a square of tracing paper stitched on. They are 'hospital supplies', to use to put a soldier's little treasures in, out of his pocket, if he is wounded and taken to hospital. There are huge stacks of them to make, and when I thought of all the W.V.S. Centres all over England making the same numbers, I could have wept. It's little things like that which seem to bring home to me the dreadful inevitableness of things, with everything prepared for a three years' war. The chintzes I sewed would have made such gay cushions or curtains – or romping children's overalls.

Wednesday, 29 November 1939
I wish sometimes I was a religious woman and could find comfort and faith in bombarding God with requests and demands. I think people must be born like that, though. I try sometimes to pray that Cliff will not have to go to France – will come out of the Army – but feel in some queer way presumptuous, and just ask for comfort and help on his journey. My next-door neighbour has every religious service on at all hours, and finds comfort in it. I wish I could do so – I would only find irritation at the loud noise. She says she prays God to strike Hitler dead. Cannot help thinking if God wanted to do that he would not have waited till Mrs Helm asked him to do so.

VITA SACKVILLE-WEST

Country Notes

September [1939]

With the prospect of devastation hanging over us, the impression
of fecundity produced by the countryside the past fortnight
strikes one as painfully ironical. All crops seemed to come to
fruition at once: the corn, the apples and the hops. These things
happen every year, but this year one noticed them more
poignantly than usual. For one thing, a number of the ordinary
farm workers had been called away to grimmer jobs, and their
place was taken by amateur improvised labour. Skinny little boys
from London raked the chaff and cavings from under the threshing machine; handsome, elegant young men waiting to be put
into uniform heaved trusses of straw from stack to cart; school-
boys climbed into apple trees and picked, for once legitimately,
the huge green cookers into bushel baskets. Everything hummed
with liveliness; the thresher hummed literally, so did the drying-
fans in the oasthouse; there was a constant burr from stackyard
and oasts; the air smelt of hops; dust-motes flew about; large
horses stood waiting patiently between the shafts of large wag-
gons; peaches and nectarines on the wall ripened so rapidly that
the blush came over them as over the cheeks of a girl; figs turned
as brown as Syrian sailors. A sudden hurry woke the somnolent
farm to life; everyone took a hand, grateful for the physical activity which puts a stop to thought; everything bore its own
particular fruit. This teeming effect has been increased by the
quantities of extra children straying all over the place, as though
country families were inordinately prolific. Swinging on gates,
smeared with blackberry juice in the lanes, they have turned the
country into a warren. Some of them, I understand, are not too
popular with their hosts and hostesses. There is one story of two
little boys, left behind to play while the farmer and his household
went out to work; on his return he found a cloud of feathers and
a squawking barnyard full of completely naked chickens.
Decidedly, being in the country is great fun.

Then there are the land girls, an unfamiliar sight in the orchards
and among the cows; picturesque in their brown dungarees, toss-
ing their short curls back and laughing. I came across two of them

picking plums; very young they were, and standing under the tree loaded with the blood-red drops, their arms lifted, the half-filled baskets on the ground beside them, they could scarcely have looked prettier in their lives than on that sunlit morning.

Black-out

In contrast to the sunlit days came the starlit nights. I could imagine nothing more desirable and mysterious than these black secret nights, were it not for the sinister intention behind them. I suppose that one should not allow the intention to impair one's appreciation of this new beauty of the starry night. The moon has gone, and nothing but stars and three planets remain within our autumn sky. Every evening I go my rounds like some night-watchman to see that the black-out is complete. It is. Not a chink reveals the life going on beneath those roofs, behind those blinded windows; love, lust, death, birth, anxiety, even gaiety. All is dark; concealed. Alone I wander, no one knowing that I prowl. It makes me feel like an animal, nocturnal, stealthy. I might be a badger or a fox. All voices are stilled as though by a hand laid over noisy mouths. The experience is a strange one, making me feel more like myself and more unlike myself, more closely united to those who share my roof yet more divorced from them, than ever I felt before. I think of all the farms and cottages spread over England, sharing this curious protective secrecy where not even a night-light may show in the room of a dying man or a woman in labour.

The black-out is inconvenient to the man drying the hops from dusk to dawn. I stroll round to the oasts, and find one door left open beneath the shadow of the staging. They have hung a green silk scarf over the central lamp, so that the glaucous light of under-seas tinges the lime-washed walls to the very colour of the hops themselves. War brings an unforeseen strangeness to these small interiors of illumination.

I continue on my rounds. The Londoners' children in the village are asleep by now in their improvised beds. The landgirls, tired out, are asleep also, their brown dungarees exchanged for striped pyjamas. The four young men whom I watched at supper, four boys at the beginning of lives probably to be lost, the boys who slung the sheaves in early morning, are asleep also. All these people gathered under various roofs are asleep.

The place I love; the country I love; the boys I love. I wander round, and towards midnight discover that the only black-out I notice is the black-out of my soul. So deep a grief and sorrow that they are not expressible in words.

CHAPTER THREE

Horizons Darken

In April and May 1940 Germany invaded Denmark, Norway, Holland, Belgium and Luxembourg. At the end of May the British Expeditionary Force was evacuated from Dunkirk; a month later France surrendered.

Because Britain was never invaded, it remained to some extent on the edge of the terrible sufferings and devastation in mainland Europe. People could not see fully the horror of what was going on in Europe: the persecution and oppression, the life under an invading power, the many millions put to death or forced to become refugees. But there were glimpses, indications, echoes.

Eye-witness accounts by English and American women in France during the summer of 1940 reverberate with shock. With their eye on the effects of war rather than its acts, they show the characteristics of women's war reporting at its best. Their standpoint is the margins of war, explicitly and democratically among ordinary people; their focus is highly angled, picking out significant detail. Even Tom Harrisson, who found little to praise in his article on 'War Books' for *Horizon* in December 1941, paused to admire Cecily Mackworth's *I Came Out Of France* for its 'epic quality and sympathy'.

Those women who did manage to leave France or other parts of Europe sometimes had exciting adventures – the usual stuff of war stories – and books such as Bessy Myers' *Captured, My Experiences as an Ambulance Driver and as a Prisoner of the Nazis* (1941) began to appear. An interesting feature of women's writing about scrapes and escapes is the way the authors often insist on their ordinariness in other circumstances. Etta Shiber, for example, was imprisoned for helping English servicemen who had been left behind after the evacuation from Dunkirk to return to England. What she did showed courage and initiative, yet she continually describes herself as a timid middle-class lady, 'an ordinary woman with no particular taste for adventure'.

Escape to England was not always the end of the story. With the threat of invasion spreading, the popular press worked up public opinion against Austrians and Germans in England, most of them victims of Nazi oppression. In the summer of 1940 nearly four thousand women were interned in segregated quarters on the Isle of Man. These were dark days, and it is heartening to find women joining in the tireless work on behalf of the refugees: among them were the MP Eleanor Rathbone, Secretary of the Parliamentary Committee on Refugees, and the Austrian Eva Kolmer, who collaborated with François Lafitte on his powerful 1940 Penguin Special, *The Internment of Aliens*.

CECILY MACKWORTH

The Power of Propaganda

It was gradually becoming apparent to what extent the German Fifth Column had been organized throughout France. The sick refugees who passed through my dispensary told me stories which, separately, meant nothing, but became significant when viewed as a whole. At every station there had been benevolent men and women waiting to give false information; nurses who had separated children from their parents and then, when inquiries were made, turned out to be unknown to any of the Red Cross organizations. Notices appeared mysteriously on the walls of town halls and churches, warning the population to leave immediately, signed with the seemingly authentic signature of the mayor. False rumours had been put about with such consistency that it became clear that they were not rumours at all, but perfectly timed propaganda. Refugees from remote corners of the south assured me with absolute conviction that the Germans had been close behind them as they left their homes. At this time it really seemed as though the world had gone mad. The feeling that it was impossible to trust anyone was extraordinarily oppressive.

KAY BOYLE

The Fall of France

26th June. Yesterday was a day of downpour, and of quiet and moving grief among the people here. There was a ceremony of mourning on the square in the rain, and the soldiers passing through lounged about as the wreath was placed on the monument of the last war's dead. Two of them turned their backs and did not salute when the French flag was raised. Afterwards the women returned quietly and sat down, raw-eyed, behind the counters of their shops. None of them have any news of their men – none; and Germany is claiming a million and a half prisoners for the duration of the war.

1st July. One feels the need badly now of seeing people, watching things, hearing things said. Every café table seems to have become a sort of refuge, and people who have never before set eyes on one another find themselves sitting down and looking into each other's faces for the answer, not understanding yet how it has happened or why it has happened, but only that we share a disastrous fate in common, and that is the fate of sudden and incredible defeat. They tell you the story of their own experiences, or the experiences of friends, or merely of people they have heard about somewhere, as if in saying these things over and over they must somehow find the explanation in the end.

POLLY PEABODY

In France, August 1940

I went to the American Red Cross to find out if anything more had been heard of my unit, which was still sitting up in Sweden, and also to offer my services in whatever capacity they might be required.

The personnel of the American Scandinavian Field Hospital I was told, were at that very moment on their way back to America.

After exchanging a few Red Cross smiles, which are enough to make milk curdle, I was given the job of ambulance driver at the

American Hospital in Neuilly, and the work consisted of transporting food and clothing to the various prison camps, to relieve in some degree the hell to which the prisoners of war were subjected.

Most of the men slept on the damp ground, were underfed and lightly clothed. They all suffered from dysentery, of which many died. Thousands of parcels were packed for prisoners, but the tragedy was that they seldom got delivered.

One day, while I was working at the hospital, a little man, all bent with age, and whose small eyes had faded with the years, appeared with a parcel for his prisoner son. He held the bundle wrapped in newspaper under his arm, and spoke with a sort of excitement:

'You know, I have come a long way to bring it – I also had to wait for hours in line before I could get in, and at my age it is not so easy, but I know it'll make him happy – poor boy.'

I asked him what was in the package. 'A steak,' he said triumphantly. I refrained from telling him that the steak would be rotten by the time it reached his son, but I informed him that all packages had been momentarily stopped: I thought he was going to cry. 'Ah! Mamzelle, he must be so hungry.' For a few minutes he stood gazing at the rumpled newspaper which the fresh meat had already stained: then without another word he turned and hobbled away.

Meanwhile, the Germans told the prisoners that at home no one was thinking of them, or cared, as they were too busy messing around with dirty politics. These conditions altered with time, and the lot of the prisoners improved: but in those August days they were shocking.

Lists of prisoners and casualties were on sale outside subway stations and on the news-stands. This was the only way in which the people of Occupied France learnt what became of their men.

I remember a woman who had apparently just bought one of these lists. She was standing on the side-walk, glancing through the long line of names, when suddenly she raised a clenched fist to her mouth to stifle a scream. For a moment she swayed: then, with the crumpled paper over her eyes, she sobbed and sobbed. The newspaper woman tried to console her, while passers-by lingered a moment and looked at her with sympathy, and went on their way shaking their heads. There was hardly a woman in

France who didn't have a brother, husband or son or other relation they couldn't account for. At first, they said, 'He is surely a prisoner.' They all clung to that hope until sometimes the bitter truth was known.

Many people stopped me to ask questions or advice, on account of the uniform I wore. I was in a store once, when a woman approached me. She had a dazed, angry expression.

'Look,' she said, 'this is what I received this morning,' and held out a dirty piece of paper, the corner torn off a full sheet. The paper bore the stamp of a Red Cross, and on it was scribbled in pencil the name of a man, his regiment, number and the two words, 'gravely wounded.' That was all. The man was her son.

The case of the prisoners of war was close to everyone's heart, and it is still the hatchet which Hitler holds over the heads of the people. 'If you don't play along with us,' they say to the French, 'you will never see your men again.'

SYLVIA LEITH-ROSS

Leaving France

There were also hours and hours spent outside the Portuguese Consulate in Toulouse. I had been into a bookseller's shop to buy a map. When no other customers were near, the bookseller leant over the counter: 'I see you are English. I, I like the English. They gave Shakespeare to the world. You must get out of France at all costs! And Mademoiselle who is with you, she is so young. You must not stay another day. Get a Portuguese visa, then perhaps the Spanish will give you a transit visa, even though the frontier is closed.'

And so the greatness of Shakespeare led us to the Portuguese Consulate where, hemmed in by the crowd, we found a Canadian doctor and his French wife, marooned as we were, and without a car.

Together, we worked our way into the house, and step by step, up the stairs. In the Consul's office, intending travellers were putting in the visas on their own passports, writing on the corner of the mantelpiece, on the windowledge, and on each other's backs. The Consul stamped them cheerfully by the hundred. We were the only British subjects. At last we got through, though what we intended doing with our visas, we had no idea.

There was just room in the Austin for Dr W. and his wife. As we drove out of Toulouse, we passed bands of young men on bicycles, lads just under military age. Each had a bundle tied to his bicycle, and each rode swiftly, head down. Where to? They probably did not know.

We had long stretches of road to ourselves. There were moments when it was difficult to remember the war, so quiet was it. Then we would come on a level-crossing and have to wait while a train went by, very slowly, full of soldiers crowded into goods vans. They also did not look as if they knew where they were going to, with their white, unshaven faces. Once we passed the remnant of a Senegalese regiment. They marched heavily, wearily, their big feet in heavy boots, covered with dust. Their faces had gone a deep leaden grey, frightening when one sees it in an African.

We drove till late, and stopped at a small inn in a wayside village. The innkeeper and his wife had little food left, but would do their best, they assured us. There was a room vacant in another house where we could sleep. They had no news to give us; refugees had passed by in great numbers, but were now lessening. Of the Spanish frontier, they knew nothing reliable, nor of what was happening on the coast. We were eating fried ham when someone mentioned Bordeaux. It was good ham, but Mrs W. said she preferred ham cured *à la façon de Bordeaux*. Madame could not agree, and defended her local method. They spoke with fervour and animation, like two artists discussing some rare method of mixing paints or varnish.

It was eleven o'clock at night; all of us were worn with mental and physical fatigue; the future was a black chasm; the present heavy with difficulty and danger. Yet these two Frenchwomen had the courage and the vigour and the integrity, to sit down and discuss, at length, the merits of two ways of curing ham. . . . For a moment, it seemed to me ridiculous, then a kind of awe came over me. In the midst of unimaginable disaster, they were being true to themselves, they were being French. Nothing could stop them from thinking that cooking was an art of importance. In the face of ruin and desolation undreamt of, they threw out the challenge. It was not cured ham they were defending, but the right of France to be herself, *envers et contre tous*. [. . .]

We turned due south to St Jean de Luz. The town was full of people milling to and fro, of abandoned cars, and mounds of luggage. The British Consul sat in a room above a café, and dealt with a throng of nationalities, which had somehow acquired British passports. He was kind and competent. There was a British ship in harbour. We were to embark at five o'clock.

Down on the quay, there was a confusion of soldiers and sailors and civilians, of lorries and ambulances, arms and stores. Every now and then, a French officer would stop one of us, and whisper: 'You are English. Can I get to England? I must go on fighting.'

ETTA SHIBER

The Indifference of the Comfortable

My only desire now was to forget all that had happened to me; but as the days went by, and the first joy of release passed, I was overcome with a new anguish – one which was associated with the period which I had hoped to put behind me. It was, oddly enough, the result of the width of the gap between my new life and the events through which I had just passed. For, all about me, I saw people leading their normal calm existences, unaware, apparently, of the importance of the enemy threat. I had been a part of the war, although a small part, and I could not regard it with detachment myself, or remain unmoved when I saw others doing so.

Sometimes I would look about me in the streets, at the carefree crowds and say to myself: 'And yet we are at war!'

For me that fact had changed a whole existence. For millions of others it had also changed – or cancelled – existence; and while those about me seemed so unhurried, I knew that other thousands were striving and dying, and that every minute lost to help them would mean for them, not sixty seconds more of discomfort, but the end of life itself.

I couldn't forget the faces of those I had left behind me – Kitty, Father Christian, Tissier, Chancel, all the others, with whom I had lived an existence so different from that I know at present. With them, almost against my own will, I had been able to save some few lives – but how many more who could be saved still remain in peril! How many in France and in other countries under the heel of the oppressor suffer, struggle, and die!

The indifference I meet everywhere frightens me. I believe in human solidarity – but so many live unconcerned with the pains of their millions of brothers under the yoke! I believe in divine justice – even in our materialistic world – but I know it works through the instrumentality of human beings sufficiently in tune with it to strive for its execution. And as I see how many there are who put their own comfort above the efforts necessary to save millions of helpless beings, I feel guilty myself – guilty for being here now, in a place of safety, busied with matters of no importance, while this clash of the forces of good and evil is shaking the world.

Yes, I am troubled by a sense of guilt. Some who are alive today may be shot tomorrow; and how can anyone rest knowing that he might be able to contribute to saving precious human lives if he is not doing so?

CYNTHIA SAUNDERS

Tribunal Day

1939

The KC* laid his black hat and coat on a red leather chair underneath the trellised window overlooking the High Street, rubbed his hands and said, 'A cold morning, Sergeant.' 'Yes, Sir, very cold,' the policeman answered. It was ten o'clock. The door opened and the interpreter came in, shook hands with the KC and the Sergeant, and said cheerfully, 'Let's turn them all down this morning and get to lunch early.'

'I'm sorry you're feeling so bloodthirsty, Miss Simmons,' the Sergeant said, 'make them think we're in Germany, eh?'

At 10.15 enter the first alien. It was quite a way from the door to the two chairs placed at a discreet distance from the little table

---

* King's Counsel

behind which the Judge sat. On his left was the Sergeant, acting as secretary, taking down everything that was said; on his right the interpreter.

'Are you Grete Schmidt?'

'Yes,' a large, homely woman replied.

'When were you born?'

'Eighteen, six, ninety-three,' came the answer in Teuton fashion, meaning June 18th, 1893.

'And when did you come to England?'

'One, five, thirty-five.'

'Are you Jewish?'

'No.'

'What is your religion?'

The buxom cook spread herself. She had wanted to say so much, but the questions came a little too fast.

'Me? I believe in the Lord, and He made the world a very big place and I don't understand why people should always be being told they must go home.'

The interpreter smiled, the Sergeant smiled and the Judge passed his hand over his mouth.

'Nevertheless, Miss Schmidt, why are you in England now?'

'Because I like England. I don't like Austria with Hitler there.'

'Have you any money over here?'

'O yes, Sir, I save.'

'In a bank, Miss Schmidt?'

'No, Sir – one's pocket is one's best friend,' and she drew out a little leather satchel with pound notes.

Miss Schmidt had excellent references and 'her lady' was outside. Exempted from internment until further notice.

Next, an elderly Jewish couple. The man limped badly, walking with a stick. He sat down with some difficulty. 'Excuse me, I am lame – the Nazis,' he said. 'I am sixty-five today, my birthday.' The Sergeant leant across and shook hands with him. 'Congratulations.' Then the old Jew broke down for a few seconds. So did his wife. Miss Simmons looked away to the window and the Judge waited patiently.

The questions began. When it came to his former profession he had a rare one. He had made the printed silk ribbons often used on wreaths. 'Hitler took my business, my grandfather founded it, you see in the concentration camp they broke my leg . . . and in the High Street my wife knows . . . but you see I have come here . . .' He was dithering helplessly. Shades of former cross-examinations.

Miss Simmons translated, adding that it would be kinder to serve, and de-restrict.

The Judge thought so, too, and asked her to translate how he hoped they would both have a peaceful time in England. They tottered out, their registration books endorsed: 'Victims of Nazi Oppression, exempt from Internment and from all restrictions applicable to enemy aliens.' A little shred of happiness for past miseries. The Tribunal had been sitting for three weeks, but it took a few seconds to recover from this.

'Next, please.'

The door opened and a very beautiful youngish German woman tripped across the floor up to the two chairs, of which she took one and lifted it firmly to the table, sitting down immediately opposite the Judge (a thing he could not bear). Miss Simmons caught the Sergeant's eye and the Judge's, but not the beautiful woman's, who was out by every means in her power to win or die. She wheeled and charmed the KC in vain. It only got her case postponed for Home Office and other files to be sent down from London.

'Only she is too like a copy-book spy to be real,' the Judge observed to Miss Simmons at luncheon.

'Next, please.'

This was an Austrian boy of 19, parlourman in the house of a Staff Captain. Yes, he waited at table (and overheard everything), no, he wasn't a refugee (and so had deliberately become Stateless), but Austria under Hitler, &c. Rather a tall story. Anyway unsuitable for employment in Staff Captain's house. Tribunal had no power to make him leave or be dismissed; only power to intern or exempt from internment with or without travelling restrictions. Interned.

Then four refugees, then luncheon, and another half-dozen, all straightforward cases.

Finally, about 4.15, the last for the day.

She spoke very little English, and answered every question in monosyllables. She was not a refugee. She had had two sisters over here in service, like herself, who had gone back to Germany shortly before the war started. Why had she stayed? No answer.

Had she deliberately stayed? Yes. Would she like to go back now?
No. Was she a member of the *Arbeitsfront*? No. Had she voted
when the German ship came? No? Why not? No answer. It was
getting late and the Tribunal was getting no further. A shame that
the last case should be so tedious. It was no use starting all over
again. Suddenly Miss Simmons had an idea. Had the young
woman any special friend in England? Yes. Who?

'My employer –'

'Are you engaged?'

'He's the father of my child.'

That, too, may be the price of refuge.

DIANA MOSLEY

Internment in Holloway

1940

The beautiful hot summer weather went on and on; the garden at
Denham was full of flowers. On Saturday afternoon I fed the
baby and put him in his pram. I took my book into the garden. A
maid appeared.

'There are some people at the door who want to speak to you,'
she said.

'What sort of people?'

'Three men and a woman.'

I knew at once they must be police. Journalists sometimes hunt
in couples, and one or two had come since M.'s* arrest asking
rude and irrelevant questions, but three men and a woman
sounded more like police. I went to the door, and a warrant for
my arrest was produced. The woman came with me while I put a
few things in a small box; 'enough for a week-end,' she said. I was
thinking about the baby and the bombing of London which, since
France had fallen, was expected hourly.

He was eleven weeks old that day. I asked where I was to be
imprisoned; I had heard of a women's prison at Aylesbury; but it

---

* Oswald Mosley, Leader of the British Union of Fascists and Diana's
husband.

was to be Holloway, therefore I decided, much as I longed to take him, that I must leave him with Nanny, who would take both babies to Rignell where they would be as safe as it was possible to be. Since, however, the policewoman had said 'a week-end', I thought I should do my best to be able to continue nursing the baby when it was over, and then wean him in the usual way. It was supposed to be bad for a baby to have a complete change of diet. I hugged the babies, and Nanny who was in tears, and was driven away.

The police motored me to London along empty roads; we were there in no time. Hoping to be able to nurse the baby again I asked my escort to stop at Bell and Croyden in Wigmore Street, the policewoman came with me and I bought a contraption called a breast pump. I should have been wiser to have got the salts and bandages which women use who do not intend to nurse their babies; I should have had far less pain. At Holloway prison the great gate opened and the car deposited me the other side of a yard.

Then came the strange procedure called in prison language 'reception'. I was locked into a wooden box like a broom cupboard. It had a seat fixed opposite the door; if you sat on it your knees touched the door. There was no window but light came in from the wire netting roof of the box. Here I remained for four hours. This was in the nature of a practical joke on the part of the prison authorities, for there was no reason why I should not have been taken straight to my cell after the usual formalities. There was nobody else arrested under Regulation 18B that day.

I collected my thoughts. My ideas about prison came from American films, and I envisaged cells of which one side would be made of iron bars, all giving on to a landing, like a zoo. The walls of my cupboard, painted a dirty cream colour, had been scribbled on by former denizens; there were a few swear words and cryptic sentences. 'Fraser is a cow,' was one. I tried to read the book I had brought with me, a pocket edition of Lytton Strachey's *Elizabeth and Essex*. It was not an ideal choice but I had snatched it up as I left my room.

After a couple of hours the door was unlocked for a moment and I was given a chipped enamel plate with a vast sandwich upon it, also an immense mug of thick china made in the shape of a bobbin with a waist but no handle, containing a hot brown liquid which I guessed was supposed to be tea though it looked more like soup. I was thirsty but dared not drink. I missed the baby in an almost unbearable way. I left the sandwich untouched. After a while I heard other prisoners arrive and being locked into the adjacent boxes, and for the first time I heard the odd noise made by women prisoners, particularly prostitutes. They shout to one another in a sort of wail that is more like song than speech. It was to become a familiar sound over the years; also the accompanying shouts of the wardresses: 'Be quiet, you women.'

After about four and a half hours in my box I was taken out to see the doctor, an unprepossessing female with dyed hair and long finger nails, varnished dark red. I told her that I had been nursing my baby but that I could look after myself, and when a bath was mentioned I said I had had one that morning which seemed to satisfy her. Then a wardress took me to F Wing.

She made me go first, an act of apparent courtesy which, like so much in prison, is not quite what it seems. Wardresses must always have their prisoners in front of them; if they were following there's no knowing what they might take it into their heads to do: run away, for example.

As she unlocked the door and we stood in the entrance to F Wing a babel of voices suddenly fell silent and a sort of gasp went up. Dozens of women, many of them in dressing gowns, were standing about in groups, most had mugs in their hands. I did not know it, but it was ten minutes before they were due to be locked in their cells for the night and for this reason they were all on the landings. They crowded round me with kind expressions of sympathy; they knew I had left a little baby and were furious on my behalf. I knew very few of them, though they were members of B.U. [...]

Before I arrived the 18Bs had decided to eat together at trestle tables set up in the space between the cells on the ground floor. They took it in turns to fetch the food in huge metal containers from the prison kitchen, and to wash up. Washing up was a nasty affair, the plates were battered enamel, the forks bent and old, there was no soap and very little hot water. As soon as I decently could I abandoned this communal style of living. I got a china plate of my own and avoided the dreadful enamel. In any case I could not eat the prison food, except for the delicious bully beef; I made my ration of this last several days, otherwise I lived on prison bread and Stilton cheese sent me by M.

LIVIA LAURENT

Internment on the Isle of Man

1940

We arrived at the camp on the Isle of Man. Compartment by
compartment we were unlocked, let out and received by a smiling, gushing lady. 'This way dear.' She had helpers who were told
where to take us. 'Three for the Hydro, six to the towers, eight to
Seaview, four to the Strand Café. You have lost your friend dear?
Never mind, you will find her again. No one gets lost here.' We
were pushed, counted, torn apart. Else and Lotte just vanished,
only by hanging on to Matilda's rucksack did I manage not to get
lost myself.

We found ourselves tramping down a lane. 'This is where you
are going to live,' a cheerful girl told us. She knocked at the door
of a boarding house. 'Two internees for you, Mrs Drinkwater.'
Mrs Drinkwater was outraged. 'I have no room. What will they
think of next,' and slammed the door in our faces. So that was
that. Back to the station, which was already deserted. The smiling
lady was just on her way home. 'Mrs Drinkwater had no room
for these two,' our guide told her. 'Mrs Drinkwater? Who is Mrs
Drinkwater? Who are you?' she wanted to know. I just looked
the other way. This was a farce. Matilda would burst in a minute,
I could see it coming. 'But they've just arrived'; the girl got flustered too. 'Ah yes, so they have, take them to the Bay View,
plenty of room there. Goodnight, you'll be happy there.' She was
gone.

The streets were quite empty already. This was the Bay View.
'Just knock at the door, all the best, goodnight,' and before we
could thank her, the girl had disappeared. We knocked. Nothing
happened. We knocked again. A face showed in a window: 'Who
are you?' 'We are new, supposed to live here!' 'The landlord is
out.' 'Can't you let us in?' 'Impossible, the door is locked. You
can't get in, we can't come out. Wait!' She was back in a second.
'Catch,' she threw us bananas, oranges, apples.

I settled down on the steps and wondered if we were going to
spend the night there. Matilda's mood suddenly changed and she
became hilarious. There were people hanging out of all the windows now; trying to be helpful, laughing, feeling sorry for us.

'You'll be put in jail for overstepping the curfew!' 'That's O.K. with me, we've just come from there. Give me Holloway anytime. At least there is a bed for everyone.' 'You've been at Holloway?' The little brunette who had thrown us the oranges looked scared. It suddenly dawned on me that most of the people here hadn't been in prison at all, they had been sent here straight away.

'There is Mr Harrison, he'll help you!' A young curly-headed clergyman was coming towards us. After much wandering about we eventually landed in a small private house with one small bed for two people. [...]

We were not all alike, and our lives differed considerably. What was, for me, the better part of a year a time of comparative contentment and inner freedom, was, for others, the most frightful strain and unhappiness. Those who lived in the big hotels and suffered from the gossip and constant malicious attacks of others, those who stayed in small houses and were used by unscrupulous landladies as maids of all work, those who were torn away from husbands and children, those who knew their families to be in the front lines of London, in the trenches of Swiss Cottage, Bloomsbury and Maida Vale, those who had not yet learned to think of themselves as removed from their own background; and all of those who were not quite consciously determined to make the best of it, at whatever cost.

There were others who liked the absence of responsibility, the fact that no decision was required of them, for some it was their first real 'holiday' as they called it, others enjoyed the easy companionship, the chance of meeting people they wouldn't have met in the ordinary course of their lives; and Mrs Becker who had kept the little haberdashery shop in a back street of Manchester was happy and proud to dry dishes, graciously handed to her by Mlle Adele, the great singer and opera star. [...]

When I left my companions that afternoon, though arranging to meet again, I knew that that companionship was over. It had been over the moment we left Holloway. It happened to everybody. I met Leni. 'How is Gretel?' They had been inseparable, always walking arm in arm. 'We quarrelled,' and a long story of Gretel's misdeeds followed. Hildegarde walked around by herself. 'Where's Rita?' 'Don't mention that name to me, I never want to see her again,' she flared up. On the small territory allotted to

4,000 people, many lonely walks were taken, many tales of horror told about the friends of yesterday. Why was this necessary? Did people's natures come out in this so-called freedom? Had they only been subdued in Holloway? The story went that a sedative had been mixed in our food there, that's why we had been so peaceful and placid in prison. Quite possible, it would make as good an explanation as any. . . .

Dame Joanna Cruickshank (the Camp Commandant) was deeply grieved to find that some of us had not been quite straight with the authorities. It was hard for her to say, but say it she must, there were some internees who had actually reverted to dishonesty in order to obtain some of their own money. Not without reluctance she found herself compelled to employ this method* which, as she fully realized, punished innocent and guilty alike. She sincerely hoped it would not have to be for long. It was as painful to her as it must have been to us. As soon as we would show ourselves worthy of her renewed trust, she would reconsider the issue. And there was something else she had meant to say to us for a long long time. Happiness was of own making; place, conditions and circumstances were of no importance. All that mattered was to be happy!

While she went on talking at great length, imploring us to be happy at all costs, I watched the people as they were listening. There was old Mrs Kaiser, a grandmother, who had brought up a large number of sons and daughters, who had been a good wife and mother, and was nearing the conclusion of a full and varied life. Being poor, she couldn't have been one of those so rightly punished for embezzling their own money, but she looked crestfallen and apologetic just the same. There was little Miss Schwarz, a Bible student, who would rather have died than infringe the slightest regulation, however ridiculous, looking sad and guilty. There were countless others, teachers, successful business women, women who had done their jobs in life as well as anybody, and who had every right to be proud, independent, and confident, looking like children in a charity school, cowed and utterly crushed. There were little murmurs of regret, someone went so far as to say 'I'll never do it again,' although I am convinced she

---

*Of stopping the billing system with local shops.

hadn't done anything at all, and the general atmosphere was unbearable.

The only failing of these women was the fact that they had the wrong kind of passport; very few of them had enemies, still less would they have indulged in any act of malice. But the fact alone was sufficient to overshadow any other consideration for their personal value, their own integrity. And they accepted it. The terrible thing was their own acceptance of it, making it possible for a technical matter to influence their character, their courage, touch their very souls. [...]

The Service Exchange – the name explains itself – presented a highly intricate system for providing and exchanging work. Those who worked full-time had the chance of making 2/7 a week, for the remainder they were given vouchers. So a teacher who worked at the school, or gave private lessons, could have a jumper knitted in return, or have her hair done, or her clothes repaired. There was a laundry working full time, a hairdressing saloon, dressmakers, toymakers, weavers, spinners, fortune tellers, people who would type for you, or write a competent English letter, others who would take your children for walks or clean your mackintosh by a special method, guaranteed Viennese; even legal advice was to be had. Gardening came under the scheme too, and everywhere you saw people working in small allotments, later on in the fields, getting ready for the spring. And a good job they made of it.

FLAVIA KINGSCOTE

Internment in Italy

1941

Soon the cold spell relaxed and early summer came to Tuscany. In the hotel garden where we were allowed to walk at will, supervised by a pleasant carabiniere, lilac and irises bloomed in profusion, and all through the night and during much of the day the song of nightingales filled the air. It would have been difficult to have chosen a better suited spot in which to recuperate from the various strains and stresses of the last month, and personally, I was glad our stay here looked like being a long one. We were all very relieved, and many of us extremely surprised, to learn our whole party was to be released when the protracted negotiations regarding our line of departure were completed. Even today I cannot understand why the Italians let us all go unquestioningly, including young men of military age, but it was enough then to know we would eventually be leaving, and for the present I sat back and enjoyed the peace and beauty of my surroundings.

We were allowed out for two hours in the morning and another two in the afternoon, during which time we were given complete freedom within the bounds of the 'campo', a disused horse-show ground resembling a football field, about fifty yards distant from our three hotels. Apart from this we were also allowed to go for walks every afternoon in groups from each hotel accompanied by detectives. These walks grew longer and less formal as the weeks passed, our escorts at first lacking enthusiasm, but gradually the novelty of going for country walks took hold of them, and instead of trudging gloomily behind us along a mile or two of tarred road they would vie with each other, each trying to take his own particular group the longest and most cross-country hike, bringing us back long after the allotted time laden with wild flowers and other trophies.

The inhabitants of Chianciano accepted us without undue excitement or curiosity. Once the novelty of our presence wore off they settled down again, and soon realized what a piece of good business we represented. It was estimated that during our four or five weeks' stay we consumed more wine and beer than is normally drunk in two years, Chianciano being, after all, a spa for heart and liver troubles. The shops did a roaring trade not only in clothes but in sweets and cigarettes which were still to be had in unlimited quantities. The people, while remaining reserved, showed a distinct friendliness towards us, and it was from their lips we learnt of the loss of the *Bismarck* long before it was officially reported in Italy. They can only have heard of the sinking from the BBC, and their manner in conveying it to us with downward-pointing thumbs and sardonic grins, left little doubt as to their satisfaction.

A POLISH REFUGEE

How it Feels to be a Refugee

1943

We brought away nothing valuable from Warsaw – but there was one thing that we did bring, or rather it brought us. That was our car. We ought not to have had it. It was only my idiotic sentimentality. When we came to the French port we had no more money to buy new tyres and we ought to have left it there. I looked at it standing abandoned on an open platform. It had grown a little dirty and worn. I remembered how we had driven it out of our own garage and I thought of the times we had been together since, over what dreadful roads we had driven, and through how many countries. I remembered how we had slept in it when we had no money to pay for a hotel. And I thought to myself, there is my good friend which not a single time has let me down, and I couldn't bear to lose it. So it came with us. It stands now in a garage, and I am still paying five shillings a week, and from time to time I have terrible rows with my husband about it. But so far I have won, and we still keep it. Sometimes I go for a little and sit in it. It is like home.

It isn't easy to be a refugee. And yet, when you have lost so much, it seems as if you are given something in exchange. We have lost our houses and our possessions. But many of us have found a stronger faith in ideas. [...] Often I have heard people say, 'You refugees are a queer lot – you seem to have lost touch with reality. You have the most impossible ideas.' Then I think not only of Chopin who wrote his music in exile, I think also of Pilsudski, who planned the new Poland in a German prison, and of Masaryk who planned in exile the new Czechoslovakia. And perhaps the greatest work of the spirit written by man in exile is the Book of Revelation, which St John wrote on the Isle of Patmos. For myself I have always believed in ideas, but never so much as now.

CHAPTER FOUR

Preparing for the Worst

The evacuation of the British Expeditionary Force from Dunkirk was followed by the Battle of Britain – the daylight dogfights between German and British planes over British soil. In the summer of 1940 Britain prepared to be invaded. Barricades, tank traps and miniature forts appeared; signposts, village and street names disappeared. An appeal to the public for weapons netted twenty thousand shotguns and pistols; these went to the Local Defence Volunteers, later known as the Home Guard.

Women sometimes felt marginalised in these fevered preparations, as they were not allowed to join the Home Guard until 1943, and then only as auxiliaries. But they were keen to do their bit: Home Guard wives proved themselves proficient at mixing Molotov cocktails – bottles filled with resin, petrol and tar to lob at invading Nazi tanks – and the MP Edith Summerskill founded the Women's Home Defence Organization to teach women how to use firearms. The novelist and playwright Margaret Kennedy made her own five-point invasion list of 'things we ought to do', which included having a large sum of money 'ready to be sewed into my stays' and a knapsack of iron rations. She prepared for mobility; the official advice was to '*stay put*'. Meanwhile the shortage of jobs for women was still acute, and a magazine article by the MP Eleanor Rathbone entitled 'The Waste of Woman-Power' was one of many protests that appeared in the press.

Invasion fears bred rumour and gossip. The government response was heavy-handed, aiming much of its propaganda at women. Two housewives gossip on a bus while Hitler and Goering sit smugly behind them in the famous 'Careless Talk Costs Lives' poster. Concern for public morale prompted Duff Cooper, head of the newly formed Ministry of Information, to invite the nation to 'join the ranks of the Silent Column', to 'fight against gloom' and 'be silent rather than say anything depressing'. His initiative was met with dismay and derision, his team surveying public morale denounced as Cooper's Snoopers. Dorothy L. Sayers helped to lead the movement against the Ministry of Information campaign, which was seen as both patronising and intrusive; by August the Ministry agreed that 'the word "morale" must not be used again'. The Queen never gave the speech written for her by A.A. Milne, in which she was to entreat her countrywomen 'to remember, when you are tempted to spread these rumours, or these ugly thoughts of hatred, just to say to yourself, "The Queen asked me herself not to. She asked *me*."'

Judging by what women published at the time, the government's fear of invasion hysteria among women were exaggerated. Or perhaps the women who made the effort to write – or who were accepted – for publication were themselves aware of the need to allay fear. Rebecca West faced the issue with characteristic directness in her article 'If The Worst Comes To The Worst'. Other writers, such as Naomi Royde Smith, were less direct, and took the sting out of rumour and gossip by playing with them.

The mood of the writing at this time seems to be one of realistic determination; this entailed closing down the emotional temperature. *England's Hour*, Vera Brittain's collection of essays on wartime London (written in 1940 and published in 1941), was much admired in America, where it was described approvingly as 'a completely unsentimental book'. In England, however, it was condemned by E.M. Delafield and others for its 'sentimental approach'. More in tune with the prevailing mood were the 'Rebuilding Britain' articles with titles like 'Hopes For The Future', urging readers to 'work to prepare for peace'. The heroine of the moment was Mary Cornish, a children's escort on the torpedoed ship *City of Benares*, who looked after six boys in an open lifeboat for over a week, and was celebrated by Elspeth Huxley in *Atlantic Ordeal*.

NESCA ROBB

The Struggle for Employment

When I first went to the [Women's Employment] Federation, early in 1940, the Emergency Register contained over nine thousand names. It did not, except in a few special cases, deal with teachers, who were held to be in a reserved occupation, or with certain categories, such as doctors and dentists, who had their town emergency schemes. Apart from these we had records of women capable of infinite varieties of work; qualified in social and domestic science, in secretarial and business experience, in the arts and sciences, as lawyers, linguists, architects, statisticians. Yet of the eager volunteers who had come forward in the preceding summer, overflowing the Marsham Street offices and leaving the interviewers breathless before their onslaught, only a tiny fraction had been absorbed into any form of national service. What indeed could they have done, during those months of torpor? This did not, however, mean that all those who, in September, had been safely in employment, were still employed in the spring. The country had been disorganized for peace without as yet being organized for war. Many businesses, from caution or necessity, had reduced their staffs. The evacuation of all kinds of concerns – business houses, schools, institutions and private families – had raised new problems for workers. Some, with special family ties, could not follow their employers; others, especially women with business or professional connexions of their own, found that their clients were dispersed and that, in the harder conditions of the day, there was little hope of finding new ones. The luxury trades and the arts were the first and hardest hit, but there was probably no single profession unaffected. Meanwhile, slowly, but to the unemployed woman very perceptibly, the cost of living began its inevitable rise.

The younger women were on the whole the lucky ones. They could join the Women's Services or the Land Army. As the younger men were the first to be called up, it was natural that their feminine contemporaries should take their places in junior posts. Most of the temporary civil servants, including practically the whole secretarial and clerical staffs of Government officers, were recruited also from the lower age groups. Even these advantages were not stable. There were long periods in which the Services stopped recruiting, in which there was no further extension of office staffs and no demand even for voluntary workers.

For the older women the position was much worse. For months on end it seemed that the country had no place for them and was completely indifferent to their problems, if indeed it realized that they had any. How some of them existed, or were expected to exist, during that time was hard to imagine. Some were entitled to unemployment benefit, but many were not; and as a rule they had heavier responsibilities than their juniors. Their age debarred them from the few forms of service that showed any wish for recruits, but there were no civilian posts for them to fill.

The class perhaps most seriously affected were the older office workers of all kinds. Hundreds of them were out of work and often in acute difficulties. Yet they could well have undertaken most of the routine Government jobs which many of them had held in the last war, and so released younger women for active work or training. The whole problem of woman power was indeed horribly bungled. It was doubtless impossible to reabsorb the new host of unemployed women into industry without some delay; but no explanation of this state of affairs, no guidance or encouragement of any kind was given by those in high places. There was no large-scale provision of training for the services that would clearly be needed later on. Every now and then the press would break out into headlines proclaiming that so many women were wanted, or that a training scheme for this or that was on the point of opening. When this happened we were invariably besieged by inquirers. Unhappily it generally proved that the women were not wanted after all; that the training scheme's opening was indefinitely postponed, or that it provided only for an infinitesimal number. Investigation seemed always to reveal some new nightmare's nest of muddle.

It was disheartening for all; for some it was excruciating. I shall not readily forget those days of the late spring and summer when things seemed to have reached complete stagnancy and one sat at one's desk feeling like the oracle of hope deferred. If one placed a candidate at that time, one felt as if one had saved a life – but how rarely could it be achieved! As a rule one could only take down the applicant's qualifications, explain, encourage and sympathize as best one could and refer her to all other possible agencies on the forlorn chance of something turning up. There were those who came back to us repeatedly after fruitless searches, each time a little more unhealthily transparent, a little bluer under the eyes and more pinched about the lips. They were marvellously uncomplaining, but the signs were clear. Fortitude is an inspiring sight, but there are few spectacles more painful than that of a fortitude that is being slowly disintegrated.

One acquired, too, an uncomfortable insight into the way in which much of women's work is underpaid. The principle of equal pay for equal work is still very far from being put in practice. That it is not generally adopted may be partly due to a belief, still widely held, that women work only for themselves and are never burdened with family responsibilities. Very few of the hundreds who came to us were without some such burden. There were widows with families to educate, wives whose husbands were invalided or out of work, single women who were supporting younger brothers and sisters, or, most often, some aged or infirm relative. It was sometimes unbelievable how many people our clients had been called upon to help out of salaries that made by no means lavish provision for one. Again, the older generation was the most affected, but the country has lost many volunteers for the Services and other war organizations because no provision is made for dependants and one cannot save much out of two-thirds of a soldier's pay. It is charming to be told, as Mr Chesterton was fond of telling us, that we are all queens and beings hallowed and apart; but the values lately set on female lives and limbs reveal a different attitude. Between the extremes of pretty speeches and flagrant unfairness there must be some mean of common sense and plain justice where women are concerned. Perhaps that is one of the things that will be discovered in the new Britain.

Another problem that was continually brought before us was that of women who for the first time in their lives wanted work and had never been trained to do anything. These were mostly middle-aged women, often mothers of families, who had hitherto been comfortably off or even rich. The war, with its tale of falling investments and ruined businesses, had thrown them suddenly into the struggle for employment. They were often charming people, intelligent and cultivated, who had probably run their homes admirably; but the fact remained that it was almost impossible to place them. The only posts for which they were positively qualified were those of house-keepers in private houses; and here again, owing to war conditions, the demand was limited. Some of them had married young and never given a thought to possible vicissitudes in the future. A great many had, however, the same story to tell. 'My parents did not think it worth while to spend money on educating the girls.' 'My father (it generally *was* father) wouldn't hear of his daughters doing anything.' These sentiments are unfortunately not yet out of date. Sometimes I wondered if parents who have deliberately stopped their daughters from training for a profession, are compelled to watch from another world the havoc they have wrought in this. It would often be a pretty Purgatory. Neither marriage nor private means give any guarantee that a woman will never have to work for her living. The instability of human fortunes is more marked than it has ever been in our lifetimes; and the scales are weighted more heavily against the unqualified. Some form of sound training and some experience of work are very necessary investments for a daughter's future. The lack of them can be a deadly handicap in time of need.

NAOMI ROYDE SMITH

Rumours

After the withdrawal from Norway, Quisling rumours ran like wildfire. My early tea was brought up one Sunday morning with the announcement that the Town Clerk had been arrested as a spy. Sleepy though I was I refused to believe this news. It was entirely untrue. There is, however, a circumstantial tale of a local clergyman's daughter who was able to denounce as a spy a British officer quartered on the vicarage. She heard him going late at night to the lavatory: but he never pulled the plug! This unEnglish behaviour excited her suspicion, she reported it, and her guest was discovered to be signalling with a flash-light from the window of the retreat.

Our best rumour, however, was a real sensation. One morning I noticed a distant smell of hot onions. As I was repainting chairs at the time I thought this might be due to some war economy in the composition of the enamel I was using – or that onions had been added to the cheese and cocoa which the daily woman requires with her elevenses. An hour later I went off to have my hair shampooed and learnt that there had been a gas alarm from Southampton. Air Raid Wardens, in gas-masks, had paraded the town, school children had been put into *their* gas-masks; the hairdresser had been told to close all the windows and warn his clients to keep their heads well into the basins. The agitation was at its height when a message came through to say that the pollution of the atmosphere was not of Enemy Origin. A local pickle factory had had a fire and onions and vinegar frying and boiling together had produced a miasma blown by the wind in our direction.

DIANA COOPER

Preparing for Invasion

After Dunkirk we talked exclusively of parachutists, of how they would come and deceive us by being dressed as nurses, monks, or nuns with collapsible bicycles concealed beneath their habits. An English uniform would have been a better disguise for the expected invaders. Orders and suggestions overwhelmed us. We must stay put (how does one do it?). We must not spread alarm or dismay (I must therefore hold my tongue). We must fill our ginger-beer empties with an explosive prescription, label it 'Molotov Cocktail' and hurl it at the invading tanks. We were advised to feed the enemy's cars with sugar to neutralise their petrol. Place-names were obliterated on roads and stations. Barricades of wagons and tree-trunks were successfully obstructing our own movements. We must 'Be like Dad and keep Mum' (very funny, we thought), and the children must not have kites or fireworks. We had killed our black-widow spiders when war came, and now the Zoo's Home Guard were trained riflemen. To have been hugged to death by a bombed-out bear would have been an anticlimax. One zebra only got a run for his money and streaked round Regent's Park pursued by the Zoo's secretary, keepers and the public. We had all given our weapons, binoculars and dainty opera-glasses to the Home Guard. In June the ringing of church-bells was stopped, so that they might ring again for invasion. It sounded a topsy-turvy order. Their silence, and the darkened houses that betrayed no cheer or welcome and were no longer symbols of shelter, affected me acutely.

A difficult suggestion that had a foolish appeal for me was to equip one's car with an all-covering armour of small pebbles between sheets of tin. This naturally never materialized and I was disappointed.

MARGARET KENNEDY

Bright Little Jokes

We are all keeping a check on our emotions. We are a little guarded in what we say for fear of inadvertently annoying people, or straining nerves already taut, or deepening the general depression. We avoid controversy or provocative sallies; what would normally be stimulating arguments might easily sharpen into quarrels just now. One tries to short-circuit emotion rather than to share it. The 'genial current of the soul' is dammed up, and we fall back on bromides and bright little jokes.

FRANCES PARTRIDGE

German Parachutists

May 13 1940
Everyone makes jokes about the likelihood of German parachutists landing in our Wiltshire fields dressed as nuns or clergymen – a good farcical subject on which to let off steam. This afternoon I was alone in the kitchen when the doorbell rang, and there on the step stood three tall bearded men who addressed me in strong German accents, and wore something between clergyman's and military dress! Aha! I thought, the parachutists already. But when they asked for Mrs Nichols I realized that it was some of the Brüderhof, a community of Christian Pacifists of all nations who live the simple life near Swindon. Curiosity was too much for me, so I asked them to have some tea. Two were very unattractive redheads with scarlet mouths above their beards. It was the maddest of mad hatter tea parties, consisting of me and these three Jesus Christs, all looking at me sweetly and speaking in gentle voices. I told them we were pacifists. 'Are you persecuted much?' they asked, rather taking the wind out of my sails. I felt as if Jesus Christ had mistaken me for John the Baptist.

NAOMI ROYDE SMITH

Rumours of Invasion

September 1940

A protean rumour which has shown itself in various forms during this month has reached here in what may be its final and true shape.

It began with a reported tocsin in Cornwall, spreading to Hampshire, heard by many and given a headline in the morning papers about three weeks ago: the Germans had landed somewhere in Dorset; in Kent; in Lincolnshire. This was officially denied. Then a whisper started that the corpses of German soldiers, in full battle dress, had been washed up all round the coast. Presently the horrid detail that each corpse had its hands tied behind its back was added. I felt that this was a sheer Quisling intended to foment indignation against the Royal Navy. Who else could have had this notion or the opportunity of doing such a thing? Then the tale grew into patent absurdity. The whole of the Channel from Weymouth to Devonport was *covered* with the corpses of stricken armies. The retailer of this piece of nonsense had pointed out to those who brought it to him that, if this were true, the entire population of the Reich must have perished, also that no corpses drowned in the North Sea would get far beyond the Straits of Dover as the tide there would wash them to and fro. After that the rumour died down, but today it has come back in a more plausible form. The Invasion had a dress rehearsal last week. The RAF attended it. The embarked *Wehr* did not like the prospect. A suspicion that this was no mere rehearsal produced a stampede. The hospitals of Northern France are now filled with German soldiers, all shot in the back by the bullets of their commanding officers.

AN ENGLISHWOMAN

An Invasion Alarm

From an Englishwoman to a friend in America, 8 September 1940

We had an invasion alarm last night. (Please, Censor, don't cut all this out; it is quite harmless and will be useless information to the enemy by the time it arrives.) Phil and I were at the flicks when just in the middle of the most exciting part of *The Thin Man* a message was flashed on the screen requiring all troops to return to their barracks at once.

We found that the invasion password had been given by telephone just before we got back. Phil seized his rifle and kit and dashed off to report at HQ.

I was just starting to wash my hair before the midnight news when the bell went and I went down to admit a very young, very solemn soldier. He announced that he had come to phone a message and stand by our phone throughout the night for further orders for his unit who were stationed in defensive positions around. I suggested that he leave his kit in the outer hall – 'No, I'll not do that.' He obviously considered that the safety of Britain hung on his every act.

So he piled his rifle, tin helmet, gas mask, etc., beside the telephone. Then he gazed dubiously at the instrument, scratched his head: 'I've never done this afore.' I said: 'What, do you mean to say you've never used a telephone?' 'Never.' I showed him which way to hold the receiver and how to dial and explained about the number being engaged. Then I went off to hear the midnight news. When I came down about 12.30 meaning to get him some food, I found him still clutching the telephone with sweat pouring from his head and not a thing happening! I got him connected up with his HQ then and stood by telling him what to say.

VERA BRITTAIN

And So – Farewell!

Towards the end of June 1940, many conscientious parents throughout England find themselves confronted with a heart-breaking dilemma.

Simultaneously with the collapse of France, the Government announces an official scheme to send thousands of British children to the Dominions. Canada, South Africa, Australia and New Zealand broadcast enthusiastic offers of hospitality. In the United States, a Committee is formed under the Chairmanship of Marshall

Field of Chicago to rescue Europe's children; it is even possible, we learn, that the adamant immigration laws may be modified in order to admit a hundred thousand boys and girls of British stock to America.

We feel certain that the Government would not sponsor so large a scheme unless it was convinced that horror and dislocation would come to this country with the downfall of Europe. The announcement of the plan seems to thousands of anxious parents a warning of 'things to come'. Earlier evacuation schemes have made no special appeal to them, for moving children from the town to the country was merely a method of redistributing the population; it assured neither safety, freedom from chaos, nor the sense of security which is the birthright of childhood. Emigration to the Dominions or America, where real freedom from war will be a gift from new territories unhampered by the evil nationalistic traditions of the quarrelsome Old World, is a proposition more hopeful and far more imaginative. The most resourceful and energetic parents decided to register their children immediately.

From the moment that the Children's Overseas Reception Board – to be known familiarly as 'Corb' – is established in the Berkeley Street offices of Messrs. Thomas Cook and Son under the Chairmanship of Geoffrey Shakespeare, Under-Secretary of State for the Dominions, a queue of parents and children begins to stretch from the office door into Piccadilly. The opportunity of safeguarding the children's future appeals equally to the small households of Mayfair and the large dockyard families from Bermondsey and Chatham.

'If we must die,' say these fathers and mothers, 'at least we intend to save the next generation.'

Sick at heart, conscious that our obligations as parents may demand a sacrifice of a kind we had never contemplated, Martin and I debate the question for a weary week-end. Richard is at school in a so-called 'safe area', but Hilary, at Swanage, has already been summoned to the air-raid shelter, and her headmaster has finally concluded that no place nearer than Canada can now offer a stable life and an uninterrupted education. We ourselves have lived in the United States for long periods during fifteen years; we have friends tested by a decade of loyal affection. Shall we not be sadly remiss as parents if we fail to take advantage of circumstances so favourable?

'It's a terrible thing to do,' I protest, unable, after twelve years of careful rearing, to face giving up the children just when their personalities are developing and their fascination is growing every day.

'You're only thinking of yourself,' Martin replies inexorably. 'It's the children's interests that matter, not your feelings.'

I agree with him miserably. 'I know that. I'm only trying to decide whether it's better for them to have danger with me or security without me. As you feel so certain, you're probably right.'

After one more night of agonised indecision, I accompany Martin to the offices of the Children's Overseas Reception Board. Two humble units in a long line of troubled questioning parents, we make our inquiries. The woman Member of Parliament who answers them happens to be a personal friend.

'Don't hesitate,' she advised us. '*Get them out!*'

She hands us several alternative application forms; one is a request for permission to make private arrangements without waiting for the government scheme to come into operation.

'Look here,' she adds, 'you could afford to pay for their passage, couldn't you?'

We admit that we could. 'The children have been to the United States before,' we continue. 'They both hold re-entry permits.'

'Well, then, there's nothing to wait for. They're in quite an exceptionally favourable position. Fix up their passages yourselves, and you'll be making room under the government scheme for two more children whose parents can't afford to send them on their own.'

We decide to take her advice and book provisional berths for Richard and Hilary, never dreaming that in three weeks' time, when the operation of the government scheme has been impeded by the loss of the French fleet and the resulting shortage of convoys, we and other middle-class parents who have acted with similar promptitude will have our distress increased by accusations that we have abused our 'class privileges' at the expense of children from state-aided schools whose interests under the scheme we believed ourselves to be serving.

When we visit the Passport Office to obtain passports for Richard and Hilary, there is certainly no evidence that the queue of parents which stretches to the end of Dartmouth Street is composed of 'wealthy escapists'. For over an hour we stand waiting in the company of an ex-army corporal, who is using his savings to send his family to a Canadian sergeant whom he knew in World War No. 1.

'Yes,' he explains, 'I'm sending the wife and kid. She don't want to go, but I tells her: "You mark my words, it'll be the only life, after this war. The boy won't 'ave 'arf a chance here, compared with over there. When it's all over," I says to her, "I'll come out and join you."' [. . .]

The morning so long dreaded has come. Last night I delayed as long as I could over drying Hilary's slim fairy-like body and brushing Richard's thick nut-brown hair. Sleepless, I looked at their sleeping faces – Richard's long dark eyelashes motionless on his cheeks, Hilary's fair serene face as unperturbed as an angel's. Modern children, endowed as though by some law of compensation with a calm emotional detachment which they cannot have inherited from their war-ridden parents of the Lost Generation, they neither fear nor even speculate about the adventure before them.

We join the waiting boat train at Euston, our luggage-laden taxicab hemmed in a long cavalcade of vehicles which threads its way laboriously through the newly barricaded entrance to the station. Just in time we board the train and discover that it is crowded with children – children of both sexes and all ages, babies whose fortunate mothers are justified in leaving an invasion-threatened country and going with them, older children who vary from five or six years old to the school ages of fourteen and fifteen. Most of them are being accompanied to the boat by their parents – miserable mothers and fathers of whom some are even now torn cruelly with indecision. On the way back to London we are to meet an unhappy father whose departing wife, right up to the moment of embarkation, announced her intention of returning to London with her boy and girl.

Like the rest of the children in the train, Richard and Hilary remain philosophical, even with regard to the dangers that they may encounter on the way to Montreal.

'Wonder if we'll meet any submarines?' speculates Richard, voicing with no inhibition of fear the secret dread that tears at our hearts, challenging our resolution, making us perpetually uncertain whether we have acted for the best. It is the parents, not the children, who are suffering; at least we can thank God for that. As the crowded train rolls inexorably onwards, the hackneyed verse of a familiar hymn seems to beat into my brain with the roar of the wheels.

> 'If Thou should'st ask me to resign
> What most I prize, it ne'er was mine.
> I only yield Thee what is Thine.
>   Thy Will be done!'

At the docks we are ushered into a large covered shed, to wait for what seem indefinite hours till the immigration officials arrive. Tired out already by the long train journey, the dozens of babies lift their voices one by one in loud wails of protest, and soon the dock resembles the parrot-house at the Zoo. Looking up and down the huge enclosure at two or three hundred weary older children sitting with mute resignation beside their suitcases, we conclude that the immigration officials cannot be fathers. At last a number of stewardesses take pity on the waiting families; they bring cartons of milk and packets of biscuits, which they offer to children and parents. Martin and I feel that the biscuits would choke us, but Richard and Hilary, seizing their supply with eager grubby hands, each zestfully consume eight biscuits and two cartons of milk.

A Canadian Pacific official approaches us.

'Are these the children who hold re-entry permits to the United States?'

Richard and Hilary move forward in proud assent. Now that the moment has come, my legs suddenly feel as though they will no longer sustain me. Oh, my darling children, is there time to call you back from salvation, even now?

With imperturbable dignity, Richard and Hilary march off beside the CPR official into the hut where the immigration officers are sitting. As we watch them from a distance, we notice a long file of girls from a Yorkshire convent school move towards the gangway, accompanied by their gentle nuns. Are these the wealthy, taking advantage of their privileges? They exist, perhaps on other liners; not many of them seem to be boarding this one.

Apparently without a qualm, the children exhibit their papers and their money. After answering several questions, they reappear with their escort.

'The only thing that worried me,' Richard confesses, 'was whether they'd let me keep the five shillings Granny gave me, as well as my ten pounds.'

'And did they, darling?'

'Yes,' chimes in Hilary. 'They didn't mind a bit. Richard said: "Have I got to give you my five shillings, because I'm only supposed to take ten pounds?" and the man said: "Never mind, sonny; we won't worry about that."'

A cold rainy wind blows suddenly over the docks. Beyond the enclosure we see now the grey-painted hulk of the anonymous liner, waiting to carry away from us the dearest possessions that are ours on earth. No – not our possessions. We never possessed them; they have always possessed themselves.

The CPR official approaches again. His manner is discreetly sympathetic.

'I'm afraid you'll have to say good-bye to the children now.'

'Very well,' we reply with outward equanimity. I remember then that I have brought no farewell gifts for either; that I was packing throughout the two hours that the children went shopping with their father. Oh, dearest Richard and Hilary – will you think of me as the careless mother who never gave you a parting present, when you bought her such a lovely bunch of scarlet carnations?

'Good-bye, Mummie! Good-bye, Daddy!'

'Good-bye, my own darlings. You'll look after Hilary, won't you, Richard? And you, sweetheart – you *will* do what Richard tells you on the boat?'

'We'll be quite all right, Mummie. Don't worry about us. We promise we'll look after ourselves till you come across too.'

'Good-bye, then, my loves!' ('*If Thou should'st ask me to resign What most I prize . . .*')

With the gallant pathetic courage of children, Richard and Hilary kiss us and leave us as calmly as though they are departing for a weekend visit to a familiar relative. Their eyes are bright; their faces do not change as they go with their guide to meet the unknown adventure.

At the entrance to the gangway, they turn and wave cheerfully. Then the tarpaulin flaps behind them, and they are gone.

ELSPETH HUXLEY

from *Atlantic Ordeal*

Mary Cornish started games. They played 'Animal, vegetable or mineral', and when that palled, 'I Spy'. But there were not so many things to be spied from a small boat in mid-Atlantic. Their companions, the boat's essentials – sail, mast, tiller, handles, a barrico of water and tins of bully; at sea the waves, spray, clouds and a few sea-birds. So many games needed paper and pencils to play. They needed concentration too, and this became harder and harder to achieve.

When games ran out, Mary Cornish started to tell stories. Dim recollections of *The Thirty-nine Steps* and *Bulldog Drummond* lingered in her mind. Now she tried to drag from her memory tattered shreds of these stories and others and to hang them on a new framework. It was a desperate task, for she was not by nature a story-teller, although fortunately a nephew had provided her with some experience of small boys' tastes. Captain Drummond was the hero: square-jawed, strong, lean, tough and fearless. In the first instalment he became deeply embroiled with a gang of Nazi spies. Aeroplanes, submarines, parachutists, secret wireless installations, master minds and cyphers were soon involved. The story reached a point where she could think of no way out for Captain Drummond, and the first instalment ended.

'Go on, Auntie – *please* go on!' they implored. They were promised more next day. Thereafter, there was no escape. The first instalment of the day, eagerly awaited, was given after the midday meal. A second instalment followed after supper – a few swigs of condensed milk sucked out of a hole punched in the tin – before settling down for the night.

To invent new episodes for Captain Drummond, twice a day, became almost a nightmare. Only the most thrilling adventures, the most hair-raising escapes, the most breathless fights, would satisfy her audience. Once, moved by a fit of nostalgia for the sight of green and growing things, Mary Cornish spoke of a garden she knew well in Devon. She described to the boys its blazing June flowers, its shady trees, the cool lawns and the smell of mown grass and moist earth; but this was not a success. The boys – although they were town dwellers who had never seen a

Devon garden – became homesick, and the older ones grew rest-less; they wanted Captain Drummond dangling from the edge of a precipice, hidden in a Nazi bomber or chasing an enemy agent across the moors at night. Only in tales of action could they alto-gether forget their thirst and hunger, their cramp and cold, and the sea. [. . .]

All day long, eyes had raked the sea in vain; ears, strained to catch the drone of aircraft engines, had heard only the pounding of waves on the boat's timbers, and the cry of gulls. Now another night had fallen and long, weary hours of cold discomfort lay ahead. It was at such moments only that the boys' spirits fell. Sometimes a half-stifled whimper would come from under the blankets, and Mary Cornish would say brusquely: 'Don't you realize that you're the heroes of a *real* adventure story? There isn't a boy in England who wouldn't give his eyes to be in your shoes! Did you ever hear of a hero who *snivelled*?'

This spartan treatment worked every time. The boys' minds were turned from self-pity to the ever-distracting subject of their home-coming, to the delight of Mum and Dad, and the awed admiration of their school-fellows. Auntie was right; heroes don't snivel.

REBECCA WEST

If the Worst Comes to the Worst

8 June 1940

If the worst comes to the worst, and the Germans invade England, many of us will be hurt and some of us will be killed. We will see other people, possibly those whom we love, being hurt and being killed. Our homes may be destroyed, and towns which are dear to us, and woods and fields which are the fond back-ground of our lives, may be horribly annulled. We may know fire as a pursuing enemy and hunger and thirst as our compan-ions, so well that sudden death becomes a friend. Well, it might be far worse.

It would be much worse, to take one possibility, if we behaved badly. We all of us are bound to feel fear during the next few weeks. Anybody who did not would be defective, as defective as the politicians who did not become alarmed by the aggression of Nazi Germany. It is a wholesome reaction. When the bowel finds that it is harbouring an irritant, it uses every muscle in its wall to expel it, and the result is colic. When the mind becomes aware that it is faced with a dangerous experience, it floods the consciousness with a disagreeable sensation, designed to warn it that it will perish if it does not organize all its resources in self-defence. Do not be ashamed of your fear. Cherish it, obey it to the point of thinking quickly and acting vigorously in the interests of your safety. But conceal it.

Conceal your fear. Act on it, get the fire-hose and the sand-buckets ready, clear the attic. But do not express it in the disagreeable form in which it came to you. Should you do so, you may be condemning yourself and all whom you love to the pangs of a perdition far worse than the malaise of fear.

For fear and pain have one important characteristic in common. Their outward and visible signs give onlookers an exaggerated impression of what the person who is ill or is afraid is suffering. Anyone who has undergone pain so severe that it has to show itself in cries and movements knows that these often overstate the degree of discomfort that is actually felt. The body is calling for help, so it makes the appeal as strongly as possible. Amateur and inexperienced nurses are constantly deceived by this overstatement into believing that their patients are being subjected to a strain greater than they can bear, and anticipating their death or mental collapse. The experienced nurse, however, knows that there is a tough core in the human being which makes it keep hold of its life and its wits till it meets the germ or suffers the mechanical injury that simply will not be denied, and she knows that in ninety-nine cases out of a hundred the patient who says 'Give me prussic acid, I want to die' lives to want nothing so much as the longest possible enjoyment of life.

Fear, like pain, looks and sounds worse than it feels. When one is afraid of being killed in an air-raid or by a parachutist, there are all sorts of considerations which our mind checks up on the other side. There is the sporting chance we all enjoy of not being hit, the hope that somehow we may be able to perform some act of disservice to the enemy, the knowledge that the military operations of which these raids will be a part should end in a victory for England and freedom from Hitler. But fear, like pain, is an appeal, made for an urgent purpose. It, too, is always an over-statement.

Therefore you should not speak the words it puts into your mouth, or let it decide the expression of your face. For there will be no experienced nurses about you to know that you are not in such a bad case as you seem. We are facing an entirely new set of events, and there are no kind seniors to look after us, who have been through it all before. We have got to find out the code of conduct proper to the moment and apply it without help. We are all novices in this situation, even our governors. Therefore we might, if our code did not include the most rigid stoicism, con-trive for ourselves a ruin which is worse than any pain we might suffer in warfare. If we say, 'We cannot bear the torture of wait-ing day after day for the bombs to drop on us', or 'We cannot bear having bombs dropped on us day after day because we are afraid of being killed', and if we say it again and again with the bogus poignancy of fear, it is possible that the Government might hear us and believe us. They might form the mistaken view that it was impossible to go on waging war when the civil population was in such a demoralized condition. They might then feel obliged to make terms with the Germans.

This would not mean peace. It would, indeed, mean that we should never know peace again, and that our children and our children's children should not see its return. Our young men would be taken from us to fight Germany's imbecile wars of aggression against Russia, America, Africa, and Asia, and when they came back to us they would have been trained in such deli-cate arts as machine-gunning civilian refugees. The rest of us would be forced to give our labour and every penny more than was needed for our bare subsistence to pay for these imbecile wars. As the background of our lives would be the fear of the concentration camp; and we would never again warm our hands at the fires of kindness and tolerance. Those of us who know Nazi Germany know that it is darkness; but we would dwell in the outer darkness which is the lot of the Czechs and the Poles today. Let us, therefore, bridge our fear and give the Government full opportunity to win the war.

And let us see to it that if the worst comes to the worst it finds us not only in command of our fear, but also beyond the power of surprise. Each of us should today examine his or her circumstances in an attempt to foretell what predicaments the war may bring us, and whether they could conceivably lead us to be a trouble to the authorities, thus conniving at our own enslavement. We should all of us go to our doors and say to ourselves, 'If the village was set on fire I should be naturally inclined to run away from it along that road. I must remember that I must not do that if there are German troops on that road, for then our troops and aircraft might be afraid to bombard it. I must find some other way; and even if there is no other way, I must not go on that road.' The problem will differ in every locality; but we must always find a like solution. Otherwise, however well we mean, we will be as dangerous as cowards and traitors.

If these most pardonable errors of startled flesh, fear and stupefaction, can in these present extraordinary circumstances compel us to guilt, there is consolation in the ease with which we can now achieve unparalleled distinction. That is a miracle: a miracle of a sort that was called to my mind the other day by a letter in *The Times* contributed by Lady Baldwin. She wrote suggesting that the flag of our patron saint, St George of Cappadocia, should be hung from every church tower in England. Excellent wife that she is, she probably wrote with the intention of forestalling those who would like to use Lord Baldwin for that purpose on their particular church tower. But her letter turned my thoughts to some inquiries I had made into the identity of our patron saint, two years ago, after I had spent a spring night wandering about the Macedonian foothills, from church to mosque and from mosque to pagan altar on the rocks, watching Christians and Moslems ask St George for children from barren wives and crops from barren lands.

He was not, as Gibbon falsely told us, 'a villainous army contractor'. Gibbon was a great man but the world is not even faintly like what he supposed. He was confusing George of Cappadocia with George of Laodicea, a thorough bad egg of a bishop who lived quite a couple of centuries later. Very little is definitely known about the true St George, who was martyred somewhere near Constantinople in the third century. The Pope Gelasius, looking into his case, could find out nothing about him and was driven to remarking tactfully that he was one of 'those saints who are justly revered by the people but whose actions are known only to God'. Yet the best scholars believed that he really existed;

and there survives in the Near East a tradition which makes it probable that there did once live an heroic and virtuous person called George of Cappadocia, who had an extraordinary adventure with a wild beast amounting to a powerful intervention on the side of life against death.

Many are the miracles that are ascribed to him. Always he is putting in his spoke in favour of this precious though often highly disagreeable entity that we call life. He was for it, he wanted more of it, he would not have it downed. Once he saw some planks by the roadside, planks that were dead wood, cut and planed; he turned them back into trees. The sap ran up their veins, branches stirred in them, they put forth green leaves. This he did because they had been lying by the roadside to be built into a house, which was not at the moment needed. The urgent requirement was a wood which good men could use as an ambush against brigands.

When we were young it seemed as if the modern world had made planks of us. We had been drained of much of our natural vitality and forbidden to grow according to our instinctive bent, we were deprived of our individuality and planed down to uniform shape so that we should fit into a standardized and mechanized world. That world has fallen to pieces. Now we are living trees again. We must rely on our own individuality, for in a time of crisis there will be nobody to tell us how to behave. Our habit of natural growth, whether we are stunted or noble, whether we are sickly or sturdy, is what counts today. If we grizzle and chatter and prefer short term safety from the bombs instead of long term safety from slavery, then we are rubbish: dead wood by the roadside, timber for a house that will never be built. But if we are a quiet shelter to all those who come within our shadow, then we shall have the dignity of the living forest, and the worst will be far from the worst. Indeed, it will be better than the best that we could have hoped for in the days before this test.

CHAPTER FIVE

The Blitz

Britain was not invaded at the end of the summer of 1940, but was heavily bombed. Between 1940 and 1941 about 43,000 civilians in Britain were killed in air raids, and about 17,000 during the rest of the war. A further 86,000 were seriously injured, and by May 1941 nearly one and a half million people had been made homeless in London alone – a far higher figure than the government had anticipated.

At the centre of the blitz women were working as Air Raid Wardens, fire-women and nurses, as drivers of ambulances and mobile canteens, and as members of voluntary organisations. These organisations could respond more flexibly to events than government agencies could, and the WVS in particular shouldered a huge amount of physical and emotional hard work. The Housewives' Section ran neighbourhood support groups, keeping records, giving food and shelter, sweeping and salvaging. At Incident Inquiry Points the WVS helped to identify casualties, to inform and comfort the bereaved.

The blitz spawned new forms of writing. In three weeks Clemence Dane put together *The Shelter Book*, 'A gathering of tales, poems, essays, notes and notions for use in shelters, tubes, basements and cellars in wartime.' It was published by the end of 1940, and the others followed suit, with reviewers recommending books for their 'shelterworthiness'.

Women writers were outspoken from the start. They described the terrible conditions in the East End of London, the shortcomings of a cumbersome bureaucracy, the looting and the nightly trekking out of city centres into the countryside to find respite from the bombing. They sympathised with the irritation people felt at the 'we can take it' attitude attributed to them by the media. But they also recognized what Barbara Nixon calls the 'dogged equanimity, which was an unspectacular form of genuine courage'.

Compared with the wartime casualty toll worldwide, the British air-raid figures were mercifully low. Women's accounts of the blitz are characterised not so much by a litany of suffering as by restless shifts of perspective and swings of mood. A heightened awareness of reality, a sense of the absurd and the theatrical – 'life is being lived temporarily on a public stage' wrote Elizabeth Bowen – these all come from the nervous tension of the time, and express it perfectly.

VIRGINIA WOOLF

Thoughts on Peace in an Air Raid

1940

The Germans were over this house last night and the night before that. Here they are again. It is a queer experience, lying in the dark and listening to the zoom of a hornet which may at any moment sting you to death. It is a sound that interrupts cool and consecutive thinking about peace. Yet it is a sound – far more than prayers and anthems – that should compel one to think about peace. Unless we can think peace into existence we – not this one body in this one bed but millions of bodies yet to be born – will lie in the same darkness and hear the same death rattle overhead. Let us think what we can do to create the only efficient air-raid shelter while the guns on the hill go pop pop pop and the searchlights finger the clouds and now and then, sometimes close at hand, sometimes far away, a bomb drops.

Up there in the sky young Englishmen and young German men are fighting each other. The defenders are men, the attackers are men. Arms are not given to Englishwomen either to fight the enemy or to defend herself. She must lie weaponless to-night. Yet if she believes that the fight going on up in the sky is a fight by the English to protect freedom, by the Germans to destroy freedom, she must fight, so far as she can, on the side of the English. How far can she fight for freedom without firearms? By making arms, or clothes or food. But there is another way of fighting for freedom without arms; we can fight with the mind. We can make ideas that will help the young Englishman who is fighting up in the sky to defeat the enemy.

But to make ideas effective, we must be able to fire them off. We must put them into action. And the hornet in the sky rouses another hornet in the mind. There was one zooming in *The Times* this morning – a woman's voice saying, 'Women have not a word to say in politics.' There is no woman in the Cabinet; nor in any responsible post. All the idea makers who are in a position to make ideas effective are men. That is a thought that damps thinking, and encourages irresponsibility. Why not bury the head in the pillow, plug the ears, and cease this futile activity of idea-making? Because there are other tables besides officer tables and conference tables. Are we not leaving the young Englishman without a weapon that might be of value to him if we give up private thinking, tea-table thinking, because it seems useless? Are we not stressing our disability because our ability exposes us perhaps to abuse, perhaps to contempt? 'I will not cease from mental fight,' Blake wrote. Mental fight means thinking against the current, not with it.

That current flows fast and furious. It issues in a spate of words from the loudspeakers and the politicians. Every day they tell us that we are a free people, fighting to defend freedom. That is the current that has whirled the young airman up into the sky and keeps him circling there among the clouds. Down here, with a roof to cover us and a gas mask handy, it is our business to puncture gas bags and discover seeds of truth. It is not true that we are free. We are both prisoners to-night – he boxed up in his machine with a gun handy; we lying in the dark with a gas mask handy. If we were free we should be out in the open, dancing, at the play, or sitting at the window talking together. What is it that prevents us? 'Hitler!' the loudspeakers cry with one voice. Who is Hitler? Who is he? Aggressiveness, tyranny, the insane love of power made manifest, they reply. Destroy that, and you will be free.

The drone of the planes is now like the sawing of a branch overhead. Round and round it goes, sawing and sawing at a branch directly above the house. Another sound begins sawing its way in the brain. 'Women of ability' – it was Lady Astor speaking in *The Times* this morning – 'are held down because of a subconscious Hitlerism in the hearts of men.' Certainly we are held down. We are equally prisoners to-night – the Englishmen in their planes, the Englishwomen in their beds. But if he stops to think he may be killed; and we too. So let us think for him. Let us try to drag up into consciousness the subconscious Hitlerism that holds us down. It is the desire for aggression; the desire to dominate and enslave. Even in the darkness we can see that made visible. We can see shop windows blazing; and women gazing; painted women; dressed-up women; women with crimson lips and crimson fingernails. They are slaves who are trying to enslave. If we could free ourselves from slavery we should free men from tyranny. Hitlers are bred by slaves.

A bomb drops. All the windows rattle. The anti-aircraft guns are getting active. Up there on the hill under a net tagged with strips of green and brown stuff to imitate the hues of autumn leaves guns are concealed. Now they all fire at once. On the nine o'clock radio we shall be told 'Forty-four enemy planes were shot down during the night, ten of them by anti-aircraft fire.' And one of the terms of peace, the loudspeakers say, is to be disarmament. There are to be no more guns, no army, no navy, no air force in the future. No more young men will be trained to fight with arms. That rouses another mind-hornet in the chambers of the brain – another quotation. 'To fight against a real enemy, to earn undying honour and glory by shooting total strangers, and to come home with my breast covered with medals and decorations, that was the summit of my hope. . . . It was for this that my whole life so far had been dedicated, my education, training, everything. . . .'

Those were the words of a young Englishman who fought in the last war. In the face of them, do the current thinkers honestly believe that by writing 'Disarmament' on a sheet of paper at a conference table they will have done all that is needful? Othello's occupation will be gone; but he will remain Othello. The young airman up in the sky is driven not only by the voices of loudspeakers; he is driven by voices in himself – ancient instincts, instincts fostered and cherished by education and tradition. Is he to be blamed for those instincts? Could we switch off the maternal instinct at the command of a table full of politicians? Suppose that imperative among the peace terms was: 'Child-bearing is to be restricted to a very small class of specially selected women,' would we submit? Should we not say, 'The maternal instinct is a woman's glory. It was for this that my whole life has been dedicated, my education, training, everything. . . .' But if it were necessary for the sake of humanity, for the peace of the world, that child-bearing should be restricted, the maternal instinct subdued, women would attempt it. Men would help them. They would honour them for their refusal to bear children. They would give them other openings for their creative power. That too must make part of our fight for freedom. We must help the young Englishmen to root out from themselves the love of medals and decorations. We must create more honourable activities for those who try to conquer in themselves their fighting instinct, their subconscious Hitlerism. We must compensate the man for the loss of his gun.

The sound of sawing overhead has increased. All the searchlights are erect. They point at a spot exactly above this roof. At any moment a bomb may fall on this very room. One, two, three, four, five, six . . . the seconds pass. The bomb did not fall. But during those seconds of suspense all thinking stopped. All feeling, save one dull dread, ceased. A nail fixed the whole being to one hard board. The emotion of fear and of hate is therefore sterile, unfertile. Directly that fear passes, the mind reaches out and instinctively revives itself by trying to create. Since the room is dark it can create only from memory. It reaches out to the memory of other Augusts – in Bayreuth, listening to Wagner; in Rome, walking over the Campagna; in London. Friends' voices come back. Scraps of poetry return. Each of those thoughts, even in memory, was far more positive, reviving, healing and creative than the dull dread made of fear and hate. Therefore if we are to compensate the young man for the loss of his glory and of his gun, we must give him access to the creative feelings. We must make happiness. We must free him from the machine. We must bring him out of his prison into the open air. But what is the use of freeing the young Englishman if the young German and the young Italian remain slaves?

The searchlights, wavering across the flat, have picked up the plane now. From this window one can see a little silver insect turning and twisting in the light. The guns go pop pop pop. Then they cease. Probably the raider was brought down behind the hill. One of the pilots landed safe in a field near here the other day. He said to his captors, speaking fairly good English, 'How glad I am that the fight is over!' Then an Englishman gave him a cigarette, and an Englishwoman made him a cup of tea. That would seem to show that if you can free the man from the machine, the seed does not fall upon altogether stony ground. The seed may be fertile.

At last all the guns have stopped firing. All the searchlights have been extinguished. The natural darkness of a summer's night returns. The innocent sounds of the country are heard again. An apple thuds to the ground. An owl hoots, winging its way from tree to tree. And some half-forgotten words of an old English writer come to mind: 'The huntsmen are up in America. . . .' Let us send these fragmentary notes to the huntsmen who are up in America, to the men and women whose sleep has not yet been broken by machine-gun fire, in the belief that they will rethink them generously and charitably, perhaps shape them into something serviceable. And now, in the shadowed half of the world, to sleep.

BARBARA NIXON

from *Raiders Overhead: The Record of a London Warden*

That day [7 September 1940] London had changed. It was not only the damage, the shattered houses and the glass in the streets, often inches deep. And it was not a melodramatic change; it was more like a drunk man suddenly sobering up when he receives tragic news. At last people realised that there was a serious war on – a war that meant visible death and destruction, not only newspaper articles and recruiting posters and war memorials. And they did not like the realisation.

For troops who have been training and waiting for months, the long-expected attack can often give a sense of relief as well as alarm. But the British public had not had any training, physical or moral, to help it to withstand the nervous strain of being bombed. The ordinary man had not cared deeply about the betrayal of Czechoslovakia at Munich, although he knew that it was shameful, but he had cared less about the Poles. If he troubled to justify the declaration of war at all, it was on technical grounds that if we continued to give way to Hitler there would soon be no allies and no battlegrounds left. The first year of the war with its 'patrol activity' in front of the Maginot Line was commonly accepted as mystifying and ridiculous, and then dismissed as other people's business. Ten days before France collapsed, when I had expressed anxiety in the local pub as to what might happen if that country gave in, my remarks were received with indignation and scorn. When the collapse came, the French and the Belgians were just 'dirty traitors.' It was as simple as that. Only one person in twenty genuinely thought that the war was anything to do with him. Indeed, enthusiastic support could hardly be expected when so many people had friends or relations in factories, who were being told to go to the lavatory for an hour, or otherwise waste their time, because there was insufficient work to do.

The newspapers told the country that London could take it. But locally there were sour comments on what journalists knew about it. If London at that stage had been bombed as heavily and continuously as Cologne and Stalingrad, one hesitates to think what might have happened. In the last war there had been the pious cliché that the strain was nearly as great for those safely in the rear as for 'the loved ones at the front.' This time it was true, and the most common saying by men, as well as women, was that this wasn't war, it was murder, they wouldn't stand for it, and so on. The loudest cry, however, was: where were the guns? Where were these defences that had been praised as impassable?

All through Sunday and Monday the East Enders drifted miserably westwards, looking for shelters; most of them had no baggage; they had lost everything; some carried pathetic and clumsy bundles of their remaining belongings; some pushed battered perambulators stacked with salvaged, broken treasures. They had nowhere to rest, nowhere to wash. In the West End attempts were made even to exclude them from some shelters. On a 38 bus in Piccadilly a wretched-looking woman with two children got in and sat down next to me; they still had blast dust in their hair and their tattered clothing; they were utterly miserable, and the lady opposite moved her seat and said, loudly, that people like that should not be allowed on buses. Fortunately, the conductor announced with promptitude that some ladies could take taxis. [. . .]

It is, perhaps, understandable that sleeping accommodation was not provided. It had, apparently, not occurred to the Government that raiding might be continuous throughout the night. One can say that it should have done so, as it certainly occurred to many ordinary citizens, at least by the time of Denmark's invasion. But the fact remains that it did not. The millions of bunks needed could hardly have been provided more quickly than they were, once the need for them was belatedly realised.

Again, the Government's argument that it was impossible to provide safety from direct, or very close, hits for the whole population was also tenable, if unpopular; and this is not the place to go into the relative strengths of the various types of shelter.

But lavatories – lighting – ventilation! For the lack of these there can be no excuse. Even if a raid is only going to last an hour, it is still frightening, and a lavatory is essential. There cannot be any argument about it. I have seen shelters which were built over the gutter, and this was left unscreened to run across the middle of the floor. In our area we were well off. There were chemical closets usually partially screened by a canvas curtain. But even so, the supervision of the cleaning of these was not adequate. Sometimes they would be left untended for days on end, and would overflow on to the floor. On one of these occasions, with difficulty, we moved the offending article outside. We had already reported it the night before. In the morning the police said that it could not stand outside in the public gaze; we said that still less could it stand inside under the public's nose. Even a regulation-minded police-sergeant could see the force of this argument, and a report went from the Station to the Town Hall and had the desired effect.

Then the question of lights. I have been told by wardens that, for the first two months, shelters in some boroughs had no light at all. We had one hurricane lamp for about fifty people. How often in the small hours, if the raid had started early, there would be a wail of 'Warden! Warden! The light's gone out!' and children would wake up and howl, women grow nervous, and the men would swear. It is expecting altogether too much of people's nerves to ask them to sit through a raid in the dark. That one paraffin lamp also provided the only heating that there was in those days. It was bitterly cold that winter, and naturally, therefore, the door was kept shut. Some of the bigger shelters had ventilation pipes, but the smaller ones that held fifty people had only the door. In some, the atmosphere of dank concrete, of stagnant air, the inevitable smell of bodies, the stench of the chemical closets was indescribable. More than once I had to stop a conversation abruptly and go outside to avoid being sick. It is begging the question to say that they must have been dirty people. Cleanliness is almost entirely dependent on the provision of material facilities. Few of us would be clean as we are if water were not laid on. Big stores and hotels in the West End provided some grand shelters, complete with amenities; but apart from these, ours were, in the early days, among the best in London.

Why did people tolerate such conditions? Since improvements have been made, newspaper columnists have often speculated on this question. Was it stupidity, or was it courageous endurance? Probably there was a little of each, but the main reason was fear. If you live in an old and rickety house that trembles at a passing bus, or at the top of a block of flats; if you have children, or are old and slow in moving; or if you were simply brought up to be nervous and uncontrolled – you are justified in being afraid. [. . .]

At night it was a dead city. The few small shops were barred and shuttered, and the blocks of flats were deserted. If there was no gunfire or drone of planes it was quieter than the countryside. Even in an open field, the soughing of a tree in the breeze, the rustle of a rat in a hedge, or the wheeze of a cow, can still be heard. But here the silence was almost tangible – a literally dead silence, in which there was no life. It was difficult to believe that this was London, whose daily uproar never sank below a steady rumble, even in the small hours. After 10.30 p.m., when the public houses turned out the few hardy regulars, the silence was complete, only broken occasionally by the echoing footsteps of a warden, or policeman, on patrol. All the population was underground. When the silence grew overpowering, we went down into a shelter to reassure ourselves that there was still some life in this deserted city. [. . .]

Locally, after the first few nights, people began to select the company they preferred, and very quickly each of our shelters developed a distinct character of its own, which was dependent to a large extent on the shelter marshal. Mrs Barker, in charge of No. 2, brought down her gramophone, and her shelter was noisy and gay. With a lusty voice she led the singing, and kept it up till three or four in the morning if it was a noisy night. When a bomb burst within earshot she roared into 'Roll out the barrel' with admirable gusto. The next shelter was in the charge of a retired post office worker with silver white hair, and they were all very nervous and quiet: they even complained about Mrs Barker's gramophone, saying that the German pilots overhead would hear the noise and drop a bomb on them all! The younger people congregated in the next one, and it became known as the courting shelter. Those in the main road had a more casual population, and that necessarily meant a percentage of drunks and fights. In the large shelter near the railway station there were frequent raucous brawls; twice, women were delivered of children; and drunken adolescents gambled, and upset the chemical closets, and indulged in every form of anti-social behaviour. [. . .]

I had been fairly confident that I could behave reasonably well under gunfire and bombing, and the first seven nights had, more or less, justified my confidence. But what I was unsure of was what my reactions to casualties would be. I had never seen a dead body, I was even squeamish about handling dead animals, and I was terrified that I might be sick when I saw my first entrails, just as some people cannot stop themselves fainting at the sight of blood. At later incidents one forgot oneself entirely in the job on hand. But on this occasion, because I was unsure of myself, I was acutely selfconscious, and, as a protection, adopted as detached an attitude as I could. I had to watch myself, as well as the objective situation.

I was not let down lightly. In the middle of the street lay the remains of a baby. It had been blown clean through the window, and had burst on striking the roadway. To my intense relief, pitiful and horrible as it was, I was not nauseated, and found a torn piece of curtain in which to wrap it.

The funerals of our fellow-wardens were a greater strain than the blitz itself. At first, the Town Hall made no official preparations for the burial of five of their service members – four wardens and one stretcher-party man – killed on duty. We made eight visits to various officials before they agreed to give municipal support to the arrangements the different families had already made. It was not that we ourselves wanted a 'fuss', but for most relatives anything that can even make a pretence that their irreparable loss was worthwhile, or that it meant something to others as well as themselves, was at least a slight softening of their bitterness. And there was bitterness. There was still no real war; it seemed we would never be fighting back, and no war could ever be won by sitting down and 'taking it' as the press still encouragingly called it.

Moreover, there had been more in the air than mere high explosive on that last Saturday raid. The same night Hess had landed in Scotland, and was being fed on chicken and grapes, the papers said, because he had broken his ankle. A legion of theories and rumours spread about: some people were optimistic and thought it meant that Germany was cracking up, most were distrustful of the 'high-ups' in this country, a very few hazarded the opinion that the Germans were going to turn against Russia and wanted us out of it. But the upshot was always the same – gloomy shrug, and 'If we're going to be sold out by Quislings in the end, why put up with all the bombing now?'

At the last moment the Town Hall authorised an official Civil Defence parade for the funerals, and lent us clean overalls for the two days. Members of all our services turned out and lined the streets, and did a slow march to the different churches five times in two days. I am sentimental, bordering on maudlin, by nature, and despite terrific efforts to think of something else, sniffed abominably. I was well jeered at for it by my old tough friends of '13,' who were evidently surprised.

But even the funerals would not go 'according to plan.' With poor Mackin's nothing would go right. He was a Communist, and at first there was delay because official stomachs could not digest the red cotton hearse cloth which his family provided, and justifiably insisted on. At the very last second, as we all about-faced, three young friends of his, who had obviously taken half an hour from work and run most of the way, arrived with a pathetic little bunch of red tulips. Despite the coachman's disapproval, they were fixed in position, and nodded and flopped proudly and jauntily in front of the grand official wreath.

When we halted at Mrs Trew's house to pick up Johnny (the one who had had the railings blown into him) the hearses became blocked in a cul-de-sac caused by débris, and took over an hour to be extricated. Then, to make up time, Mackin's hearse dashed off through North London to the crematorium at sixty miles an hour, and six of us in a stretcher-car, who were to be bearers, lost it and arrived too late. His requiem – the Internationale – as played by the organist, was unrecognisable, since the latter had never heard the tune before and had a limited mastery of his instrument. It was all dreadful. The only alleviation of one's misery was the thought that Mackin himself would have had a first-class laugh, saying that he had been a thorn in the flesh of the authorities all his life, and could still make them uncomfortable, even with his feet gone and a hole in his head.

ELIZABETH BOWEN

London, 1940

Early September morning in Oxford Street. The smell of charred dust hangs on what should be crystal pure air. Sun, just up, floods the once more innocent sky, strikes silver balloons and the intact building-tops. The whole length of Oxford Street, west to east, is empty, looks polished like a ballroom, glitters with smashed glass. Down the distances, natural mists of morning are brown with the last of smoke. Fumes still come from the shell of a shop. At this corner where the burst gas main flaming floors high made a scene like a hell in the night, you still feel heat. The silence is now the enormous thing – it appears to amaze the street. Sections and blocks have been roped off; there is no traffic; the men in the helmets say not a person may pass (but some sneak through). Besides the high explosives that did the work, this quarter has been seeded with time-bombs – so we are herded, waiting for those to go off. This is the top of Oxford Street, near where it joins the corner of Hyde Park at Marble Arch.

We people have come up out of the ground, or out from the bottom floors of the damaged houses: we now see what we heard throughout the night. Roped away from the rest of London we seem to be on an island – when shall we be taken off? Standing, as might the risen dead in the doors of tombs, in the mouths of shelters, we have nothing to do but yawn at each other or down the void of streets, meanwhile rubbing the smoke-smart deeper into our eyes with our dirty fists. . . . It has been a dirty night. The side has been ripped off one near block – the open gash is nothing but dusty, colourless. (As bodies shed blood, buildings shed mousey dust.) Up there the sun strikes a mirror over a mantelpiece; shreds of a carpet sag out over the void. An A.R.P. man, like a chamois, already runs up the debris; we stare. The charred taint thickens everyone's lips and tongues – what we want is bacon and eggs, coffee. We attempt little sorties – 'Keep BACK, please! Keep OFF the street!' The hungry try to slake down with smoking. 'PLEASE – that cigarette *out*! Main gone – gas all over the place – d'*you* want to blow up London?' Cigarette trodden guiltily into the trodden glass. We loaf on and on in our cave-mouths; the sun goes on and on up. Some of us are dressed, some of us are not: pyjama-legs show below overcoats. There are some Poles, who having lost everything all over again sit down whenever and wherever they can. They are our seniors in this experience: we cannot but watch them. There are two or three unmistakable pairs of disturbed lovers – making one think 'Oh yes, how odd – love.' There are squads of ageless 'residents' from aquarium-like private hotels just round the corner. There are the nomads of two or three nights ago who, having been bombed out of where they were, pitched on this part, to be bombed out again. There is the very old gentleman wrapped up in the blanket, who had been heard to say, humbly, between the blasts in the night, 'The truth is, I have outlived my generation . . .' We are none of us – except perhaps the Poles? – the very very poor: our predicament is not a great predicament. The lady in the fur coat has hair in two stiff little bedroomy grey plaits. She appeals for hair-pins: most of us have short hair – pins for her are extracted from one of the Poles' heads. Girls stepping further into the light look into pocket mirrors. 'Gosh,' they say remotely. Two or three people have, somehow, begun walking when one time-bomb goes off at Marble Arch. The street puffs itself empty; more glass splinters. Everyone laughs.

It is a fine morning and we are still alive.

This is the buoyant view of it – the theatrical sense of safety, the steady breath drawn. We shall be due, at to-night's siren, to feel our hearts once more tighten and sink. Soon after black-out we keep that date with fear. The howling ramping over the darkness, the lurch of the barrage opening, the obscure throb in the air. We *can* go underground – but for this to be any good you have to go very deep, and a number of us, fearful of being buried, prefer not to. Our own 'things' – tables, chairs, lamps – give one kind of confidence to us who stay in our own paper rooms. But when tonight the throb gathers over the roof we must not remember what we looked at this morning – these fuming utter glissades of ruin. No, these nights in September nowhere is pleasant. Where you stay is your own choice, how you feel is your fight.

However many people have crowded together, each has, while air whistles and solids rock, his or her accesses of solitude. We can do much for each other, but not all. Between bomb and bomb we are all together again: we all guess, more or less, what has been happening to all the others. Chatter bubbles up; or there is a cosy slumping sideways, to doze. Fear is not cumulative: each night it starts from scratch. On the other hand, resistance becomes a habit. And, better, it builds up a general fund.

Autumn seems a funny time to be bombed. By nature it is the hopeful start of the home year. The colours burning in the trees and weed-fires burning in the gardens ought to be enough. Autumn used to be a slow sentimental fête, with an edge of melancholy – the children going back to school, the evenings drawing in. Windows lit up earlier. Lanes in the country, squares in the city crisp with leaves. (This year, leaves are swept up with glass in them.) In autumn, where you live touches the heart – it is the worst time not to be living anywhere. This is the season in which to honour safety.

London feels all this this year most. To save something, she contracts round her wounds. Transport stoppages, roped-off districts, cut-off communications and 'dirty' nights now make her a city of villages – almost of village communes. Marylebone is my village. Friends who live outside it I think about but seldom see: *they* are sunk in the life of their own villages. We all have new friends: our neighbours. In Marylebone, shopping just before the black-out or making for home before the bombers begin to fill up the sky, we say, 'Well, good luck!' to each other. And every morning after the storm we go out to talk. News comes filtering through from the other villages. They say St John's Wood had it worse than we did. Camden Town, on the other hand, got off light. Chelsea, it seems, was hot again. They say they brought 'one' down on Paddington Green. Has anybody been over to Piccadilly? A man from Hampstead was here a minute ago; he said ... Mrs X is a Pimlico woman; she's quite upset. Anybody know how it was in Kilburn? Somebody had a letter from Finsbury Park.

For one bad week, we were all turned out on account of time-bombs: exiled. We camped about London in other villages. (That was how I happened to be in Oxford Street, only to be once more dislodged from there.) When we were let home again we were full of stories, spent another morning picking up all the threads. The fishmonger said he had caught sight of me buying milk in Paddington. 'What, you were there too?' I asked. 'No,' he replied, 'I've got Finchley people; I was only over in Paddington looking after a friend.' We had all detested our week away: for instance, I had been worrying about my typewriter left uncovered in the dust blowing through our suddenly-emptied house; the fishmonger had been worrying about all that fish of his in the frig. with the power off. It had been necessary for several of us to slip through the barricades from time to time in order to feed cats.

Regent's Park where I live is still, at the time of writing, closed: officially, that is to say, we are not here. Just inside the gates an unexploded bomb makes a boil in the tarmac road. Around three sides of the Park, the Regency terraces look like scenery in an empty theatre: in the silence under the shut façades a week's drift of leaves flitters up and down. At nights, at my end of my terrace, I feel as though I were sleeping in one corner of a deserted palace. I had always placed this Park among the most civilized scenes on earth; the Nash pillars look as brittle as sugar – actually, which is wonderful, they have not cracked; though several of the terraces are gutted – blown-in shutters swing loose, ceilings lie on floors and a premature decay-smell comes from the rooms. A pediment has fallen on to a lawn. Illicitly, leading the existence of ghosts, we overlook the locked park.

Through the railings I watch dahlias blaze out their colour. Leaves fill the empty deck-chairs; in the sunshine water-fowl, used to so much attention, mope round the unpeopled rim of the lake. One morning a boy on a bicycle somehow got inside and bicycled round and round the silence, whistling 'It's a Happy, Happy Day.' The tune was taken up by six soldiers digging out a bomb. Now and then everything rips across; a detonation rattles remaining windows. The R.E. 'suicide squad' detonate, somewhere in the hinterland of this park, bombs dug up elsewhere.

We have no feeling to spare.

VIRGINIA WOOLF

Autumn 1940

Friday 13 September
A strong feeling of invasion in the air. Roads crowded with
army wagons: soldiers. Just back from half day in London. Raid,
unheard by us, started outside Wimbledon. A sudden stagna-
tion. People vanished. Yet some cars went on. We decided to
visit lavatory on the hill; shut. So L. made use of tree. Pouring.
Guns in the distance. Saw a pink brick shelter. That was the
only interest of our journey – our talk with the man woman &
child who were living there. They had been bombed at
Clapham. Their house unsafe. So they hiked to Wimbledon.
Preferred this unfinished gun emplacement to a refugee over
crowded house. They had a roadmans lamp; a saucepan & cd
boil tea. The nightwatchman wdn't accept their tea; had his own.
Someone gave them a bath. In one of the Wimbledon houses
there was only a caretaker. Of course they cdn't house us. But
she was very nice – gave them a sit down. We all talked. Middle
class smartish lady on her way to Epsom regretted she cdnt
house the child. But we wdn't part with her, they said – the man
a voluble emotional Kelt, the woman placid Saxon. As long as
she's all right we dont mind. They sleep on some shavings.
Bombs had dropped on the Common. He a house painter. Very
friendly & hospitable. They liked having people in to talk. What
will they do? The man thought Hitler wd soon be over. The lady
in the cocks hat said Never. Twice we left.
More guns. Came back. At last started, keeping an eye on shelters & peoples behaviour.
Reached Russell Hotel. [. . .]

He laid rather
a thin rug on
the step for me
to sit on. An
officer looked
in. 'Making
ready for the
invasion' said
the man, as if it
were going off
in about ten
minutes.

2 October
Oh I try to imagine how one's killed by a
bomb. I've got it fairly vivid – the sensation:
but cant see anything but suffocating nonen-
tity following after. I shall think – oh I
wanted another 10 years – not this – &
shant, for once, be able to describe it. It – I
mean death; no, the scrunching & scrambling, the crushing of my bone shade in on

my very active eye & brain: the process of putting out the light, – painful? Yes. Terrifying. I suppose so – Then a swoon; a drum; two or three gulps attempting consciousness – & then, dot dot dot

ROSE MACAULAY

A Sample Corner of Total War

October 1940

Where an hour back two houses stood in this small street, there is a jumbled mountain of fallen masonry, rubble, the shattered débris of two crashed homes; beneath it lie jammed those who lived there; some of them call out, crying for rescue, others are dumb. Through the pits and craters in the rubbled mass the smell of gas seeps. Water floods the splintered street; a main has burst; dust liquefies into slimy mud. The demolition squad stumble in darkness about the ruins, sawing, hacking, drilling, heaving; stretcher bearers and ambulance drivers stand and watch. Jerry zooms and drones about the sky, still pitching them down with long whistling whooshes and thundering crashes, while the guns bark like great dogs at his heels. The moonless sky, lanced with long, sliding, crossing shafts, is a-flare with golden oranges that pitch and burst and are lost among the stars. Deep within its home a baby whimpers, and its mother faintly moans '*My baby. Oh, my poor baby. Oh, my baby. Get us out.*' The rescue squad call back. 'All right, my dear. We'll be with you in ten minutes now.' They say it at intervals for ten hours. Water and milk are passed down to those who can be reached. The rescuers work on. They are kind, skilful, patient, brave, thirsty men; they wish that a mobile canteen would turn up with hot tea or cocoa. They are friendly and polite; one of them mutters obscene oaths at Jerry as he zooms overhead, whooshes through the air, and crashes somewhere near at hand; another nudges him, indicating that a tin hat near him covers a female ambulance driver; he apologizes unnecessarily. 'Sorry, mate, didn't see you there.'

Someone is dug out; she is seventy-four, gay and loquacious; she does not cease talking as she is carried to an ambulance and driven to hospital, she is so pleased to be out. Half an hour later her married daughter is extracted; she has a grey, smeared, bruised face: she cries and is sick. 'Oh my back, my legs, my head. Oh, dear God, my children.' She is carried to an ambulance, driven away. 'The children are safe,' she is told. 'They will be out quite soon. You'll see them soon.' But she will not, for they are all dead, two boys of eleven and twelve, two babies of three and one. 'If only,' she moans, 'they didn't suffer much . . .'

Dawn is near. It grows colder. Still Jerry zooms and crashes, still the rescuers dig, saw, heave and console. 'All right, my dear, you'll be out in a jiffy.' There are only two voices to answer now; one exhausted woman's, and a baby's wail. Not much hope now for the others. At dawn the demolition squad, the ambulance drivers and the stretcher bearers are relieved by others; only inside the ruins the personnel remains the same.

'It's this every night now,' says a demolition worker, drinking a mug of cocoa on the pavement before he goes. 'This and fires.'

'There were a few casualties,' says a bland voice next day. 'But little material damage appears to have been done.'

A sample corner of total war. Elsewhere, men are being burnt alive, blinded, shot, drowned, smashed to bits when their planes crash. Civilian war deaths are no worse than those of the young men in the fighting forces; all alike are sentient human beings, dying suddenly or in agony. 'Eighteen of our planes were lost, but eight of the pilots are safe.' And ten not. Do not let us cant about 'women-and-children.' However it may be about children – and I admit that here our feelings outrun reason – it is no worse that women should be killed than men. It is all part of the blind, maniac, primitive, stupid bestiality of war, into which human beings periodically leap, spitting in civilization's face and putting her to confused rout. The alternative, here and now? No one can see any, except surrendering to the still more blind, maniac, primitive, stupid bestiality of Nazi rule over Europe, which would be to spit at and rout civilization even more earnestly.

KATE O'BRIEN

Cheffie

Yesterday someone told me that Cheffie has been killed by Hitler.

She kept a cheap restaurant on the unsuccessful side of Bloomsbury. I do not know when this restaurant began, but I have heard that Cheffie was there during the other war. She was from Derbyshire, she said, and I think she sometimes 'stunted' Derbyshire cooking. But that was never the point. The food she served was cheap and fancy, and sloppily served on fancy tables. But it was hot and you could have it at any hour of day or night, and you could have it if you didn't pay for it.

Sometimes in the evenings Cheffie wore a Spanish shawl; sometimes she wore black lace. She wore jade and coral and amber. Her hair was very black and her skin was soft, slackened leather. She was graceful, a bit too tall.

I don't know if she was wife, widow or maid, or what other name she had besides Cheffie. She seemed all right alone. She seemed complete.

Her fingers were long and strong; she was always gashing them with knives as she cut her superb, big sandwiches. You could ring up for sandwiches at any small hour, if your party was waning. She cut them and sent them round with her love. No matter if it was three a.m., and you hadn't set foot in her restaurant for a year or more. No matter if you were too grand nowadays for her shady bohemianism and her paper napkins. You were always given the impression that Cheffie didn't see through you.

She had a startling, husky voice. If she was tired it boomed below human compass – if she had had a few drinks and the young chaps, geniuses and that, who had the run of her place, were baiting her out of patience.

Sometimes she was too conversational, too friendly, what you called a bore. She had a flat upstairs, and sometimes, if people were crying or quarrelling, she took them up there, or sent them up there, to settle their trouble some way or other. Anybody could sell her any old poster or mural design or wise-crack or publicity stunt. Anyone could talk her into anything. All that was necessary was to seem unhappy or put upon. 'Dear', she said in her cracked, booming voice. 'Dear' and 'child'. I can see her going into the shelters with her jugs of coffee. I can hear her slow and not too obvious jokes. I bet she was welcome.

She was superstitious. I have been told that a few nights before she was killed a bomb fell, and everything shook in her rooms and nothing was broken. But a little Madonna on her mantelpiece that someone had given her because it looked like her fell over on its face. She did not like that. She said it was a bad omen.

A few of the unsuccessful and dreamy will remember her uneasily. A few – writers, sculptors and such – who were young lately and had hoped against hope that the world might be saved to give their slipping youth its last chance, will examine their consciences, lest they were ever superior or unkind to Cheffie – in any way she might have noticed. No doubt they were, and she noticed. But I think that it is no more than her due to guess that her bounty was as boundless as the sea. She censured no one. She fed and smiled at the liar, the cheat and the idler. She was a romantic and she died romantically.

STORM JAMESON

The Death of a Sister

24 February. It is not true that, two weeks ago, an air-raid killed my young sister; it is not true that she alone, of the five or six persons in the kitchen of the communal restaurant, was killed when a bomb demolished the place. She was a volunteer worker – a part of her war work – and when the bomb fell, since there were no other sounds, no gun-fire, she must have heard it come. It is not true that you don't hear the bomb which is going to fall near you. One of those daylight raids of single planes. Flying at a great height, they loose their bombs on some small unguarded town and make off. What are they? Young men making a practice flight? [. . .]

When old people die, surely with nothing left to want, unless it were another sunny afternoon to slip in among all those they have been gathering since childhood, one's anguish is without disbelief – even without despair. But there was so much she wanted. To see her children again; to work, to use her quick rather short fingers, young restless hands; to make plans. She planned as she moved, with the pure energy of delight. From everything of hers we touched, afterwards, it was the future sprang out. Even expecting that in a long war there would soon be no such frivolities, she had bought the cards for three more birthdays – for a boy of seven, eight, nine, and a girl five and six and seven. [. . .]

Why God, take one so filled with the future? You could have taken me and that column of the past I am becoming. Why, why? [. . .]

I have to remind myself of what has happened. There is not a nerve in my body which consents to it. And now I know that what we say of the young dead, *They shall not grow old*, says only that the agony of their solitary going away remains, unchanged by time. The future does not spring from it, as it sprang from the laid table, and from the places where, under a handkerchief or among books, she had hidden it. Nothing wears it down. And think that so many young are being hurried out of life before they have grown used to it, and this pain, this glacier, is covering Europe with its cold – where we have to live.

LORNA LEWIS

Food on Wheels

November 1940
4 a.m. . . . Not perhaps one's favourite hour for rising, especially when the All Clear hasn't gone. But here we are scrambling out of impromptu beds, loading up the mobile canteens with tea urns, milk jugs, cakes, sausage rolls, etc. Cramming stores into the vans, tea and snacks into ourselves, tin hats on to our heads. Pushing and blundering about sleepily with heavily-shaded torches, hoping to goodness that bombs and barrage won't break over us and the vans.

Then we're off for the East End shelters which the Ministry of Health has asked us to serve. Groping our way in the blackness we pause for each unfamiliar red light on the road. Maybe it's a road diversion due to a newly fallen unexploded bomb; or rubble and glass on the road from bombed houses; or a fresh crater. Anyhow, better treat all red lamps with respect.

My particular goal is down in one of dockland's poorest and

most battered quarters. This shelter holds anything from 1000 to
1200 people and is under a big warehouse. Outside its entrance
we open the side of the van, let down the counter, get out mugs
from the drawers, by the light of a very small electric lamp. Then
out of the darkness appear pale faces, the faces of men, women
and children looking up at us. The sound of distant gunfire is
drowned by coughing and a clamour of voices: 'Tea, miss. . . .
Three teas, mate, and three nice cakes . . . Tea, ma . . . Five cups
of you-an'-me, please. . . . Two very speshul teas for this lady,
dear, and a sponge cake and bar of milk chocolate and a large
woodbine.'

In this neighbourhood there's been no gas now for weeks. It is
on the emergency efforts of our and other units that many thousands of London citizens go off to their work and the dangers of
the day. From our van alone my colleague and I serve in under
three hours about four hundred cups of tea. Soon the counter
and the cash box are a mass of crumbs and stickiness, the floor is
a flood of tea drips. Washing up is done in a small bucket and is
on primitive lines; we can only hope that what the customer's
eye doesn't see the heart doesn't grieve over.

DIANA COOPER

Shelter in the Dorchester

9 September 1940

It's not really the place to sleep, the eighth floor of the Dorchester.
I never close an eye, but Papa sleeps like a baby in a pram, cheek
on hands. One hears those vile machines and the whistling and
thuds, and then one starts waiting for the next and counting the
watcher-of-the-sky's steps overhead. I cannot bear to look out of
the window. There always seem to be great fires ringed round.
The All Clear goes when light comes, and at last one sleeps for an
hour – and then one looks out on to the next day and there are no
fires, and one cannot believe that so much can have gone on and
so much yet be standing and unchanged.

There was a big row tonight between Papa and me undressing
and in different stages of nudity. Our gun was banging away outside and the thuds were hideous to hear, and I said that we *must*

go down to the basement. I had meant to all that day, and had taken precautions to stop argument such as 'I haven't got a suitable dressing-gown' by buying him a very suitable shade of blue alpaca with dark red pipings. 'I think you're too unkind,' I'd say, pulling off a stocking. 'We *can't* go down; I'm too tired. Besides it doesn't make any difference where you are.' I was beginning to cry and give in when the guns gave a particularly violent salvo and the look-out man popped his tin-hatted head in at the door saying excitedly. 'You are advised to take cover.' This was a break for me and it settled Papa, who then donned his Tarnhelm outfit with the slowness of a tortoise, and down we went. I had arranged with the management that if I achieved my purpose we could have two rest-beds in the Turkish bath. So there we slept in hygienic comfort and, to my mind, greater security. The dynamo makes a nice *Enchantress* or Clipper noise, so that you hear the bombs less, and our own big Hyde Park gun doesn't blow your head off as it does above ground. Still we are encouraged by its bombast because we feel it is some kind of answer and the noise is said to exhilarate. [. . .]

1 October

Our first funk-hole, the Turkish bath, is said to be a death-trap, so we are in the re-constructed gymnasium. Eight nice Little Bears' beds behind screens, all the camels, horses, bicycles and rowing-sculls removed. Unfortunately it has a hollow wood uncarpeted floor, three swing-doors with catches on them and the room is treated as a passage. I never get a wink, but Papa is the proverbial log. The second night a great improvement took place. We had sheets, a table and a lamp. No one else had a lamp. There was a carpet to muffle the many fewer footsteps. Conversations are conducted in whispers that take me straight back to childhood and to you – Sir George Clark asking Major Cazalet if he knows what the time is etc. No one snores. If Papa makes a sound I'm up in a flash to rearrange his position. Perhaps Lady Halifax is doing the same to His Lordship. Between 6 and 6.30 we start getting up one by one. We wait until they have all gone. They each have a flashlight to find their slippers with, and I see their monstrous forms projected caricatureishly on the ceiling magic-lanternwise. Lord Halifax is unmistakable. We never actually meet.

HILDE MARCHANT

A Journalist's Impressions of the Blitz

At the corner of the street a little general store had been broken
down. It was the sort of shop that sold everything from floor
polish to hairpins. The grocer was digging there. His apron hung
on the bedroom door above him, blown to rags but still hanging
on the hook. His credit was a heap of bills under the smashed
counter.

He was rescuing tins of pineapple, salmon, milk, peaches and
neatly stacking them on the pavement. Some had been blown
open and were mashed into the ground. As I talked to him he
unearthed a dusty card of aspirins. He jumped out of the hole and
yelled across the street.

'Hey, Alan, your mother might like these.' Then he turned
to me and said, 'Might be useful. His mother's expecting. A
bad time.'

Life circulated round this little store. People came up to the
grocer and asked if he had a tin of soup or a packet of cheese or a
tin of milk, and as he handed it out to them he said quite
solemnly, 'Put it on the account.' It was a game he was playing
with himself, for the accounts were somewhere in the hole, and he
was not even bothering to make a note of the tins he gave away.
[. . .]

The next day, they sent me to look at Madame Tussaud's wax-
works that had been hit in the back. It was the only rather numb
laugh of the grim week.

Heads, arms, legs and torsos were strewn around the Hall of
Tableaux. In one gallery models were heaped on the floor in agonising and painful positions, some with their heads at the side. A
workman was picking up the arms and legs and sorting them out
in stacks of left and right, and putting all the heads together in a
neat row. Flying glass had stuck into some of the models' faces
and a girl was picking it out with large tweezers. Hitler's nose was
chipped and Goering's magnificent white uniform was covered
with black dust. Mary Queen of Scots had left her head on the
executioner's block and her body was blown across the room
into the Tableau of Kings and Queens.

Walking through this damaged history it was impossible not to find significance in the survivals. Queen Mary sat regal and undamaged and Queen Elizabeth was still ordering the end of the Spanish Armada, even though her coronet of jewels was a little cock eyed. Napoleon was blown to pieces and I picked up pieces of Caesar's wax laurels in the far corner of the hall. [. . .]

At the street corner a Ministry of Information van was broadcasting instructions to the people . . . 'Boil all water to avoid typhoid.' Hospitals offered injections, and, sensibly, many of the people took them.

'Keep away from the centre of the city between two and five this afternoon.' The Royal Engineers were dynamiting the buildings.

Addresses were called out where hot food, blankets and first aid were available.

The people stood around listening to the voice, occasionally asking when bread was coming into the city, did typhoid injections make a child sick. There was no clamour. Just sullen resentment at the inconvenience. They had patience because they were too weary to be angry.

In one battered area I saw a shelter sign and went down to see how the shelter had withstood the bombardment. It was dark inside and a friend who was with me switched on his torch. At the end of the concrete trench the beam picked up four faces, greenish faces, so still that they looked dead.

There was a man, a woman, a boy of about fourteen, and a child of ten. We said:

'What are you doing here?' They didn't answer, and I saw the woman and child had half a pork pie in their hands. They began to eat them very slowly, with both hands to their mouths.

We talked quickly for about a minute, but still they did not answer. The man, who was blinking in the light of the torch, said very slowly:

'Don't move us out.'

We reassured him and asked why he wanted to stay there in the middle of the day.

The woman looked at me and said:

'We want to be here first for the night . . . we want a good seat tonight . . . it was crowded last night . . . my girl had to sit on my knee . . . we want a good seat.'

I stayed with them while my friend went out to find a helper.

Though it was three in the afternoon this family had not been out all day. They had not eaten, and when the eldest boy went for the pork pie they said they had kept his seat. The benches at the side were empty.

A woman from the WVS came down to persuade them to go to a rest centre, but the woman whimpered and said someone would take their place. So we wrote out slips of paper with 'Reserved' on them, and she took them for a meal. They were bomb shocked. They stumbled down the street. [. . .]

One day something quite fantastic happened. As we looked at the flats, suspended in mid-air, one of the bedroom doors opened and a young man put his head round. He stepped into the room and went carefully over to the cupboard and began to take suits from their hangers. It was as if, by some strange X-ray, we were looking through the wall of his flat into his home, for the young man was quite at ease taking the clothes from the cupboard. Once he looked out into the road and shouted to someone below:

'Which of these two?'

And the man in the road shouted back and the man made up his mind. He put several suits over his arm and then walked back to the bedroom door, opened it, walked into the corridor beyond, then carefully shut the door behind him. He had done it all so smoothly and naturally, as if there was nothing strange about walking into his flat on the third floor, with the back wall all blown away.

SYLVIA TOWNSEND WARNER

Bombs in the Country

November 1940

The house is full of feathers because when the incendiary ate up the bed it loosed great quantities of stuffing from pillows and eiderdown, quantities of which are still floating around like unwieldy gossamer. And with wet feet and cold hands and mouths full of down we exclaim to each other (through the down): Isn't it lovely to be home? Everything's so comfortable! [censored] morning we were got out of bed at [censored] bombs falling sufficiently near to wake me. If a bomb wakes me, it can be assumed that it is too close to be disregarded. When no more fell we wondered if we would make tea, then we decided we would go out in to the garden. Oh it was so lovely to go out of the house, which wore, as all houses surprised too early do, a rather surly and dishevelled expression, into that sweet night air. The sky was marbled with flat pinkish clouds, exactly like the pattern that sea makes of sand at low tide. The little river, heavy with rainfall, went by with its full hushed spinning-wheel voice; and I said to Valentine, being full of platitudes and great thoughts as one is if one wakes up too early, how extraordinary it is that one feels this profound difference between things like bombs, which one can only partially assimilate to one's experience, and things like a cloudy moonlight sky and the naked boughs of an apple tree, which are commonplaces, and part of one's ordinary being. For all its violence, war is papery-thin compared to a garden with apple trees and cabbages in it. Even when it's forced down one's throat, one can't swallow it. Whereas one goes out and eats great mouthfuls of cabbage and apple tree and moonlight. In fact, I shouldn't be surprised if in the last analysis it turns out that the horror of war is tantamount to the horror of boredom; it is the repugnance one feels to being compelled to attend to things that don't interest one.

Afterwards this lovely late moonlight turned into a sunrise with the eastern landscape banded with grey and faint golden vapours, and in the western sky a terrific tall navy blue raincloud with a rainbow climbing up it, and the elm-trees like gold inlay, and the postman coming up the drive shaking off the rain like a cat and saying that all four bombs had fallen quite close, and fallen in fields and done no harm to any one. So perish all warlike heroism: for it is undoubtedly heroic to go out on bombing raids, it is even more dangerous than going out on a horse to kill foxes. If more deeds of heroism could just fall flat there would be more hope for humanity. It is interesting how almost all working class people seem to know this without having to bother to hold it as a theory. They have almost endless fortitude, but whenever they get involved in some act of obvious or showy bravery they instantly begin to disinfect it by saying it was a bloody nuisance, or that they would never have done it if they'd had time to think, or that they've never felt such a fool in their lives. This is so marked in the eighty per cent of our population that the remaining gentry percentage have more or less to follow suit, though they very rarely achieve the true grumbling note of the working class hero malgré lui. But the essential difference goes much further when you come to think of the spectator. Working class spectators of the brave acts pour on as much disinfectant as the performers, and say that they never saw Bert run so quick, or that Alf was unlucky from a boy, always getting mixed up in things, or that his trousers will never be the same again. Gentry spectators just can't or don't attempt this, they'd as soon part with a trump.

BEATRICE WEBB

Nights of Battle, Days of Peace

20 April 1941 3 a.m. [Passfield Corner]
These last two nights have been the most fearful of the war. The Battle of Britain is raging round us. Tonight continuous bombing and gunfire have shaken the house. A huge fire has lit up. Aldershot and Farnham to the east; whilst gunfire and flares light up Bordon and the south coast. Mrs Grant is cowering downstairs in the kitchen; I find Sidney reading, but glad to have a cup of tea. Neither he nor I are perturbed; Annie wanders up and downstairs, looking out for fire bombs. I tell her that the Germans won't waste any on us in a non-built-up area; and anyway if a fire bomb falls on the house and gets through the roof, we should hear it. Meanwhile, last night, London has had a terrific attack. [. . .]

The nights of battle and days of peace are the strangest sort of life the British people have ever experienced. Just as I feel that we and our generation are, through old age, on the verge of nonexistence, so do I envisage that the present-day Great Britain and her ruling class are doomed to disappear within the next few years. Our little island will become subordinate – either to the USA and the Dominions or to Germany, or to the USSR and its new civilization, creeping over the world. As we happen to believe in the *rightness* and eventual success of Soviet Communism, we are not despondent about the future of mankind.

CHAPTER SIX

Call Up

By 1941 it was becoming clear both that production needed to be expanded dramatically and that employers were still reluctant to hire women. Under pressure from its Women's Consultative Committee, the government was forced to act, and in December 1941, for the first time in the history of this country, introduced conscription for women. This was the biggest single change that the Second World War brought to women's lives. A new world was inaugurated, with new rules and categories and terms: registration, essential work orders, reserved occupations and the definition of the mobile woman. Once called up, a woman could choose between the Services, Civil Defence, the Land Army and industry. Part-time and voluntary work were also a feature of conscription, the rules of which had to accommodate the traditional shapes of women's work and responsibilities.

Strong feelings about the conscription of women spilled into the press in the second half of 1941 and the beginning of the following year. Conflicting imperatives and advice – the good of your country versus the good of your family – clashed on the pages of magazines. Women reporters collected material for inspiring accounts of British women at war; they were joined enthusiastically by the popular J.B. Priestley. His illustrated book *British Women Go To War* came out in 1943.

During the course of the war nearly half a million women joined the Services, and many millions more put on uniforms to work in the Land Army and Civil Defence, on buses, trams and railways, in hospitals and canteens. The uniformed woman became one of the war's strongest images. She often appeared in advertisements, not just for the war effort but for products from floor polish to face powder. Not universally beloved, however, she also came top of the Daily Mail poll of wartime grouches.

As with work, so with uniform: the war might force women to adopt the ways of men, but those ways must then adapt to the ways of women. Literally, in the redesign of the ATS uniform to make it more fashionable (but 'khaki is a colour detested by every woman and makes a well-developed girl look vulgar' according to one *Times* correspondent), and imaginatively too. The new Wren rating's hat won the highest seal of approval when it caught on as a stylish shape among women generally, and versions of it in different colours filled high street shops.

Uniform for women was not just a matter of clothes. 'Whatever happens, remember to wear lipstick because it cheers the wounded' was the advice to ambulance drivers in France. Uniform could mean many different things to its wearer: a rite of passage, a sense of belonging and worth, a challenge or a threat. 'Problem: how to obtain the right degree of femininity and still look efficient' wrote one woman as she struggled with her hat. Problem solved, thought some observers, by each woman wearing her hat at a different angle. Uniform need not mean uniformity.

CORRESPONDENCE IN TIME AND TIDE

Women's War Service

20 September 1941
Sir: My daughter's case must be typical of many, though not every young girl has the pluck or the wit to cut the knots that bind her in a false position.

She was married at Christmas to a young Lieutenant and was able to find quarters in a quiet country village near his unit and to see him at frequent intervals. The call for her year came; at her interview ('a most incompetent affair', she called it) she opted for hospital work of which she had had some experience. No summons came to her; no suggestion of what she ought to do. She immediately began making independent inquiries for some hospital which would be glad to take her as a war probationer.

Far from offering encouragement, the Colonel, the Major and the Captains all assured her husband that it was 'absurd' for her to 'go before she was fetched', while the Colonel's wife and the Major's wife and the Captains' wives, with all of whom she had been on the happiest terms of friendship, tried to convince her that her eagerness to serve was 'foolish panic' and that she must not let herself be 'overwrought'.

She is a courageous, independent young woman; her answer to all the mischievous advice of her elders was: 'if the country needs the 1919s* it needs *me*, and if it needs me, I'm off.' In defiance of her entire circle she packed her boxes, found her job and is radiantly happy in it. She joined her husband on his next leave in the proud consciousness that she was doing her duty, as he his.

But is it fair to put a young girl to so severe a test?

Comb out the residential hotels and boarding houses throughout the safe areas and release the less courageous but willing young women whose seniors are advising them to wait till they are fetched. Comb out in particular the nests of camp-following parasites who are neither running houses nor rearing children, but living for jaunts and dances and cocktails at the expense of junior officers who are hard enough put to it to meet their mess-bills.

I am, etc.,

A Proud Mother

18 October 1941
Sir: Several letters have recently appeared in your paper attacking officers' wives (though why 'officers' and not NCOs' or any other wives I have been unable to discover) for not taking up full-time war service. I should like to say a word in defence both of myself and of those much maligned women whom one of your correspondents describes as 'playing bridge and knitting and gossiping and perhaps salving their consciences by doing a morning a week at a First Aid Post or a canteen'. I have found most of them willing, even anxious, to work, but held back by the surely quite natural desire to see as much as possible of their husbands before they are sent abroad or perhaps *killed on active service*. Many of these wives have children to look after, most of them are living under very difficult conditions in abominable lodgings on small pay and nearly all of them do far more than your correspondent's

---

* Women born in 1919.

'morning a week' in the way of voluntary service. One of the chief difficulties in the way of their obtaining work is the short time their husbands are stationed in one spot. I myself volunteered to work for three weeks at a time in a forestry camp whilst my husband was at sea only to be told that they didn't want 'temporary labour'. Most of the semi-permanents *do* work, and I have found that those wives whose husbands go abroad get jobs almost at once, if only for the emotional relief of having 'something to do'. This also applies to war-widows.

The women's services? In theory a wife is given leave when her husband gets it, but it does not always work out that way. For example, often the first notification a naval officer's wife has that her husband is getting leave is a telegram telling her to meet him some hundreds of miles away in a few hours' time. How can a WREN, WAAF, AT, etc. get away in time to catch the next train north, south, east or west? She can't, and if she misses it, those precious days of re-fitting or boiler-cleaning are wasted and they won't occur again for some months. In fact, leave in all branches of the services, even the Army at home, is so subject to sudden postponements, cancelling, etc., that it is almost impossible to arrange these meetings.

So, although I am now looking for a job myself, I remain unashamed to sign myself.

A Camp Follower

('A Camp Follower' seems to hold rather peculiar values. We know that the whole question of man-power is deeply exercising those responsible for our war effort. We have been told time and again that our workers are responsible for as essential a part of our war effort as is our Navy, our Army, our Air Force. We know also that we have not got nearly so many of them as we need. Yet our correspondent seems to find it quite natural that married women should put their desire to see as much of their husbands as possible before their duty to their country in its hour of grave need. If the men who are being sent overseas to fight were to take the same line, if they were to say that most of them are willing, even anxious, to fight for their country, but are held back by the surely quite natural desire to see as much as possible of their wives, would it not strike 'A Camp Follower' as being a curious and even possibly a slightly regrettable point of view? – Editor, *Time and Tide*.)

EDITH SUMMERSKILL MP

Conscription and Women

1942

In December, 1941, a National Service Bill was introduced into the House of Commons which might in other days have created a Parliamentary storm of the first magnitude. It was unprecedented for it proposed to conscript the women of the country. And yet it passed all its stages in record time, and is now on the Statute Book. [...]

The periodic upheaval occasioned by war reveals that women have individualities of their own and are not merely adjuncts of men. They have aspirations and ambitions which become apparent in war time, because only then can they enjoy a real freedom to achieve at least some part of their heart's desire. But for the Crimean War Florence Nightingale would no doubt have continued to be the dutiful daughter of highly respectable parents. Her unwomanliness was deplored by her mother who believed that a lady should be satisfied with the shelter of her father's home until she exchanged his roof for that of her husband. It wa scandalous that she should wish to nurse dirty soldiers. Women who did that were inviting trouble. And no doubt the grandfathers of those who whisper about the morals of the woman in the Services today opined that no respectable woman could become an army nurse and still preserve her chastity. [...]

Fears have been expressed that communal feeding and crèches herald the disintegration of family life after the war. Some of the worst features of home life are certainly threatened, to the dismay of the domestic Hitlers who revel in the petty dictatorships which they have established. The freedom which women are enjoying today will spell the doom of home life as enjoyed by the male who is lord and master immediately he enters his own front door. I hope that communal feeding has convinced us of the stupid waste of fuel, food and labour entailed in millions of families each day cooking their meals on millions of separate gas stoves. It must at least have shown the housewife that she is not indispensable, and that on occasions the family can feed well and cheaply, while she takes a day off to spend as she thinks fit. There is a curious belief which is shared by most men that women instinctively love cooking and washing up. A perfectly cooked meal is certainly an achievement and a woman may well experience pleasure in producing a savoury and appetising dish. But I have never known ecstasy induced by washing up.

ETHEL MANNIN

Non-Co-operation

When the time came, in July of that year, for me to register with my age-group for national service I did not do so. If they wanted me they could come and get me; as a pacifist I was not prepared to do war work, and if the refusal meant prison that, anyhow, would be an experience I had not yet had, and though I did not expect to like it any better than Reginald had it would anyhow be interesting and provide background material for a novel.

Nothing, however, happened, whether because the authorities overlooked the matter, or because they thought it not worth their while to bother with such an obvious trouble-maker, I shall never know. The authorities were sufficiently interested at the time to intercept my mail – and Reginald's. We were on 'the list' of mail set aside for 'inspection'. A friendly postman had tipped us off about it, though we were aware of it sometime before then, for our letters ceased to arrive by the morning post and when they did arrive, several posts later, bore the obvious signs of having been unofficially opened. [...]

In spite of my policy of non-co-operation over national service I did, however, volunteer for fire-watching, not under any moral compulsion but because it was rumoured that it was going to be made compulsory, and whereas I had no objection to doing it voluntarily – though I regarded it as quite futile – I had the strongest possible objection to compulsion. I applied at the post and was signed on, then, having taken a course of training, that is to say crawled round a smoke-filled hut on all fours and listened to a discourse on how to manage a stirrup-pump, I was issued with a tin helmet and allotted duty days. I understood that when I was 'on' it was my duty, as soon as the siren sounded, to put on my tin hat and run up the road to the big house which was the local firewatchers' H.Q., take a disc with the letter F imprinted on it in white paint from a box in the porch and run back home with it and hang it on my gate.

Low-minded friends thought this frightfully funny, for some reason; one of the most literary of them laughed until the tears ran down his distinguished cheeks. 'Why an F, Ethel?' he gasped. 'Why hang it on your *gate*?' F-Freddie, I explained, F-Firewatching. [...]

I hung up my F with the best of them, but inevitably there was a night when I was caught napping. There had been a 'lull', and on a night when I was supposed to be 'on' I had gone to town. It was so long since I had hung up my F that I had forgotten, on that particular night, that it was my night for F-ing, as my friends called it, and there was, of course, an alert before I got back.

STELLA ST JOHN

from *A Prisoner's Log, Holloway Prison 1943*

The prisoners are usually amazed when you say you are in for conscientious objection to war.* On the whole they are very tolerant about it, some even being sympathetic to the point of saying, 'Good luck to you. I don't hold with this war, but I wouldn't get put in here for it.' Others merely look at you as if you were mad. I only came across three women in the whole time who were really antagonistic about it. None of the officers showed that they were much opposed to us. The chaplain was the most antagonistic to me. He had no use whatever for the pacifist position and thought it anti-Christian. He did not hide the fact in private conversation or chapel service. The Methodist minister, although not a pacifist, was very sympathetic. Some of the officers thought that we should be separated from the criminal offenders. We did not agree.

---

* Stella St John was sent to prison for six weeks in 1943, for refusing to be directed into war work.

MARGARET GOLDSMITH

Conscription and Women's Pay

I have noticed one very interesting economic result of conscription, though this has nothing to do with the pay in the
services. I was first made aware of this development through the
case of a young woman who was employed with a number of
others in a large scientific organisation, the work of which is
now of national importance. The salaries paid by this organisation to their trained women research assistants was always
shockingly low, but the work was interesting and before the
war there were plenty of applicants for employment with this
firm. Then came the call-up. The first girl to be summoned
to the labour exchange was quite pleased; she rather wanted to
join one of the services, to 'be a part of her generation' as she
precociously put it.

The official at the Labour Exchange asked about her qualifications. The girl had a good science degree from London, as well as
a knowledge of languages. The woman at the Labour Exchange
was puzzled:

'Well, are you a clerk, or aren't you a clerk?' she asked.
'According to your salary you are a clerk, and therefore your
occupation is not reserved, so you must go into industry or the
A.T.S., but according to your qualifications you might be most
useful in special scientific work with the W.A.A.F.'

So the young woman went into the W.A.A.F. to train for a special job.

Actually the work with the scientific firm in which the girl had
been employed was equally useful, but the Labour Exchange,
having orders to call up 'clerks', had whisked her off before anything could be done about it.

Her employer was extremely annoyed, and stormed down to
the Labour Exchange. The situation was awkward for him.

'Miss X is essential to my work, and to the country,' he said
pompously.

'Well, she can't be,' the official at the Labour Exchange told
him blandly, 'or you'd pay her more.'

The irate employer went back to his office and, to avoid further
controversies with the Labour Exchange, he raised the salaries of

his other scientifically trained 'clerks'. His sentiments as he did so are unknown.

ZELMA KATIN

On Being Measured for my Conductress's Uniform

Now we were hurried to the clothing store, where a tailoress measured us deftly for our uniforms – jacket and skirt, trousers and overcoat. This, so far, was the most exciting part of our initiation and we all felt we were getting somewhere at last. It's extraordinary what a profound part in your and my psychology a uniform plays. [...] I think we were looking forward to donning our uniforms not only because of appearances' sake but because we wanted to be set apart from or above the rest of our sex. Then in addition there was that blessed quality about a uniform: it makes physical defects seem insignificant.

HILARY WAYNE

Dressing Up

We were marched to the Stores to be fitted out, and very lavishly fitted out. To people feeling the coupon pinch and wondering where the next pair of stockings was coming from, it was miraculous to be handed four pairs. The kitbag which was given out first was, indeed, soon overflowing with underwear of excellent quality, khaki shirts, ties, sweater and gloves. Then cap, tunic, skirt and greatcoat were tried on and critically inspected by an officer before they became one's own. Then to the 'Haberdashery' counter for studs, shoe-laces, tooth-brush, hair-brush, comb, button-cleaning equipment, shoe-brush, field dressing and housewife. Then two pairs of shoes. And the only thing to disburse at the end of this orgy of acquisition was a signature as receipt. It was difficult to manœuvre the overflowing kitbag back to the barrack-room, a considerable distance. I have never mastered the art of carrying a kitbag. It is always too heavy to hoist on to my shoulder, and if someone else did it for me it felt top-heavy and as if the contents would pour out in a shower. I found the only way, though it was unmilitary, undignified and unhygienic, was to drag it along.

I think some kindly AT helped us on that first journey. I know that the dressing-up was a very exciting experience and that it was most interesting to see the other twenty-four change from civilians into soldiers.

What effect does uniform have on those who wear it and those who do not? There is no doubt that 'dressing up' helps soldiers, as it helps actors, to play their parts. I think we not only looked different, we felt different. For one thing, I personally felt less self-conscious. I had rather dreaded sleeping with a number of women, but the very numbers and the fact that day and night we were all dressed exactly alike gave me the comfortable feeling that, whatever happened, I could not be conspicuous.

LESLIE WHATELEY

Smoking in the ATS

During March 1944, at the request of my senior officers, I issued an instruction regarding where auxiliaries must not smoke in public when in uniform. I had received various complaints and criticisms, all in the same strain, as to the bad impression created by auxiliaries smoking while walking in the street, sitting in a bus or standing on a station platform. I agreed with these criticisms, for to my way of thinking such habits looked unattractive and unfeminine in civilian clothes, and in uniform worse.

SHIRLEY JOSEPH

All Very Unsettling

War is a strange thing. The grander the uniform the more important your job must be. Values, ideals, and morals get mixed as if in a cocktail shaker. The result, for a time, is stimulating. In the shaking-up process girls who before the war were doing menial work – or what they regarded as menial work – found that they were welcomed into houses with as much enthusiasm as a conquering hero, just because they happened to wear a uniform. It was all very unsettling. The uniforms would have to come off one day.

BARBARA CARTLAND

Wedding Dresses for Service Brides

I thought the WRNS uniform very smart, the WAAF passable, and the ATS hideous. I was in the warmest sympathy with the auxiliaries who complained that they wanted to be married in white. As they had an issue of only fourteen coupons a year with which to buy handkerchiefs, it was obviously impossible. I wrote personally to Chief Controller Knox and to Air Commandant Trefusis Forbes (then Director of the WAAF) and had replies to say they had both tried to get concessions for brides, but the Board of Trade was adamant.

A year later, at a meeting of Welfare Officers in London, at which we met for the first time the new ATS Controller, Mrs L.V.L.E. Whateley, the matter was raised again, and I suggested that, if we advertised, people might be induced to sell their wedding dresses free of coupons. The Dowager Lady Loch, a local Welfare Officer for West Suffolk, remarked:

'Mrs McCorquodale must have a touching regard for human nature if she thinks she can get people to part with dresses without coupons.' Everyone else looked limp, said it was a pity, but what could we do if the Board of Trade would not change their mind? etc., etc.

I thought of the brides I had admired – of Margaret Whigham, who was mobbed by her admirers outside the Brompton Oratory when she married Charles Sweeney; or golden-voiced Mary Malcolm, wearing a medieval head-dress, as the bride of Sir Basil Bartlett; of dark, romantic Lady Pamela Berry; of Rosamund Broughton in white satin on the arm of dashing Lord Lovat; of the fair young Duchess of Norfolk in shimmering silver lamé, and I thought of the ATS brides in their ugly, ill-fitting khaki uniforms.

Of course they wanted to look lovely and glamorous on what is the most thrilling day of a woman's life. It is the one day in which they are the centre of attraction and when everyone's attention is focused on them.

And most important of all, clothes do influence a woman. Everything connected with the wedding regalia is traditional, the veil, the white dress, the bouquet, the wreath, all have their place and meaning. It is a moment of surrender, of giving one's life and happiness into another's keeping. It is difficult to feel soft, gentle and clinging in woollen stockings, clumping shoes and a collar and tie.

I was determined not to be defeated. I advertised in *The Lady* and bought two very pretty wedding dresses, one for £7 and one for £8. Both were spotless and might have come straight from the dressmaker's. Both had their wreath and veil complete. I sent them to the Chief Controller as a gift and suggested that it would be easy to get others. In reply I was asked if I would buy privately wedding dresses for an ATS pool at the War Office.

The Service bride-to-be could apply through her Company Commander for a wedding dress which was lent to her for the day. Afterwards it was returned cleaned and refurbished to be ready for the next bride of the same measurements.

I agreed to buy the dresses and got to work. I advertised in *The Lady* and in the local newspapers. In all I purchased over 70 wedding dresses for the War Office and about 40 or 50 for different RAF Commands and stations which worked under a different system, but who also wanted wedding dresses and wanted them urgently.

It meant a great deal of packing and unpacking, it meant going to inspect dresses in all sorts of places. I always knew that a wedding dress meant a lot to a woman, but even I was surprised at how much they were prepared to sacrifice for it. In mean streets, in poverty-stricken houses, a tired, down-at-heel woman would show me a lovely dress which must have cost her at least £15 or more. Sometimes when they showed me a photograph of their wedding it was hard to recognize the radiant girl in white as the same woman who stood beside me. How many dreams had been unrealized, how many hopes dashed, how many tears shed since the day that photograph was taken.

Yet not one of them regretted that expensive, useless dress.

'I hate to part with it,' they said to me, 'but it's only lying in the drawer and I'll be glad of the money.'

I was limited as to the sum I could give for the dresses, not more than £8, but sometimes I gave a little more out of my own pocket because I understood that those dresses were made of more than satin and tulle, lace and crêpe de chine; they were made of dreams, and one cannot sell dreams cheaply.

But we got heartily sick of wedding dresses in my house before I had finished. My maid helped me by pressing and cleaning them, and finally she said:

'I know one thing, if I get married, it won't be in white. I never want to see a white wedding dress again as long as I live.'

The brides, however, were pathetically grateful. For one day at least a girl who was never meant by nature to be 'a fighting unit' could forget the war, her uniform, her camp, her duties, and be a woman. A woman lovely, glamorous, and enticing, a woman to be wooed and won.

CHAPTER SEVEN

The Women's Services

The women in the Women's Land Army (WLA) and the Auxiliary Services – the Auxiliary Territorial Service (ATS), the Women's Royal Naval Service (WRNS) and the Women's Auxiliary Air Force (WAAF) – were fewer in number but much more visible than the huge numbers of women working in factories.

Controversy surrounded them. Should they fight? This sensitive issue was handled carefully in the Conscription Act: 'No woman should be liable to make use of a lethal weapon unless she signifies in writing her willingness to undertake such service.' Women were not directed to the front line of battle, but the definition of the front line might not be clear. ATS women on Anti-Aircraft batteries certainly had their hands on the trigger, and parents sometimes made 'an awful row about it', according to the Director of the ATS, Leslie Whateley. Her policy had to take public feeling into account: 'Officers were instructed never to allow anything that would cause public outcry. Girls on the batteries were all volunteers, but if their parents objected they were posted elsewhere.' Parents also worried about the living conditions provided for daughters away from home for the first time: hastily erected huts or improvised billets could be cold and primitive, and supervision inadequate.

Typical invitations to women to 'Serve in the WAAF with the men who fly' or to 'Join the Navy and free a man for the fleet' underlined the servicewoman's role as handmaiden rather than gun-toting Amazon. Her job would often be menial – the clerking, cooking or cleaning that she might have been doing anyway, but there were good opportunities for training and development, and a wide range of jobs on offer.

Women were outspoken about the Services and the Land Army. They brought a fresh eye to Service life. 'This is tripe', wrote one woman about a new Army regulation. They deplored the class-ridden anachronisms, but they welcomed the training and the chance to broaden social and educational horizons. Above all they appreciated the friendship which, for many women, was the best aspect of the war.

PHYLLIS CASTLE

A Week in the WAAFs

We were going to be made into 'good Waafs.'

Accommodation at the Grange wasn't fancy. It comprised – for fifty-five of us plus staff – three bathrooms, three W.C.'s and not one looking-glass. We slept on three-piece pallets called biscuits, and straw, sausage-shaped pillows. We kept our clothes in airmen's wooden boxes. The wretched things were painted grey and their most notable characteristic in the blacked-out semi-gas-lit gloom, which was all that we were allowed after dark, was a miraculous invisibility.

We were made to march over the innocent English countryside like young Prussians, and when we got rather out of rhythm negotiating a twisting down-hill loose stony bit of lane with hedges entwined with blackberry brambles overhanging just the height of our faces, we were loudly abused by the Senior Section Leader and commanded to whistle 'Hang out the Washing on the Siegfried Line' to keep us in step. [...]

There were eight of us in our room. There was a Cambridge girl, an elementary school teacher, an art student, two Harrods' shop assistants, a child of eighteen fresh from finishing school and presentation at Court, and an amusing tough collar-and-tie type who'd created records on the motor cycle, could take automobiles to pieces, and held a pilot's licence. The general atmosphere inclined to heartiness, especially when the flyer was about. [...]

Discipline and unquestioning obedience are, of course, first principles in the services. Orders are given with an air of God from a burning cloud, and, however impossible and preposterous, have to be carried out. Personally I was rather charmed by this. Such good exercise for the faculty of inventiveness, I thought. Discipline was rigid. I mean that. As one of my superiors pronounced over me: 'You can't be late in the services, there's no such thing – it simply doesn't exist.' (I'd just arrived half-an-hour late.) Life in the Waafs was going to be a cross between boarding school and prison, I quite saw that.

Our lectures were truly diverting. An officer would appear in the morning and talk about etiquette in the services. You were allowed to wear a pin under your tie in the army, but not in the Air Force – never in the Air Force – it simply wasn't done. That very afternoon another officer, lecturing on rations, would tell us that white bread was better for you than brown, and that fruit was an unnecessary element of diet. But we would hardly be listening to these peculiar pronouncements, we would be gazing – transfixed by the charm of the thing – at the pin under her tie.

ELSPETH HUXLEY

WAAFs in the Operation Room

1942

Round the big map sit the WAAF plotters, in their shirt-sleeves perhaps, each one armed with a long stick like a billiard-cue. When everything is quiet these plotters sit round the table, reading and writing, and knitting socks. Each girl wears earphones clamped to her head. Then you'll see an airwoman suddenly put down her knitting, lean over the map and push a counter from one square to the next. That's an enemy bomber approaching at 15,000 feet from the sea. Up above, the Controller speaks a sentence into a telephone, and a few minutes later a light comes up on a board on the wall: a fighter patrol has taken off to investigate.

The plotter moves her billiard cue again, and the counter approaches closer to our coast. Someone else on the bridge above makes a move now – a WAAF telephone operator moves a switchboard plug, a message goes back to Command, and a few minutes later the siren wails in some coastal town. For that was the birth of an air-raid warning, in an Ops. room many miles from the raided town, and it was a WAAF officer who gave the word that sets the sirens going.

And so it goes on, twenty-four hours out of the twenty-four. WAAF plotters work in four-hour shifts, night and day. They live a queer, keyed-up, underground existence on duty, and off-duty the same sort of station life as the men around them lead; sleeping thirty to a bare wooden hut probably, eating in messes with hundreds of others four good hot meals a day; a bit of PT and drill, dancing at the NAAFI, the station cinema, say, twice a week. Their job doesn't look difficult to learn, but they've got to be alert, quick, and 100 per cent reliable. One slip, one careless move, may let an enemy aircraft through, and then others will perhaps pay with their lives for that one small mistake.

CONSTANCE BABINGTON SMITH

Aerial Photography

I myself was much looking forward to seeing some German aircraft, because I was intensely keen about aviation and had been writing for *The Aeroplane* for some years before the war. But the first aerial photograph of an enemy airfield I ever saw was a disappointment and shock. It was a busy fighter base in the Pas-de-Calais, and I had to try to count the aircraft; but even under a magnifying glass the Me 109s were no bigger than pinheads, in fact rather smaller. My heart sank, and I thought 'I shall never be able to do this'. A bit later, however, we had an aircraft test which was more to my taste: we were given some good clear photographs of a dump of French aircraft which the Germans had written off at Merignac, near Bordeaux, and had to identify as many as we could, with the help of some recognition silhouettes. I thoroughly enjoyed myself, but was rather worried because when I took my list to Kendall there was one aeroplane I hadn't been able to name. Kendall smiled. 'No,' he said, 'nor can I.'

We started by looking at single prints, but were soon trying to use a stereoscope, that apparently simple optical instrument which presents exaggerated height and depth – if the 'pair' of photographs below it is set in just the right position. There were not enough stereoscopes to go round, and I realized that a 'stereo' was something important and precious. In time I borrowed one. It was an absurdly uncomplicated little gadget, like a pair of spectacles mounted in a single rectangular piece of metal, supported by four metal legs that held it a few inches above the photographs. I stood it above a pair of prints as I had seen some of the others doing. I could see two images, not one, and there really did not seem much point. It was much simpler to work with an ordinary magnifying glass. I edged the two prints backwards and forwards a bit – still two images, and then suddenly the thing happened, the images fused, and the buildings in the photograph shot up towards me so that I almost drew back. It was the same sort of feeling of triumph and wonder that I remember long ago when I first stayed up on a bicycle without someone holding on behind. From then on interpretation was much easier.

BARBARA PYM

A Wren's Diary, 1943

Wednesday 7 July
Well, the Nore Training Depot is a big North Oxford Victorian Gothic house, that looks like a Theological College – actually it was a school. I was in time for Tea Boat – afterwards changed my ration books etc. and got sheets. There was a lot of queueing and I felt a little low and strange – but not very. I have a cabin – Beehive XI – which I share with a girl of 19, my own class and quite nice. She has a long rather melancholy face and I can see her when she is older as an English gentlewoman – one of her names is Mildred. There are about fifty new pro-Wrens – most of them in teens and early twenties. I don't think there are really any of our kind of people though there are one or two pleasant ones.

Making up a bunk is difficult, especially when you have the lower one and it is fixed against the wall. You must do hospital corners and the anchor on the blue and white quilt must be the right way up.

Monday 12 July
We had Divisions and squad drill out on the grass in a fine drizzle of rain. AFS men and other Wrens drilled near us. It is quite fun except for the hanging about. I had a slight feeling of desolation, coming to myself a little and thinking but what am *I* doing here and why on earth am I standing out on the grass drilling with this curious crowd of women.

Monday 19 July
Too Many Women. Has this ever been used as a title? It would do
for my life in the Censorship or this Wren life – squashed among
them in the queue for breakfast. [...]

Tuesday 20 July
Today we were kitted. We were taken in lorries to Chatham at 8
a.m. – a great herd of us - I was standing in a mass of suitcases,
lurching all over the place as we drove very fast. My hat is lovely,
every bit as fetching as I'd hoped, but my suit rather large though
it's easier to alter that way. I have also a macintosh and greatcoat –
3 pairs of 'hose' (black), gloves, tie, 4 shirts and 9 stiff collars, and
two pairs of shoes which are surprisingly comfortable. After that
we had to get respirators. One girl and I got left behind at the
clothing store so had to hurry through the barracks – on our way
we came across a little company of Greek sailors being drilled – in
Greek. Service respirators are a good deal more comfortable than
civilian – we went in the gas chamber. Then had lunch in the
WRNS mess.

It all sounds quite simple written down like this, but it's a long
dreary business and we all looked very tired and fed up as we sat
(or lay) in dejected groups in the WRNS fo'c'sle – I wished I was
out of it all – but suddenly, drinking the dregs of a cup of indifferent coffee my spirits began to lift and when we got back I was
quite excited – I packed two large parcels of civilian clothes and
sent them off. At 4.30 we had a lecture by a Padre, but all the time
I wanted to shorten my skirt and there seemed to be so much to
do.

Wednesday 21 July
It felt funny being in uniform – more like fancy dress than anything, but I don't look too bad. Hair is a difficulty. I think I must
have mine cut.

Sunday 1 August
We had Divisions and I couldn't swing my arms properly so
Third Officer Honey had to move me. Gradually people will
begin to discover what a fake I am – how phoney is my Wrennish
façade. My Wren façade – no that makes it quite different. We had
the service outside this week – it was much nicer, though singing

was a little difficult as the harmonium accompaniment dragged rather. After that I went to the Regulating Office and made out my list for Monday. I am going to try hard to be really efficient – it doesn't come naturally to me, no use pretending it does, but it will be good for me to learn to be.

Sunday 3 October
I am reading *A Room of One's Own*. Most delightful and profound – if I had the time I would write an essay about life in the WRNS.

Officers – pay them the respect due to their uniform but otherwise assess them as people.

On Being Yourself, and how you cannot be *too* much yourself or the life wouldn't be endurable. On Friday evening I was having supper when Marion Booth, a very attractive looking MT driver came and sat by me and we talked about German and Rilke and the necessity of hanging on to the things that matter – painting for her, writing and literature for me and music, of course. This is important, otherwise you will lose yourself completely, as you do in the first week or two. '… it is much more important to be oneself than anything else.' So Virginia Woolf. I wonder what she would have made of service life.

A WREN

On Duty in Plymouth

A seventeen year old Wren writes to her father:
I am pretty sleepy at the moment as I was on duty last night and we didn't get to bed until 2 a.m., and our first trip was 6.30 this morning.

We were doing liberty trips all night out to the destroyers in the Sound. The last trip at midnight was the worst. It was blowing pretty hard, and we had to take eighty men out and many of them were not sober. Before we had even started four of them went over the side. Luckily it was moonlight so we had no difficulty in fishing for them with a boathook. I just saved a fifth from going over by catching him by his gas mask, just as he was disappearing. Luckily there was a sober A.B. up with me in the bows, and between us we managed them. It was a terrific experience, and I think I must be pretty hard boiled as it didn't worry me at all. None of them ever get fighting drunk. You have just got to treat them all like a lot of small boys.

HILARY WAYNE

Class in the ATS

Before I joined up I took my voice for granted and I suppose I did not give the question of Class a thought from one year's end to the other. Unlike the lady who put a notice in *The Times* thanking her friends 'high and low' for their sympathy, I dislike the idea of social barriers between human beings so much that it is a temptation to ignore their existence. But they exist very definitely none the less, and almost immediately in the ATS voice and class consciousness were thrust upon us.

I once had in my possession a folder issued by one of the Women's Services, setting out the different occupations open to recruits. They were divided into two classes – S. (Specialised) and G. (General) – and although I know that no such thing was intended, the folder gave us the impression that the categories labelled G., which included cooks, orderlies, messengers and so on, would absorb the socially lower entrants. From then on we privately adopted the convenient, less offensive and to others unintelligible classification 'S.' and 'G.' to differentiate those whom a former generation would unblushingly have labelled upper and lower classes respectively. I shall use these abbreviations here.

In the ATS the Gs. greatly preponderate, and although I have eaten, slept and worked most harmoniously with them, although I have liked the great majority and I know that they have liked me, I discovered that, more's the pity, there is between the classes in this country a great gulf fixed. When I have deplored the cleavage, people have said, 'Education will change that,' but there is more to it than education.

True, the first and most obvious advantage of the S. over the G. is the educated voice. It at once proclaims the privileged camp. I remember a girl saying admiringly of an officer, 'She speaks lovely.' It seemed to me strange that she recognised her own shortcoming and was apparently powerless to deal with it: but this I found to be the rule.

When I was working in the kitchen at the Training Centre I came in the course of a hunt for cleaning utensils into the vegetable room and a rather hostile group. To my enquiry as to whether they had a broom to lend me they chorused nasally, 'Naow, we haven't.'

The devil made me mimic them: 'Naow, we haven't!'

I shall never forget the reproach: 'You needn't copy us, Mrs Wayne.'

I felt very ashamed and I apologised. I think they deserved a gibe of some sort, but I was usually ultra-careful not to widen the gap between us. [...]

I hold no brief for any particular brand of voice or accent; I only record that those who speak lovely and those who don't speak different languages, and for absolutely free and equal intercourse among numbers it is essential that people speak the same language. Education may level this up, but it will take a long time.

But there is a still more potent obstacle to unrestricted social intercourse, and that is background. It must be realised that from the earliest days the lives of the G. and the S. run on completely different lines. They live in different houses, go to different schools, eat different food – the amount I spent on milk, butter and eggs alone when Hazel was young would probably have fed many a G. family: in a word, the standard is utterly different and – most vital cleavage of all – so far from being waited upon as the Ss. are, it is the Gs. and their ancestors who for generations have worked for and waited on the Ss. This has produced a relationship whose roots go back, I imagine, to the days of vassals and serfs. Satisfactory social intercourse must presuppose a more or less common background; otherwise nearly every subject is taboo. Travel, country houses, books, pictures, music, good food, opera – in a word, all the best things and the environment which takes them for granted – are outside the experience of the G., and therefore to converse about them is impossible and even to speak of them seems swanky. [...]

Of course, the Army system does nothing to help. The aloofness, the pomp and privilege of the officer, practically always S., emphasise the social gulf between him and the private soldier.

This is not the case in the American and Canadian armies, where officers and men are on much more free-and-easy terms and the men are correspondingly happier and more contented. One is reluctantly forced to the conclusion that the majority of Ss. in this country do not want to bridge the gulf, to share their privileges.

The ATS, I think, had a rare opportunity to try to make new standards, to show a burning desire to destroy artificial barriers. But its slavish imitation of the men's Army, with even less access for the G. to commissioned rank and privilege, shut out all hope of a fresh outlook. And we had the same insistence on petty detail and petty restrictions and a disregard for the larger questions of comfort and contentment. It is very significant, I think, that the great men – the Wingates and the Montgomerys – prefer to discard privilege and identify themselves with their men. We had an officer of the same calibre. Pay Parade was almost a sacred rite in the eyes of most officers: even a whisper in the waiting ranks outside the office was angrily quelled, and a tunic button undone called forth a frowning rebuke. I shall never forget my surprise when our new officer paid me – I was the last to be paid because I had been issuing savings stamps – without my hat on my head and with no salutes. It was she who refused to allow furniture to be removed from the Sergeant's room to make her own more comfortable, and it was she who, after we left Riverford, turned our room into a cheerful and attractive recreation-room for the girls and presented them with her own radio. To her, too, we owed the gas-ring in the kitchen.

It was interesting to consider whether there were any characteristics more inherent in the G. than in the S., and the result was much what one would imagine. The G. is far quicker and more capable at practical work. Now that there is so little domestic help, the S. has learned to cook and dust and sweep, and although I think she has made a very good show at it and has gained self-respect and usefulness in the process, the G. has had a long start. I can tell an S. by the way in which she takes up and handles a broom. It is the way of the amateur. The G. has a completely different technique. Her quickness and vigour are amazing. She will wash and iron her clothes, shampoo and set her hair with admirable speed and competence.

Conversely, she does not theorise. Hers is a world of action, not speculation. Even on the subject of a 'picture' or a film star it is almost impossible to start a discussion; you like or you dislike, but you do not delve.

Again, no doubt because they have for generations been the under-dogs, the Gs. are in our opinion too meek. They may grumble at bad conditions, but they accept them. The creed of the S. is rather 'Those who don't ask don't get,' and she will agitate for something better and usually get it. This attitude shocks the G. She carries self-effacement to extreme lengths. Sooner than ask for help she will risk injuring herself by over-lifting. This trait may have been encouraged by the lack of chivalry in her own class; the men at the Barracks were more willing to help us, and the S. accepts help readily because she is used to it.

At Riverford there was a high percentage of S. girls in the Motor Transport Section, and it was illuminating that they had a far pleasanter and more comfortably equipped billet than ours. People get what they'll take. [. . .]

Communal life is not everyone's taste, and the herding of the sexes is very conducive to narrowness, nerves and 'cattiness'. There was much homesickness and loneliness – Hazel* and I were constantly envied for being together. The woman soldier does not know the compensation of belonging to a regiment with its traditions, comradeship and pride. She is merely attached to a unit, without any guarantee of permanency. To girls used to independence and freedom the rules and regulations to which they are suddenly subjected are most irksome. Discipline may be good for the soul, but the adult mind prefers it diluted with common sense. And common sense does not flourish in the ATS.

It is not common sense to object, as our officer did, to our having anything but our pay-books in our pockets and forbid the carrying of a bag to take the glasses, compact, handkerchief and purse which were the minimum necessities. When I asked her what we were to do with them, she said we must carry them in our left hands! It is not common sense to issue regulations days ahead in winter that 'gloves but no greatcoats will be worn' on Church Parade, and to let people freeze in consequence. It is not common sense to allow the wearing of civilian clothes on 24-hours' leave

*Hilary Wayne's daughter.

and forbid the comfort of it in the evening when work is done. In short, it is not common sense to make of a community of sensible girls and women a constantly supervised and chivvied boarding-school.

VITA SACKVILLE-WEST

from *The Women's Land Army*

We have grown tired of hearing the Land Army described as the Cinderella of the women's services; it has a sort of self-pitying sound. But this, in many ways, it really is. Not for the Land Army are the community existence, the parades, the marchings-past, the smart drill, the eyes-right, the salutes – or very seldom. For the most part its members work isolated and in a mouse-like obscurity. Their very uniform seems to suggest a bashful camou-flage of green-and-fawn to be lost against the grass or the stubble. It is seldom that the Land-girl emerges into the streets of great cities; when she appears in public at all, it is in the village or the little country town, for by the very nature of her occupation she is rural, nor urban. Yet often in her previous occupation she has been urban enough. She has been a shop-assistant, a manicurist, a hair-dresser, a shorthand-typist, a ballet-dancer, a milliner, a man-nequin, a saleswoman, an insurance-clerk. She has worn silk stockings and high-heeled shoes, pretty frocks and jaunty hats; has had plenty of fun, being young and gay; has done her job during the working-hours, and then at the end of the day has returned to her personal life among friends or family, entertain-ment or home. At a moment's notice she has now exchanged all that; instead of her silks and georgettes she wears wool and cor-duroy and clumping boots; her working-hours seem never definitely to end, for on the land there may always be a sudden urgent call; she lives among strangers, and the jolly atmosphere of homely love or outside fun is replaced often by loneliness and boredom. She gets up at an hour when other people are still warmly asleep – and although dawn in spring or summer may be a moment one should be sorry to miss, a dingy wet morning in the winter before the light has even begun to clear the eastern sky is a very different story; she goes to bed with aching muscles after a dull evening, knowing that next morning the horrible alarm will shrill through her sleep, calling her back to her damp boots, her reeking oil-skin, and the mud and numbing cold outside. All this she has done, and is doing, so that *we* may eat. Nor has she always done it under the threat of a compulsory calling-up, but often voluntarily before her age-group was reached.

'Why did you chuck your good job before you need?'

'I just couldn't bear to see other girls in all sorts of uniform and feel I was doing nothing but sell shoes in a lovely shop.'

Whenever one is dealing with human beings in the mass, some very odd and unforeseen factors emerge. They are most revealing, and demonstrate how much at fault one was in any preconceived estimate of how people were likely to react in given circumstances. Thus it was astonishing to find that one-third of the Land Army volunteers came from London or our large industrial cities; and astonishing to note the tragic disappointment shown by those who could not be accepted for country work because they were more urgently needed elsewhere. This surprising fact does suggest that there are many townspeople who feel they would prefer the country, in complete contradiction to the popular view that the youth of today is wedded to the cities.

MARGHANITA LASKI

Our Auxiliary Women

1939

When we first heard that we were to take two land girls for training, speculation was rife. Miss Brown, the farm manager, who had had grievous experience of agricultural pupils, paying enormous premiums and apparently uninterested in agriculture, was deeply pessimistic. My brother had a wild hope that at least one of them would be a platinum blonde. I patiently expected two strapping typists whose refined voices would gradually be transformed into uproarious holloas.

It had been unanimously decided that we wouldn't have the girls living in the house. 'It would be bad for them,' we explained to each other. 'They'll have eventually to go and work for farmers whose living conditions will be totally different from ours, and it would be only kind to introduce them to that sort of thing right away.' So we arranged for them to stay with the gardener, who lived with his wife in a red-brick bungalow without electric light or running water, but 'much, much better,' we said, 'than anything they'll have to put up with later on.' We even wondered a little if we hadn't been too kind, and if they wouldn't be better off in the corrugated-iron shack of the hedger-and-ditcher. Finally we insisted firmly that we weren't responsible for their morals, 'but,' we added apprehensively, 'one does hope there won't be any trouble with the men on the place.'

The first girl arrived with her mother and the Nonesuch Blake. (We had a moment's delight at the thought of a ploughman's mother insisting on inspecting his sleeping-quarters.) This girl was seventeen years old, would have gone to Cambridge if it had not been for the war, was decisively gentry. The mother wore high-heeled shoes and admirable tweeds. She announced to Miss Brown that the car would be sent on Saturday to bring Brenda home for the week-end, and seemed to have no cognisance of the fact that an optimistic Government was paying twenty-five shillings a week for her daughter's services, and that cows have to be milked on Sundays, modern methods of breeding having as yet failed to achieve bovine recognition of the Sabbath Day.

We left Brenda to Blake and the gardener's wife and sat down to wait for the next. My brother was still uneasily hoping for his platinum blonde, but the rest of us wanted no more than a strong uneducated wench of something over twenty-five.

The second girl arrived in the course of the afternoon, and both were invited up to the house for tea. There had been considerable discussion over this, some of us enquiring whether such glimpses of *le higlif* mightn't tend to unsettle them, others retorting that it was Only Once and that we could lend them some of the six-penny Penguins we'd finished with.

There was no doubt about it, Dorothy was even more of a shock than Brenda. She said she was sixteen, but she looked an undersized twelve. Her mousy hair was tied back with a pale blue ribbon – 'Oi'm growing it ter look loike Greeta Garbo' she explained. We sat back weakly while she poured out a continuous flood of explanation.

'What Oi reely wanted wus ter be a spoi,' she said, 'but Oi couldn't find out 'ow ter set about it. Oi uster be in service, and

then Oi went to a *fête*, and there was a tent with a lady in it
taking names of girls fer the land. My, Oi wusn't 'alf sorry for 'er,
because no one went and enrolled. So Oi goes in and enrolls, and
they puts me down for a medium uniform, three soizes they 'as,
small, medium and large. They puts me down for a medium' – she
was about four feet ten, and small in proportion – 'Oi allus did
loike the idea of working on a farm. No, Oi 'aven't reely bin in
the country before. Oi come from Southampton. Oo, moi Dad,
'e's going ter be that angry when 'e foinds Oi'm 'ere. But moi
Mum, she allus lets me do jest what Oi want. You go, she sez, and
Oi'll settle yer Dad. Moind yer, 'e moight come 'ere after me, but
Oi wudn't let 'im ketch me. Oi'd run away.' She bounced vigorously on the sofa, and the chocolate-box bow flapped up and
down.

'Do you ride?' asked my brother of both girls indiscriminately.

'Oh yes,' replied Brenda, as one might say 'Naturally.' Dorothy
began, 'Oi've allus wanted ter roide. Oi'd loike ter be a cow-boy,
tomboy, moi Mum uster say. But Oi'm scared of 'orses, though
not so bad as of cows. But there, Oi'll have ter git used ter them.
Moi Dad says –' and on she went, her pallid face lit by every
facile enthusiasm of the moment.

At last I said, 'Would you both like to borrow some books?'

'Oi'm that fond of reading!' cried Dorothy readily. I took them
into the library. Brenda was soon absorbed in the shelves.
Dorothy said to me, 'You choose one fer me. 'Ave yer got one
about spois? I don't want no politics nor jography.'

I found a book called *Secret Agent*, or some such title. Dorothy
said eagerly, 'Does it give any 'ints?' and I, with the book open at
a conversation between Ludendorff, Hindenburg and von
Mackensen about strategic considerations on the eastern frontier,
unkindly said, 'Lots.' To salve my conscience I pressed on her a
book about cowboys, published by a firm strangely calling themselves The Wild West Club. Brenda had taken *The Hunting of the
Snark*. I smiled at her, then the girls went off and I returned to the
drawing-room to find the discussion in full swing.

General opinion, I found to my surprise, was distinctly in
favour of Dorothy. Brenda was felt to have behaved unfairly in
displaying undeniable erudition and gentility. There was an
uncomfortable feeling that she ought to have been asked to stay in
the house, which found expression in such phrases as, 'Do that

girl good to have to rough it.' and 'She'll soon get her airs and graces knocked out of her.' My impression of the normal sadism of women to girls going to, coming from, or at the University was fully confirmed.

Dorothy, it was agreed, was the right sort of type – *i.e..*, class – to make a success of farm-work. The opinion was, however, unanimously held that both girls were far too young to go farming, and that we didn't know what the Government was thinking about to send us mere children.

Personally, I was desperately sorry for Brenda. I saw her in the B.B.C. joviality of the gardener's family, sitting silent for lack of any conversational bridges, dubbed stuck-up and rude in the absence of any possible understanding. She was too young and too unsure of herself to seek for common ground. But I privately backed Brenda, Breeding and Blake, and felt strongly that when it came down to it education would tell.

Alas for my hopes! Next morning Brenda had left. Faced with the threshing machine she had remarked that she had meant to come to a farm where there was a real shortage of labour, and that as we had plenty of men, and in any case the work didn't appeal to her, she'd like to ring up for the car to come and fetch her. Dorothy, it was reported, was displaying great eagerness and doing splendidly, apart from a certain naïve inability to recognise the connotation of such simple words as 'shovel' and 'fork'.

So we are left with Dorothy, who is gradually learning to snap names and farm implements. Inquiries among neighbouring farmers has revealed that no one wants any land-girls ever. We train Dorothy diligently for a job in which no one is going to want to employ her, and for which she is physically unsuited.

And the family is finally and irrevocably convinced that too much education unfits a girl for life and only results in making her unbearably superior.

E.M. BARRAUD

P for Prisoner

For two months – with intermittent breaks on account of bad weather – we were threshing, and we had the help of six Italian prisoners of war. At first there was a very natural atmosphere of armed neutrality on both sides; we were unconsciously thinking of uncles, brothers, friends still out in North Africa; they were remembering their comrades – we were both remembering we were enemies. Gradually the mere fact of working together through the exigencies of the day's demands began to thaw us out. One of the men made a sparrow trap with three little slips of wood and a bit of board. David and I went and examined it, drew Stone's attention to it. Grudgingly he came to have a look at it, stared a moment, then smiled. 'Cor,' he said, 'I'm made 'undreds of them time I wer a boy,' and indeed I discovered all the village boys know the trap very well. Differ the ways of countries never so much in their more sophisticated aspects, in these simple things there is a common denominator which gives one hope that the day may come when war between the peoples of different nations will be as unthinkable as war would be nowadays between, say, Yorkshire and Lancashire.

Apparently the gangs of prisoners were sent out in alphabetical order; the surnames of all our men began with a P. They were not, therefore, all from the same unit. Two were from the crack Bersaglieri regiment, now armoured: one was an artilleryman, from a mountain unit operating on skis; the other three were infantrymen, from different regiments. They were all captured in the first few days of our advance from El Alamein, and they were all unreservedly glad to be out of the war.

Our first efforts at conversation were single words about the work. None of them spoke any English, except a hesitating 'Good morning!' and none of us had a word of Italian, except odd words from musical scores, or the titles of operas – and somehow I did not quite see how I could work in such things as 'La donna e mobile', particularly as our old mare is anything but! I had hoped one of them might speak French, but we were unlucky. Nevertheless, I found my rusty French was a bit of a help, backed up by even rustier Latin, most of it ecclesiastical, and one of the men had a tiny dictionary which helped us over the worst patches. After a day or two we had exchanged the words for the job in hand – oats, barley, wheat, chaff, sack, hay, fork, straw and the like – and even managed to pick up bits of information about each other. And somehow one feels more human when names have been exchanged and one can call a man 'Carlo' instead of plucking him by the sleeve.

Carlo was the first of them with whom I exchanged words. He told me he came from El Alamein, was an artilleryman in a ski unit, that his home was in a little Lombardy hill village where he helped on a family farm, that after the war he intended to go to join an uncle in America, that his mother was displeased with him for allowing himself to be taken prisoner, and that his father was English! Carlo was short, thick-set, dark-haired, blue-eyed, slow to speak and yet his English was soon better than any of the others. The others were content to rub along with a minimum of nouns, but Carlo painstakingly filled in his gaps with verbs and other parts of speech. It was Carlo who made the bird trap, borrowing my knife, his own having been confiscated when he was taken prisoner.

Giovanni was a shop-assistant in Sienna, a tall raw-boned fellow, fair-haired and with grey eyes. Giovanni was a fanatic, quick tempered, yet good natured and friendly as a small child. This was my first impression of him, and because of it I was a little alarmed when David one lunch time actually dared to mention the war, and our continued successes in North Africa. Giovanni, squatting on his heels, looked at him earnestly. 'Victory Italy, good!' he said. 'Victory England, good! No interest!' All he wanted, he explained, was 'Finish guerra, go 'ome.' And after lunch, as he worked beside me, he haltingly found words to tell me, driven home with gestures, how friends had been blown to pieces beside him, how one man had gone out of his mind. Giovanni had no use for Mussolini and indicated forcefully just what he would like to do to Il Duce should opportunity ever offer. It was for Giovanni I braided up straw in the various patterns Stone has taught me. He was delighted with the results and placed them carefully in his haversack, telling me he would take them back to their campo and put them in what he called the 'presepio'. This puzzled me, and finally I decided he meant some sort of museum they had got at their camp, but Christmas came soon after, and in comparing notes with them about customs in Italy and England, the word kept coming up, and at last I discovered its meaning: Giovanni was going to use my straw braids as part of the decoration of the manger they were making in the camp chapel.

EX-LANDGIRL

Landgirls' Discontents

November 1943

I was in the Land Army for eighteen months and thank God I am out of it now. My fundamental reason for resigning was that as a result of the monotony, the deadly drudgery, the entire lack of intelligent instruction, the lack of money, the loneliness and the apathy which one inevitably fell into after a couple of months, I felt myself slipping into a moral decline. [. . .] The only outlet was to pub crawl or to pick up a nice-looking American soldier. Reading, somehow, or even attending a lecture, was a terrific mental effort after a physically strenuous day even if it was available. All one yearned for was having a good time. It seemed the only panacea for the drudgery of our daily life.

I admit all Land Army girls do not have these dead-end, deadly jobs, but I can safely say that the majority of them do. Surely it is up to the Land Army to direct these unspent energies into the right channels. But what do they do – officially – practically nothing. There are, it is true, such bodies known as Welfare Committees. I had the honour – as a Landgirl – to be asked to sit on one. One look at those women on that Committee was enough for me. They had no idea of the job they were tackling. They looked upon us, mentally, as the servant girl type. The Committee consisted for the most part of already overworked members of the Country Committee, District Representatives (usually aged and charming spinster ladies not conversant with the facts of life, who once a month made vague and diffident enquiries as to whether we were getting a bath once a week and if we would like another pair of shoes) and, perhaps, an elderly clergyman's wife. They had no funds beyond the money which had been raised at a few dances got up by some hostel or other. They had no experience in welfare work; they were the type of woman who has no real understanding of the young girl of today or how to tackle the problems of wartime morale. On psychology, I can safely say they had never read a book.

The war has been on for over four years now, and I think, without prejudice, the Land Army is the most neglected of all the military and civilian Services and Organisations. In most cases the

Land Army girl is doing a bigger job of work than many women working in factories or in the Services; she works longer hours and earns much less money; but, nevertheless, she is the most neglected. I have known young girls of 17 or 18 sent down from the north of England to farms in the extreme south-west of England, having never left home before. They were put in private billets (not hostels where they would, perhaps, have got some older girl to look after them), with no supervision whatsoever, and I have seen them pick up the inevitable American soldier with the inevitable pub crawling and hedge crawling and all the rest of it following in due course. I consider it a damned shame that no one cares what happens to the Land Army girl now, or after the war.

CHAPTER EIGHT

Other War Work

By 1943 women between the ages of eighteen and fifty were being directed into war work. By then at least 80 per cent of married women and 90 per cent of single women were contributing to the war effort in some way, whether in a full-time, part-time or voluntary job. The Services accounted for much less than a tenth of these millions of working women: other areas, both traditional and new, made their demands too. More nurses and welfare workers were needed, to deal directly with war's bloody and painful aspects. A variety of exciting jobs beckoned adventurous young women and bored housewives, as the small selection in this chapter shows; and women took to their canal-boats, Tiger Moth planes and tractors with zest. Radio talks featured women describing their exotic new jobs: smashing up motor cars, harvesting nettles, organising baths for the troops and so on. Most women, however, would have to go into munitions, making weapons and aeroplanes for the war.

These women knew the war at its least glamorous. Shifts were long – a twelve hour working day was not uncommon. Factories were often difficult to get to and conditions in them primitive. Then there would be the rest of life to fit in: the shopping, housework, cooking and childcare arrangements. No wonder absenteeism was common. There was also opposition from employers and workers alike as women moved into hitherto all-male preserves.

Women had always done voluntary work, but never before or again on the scale it reached during the war. Many of the social services we now expect from the State were provided, indeed sometimes invented by voluntary organisations, and in particular the Women's Voluntary Services. Founded by Lady Reading in 1938, by the end of the war the WVS had a membership of over a million. WVS woman was easy to ridicule, the archetype of the bossy female beloved of cartoonists. It was easy too, to underestimate the hard work, the skill and care that went into schemes for evacuating, clothing, feeding, salvaging – for whatever the need of the moment was.

All these different contributions to the war effort had to be recorded and acknowledged. Women were commissioned to provide reports like Celia Fremlin's *War Factory* for Mass Observation and Rumer Godden's description of WVS work in Bengal. The workers themselves were also keen to put their new experiences into words. Susan Woolfitt, for example, gives an enthusiastic and engrossing account of the year she spent on narrow-boats, carrying cargoes on Britain's canals. She was one of many women who wanted to describe the effects that the work had on them; and sometimes they found the work itself so fascinating that they wanted to capture its every detail.

BRENDA MCBRYDE

Nursing in France 1944

The Resuscitation department formed one arm of a U-shaped arrangement of tents with the theatre as a bridge leading to a surgical ward. It was floored with a heavy tarpaulin groundsheet and stacked with trestles to support the stretchers of wounded as they arrived from the ambulances. Here the men were given intensive treatment for shock until they were sufficiently restored to undergo operation, after which they passed straight from the theatre to the wards.

At the entrance to Resus., was the treatment area, a table covered by a sheet on which were laid trays of instruments, syringes, sterilisers, etc. Upended wooden boxes provided shelves for medicines and dressings; splints were stacked in a clean dustbin, and large, wooden chests contained the transfusion apparatus. On the other side of the entrance was a makeshift desk which bore the Admission Book and an array of requisition forms for diets, dispensary, replacements and repairs, extra blankets, pillows.

Thirty casualties had been admitted into Resus., during the night, all but two of whom had now been operated on and transferred to the adjoining ward. The two sisters from the 81st who were going off duty now handed over these remaining casualties, and wearily made for breakfast and bed, leaving Audrey and me in charge.

The two men lying so still on their stretchers with eyes closed were from the 7th Armoured Division. Both had been badly wounded in an abortive attempt to take an enemy pillbox. They had lost a great deal of blood but were now beginning to respond to the transfusions which had gone on all night. We were registering their blood pressures when one of our own surgeons from the 75th, Major MacPherson, a Canadian, came in.

He raised sandy eyebrows towards us. 'You settled in all right?' He felt under the grey blankets of one of the stretchers for a pulse and bent down close to the soldier's pale face. 'We'll get you to the theatre presently, son. Fix up that leg. OK?'

The soldier, who had a huge gunshot wound of thigh, made an almost imperceptible movement of his eyelids. He was swinging between reality and unconsciousness. We went to the desk to check his transfusion chart.

'Give him saline next and we'll do him first on the list.' Major MacPherson sighed and lowered his voice. 'I'm not looking forward to operating in that tent.'

With Sister Agate in charge, he would not even notice that the theatre was a tent.

'Sir.' George Easton, the Resuscitation orderly attached to the 81st, stood at the tent entrance. We turned at the urgency in his voice. 'Convoy of wounded on the way.'

'Inform Lt. Colonel Harding, i/c 75th Surgical Division,' Major MacPherson said sharply and went to the door as a string of ambulances went by on their way to Reception.

The taking of Tilly-sur-Seulles on 18th June had been a great victory for XXX Corps. Now, five days later, they were meeting stiff resistance in the high ground south of Tilly. This battle was being translated to us in a grim toll of casualties.

We entered the names of many famous regiments into the Admission Book that day: the Staffordshire Yeomanry, 4th Wilts, Dorsets, Green Howards, and East Yorks, men of the 7th Armoured Division and 50 (Northumbrian) Division. Most of their proud uniform, stiff with blood and caked in mud, had to be cut from them. We sliced the tough boots with razors to release shattered feet. The stretcher bearers came again and again until every trestle was occupied and the floor crammed so that there was barely room to put a foot or kneel between the stretchers. Audrey and I accompanied Lt. Colonel Harding and Major MacPherson as they went from one man to the next, assessing his condition and setting up transfusions.

In the trauma of that first day, everything I had learnt during four hard years of training suddenly made sense. My hands had a sure and certain skill and my brain was unflustered as I replaced dressings over gaping wounds, gave injections of morphia and the new wonder drug, penicillin, charted blood pressures. I began to see, for the first time, that the disciplines of the training school were a necessary part of the whole. That tent, full of men, reeking of blood, was where I was needed. These men, whose clammy bodies overpowered me with the nauseous sweet smell of shock were my fulfilment, since they could no longer help themselves.

LENA K. CHIVERS

Night Duty

5 August 1944
The latest convoy of wounded at our casualty clearing station in Southern England had been settled in bed. The men who had been to the operating theatre were back in the ward, the dressings had been finished, the plasters fixed, the first round of medicines and drugs administered. The screens were put round the bed of the Fighting French Commando who seemed likely to die.

Blood was slowly dripping into the veins of four of the men. The field ambulance cards tied to the bedrails of two soldiers were marked 'Gas gangrene test positive'. You could smell that without looking at the cards; it is a smell you can't confuse with anything else – a special sweet and evil stench, less sweet than the smell of death, more penetrating than that of stopped-up drains.

I started to tidy up. We had undressed the men quickly and left their uniform on the floor by each bed. If it was not badly soiled you folded it up and put it in the lockers, but if the articles were torn or blood-stained you emptied the pockets and put them in a pile for the orderlies to carry away.

I started by Sergeant Davies' bed. I thought he was asleep and I was very quiet with his things. It must have been raining in

Normandy – you could tell he had been lying on his side in the mud. I took the flat, wet cigarettes out of his trouser pockets – and his shaving things, a comb, a small steel mirror and half a dozen boiled sweets. I put his wallet and his pay-book and the crumpled photo of his wife on his locker. He opened his eyes as I moved away with the uniform. 'Nurse', he said, 'couldn't I keep my rat? Could you cut it off for me?'

With his uninjured arm he pointed to the divisional insignia on the sleeve of his tunic – a jerboa or desert rat, the badge of the Seventh Armoured Division, which had been nicknamed the 'desert rats' in North Africa.

'I had the same one in Tobruk,' he said. 'He brought me luck. I cut him off my tropical uniform and sewed it on this lot. I shall want him next time.'

I cut the stitches with my surgical scissors and put the badge on the locker. 'Thanks, Nurse.' And he started to tell me why the Seventh was the best armoured division in the British Army.

But there was no time to listen. The ward had to be made tidy quickly. Boots and tin helmets had to be tidied together under the beds, and the rest either inside the lockers or in the pile in the corner. It was getting to be quite a big pile – black berets of the Armoured Corps, tunics of the glider troops with their badge of a blue winged horse on a dark red ground, or the parachutists' badge of a white parachute with pale blue wings, often the red shield and blue cross of the Eighth Army, and several times the ribbon of the Africa Star, the shoulder flashes of Commandos, of Royal Marines, of the R.A.S.C. . . .

There seemed plenty to do during the night. There were some four-hourly drugs to be given, and fomentations, and drinks, and pillows to be changed around. Men with new plaster splints found it difficult to get comfortable. You often had to put a pillow or a sandbag in a most unexpected place to give a man relief. Sergeant Davies insisted on telling the man opposite why he would never even consider serving in anything other than the 7th Armoured Division. But the man opposite who was in the Lincolns, just turned over and snored.

We had rather a bad night with Evans. He was a South Wales miner, who had volunteered at the beginning of the war and managed to get himself into the Royal Engineers. We had sent for his wife because he had been put on the danger list. They had taken his foot off that afternoon. His wife just sat and smiled at him and then when she couldn't smile any more, she went into the kitchen and cried. Every time this happened one or other of us made her a cup of tea, and then she went back to him and smiled again.

After midnight everybody seemed settled. Although I had been on night duty for a long time there always seemed something strange and almost theatrical about the ward at these quiet times in the early hours of the morning. Perhaps it was the look of the place – the shaded lights, the two long rows of beds with their bright blue counterpanes, some of their silhouettes looking freakish because of the bed cradles and the bed blocks; and then the men were lying in such a variety of positions, often with their limbs stuck out at queer angles in the plaster splints or sometimes slung on to frames and hung with weights and pulleys; the light caught the glass flasks of blood which was still dripping slowly into the four bad cases. They were asleep and completely unconcerned about what was going on. The pile of dirty uniforms lay in the corner like the discarded costumes of a crowd of players.

THE DOWAGER MARCHIONESS OF READING

Women's Voluntary Services

1945

The flood tide of 100,000 enrolments which nearly swamped all Centres in September, 1939, dropped gradually to a low level record of 12,000 enrolments in January, 1940, to be raised to 20,000 in one month by the invasion of Norway and 61,000 by the fall of France. Out of this army of women, many of whom had no experience either in administration or in the practical duties they were expected to perform, the staffs of WVS Regional Offices and Centres fashioned an implement of Civil Defence which proved infinitely flexible, so that it could meet any local emergency in the way best suited to overcome it, and yet consistent enough in policy and organization to merit the confidence of the Central Government and the Local Authorities. There were no precedents for a voluntary organization working under the orders of Local Authorities and yet controlled by a national headquarters in close touch with the Government, but this very lack meant that there were practically no restrictions on what such an organization could do. When the urgent necessity for increasing the provisions for the welfare of serving men during the first winter of the war led WVS to open canteens in places where the appropriate organizations lacked personnel and equipment to do so, the Ministry of Home Security ruled that WVS could properly undertake *any* work, arising out of the war, which might be asked of it by a Government Department. Since then WVS has worked for almost every Government Department, but hardly ever did a new undertaking start at the suggestion of Headquarters; almost always it has been found necessary and tried out in some Centre first, and as the experiment proved itself so was it adopted nationally.

The German delay in opening an attack in the west, whether by land or air, made the development of WVS follow an unexpected course. Evacuation and not ARP dominated the work during the first year. Evacuation called into play every faculty most strongly marked in women, quick intuition of difficulties, a gift for improvization in domestic planning and a pride in the improved appearance of children placed under their care. A million and a quarter mothers and children moved into the country districts in September, 1939, and, without the devoted help of volunteers, most of whom were WVS members or worked in close co-operation with WVS, the scheme could not have achieved even partial success. Failures are always more vocal than successes and the difficulty of absorbing some types of evacuee into private billets needs no description – we have all heard enough about them! What we are more likely to forget are the thousands of cases in which volunteers, working as Assistant Billeting Officers, found homes in which evacuated children settled happily, if not on their first arrival then after tireless efforts had found the right combination of temperaments.

The clothing of evacuated children whose parents could not send them adequate garments absorbed most of the energies of WVS during the first winter, and it was this urgent need for clothing which first led the American Red Cross Society to send goods for the relief of civilian distress to WVS. Their representatives visited England during the early part of 1940 and found that WVS was everywhere in touch with the needs of the evacuees as well as possessing a central organization which could collate the results of local experience and estimate future needs. In August, 1940, the American Red Cross appointed WVS to be their distributing agents for all goods that they were sending to Britain for the relief of civilian distress and, since then, WVS has distributed on their behalf goods valued at many million pounds. This steady flow of supplies from the United States was amply supported by gifts from organizations and private donors in the Dominions and Colonies of the British Empire and from sympathizers in all free countries. [. . .]

If most forms of WVS work started with evacuation they found their apogee in the heavy raids. Outside London the majority of Rest Centres were staffed, wholly or in part, by WVS while members worked tirelessly in Clothing Depots, Emergency Feeding Centres, Administrative Centres and Information Bureaux which brought help to the bombed-out. The members of the Housewives Section, with their minimum of training and their maximum of common sense, brought a feeling of self-reliance and mutual help into almost every street. Mobile canteens, many of them bought through the Civil Defence Canteen Trust which was inaugurated, at the suggestion of WVS, in November, 1939, were the first line of defence in emergency feeding. When the provincial cities became targets for concentrated attacks, these canteens were called in support from all over the country and their teams made long journeys, over unfamiliar roads which were sometimes frozen, or blocked with bombs, to a rendezvous at dawn in a stricken city. Here they worked day and night, feeding firemen and rescue squads who could not leave their work even to go in search of food, and people who had either lost their homes or all means of cooking in them. [. . .] The influence upon our national life of the million women who, through WVS, have learned to take a wider view of their duties as citizens will be considerable. There are three essential characteristics of WVS work:–

First, that WVS has been able to tackle anything and, when one need passed, to switch its resources of trained woman power on to the next job without alterations to a rigid constitution, whether the change was temporary, like the rush of issuing ration books, or a permanent change in the emphasis of the country's needs, and has thus never wasted that most important raw material of war effort, the intelligent service of volunteers, on stand-by duties.

Secondly, without distinction of religion, class or politics WVS has given a sense of responsibility to women who had never thought of influencing the life of the community beyond their own doorsteps. They have found happiness in helping, not only their neighbours during emergencies of peace or war, but also the stranger within their gates.

And thirdly, they have also learnt something of the intricacies of Local Government; in fact, WVS, through the work it has done, through the integrity of service it has given, and through its readiness to try and help in a really orderly and sympathetic way, has become the hyphen between officialdom and ordinary human beings. A working woman once said that voluntary public service had been the prerogative of the wealthy until WVS brought it within the scope of all. That contribution must not – and will not – be lost. .

NELLA LAST

The WVS Canteen

Thursday, 28 August 1941

There was a ring and Mrs Thompson, our canteen head, was at the door. She had come to tell me that we will have the two new American mobile canteens any time now, as well as our own Jolly Roger, and also a 'first grade' canteen for the soldiers. She wants me to give an afternoon and/or evening as advisory cook. She says I'll not have to work really hard, only overlook and give advice on economical and tasty oddments. Mrs Diss, who has taken over as head of WVS, had sent her. It's what I've always wanted to do – I am realising more each day what a knack of dodging and cooking and managing I possess, and my careful economies are things to pass on, not hide as I used to! She stressed the point that I would not have hard work to do, and I said, 'I'll do my share like the others.' But she said, 'Mrs Diss said you do more than your share at Hospital Supply, and it's too bad to ask you to do more.'

When she had gone out, my husband said, 'You know, you amaze me really, when I think of the wretched health you had just before the war, and how long it took you to recover from that nervous breakdown.' I said, 'Well, I'm in rhythm now, instead of always fighting against things' – but stopped when I saw the hurt, surprised look on his face. He never realises – and never could – that the years when I had to sit quiet and always do everything he liked, and *never* the things he did not, were slavery years of mind and body. [. . .]

Friday, 26 September 1941

We managed very well at the canteen, considering we were fresh to the place and there is a shortage of crocks etc. I prepared salmon paste and sardine paste, and a boiled tongue was brought in. It was all sandwiches or pies this afternoon – it's at night that there is a run on cooked bits, like sausage and mash or eggs and chips. It will be a grand place when we get going, for there is a nice room for reading and writing, a billiard-table and dart-board, and servicemen are encouraged to bring their wives. I will try and cook oddments at home, and think up fresh recipes to keep the menu list attractive. We are giving good value: a plate of tomato sandwiches (four slices off a loaf, spread with marge and butter), two large cakes and a breakfast cup of tea came to 8d.

Friday, 3 October 1941

They are a grand lot on my shift at the canteen. They say, 'Just tell us what to do and we will do it,' and then scurry and hurry round. I'm very lucky to have such good helpers. I've shown one woman how to make potato cakes, and another says she is going to practise making waffles at home, ready for next Friday.

I get many a chuckle at myself nowadays – no hiding away my dodges and strict economies as I used to. Instead, I broadcast 'how little fat', or 'how economical' my bits and bobs of recipes are. And Gran's old recipes are going the rounds. Her piccalilli and chutney are pronounced 'marvellous'. I had no time to copy out a recipe one day, and hurriedly pushed my old tattered recipe book in my basket, to do it at the Centre. I got on with my job, and when I went into the office, a chorus of 'Would you mind me taking a recipe for . . .' greeted me. It's childish of me, I know, but

it gives me such a warm feeling to find I've anything people want.
I've not a lot to give, and I do so like giving.

JOAN BRIGHT ASTLEY

Women at the War Office

Women were expendable in the War Office in those early days as
they sat at their typing-tables, guarded by lady supervisors, with
eagle eye and scratching pen, who noted their movements and
checked as to whether 'Colonel B. has had Miss K. recently', or
whether some other girl should have the dubious privilege. None
of us, no female, was allowed to carry the red-lettered 'Top Secret
Officers Only' files; it was a daunting experience to me at the time
of Dunkirk – when even the tea-trolley stood silent and the jokes
had ended – to be asked by a furious brigadier: 'Can't you *read*?'
as he pointed at the 'Top Secret Officers Only' file in my hand.

FRANCES PARTRIDGE

A Cook Leaves

11 May 1941
When Joan brought in the green tea this evening after dinner, she
gasped and said, 'Mrs Partridge, I want to leave and do war work,
as Tim's being sent abroad.' I went with her into the kitchen,
where she told me that he was going in about three weeks' time,
and she felt she couldn't bear it unless she was hard at work all
day, so she had been to an aeroplane factory in Newbury to see if
they would take her on. I didn't know how to show her how
sorry I was without upsetting her more, her white face and
breathless voice were so pitiful. I came back to the sitting-room so
struck by Joan's tragedy that I felt on the verge of tears, and neither
R. nor I could read or think of anything else for some time. Here
was something absolutely good (Joan's relation with Tim) and it
has been struck, and is crumbling away so rapidly that she has to
try and drown her misery in the rumble and crash of machinery.
And of course it is the happiness of not one but hundreds of Joans

and hundreds of Gunner Robinsons, thousands, millions I should say – of all nationalities – that is to be sacrificed in this awful pandemonium. R. went to talk to her. We were both too upset to read.

The ducklings were put out this morning in a run on the lawn and we spent some time watching them. Our life gets more domestic and agricultural and when Joan goes it may get more so. If only I could cook!

VERE HODGSON

A Munitions Procession

September 1941
Cath and I went to see the wonderful munitions procession lining up in Hagley Road. It was to attract women to the factories. All firms sent contingents in marvellously coloured overalls – on lorries containing parts of Spitfires etc. with the words: We Made These.

There never was such a talkative procession – they chattered like magpies all the time. One lorry had elderly women. We are all between 60 and 80 . . . we are still working – why aren't you? How happy they all looked. They insisted on a lorry being provided for them, otherwise they said they would walk – but left out they would not be. There were some wonderful Tanks – the fastest in the world. It was a mile long, with a donkey to finish up with!

AMABEL WILLIAMS-ELLIS

Factory Work

In two big steel-mills and in a third factory where they worked in brass there were women and girls in every department, except at the rolling-mills and furnaces. In the steel-mills there were 5 or 6 men to every woman, but these two factories were so big that there were over 2,000 women in one firm. Plenty of them worked with the red-hot metal too; and in the brass-works 'hot pressing' was done by women waited on by young girls.

A long bar of brass as thick as a woman's forearm had been cut into six-inch lengths. Besides Mrs Knowles (in a dark bib-and-brace suit over a pink satin blouse) stands a gas oven on long legs and with an open front, the licking flames giving out an intense heat. This oven is fed from behind by Florrie, who fetches the short brass bars and rattles them down a hopper. With a long pair of tongs Mrs Knowles takes one of the bits of brass – its once-sharp edges blurred because it is nearly white hot. She puts it under the green-painted hood of the press and pulls a lever, which brings the mould stamp heavily down. She leaves the metal in for a moment (the work has its own special rhythm); then, as she releases the press, the rough form of what will be the nose of a shell tumbles, still burning hot, into a hopper below. There is a row of these presses, and the noise is so loud that it is impossible to talk. Mrs Knowles' face gleams with perspiration. Now and then she moves for a moment out of range of the heat to get a drink from a jug of water.

INEZ HOLDEN

Night Shift

It was strange the way the talk could go on. We worked on nine and a half hour shifts for six nights a week; it was true we had one hour each night off for a meal, but it was difficult to get any food; then, it meant a long wait at the food counter, fetching plates backwards and forwards from the cooking stove to the benches where we sat to eat. No one spoke much during the one-hour break. Many of the workers were tired when they reached the factory; we worked all the time we were there, and yet conversation crept in – cut-up scraps of conversation between the times of fixing up a machine, counting pieces of work and waiting for a new drill or tap to be fixed in the machine. But even in prisons, where there are more difficulties, the chatter gets through; words are sent out from the side of the mouth in chapel between the snatches of hymns. [...]

A young day-shift engineer who had just come off Home Guard duty was talking to Nan at one of the lathes near the end of the centre work bench. She had been laughing as she worked and listened to his talk, but now her face wore an ill-at-ease expression. The Home Guard boy was leaning over the machinery like a caricature of a drunken guardsman breathing down a barmaid's neck, and then suddenly Nan slapped his face, quick as a cat at play. Nan's slap was not a hard hit, but it was a boomerang blow, so speedily sent and quick to return that it was difficult for the boy to be sure that Nan's hand had ever left the lathe. He went on talking as if nothing had happened, but the memory of the slap stayed like a brake on the back of his mind.

CONSTANCE REAVELEY

The Machine and the Mind

When I began to work a capstan, I enjoyed it greatly, though it was a strange transition from a don's life. I tried to analyse this pleasure, and seemed to become aware of a number of heterogeneous gratifications. I felt a strong sense of virtue in carrying out repeatedly and exactly the simple processes I had been taught, the small child's smug satisfaction in obedience. I liked the sense of safety, of being looked after, when my machine was set for me and I had nothing to do but pull the levers and turn the wheels. It was flattering, and gave one a sense of power, to have so intricate and expensive an instrument under one's hands, and I loved it for working for me. I was a little surprised at first to find that I didn't resent getting my hands messy with the brown oil that lubricated the machine; the release of the inhibition against dirt gave a faint sense of illicit freedom. I liked being allowed to destroy something, that is to grind away parts of the solid bar which was to be made into a screw. I even more enjoyed making something, the little screw which fell into my hands as the parting-tool finished its work. I liked reaching certain figures in output, 20, 50, 100, 120 and so on. Substantial output was pleasing in itself. When I was cutting away one small surface, I sometimes omitted to flick over the lubricant; the thought came that if I were a dentist, and let my tool get heated in that way, I should hurt someone; this gave me an agreeable sense of power. As I got more accustomed to the job I enjoyed conforming my movements to a rhythmical pattern; rhythm is economical of time as well as delightful. I have no idea whether these primitive sensations are common. They faded out as I got more used to the work. It is not easy to get working people to analyse their own minds, especially in relation to their everyday experience; I could not find out what other people felt.

I was not left on a capstan for long, but was moved to a grinding-machine. I enjoyed this too; a certain deftness was needed, and some judgement. I enjoyed improving my speed, and the shining silver of the ground surface. As the novice's pleasure in simple performance wore off, I became interested in other matters. I watched the life of the factory. I thought a good deal went on that ought to be more widely known about and understood. I thought I should write to the Bishop, and urge that young men in training for Holy Orders should work for six months or so in a factory (or a mine or a shop) to get an insight for themselves into the way people live and work; the young are generous enough for anything when once they get an idea into their heads. Again, it seemed to me that the girls I knew at the works needed a better literature to feed their minds. Fiction, like poetry, should be an interpretation and criticism of life; the stories they were reading were nothing but wish-fulfilment fantasy, and they got sick of them. I thought I would write to the head of a women's college, and suggest that a girl who wanted to write, and would work in a factory for a few months, could produce stories for factory girls about factory girls, which would give them a lot more interest than anything there is on the market for them at present. And if the stories were illustrated by an artist who had spent some time in a factory, factory people might begin to feel that their experience is part of the common life; I must get in touch with an artist.

I did none of these things. There was no time. I realised that if you have ten hours a day for thinking of things to do and only two or three very weary ones for doing them, you either become accustomed to unfulfilled purpose, to fantasy-thinking uncorrected by experiment in the real world, or else you give up making plans.

Like many other people I chose the second alternative. I was getting very tired. I found at this third stage that the time passed in day-dreaming and brooding. It is very difficult to remember or analyse day-dreams. They seem to be at the mercy of emotion and your emotions seem to be much influenced by the way you spent your last leisure; you remember what you said and what he said, and invent long conversations that never were and never will be; more brilliant than real conversations, of course. Or if your leisure had very little in it, your mind wanders forward. If you are very tired, you may become preoccupied with grievances, or imaginary grievances; will the charge-hand refuse to give you an early pass, or will he put you back on the machine you most dislike? When you are tired, which is most of the time, your thoughts repeat themselves as your machine repeats its process; you can't disengage yourself from them. You are imprisoned in your own imagination for hours on end, tied to some idea which has associated itself with the succession of the job. Nothing happens to break into the helpless cycle of these thoughts.

I went and consulted a tool-maker friend of mine and his wife. I asked them whether this fatiguing and sometimes unpleasant repetition of useless thoughts happens to every one who works a machine. 'No,' they said, 'you have an active mind. Many women haven't. They don't think of anything.'

CELIA FREMLIN

Lack of Interest in Working for the War Effort

It is felt by the management that one of the big problems of this type of factory is that the work seems superficially to be so remote from the war; that it is not of obvious immediate use, like making bullets and shells. They feel that lack of interest in the work is largely due to this – that the girls do not feel they are contributing directly to the war. And a good deal of trouble has been taken to emphasize and publicise the importance of the work for the war effort.

As far as the machine shop is concerned, however, evidence goes to show that some of this anxiety is misdirected. The trouble there is not that the girls do not realize that their work is important to the war, but that the majority of them are so little *interested in the war that they do not care whether their work is important to it or not*. As in so many country places, to the women at least, the war is simply a thing that happens, like a thunderstorm or an earthquake, and victory is similarly a thing that will happen. All that can be done is to hope that it will happen soon, as one hopes for fine weather. The idea that anything one does or doesn't do oneself can possibly have any bearing on it all, comes very slowly.

This attitude to the war was illustrated by a small study of newspaper reading in the canteen. Every day for a fortnight at the end of February, an observer brought a copy of the *Daily Mirror* into the canteen and handed it round among immediate neighbours (about a dozen usually had some kind of a look at it), and noted down afterwards all the items in the paper that had attracted any comments of any kind. During the whole of this period there was a total of not more than four remarks about the war news at all, and these were of the briefest. Here is a typical set of reactions to looking at the paper – the particular day being February 26th, the day when a Cripps speech was headlined all over the front page:

> 'What's your birthday, Peg?'
> 'June. First half of June. What's it say?'
> '"No great excitements, but a pleasant, easy-going sort of day."'
> '(*Laughs*) Easy-going! I work till eight o'clock, and don't get home till half-past nine! Good thing they say there's no excitement, anyway.'
> 'What's yours, Lil?'

And so on, until the birthdays of most of the girls within hearing have been accounted for. Then they start looking at the other pages:

> 'Isn't that a nice one? Look, the Queen talking to someone in a factory. It's nice, isn't it. It flatters her.'
> 'What's that about the ATS pyjamas? They don't get no coupons, do they, in the ATS?'
> 'It says they can get them without now, or something. I wouldn't mind being in the ATS, would you? Better than here.'

Interest flags, and there is no more talk about the paper. One girl goes on looking languidly up and down the middle page until one of the men from another table comes and borrows it.

This negative attitude to the war is to a large extent character-istic of all country districts, but it is even more strongly marked among factory workers like these than among the rest of the pop-ulation in the area. For, paradoxical as it may seem, life in a twelve-hours-a-day war factory makes one feel further removed from the war than one could in any other type of life.

AMABEL WILLIAMS-ELLIS

Hostels and Girls

Each hostel holds a thousand women and girls; there are four, five, sometimes seven, hostels in a group; there are four or five such groups in England and Wales, perhaps more – there is offi-cial reticence regarding that, on security grounds. Everywhere the routine is much the same, for the factories work night and day and three shifts of human beings must minister. The girls climb into a row of waiting 'buses, clock in at the factory, work, eat during the brief factory break, climb into their 'buses again and back to the hostel for another meal, rest and bed.

It was with the expectation of finding something rigid, mechan-ical, even monstrous, and tolerable only as a war necessity, that I went and looked at seven such hostels, staying three days in one of them. There would, of course, I knew, be a certain decency (the large numbers allotted to 'welfare' was a feature), and some attempt would be made to amuse the poor conscripts. A fellow-visitor had similar anticipations. 'Till a cum a made sure t' place must be a barracks wi' so many! Many a time, puttin' t' dinner on t' table in Bradford a near cried thinking of our Maudie alone in such a place!' Invited to stay and to see for ourselves, Mrs Hawks and I entirely revised our opinions. There are hostels that I have not seen, but of the seven (in two different parts of the country) that I have visited I can report that they are the nicest of clubs, that they represent real and varied experiments in communal living, and that the atmosphere is comparable to that of a summer-school or of a well-organised one-class cruise.

The source of hostel atmosphere is twofold. In the first place, each of those visited had been handed over for administration either to the Workers' Travel Association or to the Co-operative

Holiday Guild, that is to people used to having to please and amuse their public, but also with a sense of social responsibility – some of their public have always wanted to enlarge their horizons. Men as well as women do this work. In the second place, first-rate architects with a real cultural background have been responsible for lay-out and decorative detail; architects, moreover, with the soundest and most modern views on plumbing. The war forced an austerity on the architects that they (and I) enjoyed: but, had the hostels not been a war-time measure, no doubt a little of what one might call 'Sickertism' would have pleased the residents. Residents agree that the hostels are bright and pretty, that the chairs are comfortable and the little bedrooms for two beautifully planned. The state of the light-coloured decorations and curtains after six months of use (three-shift use) show that they have been, on balance, approved. (Experience is that people are not so reasonable and responsible in their care of material objects unless they like them.) Girls and women have come, or been drafted, to these hostels from all over the place and, had this interesting social experiment not been a by-product of war, it would have been interesting to see whether some of the home-sickness of most residents' first weeks could have been prevented by the actual framework within which the life of the place moves.

One homesick girl from Belfast spoke as if she were in a sense impatient with herself at not being able to take more advantage of many things the hostel had to offer. It was hard to be precise as to what was the matter; the other girls just said she would 'get used to it.' What was it, besides her familiar friends, that she missed? She could not put her finger on it, but remarked that, though the food was nice and there was plenty of it, she couldn't have a cup of tea just when she thought she would, and that, though all the buildings were kept so nice and warm, there wasn't a fire to poke. In peace-time this could have been remedied, not by the administration but by the architects, which might, or might not, have helped her. The size of the place and the many contacts were a relief to some. A London woman of about fifty (small, rather drooping with a singular look of sadness and resolution) told me that just now she could not stand either her own home or someone else's. She had been widowed by the last war and left with a little boy of two. This only son had now been eighteen months in

Africa. 'Always been plenty of time for something to happen between his writing and me getting it. Time passes best here.'

MOLLIE PANTER-DOWNES

War Work for Wives

31 January 1943

Wives of all sorts of men come within the scope of the new Bevin regulations, which are to take effect shortly. These, in addition to providing a close check on possibly slippery female labor by insisting that employers notify the Labour Exchange when a woman worker leaves them, will direct all childless married women under forty-five to take part-time jobs within a reasonable distance from their homes. Housewives have been, oddly enough, officially designated one of the 'unoccupied classes,' but it looks as though the days of many of them are not going to be so very leisured in the future. Tapping this last great reservoir of female labor is the follow-up of a recent drive to make it harder for women not only to get out of war service but to choose what form their service should take. Girls who are affected by the new call-up of nineteen-year-olds can no longer decide that they look better in Navy blue than in khaki and act accordingly, for they are being put willy-nilly into whatever service is shortest of recruits. It has also been ruled that once a girl joins a service, she cannot duck out after the fortnight probationary period because she finds the service life doesn't suit her. The effect of the demands Mr Bevin has made on the personnel of retail business is already visible in some of the shops – notably in one on Regent Street where customers in the neckwear department were seen the other day timidly selecting purchases with the help of a commanding, white-haired dowager in a velvet train.

ZELMA KATIN

First Day on the Trams

At 3.30 I awoke suddenly, my eyes rimmed and my head dull. I was troubled with uncertainty. Was it I who was going to dress up in conductor's uniform, run down to the tram depot in the black-out, shout 'Fares please', punch tickets, and chaff other conductresses in a canteen? Was this woman in navy blue myself? There must be two 'I's': the original 'I' is a married suburban woman who once studied botany in a university college, speaks with a southern intonation, confines herself to her house, and belongs to the petit bourgeoisie. She must have indulged in a burst of dichotomy and procreated another 'I' – an aggressive woman in uniform who sharply orders people about, has swear words and lewd jokes thrown at her, works amid rush and noise, fumbles and stumbles about in the blackout, and has filthy hands and a grimy neck.

MARY DE BUNSEN

A Hen among the Eagles

I was rung up and asked to get in touch with a firm of aircraft dealers. It appeared that they wanted a ferry pilot, and somebody had recommended me.

Trying to disguise my enthusiasm, I telephoned to them at once and expressed my willingness to collect a couple of Tiger Moths from Manchester and fly them south to an aerodrome which I will call Stoney, to be dismantled for export.

I went to Stanford's to try and get the 4-mile-to-inch Ordnance Survey maps of the North Midlands, and was told that aviation maps were no longer on sale to the public. So, just for fun, and knowing that it would be quite futile, I went to the Air Ministry and was ushered into the presence of the OC Maps (I do not know his official title). He listened patiently while I explained that I was an unattached civilian, suddenly called upon to fly what would doubtless prove to be a circuitous and complicated route, beset with balloons, Heinkels and all sorts of unknown hazards, and that it would tend to minimize the confusion I should cause in the process if I could be provided with some sort of adequate map.

He shook his head sadly. Now if I were another department of the Air Ministry, or an official body, it would be quite different; but there existed no mechanism whatever by which an aviation map could be issued to an unattached civilian. I should have to chance the balloons. [. . .]

The Tiger Moth was standing out on the tarmac, painted bright red with silver wings, creaking and straining a little in the wind and looking as tigerish as even a mild and biddable aeroplane sometimes can. I remembered with disfavour the liveliness of small biplanes in gusty weather. Inwardly I was experiencing all the usual symptoms of stage fright, while outwardly playing the part of the Experienced Old Hand. [. . .]

The Tiger Moth left the ground somewhat prematurely on a strong gust of wind; but, finding itself in the air, was good enough to remain there while I held the nose level to get up a bit of speed. I watched the air-speed indicator and climbed at a safe 75 miles an hour through a very bumpy layer of air. They told me afterwards that I appeared to be chucked about a good deal in the first few hundred feet. At about a thousand feet, things quietened down a bit and I looked round to get my bearings. The weather was squally, with a chance of thunder and excellent visibility, except in local rainstorms, when it was liable to shut down to under a mile.

Manchester, true to tradition, was enveloped in a yellow, smoky haze, filled with monstrous floating shapes: the barrage balloons I had regarded hitherto with such affection and which now took on an unfamiliar and menacing aspect. Heavy clouds hung over us and a rainstorm hid the southern horizon. Beneath me lay the cemeteries which are a permanent reminder of the transitoriness of life to all who enter or leave this aerodrome on wings.

I crossed a canal and arrived over Altrincham, from which radiated the usual network of railways. It was essential, in order to check up on my doubtful compass, to discover which was which; but on my 10-mile map they were small and difficult to identify. I started circling, and focused all my attention on the map; but every time I fixed my eyes upon it, the aeroplane tried to stand upon its head, and had to be retrieved from some unconventional attitude.

I set out eventually along a railway which, though uncertain, appeared to agree with my compass course. I verified it finally by referring to a fairly large-scale motor map, which was not very helpful about railways, but clearly marked two small but unmistakable reservoirs.

Without any further difficulty, I arrived, in about half an hour, at Stoke-on-Trent, which was shrouded in the usual industrial haze blended with the outskirts of a heavy shower. Here it was necessary to get on to a new bearing, and, once again, to find a railway line or other identifiable landmark on which I could check for drift. Somebody must have taken the aerodrome away and hidden it, because next time I passed that way, on the second ferry trip, it was right there, staring me in the face. Anyway, this time I started off with insufficient evidence along the *wrong* railway line, and when I had discovered this, made my first mistake. I should have retraced my steps to Stoke and tried again. But time seemed all-important, and I was perhaps too conscious of the existence of the Observer Corps, for whom I was doubtless providing a sort of field-day. If I turned back it might upset everybody's calculations. It felt better to appear to be going somewhere definite. So I went on. [...]

All at once a gigantic mare's nest of an aerial obstruction reared its ugly head on the horizon. I remembered a once-famous Notice to Airmen which drew attention to the presence, in the neighbourhood of Rugby, of a group of X wireless masts X feet high, and after enlarging on their size and number, concluded naively with the words, 'These constitute a danger to aircraft'.

'If that,' I reflected, 'does not constitute a danger to aircraft, I will eat my hat. This must be Rugby.' It was. I was found. What is more, after being lost for the best part of an hour, I was within about three miles of my intended course.

It was at this juncture that I was aware of a curious sensation in my throat; a sort of intermittent vibration accompanied by a buzzing in the ears. Suddenly I discovered the cause of it. I was singing Christmas carols. I was happy; I had been lost and was found, and God was in his heaven and all was right with the world.

I soon got on to the country covered by my large-scale map, and after that it was plain sailing. I had seen a few aeroplanes, too far away to identify, and once a Blenheim flashed underneath me much too close, clearly demonstrating the effectiveness of camouflage. I altered course and flew round a couple of opaque rainstorms. The clouds broke up gradually and sun flooded a suddenly friendly and welcoming countryside. Cloud shadows lent life and movement to the rolling grasslands. Below, grasshoppers

were chirping and larks singing, and I, had I his voice and opportunities, could have outsung the lark. The violent bumps of the
early part of the flight had given place to a gentle rocking lullaby.
These moments, when engine noise and vibration are drowned in
a vast inward peace, are the joy and solace of the pilot.

My watch showed two hours in the air, and there before me lay
my destination, and my troubles were seemingly over. It
remained only to get down – a simple matter.

The one element in the flight which had so far given no cause
for anxiety or complaint was the aeroplane. She had been a perfect
lady, had humoured my harshness, and responded willingly to my
lightest touch. Losing height gradually at half-throttle, I opened
up again at 1000 feet for a preliminary circuit. I had been
expressly told that failure to circle for identification might mean
that I should be shot at. But perhaps she smelt her stable and was
in a hurry to get down; for the engine only picked up on two
cylinders and the whole contraption felt like shaking itself to bits.
I made an attempt to stagger round, just to fulfil the regulations,
but the aeroplane had decided otherwise, and so I put her down
very hurriedly in the middle of the aerodrome, making one of
those accidentally perfect landings which would be so impressive
if one could succeed in bringing them off every time.

I taxied in, and was received at the point of the bayonet by a
detachment of grinning soldiery, who allowed me to alight on
production of my identity card, which was in my handbag in the
luggage locker. Happy and rather dazed, I went off and drafted a
telegram to my employers: 'G-AFZD delivered Stoney this
morning, returning Manchester for G-AFYA.' One day I should
write the saga that lay behind that bald statement. For the present
let them take it for granted, as I hoped they would. Honour was
satisfied and I should have something to tell my grandchildren.

'What did you do in the war, Granny?'
'Why, dears' (casually), 'I was a pilot.'
'Oh, *tell* us . . .!'

Dreaming new dreams, and with an older one fulfilled, I took the
train back to Manchester.

SUSAN WOOLFITT

Work on a Narrow Boat for Inland Waterways

One of the clearest impressions I have of those early days is of the exhilarating feeling on waking up each morning, *longing* for what the day would bring forth. For five years life had been a matter of just getting through the day as best one could; rations, mending, fuel restrictions, queues . . . all the innumerable irritations that made up the daily round. Now that was all a thing of the past; there was very little waiting about and so far no signs of rules and regulations . . . instead there was a permanent rush, activity, a job to be done under my nose, here in the boats; a question of ropes, tillers, judgment of eye and hand, movement, novelty and excitement.

For it *was* exciting – it was thrilling and I was enjoying every second of it, even though I was being clumsy and ignorant and inefficient. It was all new: sights, sounds, people, drill, clothes, food . . . the whole pattern had changed and I felt as though an enormous double window had been flung open, allowing me to breathe in great gulps of fresh air, while away in the distance a huge and unknown country lay at my feet.

Another thing, which other housewives will perhaps understand, was the perfectly blissful sensation of being bossed about by someone else, for a change! Thinking for the family all day and every day in war-time left you more exhausted than you knew, till you got away from it. It was really heavenly to be given orders and not be expected – in those early days – to think for myself or make decisions for other people. [. . .]

Have I made it plain what a wonderful job this was, what a superb piece of escapism, while yet doing war-work? There was no time in a beginner's mind for anything but the work on hand; so much learning left no energy or mental space for speculation, no matter how important it may have seemed a month before. Not for us was the misery of listening to the news four times a day and pondering the result of a reported battle; of standing in queues for food; of doing all the housework without domestic help; of trying to keep up one's personal appearance on forty-eight coupons a year, and of all the other little fidgeting things that had got many housewives so completely down.

In case I sound very unpatriotic, I would point out that we *were* conscious that the war was still on, and that in our own line of country we were doing what we could to help win it. If in so doing we could also escape from it what more, short of victory, could anyone ask?

I went home for a week's leave at the end of this trip feeling as if a tornado had blown through my body and mind, tearing away all the cobwebs with which I had been hung for years, and leaving me revitalised and vibrating with life and new hope.

My friends thought I looked very dirty; they were right, I was filthy; my hands were a disgrace and a tribulation, my hair looked as if the mice had been in it, and all my movements were big and clumsy and my table manners appalling. I had put on a lot of weight and my eyes had a great many new, and grimy, lines around them from being constantly screwed up and looking into the distance, and I suspect, though nobody was unkind enough to say it, that I was frightfully hearty.

What the outside world could not see were the pictures in my mind, which will always be there; the warmth in my heart which comes from feeling that you fit into something; the delight in using my whole body to do my job and not only my feet and hands; the comradeship that I had found, the comradeship of people all doing the same difficult work and sharing the same hardships; and finally, the pleasure of resting my tired body in the knowledge that soon I should be going back to start it all once more.

NAOMI MITCHISON

Tractor Driving

Tuesday 15 April 1941

Lachie was taking over Jo [the horse] and the harrow, to go over the field wherever the cultivator had passed. Duncan had done about half [with his tractor]; I went over and he showed me how to work it, and went round with me a couple of times. Then said he must be going, asked if I thought I could take it on. Of course I said I would, though I was doubtful really; but I felt a nasty kind of pleasure because Anne, anyhow, wasn't able! But the first round had jolted me about, so that I almost pitched out; my skirt kept on working up past my knees, and I was always bruising the inside of my knees on the steering wheel; it was like nothing so much as steering a ship in rough weather. The hints were supposed to be filled in, but they were awfully rough to cross. At first I was rather frightened of the slope at the bottom but soon found that the tractor didn't run away. It was a job to turn, one had to make a wide circle usually over the cultivated part. It rocked, and sometimes gathered clods; then I had to back, to get them out of the teeth of the cultivator. Once I stopped the engine accidentally, by not accelerating enough on the slope up. [...]

It was grand, though, after a bit, when I decided I wasn't going to fall our after all, and had got reconciled to the bruises, and used to the feel of the engine. The tractor was so powerful, and it was fun making a new break, judging how to turn and so on. I got it all turned over, and then undid the cultivator and turned the tractor, which now bounded along, down the grass edge of the field ... Lachie picked up my notebook which I had dropped and was about to run over and gave it to me, grinning. Gingerly I got out of the gate and turned down the drive. There was no horn, but I was making a lot of noise. I got on to the road and into the top; one is much higher up than in a car, able to look over hedges. I pulled my skirt down and chugged along and wished people could see me, I was so pleased. Several did – the doctor shook his fist at me, he always thinks I'm doing rash things.

DIANA COOPER

Making Camouflage Nets

The making of camouflage-nets seemed to have no appeal for war-hands, with its 1*s.* 6*d.* an hour and no music while you worked. This curious and useful task had dumped itself on the top floor of the Army & Navy Stores, so there I clocked in for the full working day. There were erected large open frames of wood like Gobelins tapestry equipment, on which tarred nets were stretched. To each frame were allocated two women, face to face through the trellis, both supplied with foliage-coloured strips of canvas. We would thread and knot them in roughly symmetrical patterns. I began as a time-worker opposite a calm middle-aged lady who, as the long hours ticked peacefully away, told me much of her past life and her aspirations. Older than me, she was far nobler. As war-effort she had resolved to learn Esperanto and hieroglyphs that, thus armed, she might be ready to follow the invading armies across the sea into countries where, not knowing their vulgar tongues, she could still be useful. The rest of us were a bit cretinous, dregs in fact, without zest or much morale.

Efficiency at the hand-destroying job was quickly learned and I put myself on to piece-work. With no union this was allowed, and oh, the difference in production! The three or four of us on piece-work brought our sandwiches and pots of yoghourt and ate our snacks gaily enough on a bank of bogus woodland. Half our time was spent dodging bottle-necks, pursuing nets and strips that held us up by not appearing when they were wanted. We naturally turned out twice as many 'camouflages' as did lethargic 'timers' who gave most of the day to queuing up for cups of tea or the lavatory, and to snatching ten-minutes breaks for a fag on the balcony, generally falling into a watch and thence into a weakness.

DOROTHEA RUSSELL

Music for All

One day in 1940 a friend told me that the Air Force men from the Canal on leave in Cairo usually returned before their leave had expired because Cairo was a hateful place and there was nothing to do there. He said: 'You have done nothing for these men.' Having opened the first Welfare Club very early in the War I was rather piqued and said that I thought we had done a lot, but he replied: 'Nothing but food, lunch and beer, buns and tea; these are intelligent men, they want something for the mind.' So I said: 'All right, I'll do something.'

It seemed to me that we had to give men what they could not find already in Cairo, and that was quiet, and something to occupy their time. Men did not want to sight-see or to walk the streets all day or go to variety shows every night. The existing clubs, except for one excellent library, were all overcrowded and mostly (including my own Tipperary) trying to be as cheap as possible. I planned to have a centre entirely cultural and high-brow, with classical music its main attraction and with all the amenities of a first class London or provincial-town club under one roof on which a man could base himself for the day.

I believed that men wanted comfort and homeliness combined with attractive surroundings and above all quiet and space, and that they would willingly pay for this. An entrance fee would keep out the merely curious. And it was to be for all ranks, men and women, and their guests. There was a great deal of opposition to this in the more conventional army circles, but I knew what this would mean, especially to Imperial and Colonial troops, and eventually I was given a free hand. I called the club 'Music for All'.

At first, the Executive Committee of the Co-ordinating Council, which had the spending of the British Colony's War Fund, turned it down. They said it was a lovely idea, but quite unpractical, it would never work, they could not subsidise such a club for a mere couple of hundred men a week! (nearly a *million and a half* have been through 'Music for All', and over 3,000 men have visited it in one day.) They said I could not find a building, that I could not get an audience, nor the musicians, nor, they added, could I possibly run it. They would have to get a first class man out from home on a large salary! They simply hated to disappoint me but it could never be a success.

I did not despair, but the more I thought about it the more sure I was that my scheme was what was wanted and that if only I could get the money it would succeed. I cast around to see from where the finance would be forthcoming, but I am not one of those people who can persuade others to put up money for their schemes. I returned to the charge and this time decided to try General Auchinleck. I knew that if I approached him in the ordin-ary way he would be bound to refer the matter to my own masters again, so I asked him to dine one night and got him so interested that he told me to send my scheme and budget in to him, and a fortnight later I received a letter saying he had given orders for the necessary credit. I asked for £5,000 and spent £20,000.

Mrs Besly (who has worked with me since September, 1938) and I went ahead on our great adventure. To start off, we had the most extraordinary piece of luck, for I heard of the one utterly perfect room in all Cairo (holding 730 seats) and within three days of seeing it we had taken it at a large rent and surrender price, for we had to buy out a cinema. Then our troubles started. Everything that could go wrong went wrong, prices doubled, materials became unprocurable, transport non-existent. After seven weeks of gruelling work, gutting, building, furnishing, painting, we were due to open with a Palestine Orchestra concert at 6 p.m. on November 19th, 1941. At midday there was still scaffolding up to the immensely high ceiling and not a chair in the place, but we were ready and led off with a great splash.

For months we had a most anxious time. Our day began at 9 a.m. and generally ended at 11 p.m. for in the beginning we had to be there all day and to attend to everything ourselves. Gradually a staff was formed and trained mainly out of complete amateurs. The only exception was the Musical Director, first a distinguished local musician, later an Air Force man, Clifford Harker, formerly sub-organist of Newcastle Cathedral. We started with only our big Music Room Lounge and a temporary kitchen; we began with a concert every night and a trio which played twice a day, and we went on from event to event till we now have four musical as well as many cultural programmes every day. No one wanted to run our lectures for us till at last the Acting Dean of the American University, Dr Worth Howard, took them over; someone organised chess, someone bridge. Eventually we began a small tentative library in a corner of our Entrance Hall; now this has a large room to itself and has 1,100 books out at a time. My old friend Monsieur Groppi (famous name in Cairo) took on the restaurant at his own risk, and was a staunch supporter through a most anxious and difficult time, telling me not to worry if the restaurant lost money for he would still carry on.

No one can imagine the worry and the anxiety. We were really working in the dark for no one had any experience of such a centre. Were we on the right lines? Was this really what men wanted? Was I right, on insisting on my opinion in the face of the disbelief of almost the whole of the Welfare Council? We felt our way as to what was suited to what day, to what time of the day; the stationary people in Cairo liked one type of thing, leave men another; so many factors had to be carefully balanced. You cannot please everybody and one of the things we had to learn was when to ignore complaints and requests, and when to pay attention to them. We stuck it out in spite of losing £500 a month for the first two months – in spite of the long faces of my Council who used to come and tell me I must have variety, I must have dances, I *must* make it pay. Keeping going in this difficult time was complicated by the extreme fatigue of long hours and much responsibility. Daily returns were scrutinised, analysed, losses were cut, large expenditure embarked on and debt incurred. £20,000 on overheads, over and above running expenses, has all come out of takings up to date. Trial and error succeeded trial and error until at last we arrived at what was really wanted. Tremendous encouragement from the men themselves kept us at it; letters that I shall never forget came to us in the office telling us what 'Music for All' meant to many of them.

A man can spend the whole day here for 7 1/2 d. Once he is inside he goes where he will, listens to what he likes. He pays only for his bath, food and library books. We can pack the hall holding 730 people for gramophone or live music programmes, for a musical lecture, for Chamber music for which at first we could hardly get an audience. Many men have told us that they did not know what classical music was until they came one night out of curiosity, eventually to take out a subscription ticket and to come many days a week. People have heard Britten, Stravinsky, Hindemith, for the first time in 'Music for All.' Many men had never heard an opera until something took them to one of our gramophone opera evenings, and we sometimes have such crowds for these performances that we have to close the main doors two hours before. We have proved that this is the kind of thing people hunger for, that you must not talk down, that you can afford to be very highbrow, and that if you are, you will be a great popular success.

JOYCE GRENFELL

Entertaining the Troops

Jerusalem, Sunday, October 7, 1944
To No. 16 Gen. Hosp. after lunch. Two TB wards. It was good. Hard work in the first one for sound as there were constant alcoves and pillars and one was continually having to move so

that they could all see and hear – if possible. Hosps. are my dish all right. I really do know how to do this part of the job, I think. But if only there were more *time*. We could have spent the whole day in each ward talking – telling them about home. One man, from Edinburgh, asked about food. I said it was better there, much. Which is true. He asked me if I was saying so to comfort him – 'propaganda?' or if it was really true? They are wary out here and worried too. Many of the men I sang to yesterday have less than a year to live. They have all been told. No sign of depression, only a rather agonising wideness and clarity of eye that unbuttoned me. A young sailor, a Geordie, sat cross-legged on his bed leaning forward so's not to miss a trick and when he laughed he slapped himself and rocked. Another got such giggles at 'Ernie' that he pulled the sheets over his head to control himself. A surging of feeling pours over me about the whole thing and I wish I knew and could do more. The way they thank one afterwards is undoing. Scotch scones for tea and a visit to a nice depressed Welsh officer from Bangor who said he'd listened in to me. In the last ward, lit by the low sun and therefore lovely to look at, with the men lying and sprawling on red-blanketed beds in a white ward, zinnias burning in bowls at intervals and a dusty green of olive trees seen through the window – in the last ward there was a very young Indian lying alone in a little room at the end. He made a beautiful design – lying on a very white bed hung with snowy mosquito curtains, his lovely face and long boy's arms dark in contrast. He smiled a gentle smile and spoke in perfect English to say it had been 'so nice'. [...]

Poona, Saturday, December 9, 1944
Did four shows yesterday. TB officers at midday, surgicals at 2, neuros at 3, and TB other ranks at 6.30. I'd forgotten how heart-breaking this job can be unless one disciplines oneself and keeps things quite clear in one's mind. The first impact here yesterday was a bit much. The last show of the day was in an enormous TB ward. Most of them were able to move up to one end and it wasn't bad for sound. They were a very tragic lot and I was haunted by their unseen homes and families. No sentimental stuff in there. [...] Except a request for 'I'll be seeing you'. One can't – or I can't – bear to sing songs like 'Someday' or 'All my tomorrows' to people who have no future.

CLEMENTINE CHURCHILL

from *My Visit to Russia*

It was in the autumn of 1941 that the British Red Cross Aid to Russia Fund was started. The might of the German armies, intoxicated by their victories in Europe, had been flung in wanton aggression against the Russian people on June 22 of that year. We in Britain were filled with admiration at the heroic resistance put up by the men and women – and the children even – of the USSR. We were shocked by the stories of the desolation and misery brought to the brave Russian people by Hitler's hordes. The calculated cruelty and barbarism of the Nazis were carried to new excesses in the invasion of Russia. We wanted to flash a signal of friendship and comradeship across the wastes of subjugated Europe to these men and women in their bitter ordeal. Above all, we were eager to do something practical to relieve their sufferings. Our hearts were with the Russian soldiers and with the civil population of the over-run territories. We knew how grievously the hospital facilities must be taxed. We thought of the numberless wounded lying on the battlefields. When we heard that medical supplies were running short, that doctors and nurses were working until they dropped with fatigue, we guessed what that meant in terms of human suffering.

It was in this mood that the idea of a special appeal for Russia's needs was born. I was proud, indeed, to become founder and head of the Red Cross Aid to Russia Fund. The British people saw in this Fund an opportunity for expressing their emotions of admiration and sympathy for the Russian people in their struggle. By Christmas, 1941, they had contributed £1,000,000. By the end of last year (1944) the Fund exceeded £6,000,000. It is now over £7,000,000.

It represents a great act of practical friendship which must surely affect the relationship of our two countries for many years to come. Friendship is a creative and life-giving quality, and throughout my visit to Russia I was conscious of the wonderful kindliness of feeling towards us which the operations of this Fund has evoked.

Many people in Britain may have looked upon my journey to Russia as the climax and culmination of the work of the Aid to

Russia Fund. To me it is only a beginning. I do not mean from a monetary point of view, but as the beginning of a closer relationship between the Soviet Red Cross and the British Red Cross Society. I feel that this is a priceless foundation on which to build for the future. People draw very close to one another through the communion of suffering. Men and women in London and the other blitzed cities of Britain felt a swift, instinctive response to the ordeal of Leningrad and the agony of Stalingrad. We saw how human nature could transcend all the obstacles of different language, different customs and geographical distance when Russian cities and British cities were linked together in a common valour of resistance to the same implacable enemy.

RUMER GODDEN

Every Monday in Calcutta

Every Monday night you may see a queue stretching far out of the doors of a certain RAF canteen in Calcutta. Every Monday night the canteen counters are cleared, except for the urns of tea; everyone is waiting.

Towards half past six a car appears and draws up outside the canteen; from it a lady and Indian servant in white get out and begin to unload trays, plates, bundles, baskets, everything for a cold supper she has brought to serve two hundred men; this is a supper such as she would serve herself to honoured guests in her own house; it is served on her own crockery by herself and her own servants at her own expense in her own way.

The men start to file past the counter when she has set it out with flowers, silver, and bowls and dishes of the beautiful food. The supper begins with cold chicken and ham pie, sliced tongue, sliced beef, potatoes stuffed with cheese, or egg, or tomato; with several kinds of salad and celery; with French rolls and butter. Next there is apple tart and whipped cream or cold coffee soufflé. As the canteen cannot serve food entirely free a nominal sum of An 1 is charged for a helping. After supper this lady makes coffee in a giant Percolator and sends round with it cream, cakes, éclairs, meringues, cigarettes, and chocolates, while, from a selection of her own records, a gramophone concert is amplified to fill the whole room.

The evening lasts from 6.30 to 9.30 when she packs up and drives away to return again next Monday; and this has been going on since 1942 – every Monday night.

MARY TREVELYAN

Welfare Work with the Soldiers

Belgium 1944

My work is to be in charge of the programme at this hotel, a peace-time luxury hotel called the Hotel Albert 1er, but already known to thousands of soldiers as the Albert. Three times a week four hundred soldiers arrive at the Albert, and four hundred are leaving at the same time, so that we have 1,200 guests in the course of one week. [. . .]

All the men who come here seem quite blissfully happy and are full of praise for what they call 'the wonderful organization.' They immensely appreciate small touches, such as lovely flowers in the lounge, or the tea-time orchestra which plays for three hours daily, or the way the waiters in the dining-hall call them 'sir' and light their cigarettes for them. It is a long time since they have been able to live as individuals, free to do what they like and treated as persons, not as units in a crowd. [. . .]

We are working out some very definite views about sympathy. It is impossible not to be moved by these men and you'll perhaps think I am becoming very sentimental, but all the same I don't believe that we really help them by giving them too much sympathy. Coming here and stopping suddenly, as they do here, has certain dangers, not least because in so short a time they have to go back to the nightmare. Very often a group will pool their experiences for our benefit, as we sit talking over a cup of tea in the evening and we find ourselves surrounded by white-faced men and boys who have lived for months very close to death. I am beginning to find that a small remark as to their toughness, a hint of admiration, not given seriously enough to embarrass them, will make a whole group stiffen up again. I am putting this very badly, but I believe that is one of the small ways in which we can try, in a very amateur way, what I call mental rehabilitation. If we sent them back feeling sorry for themselves, and heaven knows they've every right to be that, we should make things harder instead of easier. Since they are in the thing and are determined to see it through, then they've got to be helped to go back to it with as stout a heart as possible.

CHAPTER NINE

Watching, Waiting, Praying

In terms of the number of people who lost their lives or were wounded in the Second World War, British casualty figures were low. But that did not lessen the anxiety of all the mothers and wives, sisters and friends. Separation was a fact of war, and there would always be worry for whoever you were separated from, as well as sadness for their absence. The new friendships which women said they enjoyed during the war could be supportive, but in public women's responses to wartime tension tended towards the stiff upper lip, the 'I Cope' which was the FANY motto. Kind offers of sympathy might be rebuffed as women wanted to keep control of their emotions: 'One can't afford to break down often,' observed Clara Milburn as she waited to hear about her son's fate after Dunkirk. Hearing that her husband had been shot down, Esther Terry Wright brusquely rejected the landlady's kind gesture: 'I did not feel that it was her affair at all.' Emotional release had to be temporary and private. Women remarked on the increase of crying in the darkness of the cinema.

Anxiety about the well-being of others was not the only thing which made the war difficult for women to think about. A nation at war must think aggressively, and this does not come easily to women. How to think about the enemy, how to think about forgiveness: these problems exercised women during the war. In this chapter Sybil Dobbie and Margaret Lane contemplate the mothers of dead German and Italian airmen in their 'stricken homes'; Betty Miller meditates on the extraordinary relation we have with our enemies in times of war, and Dorothy L. Sayers concludes her thoughtful essay, 'Forgiveness is a difficult matter.'

Women are supposed to be peace-makers, and Lily Montagu firmly rejected the urge towards hatred and revenge in the aftermath of the raid on her synagogue. With the failure of peace-making, however, many women were troubled by feelings of guilt. They had failed to keep the peace, and were involved in the processes of destruction. Vere Hodgson, a welfare worker attached to a religious community in Holland Park, expressed these feelings when she imagined 'all our ancestors looking down reproachfully saying: "You have failed your trust"'.

Words could comfort, offer support, provide expression, give consolation. Special wartime prayers for women were published; poetry and prophecy were popular. Public utterance sometimes came more readily than more personal intimate expressions of feeling. Although women are generally supposed to be better at expressing their emotions than men, women too arrive at a point where words fail. Helen Waddell wrote a beautiful epitaph for her nephew, but the letter of condolence to her sister began with the words 'I can't write.'

CLARA MILBURN

Waiting for News of a Son after Dunkirk

Friday 31 May (1940)
The longest day ever! Every time the telephone rang one expected news. Mrs Carter came in at 10 a.m. to say that she had heard through Major Cox that two days before our men of the 1/7th Battalion Royal Warwickshire Regiment were safe. We were so happy to hear this, but later, on ringing up one another, we found each had heard something of the kind and no-one seemed to set great store by it. So our spirits went down and down and the day wore slowly on. We worked in the garden and, lest we should not hear the telephone, we gave our big bell to Mrs Biggs at the telephone exchange next to us to ring for us while Kate was out. After supper a walk with Twink in an endeavour to calm and compose oneself in the tranquil fields, so rich in their late spring growth.

Saturday 1 June
Still no news . . .

Wednesday 5 June
A glorious day with a strong cool breeze to temper the heat. We decided to spring-clean the hut in the garden and there came across the little car Alan made and the box of motor trial trophies put away at the beginning of the war. This, on top of a restless night, was too much altogether, and to cry a bit relieved the tension. Mrs Gorton came then, full of sympathy, and her embrace set us both weeping. But it was a case of pulling oneself together. One can't afford to break down often.

Thursday 6 June
Still perfect hot weather. I never remember such a lovely spell, and the mornings are just grand.

The telephone rings at intervals all day with rumours and snippets of news from one or another, but nothing definite about our boys. As we sat down to dinner tonight, very tired and thirsty after digging and hoeing, Mrs Cutler rang up. She is just an acquaintance in Balsall Common whom I knew through billeting. But she said: 'Mrs Milburn, I am going to Olton Monastery tomorrow and I am having candles lit and prayers said for the safe return of your son'. Surprised and touched, I could scarcely answer properly before the voice said 'Goodnight'. The kindness and sympathy everywhere is wonderful. After dinner a rest and then, as we were about to continue our gardening, Harry and Ethel Spencer came, and she and I talked of Nevill and Alan, both thinking of them as our 'little boys' – mothers always do – and wiping away a tear or two. How drawn together we all are these dark days. Tonight, as they left, we all kissed each other like brothers and sisters. It is good to have so many real friends. [. . .]

Friday 7th June
When I was writing a few notes this afternoon I heard Twink bark and a voice called out 'Can I come in?' It was Mrs Winser. She soon told me that they felt they had real confirmation now that Philip is killed, and I felt how splendidly brave and calm she is. So we talked a little together about our boys and she has the

feeling that the dreadful anxiety is over and that it is even comforting to know the worst.

Cooper from the garage reports that a man named Smith in Alan's platoon saw him near Dunkirk, but one wants to see the man and hear his story. The 1/7th seem to have held the line against great odds before the real evacuation took place. And so the days go by with hopes rising and falling, the telephone ringing and still no definite or genuine news.

Saturday 8th June

Tales of the gallantry of Dunkirk are still pouring in and the thought of the beach and the men in the open sand dunes waiting, waiting to embark, perhaps for 24 hours and then to be told they will have to wait another 24, is haunting to the imagination. The stories of bombing and machine-gunning are so terrible, with no cover for the troops.

Sunday 9th June

I was up early for church, but disturbed by the very kind questioning of one and another.

A message from Harry Spencer about a man of the 1/7th Bn. R.W.R. at Meriden sent us dashing over there just before supper to get news of Alan from him. The woman from a small shop brought him to talk to us in the car. He saw Alan a fortnight ago and was sure he was a prisoner. The man himself was in the evacuation, but said Alan was probably captured the day before King Leopold's capitulation – May 27th. We went back for supper and then Ethne Green rang up to say that Ivan Woodcock was home and reported that Alan was a prisoner of war and was surprised that we did not know this. Jack went round to see him and gleaned a little more of the same story. Though we dare not take this as authentic, somehow it seemed more hopeful and we went to bed and slept well, thankful for a quiet night. [. . .]

Monday 10th June

A telegram from the War Office arrived saying that Alan's unit reported him as believed missing. This may fit in with the story of the capture. Oh, what a long and weary business it seems. Still we ring up other parents and wives and we are all just hanging on.

Tuesday 11th June

A letter arrived today from Major Cox describing the action in which he thinks it likely Alan and his colleague Purchas (who was wounded) and 40 men were taken prisoner. A farmhouse where Major Cox and his men were taking up station could not be vacated for a moment because of 'murderous machine-gun fire'. Later, after a counter-attack, they went to look for Purchas and Alan and for men who were placed earlier in a house 200 yards away. But nothing was to be seen of them at all, and so it was concluded that they had been taken prisoner.

One's mind seems numbed, and the last day or two I go on, keeping on the surface of things as it were, lest I go down and be drowned. Every moment Alan is in my thoughts, every hour I send out my love to him – and wonder and wonder. This queer unreal world, carrying on in some ways here just as before, with this gorgeous weather and summer heat heartening us, and yet most other things so sombre and heartbreaking. [...]

Monday 1st July

The raiders were over last night and I was glad we did not have them. A morning full of household jobs and oddments of tidying, washing and putting away – a typical Monday morning. Still longing to have some word of Alan. Everyone asks and still we say: 'No news.' Always is one thinking of him, wondering whether he still lives and, if so, whether he is well, where he is, what he does all day, what discomforts he is suffering. If ... if ... And so the days go by. Always one works and works and occupies oneself from morning till night, getting up at 7.30, breakfast at 8, seeing Jack off at the gates and closing them about 8.40, working in house and garden, going out into the village, walking Twink, once a week going to Leamington, sewing at Berkswell Rectory on Tuesdays, occasional WI and MU meetings, always something to do. [...]

Tuesday 16th July

About 5.30 I sauntered rather heavily off through the field at the back to take Twink for his walk. When I was well away, I heard Jack calling and saw him waving to me from the hedge. 'It can't be a telegram about Alan!' I thought, so I crammed that thought back and we met in the middle of the field. 'Kate has just had a telegram over the phone for us from the War Office. Alan is a prisoner of war,' he said. There and then, saying 'Thank God', we embraced each other for sheer joy at the good news. Oh, how delighted we were to hear at last that he is alive – and apparently unwounded.

Well, Twink and I went through the fields and then I came home to telegraph and telephone messages round to all the very kind friends who had so often inquired, or even shown their sympathy by their one expression and then their silence. Everybody has been so sweet and kind, it was almost too much to bear. Even the garage proprietor, Mr Cooper, said: 'We thought a lot of him.' After a very busy evening it is 11.30 and, with a heart full of thankfulness, I hope to sleep.

My darling dear, you are alive!

ESTHER TERRY WRIGHT

A Husband is Shot Down

Perhaps if he had known, S. would have come to the telephone, as I had always imagined someone kindly and discreet would do. As it was, when I rang at midday to see if David was feeling unsettled too, it was an airman who said: "'E's one of the one's o've come down.'

That is how it happens.

I tried saying that I was Mrs Lachasse, hoping for something better, because for all it was a busy morning, that seemed a bad way of breaking news; and so by degrees I found that David was in hospital in a place that sounded like the Highlands of Scotland. If I would ring again in an hour and a half they might be able to tell me more.

I was in the police-station ringing up. I tried to get a car, but no one would help. I told them at the garages that I had a husband who had been shot down, but that made no difference. I managed to find a willing driver at last, and I said I would ring again, then I went and told Mother; and we packed our things.

The little landlady peered up at me with a nervous grin and said: 'I'm sorry about your trouble.' I hope I was not short with her, but I did not feel that it was her affair at all.

I waited until the hour and a half had passed exactly, and this time they sent F. to the telephone. He had been at the party. He was someone I knew. He told me David had come down by parachute and was burnt. They had taken him to hospital and he had been on the table for examination, and that was all they knew. I said to F.: 'He's not going to die or anything?' F. said: 'Nothing like that.'

To leave the subject, I asked F. who else had been shot down. He said nothing, and I cursed myself for being gauche.

Much later on, an Army colonel who had seen it described B.'s end as graphically as anyone could have wished.

After quite a long time I decided that David might be alive, and might even go on living, for all the journey to him was so long. Nothing was very real on that long drive: it was like the morning after a sleepless night, when your senses are doubly alert and yet register very little. I had two packets of cigarettes in the car. Mother sat in the front with the driver. Once we stopped and she bought fresh sandwiches, and while we waited for her, I told the driver what our journey was for. He listened to me, and then he told me how he had had to abandon the car that morning to a dive-bombing attack in a main street; and here they both were safe after all.

When we were getting near the hospital I asked Mother if she would mind my going in alone. If there was any drama about, I would see it through better by myself.

Mother had already decided that for herself. I left her in the car, and when she had what news there was, she drove away to find beds for us.

They put me in the master's office and left me alone. There was a letter on the desk addressed to me, and so I read it:

'Dear Madam,
'I am writing to confirm my telephone conversation of this after-noon's date, stating that your husband, Pilot Officer D.W. Lachasse, is very ill in the above Hospital. You may visit at any time you wish to come.'

On paper, the message was sinister. It did not cheer me at all. It took David from me, just like that, and made him a part of the hospital, and so a part of a government scheme, as the Air Force had never done. I had plenty of time to think things in that hot little office.

After a very long time, the master came in. I had expected something dignified; and here was a little bald North Country man with protruding eyes, and a grocer's confidential manner. I told him that I had seen the letter, and I waited. He said that David was very badly burnt, but 'nothing that won't get better,' he said. He seemed to be sizing me up. He told me how they had watched him come down by parachute that morning, and how the air had been so still that it had taken him twenty minutes to come. And how they had him on the table a quarter of an hour after he landed. I asked tentatively if I might see him. The telephone-bell rang before the little man could answer. Because I was listening acutely, I heard his voice change, as he said very quietly: 'Leave it to me.' He would turn round now and tell me that after all I had come too late. I wished it might have been someone else, and not this funny little man, and I was thinking how I would ask in a hurry if I might see one of the doctors, before he could get the words out and have it all over when, down the telephone, he began describing the morning's excitements: 'It was *hell on earth!*' he boasted.

He rang off at last, and now we went in the strong sun across the courtyard and round a pile of new sandbags into a cool corridor that they darkened. The master told me that we should be here for seven weeks. Then, it seemed an unbearably long time. And yet the implication that we should leave at all was cheering.

We found a doctor in the corridor inside standing as I knew by David's door. The master left us – so that I might be prepared, I knew. The doctor was immensely tall. He wore a navy flannel suit with a loud white stripe, and a bad tie. When he talked, he blinked down at me. He told me, as the master had done, that I should find David purple. I made lighter of that than I felt; and said that I had seen such things, because years before I had a burnt brother in a lint mask. He said that his eyebrows were gone; and in the same mood of unreal brightness that had prompted my question to F. on the telephone, I made some fatuous remark about how proud he had been of those eyebrows. But successful conversation was surely not expected of me, and after all this, I was let into the room.

David was lying on the bed. The newness of his accident was a sensation in the room. He himself was something brand new and very real. I saw him just for a moment, his face and his arms purple with fresh dye, and very swollen. I thought he had no eyes; and I thought they had not told me that, but had left me to find out quietly for myself; and, curiously, how wise they were. Behind all this was David. I saw then, as I cannot see now, how we should manage his blindness. (The Irish colonel spat out later on, at his lunch-table, that without his eyes he would have been better dead.) The master was in the doorway, and I looked for his permission, and kissed David, and said the things I had ready to say. His lips were very red against the purple.

He told me how the hood had jammed and trapped him; and how after a long time he had remembered me, and got it open. N.R. said afterwards that it could not have been more than six seconds.

A nurse brought the wings and buttons and the buckle off his tunic. I made out a receipt for them and signed it; and she said it was all right and took it away. A wire came to say that I was on my way. There was a baby crying all the time. The sunlight was white and harsh outside the window. The baby cried and cried. After a time I got up and closed the window, and made the room my home.

AUDREY DEACON

A Wren's Diary, 1944

Monday 1 May
Today I was sent for from Tidworth Military Families Hospital where Terry[1] has been taken after an accident. When I arrived I found he had been hit in the neck by a splinter from a PIAT[2] during a practice shoot. It struck the carotid artery, and he lost a lot of blood. They gave him a transfusion, but his condition was still serious. [. . .]

---

1. Her husband of a year.
2. Anti-tank projectile.

(After initially making a good recovery and going home to Plymouth on convalescent leave, Terry was suddenly taken ill and had to be operated on for a blood clot on the brain.)

Sunday 5 June

I went in on my way home: he was still not out of the anaesthetic. I rang up about quarter past nine: Sister said his condition was critical and could not well be worse, and asked me to spend the night at the hospital. I went back again with Warick, and saw Terry for a moment. He looked rather dreadful, with his hair shaved off, and his face very white. He was still not conscious, but they said he was coming round from the anaesthetic. He was breathing very heavily.

Monday 6 June

I slept in an empty ward – or rather stayed awake most of the time. Soon after six I was brought a cup of tea, and then Sister came in and said he was worse, especially during the last hour. I went down and saw him: he was terribly white, and his breathing was terrifying – a kind of snort on the in breath and a rattle on the out – quick and short, and very loud.

For a few moments I felt faint, but afterwards I found Sister and got her to ask the RSO[3] to see him again. He told me that Terry's condition was very grave. Sister rang up his home and mine.

I went back and dressed. Soon after that I was told that Warick had arrived. We waited a little, and then Sister asked us to go to the ward. Then she said 'I'm afraid he has just died.' He had never regained consciousness.

We came home then.

Everybody has been very kind. The SO[4] sent Joy out to say how sorry they all were.

But it doesn't help. I just don't know how to start again. I had looked to Terry for support and comfort for so long: absolutely everything was bound up with him. He was so very sweet: he always understood, whatever I said.

---

3. Resident Surgical Officer.
4. Signal Officer.

MARY BROOKES

'Missing – Believed Killed'

On 18 November 1940 I received a telegram stating that the *Beaverford* had been sunk and that my husband was reported 'Missing – believed killed'. At that time I was living with his mother and sister at Weybridge and for many weeks we tuned in to Radio Hamburg at 7.30 each night. This was because the traitor William Joyce, nick-named Lord Haw-Haw, broadcast a daily propaganda talk in English, finishing with a list of British ships sunk by the Germans and names of survivors who had been picked up and taken prisoners of war. The radio reception was poor but we forced ourselves to listen to that detestable voice in desperate hope.

My Christmas 1940 was bleak and made even worse by a postal delivery on Christmas Eve of a returned batch of my own letters to my husband. These had arrived in Canada too late for him to have received them before the ship sailed for home. [...]

11.10.43 It was at this time that I finally had to come to terms with the fact that my husband had really died in the *Beaverford* sinking. This came about due to a newspaper article in a London evening paper being sent to me by a friend. We seldom saw any newspapers at this time, but relied on the radio or on the cinema newsreels to keep up with current events. The article described the last desperate fight and the sinking of the *Beaverford* as witnessed by the Captain of the last escaping ship of the convoy. Apparently the naval escort, i.e. the *Jervis Bay* had gone down gallantly twenty minutes after the initial German attack. The *Beaverford*, with its paltry few guns had kept the German raider at bay for five hours, enabling most of the convoy to escape before being sunk by a direct hit by the German raider.

The last official notification, 29/3/41, from the General Register and Record Office of Shipping and Seamen had stated that 'Warwick T. Brookes is supposed to have died on November 5 1940.' That word SUPPOSED had sustained my hopes, for never at any time had I been informed that, quite categorically, all the crew had perished. This news in 1943 had quite a shattering effect

on my morale and I felt unable to consider further courses of
any kind.* I was granted nine days compassionate leave and told
to think about my future.

It was pure coincidence that during my leave I was invited,
together with my husband's mother and sister, to attend a
memorial service for the crew of the *Beaverford* at Downhills
Central School, Tottenham. This was held because the ship had
been adopted by the school and my husband had been in charge
of correspondence between the crew and the children. Early
in 1939 I had visited the school with him and met the staff
and pupils.

HELEN WADDELL

On the Death of a Nephew

1942

My darling – and my darling Mollie who was his mother too –.

I can't write. He sits waiting on the settee in O.K.'s room, he
walks into the Escargot, he watches O.K. make salad dressing, he
stands in the hall getting into his overcoat, always that tilt at the
corner of his eyelid, that far-back smiling.

... The wire came about the same time as the last news about
Jack, we were still at the office, just about to go home. I did two
things which have gone to *The Times*, but I am so scared you will
hate them. The notice is just as Daddy wished, but I added two lines
from the Greek anthology:

'Morning star among the living:
Evening star among the dead.'

Then I began writing a note to go under 'Fallen Officers' but the
only way I could do it to make it effective seemed to me to link it
with his friend. F.A. Voigt said that with one so young, it seemed to
him better to dwell rather on the two comrades-in-arms, and

* Mary Brooks was due to go on an ATS course.

somehow I thought Willie McGrath had no one to speak for him. Do forgive me if you think I have let you down.

MARGARET LANE

The Wreckage Wind

1944

We heard that the body of a German airman had been washed up somewhere near Slyne Head.* Word went along the beaches, but the coastguards were prompt and Slyne Head is difficult to reach when the big winds are blowing, so nobody saw the body taken up or knew what had become of it. It was only one of the many strange, useless or macabre objects which come in with the wreckage wind from the south-west. Perhaps a week after the news of the drowned man we heard that he had been buried in the Protestant cemetery. Nobody took much interest. The Protestant cemetery is a dead area, without character; nobody goes there, and you could spend years in the place without once seeing the derelict gates unlocked or hearing that the silent church had ever been opened. The graveyard itself is only a handful of graves, with here and there is a forbidding granite memorial to prove that Protestants have actually lived and died. Nobody ever cuts the grass; it is neglected; living attention is focused on the Catholic church at the other end of the village, and local funerals wind out to the ancient rabbit-rotten sandy graveyard at the edge of the beach. Looking over the stone wall one could hardly tell that the shaggy turf had been disturbed and another mound added, and soon the tough sea grass and the nettles together were covering the scars.

Some time later, when we were buying sago and bootlaces in the post office, a smart green motor car scattered the chickens in the doorway and a young chauffeur in foreign-looking uniform came in and saluted Mrs Doyle at her counter. In polite unnatural English he confirmed the name of the village and then begged to be directed to

---

*   On the west coast of Ireland, which was neutral in the Second World War.

the Protestant cemetery. He had passed it, Mrs Doyle said, and she went outside the door with him and pointed. The car reversed, giving us a view of a massive muffled figure in the back seat, and slid smoothly away down the road by which it had come.

'That would be the German Minister,' said Mrs Doyle. 'That was a German uniform he was wearing.'

'Oh, surely that was a chauffeur, Mrs Doyle? Perhaps the Minister is the one in the back of the car.'

'Ah, not at all. That was a woman he had with him, a big, stout woman. Never fear, that was the Minister himself in his German uniform. He will be visiting the grave.'

Amused by our ignorance she showed her yellow teeth at us and retired into her lair behind the post office partition.

Curious, we went into the sun-bright road and stared after the green car. At the cemetery gate the chauffeur had opened the door for a big man in a long overcoat, and now had reached a large white cardboard box out of the boot and was opening that, too. What could they be doing? We idled shamefacedly after them, wheeling our bicycles, turned down the rough track at the corner of the cemetery and came to a casual standstill at a gap in the wall.

Someone, perhaps the old woman from the cottage opposite, had unlocked the gate, for the big man and his chauffeur were inside, stepping irresolutely about in the rough grass with the air of distaste. The chauffeur carried a flat laurel wreath tied with a red ribbon in his left hand. Presently they found what they were looking for, and the chauffeur handed the wreath to the big man and fell back several paces. The man laid the wreath on the hummock, removed his hat for a second, put it on again, unbuttoned the breast of his overcoat and drew out a small flat camera suspended round his neck on a leather strap. The chauffeur strolled away and smoked a cigarette in the road.

The big man fiddled with his camera for a bit and held it up to his eye. Then he snapped up the leather case and went back to the car, buttoning his coat. The chauffeur trod on his cigarette and opened the door, and in a moment we heard it slam and saw the car slide off and grow small along the flat, white, narrow road and finally lost itself in the low-lying purple and green distance between the potato-fields and the sea.

When everything was quite still again, and we were fairly sure that nobody would see us, we climbed through the gap in the wall and went with a sense of guilt to look at the grave. I think we had a vague feeling that we should discover something; that there would be a card tied to the wreath, perhaps, with a name on it; that the diplomat with the camera must have left some clue to identify the nameless body beneath the grass. But no: there was nothing tied to the wreath but the red ribbon. Had these official visitors, then, known no more of him than we did?

We stood and stared at the grave in uneasy silence. How strange, how lonely, how cold to lie in the indifferent Protestant cemetery to which the sea has brought you. We are your mourners, alien, impersonal; we do not know you. We suppose only that you were young; that you were lost, and saw the strange coast with dismay, perhaps with horror; that you knew the coldness of its sea before you died, and were carried unresisting into the long weeds and the rocks, guided by the wreckage wind through the fringed barriers. Nobody will ever know your thoughts; and in some German home, eventually, that snapshot will arrive, bearing its routine message, and be slid slowly under the glass of a photograph on the mantelpiece – the photograph of a young man in uniform who may not even be you, but what difference will that make? He will be dead like you – you will have that in common. The same symbol will serve to console any mother or wife. It will comfort them to have proof of your Protestant burial.

SYBIL DOBBIE

Air Raids on Malta

One day a small metal receptacle, tightly screwed up, came down on a little parachute during a raid. Round the edge of it was printed in English, 'We promise on our honour that there is no high explosive in this.' A guard was therefore immediately mounted near it and a summons sent to the bomb-disposal officer, but when it was opened up the promise proved to be true, for it contained only some shaving things, a spongebag, toothbrush, one or two photographs and personal things, and the identity card of a certain German pilot shot down over Malta a few days before. There was also a note in English, saying, 'Please give these to Lieutenant – and tell him not to go flying

again without his identity card.' It was a strange, almost school-
boyish gesture from the dour and serious-minded Luftwaffe.
Only they did not know that their comrade had been killed in
the battle.

In the course of my work I used to see a good many communications from the International Red Cross asking for information
about German and Italian airmen missing after attacks on Malta.
These communications proved more than anything else could do
how many more planes were failing to return to Sicily than we
had known, for very rarely could the missing men be identified.
Occasionally it was known they had been killed. Such information as could be collected was sent to the Red Cross, but through
the bare typewritten form one seemed to catch glimpses of
stricken homes, of heart-broken, waiting wives and mothers. And
one could imagine similar forms being sent to Germany and Italy
and containing the names of British airmen. All over the world, in
many languages, that cry is going up: 'Where is he? What happened to him? I could bear anything if only I *knew*.' The causes
of war are national, financial, commercial, what you will. But the
results of war, the pain and sorrow and bereavement, are international and universal.

BETTY MILLER

Meditations of a Fifth Columnist

Love your enemies is one of those precepts whose motive force,
like a foreign currency, is instantly frozen in time of war. The
State demands of us, an additional income-tax as it were, a ready
and sustained flow of hatred. This emotional expenditure is
required of us at a time when we are, in fact, and at other levels of
consciousness, pre-eminently occupied with the thought of the
enemy: actively, or through the youthful limbs of sons or brothers,
seeking him out; searching him, body and spirit, in order to grap-
ple with him in the passionate embrace, the bitter partnership of
death. He is, in other words (and this is the reverse of the official
medallion) closer to us, more intimately a part of our own being
during time of war than at any other period in our relationship
with him. It is when we are officially at war, therefore, that we

are, unofficially, most susceptible to each other's influence. No longer a mere business of cultural acquaintance, already the illicit issue of our union – our mutual progeny of dead, our still-born – lie farmed out in their cemeteries: honoured by the living: by life, peremptorily disowned.

EVELYN UNDERHILL

Two War-Time Prayers

Let us so confess to God with shame our own great share in the guilt of war; our pride and possessiveness; our spirit of criticism and lack of generosity; our unworthy fears and suspicions; all that prevents the spread of love and the triumph of his peace; and let us ask for his forgiveness.

O Lord Jesus Christ, because thou hast taught us to love our enemies, we pray for all the German people. Change the hearts of those who rule them. Show them thy will, and turn their minds to justice, truth and peace. Have pity on them in all that they must suffer in this war. Especially we pray for all the children of Germany, to thee who didst become a child for our sake. Keep them by thy power and grant that they may grow up into a new world of peace and brotherly love; for thy Name's sake. Amen.

LILY MONTAGU

In Memory of Our Dead

As I left Whitefields* after our beautiful service on Saturday April 19th, a man pressed my hand in a kindly sympathetic way, and

---

* Whitefields Tabernacle, the London church where Lily Montagu held religious services after her synagogue was bombed and twenty-seven members killed.

said, 'All right, Miss Montagu, we shall have our revenge!' If he meant that a Berlin woman who had given her life to some piece of work for nearly fifty years should experience my kind of heartache when she saw the outward shell destroyed in a few minutes, if he meant that another woman should see the place shattered which had echoed night after night for twenty-seven years with the joyous sounds of young people bent on recreation and education, and revelling in activity; if he meant this, then indeed he offered me a poor form of consolation. In memory of our dead, I would urge you to cast hatred out of your hearts, as hatred is destructive, and through hatred we lose our standards and aspirations. We love our country, our England, and insist that she must never do the dastardly things which the Nazis are doing today. If she does yield to the popular cries of revenge, she will have to lower her standards, until they cannot be distinguished from Nazi standards. Not so can our dear ones be honoured. By their graves, we dedicate ourselves to the uplifting of our thoughts and feelings, to the purification of our conduct, to the furthering of deeds of love, mercy and goodness.

DOROTHY L. SAYERS

Forgiveness and the Enemy

1941

Forgiveness is a very difficult matter. [...] Are there not crimes which are unforgivable? or which, we at any rate, find we cannot bring ourselves to forgive? At the present moment, that is a question which we are bound to ask ourselves. And it is here, especially, that we must make a great effort to clear our minds of clutter. The issue is not really affected by arguments about who began first, or whether bombs or blockade are the more legitimate weapon to use against women and children, or whether a civilian is a military objective; nor need we object that no amount of forgiveness will do away with the consequences of the crimes – since we have already seen that forgiveness is not incompatible with consequence. The real question is this: When the war comes to an end, is there going to be anything in our minds, or in the minds of the enemy, that will prevent the re-establishment of a right relationship?

That relationship need not necessarily be one of equal power on either side, and it need not exclude proper preventive measures against a renewal of the conflict – those considerations are again irrelevant. Are there any crimes that in themselves make forgiveness and right relations impossible? [. . .]

I do not know that we are in any position to judge our neighbours. But let us suppose that we ourselves are. [. . .] ready to greet repentance with open arms and re-establish with our enemies a relationship in which old wrongs are as though they had never been. What are we to do with those who cannot accept pardon when it is offered? And with those who have been corrupted from the cradle? Here, if anywhere, is the unforgivable – not in murdered citizens, ruined homes, broken churches, fire, sword, famine, pestilence, tortures, concentration camps and the enslavement of populations, but in the corruption of a whole generation, brought up to take a devil of destruction for the God of creation and to dedicate their noblest powers to the worship of that savage altar. If for the guilty there remains only the judgment of the millstone and the deep sea, we still have to ask ourselves: What are we to do with these innocents? [. . .] Forgiveness is a difficult matter, and no man living is wholly innocent or wholly guilty.

CHAPTER TEN

Living Through The War

Losses at sea, in North Africa and the Far East meant that the middle years of the war saw many setbacks abroad. At home rationing arrived. Food rationing had begun in 1940, a complicated system of coupons and points which reached its tightest in 1942. People did not go hungry, but food could be monotonous and stodgy.

Clothes rationing started in June 1941, with the Board of Trade directing a patronising campaign at women. 'One of its officials,' wrote Mollie Panter-Downes for the *New Yorker*, 'goes on the air now and then in a dialogue with a young lady announcer of the BBC, in which he makes a point of such admonitions as "Cut your cloth according to your coupons" and "Never coupon today what you can put off till tomorrow." The young lady always acts as a stooge who has done all the wrong things, frittering away her precious coupons on nonessentials like bathing suits.' In 1942 'Austerity Regulations' limited shapes, designs and trimmings in order to save textiles, and Utility clothes were introduced to ensure that there was enough reasonable clothing at controlled prices. Home dressmaking became popular – or perhaps necessary would be more accurate – and skirt lengths crept up. Waiting to meet her husband at the station at the end of the war, Diana Hopkinson caught a glimpse of herself in a long mirror: 'I saw that my petticoat showed at least three inches below my frock. Skirts had grown so much shorter since I had last worn it.'

British women recognized that, compared to the suffering on mainland Europe, their trials were small. For most it was a time not so much of severe hardship as of tiredness and boredom – 'that unspectacular product of war' as Hilary Wayne called it – and of the expense of an unusual amount of effort just to keep going. 'Nothing happens easily any more,' wrote Rebecca West. Women were keen to chronicle all the large and especially the small changes of wartime life as they happened. Mollie Panter-Downes sent a series of fortnightly reports to the *New Yorker* throughout the war, superb 'Letters from London' which bring the daily details of war vividly to life. Gertrude Stein's diary of life in Occupied France had to be kept hidden, and await the end of the war for publication.

Women recorded the shifts in domestic and social behaviour, usually with tolerance and sometimes with hope for the future, as Winifred Williams showed in her enthusiastic conversion to British Restaurants. Later accounts of wartime Britain might be more open about disaffection or crime, or more direct in criticising the way the country was being run. The writing of the time had the particular task of getting its writer and readers *through* that time. How it set about doing it is part of its meaning for us now.

NELLA LAST

The Changes War Brings to Women

Thursday, 14 March 1940
I reflected tonight on the changes the war had brought. I always used to worry and flutter round when I saw my husband working up for a mood; but now I just say calmly, 'Really dear, you *should* try and act as if you were a grown man and not a child of ten, and if you want to be awkward, I shall go out – ALONE!' I told him he had better take his lunch on Thursday, and several times I've not had tea quite ready when he has come in, on a Tuesday or Thursday, and I've felt quite unconcerned. He told me rather wistfully I was 'not so sweet' since I'd been down at the Centre, and I said, 'Well! Who wants a woman of fifty to be sweet, anyway? And besides, I suit *me* a *lot* better!'

Arthur said last time he was here that I had altered, and when I asked how, he said, 'You are like your photo taken a year last Christmas. It was quite a good photo except for the look in the eyes, which looked sad' – I've always had 'laughing eyes'. I notice the same rather subdued look in a lot of women's eyes. And yet we laugh a lot at the Centre, and I know I laugh and clown more than I've done since I was a girl. Perhaps the 'quiet look' is a hangover from nights when we lie quiet and still, and all the worries and unhappy thoughts we have put away in the day come and bring all their friends and relations!

Monday, 18 March 1940
As the account of the Fins' exodus came over the wireless, I looked round at my cushions, lampshades and rug with their uncounted hours of effort, at Gran's old tea-set in the cabinet, at my bits of brass and the bowl of golden yellow tulips, and thought of the anguish of mind it would be for me to crowd a few essentials on to a handcart and leave my bits of treasures. My heart ached for the Finnish women and such a WHY? seemed to wrap me round. I think my mind must be a bit limited, for I always seem to think – or try to think – of cause and effect, but the dreadfulness of the punishment meted out to Poles and Fins and Jews leaves me feeling so puzzled.

Sometimes I find myself admiring afresh my smooth panelled hall, my wide windows, my honey-coloured tiled fireplace, with a wonder which is like reverence that I can keep them, while other women – no different from me – see ruin and desolation to their loved homes. It's so *wrong*. The thought of all the suffering and loss makes me feel so little and futile, for it would take an army of workers and helpers to do much to help. I will be thankful when our airplane carrier goes. It's an ever-present care and worry in all our minds, for there is an unspoken fear that bombers will come to try and destroy it, and the spoken hope is that it gets away safely without being torpedoed or mined. [. . .]

Sunday, 29 November 1942
I listened to Churchill with a shadow on my heart. It's bad enough to think privately all that he said, without hearing it on the wireless – to see the long, hard and bitter road, to feel the shadows deepen rather than lighten, to envy the ones who think that Germany will collapse in the spring, to have in mind always the slave labour, the resources of rich Europe, to remember Goebbels' words that whoever starved, it would not be Germany. I thought of all the boys and men out East. How long will it be before they come home? It's bad enough for mothers – but what of the young wives? I felt my hands go clammy and damp, and I

put my toy rabbit down. I looked at his foolish little face, such an odd weapon to be fighting with. I never thought my dollies and soft toys could be used in my wartime scheme of life. I don't envy people with money as I used to do, for most of them want it all for themselves; it's best to have a little gift of making things. Three and a half-ton bombs on Italy. I'm sorry it has to be. I like Italian people. I wonder what would happen if they revolted. I've read a lot of nasty things about the Fascists, and I wonder if there are a lot in comparison to the 'nice' Italians. [. . .]

Saturday, 5 December 1942
One of our helpers had a WAAF call for her, who used to be billeted with her before being moved into huts. She was such a nice refined girl, evidently well educated, and we chatted for a while. I said I hoped they had heating in the hut. She said, 'Ah yes, but not officially – we pinch the coal off a nearby dump.' We laughed, and then she went on, 'I'm rather shocked, really, at my attitude to other people's property – at the light "what's yours is mine" attitude of *all* of us – from coal to clean knickers, from handkerchiefs to stamps, and so on. If we haven't anything of our own, we just take someone else's!' It set me on a train of thought. I thought of all the good scrubbing-brushes and pan-brushes that had gone from the canteen, and the soap from the Centre.

    One thing led to another, and I thought of other little changes, both in myself and friends. Of our slaphappy way of 'doing the bits that showed most', making beds soon after rising, without the turning and airing we once thought so needful: now, in my rush out on two mornings a week, they are lucky to be straightened. I saw pillow-slips and towels, even underclothes, scrutinised to see if they were *quite* soiled – or would they do another day, or week? I saw myself putting on a dress, working all day at the Centre and then having neither time nor energy to change when I got in – just a quick wash, and a house-dress in a gay print, as I cooked tea. I thought of a stack of dirty crocks to tackle after tea, of pictures and furniture that were once polished every week, and now got done when I had the time. I wondered if people would *ever* go back to the old ways. I cannot see women settling to trivial ways – women who have done worthwhile things.

E. DOREEN IDLE

Social Life in the East End of London

Through the exigencies of domestic affairs certain social conventions have been broken down. Neighbours of either sex frequently throw in their lot together. A woman will live with her neighbour who is a small shopkeeper, looking after his domestic affairs; a man and a women who work together during the day will also share their home arrangements and their shelter; those who are the sole remaining members of evacuated families pool their domestic resources. There are innumerable variations of this kind of association, and from what I have seen, they are extremely happy and successful, founded as they are on those qualities of neighbourliness which are only to be found at their best among the working classes. [...]

Shops now serve a more distinctly recreational function than before in the sparsely populated districts, for old women collect there, pull out the boxes and sit down for a chat, whether they have shopping to do or not. And I am told that the isolation and lack of local event during the summer of 1941 reduced topics of conversation to the rock bottom of monotony.

CORRESPONDENCE IN TIME AND TIDE

Cigarettes – for Men Only

July 5 1941
SIR: While bicycling round the town this afternoon, I saw a placard in a tobacconist's window, in fact three placards all screaming to the populace that Gentlemen only will be served with cigarettes.

Boiling with rage I returned to duty (in a boys' school where I teach the rising male generation) and entered the common room. Amid complacent laughter the masters told me that this action was not only legal but patriotic.

Hitherto I have suffered no disadvantage from being a woman, but today my eyes have been opened to the ignorant prejudices still abroad, but it would seem that often women themselves are to blame for taking them as a matter of course. I know many who do. The matron and I (both non-smokers but neither of us a bitch in a manger) hope to end this state of affairs here.

I am, etc.,

SCHOOLIE

(There is no official backing for an improvized tobacco rationing system which precludes women from buying cigarettes. Where individual tobacconists take it upon themselves to make this differentiation it is to be hoped that the local population will take steps to put an end to it with as much vigour as our correspondent. The practice is all the more unattractive for being Nazi-inspired. In Germany women *are* unable to buy cigarettes. The veto is a characteristic example of the position of women under the Nazi régime. – EDITOR, *TIME AND TIDE*.)

MOLLIE PANTER-DOWNES

Rationing

June 1 1941

Something unforeseen to the public was sprung this morning when the President of the Board of Trade came on the air to announce the imminent rationing of clothes, thereby ruining the Sunday-breakfast appetites of millions of women who regretted not having bought that little outfit they'd dithered about the other day. Sixty-six coupons are to be the basic ration for twelve months, no matter where you shop, which sounds all right until you realize that you must fork out, for example, seven coupons just for a washable frock and five for a sweater. To get a pair of pants, a man will have to turn in eight; if he's a Scot and fancies a kilt, he need part with only six. It was prosaically announced that the spare page of margarine coupons in the Englishman's food-ration book is to be used for clothing until the authorities get around to issuing separate clothing books, which should give couturiers an elegant shudder. No one quite knows how this is going to work out or how the officials plan to prevent a bootleg smock or two from changing hands quietly under the counter, but it is certain that this new step will mean the writing off of hundreds of small businesses which have bravely struggled along against the blitz and the disappearance of their best clients to the country.

The country is where millions on unmoneyed as well as moneyed Londoners usually count on going for an annual Whitmonday excursion, but this year a stroll to look at the sheepshearing now giving a bucolic air to Hyde Park is probably the nearest most will get to it. The usual jaunts to the seaside are impossible, even for those who can take the time off, because most accessible bits of ocean are in defence areas prohibited to casual tripper traffic, which, anyway, has been severely curtailed by the recent further cut in the gasoline ration. It is hoped by aggrieved civilians that something equally tough is going to be done about Army gasoline, which apparently isn't stinted, judging by the sorties of lorries sent on unessential journeys that a dispatch rider on a motorcycle could perform just as well at a fraction of the expense for fuel.

Motorists, gloomily counting their diminished gasoline coupons this month, were cheered by finding a memorandum from the Ministry of Transport tucked inside the book. It gives instructions for the immobilization of cars in the event of invasion. The magneto and the fuel-injection pump must be smashed with a hammer, and in case non-mechanical owners should stand gaping and wondering which of the silly-looking things to smash first, the pamphlet recommends gently that 'they should go to the nearest garage at once to find out.'

August 10
The classic English topic of conversation, the weather, has vanished for the duration and now would be good for animated chat only in the event of a brisk Biblical shower – of oranges, cheese, cornflakes, and prunes instead of manna. Everyone talks about food. An astonishing amount of people's time is occupied by discussing ways and means of making rations go further, thinking up ingenious substitutes for unprocurable commodities and trying to scrounge a little extra of whatever luxury one particularly yearns for. Nearly everybody now and then finds himself thinking of some kind of food to which in peacetime he never gave a second thought. Strong men, for instance, who normally wouldn't touch a piece of candy from one end of the year to the other now brood over the idea of milk chocolate with morbid passion. No matter how comparatively well one eats, deficiencies in diet lead to occasional empty moments which the individual mentally fills in to his

own liking with filet mignon, plumcake, or a dish of ham and eggs.

Quite a lot of Americans in London, who earlier in the war irritably curbed a tendency of anxious families at home to shower them with things like tinned butter, are wishing they hadn't been so hasty. Since Americans here are not allowed to write home and ask for what they want, all they can do is pen effusive thanks for the delicious ham or whatever (which actually was never sent) and trust to their dear ones' sagacity to put two and two together. The official attitude toward food parcels is divided between reluctance to check these friendly impulses and a wish that precious shipping space could be left clear for bulk consignments, which would benefit the many instead of the few.

On the whole, the food situation, although it's far from good, is a long way from being desperate. The average number of calories which each member of the population consumed during the first year of the war was only one per cent lower than it was in peacetime and it is expected that it will be no lower this year. Those feelings of emptiness are more the result of turning rather suddenly to a thinner diet; obviously, a nation which once consumed a lot of meat and fats can't switch abruptly to vegetables and cereals without experiencing discomfort under the waistband. The urban poor come off the worst, owing to their distaste for such substitutes (the unshakable aversion of cockney evacuees to green-stuffs is the bane of many a communal feeding centre) and to their habitual partiality for delicacies like tinned salmon, condensed milk, and endless cups of tea, all of which are difficult or impossible to procure. The rural poor do a good deal better because they grow a lot of vegetables, generally keep a few chickens, and poach a rabbit or two when they're lucky. The more moneyed classes are able to buy trimmings to furbish up the dull, basic necessities, but anything substantial beyond those necessities is becoming increasingly hard to come by, money or no.

The shelves of, say Fortnum & Mason are dazzling at first sight, but closer inspection reveals that the bulk of the displays consist of sauces, chutneys, and other condiments, which don't go far toward assuaging the appetite unless accompanied by a good slab of fish, flesh, or fowl. At the moment, fowls have practically disappeared from legal markets because poultry farmers prefer to sell at black-market prices rather than at the government-controlled figure.

Fish is expensive, and the meat ration is such that a small family probably gets no more than a modest joint once a week. Horse-flesh is on sale, ostensibly for dogs, but possibly appears incognito in many of the cooked foods which shops offer for human consumption. Eggs are rationed at the rate of one a week to a person and often turn up stamped with a cryptic blue hieroglyph which pessimists say is a Chinese character indicative of age. Vegetables are plentiful; Londoners dug for victory so manfully this spring that scarlet runners in every back yard seem to be trying to strangle the house, and for the time being there is a greater danger of being hit by a marrow falling off the roof of an air-raid shelter than of being struck by a bomb. Among unrationed foods, the following are likely to elicit a regretful no from one's shopkeeper: breakfast cereals, tinned and dried fruits, olive oil, tinned fish and soups, jellies, biscuits, lemons, lime juice, honey, chocolate, and macaroni and every other variety of pasta.

Now that marketing has become one long dialogue of queries and negative answers, the job of feeding a family is one which requires ingenuity, stamina, and endless time. The time factor has been sympathetically studied by the authorities in their drive to get women into line in the war industries. Some of the factories solve the problem by letting married women off for a couple of hours during the morning so that they can do their household shopping. In certain towns, food shops are trying out a scheme of reserving a proportion of their goods for war workers who can only get in late and would otherwise find everything sold out. The housekeeping difficulties of families in which both husband and wife go to work every day are simplified to some extent by the government-run chain of British Restaurants, of which there are now six hundred operating – two hundred and fifty of them in the London area – and about four hundred more under way. These restaurants, which were originally planned for bombed-out people and workingmen who didn't have the use of a works canteen, serve a good meal of meat, dessert, and a cup of tea for a shilling. The amount of meat served to customers at a British Restaurant or at a West End place like the Savoy is the same one-penny-worth a head, though the Savoy may add a few champignons.

Lately, there has been an acute shortage of beer, which is a big hardship to the workingman. Except in bars, hard liquor is equally difficult to buy. Often chagrined customers, after pointing wrathfully to displays of Scotch and rye in a shop window, discover that the bottles are dummies. The resulting skepticism about the nature of things sometimes has unfortunate results, as when a housewife stared coldly at a mound of lemons in her greengrocer's shop under the gloomy impression that they were hollow papier-mâché mockeries. She discovered later, after they were all gone, that they were part of a crate of the genuine article which had just come in that morning.

BRYHER

Camel Hair Coats

I opened the newspaper one April morning [in 1942] to find that the Zoo was offering to sell clippings from their camels' coats without coupons. [. . .] I dashed off alone at lunch hour. Eventually a man arrived, looking puzzled but otherwise affable. Yes, he assured me, they combed the beasts regularly to keep their coats from becoming matted and a firm had previously collected these combings, he did not know for what purpose, could it have been for brushes? 'I've got two sacks of Droms and five of Bacs.' He meant, I presumed, Dromedaries and Bactrians but how impolite, even in wartime, not to refer to his charges by their full names. [. . .]

'Had I a bag?'

In my enthusiasm I had forgotten this precaution.

Well, he would see what he could do. He hailed a friend and left me alone with the animals. They ignored me. It seemed ages before he returned with a sack full of combings and then he actually helped me to find a taxi at the gate.

'Stinks, it does!' The driver slammed a window shut and we charged rather than proceeded decorously through the empty streets to Lowndes Square.

'You can't keep that stuff here,' was Hilda's unenthusiastic reception, 'see if they will let you store it in the basement.'

'But it's camel and off coupons.'

Hilda slammed the door and it was only after much discussion that I was able to find a corner for my sack at the side of the baggage room. People would not realize that if conditions got worse I was a public benefactor. [. . .]

A resident at Lowndes complained about a curious smell in the basement, could it be the new gas? I got Mrs Ash to help me pack the clippings inside paper that we had drenched with disinfectant and posted them to Scotland. I heard no more for six months. Then without warning six skeins of rough and prickly wool, together with a startlingly small bill arrived with the morning post.

Our winter clothes were already thin with wear but I cannot pretend the wool was a success. I shared it eventually with Osbert [Sitwell]. He had a coat made that he gave later to a gamekeeper, then doing night watches. I have always felt the cold terribly but my jacket was too hot even for me and I passed it on to a farming friend to wear during the lambing season.

MRS ROBERT HENREY

Piccadilly Circus, Easter 1942

The plinth of Eros was now covered with yellow and blue posters bearing the words: 'Save in War Savings.' Underneath the lettering were pictures of sailors signalling the message with flags.

I stood watching the throb of the Circus a moment from the steps of Swan & Edgar's. [...]

Behind us the big shop window had paper crocuses growing from green matting among the gloves and stockings. At the entrance to the underground, the newspaper sellers, with their backs against the square brick police shelter on the kerb, were crying out the evening papers. On the other side of the Circus, between Etam and Shaftesbury Avenue, and below the huge Guinness clock, the empty shop where, the preceding month, collections were made for Warship Week, was now taken over by the Ministry of Food to teach housewives how to make the best of the new national flour.

In another forty-eight hours the white loaf was to disappear until the end of the war. The significance of this momentous decision had not yet quite dawned upon the public. They had taken the white loaf for granted during two and a half years of war. Most of this time we were the only nation in Europe to enjoy this inestimable privilege. We could buy as much white bread as we liked while people on the Continent queued up for a black substitute. Some, like the Spanish and the Greeks, had no bread at all. Even now we were not to be pitied, for the national flour, though no longer white, was to be excellent, though there was no telling what the future might bring.

Outside the shop where these lessons for housewives were to be given, was displayed a huge coloured canvas portraying an Atlantic convoy with the words:

'National Flour Saves Shipping'. [...] I turned into Rupert Street, which leads across Shaftesbury Avenue into Berwick Market. A big van stood outside the kitchen entrance of the Corner House, and a series of white-coated assistants were unloading tray upon tray of crisp, warm French loaves. They smelt good, and they were still white. It was the last baking.

SYLVIA TOWNSEND WARNER

The New Austerity

1942

I have just come in, wet as a water-rat, from carrying the washing to its local depot. No more vans coming to the door now, in this new austerity of petrol. One carries most of one's things, and also one carries bits of newspaper to wrap them in – unless one chooses to be perfectly natural and walk around clutching a nude fish. On the whole it all seems to save a lot of trouble and mental wear and tear. One can't visit, or be visited, that is very nice and makes one feel unusually warmly about one's acquaintances. House-keeping is child's play when one just buys what one can get. I don't at all object to being simplified, and personally I feel domesticity just slipping off me. It is a choice. Either one can let it go or one can intensify it. The people who intensify it seem to get quite a lot of interest out of that, too, and are as preoccupied as pirates. There is a great deal of release in hardship, people slide out on one side or the other, according to their natures.

For a long time we wondered what we should do when we had no more stockings, now we wonder how we shall keep our last pair of stockings up when there is no more elastic. Valentine has a theory that it can be done with little tabs of adhesive tape. It worries me, I must admit, a good deal. My work takes me much among clergymen, so I must have stockings and I must keep them up. Unless the church throws itself open to women, and I can become a dean and wear gaiters it seems to me I shall have to give up my work. Why my work takes me so much among clergymen is because it takes me into villages, where clergymen still abound. They are not even rationed yet, there is one to every village. The last one I saw combined being a clergyman with what is called being a village leader. That is to say, if his village were cut off from the world by invasion, he would then have to take charge of a lot of things like deciding whether cows should be milked or slaughtered, scorched cows policy, and whether Mrs Tomkins of the local first aid should or should not have priority over Mrs Bumkin of the local air raid precautions. When asked if he was village leader he hesitated before replying, and then explained that he did not care to spread the news as he had heard that village leaders would be the first people to be shot by the Germans, so naturally he did not want too many people to know about it. I thought this very nice and natural of him. It is becoming my belief that if our local villages were invaded, nobody would have time to notice the enemy, they would all be too busy taking sides over Mrs Tomkins and Mrs Bumkin, and storming the village hall, that is to say if the local first aid is in possession the emergency cooking squad will be storming it from one side and the ARP personnel from another, and the boy scouts will be making their way in by the chimney and the home guards will be tunnelling in from below. There is not enough accommodation in our villages for all the things that are going on, or may be going on. Often, too, there is not enough personnel for all the various patriotic doings. I know many people who are in charge of so many different activities that the whole of their faculties will be absorbed in vetoing as one person what they wish to carry out as another. Valentine's mother is a case in point. In her ardour for service she has undertaken the charge of so many things that as far as I can reckon she will be essential in five different places at once; and as she attains terrific velocity, fells whatever stands in her path, and is permanently fitted with a screaming device like a German bomb, she will create incalculable havoc amid both defenders and attackers, besides spraining her ankle and getting very much out of breath. I often think that Mrs Ackland is the

real reason why Hitler has not yet tried a landing on the East
Coast. She thinks so, too.

It is very odd to look at all these poor consequential idiots and
remember that war might at any moment make real mincemeat of
them. Even under the shadow of death man walketh in a vain
shadow. People often mention with surprise the flippant behaviour of animals in the face of death, how the live frisks over the
dead animal and doesn't seem to know it's there. I don't know
why they find it surprising, for in the next breath they are doing
it themselves.

EDITH OLIVIER

Shopping Bag and Food Queue

1943

There are two phrases which will be for ever inscribed on the
hearts of wartime housekeepers – Shopping Bag and Food Queue.
Lord Woolton has decreed that 'man shall not live by bread
alone', but I think he favours woman living by the Queue and the
Shopping Bag. For it is no use getting into a food queue, or into
a bus queue which will land you in one, unless you possess a
shopping bag. Without that, you must carry home a miscel-
laneous collection of onions, cabbages, fish, and tea cakes in your
pockets, for the salvage minister will not let you have any paper.

So every woman now owns a shopping bag, and she is jealously
possessive about it. At first, these bags were brilliant and striking
looking objects – in vivid colours and jazz designs; but as the
war years roll on, and cleaning materials grow hard to come by,
they all decline to the same level of dusty duskiness, reminiscent
of two colours fashionable in my youth – Elephant's Breath and
Desert Sand.

On the morning when the ration cards for the new week come
into effect, there is often a certain amount of well-mannered alter-
cation as to whether or not a landlady and lodger may each
borrow the other's bag. The winner of this friendly debate now
hangs it on her arm, draws on a rather sorry-looking pair of
Wellington boots, and sallies forth to shop. Other housekeepers
are doing the same. The first two meet with cordial greetings,

and proceed together up the road, talking about food. Another be-bagged figure is now seen approaching. The greetings become less cordial; and indeed they die away altogether, as it becomes clear that quite a number of women are on the same quest. They all hope to catch the early-morning bus to the market town.

Then begins the first queue. It is a bus queue, and queues of that breed are usually very friendly, but not so this early one. It stirs some of the evil passions of the human heart, for it is plainly about to develop into a food queue. Everyone wants to travel by this bus, so as to arrive in time to give its passengers the first pick of the market stalls, and there may not be seats for all. It is all very well for people who live at the extreme limit of the bus journey. There is certain to be room for them. But at every village on the road a little group is waiting by the post office. At first these groups are easily absorbed, but as the bus gets nearer the town, every cubic inch of space has been filled up, till there is no hope at all for people like ourselves, who live only a mile or two from the market. At last the bus appears round the corner. Futile umbrellas hail it, though these are obviously unnecessary, as the driver can plainly see the little crowd which now sways uncertainly into the road. He quickens his pace, and the bus rattles heartlessly by.

This common misfortune draws the rebuffed travellers together. They will no longer be rivals in that first picking over of the market stalls, so they have lost the angry sensation of a food queue, and are merely a defeated bus queue. They consult together. The tough ones resolve to make the best of it, and to walk. Others give up altogether and walk home; while the remaining few form themselves into a gaggle to gossip in the shelter till the next bus comes, an hour later.

VERE HODGSON

The Struggle for an Onion

17 September 1942

Such a struggle to get an onion. Tried the Old Pole (her greengrocer). None. Went to Mr Bybest – he had a few, but they were all booked. I took his refusal humbly, and bought a pound of carrots and a stick of celery, thinking sadly of the onion. I could see an idea was germinating in the man's mind, so lingered on. Finally I won without saying any more – a voice murmured: 'If you only want it for flavouring, I will let you have one.' Pouring thanks and blessings on his head I walked away triumphant. A victory indeed!

JANE GORDON

Sanitary Towels

We passed a woman proudly holding a navy-blue carton clearly marked Kotex.

'Women have lost all sense of refinement,' Rosemary announced, and added, 'That is most unladylike.'

I said: 'Well, considering those things have been practically unobtainable for months, and there has even been a question about it in the House, I suppose she thinks she is being very lady-like to find a box.'

WINIFRED WILLIAMS

At a British Restaurant

1942

Hundreds of men and women were standing on the stairs leading to the basement. They read newspapers, they chatted, they seemed strangely amiable. Well, I thought, viewing the lake of heads, Lord Woolton has got himself into a nice mess! He provides restaurants for the workers and they have to spend their lunch hour queuing. I shall be eating, if I am lucky, in half-an-hour, I thought. [. . .]

I was mistaken. We got through in seven minutes. I stood at the counter with my small wooden tray, and food was being piled on it in three surprising tiers. There'll be no empty seat now, I thought: but there was.

It was quite a pleasant place, too, with yellow walls and small square tables and shiny chairs. I sat beside two workmen who swallowed food and news simultaneously (steamed ginger pudding, the *Daily Herald* and the *Daily Express*): a pretty girl in pretty clothes joined us. Black coats and blue overalls seemed to mingle without being aware of their difference in status. This is a very democratic place, I thought, looking to see what my neighbour's paper was saying about Stalingrad.

Conversations were continuing everywhere. Apparently people treated the place as a club. [...] Soon the two workmen were piling their empty dishes on to the trays and taking them back to the counter. Everybody, I noticed, carried his plates and spoons there: apparently it was undemocratic to leave them on the tables. Well, I thought, Lord Woolton seems to be educating people as well as feeding them.

And as I drank my penny cup of tea I was dreaming – of People's Restaurants of the future, when the war is over and won, of finely-decorated buildings with paintings hung on the pale walls, of a gay democracy eating delicious lunches at a price the poorest could afford. The Minister of Food has built something bigger and better than he knows: having once given restaurants to the people will he, when the war is over, snatch them for ever away?

And having thrown up thousands of fine civic restaurants throughout the land, I started building new schools and new factories, blocks of workers' flats, terraces of shapely houses, fine city streets. And why not? I asked myself, striding to the counter with my tray, looking at the vigorous faces of the workers around me. Why not? They will never again be able to tell us we haven't the cash. For a country that can finance this sort of war can pay for that sort of peace.

FRANCES PARTRIDGE

Beige World

24 August 1943

We joined a swelling stream of the citizens of Swindon, all following a series of notices marked 'British Restaurant', to a huge elephant-house, where thousands and thousands of human beings were eating as we did an enormous all-beige meal, starting with beige soup thickened to the consistency of paste, followed by beige mince full of lumps and garnished with beige beans and a few beige potatoes, thin beige apple stew and a sort of skilly. Very satisfying

and crushing, and calling up a vision of our future Planned World –
all beige also.

VERILY ANDERSON

Respectable Looting

The blitz had played some queer tricks with its victims. Into our
garden had been blown a broken lawn-sprinkler, which we converted into a standard-lamp for our drawing-room. Beside it lay
a linen-basket which we bent back into shape and painted a nice
shade of crimson and cream. From other gardens, sometimes digging a little to unearth them, I collected curtain-rods and rings
and coat-hooks and other things needed, but impossible to buy
then, for moving into a new house. Donald was too law-abiding
to relish this pilfering as I did, but he ceased grumbling when we
had got our loot safely into the house. And he took an attractive
pleasure in restoring it to a usable state.

A nursery fire-guard was something impossible to find in any
shop. The day I stepped out of a bombed site with one in my arms,
I walked straight into a policeman. I thought instantly of the
notices saying that looters might be shot. The policeman shook his
head in a disappointed way, as though he expected better of me.

'I know,' I said. 'I'm ready. You can shoot me.'

'It's not that, miss,' he said. 'I've had my eye on it to take home
after dark for my own toddler.'

'Take it,' I said, holding it out to him. I knew now what thieves
meant by *hot*.

'No, miss,' he said sadly. 'You got it first.' And he continued on
his beat.

MOLLIE PANTER-DOWNES

The Fourth Christmas of the War

December 27 1942
It's now reasonable to suppose that this fourth Christmas of the
war may be remembered as the one which brought the phrase

"after the war" back into active circulation. Certainly one hears it being used far more frequently and confidently now than for some time past. People talk about the end of the war as though it were a perfectly matter-of-fact objective on the horizon and not just a nice pipe dream.

The recent holiday season, besides being the brightest as far as outlook goes which this country has had since the horrors started in Europe, is also likely to linger in the public's memory less cheerfully as one of the most expensive which ever bore down upon the pocketbook. The cost of all traditional garnishings which weren't price controlled, from mistletoe to food and drink, soared alarmingly during the last few days before Christmas. The toy racket tardily drew stern official attention, rather too late to do much good for parents who had already in desperation shelled out high prices for shoddy rubbish.

One of the gayer manifestations of the festive spirit has been the bower of tents and greenery which suddenly blossomed in the sombre, gutted shell of John Lewis's bombed Oxford Street store. This was a Potato Christmas Fair, sponsored by Potato Pete, a creation of the Ministry of Food's propaganda department to make starch-stodged Britons eat even more home-grown tubers and go slow on the imported wheat loaf. The show was visited on its opening day by Lord Woolton, by a baby elephant called Comet, who proved too heavy (perhaps from too much patriotic spud-eating) to be able to negotiate the wooden gangway down into the wrecked basement, and by hordes of the public who dutifully received hot baked potatoes from Father Christmas and signed a visitors' book beneath the vow 'I promise as my Christmas gift to the sailors who have to bring our bread that I will do all I can to eat home-grown potatoes instead.'

GERTRUDE STEIN

Life in France

During the Spanish–American war there were food scandals, and in the Boer war there were concentration camps where they had nothing to eat, and all that is natural enough. The concentration camps for the Boers excited us all, nobody knew then how everybody was finally that is everybody in Europe was finally not going to have anything to eat. There was famine in China even in Russia and there was famine in India and every one then in the time of the Boer war and before and after was very much excited about it but now here in 1943 not having anything to eat enough to eat, having what you can eat, buying eating black, that is black traffic, thinking about eating, everybody on the road bicycling or walking with a pack on their back or a basket in the hand, or a big bundle on the bicycle, hoping for provisions, somewhere in the country there would be an egg or something or something, and perhaps you will get that something. One day I was out walking, well naturally I had a basket and big prospects and hopes and I met a nice gentle little bourgeoise from Belley, and it was spring time and she had a very charming and quite large bouquet of flowers very beautifully arranged in her hand and I said what a charming bouquet of flowers, yes she said eyeing the bouquet carefully, yes, I have been in the country to visit some relations, and I had hoped, I had hoped perhaps for an egg, perhaps even perhaps for a chicken, and she heaved a little breath they gave me these flowers. They are very charming flowers I said, yes she said, and we said good-bye and went each one on our way. There are so many people in prison because they sell what they should not sell, and yet, well and yet, I met Roselyn I said you are looking very well, the restrictions do not seem to have had any effect on you, well said Roselyn, one finds things. Roselyn, I said, you indulging in black traffic, mais non, she said of course I would not, to find something is one thing, to indulge in black traffic is quite another thing. Explain the difference to me I said. Well said Roselyn, to find is when you find a small amount any day at a reasonable price which will just augment your diet and keep you healthy. Black traffic is when you pay a very large sum for a large amount of food, that is the difference. And she is right that is a difference and we all all day and every day go about and in every way we do or do not find something that helps the day along. As Madame Pierlot said, you do not buy now-a-days only with money you buy with your personality. Jo Davidson used to say that you always had to sell your personality, but now it is not a question of selling it is a question of buying by personality. Nothing is sadder these days than people who never make friends, they poor dears have nothing to eat, neither do the indiscreet, and yet almost everybody does eat. Almost everybody, almost, it comes hardest on middle-aged men, not women they resist better but middle-aged men, without wine and cheese, they get thinner and thinner and thinner. We women of a certain age, we reduce to a certain place and then we seem to get along all right, but the middle-aged men get thin, and thinner and thinner. Naturally those that had been fat. Oh dear me. [. . .]

It's funny about honey, you always eat honey during a war, so much honey, there is no sugar, there never is sugar during a war, the first thing to disappear is sugar, after that butter, but butter can always be had but not sugar, no not sugar so during a war you always eat honey quantities of honey, really more honey than you used to eat sugar, and you find honey so much better than sugar, better in itself and better in apple sauce, in all desserts so much better and then peace is upon us and no one eats honey any more, they find it too sweet and too cloying and too heavy, it was like this in the last war '14–'18 and it is like this in this war, wars are like that, it is funny but wars are like that. [. . .]

I had to buy a jar of jam.

You have to buy what you do not want to buy in order to buy what you do want to buy. That is if you have nothing to trade and a good many of us have nothing to trade. Of course if you are a farmer it is all right you have lots to trade but if you are not a farmer then you have nothing to trade. Once when we were in Bilignin during the winter we wanted to buy some eggs and nobody wanted to sell us any because all the eggs their chickens lay they wanted to eat themselves, which was natural enough, and Madame Roux said can we find nothing to trade that is not to trade but to induce them to sell eggs to us, at last we found something, and it was our dish-water. Madame Roux had the habit of carrying off the dish-water to give to a neighbour who was fattening a pig, and there was very little milk with which to fatten pigs, dish-water was considerable of a help, this was in the worst days, '41–'42, in '43 life began to be easier, well anyway Alice Toklas said to Madame Roux, no we will not give away our dish-water, if the neighbour wants it she has in return to be willing to sell us a certain quantity of eggs. So Madame Roux went to the neighbour and told her she could have the family dish-water only under the condition of our having the privilege of buying from her a certain quantity of eggs, well she wanted the dish-water and we bought the eggs, but alas she killed the pig at Christmas, and everybody killed their pig at Christmas and so there was no need any longer of dish-water to fatten the pigs and so our right to buy eggs was over, we had not had the idea of making the bargain for longer. [. . .]

There are little things to, little like an inch on the end of one's nose, and that is tobacco. I do not smoke but Alice Toklas does and she has to she just has to if not well anyway she just has to. So when cards came in cards for tobacco and they only were giving them to men, women were not being encouraged to smoke not by the government and so what to do, well the tobacconist and I agreed that since they did not ask if you were a woman, you just inscribed yourself we would do so with initials and who would know, well that worked for a whole year and helped out by an occasional friend Alice Toklas did not do so badly and then the next year they had regular cards and they had to be regular no initials did not do and what could she do, we did several things but none of them quite enough. Alice Toklas found it very hard to bear, boys of eighteen had a right to chocolate and they had a right to cigarettes too, that did seem unjust, either they were too young or too old to eat chocolate that was not reasonable but as foreigners even if not yet enemies we had no right to protest, so we tried everything, and one way and another way we got a few cigarettes, here and there and in one way and in another way and friends brought some from Switzerland you could go to Switzerland then and come out again and there were some but not enough far from enough, and then a friend found a sergeant in the French army who would sell some that the army gave them and some more too and soon Alice Toklas had enough quite enough, and then we invaded North Africa and the French army was disbanded and the sergeant went away and it was a trying moment and then the Italian army came and that was fine, why the Italian army had so many cigarettes I do not know mysteriously the German army has not, but anyway whatever the way it was done the Italian army had them by the ton very nice little cigarettes they were too and the Italians loved to sell them, and everybody bought them and all the smokers were happy again. And then the poor Italians had to go away, just suddenly and although everybody had a supply it was not a big enough one and something had to be done. In this part of the country tobacco was always grown, it has a climate that seems to suit tobacco one would not think so because it is mountainous and has a cold winter and a not too hot summer but it does seem to suit tobacco, and now everybody began to grow tobacco in their garden anybody and there were some who grew a very good cigarette tobacco and they were ready to sell us several pounds of it and I learned to roll cigarettes with a little machine everybody bought and mysteriously there was no lack of cigarette paper, everything is mysterious in this kind of war and that there is no paper but there is no lack of cigarette paper and so everybody and Alice Toklas was happy again. That is here, in other parts of France where tobacco will not grow they were not so happy.

CHAPTER ELEVEN

Love, Sex and Immorality

Women's sexuality was a fraught topic during the war, a matter for public debate and difficult private decisions. The war added urgency and eroticism to sexual relationships; it heightened romance, sentiment and feelings of obligation. It also forced couples apart and brought lonely servicemen from overseas to Britain.

Wartime weddings reached a peak in 1939–40 and the birthrate rose dramatically from 1942 onwards. But illegitimacy was also on the increase, as were divorce and venereal disease. Charges of immorality were thrown at women in the services. Rumours spread, and parents worried about their young daughters away from home, either in the services or living in the huge hostels for factory workers. The government responded in 1941 by setting up a committee of inquiry under Violet Markham. This committee toured the country, and found no evidence to back up the allegations of immorality.

Women's magazines naturally preached fidelity and celibacy to the wives and girlfriends of men serving overseas, assuring them that these were important contributions to the war effort. In the name of this cause the magazines also – and more realistically – urged restraint upon those who had lapsed. Women were told to think very carefully about the 'untold harm' which could be done by 'wretched "confessions"'.

Lovers were among the most dedicated writers of the war, and the most prolific. Bill Cook and Helen Appleton exchanged 6,000 letters while he was serving overseas as an army chaplain. (They married in 1945 and published some of their letters in *Khaki Parish*, 1988.) They were exceptional correspondents, but many couples wrote to each other twice a week. Mavis Bunyan even wrote to her RAF husband twice within six hours of his departure overseas in 1943, and dispensed with paragraphing to make the best use of space in airletters and airgraphs. The private letters which women, fully aware of the censor's eye on all mail going overseas, wrote to their lovers and husbands were sometimes surprisingly uninhibited in their discussions of love and sex – an aspect of women's war writing not very visible in the public domain until some years later.

ZELMA KATIN

The Sight of a Girl in Uniform

To many people – perhaps because they suffer from sexual frustration – the sight of any girl in any kind of uniform, even Salvation Army uniform, at once suggests immorality. So firmly has this legend taken hold that bus and tram conductresses, because they come into contact with the general public more than other groups of uniformed women, and because each forms a working team with a man, are singled out for special blackening of character. Numbers of passengers believe that the last act of a conductress and her driver or motorman each night before going home is the exercise of sexual intercourse. When, occasionally, a conductress is seen misbehaving, her guilt is considered indisputable evidence of the state of morals in the industry. I have noticed the suspicion on women's faces when, passing me while the tram is waiting at a terminus, they observe me enjoying a cigarette with the motorman.

JOYCE GRENFELL

Easy to Get

Wednesday October 25th 1944, Beirut
Viola and I have been wearing our 'glamorous' ENSA uniforms for the journeys and they do save our clothes but not our faces. Whenever I wear the uniform I get the 'hi-babe' looks, approach and conversation with the soldiers. I never meet with anything but extremely friendly and easy manners when I'm in my ordinary clothes. Even though we turn our ENSA tabs under they seem to recognize the uniform and out here ENSA stands for 'easy to get' and I resent it deeply.

MAUREEN WELLS

Immoral Englishwomen

4 March 1942

Mummy and I had a visitor yesterday. Catherine is the bossy WAAF officer daughter of one of Mummy's old school friends. She is a strong believer in free love for young girls and practises it. A year ago she fell most passionately in love with her commanding officer, a married man with a son of three, and they've been living together. She brought him down here once and I've never seen such a selfish, disagreeable-looking individual.

The next time she came she told me what a fool I was not to follow in her footsteps – wasting my youth etc etc. I brought up all sorts of arguments but she was firmly convinced in her mind that I was an old-fashioned boop, a relic from the Victorian era. 'My dear, I assure you that 75 per cent of the Waafs will never see virginity again, and what's wrong? The men must go with somebody and the authorities prefer that they go with the Waafs, who are medically examined, rather than the women of the town.'

I gave up. [. . .]

August 1943

The Yanks are saying that Englishwomen are the most immoral in the world. Marie Thornton met a young US Army air corps officer in a train the other evening and he saw her to Ashley House where she was going to stay the night. As they said goodbye he asked 'Don't you want to sleep with me?' After Marie's strong answer he said 'I'm awfully sorry, only you see I've been over here a month now and you're the first girl I've met who hasn't wanted an affair.'

PAMELA RUFFONI

Italian Prisoners and Landgirls

Autumn 1943. The mob of Italians were not wanted and only three came. We were stacking a hay-rick, three Italians, three girls, and then things started happening. Two in long kisses, and then the other two started larking and throwing hay which smothered the remaining Italian and myself. Hmmm good job I'm a little tough and have a few wits, anyway Rene came to my rescue. I thought everything appalling and disgusting, yet how sorry for those fellows I feel, prisoners for nearly three years, a girl on a haystack must be a very tempting proposition with no one around. I had been talking with the Italian who palled up with me, but I realized after this instance 'give an inch take a yard'. Even afterwards I could not refrain from talking to him, because I think he knew what I was; and in broken English said 'me like you, you serious.' But I can't get over the fact, him having a wife and baby, and giving me a picture of St Anthony.

JENNY NICHOLSON
Sensible People

Naturally with such a vast cross-section of British womanhood as there was in each of the services there were bound to be individuals whose standard of behaviour wasn't up to the average scratch. But service life didn't breed them. They arrived like that. Happily, behaving well was a good deal more contagious than the other thing, so once a brazen hussy found herself separated from her home-town gang of brazen hussies and among a number of sensible people, the tendency was for her to grow noticeably more subdued as time dragged on. It was certainly true to say that the women who entered the service like driven snow and were turned cheap and nasty by it were exceptional.

VERA LAUGHTON MATHEWS
Wrens and Contraceptives

At one station an innocent WRNS Officer asked in sick bay what these prophylactic packets were. She was duly informed by the Sister, who added that they were in great demand before a dance. The Officer, in telling me, said, 'My heart stood still because I knew the bulk of the girls at the dances were my Wrens.'

There were even some who would have liked to see contraceptives made available for the Wrens. An Admiral in a very high place, with daughters serving, actually tackled Dr Rewcastle on the subject, adding: 'I am not approaching the Director as I know she would not agree with it.' I had my compliments. Dr Rewcastle, without entering into the question of ethics, quietly answered that there was no indication that such a policy was necessary and then with her usual loyalty came straight to me.

FREYA STARK

The Generous Heart

It is, I think, an ungenerous heart that does not give itself in wartime, when men's mere physical hunger for women is so great. (This incidentally, may be the chief virtue for the semimilitary female services, though obviously not one for publication.)

VERILY ANDERSON

A FANY Gets a Proposal

The ten, or so, occupants of the carriage drew together and sought comfort in conversation. Encouraged by a lively young Marine major, we shared sandwiches and played rummy with a pack of cards produced by an elderly naval rating. The major spread newspapers over our knees and, when that failed to warm us, passed round his flask of brandy. Only a sedate girl in civilian clothes refused to join in; but soon the cold and the long waits drove her to accept a warming sip. When at last we reached London, we felt we had been through so much together that it was almost painful to part. The Marine major and I were the last out onto the platform.

'Come on, Fanny,' he said, 'let's go into the hotel and have a civilized sandwich.' He picked up my bag and carried it with him into the station hotel.

'First I must telephone some friends to see if I can spend the night with them,' I said. 'It's too late to get a train down to Sussex.'

I telephoned Elizabeth's parents, who told me they could give me a bed for the night.

When I joined the major in the cocktail bar he seemed quite different from the life-and-soul of the railway carriage.

He looked younger and quieter. We sat down with sandwiches and drinks and exchanged life stories. He was twenty-five and the youngest of four brothers. He, too, was the child of a parson.

'I say, Fanny,' he said suddenly, 'I like you awfully. Will you marry me?'

I laughed.

'Honestly. I want to marry a nice girl like you that I can let my hair down with, and yet who looks all right in public. I expect I can get some sort of a job after the war – trying shoes on people or something.'

'How nice of you,' I said, 'but —'

'Then will you come and dance with me at the Four Hundred tonight?'

'I'd love to, but I've already made a plan to go straight to some friends where I'm staying the night.'

'Pity,' said the major. He got me a taxi. 'I'll be at my club. The Junior Carlton. Ring me in the morning. I'll want to know how you are. You seem to have forgotten you only came out of hospital [with German measles] today.'

I had. The taxi crawled along the icy streets in the black-out, and I realized that neither of us knew what the other's real name was.

FLORENCE SHARP

A Street Sweeper's Proposals

You'd be surprised how many proposals I've had since I've been sweeping. Norwegians, Dutch, and all sorts. I could have been married hundreds of times. Of course, I don't entertain them. I just have a drink and say, 'Yes', and all that kind of thing. 'I'll see you tomorrow'. As a matter of fact, only today I had a proposal from an American sailor. He said: 'I'll marry you', he said, 'and you can come out to America with me'. He meant it. 'Well', I said, 'I'll think it over'. That boy liked me because I was a worker. You know, it's very funny. You go in anywhere, and you'll always find people will fall for a worker. I don't want to get married again: I've got no interest in men. I don't know why. I just don't bother about them. They're very nice to me. Most men treat me with respect. They treat me like a boy, as a matter of fact. Even before I had my uniform it was just the same. But nowadays, you go in anywhere with your uniform on and the men will say, 'Will you have a drink, Florence?' It's just the thought that you're doing something for your country. They think something of you.

I remember there was one nice Norwegian who gave me a watch. He was a very very nice man, if anybody wanted to settle down, but I couldn't be bothered to marry him. I really couldn't be bothered with a man round me. Then there was a Dutch cook once. He was a merchant seaman. After every trip he used to bring me a beautiful long loaf, the kind that mother makes, with currants and things. He used to bring me one every month all through the winter. He made it on his ship, and he used to say: 'I've put three eggs in it'. He wanted to marry me too, but I can cook and all, you know, so I didn't want to marry him.

DIANA HOPKINSON

A Letter to a Husband in North Africa

1943

You speak truthfully when you write to comfort me for our separation by saying that we have been lucky compared to many lovers. I know that. Also that we have learnt to value each other even more through separation and have reached greater unity that way as men do in battle. Those are comforting weapons when the battle against the depression and hopelessness of our separation gets me down. No – I know it is *not* hopelessness and agree with you that we can see some pattern for the future, though when you mention some small part in our future, like reading *Finnegans Wake* together, my heart leaps both with excitement at the prospect of once more spending winter evenings with you and hesitates because it is tempting the fates even to mention the possibility.

MAVIS BUNYAN

Letters to a Husband

No.1
Blackpool 25 October 1943
My beloved,
I do not really want to write this now because it will bring to me all I am trying so hard to block out. Maybe though you will receive it before you leave England if I post it right away. Somehow I cannot believe you will not be in to tea with me and we are not going out together this evening. I was so afraid I would not see you before the train went when it got so late, but I prayed so awfully hard to see you and I did. How I wish the next week were over. I shall not mind so much when I get amongst the family again but the next week is going to be so full of loneliness without you. I never thought anyone would ever mean my whole life's happiness, like you do. You seem to have grown right into me, I am incomplete without you by my side. Now I am crying again, just what I am afraid of. Letter No. 1., I wonder where you will be when you receive it, and how many I shall have written by the time I see you again? It was awful, seeing you as just a number amongst all those boys, knowing you had to go, and there was nothing we could do about it. To them just a number, but to me my whole life and happiness. I just feel right now that I can't face it, I feel I'll just go silly with wanting to see you. I know I will get by though. It is awful to think of the months without you. I would not mind so much if I could hear from you every day like I used to, but maybe having to wait months for letters makes it seem worse. To say 'I love you' seems rather superfluous doesn't it my beloved because you know the depths of my feeling for you. I do love you beyond all doubt, you mean so much to me. Every evening when the pips go for the news I will be thinking of you, sending an 'I love you' and a 'God bless'. It is two hours and a half since I had your last kiss and 'I love you'. It seems so long. Last night seems ages away. I cannot begin to say how much I am

wanting you, my whole body seems so empty. I am now only existing until you come back to me. God bless you and take care of you my precious boy, I love you beyond everything. I am praying so hard for you – and courage too.

Your ever-loving wife,
Mavis

No.5
Wimbledon 28 October 1943
My always beloved,
It is nine o'clock and here is my 'I love you'. Darling I do love you so terribly much, I have been feeling so ill these last days. It is only the effect of my mind on my body, I don't think I shall be the same until you come back to me. It is only your presence that can bring that sparkle to my eyes and give that air of 'joie de vivre' to my body. I shall not be my real self until you are once again part of me in body as well as spirit. I must have your presence to give me happiness and a will to enjoy living. Today I brought back from Southfields all your letters. They will help me over the time until I start receiving mail from you again. I have read a few this evening. A couple written before we were married and a few whilst we were waiting for 'Sunny Jim'. I wish the bell would ring now and you would be there when I opened the door, I am almost willing it. It is funny, but I cannot give up hope of you coming again, I want you so much. I never dreamt that anyone could grow to be the difference between having the world and losing it. I am so glad I have baby, the little tinker. She has been dropping things from her pram, so I said 'naughty' in what was meant to be a fierce tone. The little scamp promptly crinkled her face in a huge grin and I had to laugh. Looking at her now it seems difficult to connect her with the funny little bundle in the nursing home.

I am terribly tired even though it is only 9.35. The fire is getting low too and Lesley is shouting for her supper. I have lots to do to get ready for Torquay but I have been lazy all evening. This morning when I looked out of the window I had a shock. In the fortnight since I left here, winter has come. The sunflowers and daisies are all dead and the trees are bare. I really must go now. I love you beloved for always, and ever and a day after that.

Yours for always, and God bless,
Woodenhead

No.176

Torquay 25 June 1944
My beloved boy,
Today it is eight months since I saw your dearly beloved face and in that time my love and longing for you has increased to such a desperate need. It is becoming so overpowering that I have no will or wish to do anything. Today has been so miserable, I am glad I had to work this Sunday. It looks as though the rain has come to stay for a few days.

26.6.44

Lesley woke up darling so I had to stop and am finishing this before I get up. Your 130 letter has just come and I do love you so very dearly. You are a wicked boy to say I would soon be in my birthday suit if you were here. Do you know darling, the more I live with me the more I puzzle me. I just do not make sense . . . When I say I want all the 'loving' things that we did, it is not my body that is doing the wanting but my mind. I wonder if you will understand. The one thing I want physically is just to be held tight to you and to know that my arms are around your neck, never to let you go from me again. When I say that I want your caresses and to have you close to me it is because I know that I loved all those things when you were here and if I were having them again it would mean that you were here with me. I could never let anyone else share our glorious oneness. All I feel physically is a great emptiness and a longing that sometimes verges on a physical pain. This is what puzzles me though. I love to read of you wanting me because with us physical loving springs from our love of each other. I love it too because it is a memory of all we have been to each other and makes me feel as well as know, that I am your wife and we belong to each other for always unless God decrees otherwise. I am even thinking often of nice clothes, especially pretty nightgowns, so that I can 'lure' you and make you want me and love me lots. This is what is so silly though. Sometimes, something akin to terror comes over me in a wave. I know in my heart that directly I have your first kiss I shall want you never to stop kissing me, but I shall be so terribly shy darling you will have to be patient with me if I am silly. No wonder you once called me a dutch girl. I guess when you come back to me everything will take care of itself, and I will not even think of being shy because my longing for you is so passionate. I do love you so my most precious boy. Lesley has just come up, she looks so sweet. Heavens, she has my handbag. I do so wish I could see you with our baby, 'cos then I would be seeing you too. I do wish you could see her though, as she toddles around the house. You should see the mess this room is in, everything on the floor. My clothes, a pile of nappies, and everything from my handbag. Golly what a mess, but she seems to be having fun. I love you dearly beloved for always.

Just yours always, Mavis

CHAPTER TWELVE

Consolations

A woman provided the words for one of the war's first messages of consolation. Minnie Haskins, a retired lecturer from the London School of Economics, wrote the poem quoted by the King in his Christmas Broadcast to the Empire at the end of 1939:

> And I said to the man who stood at
> the gate of the year: 'Give me a light
> that I may tread safely into the unknown.'
> And he replied:
> 'Go out into the darkness and put
> your hand into the Hand of God. That
> shall be to you better than light and
> safer than a known way.'

These lines, with their image of the comforting presence, consoled many women. They quoted the poem to themselves and others, in diaries and letters. The King's choice, suggested to him by the Queen, was a happy one: the Royal Family seemed to fill the role of the comforting presence naturally. 'Bess is really a tip-topper', wrote Margaret Kennedy. 'The woman can't help doing the right thing: smiles and makes little jokes when little jokes are wanted, and bursts into floods of tears when tears are the only comment.'

Making do and improvising, the new skills enforced by dreary austerity as well as sudden catastrophe, were embraced by women willing to turn necessary evil into challenge and virtue. Having to improvise could provide a spur to fresh energy and invention, and this could be a powerful source of satisfaction. Constance Goddard, a farmer in the Dales, was touched by one particular demonstration at her village Make Do and Men lectures:

> A Make Do that aroused a good deal of interest was the conversion
> of a clothes-basket into a cradle. All the women inspected that

and purred over the tiny mattress made out of chaff that could be so easily renewed, and the tiny blankets cut from shrunken vests. There was a little down quilt too, filled with feathers from someone's ducks. This was quilted in a daisy pattern and the material was cut from a wedding dress. I thought the baby that slept in that little cradle would be happy, so much love had gone to the making and lining of that little nest.

Consolation itself often had to be an improvised affair. The solace and pleasures which women found for themselves and others were a wonderfully diverse mixture of formal and informal, new and traditional, material and spiritual. As this chapter shows, ghosts, Dorchester teas, riding in the lifts of shops and dancing on the tops of tables all played their part in getting women through the war.

Finding and making forms of consolation out of the war itself became an important strand of women's wartime writing. Some got satisfaction in looking at the war as a glorious and heroic enterprise. Many more preferred to see it as an unpleasant obligation, but even before the war ended there was a fond nostalgia for the spirit of Dunkirk and the Battle of Britain. Looking wearily back over the last 'five gruelling years' in 1945, Freda Bruce Lockhart cheered herself with memories of the 'morning glory' and 'deep patriotic pride' of 1940. One of the most frequently repeated commonplaces of the war was the consolation that, in Stella Bowen's words, 'we are getting nicer all the time'.

F. TENNYSON JESSE

The Ecstasy of the Fighter Pilot

October 1939

Jim Hodge has, in his Spitfire, brought down one of the German raiders over the Firth of Forth, which has made us all feel very elated. I can imagine what *his* elation must have been – he is quite a fearless person – on a brilliantly sunny day, flying and fighting over that glorious stretch of water and shooting down his enemy. I think it will be a bad day for humanity when something as primitive as the emotion he must have felt ceases to spring to life in a man's heart because of over-civilisation. I know that this is difficult to square with one's horror of war, and one's wish that there may be no more wars, but there is always a danger of losing certain high qualities in getting rid of certain fundamental ones. Man is not simple, and only the very simple-minded think he is. There are those who distinguish between love and lust – and, indeed, at the extremes of both it is possible to do so. But love is the more beautiful for the lust that is inextricably mingled with it, and the same thing, I think, applies to the high qualities of a fighting man in relation to the ecstasy of the hunt and the kill, even when the quarry is another human being.

E.M. DELAFIELD

The British Sense of Humour

13 July 1940

It is very important that people in England should notice, and remember, the value of laughter just now, and in the utterly horrible days and nights that probably lie ahead of us. There are – and we all know it – things waiting round the corner for us and – how much harder to bear! – for those whom we love, that can, in essence, be nothing but unspeakably dreadful. But there are also – and there always will be – aspects of anything and everything at which it will be possible to laugh, if we have the high courage and unselfishness to do so.

Most of us have said, on one occasion or another – 'if it hadn't been so awful, one could almost have laughed.'

It is most likely going to be very awful indeed – but if there is anything at which 'one' can almost laugh – *and there will be* – 'one' must do so – and not 'almost' either. [. . .]

It has never been easy to make a good job of everyday life, and it is immeasurably harder now. Men and their wives are being separated; all, in varying degrees, are exposed to danger and suffering, children are either in peril or else being sent away half across the world – and without return tickets either – homes are menaced with possible invasion and all-too-certain taxation – and some hundreds of minor complications of housekeeping have descended, like a plague of small but omnipresent locusts, to play hourly upon the already exasperated nerves of women.

Each single one of us must evolve an inner scheme of defence to hold on to and use, if necessary, ten thousands times a day, to ensure that neither a part nor the whole of this, is to get us down.

I am absolutely certain that one of the main bulwarks in that scheme of defence is the cultivation of a sense of humour. Never, never, let us say or feel that 'this is getting beyond a joke.'

A journalist recently, giving an eye-witness account of the last stand of a British Regiment at St Valéry, wrote:

'We saw one Sergeant taking his men to cover against the shelling in front of the barricades. He was leading them in song, and making them laugh . . . The minute the shelling stopped, they were at the barricades again.'

He was leading them in song, *and making them laugh* – and next minute, they were at the barricades again.

Good enough, isn't it?

PRINCESS ELIZABETH

Broadcast to the Children of the Empire

October 1940
The following message to the children of the empire at home and overseas was broadcast in the Children's Hour on October 13 by HRH Princess Elizabeth. This broadcast inaugurated the B.B.C.'s North American service for children evacuated to Canada and the United States.

In wishing you all 'good evening' I feel that I am speaking to friends and companions who have shared with my sister and myself many a happy Children's Hour.

Thousands of you in this country have had to leave your homes and be separated from your fathers and mothers. My sister, Margaret Rose, and I feel so much for you as we know from experience what it means to be away from those we love most of all. To you, living in new surroundings, we send a message of true sympathy and at the same time we should like to thank the kind people who have welcomed you to their homes in the country.

All of us children who are still at home think continually of our friends and relations who have gone overseas – who have travelled thousands of miles to find a war-time home and a kindly welcome in Canada, Australia, New Zealand, South Africa and the United States of America. My sister and I feel we know quite a lot about these countries. Our father and mother have so often talked to us of their visits to different parts of the world, so it is not difficult for us to picture the sort of life you are all leading, and to think of all the new sights you must be seeing, and the adventures you must be having. But I am sure that you too are often thinking of the Old Country. I know you won't forget us: it is just because we are not forgetting you that I want, on behalf of all the children at home, to send you our love and best wishes – to you, and to your kind hosts as well.

Before I finish I can truthfully say to you all that we children at home are full of cheerfulness and courage. We are trying to do all we can to help our gallant sailors, soldiers and airmen, and we are trying, too, to bear our own share of the danger and sadness of war. We know, every one of us, that in the end all will be well; for God will care for us and give us victory and peace. And when peace comes, remember it will be for us, the children of today, to make the world of tomorrow a better and happier place.

My sister is by my side and we are both going to say good-night to you. Come on, Margaret. (*Princess Margaret Rose then said:* 'Good night, children'.) Good night, and good luck to you all.

MARGERY PERHAM

Christmas in Dockland

January 1941

Christmas morning, 3 a.m. in the shelter under the Church. It's a shelter-de-luxe, this, compared with most, but even here, as night goes on, the air becomes thick with the sticky smell of unwashed bodies and bedding. Three hundred pairs of lungs use and use again their small ration of air. The lights are on, and fall upon the stacked humanity in the bunks and the garish decorations looped over them. Many sleepers snore with great power: sometimes there is a word or a groan. In the babies' corner little pink forms lie in the dainty cribs they owe to American kindness. Above them presides a lighted Christmas tree.

Christmas Day, and dinner-time. The shelterers have come up from their refuge into the hall above, and sit at the long decorated tables. Turkey, sausage and Christmas pudding are served to them, the solid realisation of an idea conceived in Hollywood. Undergraduates, male and female, pacifists, responsible matrons from among the shelterers, social workers, permanent and migratory, wait on them with the scrambling eagerness of beginners. The feasters do their part stolidly amidst the altruistic bustle; dockers, labourers, city office-boys and charwomen, factory-hands. They pull their crackers and wear their caps and accept their cigarettes. Of what are they thinking? Of the donors in Hollywood? Of their broken houses? Of their evacuated children? Difficult to say. They seem only half aware of what 'they' are trying to do for them. Most of them seem to accept 'their' services as fatalistically as the bombs.

Christmas evening. There is a pantomime in the shelter. *Cinderella*. It is a home product. One of the clergy has written it – perhaps not up to the highest Hollywood, but admirable for its purpose, none the less; another plays the buffoon most excellently. The pantomime is true to tradition with its topical jokes and its knock-about fun. The ugly sisters, with the properly improper display of underwear, monopolize the cellar in an air-raid, and Cinderella is sent to sit, not in the cinders, but on the roof as spotter. At the royal ball it is not her slipper but her gas-mask that she leaves behind. Hitler is requisitioned to take the part of the bad fairy and appears at intervals in a flash of green spot-light to the music of the sirens, only to be worsted by two clowns with more than professional vigour. Ministers and officials who make wonderful promises about shelter reform get their share of caricature. 'Where's Mrs Brown? I want to see her at once.' 'She's just gone off on the Government evacuation scheme.' 'Oh, that's all right. She'll be back tomorrow.' The audience, perched thickly on its bunks, screams with delight. It catches up other jests too personal and local for the stranger. It joins with strength in the chorus of the dominant song:

There'll always be a Christmas
Whate'er the year may be,
So let old Nasty try his tricks,
He won't stop you and me!

ROSE MACAULAY

Consolations of the War

January 1941

In this horrid business of war, the brightest spots can only be rather melancholy consolations. It is, of course, an extremely horrid business; a grotesquely barbarous, uncivilized, inhumane and crazy way of life to have had forced on us by a set of gangsters who are making us use their own weapons and practise their own horrid incivilities – as if we were jungle savages like themselves instead of twentieth-century men and women who had hoped war to be for ever outlawed. That is the worst outrage that the gangsters have perpetrated on us – forcing us to adopt their own shockingly bad manners. For war, of course, is as revolting an example of bad manners as can well be imagined. We do not think it is a grand life; as a member of the House of Commons remarked lately, we think it is a perfectly beastly life, only to be endured because the things we are fighting against are still more beastly. So its consolations are rather small stars in a pretty murky night.

Well, then, as to these consolations. You begin each day by waking up alive (so far) and a little surprised sometimes to be so. Each extra day, I mean, is not a matter of course, but a gift we had not necessarily counted on having. Your windows and crockery may have got smashed in the night, bits of our walls and ceilings may have fallen down, your house or apartment may be in varying stages of dilapidation or even ruin, but you are indubitably alive.

If you do wake alive, you may enjoy – when you go out – observing the fresh ruins, if any, and if ruins are to your taste. Of course no one wants ruins, but it is no use pretending that those made last night are not interesting next day. I sometimes think how greatly our eighteenth-century ancestors would have enjoyed them. They paid architects to build picturesque ruins in their parks and gardens; we have hordes of ruin-makers who nightly do it for free. We stroll out, then, and see the sights; here is a jumbled pile which was a house, and dangling poised at its very top, high above the street, is a large bath and broken lavatory basin and seat. There – round the next corner, not so far away from my own flat – is the ruin of a house with a little Austin car poised on its summit, blown up there from its garage by blast. The demolition workers fetch it down and stand it in the street, a little battered and thick in grey dust, in which someone inscribes the legend: 'For Sale, Good Condition. One Owner Only.' I've been told that there is to be seen somewhere a trolley-bus which has climbed on to the top of a house, but I cannot find anyone who has actually seen this.

From such bizarre spectacles one must get what interest one can, among the tragedies of smashed homes and broken glories of architecture. Some hopeful souls imagine to themselves the nobler, seemlier buildings which will one day, so they hope, take the place of the destroyed. This cannot always be done, of course; not when we lose our medieval Guildhall, our Wren churches, and (worse) those all too few churches which survived a much earlier fire in 1666 – churches such as St. Giles', Cripplegate, where Milton is commemorated, and the lovely All Hallows by the Tower. There is no pleasure to be derived from the destruction of All Hallows, unless you are so malicious as to feel a little relief that the corner of its interior which was modernised and sentimentalised to commemorate the last war has perished with the rest. Ruin is indiscriminate and stupid; it falls on beautiful and ugly, noble and mean, with the most impartial injustice. On the whole, these ruins depress; you have to look a long time and with great determination for their brighter spots.

For aesthetic pleasure, you must wait until dark. London nights, once garish, have become beautiful: black, with tiny lights like glow-worms faintly piercing the blackness – and on a clear night the stars. Or, on a moony night, magically black and silver, an ivory city sharp with shadows and deep lanes of night. And always the long lances of light that sweep the skies, crossing, seeking, probing. Suddenly the quiet is shattered by a long howling as of wolves on the trail; again and again the uncanny wail rises and drops; it ceases, and after a minute or two comes that deep drone of bombing planes: flashes begin, and crashes; the sky is aflare with golden fruits that burst and are lost in the stars. Sometimes the heavens blaze red, in east, west, or centre – or everywhere at once. Buildings are outlined against fire. Here a water-main has burst, and a great lake floods a street below a mountain of ruins; a gas-main, too, has burst, and flames leap roaring to the sky, mirrored in the water. Oh, what a scene! as Horace Walpole said of the fall of the Bastille. Above it, the enemy zooms malevolently, pitching them down with loud whistling whooshes and thundering crashes, while the guns bark like great dogs at his heels. And I say nothing for this horrid scene, except that, aesthetically, it has a kind of lurid and infernal beauty. And that, if your job calls you out to it, as mine sometimes does, you do at least get an eyeful, and see something you don't see as a rule in the London streets.

Another thing you get is a sense of friendly companionship. The men and women working together among fire and bombs – firemen, ambulance drivers, rescue squads, wardens – they have a new comradeship, which overrides class and sex. The words 'mate' and 'chum' are grown common forms of address. That is pleasant; we don't in normal times, in this rather stiff and shy country, get enough of it; it's more like the western states of America, with their companionable 'brother' and 'sister'. This greater friendliness extends beyond the air-raid workers to people in general; you meet it in the streets, in trains, buses, and shops; and (I am told by those who frequent them) you meet it in shelters, too. Perhaps especially there.

Shelters we must count among the major consolations of war. They are quite a new pleasure, and are among the town amenities most missed by evacuees to the country. They have taken the place of the cinema as an essential of the good life. I know of one woman – by profession she is a charwoman – who goes to her favourite shelter (I'm told that they differ as greatly as cinemas do) every evening at seven o'clock. She stays there until eleven, when, bombs or no bombs, she goes home to bed. Evening travellers by the underground trains may see the shelterers in the subway stations, dossing down for the night on rugs and pillows and wooden bunks, with canteen workers selling tea and chocolate. Often they have concerts and other entertainments, and sometimes distinguished persons to visit them ... but I don't think this can be very wholesome, for it seems to start them being a little smug, and shouting 'We can take it!' – which is an irritating cry, since it is hard to see what else any of us can do but take it, whether above ground or below. Still, if it cheers them up ... Anyhow, shelter life has, I think, come to stay; even in the peace (if any), this odd, communal, troglodyte life led nightly by so many Londoners will, I prophesy, go on; it must save so much trouble.

Being saved trouble is always a major pleasure, of course; and wartime saves us trouble in more ways than one. Clothes, for example. It doesn't matter now much what anyone wears; women can go about London in slacks; silk stockings are definitely off, and to wear warm woollen ones and thick brogues or boots in town as well as country is a pleasure that formerly only the strong-minded allowed themselves, but that now even the shy may safely adopt. Evening clothes, too, are seldom seen. The typical Englishman is said to derive pleasure from dressing in a stiff shirt for his dinner each night when living alone in a jungle; he may enjoy this piquant contrast between his surroundings and his clothes, but you can take it from me that he and his sisters enjoy more never dressing for dinner in wartime London. It saves trouble, money, time, and gives us a lazy, go-as-you-please feeling that I find most agreeable. I only wish I could think that the fashion would outlast the war, and not give place to some terrific reaction into formal smartness.

Then, coming back to aesthetic pleasures, the pageant of life is enormously enriched by the presence of so many foreigners in our midst. So far as civilian foreigners go, many of them were promptly interned last summer, as you know, some quite unjustly. But slowly – far too slowly – that injustice is being put right. In any case, the uniforms of Polish solders mingle with those of Czechs, Norwegians, Dutch and Free French; women from the Central European countries with handkerchiefs tied about their heads embellish the streets. And not only foreigners. Driving in the country, you are continually hailed by the rich accents of young men in battle-dress from Alberta or Montreal, who seldom know where they are and always want to go somewhere else. They are, as a rule, enormously charming.

I will end with a consolation not aesthetic but psychological; the gratifying feeling that we have the sympathy of the best people: that is to say, the best nations, and the better people of the temporarily less good nations. We haven't had it in all our wars, and rightly. We have by no means always had the sympathy and goodwill of the American people; and the fact that we have it now gives us an enormous amount of support and satisfaction. Sympathy and mutual trust have been cemented by a common hatred of this horrid business of Nazism. We have grown into a relationship of which President Roosevelt can say: 'There was no treaty, no written agreement – but there was a feeling, which has proved correct, that as neighbours we could settle our disputes peacefully. There will be no bottleneck in our determination to aid Britain.'

When I cast my mind back to the earlier history of our relationship, and its stormy beginning, I cannot help recalling Patrick Henry's words of defiance flung at us across the Atlantic in 1775: . . . 'Is life so dear or peace so sweet as to be purchased at the price of chains and slavery? Forbid it, Almighty God. Give me liberty or give me death'.

I think Patrick Henry would now be on our side, and would use those words with a different reference. Among the consolations of war, this community of purpose and ideals with the kind of people with whom community is worth having, ranks high. I think really I should have mentioned it first.

BERTA GEISSMAR

At an English Concert

During the Christmas of 1942 I had an experience which symbolized for me the difference between life in Germany as I had witnessed it since 1933, and life in England. The traditional 'Carol-concert' of the Royal Choral Society under the direction of Dr Malcolm Sargent was sold out. I asked Dr Sargent whether he could get me in, as I wished my mother to hear for once the full Albert Hall singing the lovely age-old Christmas carols. He sent me two seats in his box and I sat down with my mother. Suddenly the door opened, and a lady in grey asked whether this was Dr Sargent's' box. We immediately recognized Mrs Churchill. She was with her daughter, who was in the uniform of the ATS, and smilingly tried to prevent us from giving her the front seats in the box.

With what a tremendous panoply and show Frau Goebbels or Frau Emmy Goering would have surrounded themselves on a similar occasion! But here was the wife of the British Prime Minister, bearing a proud and historic name, quietly slipping in to share a box with two refugees. This was democracy: this was England.

C.A. LEJEUNE

The Career of Gone With the Wind

After two and a half years in London, *Gone With the Wind* was generally released. It would be graceless and irresponsible to let the occasion pass without remark. The career of *Gone With the Wind* is the current counterpart of the success of 'Chu Chin Chow' during the last war. Novelists and social commentators are noting it down conscientiously, I trust, in their little books. It is as much a part of the issue of London life in wartime as the foreign uniforms in the streets, the altered skyline, and the friendly square gardens now open to the casual strollers.

Gone With the Wind arrived in London one April afternoon in 1940, when Narvik seemed the hub of the world, and errand boys were whistling 'Over the Rainbow.' Messrs Metro-Goldwyn-Mayer, who owned the piece, suggested, with incredible daring, that it might run until Christmas, unless, of course, the air-war should come to England and bombs fall in Piccadilly. That was roughly eight hundred and forty days – I had almost written years – two thousand five hundred performances ago, and when I passed through Leicester Square last week the 'house full' boards were out, the queue was still waiting patiently round the block.

Gone With the Wind has survived, and in its own way helped to lighten, the burden of the worst succession of news this country has had to bear since the Napoleonic wars. Through the Norway campaign, the invasion of the Low Countries, and the fall of France, through Dunkirk and the Battle of Britain, through an autumn, winter, and spring of savage air-attack, through the Greek campaign, the Libyan campaigns, and the assault on Russia, through Pearl Harbour and Hongkong and Singapore, through the Battle of the

Atlantic and the Battle of the Pacific, through Rommel's drive to Egypt and von Bock's drive to the Caucasus, the sturdy British citizen has taken his place in line to find out what happened to Scarlett O'Hara in a war that is as remote as Agamemnon's brush with Troy.

What is the secret of *Gone With the Wind*'s success? It does not seem to me the greatest film ever made. It has not, to my mind, the sharp, emotional appeal of *Mrs Miniver*, the magic of *Snow White* and *Bambi*, the fertile invention of *Citizen Kane*, the brilliance of *Kermesse Heroique*, the elemental force of *The Grapes of Wrath*. It is not even the longest film ever made; I am told it would seem a mere trailer to the shows one might see in China. It provides a tremendous experience, but one which its title significantly describes. It passes. The very dispassion with which it can be examined indicates its weakness – that it lacks – shall we say? – heart, the high, noble, memorable emotion one associates with great drama.

Few people who have seen it admit – or have admitted to me – that it is their favourite film, and yet few would appear to feel defrauded in any way, few would seem to wish to have foregone the experience. I have no doubt that when it opens outside London the queues will equal those in Leicester Square. Why? Millions of people, I know, have read the book, but you cannot persuade me that the queues are preponderantly made up of Margaret Mitchell lovers.

It is my own fancy that the very characteristics which limit *Gone With the Wind* as a work of art, the qualities in which it falls short of lasting worth, make it a proper and comfortable recreation for the times. There is a closer relation between pastime and the time in which it is passed than most people realize. 'The larger music, the more majestic length of verse called epics, the exact in sculpture, the classic drama, the most absolute kinds of wine, require a perfect harmony of circumstance for their appreciation' as Hilaire Belloc wrote in 'The Path to Rome.' In such days as these, when there is but little harmony and content in our own souls, the need is for something simpler, more varied, more immediate in its effects. A mind that is heavy and disturbed does not want to reach very high or delve very deep. It wants to be carried along, distracted by many and even little things. Great emotion at such a time is painful and dangerous.

For this reason, I think, *Gone With the Wind* just suits our war-time mood. It is a prodigal film, generous to overflowing with facile events. It has, alike with the book from which it is so faithfully drawn, an impersonal narrative style which evokes violence without pain. There is enough catastrophe in *Gone With the Wind* to make the last act of 'Hamlet' seem a jest. But catastrophe without contemplation is no tragedy, and even amongst all these dead and dying, our emotions are seldom overtried.

What audiences will find in *Gone With the Wind* is a graphic account of personal doings and relationships, intimate details of this meeting and that quarrel, the gossip of a dozen homes, and the confidences of a host of interesting people. The film has a hundred different stories, each in its different way absorbing. Each receives and exacts the same engrossed attention, whether it be the Civil War or a domestic tiff, the birth of a nation or the birth of a baby. *Gone With the Wind* runs for three hours and forty minutes, or twice as long as many finer pictures. But few people, anxious to hear what happens to Scarlett O'Hara and Rhett and Melanie, carried along on a wave of sound and colour, and conscious only of the blessed distraction it gives them, will find this enormous picture overlong.

ANNA NEAGLE

The Yellow Canary

My part [in *The Yellow Canary*] was a great change for me. The daughter of parents prominent in the War Office and WVS, I appeared to be spying for the Nazis. It was not until the last few moments of the film that it became clear that I was, in fact, doing secret intelligence work for the WRNS. Richard Greene was released from the Army to play in it with me. I was so busy that I did not see the finished film for nearly a year. Then I caught up with a matinee performance in Newcastle.

Sitting in front of me were two ladies, one very elderly and rather deaf, so that her companion was constantly explaining what the film was about, to the accompaniment of low moans from her elderly friend. 'Oh no. Tch-tch,' she muttered. 'Oh dear me *no*, Anna Neagle would never do that.'

When I finally appeared in my WRNS uniform, and all was made clear, she gave a very relieved sigh. 'There,' she said, turning in triumph to her patient neighbour, 'I *told* you Anna Neagle wouldn't do things like that.'

RACHEL KNAPPETT

The Landolettes

We were running at that time, a concert party known as The Landolettes. The performers were all landgirls working on surrounding farms. They thought the best way of ending an eight-hour day pottering about the wet winter fields, was to cycle through the long dark evenings and meet together to learn tap dancing. Marjorie taught us, and when we were good enough, the girls thought it great fun to undertake engagements in out-of-the-way spots, reachable only by bicycle, with their costumes packed in suitcases on the carriers. In extraordinary dressing-rooms piled high with cups and saucers and tea urns, where worthy local ladies were preparing suppers for the audience, we would throw off our heavy boots, don skimpy cabaret costumes and perform on remarkable stages made of tables which bent and groaned under the appalling weight of fourteen hefty landolettes.

BARBARA CARTLAND

A Reassuring Ghost

A friend of mine in the ATS who was billeted in Dunstable in an old house had a strange experience. She dreamt that she awoke and saw standing at the foot of her bed a middle-aged man wearing the knee-breeches and brocade coat of Nelson's time.

For a moment she was frightened, then the man said to her peremptorily as if she were the intruder:

'Why are you here?'

'Because I am a soldier.'

As she said the words my friend was conscious that she used them deliberately so that the man should understand.

'A woman . . . a soldier?' came the exclamation in astonishment.

'Yes.'

'Then England must be in danger again!'

'Yes, terrible danger.'

The man smiled.

'Do not be afraid,' he said reassuringly; 'if England needs help it is always there.'

'Where?' my friend asked, and knew as she put the question that it was important.

The man turned towards the window as if he were listening, and there came the tramp, tramp of marching feet.

'In the hearts of her people lies England's strength,' he said quietly, and the dream faded.

JANE GORDON

The Church and the Ritz

On my way home I stopped at St Mary's Church. Ever since the Dunkirk days I had acquired the habit of going in for a few minutes on my way to and from the hospital. Today when I slipped into the pew and knelt, I could think of nothing to say. The steel hat and gas-bag slung at my back felt heavy and awkward as they clumped against the woodwork of the pew. My stiff uniform belt dug into me; and before I knew what I was doing my face was clammy with tears and I could feel my nose getting red. The very plain figure of Christ in the centre of the ugly stained-glass windows, high up at the back of the altar, gazed down on me in a friendly way, but after a few moments I stood up feeling too discouraged to bother about anything, even a small prayer. So I went home, changed into my best suit, took extra trouble with my make-up, and joined Charles for luncheon at the Ritz.

VERE HODGSON

Tea at the Dorchester

15 October 1944

I have felt for some time that after three months and more of Fly Bombs, I wanted some new experience of an exciting nature. So I fixed with a friend, who seems to know every hotel there is, to go to the Dorchester for tea. We knew we could not afford a dinner. I have so often longed to enter the best hotel in London. So garbed in my best, I stepped forth. We turned first into the Grosvenor, but it said 6/6d, which we thought beyond us a bit. And we did not want to dance. So we entered a great soft carpeted lounge in the Dorchester, and sank down into some nice armchairs in an alcove. A distinguished looking waiter asked us if we wanted tea – in which case we must wait until 4 p.m.

We smoked and looked round. A few people drifted in. A naval officer had drink after drink, and seemed worried. The little page boy in buttons came hurrying in with a message. Perhaps he had been let down.

At 4 p.m. a very inferior tea was served to us. Sandwiches, thin and beautifully cut, but the insides had no flavour of any kind at all. I think it was just soya bean. Waiter then appeared with a tray full of cakes and pastry – we were allowed two. They were awful. The cups were plain white – I expect all their own were broken. The lounge filled. Several officers. One private. Finally a society beauty swept in. She was in black, with feathers in her hat. Seeing no corner seat she flowed back to the centre of the room, nearly knocking a man over. They sat down and soon were both absorbed in newspapers. Obviously a husband and wife.

At a quarter to five we asked for our bill, and felt lucky to get out at 4/6d each, for a tea the like of which I should have been ashamed to serve in my flat. But I had had tea at the Dorchester, and that is another ambition satisfied.

Had a lovely stroll back through the Park, as I considered we could not afford the bus. I prepared a very nice dinner . . . chops, potatoes and tomatoes. For cocktails – Auntie's own ginger wine. For sherry – Government lemon squash, and for port – more ginger wine. All much better than the Dorchester would have provided!

HILARY WAYNE

The Solace of Shops

Floating day after day from basement to ground floor, from ground floor to first floor, second floor, third floor, on the escalator, I look down on the departments and begin to appreciate their subtle methods of enticement. I realize how stimulating colour is: a cascade of scarlet silk here, a blaze of artificial flowers there, clusters of gay scarves and glittering bottles of creams and cosmetics, catch the tired eye and light up the tired mind. Movement, too, is exciting. The escalator is too sluggish, but the flash of the lift registering the progress of its journey in rapidly changing lighted figures brings life to that end of the shop. The short swift flight in the lift releases energy and sends the customer out more reckless for the adventure of spending. I begin to see that the shop is more than a place in which to buy things. Long ago, before the days of coupons and war work, its allurements used to be the main temptation of idle women. Now the choosing of a coat or dress seems to be a family affair, and in a world where there is little free entertainment even the escalator is an event in the life of a child.

ELIZABETH BOWEN

Calico Windows

1944

Calico windows are something new – in a summer bare of fashions, 'crazes' or toys. They pitch home life in a hitherto unknown mood. In the theatrical sense, they rank as 'effects' of the first order. They cast on your ceiling, if you have a ceiling left, a blind white light, at once dull and dazzling, so that your waking thought every morning continues to be, 'Why, it must have snowed!' They lighten and darken slowly: inside calico windows it might be any time of year, any time of day. Through their panes you hear, with unexpected distinctness, steps, voices and the orchestration of traffic from the unseen outside world. (Talkers outside a calico window should be discreet.) Glass lets in light and keeps out sound; calico keeps out (most) light and lets sound in. The inside of your house, stripped of rugs, cushions and curtains, reverberates.

Few of these new-fashion windows are made to open: you cannot have everything. However, the sashes of those that do fly up with ghostly lightness, almost before you touch, showing you summer still outside.

This cotton and cardboard 1944 summer home, inside the shell of the old home, is fascinating. With what magic rapidity was it improvised and tacked together by the kind workman. The blast of the buzz bomb marked the end of the former phase. The dreamlike next phase began with the arrival of workmen. As though just hatched, or dropped from the skies, these swarmed in their dozens in your street. Soon they had disappeared, without trouble, inside the blasted-open front doors – yours having its share. So many and so alike were the workmen that, still dazed, you failed to distinguish one from the other, and only attempted to guess their number when it came to finding cups for their tea. They were at it almost before you knew they were there – smashing out what was left of glass, smashing down what was left of plaster, wrenching out sagging frames and disjointed doors. The noise they made at their beginning, if just less, was more protracted than that of the explosion. But nothing makes you feel calmer than being taken in hand.

Coughing in the fog of dust they had raised, scrunching over chips of glass on the floors, the workmen, godlike, proceeded towards their next stage, that of sweeping, hauling, measuring, hammering. Only just pausing, they listened patronizingly to other buzz bombs passing across the sky: you knew nothing more could happen while they were with you. To watch them filled your post-blast blankness; to watch them made you feel you were doing something yourself; and to know that *you* were not paying them was most heartening.

The calico for the windows arrived in bales, along with the felt and boarding. Workmen carrying these in wove their way between workmen carrying rubble out. The rubble was tipped from baskets on to a mounting mountain outside your doors; and the mountain was by-passed by still more workmen with tarpaulins with which to drape your roof – these last disappeared upstairs and, for all you knew, never came down again.

The whole scene was one of rhythm and, soon, of order. Watching the bold creation shape itself, you exclaimed, 'Of course, of course!' The light new window-frames, primitive as a child's drawing, which have been constructed out on the pavement, are now fitted into the old windows. The outside world disappears. The workmen's are the first faces you see in this to-be-familiar calico light. You have now been tied up, sealed up, inside a tense white parcel. The workmen see it is good. They go.

You are left alone with your new sensations. The extraordinary is only at the beginning of its long reign. So many footprints are in the dust that you lose track of your own; you lose track of yourself, and you do not care. The peace of absolute dislocation from everything you have been and done settles down. The old plan for living has been erased, and you do not miss it. Solicitous for the safety of your belongings, the considerate workmen have hidden everything: the lamps are in the hat-cupboard; the telephone has been rolled up inside a mattress; your place in the book you were reading when the bomb went off has been religiously marked with a leg that blew off the sofa; more books are in the bath. And everything seems very well where it is. Especially does it seem good that the position of the telephone makes it impossible for you to tell anyone what has happened, or to reply if anyone asks you. Already you feel secretive about your pleasure at the dawn of this new, timeless era of calico.

And next door? For you are not the only one. You run in to ask how the next-doors sustained the blast, but how they feel inside their white box is a more intimate question. Next door – now that you come to listen – sounds remarkably silent: can they have gone to the country? If so, have they any notion how much they miss? Next-door-but-one, and next door to that, add their quota to the deserted silence.

No doubt, however, everyone else, like you, is standing still, taking stock, looking round. Now you think, you find you are making no noise yourself – they probably think you have gone away.

But perhaps as that first dusk falls your curiosity heightens, till you go out to make a reconnaissance. Your street, chequered over with black and white, looks somehow coquettish and self-conscious. Going farther, you are perhaps diminished by finding your entire neighbourhood endowed with this striking new thing in panes. Seen from the outside, all the way down a street, calico windows lose tone. You begin to wonder, inimically, how long these good people's windows will stay clean, and what they will look like when they no longer are. Now, in this hour before black-out, lights flower behind the criss-crossed frames. Do that young couple realize, or should you tell them, that they perform a shadow-play on a screen? No polite person stares in at a lighted window, but what is to stop you staring at calico?

Back home, you remember you have no black-out. You grope to bed in the calico-muffled dark.

Those first twenty-four hours are only the sharp-edged beginning of the mood. You must live, of course; you must pick up at least some of the pattern; you must at least play house. You discover that what turned on, turns on still – hot water, wireless, electric light. Whether willing or not, you disinter the telephone from the mattress, to explain you are quite safe, perfectly all right, happy; and to learn, from the pause on the wire, that you are disbelieved.

But everything comes from a distance; nothing disturbs you. Each time you return home, shutting the door behind you, you re-enter the mood. The hush of light, the transit of outdoor sounds, the bareness in here become familiar without losing their spell. Life here – life in a blasted, patched-up house – is *not* life, you have been indignantly told. What is it, then – a dream? We are, whatever else we may be, creatures of our own senses, varying with their food. Is this different food for our senses making us different creatures?

This tense, mild, soporific indoor whiteness, with, outside, the thunder of world events, sets the note of the summer for Southern England. I say to myself, all my life when I see a calico window, I shall be back in summer 1944. Then I remember – when war is over, there will be no more of this nonsense; we shall look out through glass. May the world be fair!

CHAPTER THIRTEEN

Speaking Out

Women were in the vanguard of European writers who protested against Hitler. Books from Germany and Poland were widely reviewed and discussed, in particular Irmgard Litten's highly praised *A Mother Fights Hitler* (1940), a dispassionate report of her five year struggle and failure to save her lawyer son from Nazi persecution.

More openly emotional were the messages going to and from America. A stream of British books with uplifting titles bombarded America before her entry into the war at the end of 1941: F. Tennyson Jesse's *London Front*, Margaret Kennedy's *Where Stands a Wingèd Sentry*, Vera Brittain's *England's Hour*. These writers were among many who saw that they had an important function in cementing the special Anglo-American relations that held throughout the war. Americans had to be thanked for the massive aid they were sending across the Atlantic, and to be encouraged in pro-British sentiments. The mothers, wives and girlfriends of American GIs stationed in Britain needed reassurance that they were being well looked after.

American women journalists toured Britain and reported on their findings, as did the wives of visiting politicians, notably Eleanor Roosevelt. Sometimes it seemed as if rumours were being countered. 'People look healthy ... thinnish, firm and fit', wrote one American woman to her daughter in 1942. Her eagle eye spotted 'a good deal of handholding between soldiers and their girls, but nothing more'. The fervent anti-Nazi journalist Dorothy Thompson wrote and broadcast frequently to both English and American women. Her 'tributes' to the women of Britain were an explicit attempt to bring the war closer to Americans, to 'make the women of America *imagine* the women of Britain'.

A group of Scottish women were so moved by the plight of their sisters in Leningrad (now St Petersburg) that they compiled an album of messages of support. This album, with its letters, postcards of Scottish towns and six thousand signatures, was sent to Russia in December 1941. In 1943, when the siege of Leningrad was in its third year, the Leningrad Album arrived in Scotland, a beautifully illustrated reply from the Russian women.

Throughout the war women continued to speak and write about the sufferings in Europe. They wrote on behalf of the Jews, and on behalf of starving children. They also spoke out against the mass bombing of civilian targets and in favour of peace, and not always to deaf ears. Although Vera Brittain had some of her *Letters to Peace-Lovers* returned to her (once with the message 'We're all too busy doing our bit to bother with such nonsense'), her 1942 pacifist pamphlet 'Humiliation with Honour' sold ten thousand copies by February 1943.

QUEEN ELIZABETH

The Mark of the Good Neighbour

The Queen's Message to the Women of America August 1941
It is just over two years since I spoke to the American people, and my purpose then was to thank countless friends for much kindness. It is to those same friends and of even greater kindness that I want to speak today. We, like yourselves, love peace and have not devoted the years behind us to the planning of death and destruction. As yet, save in the valour of our people, we have not matched our enemies, and it is only now that we are beginning to marshal around us in their full strength the devotion and resources of our great British family of nations which will, in the end, please God, assuredly prevail.

Through these waiting months, a heavy burden is being borne by our people. As I go amongst them, I marvel at their unshakable constancy. In many cities, their homes lie in ruins, as do many of those ancient buildings which you know and love hardly less than we do ourselves. Women and children have been killed, and even the sufferers in hospitals have not been spared. Yet hardship has only steeled our hearts and strengthened our resolution. Wherever I go I see bright eyes and smiling faces, for though our road is stony and hard, it is straight, and we know that we fight in a great cause.

It is not our way in dark days to turn for support to others, but even had we been minded so to do your instant help would have forestalled us. The warmth and sympathy of American generosity have touched beyond measure the hearts of all of us living and fighting in these islands. We can, and shall, never forget that in the hour of our greatest need you came forward with clothing for the homeless, food for the hungry, comfort for those who were sorely afflicted. Canteens, ambulances and medical supplies have come in an unceasing flow from the United States. I find it hard to tell you of our gratitude in adequate terms, though I ask you to believe that it is deep and sincere beyond expression. Unless you have seen as I have seen, just how your gifts have been put to use, you cannot know, perhaps, the solace which you have brought to the men and women of Britain, who are suffering and toiling in the cause of freedom.

Here in Britain our women are working in factory and field, turning the lathes and gathering the harvest, for we must have food as well as munitions. Their courage is magnificent; their endurance amazing. I have seen them in many different activities. They are serving in their thousands with the Navy, Army and Air Force, driving heavy lorries, cooking, ciphering, typing, and every one of them working cheerfully and bravely under all conditions. Many are on the land, our precious soil, driving the plough and making a grand job of it. Others are air-raid wardens or ambulance drivers, thousands of undaunted women who quietly and calmly face the terrors of the night bombings, bringing strength and courage to the people they protect and help.

I must say a special word for the nurses, those wonderful women whose devotion, whose heroism will never be forgotten. In the black horror of a bombed hospital they never falter, and though often wounded think always of their patients and never of themselves. And I need not remind you, who set as much store by your home life as we do, how great are the difficulties which our housewives have to face nowadays and how gallantly they are tackling them.

I could continue the list almost indefinitely, so manifold is the service which our women in Britain are giving, but I want to tell you that whatever the nature of their daily, or nightly, tasks, they are cheered by the evidence of your help for them. We like to picture you knitting on your porches, serving in your committee rooms, and helping in a hundred ways to bring relief to our civilian garrison here. So I speak for us all in Britain in thanking all of you in America. I feel I should like to send a special message of thanks to American women. It gives us strength to know that you have not been content to pass us by on the other side. To us, in the time of our tribulation, you have surely shown that compassion which has been for two thousand years the mark of the Good Neighbour. Believe me – and I'm speaking for millions of us who know the bitter, but also proud sorrow of war – we are grateful. We shall not forget your sacrifice. The sympathy which inspired it springs not only from our common speech and the traditions which we share with you, but even more from our common ideals. To you tyranny is as hateful as it is to us. To you, the things for which we will fight to the death are no less sacred, and, to my mind at any rate, your generosity is born of your conviction that we fight to save a cause which is yours no less than ours, of your high resolve that, however great the cost and however long the struggle, justice and freedom, human dignity and kindness shall not perish from the earth. I look to the day when we shall go forward hand in hand to build a better, kinder and happier world for our children.

May God bless you all.

THE GREENHILL KNITTING CIRCLE

A Message to the Women of Leningrad

Dear Women of Leningrad,

We are glad of this opportunity of expressing our gratitude to your country and our admiration of the terrific battle you are waging against our common foe, the enemy of all progress and humanity.

We are horrified at the suffering brought on the people of Europe by fascism but we know that Britain and Russia and America together will eventually defeat this fascist horror. Fighting together we can do it.

The women here will 'do our own bit' to the best of our ability and we look forward with you to the time when we shall build a new world of peace and goodwill amongst men and women the world over.

With our best wishes to our splendid ally.

From the women of Greenhill Knitting Circle, Coatbridge.

LUCY OLBROMSKA

Poland's Women Appeal to the Conscience of the World

July 1941

The other day I read a letter from a Polish mother to her son in England. Here is a literal translation of what this Polish mother, veteran of one Polish war, robbed in another of her husband and her children, enduring the bitterest hardships, looking on at the transformation of her country and home into one vast concentration camp, writes:

'My little son, far from me, irreplaceable. We are scattered through the world like leaves from a tree. It is autumn again. I too am like the bare tree that has lost all its green leaves. My branches are empty. Oh my children! My littlest one, how glad I am that you are with your brother. How glad I am! Grow up strong and learn your lessons. How I live you probably both know. I have sold the piano and with that I bought a little coal. Your father's high boots I traded for potatoes and flour. The money I got for the cupboard with the mirror was enough for me for a month. There is very little left for sale. I work how I can. I get some food from the Polish Red Cross. I live by faith and longing. My dearest ones, may God keep you. My longing for you accompanies you throughout the world.'

But victory will come. And a day will also come, when there will be another International Congress of Women and before that Congress they, the women of Poland, are going to stand. They are going to say: 'We stood first in the fight for freedom. We stood, and endured, alone. How have privileged women of freer continents stood behind us? What protests, what efforts, have other women made before the spectacle of our long agony and humiliation? Yes, and before the spectacle of our magnificent and prolonged and never-to-be-abandoned resistance?'

What answer will they get?

BLANCHE E.C. DUGDALE

All Ye that Pass By

December 1942

In March 1942, Himmler visited Poland, and decreed that by the end of this year 50 per cent of the Jewish population should be 'exterminated' – in plain English, put to death – and the pace seems to have been hastened since. Now the German programme demands the disappearance of all Jews, men, women and children, natives of occupied Poland or deportees from Western or Central Europe. Mass-murders on a scale unheard-of since the dawn of civilization began immediately after the order was issued. At first the details of these were hardly believed, even in quarters capable of judging the reliability of the news that percolated from behind the dreadful barriers of the 'sealed ghettos' all over the country. But the accounts were confirmed again and again, and it became evident to those who received them that the German genius for organization was being applied methodically to the slaughter of Jews. Nevertheless, it was not until the Gestapo Chief reviewed the results in person this summer that Nazi efficiency reached its peak. The exact date of highest achievement, in the Warsaw ghetto, the biggest of all, was July 24th, 1942, when ten thousand Jews were assembled for so-called deportation. The curve then declined for some time to seven thousand a day. By September 1st some 250,000 people had disappeared. For that month 120,000 Jewish ration-cards were distributed in the Warsaw ghetto (entitling the possessor to a pound of bread per week and very little else). For October only 40,000 such cards were deemed necessary. Now the Warsaw 'deportations' sink as low as three thousand persons in a day. Before I go on to give an idea of what happens to them, the origins of these appalling reports must be named. There is a spontaneous reaction against 'atrocity-stories' and a desire to believe them exaggerated, which is rooted as much in the healthier forms of incredulity as in the instinct to spare oneself pain. But my facts and figures are quoted primarily from documents issued by the Polish Ministry of Information in London dated December 1st.

If support were needed it could be found in a speech delivered recently in New York by Dr Stephen Wise, the well-known

Jewish leader, based on information given him by the State Department in Washington. No room seems to be left for doubting the reports, tallying as they do with things known to responsible Jewish bodies in the Allied countries. The facts do indeed surpass imagination. Here is one sample from the Polish Government Report. It describes what happens after the daily quota of victims has been assembled at the clearing-stations. They are carried off to death with the 'maximum of suffering'. A hundred people of both sexes and all ages are packed into trucks that would hold forty and the floors covered with unslaked lime. To enhance the effect of this, the deportees may be ordered to take off their boots. The trucks are sealed before they are started on their journey to the camps of execution at Belzec, Sobibor and Treblinka, places east of Warsaw. There the Polish peasantry can hardly endure the continual stench of putrefying flesh, for when the trucks are opened they reveal a mass of the dead and dying, standing upright for lack of room to fall down. Those who still breathe are shot, electrocuted or gassed. [...]

These things have been happening all through this November of cheerful memory. They are happening now. Scepticism cannot much longer serve as excuse for inaction, as the burden of providing proof shifts from those who believe that such crimes are being committed to those who refuse credence. So the question arises of what to do, or rather of whether there is anything that can be done while the war lasts. Certain it seems that Polish Jewry will be beyond help if the murder-campaign cannot be stopped before the war ends. But the spectre of defeat may already be lying in wait for the German people. Now is the time to enlist its help, for the argument of fear is one which Germans understand more than most.

The United Nations have sworn to exact full retribution for war crimes. Let them now repeat the pledge with specific reference to the Jews in occupied countries, and so remove any possible idea that atrocities against Jews will be punished less severely than those against peoples who are not in a minority everywhere. [...] It would be a shameful thing if the British Government, Parliament and nation were to remain supine or mere critics of what others try to do on behalf of tortured people. [...] The jaws of the trap are not closed everywhere – at any rate not yet. Palestine is not the only place within the British Empire where safety awaits those who succeed in escaping. Men who do not open doors to those who are hunted by murderers participate in the crime.

ANNA NEY

Anti-Semitism

April 1943

Anti-semitism, unfortunately, has lately become a popular feature, and every now and then we find in the press an attempt to explain the growth of this evil by one or another fault of the Jews, or even more often, by the faults of 'the foreign Jews' ...

A whole nation is being exterminated amidst so-called civilized peoples. There is nothing and nobody to stop or at least to try to stop it. (I should like at this point to pay high tribute to the leaders of the Churches together with the few other personalities who try to stir up public opinion in favour of the persecuted and advocate before the Government an effective help for the Jewish victims.) The Jews have no country, no government, no representative. If they had had, this country, this government, this representative of theirs would have saved them in time before hell was reached. There was no such preventive action. The early Christians had no backing either and were therefore attacked and made responsible for all the evil like the Jews are to-day. But is there really no prospect of destroying anti-semitism? I think anti-semitism is a mental disease like many others not yet recognized by us as such and it would lead me to a study of psycho-pathology to discuss the possible prospects of its curing. But let me tell you one thing which I know for certain about the average anti-semite, the man in the street or, more precisely, the woman in the home; the worried, the tired, the cross and envious housewife. If she were shown reality, if she could witness a farewell scene between Jewish parents and children sent apart to death; if she could hear the voices of the massacred, if she could see the eyes of children in agony, eyes and voices which God, not men, will account for: if the housewife of Hampstead or Vienna, Chicago or Melbourne would have been confronted with them: do you think she still would envy chickens and fur coats? Her heart would be filled with terror and her only wish would be – to help the victims. But as long as she does not see, she does not think. And her imagination does not go beyond the narrow horizon of the jealousies of her street.

MARGERY WITHERS

Children Under Hitler

February 1943

The story of children inside Europe to-day is not for the squeamish. A Greek officer said in a broadcast recently: 'In Athens one morning last winter I was standing in a street near Omonia Square. I had noticed one of the German bread lorries, for Germans only, parked by the pavement. It was the same with all their food lorries. They used to leave them about in the street while the population was starving. The grown-ups stood it very well, but it was heart-breaking to see the children staring at the good things they could not have. This particular morning I suddenly heard firing. I ran back to see what was happening. What I saw was a little child – he might have been seven or ten – lying face downwards in the road. In front of him he had been holding a loaf which he had managed to take from the lorry when he thought no one was looking. The loaf stuck out a little way from under his body. He had three shots in his back.'

The docks in Greek ports are crowded with children begging for food. You can see them near restaurants and canteens, searching in dustbins and gutters for anything they can possibly eat. Many of them are so swollen and weak from hunger that they can only drag themselves miserably along the pavement or lie whimpering in some corner. Sometimes they stop whimpering and lie quietly for hours as if they were asleep, until someone realizes that it is not sleep this time, but death. A report from the Athens Child Welfare Service said that nine out of ten babies in the city died before they were six months old because their mothers were too starved to feed them. A young Greek mother writes: 'My baby died. I couldn't get any proper food for her. What can you give to a tiny baby – grass or cabbage?'

VERA BRITTAIN

from *Seed of Chaos: What Mass Bombing Really Means*

April 1944

The purpose of this Book is to inquire how far the British people understand and approve of the policy of 'obliteration bombing' now being inflicted upon the civilians of enemy and enemy-occupied countries (including numbers of young children born since the outbreak of war) by ourselves and the United States. The propagandist press descriptions of this bombing and its results skilfully conceal their real meaning from the normally unimaginative reader by such carefully chosen phrases as 'softening-up' an area, 'neutralising the target', 'area bombing', 'saturating the defences,' and 'blanketing an industrial district'.* [. . .]

'I wouldn't wish this trouble on any other woman!' cries the young mother in A. Burton Cooper's Lancashire play, *We Are the People*, after her small boy has been blown to pieces by a daytime bomb on a local playground. And that, I believe, is the normal reaction of every decent person, once real knowledge has come to him or her through individual suffering.

It is because I want you, the readers of this book, to have such knowledge, so far as facts ascertained from sources available under wartime conditions can give it to you, that I am going to describe, with references to my sources of information, what our bombing policy means to those who have to endure its results. I shall have to quote some horrible details, but these are not included from sensational motives. They are given in order that you who read may realize exactly what the citizens of one Christian country are doing to the men, women and children of another. Only when you know these facts are you in a position to say whether or not you approve. If you do not approve, it is for you to make known your objection – *remembering always that it*

---

* The use of soporific words to soothe or divert the natural human emotions of horror and pity is a characteristic and disturbing feature of this war.

*is the infliction of suffering, far more than its endurance, which
morally damages the soul of a nation.* [...]

Apart from all that we have done to Italy and to German occupied countries, our reprisals mean that on Germany alone, up to
the end of October, 1943, we had already inflicted more than
twenty-four times the amount of suffering that we had endured.
No doubt there are many non-adult minds which find reason for
satisfaction in the anguish that we have caused to the enemy. But
others will reflect more responsibly that each one of those million
dead (to say nothing of the injured and seven million homeless)
have relatives and friends who will remember.

CHAPTER FOURTEEN

Recording the War

Women recorded the war for public as well as private purposes. British women war correspondents were not allowed near the front; the rules were stricter for them than for American newspaper-women. The communist Charlotte Haldane was one of the few exceptions, and her account here is a striking example of how the experience of recording the war could force writers to revise their preconceptions.

The war split up families in unprecedented ways, as people were mobilised for war work and service overseas. Between 1939 and 1945 nearly thirty-five million changes of address were recorded, in a civilian population of about thirty-eight million. As leave and telephone calls were expensive and difficult, it was primarily through their letters that women hoped to keep their families together in this last golden age of letter writing. If recording the war was the duty of the historian, it could also be a conversation with a friend, an act of love.

Magazines and radio broadcasts urged women to send daily and weekly letters to servicemen away from home. For these women writing to their men, Daphne du Maurier had some firm advice in her *Good Housekeeping* article of September 1940: 'There must be no weakness in these letters of ours, no poor and pitiful hinting at despair. We must be strong and confident, and full of faith.' In 1941 the Post Office introduced the airgraph for overseas letters, which would be photographed on to microfilm, and enlarged and printed on arrival. Between 1941 and 1945 the Post Office transmitted over three hundred and fifty million of these airgraphs.

As well as the internalised censor urging strength and confidence, the figure of the official Censor also had to be considered. Letters coming from and going abroad passed through the Censor's Office, and would probably be read by women who made up the majority of the Censorship staff. 'I find the work very interesting,' wrote Barbara Pym in 1942 about the Censor's Office in Bristol, 'though the secrecy is rather annoying as I can't talk about it or share jokes with any except my colleagues.' Internees were further constrained in what they might say, according to Livia Laurent: 'An internee is permitted only twenty-four lines in a letter, and we had to use prisoner of war paper, on which the pen stuck every time we became intense.'

CHARLOTTE HALDANE

Russian War Correspondent

I was living in the Swiss Cottage flat in June, 1941, when, without any declaration of war, Hitler launched his attack against the Soviet Union. I immediately felt an ardent desire to go there as a war correspondent, partly to round off my experiences in Spain and China, but chiefly because I was filled with a passionate urge to help the Russian comrades in their great and glorious resistance. [. . .]

My unshakeable enthusiasm and utterly uncritical attitude during this trip did nothing to allay the annoyance of my colleagues. On one occasion two of them with whom, much to their dissatisfaction, I shared a car, attacked me with such verbal violence that it amounted to a blunt accusation of being a traitor to my own country. They were in a particularly black mood on account of a small incident that had occurred during the morning. We had been taken to view a dump of allegedly captured German war material; gun carriages, and other small transport stuff. When we had examined it, one of my companions re-entered the car, livid with anger. On my asking the reason for his annoyance, he replied: 'Next time they show us "captured" German war material they might have the elementary intelligence to remove the stamp of the Stalin motor factory from the hub of the wheels!'

This incident made a bad impression on me, too, from a different point of view. I thought it stupid and careless of the Russians to allow themselves to be found out in so blatant and simple a trick. Either they did not realize that if they put on a show for the correspondents it should be sufficiently convincing to impress them, or they were gratuitously insulting the intelligence of men who prided themselves on their professional sharpness of observation, and who would not easily forgive such clumsy deception.

However, a far greater shock was in store for me.

During the tour we spent a night in a military camp near a little town called Dorogobuzh. This had been very badly blitzed by the Luftwaffe in the German advance a few weeks previously. The place was practically in ruins. The Russians made a great show of it, as an example of ruthless German bombing. To the British visitors, it was no novelty. We had seen devastation on an equal scale in our own home towns, on our own doorsteps. But to the Americans, in the autumn of 1941, it was an impressive sight. Most of them, before coming to Russia, had not been in England, and at that time had no conception of the punishment Britain was taking, night after night. Among the American party were Erskine Caldwell, author of *Tobacco Road*, and his wife, the photographer, Margaret Bourke-White, who enjoyed particular favour with the Soviet authorities. She had been given permission to take all the photographs she wanted, and special facilities were put at her disposal. She was anxious to obtain some good shots of devastated Dorogobuzh, and its suffering inhabitants. She was going to get them one morning at dawn. She allowed me to accompany her, as I, too, wanted to see the ruins, for comparison's sake. We set off in a car, accompanied by a uniformed NKVD man. A needle-sharp wind was blowing, and a fine drizzle was falling. We stopped the car in the main street and waited for sufficient daylight, as visibility was extremely bad. It was about six o'clock in the morning. The place was completely deserted, except for an old peasant woman, in a dark shawl, hurrying along, bent against the wind and rain. Mrs Bourke-White wanted a shot of this pathetic picture, and asked the NKVD man to stop the woman. This he vigorously refused to do. He pointed out, politely but firmly, that it was forbidden to photograph citizens of the Soviet Union, except in Moscow. But he obligingly volunteered to pose for the photograph himself, and did so, standing patiently against one of the ruined buildings until it had been taken. As we sat in the car, waiting for the light, the sad silence was suddenly broken by the distant tramp of many feet; it was more like a shuffle than a tramp. As it came closer, we peered out to see the cause of it. Along the straight cobbled road came an amazing procession. There were about two hundred men, peasants. They carried primitive agricultural implements. They were in rags. Their long, fair, unkempt hair fell to their shoulders. Their legs and feet were encased in ragged puttees and straw sandals. Each man had a string around his neck, from which hung, at the back, a small sack, containing a hunk of bread. At first I thought they must be prisoners, but no guards were visible, either at the head or the tail of the procession. The men, roughly between the ages of sixty and sixteen, trudged along in absolute silence, their faces pinched, pale, and wan, their eyes on the ground, not even lifted to gaze at the large opulent car, with the two foreign women and the NKVD man. When we asked him who or what they were, he merely answered: 'I don't know,' and said no more. Never, on any of my travels, had I seen such a forlornly tragic sight, human beings registering such complete and final hopelessness. So they passed, in silence and mystery. After about ten minutes, another procession, a smaller one, followed them. It consisted exclusively of women, also carrying agricultural implements, with the sacks of bread hanging down their backs, their heads and faces bent against the wind, also completely silent. The whole picture might have been a nightmare. It was certainly not the kind that is transmitted abroad by VOKS for foreign propaganda purposes.

My first reaction to the scene was one of the deepest pity and sorrow for these utterly disconsolate unfortunates. But it was followed by a fierce sense of guilt and shame. I saw myself at home, on CP platforms, making impassioned speeches, from a sincere conviction, to the British people, exalting the great and glorious Soviet Union, home of every toiler, the hope of the workers of the world. The scene I had just witnessed, more tragic and powerful than any engraving to Dante's Inferno by Doré or Blake, seemed to mock my facile and naive optimism, my wishful dreaming, and to accuse me of bearing false witness to my own people.

F. TENNYSON JESSE

The Right to Speak

27 April 1941 [after a heavy blitz on London]
There is one great advantage for civilians, particularly for women, in this war, we have a right to speak because we are all in danger,

we can speak without laying ourselves open to the accusation of being armchair critics or of having no right to speak because it is only the young men who go out and fight who are taking risks.

BARBARA NIXON

Biased Reporting

On one of the March [1941] raids the Café de Paris was hit. The melodramatic nature of the incident caught the fancy of the reporters, and for three days the papers were full of the gallantries of expensive girls who had torn their expensive dance frocks into strips to make bandages. The reporters seemed surprised; but the most light-headed society girl would not refuse a strip of her skirt in such circumstances. Even 40 guineas cannot weigh against another's life-blood. It was a gory incident, but the same week another dance-hall a mile to the east of us was hit and there were nearly 200 casualties. This time there were only 10/6 frocks and a few lines in the paper followed by 'It is feared there were several casualties'. Local feeling was rather bitter. At the end of the week one or two papers which had actually implied that it was a commendable thing to go to the Café de Paris, for instance, and thereby show that the air-blitz was not affecting West End morale, now said that to go to a local 'hop' was irresponsible and flippant.

CLARA MILBURN

Writing to a Prisoner-of-War Son

Wednesday 24 July [1940]
A letter from the War Office Casualty Branch giving us Alan's address: 'Stalag XXA', Germany. That cheered us a bit, for now we can write to him. And, of course, it was not long before I wrote him a stilted little letter on a single sheet of notepaper, which is all one may do at a time. One can write as often as one likes – but how little one can really say! For one thing, news is scarce when one cuts out the war, and one may not say anything to give any information to the enemy. So things have to be carefully sifted till

there is very little said. However one can send love and give facts in a veiled way, as I did today when I wrote: 'Little Bert Austin takes your father to his daily work', which meant 'Father has an Austin 7 to drive into Coventry, where he has taken a job at the Labour Exchange'. And then continued: 'and Maria stays with me at Burleigh. She is as good a girl as ever and behaves nicely, so I am glad to have her with me'. That meant: 'I have the Rover car for my use', because we call the Rover 'Maria'. He knows that and will put two and two together.

NELLA LAST

Where Do the Letters Go?

Tuesday, 25 August 1942
It will be six weeks on Monday since Cliff sailed. I wonder if he has reached his journey's end. A letter and an air mail card gave me a sadness, for he has not had any of my letters for a while. Where do they all go, I wonder? I send an airgraph nearly every week, and a long letter every three or four weeks – a 'diary' letter. I write the ones to Cliff and Arthur in that way now, so as not to forget any little incident that may interest them. I've four pads going at once, in an old stiff book-back to write on: always writing, always trying to interest and amuse my boys, and where do they go? And all the letters I hear of that go missing – surely all of them cannot be destroyed by 'enemy action'? A little sad-hearted wife said to me one day, 'It makes me wonder if they bother to take any letters out of the country. I write twice a week and rarely hear from Bert, who I know does the same. But when he does write, he always says the same – "Still no letter from home."'

VERE HODGSON

A Diary is Passed Round

21 August 1942
Excitement over the mulberry tree in the next garden – house unoccupied. Along with various others our caretaker raided the fruit. A

policeman came to know if we were allowing our Printing Works boys over the wall. The Manager swept him off the premises. We suspected he wanted a mulberry pie for himself. Our lady gardener, also, is a formidable person, and would rout Scotland Yard, if they interfered with her. The net result was a Mulberry Pie for all. Excellent – something between a raspberry and blackberry, only sharper. The moral side appealed to me. If I had been caught I should have appealed to Lord Woolton himself, saying it was against the national interest to let fruit rot on the trees. Our conscience is clear, for we have tried to get in touch with the owner. [...]

5th March 1944
Gratifying letter from John Fossett: 'Very many thanks for two instalments of diary. Joan and I derived hours of pleasure from reading it aloud to each other. How we laughed about the Mulberry Tree. We passed it over to the RAF and how they enjoyed it. It seemed like being at home again as we lived through your experiences.' He was in South Africa.

SYLVIA TOWNSEND WARNER

The Censor

November 1940
Do you ever think of the Censor? I don't mean from the point of view of muttonising your language, for it's obvious you don't do that. But do you ever think of him as roomfulls of ladies and gentlemen, all engaged in the embarrassing occupation of reading other people's letters? What will they do when they can't be censors any longer (for they can't all become village postmistresses or go into the CID)? Will they pine and languish, and feel themselves suddenly cut off from humanity? Or will they spend the evening of their days reading Madame de Sévigné and the Reverend Leman White (I think he was called that; anyway, he loads the shelves of every second-hand bookshop, letters to ladies about their souls)? Or will they demonstrate their freedom by never opening another envelope, not even envelopes addressed to them, whitey brown envelopes marked On His Majesty's Service and containing income tax demands? Valentine had a terrible time

when we got back a year ago, yearning to go into the censor's department. She has always been perfectly shameless about reading letters not meant for her, and, as she said, she was ideally suited for the work by never having much inclination to answer letters back.

C.A. LEJEUNE

Cinema and the Prose of War

It seems tolerably clear by now that the best thing the war is likely to draw out in the cinema is not poetry but prose: no masterpiece, but a number of small, candid snapshots of the soul of the people. This is probably as it must be, for war in these days is not a divided thing; they no longer fight battles in one parish and contemplate them in the next; there is no hermitage for the non-combatant in which he can refine, in sound or picture, the thoughts that have come to him from the battle-front; nor is there, indeed, in any real sense a non-combatant. To create or to savour the larger forms of art requires leisure of mind, and *that* is a thing we have not, neither by ten minutes nor by ten hours. But when a man's mood is disturbed, he is quicker to catch the mood of others. Human beings, rather than abstractions, are a necessity to him. He needs people; he sees people more clearly than ever before; if he has the talent he can sketch them with a remarkable fidelity.

The best film to come out of the war yet – for *Citizen Kane* was made when America was technically at peace – is a group-portrait, Noel Coward's *In Which We Serve*. In their more deliberately functional way, too, the documentary directors have made an acute study of men and women at war. Some historian of the future, with more leisure and serenity than we have, will be able to base a superb film drama on the faces and impressions recorded for him in the moment of action.

Now a new film adds to the collection of discerning wartime sketches. *The Gentle Sex* is a story of seven girls in the ATS. It isn't much of a story, if by story you understand excitement, magnitude, crisis, and a nice shiny medal at the end of it. These seven girls, with different backgrounds, different types of schooling, different codes, and different accents, simply go through their common training and do their jobs in company with thousands of others. Just a little emerges of their private lives, not much. Just a hint, but only a hint, is given of their future. The film is straitly concerned with their day-by-day experiences in the ATS – the humours and rigours of training, the physical weariness of night-driving, the easy fellowship, the sudden flare-ups of frayed nerves, the thought of marriage, so rigidly repressed, so irresistibly crowding to the surface.

The Gentle Sex was written by a woman and has a woman's understanding of women. It is acted by Rosamund John, Lilli Palmer, Joyce Howard, Jean Gillie, Joan Gates, Joan Greenwood, and Barbara Waring with a give-and-take that excites one's admiration. Leslie Howard directed, appears as a Back at the opening, and intervenes with a whimsical, speculative commentary. Mere men who turn up here and there are played by John Laurie, Jimmy Hanley, and John Justin, in two out of three cases with a nice sense of their blundering intrusion. A pleasantly ironic touch is provided by a Victorian sampler, bidding women cultivate 'a spirit of modesty, humility, obedience, and submission.' The film's most subtle irony may possibly be an unintended one – a cross-stitch credit to the War Office and the ATS.

CHAPTER FIFTEEN

The Last Year

The end of the war was a long time coming. The Allied invasion of France began on D Day, 6 June 1944, but the German surrender didn't come until nearly a year later, on 7 May 1945. The war in the Far East continued until the Japanese surrender on 14 August 1945.

In Britain the last year of the war was made worse by two new German weapons, the VIs – pilotless planes often referred to as doodlebugs – and later the V2 rockets. Freya Stark, who had been abroad working for the Ministry of Information in the Middle East, passed through London and was able to give a traveller's eye view of the new phenomenon of the doodlebug.

The end of the war had been in people's sights from the early days. Women wondered whether their lives would return to prewar patterns of marriage and home, or whether some of the changes had come to stay. Discussions about the shape of postwar society had been fuelled by the publication of the Beveridge Report in December 1942. On the whole optimism prevailed with hopes for the birth of the welfare state, although there were some gloomy predictions of a drop in women's employment once the men were demobbed.

For many of the women who had started their diaries in September 1939, VE Day on 8 May presented itself as the obvious closing entry, an epilogue of relaxed spontaneity. But even as they celebrated, many women felt the need to remember those who suffered or died. As facts emerged from mainland Europe about the concentration camps and the terrible devastation caused by the war, Rebecca West was not the only one to feel that 'their celebrations might be ironical ... We sang, we danced until midnight, but we knew that we were on the edge of doom unless the whole of humanity walked carefully.'

ZELMA KATIN

Long Days on the Trams

Summer days. [. . .] Work became harder, hotter and more tiring. My feet swelled, I acquired painful corns, and I took to wearing my son's shoes, because they were so much larger than my own. But there were compensations. There were the compensations not only of the vistas but of a temporary farewell to the blackout, of natural light for punching tickets and giving change, of cool dawns for the early shifts, of lengthened shopping hours which gave me a fairer chance to compete with full-time housewives, and of raw green salads for my meals at home.

My hands were burnt a nut brown. I rolled my sleeves up to the elbows and took my fares. Inspectors opened their eyes a little wider when they saw my bare arms but said nothing. 'Do you want a fight then?' said a passenger. Others said, 'Are you sweating lass?' 'Is the washing nearly done?' 'You do look cool, miss.' But not one conductress or motorman followed suit. [. . .]

I am glad I have dome this kind of war work, proud that I still have the moral and physical energy to follow it and I hope that out of this experience I shall have gained a new understanding of life, people and marriage. Like millions of men and women in uniform I cannot pretend I am liking it. Perhaps the sacrifice and hardship are giving us a strength which will enrich us in the future and toughen us for the struggle which lies ahead.

I will confess that I am thinking not only of a future for humanity but a future for myself. I want to lie in bed until eight o'clock, to eat a meal slowly, to sweep the floors when they are dirty, to sit in front of the fire, to walk on the hills, to go shopping of an afternoon, to gossip at odd minutes.

FREYA STARK

The Doodlebug

21 July 1944

Something very curious has happened here with these great robots. One has gone back into those ages when men saw the

Inevitable take on a visible shape and recognised their gods, unpersuadable, unreasonable in human ways, full of fascination and terror. I have a window facing the direction from which they come and spent an hour or so watching them last night – about midnight the sky still green with twilight faint and straight like faded streaks in old silk. Then the little droning things began far off, the houses mauve and dark within their outlines: we looked like an uninhabited city and the drone came nearer, it is quite slow, you hear it from so far. The sky had a few clouds, their high tips touched with light. And at last, the drumming loud now like an orchestra working up to the opening of a ballet, the fireball came skimming above the houses whose chimneys seemed to darken under her feet. (Everyone I ask tells me they think of it as feminine.) She did not give one the feeling of being wicked, but rather as if she were a planet or other creature of the natural forces, which has wilfully left its own cited circuit and gone wandering, and the destruction comes merely as a result of her unsuitability to the general surroundings. When she comes near, you hear the brazen flapping of her garments, you see that she is shod with flames or perhaps 'makes the cold air fire'. Shelley could have described her, and the Greeks would have known her ancestry. She went off, hurrying over the human world that cowered as she came, until she touched it far away across the houses, in a noise of death that seemed to fall like a stone into the stillness. It is a strange life, and a strange feeling of fear which, like a touch of black, sets off all the other colours. I would not be missing it for anything, nor the sight of London now, very gallant.

INEZ HOLDEN

The Flying Bombs

10 July 1944
At the hairdressers the girl who washed my hair said that on Sunday she and her husband had gone round to tidy up her father's flat which had been blasted by bomb damage. They got the place into working order for him and started back home. At the end of the road wardens and firemen were still clearing up the street and from the windows of a big block of flats the people

looked down on to the street scene. 'They weren't sightseers, you understand,' she said, 'only ordinary people looking out at the fire engines. There were old women and children, girls and soldiers on leave.' Then suddenly she had seen the pilotless plane descending in an arc curve at great speed. She called out to her husband and flung her arms round a pillar box. Her husband had thrown her down the area steps and fallen after her. They heard the glass come crashing in around the area and when she looked up she saw her father running down the street waving his arms and calling out, 'My children were there.' The girl told me, 'All the time I see those people in my mind, with the plane coming down on to the roof and they not knowing anything about it.' She said several times, 'All those people – all those people. I don't seem able to forget them – all those people.'

VITA SACKVILLE-WEST

The Future of the Landgirl

When the Land Army was disbanded after the last war, many members took advantage of the free passage to the Dominions offered to ex-service women. It is much to be hoped that the same thing may happen again. It seems likely that it will, for young women today are far more enterprising and adventurous then they were even in 1919, and what could be more desirable than that the stock of these fine girls should mix with their consanguineous friends in Canada, Australia, New Zealand? . . . I can visualise a new 'Mayflower', blossoming on every deck with the waving hands of a new sort of pioneer, a sort which would have astonished our Mayflower forefathers whose women were encumbered by huge skirts and tight stomachers, and encumbered even more by the convenient prejudices established by man for the control of his subservient woman. My new Mayflower carries a different muster. It carries gay young creatures, untrammelled by bulky clothes; legs are allowed to appear as legs, breeched and gaitered; the soft loose jersey replaces the whaleboned bodice, the elastic belt replaces the rigidity of the unnatural corset. And above all the liberty of the spirit replaces the rigidity of the conventional mind.

By the way, a strange idea appears to exist among Landgirls, to the effect that they may be *compelled* to 'go abroad' after the war. Let me contradict this idea emphatically and at once. Land Army officials are much puzzled to know how it can have got about. If a girl wants to go either into liberated Europe or into the colonies or Dominions, it will be entirely by her own choice. The idea of compulsion is without any foundation whatsoever, it just waves vaguely about in the air, and has roots only in the minds of those who like to believe in any stray bit of gossip they may have heard or may perhaps have read in some irresponsible newspaper.

VERE HODGSON

VE Day, 8 May 1945

Victory in Europe Day, Tuesday 8th
Today we have been celebrating! Thunderstorms in the night. No one slept much for excitement. But the sun shone warm, and it has been a Glorious Day.

Kit and I reached St Paul's about 11 a.m. One service was in progress, but another was soon due to begin. All through I continued to give thanks for our great deliverance. We had a splendid view of the Lord Mayor of London walking down the aisle, and his Chain of Office seemed to glitter with diamonds. The Choir sang the *Te Deum*. All the little boys were back. We sang all three verses of the National Anthem with great firmness, confounding their politics with tremendous enthusiasm.

Lovely and warm outside. We thought of the wonderful fire-watchers the Cathedral has had. They held their own Service. I remembered that Sunday when I walked past it, smoking ruins around, and a few weary firemen gathering their apparatus together.

We sauntered down to the River, and ate our lunch above the Temple stairs, near the *Discovery*. Carefree after so many years of anxiety. Then along to Westminster and Whitehall. We stood in Parliament St. What a squash! The buses scraped within an inch of us, and the horses of the mounted police rubbed their flanks against us.

Precisely at 3 p.m. Big Ben's chimes told us the moment was about to begin. All traffic stopped. The mounted policeman wiped the sweat from his brow. All was still. How wonderful to be standing in Whitehall, in the shadow of the House of Commons, listening to That Voice which had steered us from our darkest hours to the daylight of deliverance. No words can express what we owe him. He mentioned the Channel Islands to tremendous cheers. Kit was thrilled that they should be specially mentioned on such an occasion. She has not heard from her father for eleven months.

By now we were exhausted with heat and standing. Heaps of people on bicycles. There was a tandem – Mother, Father and Baby. Spectators were horrified at the position of this tiny mite, with a great bus towering above it – but the baby did not worry. We reached Downing St with a great effort. But I could no more. We had heard him speak.

The tube at Trafalgar Square was impossible of entrance, so we walked along Pall Mall. Cars passed us with people riding on the hoods and the bonnets. Everyone was just letting themselves go. We were glad to get to the flat for a cup of tea!

In the evening we had our own party. We were quite a United Nations. A Russian, a Swiss, a Channel Islander, a Scot-cum-Welsh and me, a true-blue English Midlander. We had ersatz champagne. Tinned grapefruit. Salad. Tongue. Tin of crayfish – and a Plum Pudding. All of us had been saving these viands up for a long time. All beautifully prepared by Miss Cameron. It was in Barishnikov's garden flat, which is bigger than mine. We had lovely coffee, and then he produced his pièce de resistance, some 1898 port . . . or some such date. We drank numerous Toasts . . . Churchill, Stalin, Auntie Nell, Kit's father in Guernsey . . . then the men drank to us.

We listened to the radio, and just tuned in to the moment when Mr Churchill came out in his Siren suit and conducted *Land of Hope and Glory*. He was wearing a black Homburg Hat. What a lad! He was cheered to the echo. God bless him!

MARGARET CRISP

VE Day in Hospital

VE Day, for which we had all waited so eagerly and which had been made possible by the men who were now in our care, would

have passed in a manner no different from any other day, but for
the efforts of individual nurses. A dance had been arranged for the
nursing staff and medical staff, and all the patients who were able
were allowed to go on four days' leave; but nobody bothered to
think of the very lonely bed-patients left behind in a half-empty
ward, the lads who had risked their lives, given their young limbs,
and sacrificed their health so that others could celebrate this occasion. Sounds of distant laughter, community singing, and a dance
band's blare reached the ears of those almost forgotten men in a
war now nearly won.

GRACIE FIELDS

The End of the War in the Far East •

Piva, Bougainville, 16 August 1945

My Dear All

Here we are on the day of celebration – this morning I sang
The Lord's Prayer at thanksgiving service, and it was very impressive.

I've now given five small concerts in five different hospital
wards, and tonight we give a big show to about fifteen thousand – about ten thousand American boys will also be there. My
pianist's young lady is a Gilbert and Sullivan opera singer and she
does her bit, also a squeeze-box hurdy-gurdy boy to play a few
tunes, and a man singer, and we do the old servant sketch when
and where it's possible.

It's dreadfully sticky hot, it is all jungle and so different to all
the other theatres of war I've sung in. You can just imagine what
the poor lads have gone through and it's usually raining, something awful sometimes, easily six inches of rain. We are lucky, it's
fine for us today, they say it rains every afternoon. The boys are
so very happy it's all over, they're all shouting HTM – Home to
Mom, boys!

CHAPTER SIXTEEN

The End of the War

Although the Allies won the war, the atom bombs dropped on Hiroshima and Nagasaki, and the evidence of the Holocaust, cast long shadows over their victory. At home, in what Mollie Panter-Downes called 'this island of tired people', many women who had kept going during the six years of war now found themselves suffering from exhaustion. Frances Partridge's friend Julia Strachey wrote to her in May 1945 that 'the dynamic principle has given way and one feels like a printed page, a sheet of newspaper or a pressed dried grass'. More prosaically, Sylvia Townsend Warner wrote at the beginning of 1946, 'No one feels well or happy just now.'

This was a time of return, readjustment, rehabilitation. Nurses and welfare workers worked with survivors from the concentration camps, and helped returning prisoners of war on their journey back home. Women working in factories and forces alike faced the prospect of demobilization, sometimes with relief and sometimes with no enthusiasm at all. For some though, the future offered an exciting new world: seventy thousand GI brides set sail for America.

Women were strongly represented among the journalists, observers and war artists who entered Germany and German-occupied countries at the end of the war. The shock was intense. 'I remember every detail of Dachau,' wrote Martha Gellhorn years later, 'and probably will as long as I live.' Recording what they saw forced a particular sort of attention, a slowing of the narrative to an appalled standstill. At the War Crimes Trials in Nuremberg too, women recognized that they were witnesses to a devastating history.

MOLLIE PANTER-DOWNES

The Power of Photography

29 April 1945

If the San Francisco Conference is the big worry of the moment, the big sensation, which also has to do with the future, because it brings up the subject of our treatment of the conquered, is the revelation of the horrors of the German concentration camps. It has taken the camera to bring home to the slow, good-natured, skeptical British what, as various liberal journals have tartly pointed out, the pens of their correspondents have been unsuccessfully trying to bring home to them since as far back as 1933. Millions of comfortable families, too kind and too lazy in those days to make the effort to believe what they conveniently looked upon as a newspaper propaganda stunt, now believe the horrifying, irrefutable evidence that even blurred printing on poor war-time paper has made all too clear. There are long queues of people waiting silently wherever the photographs are on exhibition. The shock to the public has been enormous, and lots of hitherto moderate people are wondering uncomfortably whether they will agree, after all, with Lord Vansittart's ruthless views on a hard peace. While the violent revulsion has not produced any particularly helpful answers to the question of what is to be done with the Germans, it has suggested one or two things that might not be done with them. Plenty of angry Englishmen would like to know that German prisoners of war here would no longer draw double the rations a civilian gets. After photographs of Buchenwald's walking skeletons, Britons were understandably incensed by the thought of Nazis growing plump in English prison camps. If, as some people think, the sudden piling on of the horrors is an attempt to prepare the British and American publics for the stiff terms Moscow seems determined to impose on Germany, it has certainly succeeded here. Whatever the Russians ask, it will not be enough to wipe Buchenwald and the rest from shocked British minds.

MARTHA GELLHORN

Dachau

May 1945

We came out of Germany in a C–47 carrying American prisoners of war. The planes were lined up on the grass field at Regensburg and the passengers waited, sitting in the shade under the wings. They would not leave the planes; this was a trip no one was going to miss. When the crew chief said all aboard, we got in as if we were escaping from a fire. No one looked out the windows as we flew over Germany. No one ever wanted to see Germany again. They turned away from it, with hatred and sickness. At first they did not talk, but when it became real that Germany was behind forever they began talking of their prisons. We did not comment on the Germans; they are past words, there is nothing to say. 'No one will believe us,' a soldier said. They agreed on that; no one would believe them.

'Where were you captured, miss?' a soldier asked.

'I'm only bumming a ride; I've been down to see Dachau.'

One of the men said suddenly, 'We got to talk about it. We got to talk about it, if anyone believes us or not.'

Behind the barbed wire and the electric fence, the skeletons sat in the sun and searched themselves for lice. They have no age and no faces; they all look alike and like nothing you will ever see if you are lucky. We crossed the wide, crowded, dusty compound between the prison barracks and went to the hospital. In the hall sat more of the skeletons, and from them came the smell of disease and death. They watched us but did not move; no expression shows on a face that is only yellowish, stubbly skin, stretched across bone. What had been a man dragged himself into the doctor's office; he was a Pole and he was about six feet tall and he weighed less than a hundred pounds and he wore a striped prison shirt, a pair of unlaced boots, and a blanket which he tried to hold around his legs. His eyes were large and strange and stood out from his face, and his jawbone seemed to be cutting through his skin. He had come to Dachau from Buchenwald on the last death transport. There were fifty boxcars of his dead travelling companions still on the siding outside the camp, and for the last three days the American Army had forced Dachau civilians to bury these dead. When this transport had arrived, the German guards locked the men, women and children in the boxcars and there they slowly died of hunger and thirst and suffocation. They screamed and they tried to fight their way out; from time to time, the guards fired into the cars to stop the noise.

This man had survived; he was found under a pile of dead. Now he stood on the bones that were his legs and talked and suddenly he wept. 'Everyone is dead,' he said, and the face that was not a face twisted with pain or sorrow or horror. 'No one is left. Everyone is dead. I cannot help myself. Here I am and I am finished and cannot help myself. Everyone is dead.'

The Polish doctor who had been a prisoner here for five years said, 'In four weeks, you will be a young man again. You will be fine.'

Perhaps his body will live and take strength, but one cannot believe that his eyes will ever be like other people's eyes.

The doctor spoke with great detachment about the things he had watched in this hospital. He had watched them and there was nothing he could do to stop them. The prisoners talked in the same way – quietly, with a strange little smile as if they apologized for talking of such loathsome things to someone who lived in a real world and could hardly be expected to understand Dachau.

'The Germans made here some unusual experiments,' the doctor said. 'They wished to see how long an aviator could go without oxygen, how high in the sky he could go. So they had a closed car from which they pumped the oxygen. It is a quick death,' he said. 'It does not take more than fifteen minutes, but it is a hard death. They killed not so many people, only eight hundred in that experiment. It was found that no one can live above thirty-six thousand feet altitude without oxygen.'

'Whom did they choose for this experiment?' I asked.

'Any prisoner,' he said, 'so long as he was healthy. They picked the strongest. The mortality was one hundred per cent, of course.'

'It is very interesting, is it not?' said another Polish doctor.

We did not look at each other. I do not know how to explain it, but aside from the terrible anger you feel, you are ashamed. You are ashamed for mankind.

'There was also the experiment of the water,' said the first doctor. 'This was to see how long pilots could survive when they were shot down over water, like the Channel, let us say. For that, the German doctors put the prisoners in great vats and they stood in water up to their necks. It was found that the human body can resist for two and a half hours in water eight degrees below zero. They killed six hundred people in this experiment. Sometimes a man had to suffer three times, for he fainted early in the experiment, and then he was revived and a few days later the experiment was again undertaken.'

'Didn't they scream, didn't they cry out?'

He smiled at that question. 'There was no use in this place for a man to scream or cry out. It was no use for any man ever.'

A colleague of the Polish doctor came in; he was the one who knew about the malaria experiments. The German doctor, who was chief of the Army's tropical medicine research, used Dachau as an experimental station. He was attempting to find a way to immunize German soldiers against malaria. To that end, he inoculated eleven thousand prisoners with tertiary malaria. The death rate from the malaria was not too heavy; it simply meant that these prisoners, weakened by fever, died more quickly afterward from hunger. However, in one day three men died of overdoses of Pyramidon, with which, for some unknown reason, the Germans were then experimenting. No immunization for malaria was ever found.

Down the hall, in the surgery, the Polish surgeon got out the record book to look up some data on operations performed by the SS doctors. These were castration and sterilization operations. The prisoner was forced to sign a paper beforehand, saying that he willingly understood this self-destruction. Jews and gypsies were castrated; any foreign slave laborer who had had relations with a German woman was sterilized. The German women were sent to other concentration camps.

The Polish surgeon had only his four front upper teeth left, the others on both sides having been knocked out by a guard one day, because the guard felt like breaking teeth. This act did not seem a matter of surprise to the doctor or to anyone else. No brutality could surprise them any more. They were used to a systematic cruelty that had gone on, in this concentration camp, for twelve years.

The surgeon mentioned another experiment, really a very bad one, he said, and obviously quite useless. The guinea pigs were Polish priests. (Over two thousand priests passed through

Dachau; one thousand are alive.) The German doctors injected streptococci germs in the upper leg of the prisoners, between the muscle and the bone. An extensive abscess formed, accompanied by fever and extreme pain. The Polish doctor knew of more than a hundred cases treated in this way; there may have been more. He had a record of thirty-one deaths, but it took usually from two to three months of ceaseless pain before the patient died, and all of them died after several operations performed during the last few days of their life. The operations were a further experiment, to see if a dying man could be saved; but the answer was that he could not. Some prisoners recovered entirely, but there were others who were now moving around the camp, as best they could, crippled for life.

Then, because I could listen to no more, my guide, a German Socialist who had been a prisoner in Dachau for ten and a half years, took me across the compound to the jail. In Dachau, if you want to rest from one horror you go and see another. The jail was a long clean building with small white cells in it. Here lived the people whom the prisoners called the NN. NN stands for *Nacht und Nebel*, which means night and mist. Translated into less romantic terms, this means that the prisoners in these cells never saw a human being, were never allowed to speak to anyone, were never taken out into the sun and the air. They lived in solitary confinement on water soup and a slice of bread, which was the camp diet. There was of course the danger of going mad. But one never knew what happened to them in the years of their silence. And on the Friday before the Sunday when the Americans entered Dachau, eight thousand men were removed by the SS on a final death transport. Among these were all the prisoners from the solitary cells. None of these men has been heard of since. Now in the clean empty building a woman, alone in a cell, screamed for a long time on one terrible note, was silent for a moment, and screamed again. She had gone mad in the last few days; we came too late for her.

In Dachau if a prisoner was found with a cigarette butt in his pocket he received twenty-five to fifty lashes with a bull whip. If he failed to stand at attention with his hat off, six feet away from any SS trooper who happened to pass, he had his hands tied behind his back and he was hung by his bound hands from a hook on the wall for an hour. If he did any other little thing which displeased the jailers he was put in the box. The box is the size of a telephone booth. It is so constructed that being in it alone a man cannot sit down, or kneel down, or of course lie down. It was usual to put four men in it together. Here they stood for three days and nights without food or water or any form of sanitation. Afterward they went back to the sixteen-hour day of labor and the diet of water soup and a slice of bread like soft gray cement.

What had killed most of these people was hunger; starvation was simply routine. A man worked those incredible hours on that diet and lived in such overcrowding as cannot be imagined, the bodies packed into airless barracks, and woke each morning weaker, waiting for his death. It is not known how many people died in this camp in the twelve years of its existence, but at least forty-five thousand are known to have died in the last three years. Last February and March, two thousand were killed in the gas chamber because, though they were too weak to work, they did not have the grace to die; so it was arranged for them.

The gas chamber is part of the crematorium. The crematorium is a brick building outside the camp compound, standing in a grove of pine trees. A Polish priest had attached himself to us and as we walked there he said, 'I started to die twice of starvation but I was very lucky. I got a job as a mason when we were building this crematorium, so I received a little more food, and that way I did not die.' Then he said, 'Have you seen our chapel, madame?' I said I had not, and my guide said I could not; it was within the zone where the two thousand typhus cases were more or less isolated. 'It is a pity,' the priest said. 'We finally got a chapel and we had Holy Mass there almost every Sunday. There are very beautiful murals. The man who painted them died of hunger two months ago.'

Now we were at the crematorium. 'You will put a handkerchief over your nose,' the guide said. There, suddenly, but never to be believed, were the bodies of the dead. They were everywhere. There were piles of them inside the oven room, but the SS had not had time to burn them. They were piled outside the door and alongside the building. They were all naked, and behind the crematorium the ragged clothing of the dead was neatly stacked, shirts, jackets, trousers, shoes, awaiting sterilization and further use. The clothing was handled with order, but the bodies were dumped like garbage, rotting in the sun, yellow and nothing but bones, bones grown huge because there was no flesh to cover them, hideous, terrible, agonizing bones, and the unendurable smell of death.

We have all seen a great deal now; we have seen too many wars and too much violent dying; we have seen hospitals, bloody and messy as butcher shops; we have seen the dead like bundles lying on all the roads of half the earth. But nowhere was there anything like this. Nothing about war was ever as insanely wicked as these starved and outraged, naked, nameless dead. Behind one pile of dead lay the clothed healthy bodies of the German soldiers who had been found in this camp. They were shot at once when the American Army entered. And for the first time anywhere one could look at a dead man with gladness.

Just behind the crematorium stood the fine big modern hot-houses. Here the prisoners grew the flowers that the SS officers loved. Next to the hothouses were the vegetable gardens, and very rich ones too, where the starving prisoners cultivated the vitamin foods that kept the SS strong. But if a man, dying of hunger, furtively pulled up and gorged himself on a head of lettuce, he would be beaten until he was unconscious. In front of the crematorium, separated from it by a stretch of garden, stood a long row of well-built, commodious homes. The families of the SS officers lived here; their wives and children lived here quite happily, while the chimneys of the crematorium poured out unending smoke heavy with human ashes.

The American soldier in the plane said, 'We got to talk about it.' You cannot talk about it very well because there is a kind of shock that sets in and makes it almost unbearable to remember what you have seen. I have not talked about the women who were moved to Dachau three weeks ago from their own concentration camps. Their crime was that they were Jewish. There was a lovely girl from Budapest, who somehow was still lovely, and the woman with mad eyes who had watched her sister walk into the gas chamber at Auschwitz and been held back and refused the right to die with her sister, and the Austrian woman who pointed out calmly that they all had only the sleazy dresses they wore on their backs, they had never had anything more, and that they worked outdoors sixteen hours a day too in the long winters, and that they too were 'corrected,' as the Germans say, for any offense, real or imaginary.

I have not talked about how it was the day the American Army arrived, though the prisoners told me. In their joy to be free, and longing to see their friends who had come at last, many prisoners rushed to the fence and died electrocuted. There were those who died cheering, because that effort of happiness was more than their bodies could endure. There were those who died because now they had food, and they ate before they could be stopped, and it killed them. I do not know words to describe the men who have survived this horror for years, three years, five years, ten years, and whose minds are as clear and unafraid as the day they entered.

I was in Dachau when the German armies surrendered unconditionally to the Allies. The same half-naked skeleton who had been dug out of the death train shuffled back into the doctor's office. He said something in Polish; his voice was no stronger than a whisper. The Polish doctor clapped his hands gently and said, 'Bravo.' I asked what they were talking about.

'The war is over,' the doctor said. 'Germany is defeated.'

We sat in that room, in that accursed cemetery prison, and no one had anything more to say. Still, Dachau seemed to me the most suitable place in Europe to hear the news of victory. For surely this war was made to abolish Dachau, and all the other places like Dachau, and everything that Dachau stood for, and to abolish it forever.

MAVIS TATE MP

More on Buchenwald

May 1945

Millions of people will in the last few days have seen films of the German internment camps at Buchenwald and Belsen. They will think they have gained some impression of the conditions under which thousands of people died who had committed no crime and faced no trial. After having studied every available photograph and been to all the films on what are now known as the 'horror camps', I can say without any hesitation whatever that they give but a very faint impression of the reality. [...] Photographs, if they shock one, shock through the eyes; one is not shocked through any other sense. In fact, while it is possible to photograph some of the results of suffering, there are no means by which suffering itself can be photographed. [. . .]

The so-called children in the camp present a tremendous problem. They speak with utter calm of having seen their relations shot or removed to be put into a gas-chamber. They have many of them lived their most formative years knowing only cruelty, squalor and want in its extreme forms, and they give the impression – and none can wonder at it – of callousness and of lack of interest in anything beyond personal preservation. Those who have survived are tough, and will be unlikely to prove a centre of stability or of kindliness wherever they settle. They should be under care and guidance of a high order for a time and not let loose lonely and stateless in a distraught Europe.

Some German civilians from Weimar were visiting the camp when we were there, but one woman only did I see who appeared genuinely upset. When I said to her, 'Well you have behaved in a wonderful way under Hitler, have you not?' she burst into tears and said, 'I am ashamed of being a German.' The citizens of Weimar in the main looked anything but cowed. They have never been bombed – their land has been cultivated to the last inch with the help of slave labour, and they look well-fed, truculent and aggressive. I repeatedly said to my fellow delegates that I was deeply shocked by the faces of many of the German women in Weimar. They were cruel and hard beyond belief, and I had seen none like them anywhere – until I looked at the photographs of the women guards of Belsen camp.

MARY KESSELL

German Diary by a War Artist

August–October 1945
Berlin
Berlin smells of death. Incredible, like a million-year-old ruin, so silent that crickets sing and one can hear them, with pale figures creeping around cutting trees, hidden in dark. Pools of water, pale in moonlight, and white ruins like great teeth bared. Oh, unforgettable smell of thousands of dead. Burnt-out cars and

tanks in the gutters, and mile on mile on mile where no one lives or can ever live again, just smelling, and there the cricket sings.

Across a desert of sand and fossilised trees to the Reichstag. A noble grey-green ruin, splintered by battle, the last stand in Berlin. Ruins so vast surrounding it that it seemed as if it had been there for decades, and such stillness. One American soldier was reading or looking at the Russian names chalked and painted everywhere. Great candelabras strewed the floor of the Banqueting Hall, and things flapped from bits of wire and made fluttering noises. It was as silent as the grave. We walked through miles of beautiful ruins, and I decided that this must be my first painting. At the door as we left was an old woman with a dirty piece of rag. She asked us to let her wipe the dust from our shoes, but somehow we couldn't let her do it.

Then on to the Chancellery. This is in the Russian zone. Russians are racing up and down in looted cars, using hooters all the time, like children. The noise is terrific. There is a notice outside the Chancellery. 'Open on Sundays only, 2–4.' A grimy looking policeman is sitting on an old sofa outside. We just walk past him. He gets off and salutes us and in we go. Dear God, if only all the world could see this. It's vast, endless. Here is where all the plans were made, huge filing cabinets unhinged, papers like snow to walk upon. Chairs with all the stuffing gone tipped up on steps. Paper everywhere. A Russian soldier came out wiping his lips. In a minute a German woman left, and went the other way. The paper serves as a bed: the price, a cigarette or some sugar candy. The Chancellery a brothel, run by nobody, but everybody goes there. I helped myself to notepaper and envelopes from the room upstairs, in which were hundreds of torn mutilated photographs of Hitler.

LAURA KNIGHT

From My Nuremberg Diary

On the 5th January, 1946, I was sent there [to the Nuremberg War Trials] by the War Office to do British Government war records. [. . .]

Several of the defendants have now become aware that I am picturing them; Hess again looked up at me with his mad stare. The blacks of his deep set eyes are so big that they don't show any of the white eye-ball.

Sometimes, for a rest from my own work, I put my drawing materials down and hold the earphones to my ears. In my opinion, Maxwell Fyfe is outstanding in the masterly composition of his matter; few of the other prosecutors possess his clarity. Again and again, the theatre comes to mind: 'good lines', 'bad lines', 'good diction', 'bad diction'.

Aloof as I am, alone at work in my box – not a participant in what is taking place – I need to remind myself that the drama being enacted before me does not belong to the theatrical stage, that the performing cast in the dock do not put all matter aside at the drop of the curtain, go straight to their dressing rooms and take off their make-up. At the close of still another day's session, again I peered through that slit of a window in the steel-bound door and watched the prisoners, each with a US army Snowdrop between him and the next, despairingly mount the wire-netted stairway to their cells.

I have again had an interrupted day's work. I only have the use of my box by the grace of the people who own it, a USA broadcasting company. The US press and photographers often come into focus, and click their cameras at me. Once I was a perfect picture of a German sausage, my fur coat covered with a travelling rug wound round from head to foot with rope. The outer door, leading to an unheated passage-way, had lost its handle and the thermometer was way below zero.

While working this morning I become aware of tension in court; you don't need headphones to know when something damning is taking place. Documentary evidence is produced of Doenitz having given orders to German submarine officers to annihilate ships and crews. He had actually written this in his diary – and the extraordinary thing was that he looks as ordinary as any other man you would meet in the streets.

The clock strikes eleven and, as on any other morning, the prisoners munch biscuits, stand and bend their stiffened joints, discuss points in question with the calm of actors at rehearsal. A Snowdrop, in enmity as frigid as a block of ice, pours out a drink of water for von Papen, who has to lean over the barrier to reach it.

Eleven-fifteen: the judges return, everyone resumes their seats, the Snowdrops line up again behind their prisoners. Today, as the hours pass monotonously by, one of the Snowdrops faints – passes right out, to fall without bending a joint against the wainscoating behind – and, stiff as a log of wood, is carried out.

The smell of peppermint chewing-gum prevails. All is today as it will be tomorrow, and the day after that: Snowdrops on duty everywhere, even under the bare rafters in the passage-way outside my box; icy draughts. [. . .] home-sick? . . . yah! Texas? . . . California? They long for sympathy, for someone to talk to and to look at their snaps of wives, mothers and children, carried in their breast-pockets. I haven't the heart to tell them that I can't concentrate on my work and talk as well.

REBECCA WEST

Nuremberg

The Germans listened to the closing speeches made by Mr Justice Jackson and Sir Hartley Shawcross, and were openly shamed by their new-minted indignation. When Mr Justice Jackson brought his speech to an end by pointing a forefinger at each of the defendants in turn and denounced his specific share in the Nazi crime, all of them winced, except old Streicher, who munched and mumbled away in some private and probably extremely objectionable dream, and Schacht, who became stiffer than ever, stiff as an iron stag in the garden of an old house. It was not surprising that all the rest were abashed, for the speech showed the civilized good sense against which they had conspired, and it was patently admirable, patently a pattern of the material necessary to the salvation of peoples. It is to be regretted that one phrase in it may be read by posterity as falling beneath the level of its context, because it has a particular significance to all those who attended the Nuremberg trial. 'Goering,' said Mr Justice Jackson, 'stuck a pudgy finger in every pie.' The courtroom was not small, but it was full of Goering's fingers. His soft and white and spongy hands were for ever smoothing his curiously abundant brown hair, or covering his wide mouth while his plotting eyes looked facetiously around, or weaving impudent gestures of innocence in the air. The other men in the dock broke into sudden and relieved laughter at the phrase. Goering was plainly angered, though less by the phrase than by their laughter.

But the next day, when Sir Hartley Shawcross closed the British case, there was no laughter at all. His speech was not so shapely and so decorative as Mr Justice Jackson's, for English rhetoric has crossed the Atlantic in this century and is now more at home in the United States than on its native ground, and he spoke at greater length and stopped more legal holes. But his words were full of a living pity, which gave the men in the box their worst hour. The feminine Shirach achieved a gesture that was touching. He listened attentively to what Sir Hartley had to say of his activities as a Youth Leader; and when he heard him go on to speak of his responsibility for the deportation of forty thousand Soviet children he put up his delicate hand and lifted off the circlet of his headphones, laying it down very quietly on the ledge before him. It seemed possible that he had indeed the soul of a governess, that he was indeed Jane Eyre, and had been perverted by a Mr Rochester who, disappearing into self-kindled flames, had left him disenchanted and the prey of a prim but inextinguishable remorse. And when Sir Hartley quoted the deposition of a witness who had described a Jewish father who, standing with his little son in front of a firing squad, 'pointed to the sky, stroked his head, and seemed to explain something to the boy', all the defendants wriggled on their seats, like children rated by a schoolmaster, while their faces grew old.

MARY TREVELYAN

Prisoners of War

Belgium, April 1945
The Canteen has become the central meeting-place for everybody, officers and men alike, which is just as it should be. There are always long queues at the counters for tea, buns, sweets, cigarettes and, greatest luxury of all, chopped-up pieces of chocolate. And, not least in demand, liver salts, which are the quickest way of doing something to recover from eating again. The Canteen is never empty. Most of the green arm-chairs in the far corner,

where it is a little quieter, are filled with sleeping men, their heads thrown back in complete exhaustion and their faces, when asleep, showing a grim picture of their past sufferings. Some are absorbed in magazines and newspapers, trying to catch up with the world. The writing-tables are always occupied. Some are scribbling away for dear life, pouring out pent-up excitement and emotion. Others sit, pen in hand, unable to find words, staring at the sheet of paper, putting down a few words, then throwing the paper away. There are always some noisy, cheerful groups, exchanging experiences or making plans for the future. But many just sit silent, staring into space, nibbling a bun, sipping a little tea, then getting up restlessly and going to another table.

We have tried all sorts of entertainment, for many of them ask if there is a show in the evening, but we find they are not yet in a state to take in anything. Community singing is no good, co-medians are much too quick for them to take in, singers they like, but do not bother to applaud. So, after trial and error, we have now arranged for a series of small dance-bands who play morning and evening in the Canteen and a military band which plays in the barrack square in the afternoons. They just need a little music going on, old tunes of five years ago are best, and they hum and whistle a bit.

THEODORA FITZGIBBON

GI Bride

From the moment the Embassy sent me four labels, three for my luggage and one to tie on the lapel of my coat, with a covering letter enclosing my 'orders', everything promised to be unusual. I had become that unlikely person for me, a 'GI bride'. [. . .]

I arrived at Waterloo Station, labelled and with my luggage, on 14 March 1946. My grandmother had pressed five pounds into my hand and a bottle of whisky for the journey. A porter said to me: 'You a bride, miss?' which rather amused me as I had at that time been married for two years. He led me to a special train which was to take us all, not to the boat, but to an army camp at Tidworth on Salisbury Plain. I settled in the first compartment I came to, and watched the leave-takings of the other 'brides'. One fond mother produced a hot-water bottle which was disdainfully handed back with the message that 'where I'm going to everything's properly heated'. I wondered if it was.

The unheated train rattled slowly through the London suburbs. In Middlesex the first sign of fields appeared and I noticed a rather pretty farmhouse in the middle of a field, the small town about a mile away to the left. My reverie was disturbed by a dark girl, well wrapped in a travelling rug, sitting opposite me.

'My, I wouldn't like to live in that isolated spot,' she said in a very false American accent. I asked her where she was going to in America.

'Montana,' she replied calmly. I hadn't the heart to disillusion her.

It was dark when we arrived at Tidworth Camp. We were helped out of the bus by shadowy male figures. I heard the girl in front of me say, 'Thank you,' but as she came into the lamplight she wheeled round to me and cried:

'My mother would be furious with me if she knew I'd said thank you to a German.'

I saw then that our assistants were German prisoners. From then on the German prisoners looked after us entirely. In the bare room I shared with sixteen other 'brides', Fritz or Hans stood while we made our beds and commiserated with us for the dust on the bare wooden boards. They cooked for us and served the food into our tin trays. We were frequently told over loudspeakers that we mustn't fraternize with them. My limited knowledge of German was a great nuisance as I found myself let in for many things. In this barrack room was a central oldfashioned coke stove around which we huddled in the evenings. I shared Grandmother's whisky with a chosen few.

It was all nightmarish. The beds were as hard as boards, the food uneatable, there were two baths only in an outhouse between two hundred of us. Also the American Army's passion for youth was a bit overwhelming: only one other girl apart from myself was in her middle twenties, all the others were teenagers, with the exception of one rather jolly old lady of about fifty, whom I took to be a relic of 1918.

We were not allowed out of the perimeter at all, and the Red Cross 'rest' room was built to hold about a quarter of us. The two public telephones it housed were besieged at all hours by long queues of girls shouting inanities like 'and we had tinned peaches for dinner' down the mouthpiece. Most of the time you couldn't get through, and if you did you couldn't hear what was said at the other end because of the noise in the 'rest' room. . .

During the ten-day voyage I became an information bureau. Because I had been to America before I was expected to know in detail about all the cities and towns of every state. They seldom got my name right. Usually I was called Bedelia after the heroine of a current film; they knew it was long and ended with an 'a', that was all. I used to wonder and worry a little as to how some of them would make out, they had such odd ideas of what they were going to. One very pretty Welsh girl would spend long hours on her bunk gazing at her husband's photograph, which I thought omened well, until she confided that she had always hated tall men and her husband was six feet five inches. She wondered whether *it* was worth it; *it* being that she loved her busy home port of Cardiff and she was going to a box number in Iowa. There were large notices over the ship saying: *Orientation Meetings*, with an arrow afterwards. The lieutenant in charge of the meetings told me of the poor attendances. I inquired among the girls and found that most of them thought that if they went to the meetings they would come out resembling Geisha girls.

JANE GORDON

The End of the Black-Out

Nothing appeared to have changed, and I think we were still half consciously listening for an alert or the sound of a flying bomb or a rocket. Then one afternoon when we had finished extracting teeth in the operating theatre, I was cleaning the dental instruments in casualty and overhead on the roof workmen were moving about. I paid no particular attention until suddenly the tarpaulin was pulled off the glass part of our roof and the whole of casualty was flooded with sunshine. After so many years of darkness the effect of this unexpected daylight was like a miracle. Sister had just walked into casualty and I turned towards her. For a long moment she stood looking upwards at the sunlight streaming through the window – then her eyes met mine and her face wore the strangest expression.

CLARA MILBURN

The Return of a Prisoner-of-War Son

Wednesday 9th May 1945
A Day of Days!

This morning at 9.15 the telephone rang and a voice said: 'I've got a very nice telegram for you. You are Milburn, Burleigh, Balsall Common 29?'

'Yes,' I said.

The voice said: 'This is the telegram. "Arrived safely. Coming soon. Alan".'

I nearly leapt to the ceiling and rushed to the bottom of the stairs. 'We've got the right telegram at last!' I cried.

And then all three of us, Jack in bed, Kate nearby and myself all choky, shed a tear or two. We were living again, after five-and-a-half years!

At 11.15 a.m. the telephone rang again and it was a long-distance call. 'Is that Burleigh, Balsall Common?'

'Yes! Is that Alan?' I said.

'Yes.'

And then I said: 'Oh, bless you, my darling.' And off went Alan into a description of his leaving Germany and arriving here, ending by saying he might arrive late tonight or early tomorrow and would ring up again later, and so we said 'Goodbye'.

I wrote 19 postcards and one letter, had three or four long-distance telephone calls and about two dozen others during the day. I made two long-distance calls, and when I asked for a third the operator said: 'You're keeping me busy.'

'Yes,' I said, 'this is a thrilling day.'

'Something special?'

'Yes, my son has arrived in England after five years as a prisoner of war.'

'Exeter,' said the operator's voice, and then to me: 'Was he in Germany?'

'Yes.'

'He'll be glad to get home – there you are, call out, please. They're waiting.'

Such mateyness, it is amusing.

CONSTANCE GODDARD

The Whirlwind of War

1945

I sat up late that night for I could not have slept. My mind was running round in circles. I remembered the day war was declared, the day we worked in the hayfield on a Sunday and the whirlwind caught up the hay and carried it far and wide.

The whirlwind of war had caught up all our lives and tossed them into the air, they had been swept to and fro by eddying currents and dropped again in the same field. But was it the same field? The old landmarks had disappeared and the new ones were not yet clearly defined.

NOTES ON THE AUTHORS

MARGERY ALLINGHAM (1901–1966), detective novelist, helped organise evacuation and billeting in her Essex village, Tolleshunt D'Arcy. She wrote *The Oaken Heart* (1941) about her village in wartime for her American publisher, but it was more popular in England.

VERILY ANDERSON (b. 1915), writer, joined FANYs soon after Munich. She left a year into the war to marry and bring up a family, and lived in London during the blitz.

JOAN BRIGHT ASTLEY (b. 1910) worked as a secretary and joined the War Office in 1939. From 1941 she was responsible for a special information centre in the War Cabinet Offices in London; she was also administrative officer for the British delegation at Teheran, Yalta and Potsdam.

ENID BARRAUD (b. 1904) worked as a landgirl on a farm in East Anglia. After three and a half years she was dismissed, and her job given to Italian POWs.

ELIZABETH BOWEN (1899–1973), Anglo-Irish novelist, lived in London throughout the war. She worked for the Ministry of Information, and at night as an air-raid warden. Her novel *The Heat of the Day* (1949) is about wartime London.

KAY BOYLE (1902–1993), American novelist, poet, editor and translator, lived in the French Alps with her family until 1941, and helped Jews wanting to acquire US visas. On her return to America she worked for the war effort and wrote about conditions in Europe.

VERA BRITTAIN (1893–1970), writer and pacifist, worked tirelessly for pacifism during the war, lecturing and publishing, including her *Letters to Peace-Lovers*. Her 1944 pamphlet *Seed of Chaos* was almost the only public protest against the obliteration bombing of German cities.

MARY BROOKES (b. 1918) married a merchant seaman in October 1939. He was reported 'missing, believed killed' in November 1940. In 1943 she was conscripted into the ATS, where she served in a clerical capacity.

BRYHER (Annie Winifred Ellerman, 1894–1983), novelist, poet and patron of the arts, came to London from Switzerland in 1940. She shared a flat in Lowndes Square with the Imagist poet H.D. (Hilda Doolittle). Her novel *Beowulf* (1956) is set in wartime London.

MAVIS BUNYAN (b. 1923) worked for the Prudential, looked after her small daughter, and took a job as a bus conductress. She and her husband celebrated their golden wedding in 1992.

BARBARA CARTLAND (b. 1901), best-selling romantic novelist, involved herself in a huge variety of charity and welfare work. She was Lady Welfare Officer and Librarian to all services in Bedfordshire.

PHYLLIS CASTLE (b. 1909) worked for the BBC, joined the WAAFs but was deemed unsuitable; she then joined the Women's Land Army.

LENA K. CHIVERS, biographical information unobtainable.

CLEMENTINE CHURCHILL (1885–1977), married to the Prime Minister Winston Churchill, raised nearly seven million pounds for her Aid to Russia Fund. She went to Russia on a goodwill visit in April 1945.

DIANA COOPER (1892–1986), married to Duff Cooper, head of the Ministry of Information, helped in a YMCA canteen and became a keen dairy farmer in Sussex. She travelled with her husband, then Chancellor of the Duchy of Lancaster, on his missions to Asia, Australia and Algiers.

VIRGINIA COWLES (1910–1983), American journalist and war correspondent, reported for the *Sunday Times* on the war in Finland, Russia, Germany, Poland, Czechoslovakia, Paris and North Africa. She witnessed the entry of the German Army into Czechoslovakia, got arrested by the Gestapo and had to argue her way out.

MARGARET CRISP took up nursing in 1942, on hearing of the big allied raids over Cologne and Essen, and feeling that she wanted to 'help mend the ravages of war'.

AUDREY DEACON (b. 1917) joined the WRNS in 1939 and was promoted to Acting First Officer, in charge of the Commander-in-Chief's Cypher Office in Plymouth in 1944. She married in April 1943; her husband died in June 1944.

MARY DE BUNSEN (1910–1982) joined the Auxiliary Fire Service when war broke out, but left to test-fly Tiger Moth planes. She then joined the Air Transport Auxiliary, ferrying planes round the country.

E.M. DELAFIELD (Edmée Elizabeth Monica de la Pasture, 1890–1943), novelist and short story writer, lived in Devon during the war and lectured for the Ministry of Information. She was also involved with the work of the Women's Institutes. *The Provincial Lady in Wartime* (1940) is set in London in the first three months of the war.

SYBIL DOBBIE (1908–1973) did intelligence work before and during the war. She joined her parents on the besieged island of Malta, where her father was Governor, and worked as his private secretary.

BLANCHE E.C. DUGDALE (1880–1948) worked throughout the war at the Jewish Agency and Zionist Federation headquarters in London, and was the Zionist movement's principal liaison with the British Cabinet.

ELIZABETH, PRINCESS (b. 1926) persuaded her parents to allow her to train as a driver in the ATS. She learned to drive and maintain staff cars, lorries and ambulances.

ELIZABETH, QUEEN (b. 1900) refused to leave London during the blitz, even though Buckingham Palace was hit by bombs. She toured bombed-out areas in London and other cities, giving comfort to many.

GRACIE FIELDS (1898–1979), popular singer and comedienne, went to America at the beginning of the war with her husband, who would have been interned because of his Italian background. She raised huge sums in America for the British war effort, and toured widely entertaining British troops.

THEODORA FITZGIBBON (1916–1991), model, actress and cookery writer, left Paris in 1940 just ahead of the advancing Germans. She bicycled to Bordeaux on her own and caught one of the last boats back to England.

CELIA FREMLIN (b. 1914), crime writer, worked for Mass Observation, first as a volunteer and then full-time. Called up in 1942, she was sent to a factory where she disguised her note-taking for Mass Observation as letter-writing.

BELLA FROMM, German diplomatic columnist on a Berlin newspaper, emigrated to New York in 1938. There she worked as a glovemaker, cook, waitress and typist. The Gestapo followed her to New York and she had the protection of two US bodyguards.

BERTA GEISSMAR (b. 1892), German Jewish musicologist and personal assistant to the conductor Wilhelm Furtwangler. Forced to leave Germany in 1938, she was befriended by Sir Thomas Beecham and worked with the London Philharmonic Orchestra.

MARTHA GELLHORN (b. 1908), distinguished American war correspondent and novelist, wrote for the American magazine *Collier's* during the war. She travelled widely and reported from Finland, China, England, Italy, France and Germany.

CONSTANCE FELICITY GODDARD ran a farm single-handedly in the Dales, where she took in an assortment of evacuees and helpers.

RUMER GODDEN (b. 1907), novelist, children's writer and poet, struggled to provide a home for herself and her two young daughters in a remote part of India. She trained as an Auxiliary nurse in case the war should reach India.

MARGARET GOLDSMITH (b. 1894 or 1897), American journalist, biographer and novelist, settled in Berlin then moved to London, where she worked as a literary agent.

JANE GORDON was a nurse in a children's hospital in Paddington. She was married to the writer Charles Graves.

JOYCE GRENFELL (1910–1979), writer, singer and entertainer, worked for ENSA. She and her accompanist Viola Tunnard toured military hospitals in the Mediterranean, the Middle East and India.

CHARLOTTE HALDANE (d. 1969), journalist, was employed by the *Daily Sketch* to visit Moscow and report on the Soviet Union at war. She subsequently broke with the Communist Party.

MRS ROBERT HENREY (Madeleine, b. 1906), columnist, novelist and short story writer, published a series of autobiographical accounts of her life in wartime London, including *A Village in Piccadilly* (1943) and *The Incredible City* (1944).

VERE HODGSON, welfare worker, was attached to a philanthropic and religious community in Holland Park, London. She worked at a night shelter for homeless women in Lambeth, and with families in Notting Hill. She wrote her diary when on fire-watch.

INEZ HOLDEN, documentary journalist and writer, had a variety of wartime jobs in aircraft and Royal Ordnance factories, Civil Defence and the Red Cross. She was sent to report on the Nuremberg trials.

DIANA HOPKINSON (b. 1912) worked for the Czech Refugee Trust. She married in 1939 and had a son; her husband was abroad in the Army for three years.

ELSPETH HUXLEY (b. 1907), novelist, biographer and travel writer, worked for the BBC during the war. Starting in the news talks section (short morale-boosting talks after the news), she then became liaison officer with the Colonial Office, passing on and presenting news about the war efforts in remote cut-off colonies.

E. DOREEN IDLE, researched wartime conditions in West Ham on behalf of the Fabian Society and the Ethical Union. West Ham was particularly badly hit during the air raids on the London docks in September 1940.

STORM JAMESON (1891–1986), novelist, essayist and fervent anti-Fascist, was President of the English branch of PEN during the war, and worked vigorously on behalf of refugee writers. The name she used for her autobiography, Mary Hervey Russell, is adapted from her series of novels *The Mirror in Darkness*.

F. TENNYSON JESSE (1889–1958), novelist, playwright and criminologist, lived in St John's Wood, London, and collected the letters that she and her husband wrote to friends in America into two books.

SHIRLEY JOSEPH volunteered for the Land Army 'for the sake of the experience' and stayed for a year.

ZELMA KATIN (b. around 1900) married at twenty-two and could not find work for the next eighteen years, until she was called up for war work. She worked on the trams in Sheffield, earning the nickname 'The Red Conductress' for her socialist views.

MARGARET KENNEDY (1896–1967), novelist, took her three children to a Cornish village for the war, but travelled back and forth to London to visit her husband. Their home was destroyed by a bomb.

MARY KESSELL (b. 1914), painter, mural decorator and illustrator, worked in Germany in 1945 as an official war artist.

FLAVIA KINGSCOTE was interned in Tuscany, Italy, during the spring and early summer of 1941, before being sent back to England.

RACHEL KNAPPETT worked as a landgirl in South West Lancashire.

LAURA KNIGHT (1877–1970), artist, was frequently commissioned by the War Artists Advisory Committee, often for portraits of women military medallists or for pictures of women doing war work on balloon sites and in factories. The picture she was commissioned to paint of the Nuremberg trials is in the Imperial War Museum, London.

MARGARET LANE (1907–1994), journalist, novelist and biographer, lived in Hampshire during the war.

MARGHANITA LASKI (1915–1988), novelist, journalist and broadcaster, had two children during the war. She also nursed, ran a dairy farm, worked in Intelligence and wrote her first novel.

NELLA LAST (1890–1968), a housewife and mother in the shipbuilding town of Barrow-in-Furness in Lancashire, joined the WVS and worked on mobile canteens. She started writing her diary for Mass Observation in September 1939 and continued for nearly thirty years.

LIVIA LAURENT, poet and translator, came to England from Germany as a girl. She was interned in July 1940, first in Holloway Jail and then on the Isle of Man. She was released in 1941.

ROSAMOND LEHMANN (1901–1990), novelist, translator and short story writer, took her two small children to live with her mother after her marriage failed. She became a reader for her brother John Lehmann, editor of the magazine *New Writing*, and contributed the short stories later collected in *The Gypsy's Baby* (1946).

SYLVIA LEITH-ROSS (1883–1980), expert on Nigeria, joined the British Committee for the French Red Cross and was sent to Paris in December

1939. Back in England she worked with refugees before returning to Nigeria in 1941 to assist the wartime colonial administration.

C.A. LEJEUNE (Caroline, 1897–1973) was film critic for *The Observer* during the war.

LORNA LEWIS drove a van for the Red Cross in France in June 1940. During the blitz she worked in London on a mobile canteen.

ROSE MACAULAY (1881–1958), novelist, travel writer, broadcaster and critic, joined the London Auxiliary Ambulance Service as a part-time driver. Her flat with all her books and papers was destroyed in the blitz; replacement copies of some of her favourite books were sent to her by complete strangers. She spent some of the war in Portugal, researching *They Went to Portugal* (1946).

BRENDA MCBRYDE (b. 1918), a nurse and writer, joined the Queen Alexandra's Imperial Nursing Service Reserve in 1943. She served in the invasion of Normandy in 1944, and subsequently in Belgium, Holland and Germany.

CICELY MCCALL, biographical information unobtainable.

CECILY MACKWORTH fled from Paris as the Germans entered in 1940. She worked for the Red Cross in France, before escaping to England via Spain and Portugal. She joined the Free French at their Headquarters in London, then lectured for the Army Bureau of Current Affairs in factories and hostels.

ETHEL MANNIN (1900–1984), novelist, essayist and pacifist, steadily produced a novel a year during the war. Her criticism of the Soviet Union, which she had visited in 1936, was not well received.

HILDE MARCHANT (1916–1970), star reporter on the *Daily Express*, travelled to France, Poland and Sweden, but specialised in home front reporting. Winston Churchill was so impressed by her report on the Coventry blitz that he asked for copies to be sent to British Embassies worldwide.

VERA LAUGHTON MATHEWS (1888–1959), Director of the WRNS, which she had joined the day it was formed in 1917. It was said she knew every one of her officers.

CLARA MILBURN (1883–1961), housewife and mother from Burleigh near Coventry, filled fifteen exercise books with her daily diary of 'Burleigh in Wartime'. She included letters, telegrams, maps and newspaper cuttings.

BETTY MILLER (1910–1965), novelist and biographer, moved round the country with her two young children and her husband, a major in the RAMC.

NAOMI MITCHISON (b. 1897), novelist, traveller, socialist and feminist, moved to Carradale in the West of Scotland in 1937. Here she farmed and entered closely into the life and work of the community.

LILY MONTAGU (1873–1963), social worker and pioneer in the establishment of Liberal Judaism, ran the West Central Girls' Club in London, and was presiding Magistrate at Chelsea Juvenile Court.

DIANA MOSLEY (b. 1910), married to Oswald Mosley, leader of the British Union of Fascists, was interned in Holloway Jail in 1940, under Defence Regulation 18b which gave the government the right to imprison anyone who was a member of the British Union. In 1941 she was allowed to share a house with her husband in the prison grounds; they were released in 1943.

ANNA NEAGLE (1904–1986), actress, toured Britain and Europe for ENSA. She was famous for her portrayal of wartime heroines.

ANNA NEY (Josephine Pasternak, 1900–1993), Russian poet and philosopher, left Moscow for Berlin in 1921, and moved to Oxford in 1938. The writer Boris Pasternak was her brother, and the painter Leonid her father.

JENNY NICHOLSON served as a Public Relations Officer in the WAAF. She wrote scripts for servicewomen on radio programmes such as the weekly 'Women At War' series, and 'In Town Tonight'.

BARBARA NIXON became an air raid warden in May 1940, and worked through the London blitz. She later became an ARP instructor and lecturer on Civil Defence.

KATE O'BRIEN (1897–1974), Irish novelist and playwright, lived in London during the war. *The Last of Summer* (1940) describes County Clare just before the outbreak of war.

LUCY OLBROMSKA, biographical information unobtainable.

EDITH OLIVIER (1879–1948), novelist and biographer, lived with her sister in the Dairy House at Wilton, Wiltshire. She was mayor of Wilton for several terms.

MOLLIE PANTER-DOWNES (b. 1906), novelist and journalist, wrote her superb fortnightly *Letter from London* for the *New Yorker*, starting in September 1939 and continuing throughout the war. Her novel *One Fine Day* (1946) is about the aftermath of war.

FRANCES PARTRIDGE (b. 1900), diarist, pacifist and member of the Bloomsbury group, spent the war in the country at Ham Spray House in Wiltshire, with her husband Ralph (a conscientious objector), her young son and various guests.

POLLY PEABODY (b. 1917) worked in an ambulance unit for the American Red Cross in Europe. She lived in occupied Paris, then escaped via Spain and Portugal to London, where she worked as a war corres_pondent in the blitz.

MARGERY PERHAM (1895–1982), expert on African affairs and colonial administration, was the first Fellow of Nuffield College Oxford in 1939.

BARBARA PYM (1913–1980), novelist, worked as a postal censor; in 1943 she joined the WRNS and served in England and Italy.

STELLA, DOWAGER MARCHIONESS OF READING (1894–1971), founder and chairman of the WVS (which became the WRVS in 1966), supervised the huge amount of administration involved in the WVS. She also spent much time touring the country to recruit, inspire and encourage individual members.

CONSTANCE REAVELEY, a lecturer in political philosophy, worked in various factories as machine operative, progress chaser and welfare officer.

NESCA ROBB (1906–1976), author and poet, worked in London as a temporary civil servant for the Women's Employment Federation, an employment register for professional women.

PAMELA RUFFONI (Pamela Moore) joined the Land Army in 1943. She was engaged and later married to a conscientious objector born of Italian parents.

DOROTHEA RUSSELL, army welfare worker, opened and ran the Tipperary Club for servicemen in Cairo in 1939. She started 'Music for All' in 1941.

VITA SACKVILLE-WEST (1892–1962), novelist, poet and gardening expert, spent the war at Sissinghurst Castle in Kent. She helped to organize the Women's Land Army in her area.

STELLA ST JOHN, vet and welfare worker, drove an ambulance voluntarily. She refused, however, to be directed compulsorily into war work, and was sent to prison for six weeks in 1943.

CYNTHIA SAUNDERS, biographical information unobtainable.

DOROTHY L. SAYERS (1893–1957), novelist and playwright, broadcast and lectured for the war effort. Between 1940 and 1943 she worked on the controversial but successful *Man Born To Be King*, a twelve-part dramatization of the life of Christ for BBC Children's Hour.

FLORENCE SHARP, biographical information unobtainable.

ETTA SHIBER, an American widow living in Paris, did welfare work with French soldiers. Imprisoned by the Gestapo for providing escape routes for British servicemen, she was exchanged for the German spy Johanna Hofmann.

CONSTANCE BABINGTON SMITH (b. 1912), journalist and biographer, served with the WAAF and specialized in aerial reconnaissance. She started the aircraft interpretation section, vital for intelligence of enemy activity, including the new V weapons.

NAOMI ROYDE SMITH (1875–1964), novelist, biographer, playwright and literary critic, lived in Winchester during the war.

STEVIE SMITH (1902–1971), poet and novelist, was employed full-time as a secretary at Newnes, the publishers. She did much reviewing, as well as fire-watching.

FREYA STARK (1893–1993), traveller and writer, worked as a South Arabia (Middle East) expert for the Ministry of Information. In Egypt she founded the Pro-British Brothers and Sisters of Freedom in order to combat German influence. Besieged in the British embassy in Bahgdad in 1941, she compiled daily news bulletins for the Embassy from foreign radio stations. She also travelled to America and India.

GERTRUDE STEIN (1874–1946), American author, lived with Alice B. Toklas in the French village of Culoz, throughout the German occupation. She returned to her Paris apartment in November 1944.

JAN STRUTHER (Joyce Maxtone Graham, 1901–1953) spent the war years with her children in America, where she lectured extensively for the benefit of British War Relief. Mrs Miniver first appeared on the Court page of *The Times* in a series of sketches of family life.

EDITH SUMMERSKILL (1901–1980), Labour MP, doctor and campaigner on women's issues, served on the 1942 government enquiry into the women's services. In 1945 she was under-secretary at the Ministry of Food.

MAVIS TATE (1893–1947), Conservative MP and champion of women's causes, visited factories to investigate the conditions of women workers. In 1945 she was the only woman in the party of MPs visiting German concentration camps, a visit which affected her deeply.

MARY TREVELYAN, founder and governor of international Students' House London, served on the YMCA Programme Staff with the Army in Belgium 1944–45. She worked on reconstruction surveys in Greece and the East.

EVELYN UNDERHILL (1875–1941), poet and writer on mysticism, joined the Anglican Pacifist Fellowship and wrote an uncompromising pamphlet 'The Church and War' (1940). She believed that 'the Church cannot acquiesce in war'.

HELEN WADDELL (1889–1965), medievalist scholar and poet, lived in London and worked for Constable's, the publisher. She was the assistant editor of the magazine the *Nineteenth Century*.

SYLVIA TOWNSEND WARNER (1893–1978), novelist, spent much of the war in Dorset with Valentine Ackland. She worked for the WVS and did much lecturing for the WEA, the Labour Party and the forces. She also learned rifle-shooting and grenade-throwing.

HILARY WAYNE joined the ATS with her daughter by lying about both their ages. Hilary was fifty-six but said she was forty-two; her daughter Hazel was fifteen but said she was eighteen. They both trained as cooks.

BEATRICE WEBB (1858–1943), socialist and co-founder of the Fabian Society, was living in retirement at Passfield Corner, Liphook. She continued to write her diary until a few days before her death.

MAUREEN WELLS (b. 1921) worked as a billeting officer before volunteering for the WRNS. She joined a small group of Wren couriers, then became a stoker and served at invasion bases in the Portsmouth area.

REBECCA WEST (Cicily Isabel Fairfield, 1892–1983), novelist, essayist, critic and feminist, published *Black Lamb and Grey Falcon* in 1941, a major study of Yugoslavia. She superintended British broadcast talks to Yugoslavia, and went to Nuremberg to cover the war trials.

LESLIE WHATELEY (1899–1987), Director of the ATS 1943–46, battled hard to improve the public image of the ATS and the living conditions of its members.

WINIFRED WILLIAMS contributed a series of articles to *Time and Tide* on wartime life in the industrial north of England.

AMABEL WILLIAMS-ELLIS (1894–1984), author and journalist, married to the architect Clough Williams-Ellis, spent the war in North Wales. She took in evacuees and toured war factories to investigate women's working conditions. Her pamphlet 'Women in War Factories' was used by the Ministry of Information.

MARGERY WITHERS, biographical information unobtainable.

VIRGINIA WOOLF (1882–1941), novelist and critic, published her anti-war *Three Guineas* in 1938. The Woolfs' London house was severely damaged by bombs and they lived mainly at Rodmell near the Sussex coast, often disturbed by enemy planes and bombs.

SUSAN WOOLFITT (1907–1978) worked on narrow-boats for a year. Three-women crews managed pairs of boats, which carried cargo on England's extensive system of canals and waterways.

ESTHER TERRY WRIGHT married an RAF pilot and had to find 'forty different roofs in fourteen months' in order to keep up with him on his frequent postings. He was shot down in September 1940 and badly burnt, but back flying the next year.

Acknowledgements and Sources

My thanks for help in compiling this anthology go especially to all those authors and their relatives who responded so generously and patiently to my requests and queries. I would also like to thank the staff at the London Library, the Roehampton Institute Library and the Imperial War Museum for their help, and Lynn Knight, Cathy Wells Cole and Nick Hartley for their invaluable advice and support.

Permission to reprint copyright material in this book is gratefully acknowledged. Apologies are offered to those copyright-holders whom it has proved impossible to locate.

Her Majesty The Queen: the text of the broadcast originally printed in the *Listener*, 17 October 1940, reprinted by gracious permission of Her Majesty the Queen.

Her Majesty Queen Elizabeth The Queen Mother: the text of the broadcast originally printed in the *Listener*, 14 August 1941, reprinted with the kind agreement of Her Majesty Queen Elizabeth The Queen Mother.

Margery Allingham: extracts from *The Oaken Heart*, copyright © Margery Allingham, Michael Joseph, 1941, reproduced by permission of Curtis Brown Ltd, London, on behalf of P. & M. Youngman Carter Ltd.

Verily Anderson: extracts from *Spam Tomorrow*, Rupert Hart-Davis, 1956, reprinted by permission of the author.

Joan Bright Astley: an extract from *The Inner Circle, A View of War at the Top*, Hutchinson, 1971.

E.M. Barraud: an extract from *Set my Hand upon the Plough*, Littlebury & Co Ltd, The Worcester Press, Worcester, 1945.

Elizabeth Bowen: 'Calico Windows' from *Soho Centenary*, Hutchinson, 1944, and 'London, 1940' from *Collected Impressions*, copyright © Elizabeth Bowen, Longmans, 1950, reprinted by permission of Curtis Brown Ltd, London.

Kay Boyle: an extract from *Primer for Combat*, Faber, 1943.

Vera Brittain: extracts from *England's Hour*, Macmillan, 1941, and from *Seed of Chaos: What Mass Bombing Really Means*, published for the Bombing Restriction Committee by New Vision Publishing Co, April

Gracie Fields: an extract from the Papers of Gracie Fields, Department of Documents, the Imperial War Museum, reprinted by permission of Grace Orbell and the Trustees of the Imperial War Museum.

Theodora FitzGibbon: extracts from *With Love*, Century Publishing, 1982, reprinted by permission of David Higham Associates Ltd.

Celia Fremlin: an extract from *War Factory*, 1943, reprinted by Century Hutchinson, 1987, copyright © the Trustees of the Mass Observation Archive, University of Sussex, reprinted by permission of Curtis Brown Ltd.

Bella Fromm: an extract from 'Blood and Banquets', *Harper's Magazine*, October 1942.

Berta Geissmar: an extract from *The Baton and the Jackboot*, Hamish Hamilton, 1944.

Martha Gellhorn: 'Dachau' from *The Face of War*, Rupert Hart-Davis, 1959, reprinted by permission of Aitken & Stone Ltd.

Constance Goddard: an extract from *Come Wind, Come Weather*, Jonathan Cape, 1945.

Rumer Godden: extract from *Bengal Journey, A Story of the Part Played by Women in the Province 1939–1945*, copyright © Rumer Godden, 1945, published by Longmans, 1945, reprinted by permission of Curtis Brown Ltd, London, on behalf of Rumer Godden.

Margaret Goldsmith: an extract from *Women at War*, Lindsay Drummond, 1943.

Jane Gordon: extracts from *Married to Charles*, William Heinemann Ltd, 1950, reprinted by permission of Reed International.

The Greenhill Knitting Circle: letter printed in *Dear Allies ...*, *A Story of Women in Monklands and Besieged Leningrad* by Margaret Henderson, Monklands District Libraries, 1988, reprinted by permission of Monklands District Council.

Joyce Grenfell: extracts from *The Time of My Life* ed J. Roose-Evans, Hodder & Stoughton, 1989, copyright © Reginald Grenfell and James Roose Evans, reprinted by permission of Richard Scott Simon Ltd.

Charlotte Haldane: extracts from *Truth Will Out*, Weidenfeld & Nicolson, 1949.

Mrs Robert Henrey: an extract from *A Village in Piccadilly*, J.M. Dent & Sons, 1952, reprinted by permission of the author.

Vere Hodgson: extracts from *Few Eggs and No Oranges, A Diary Showing how Unimportant People in London and Birmingham Lived through the War Years 1939–1945*, Dobson Books Ltd, 1976, reprinted by permission of Dobson Books Ltd.

Inez Holden: an extract from *Night Shift*, published by John Lane, The Bodley Head, 1941, and an extract from 'Summer Journal' originally

and Nation, 25 November 1944, reprinted by permission of Cover Stories.

Marghanita Laski: 'Our Auxiliary Women', the *Spectator*, 22 December 1939, reprinted by permission of David Higham Associates.

Nella Last: extracts from *Nella Last's War, A Mother's Diary 1939–1945* eds Richard Broad and Suzie Fleming, Falling Wall Press, Bristol, 1981, reprinted by permission of Falling Wall Press.

Livia Laurent: extracts from *A Tale of Internment*, George Allen & Unwin, 1942.

Rosamond Lehmann: extracts from 'A Charming Person', the *Spectator*, 10 November 1939, reprinted by permission of the Society of Authors as the Literary Representative of the Estate of Rosamond Lehmann.

Sylvia Leith-Ross: an extract from *Cocks in the Dawn*, Hutchinson, 1944.

C.A. Lejeune: extracts from *Chestnuts In Her Lap*, published by Phoenix House Ltd, 1947, reprinted by permission of Carcanet Press Ltd.

Lorna Lewis: extract from 'Food on Wheels', *Time and Tide*, 2 November 1940.

Rose Macaulay: an extract from 'Notes on the Way', *Time and Tide*, 5 October 1940, and 'Consolations of the War', the *Listener*, 16 January 1941, reprinted by permission of the Peters Fraser & Dunlop Group.

Brenda McBryde: extract from *A Nurse's War*, Chatto & Windus, 1979, reprinted by permission of the David Grossmann Literary Agency Ltd on behalf of the author.

Cicely McCall: an extract from *Women's Institutes*, Collins, 1943.

Cecily Mackworth: extracts from *I Came Out Of France*, Routledge, 1941, reprinted by permission of International Thomson Publishing Services.

Ethel Mannin: extracts from *Brief Voices*, Hutchinson, 1959.

Hilde Marchant: extracts from *Women and Children Last*, Gollancz, 1941.

Vera Laughton Mathews: extracts from *Blue Tapestry*, Hollis & Carter, 1948.

Clara Milburn: extracts from *Mrs Milburn's Diaries, An Englishwoman's Day-To-Day Reflections 1939–1945*, Harrap, 1979, reprinted by permission of Peter Donnelly and Judy Milburn.

Betty Miller: an extract from 'Notes for an Unwritten Autobiography' *Modern Reading* No 13, 1945, reprinted by permission of Jonathan and Sarah Miller.

Naomi Mitchison: an extract from *Among You Taking Notes ...*, *The Wartime Diary of Naomi Mitchison 1939–1945* ed D. Sheridan, Gollancz, 1985, reprinted by permission of David Higham Associates Ltd.

Lily Montagu: an extract from 'Club Letter No 26, May 1941' (to the

Cambridge University Press, 1942, reprinted by permission of Cambridge University Press.

Naomi Royde Smith: extracts from *Outside Information, Being a Diary of Rumours*, Macmillan, 1941, reprinted by permission of Macmillan London.

Pamela Ruffoni: an extract from the Papers of Mrs Pamela Ruffoni, Department of Documents, the Imperial War Museum, reprinted by permission of the Trustees of the Imperial War Museum.

Dorothea Russell: 'Music for All', *Convoy 5*, 1946.

Vita Sackville-West: 'Country Notes', the *New Statesman and Nation*, 23 September 1939, copyright © Vita Sackville-West, 1939, and extracts from the *Women's Land Army* copyright © Vita Sackville-West, 1944, Michael Joseph, 1944, reprinted by permission of Curtis Brown Ltd, London, on behalf of the Estate of Vita Sackville-West.

Stella St. John: an extract from *A Prisoner's Log, Holloway Prison in 1943*, the Howard League for Penal Reform, 1944, reprinted by permission of the Howard League for Penal Reform.

Cynthia Saunders: 'Tribunal Day' the *Spectator*, 17 November 1939, reprinted by permission of the *Spectator*.

Dorothy L. Sayers: extracts from 'Forgiveness and the Enemy', the *Fortnightly*, April 1941, reprinted by permission of David Higham Associates Ltd.

Florence Sharp: an extract from "'Sparrow Starvers' of Soho", the *Listener*, 8 April 1943.

Etta Shiber: an extract from *Paris Underground*, George Harrap, 1944.

Stevie Smith: an extract from 'Mosaic', *Eve's Journal*, 1939, reprinted in *Me Again, the Uncollected Writings of Stevie Smith* copyright © James McGibbon, Virago Press, 1983, reprinted by permission of Virago Press Ltd.

Constance Babington Smith: an extract from *Evidence in Camera, The Story of Photographic Intelligence*, Chatto & Windus, 1957, reprinted by permission of the Peters Fraser & Dunlop Group Ltd.

Freya Stark: an extract (reproduced on p. 536) from *Dust in the Lion's Paw, Autobiography 1939–1946*, John Murray, 1961, reprinted by permission of John Murray (Publishers) Ltd, and an extract from *Letters, Vol 5 1943–1946* ed Lucy Moorhead, Michael Russell, 1978.

Gertrude Stein: extracts from *Wars I Have Seen*, Batsford, 1945, reprinted by permission of David Higham Associates Ltd.

Jan Struther: an extract from *Mrs Miniver* 1939, reprinted by Virago Press, 1989, reprinted by permission of Virago Press Ltd.

Edith Summerskill: extracts from 'Conscription and Women', the *Fortnightly*, March 1942, reprinted by permission of David Higham Associates Ltd.

Mavis Tate: an extract from 'More on Buchenwald', the *Spectator*, 4 May 1945, reprinted by permission of the *Spectator*.

Time and Tide: Correspondence on 'Women's War Service', September–October 1941, and Correspondence on 'Cigarettes – for Men Only', 5 July 1941.

Mary Trevelyan: extracts from *I'll Walk Beside You, Letters from Belgium September 1944–May 1945*, Longmans, 1946, reprinted by permission of David Higham Associates Ltd.

Evelyn Underhill: prayers from *A Service of Prayer for Use in War-Time*, Church Literature Association 1939.

Helen Waddell: an extract from a letter by Helen Waddell in *Helen Waddell, A Life* by D. Felicitas Corrigan, published by Gollancz, 1990, reprinted by permission of David Bolt Associates.

Sylvia Townsend Warner: extracts from Sylvia Townsend Warner's *Letters* ed W. Maxwell, Chatto & Windus, 1982, reprinted by permission of Susanna Pinney and William Maxwell.

Hilary Wayne: extracts from *Two Odd Soldiers*, George Allen & Unwin, 1946.

Beatrice Webb: extracts from *The Diary of Beatrice Webb, Vol IV, 1924–1943, The Wheel of Life*, eds Norman and Jeanne MacKenzie, Virago Press, 1985, reprinted by permission of Virago Press Ltd and the Trustees of the LSE.

Maureen Wells: extracts from *Entertaining Eric, Letters from the Home Front 1941–1944*, the Imperial War Museum, 1988, reprinted by permission of the author and the Trustees of the Imperial War Museum.

Rebecca West: 'If the Worst Comes to the Worst', *Time and Tide*, 8 June 1940, and an extract from 'Greenhouse with Cyclamens', 1946, collected in *A Train of Powder*, Macmillan, 1955, reprinted by permission of the Peters Fraser & Dunlop Group Ltd.

Leslie Whateley: an extract from *As Thoughts Survive*, Hutchinson, 1949.

Winifred Williams: an extract from 'Northern City at Noon', *Time and Tide*, 24 October 1942.

Amabel Williams-Ellis: an extract from *Women in War Factories*, Gollancz, 1943, and extracts from 'Hostels and Girls' originally printed in the *Spectator*, 24 July 1942, reprinted by permission of the Peters Fraser & Dunlop Group Ltd.

Margery Withers: an extract from 'Children Under Hitler', the *Listener*, 18 February 1943.

Virginia Woolf: 'Thoughts on Peace in an Air Raid' (originally written in August 1940 for an American symposium on current affairs concerning women), from *The Death of the Moth and Other Essays*, The Hogarth Press, 1942, and extracts from *The Diary of Virginia Woolf, Vol V*

1936–1941, ed A.O. Bell, The Hogarth Press, 1984, reprinted by permission of the Random Century Group on behalf of the Estate of Virginia Woolf.

Susan Woolfitt: extracts from *Idle Women*, 1947, reprinted M.&M. Baldwin, Cleobury, Mortimer, Shropshire, 1986, reprinted by permission of Harriet Graham and Adam Woolfitt.

A Wren: letter reproduced in *Blue Tapestry* by Vera Laughton Mathews, Hollis and Carter Ltd, London, 1948.

Esther Terry Wright: extract from *Pilot's Wife's Tale, the Diary of a Camp-Follower*, John Lane, The Bodley Head, 1942, reprinted by permission of the Random Century Group.

Suggestions for further reading

Braybon, Gail and Summerfield, Penny, *Out of the Cage*, Pandora 1987.

Calder, Angus, *The People's War*, 1969, rpt. Pimlico 1992.

Henderson, Margaret, *Dear Allies . . . A Story of Women in Monklands and Besieged Leningrad*, Monklands District Libraries 1988.

Lumley, Joanna, *Forces Sweethearts*, Bloomsbury Publishing 1993.

McBryde, Brenda, *Quiet Heroines*, 1985, rpt Cakebreads Publications, Saffron Walden, Essex 1989.

Minns, Raynes, *Bombers and Mash*, Virago 1980.

Sebba, Anne, *Battling for News: The Rise of the Woman Reporter*, Hodder and Stoughton 1994.

Sheridan, Dorothy, ed., *Wartime Women*, Heinemann 1990.

Taylor, Eric, *Women Who Went to War 1938–1946*, Grafton Books 1989.

Waller, Jane and Vaughan-Rees, Michael, *Women in Wartime*, Macdonald Optima 1987.

Waller, Jane and Vaughan-Rees, Michael, *Women in Uniform 1939–1945*, Macmillan 1989.

Waller, Jane and Vaughan-Rees, Michael, *Blitz*, Macdonald Optima 1990.

Warner, Lavinia and Sandilands, John, *Women Beyond the Wire*, Michael Joseph 1982.